SCARLET
TIDES

Scarlet Tides

THE MOONTIDE QUARTET

DAVID HAIR

Jo Fletcher

New York • London

Jo Fletcher Books
An imprint of Quercus
New York • London

ISBN 978-1-62365-829-8

Library of Congress Control Number: 2014945600

Distributed in the United States and Canada by
Hachette Book Group
237 Park Avenue
New York, NY 10017

Manufactured in the United States

10 9 8 7 6 5 4 3 2 1

www.quercus.com

Contents

This book is dedicated to Mark Fry;
lifelong friend, best man, free-spirit
and all-round good guy.

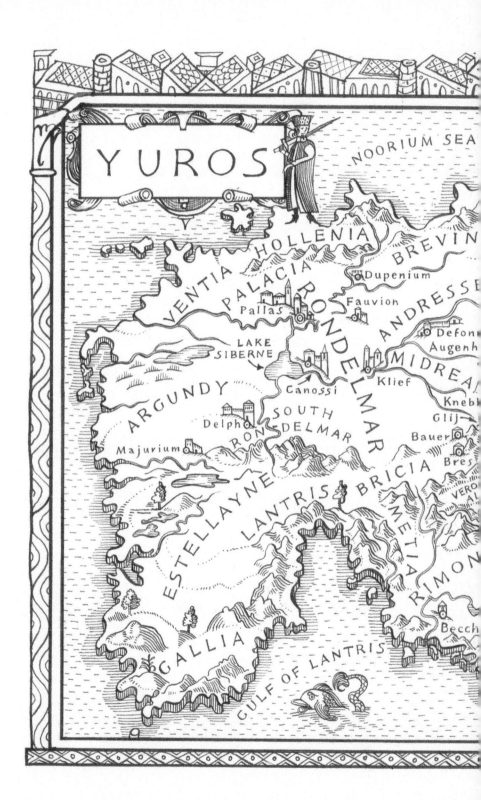

YUROS

NOORIUM SEA

VENTIA

HOLLENIA

PALACIA

BREVIN

Dupenium

Pallas

RONDELMAR

Fauvion

ANDRESSE

Defon

Augenh

LAKE
SIBERNE

MIDREA

Klief

Canossi

Knebl

ARGUNDY

SOUTH

Glij

Delpho

RON-

DELMAR

Bauer

Majurium

-DELMAR

Bres

LANTRIS

BRICIA

VERO

AL

ESTELLAYNE

METIA

RIMON

GALLIA

GULF OF LANTRIS

Becch

ICE WASTES

MIRODEAN ICE SEA

SCHLESSEN

SOUTH
SCHLESSEN
(BUNAVIA)

SYDIA

DRON
LLEY
BREKAELLEN
VALLEY

Collistein

OROS

Lukhazan

Dusheim
Spinitius

Norostein

VERELON

ILACIA

Cypinos

Thantis

GULF OF SILIUM

Pontus

Northpoint

0   500M

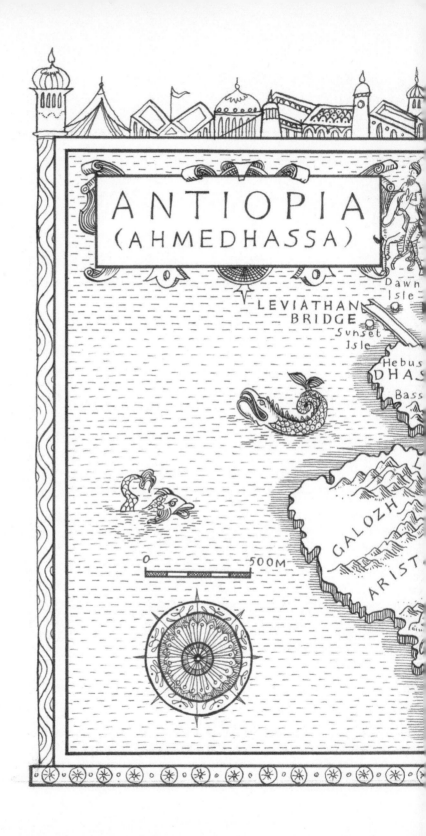

ANTIOPIA
(AHMEDHASSA)

LEVIATHAN
BRIDGE

Dawn
Isle

Sunset
Isle

Hebus
DHAS

Bass

GALOZH

ARIST

0   500M

L

GULF OF MIROBEZ

Hytel

Lybis Loctis
ochena
Riban Forensa
VON HARKUM
oz Intemsa
Krak Hallikut
Istabad
Galataz KESH MIROBEZ
Sagostabad Shaliyah Ghosh
edishar Peroz EASTERN
bad Vida KESH
Barakabad DESERT
Khotriawal
Gujati GATIOCH
TAN SITHARDHA Ullakesh
DESERT
ASHIR NIMTAYA
ETERNAL
MOUNTAINS
Kankriti-
pur Teshwallabad
BALAYAN
UNTAINS
Tuklabad Baranasi

LAKH

sjidabad Jeslamabad

Dili

NOORIUM SEA

RONDELMAR

SCHLESS

ARGUNDY

NOROS

SILACIA

ESTELLAYNE

RIMONI

GULF OF

GALLIA

GULF OF LANTRIS

OCEANUS

YUROS

URTE
C. 927

0   1000M

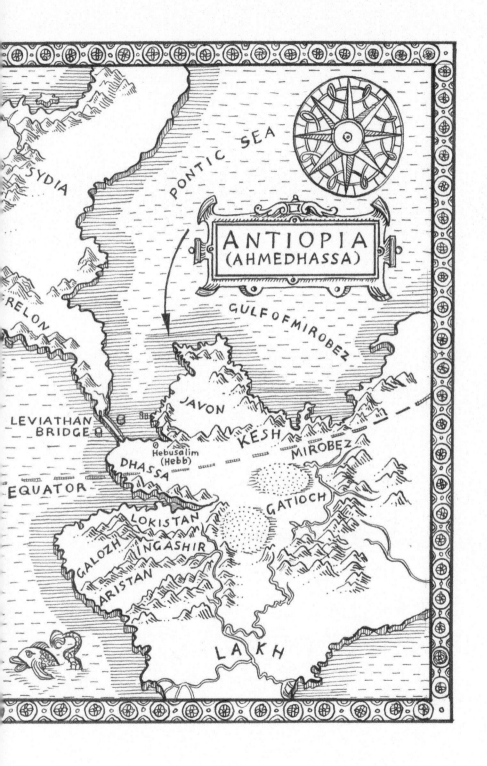

PROLOGUE

THE VEXATIONS OF EMPEROR CONSTANT (PART TWO)

The Imperial Dynasty

The Blessed Three Hundred, though reveling in their god-like powers and fresh from destroying a Rimoni legion, were cast into confusion by the death of their charismatic spiritual guide Johan "Corineus" Corin. His murder at the hands of his sister, Corinea, had horrified his followers, and left them with an immediate problem: who would succeed the man who had bequeathed them the gnosis?

But Ganitius, Corineus's loyal "fixer," and Baramitius, whose potions had opened the gateway to the gnosis, acted quickly to ensure the future of the group. Uniting behind the nobleman Mikal Sertain, they established a new leadership that saw Sertain anointed Corineus's successor, the successful destruction of the bewildered Rimoni armies, and the installment of the Sacrecour dynasty that still rules Pallas and the empire today.

Why Sertain? Because his family were well-moneyed.

ORDO COSTRUO COLLEGIATE, PONTUS

Pallas, Rondelmar
Summer 927
1 Year until the Moontide

One year until the Moontide. It seemed like no time at all.

Gurvon Gyle studied the faces about him anew as they settled back into their seats. Over the last hour, the atmosphere of the room had changed. His plan for the conquest of Javon had been agreed, but that was just the first step. The rest of this meeting would be more contentious, and test the ability of this group of people to work together. He smoothed the sleeve of his rough dun-colored shirt, wondering if his plans for Javon would go as intended.

When does anything ever go as planned?

To his left, fellow Noroman Belonius Vult, Governor of Norostein, was riffling through his notes as he prepared to speak again. He was clad in the finest cloth, of silver and blue. His noble visage spoke of wisdom and secret knowledge, like some legendary guide to the future; appropriate, Gyle thought, as their plans were set to shape the world for years to come. Five others shared the meeting chamber deep within the Imperial Court in Pallas: the four men and one woman were all Rondian, and among the most powerful people in the known world.

It was only natural to look first at the emperor. He was a young man still. Though he ruled the greatest empire in history, the crown did not weigh easily upon his brow and he looked shrunken in his glittering robes. He was sour-faced, with flawless pale skin and wispy facial hair, and his nose twitched constantly as he looked about him, as if he imagined himself surrounded by enemies. As well he might: he had ascended after the premature death of his father and the incarceration of his elder sister. Intrigue festered in his court.

The emperor's nervous eyes were drawn most often to the woman at his right hand: his mother. Mater-Imperia Lucia Fasterius-Sacrecour did not look frightening, but it was her machinations that had brought her favorite—and most pliable—child to the throne of Rondelmar. With a serene face and simple taste in clothing, she was outwardly the picture of a devout and matronly woman. Yesterday, in a vast ceremony before the massed populace of Pallas, she had been made a Living Saint, but no one then had seen any sign of her chilling and callous intellect. Gyle had witnessed enough evidence of her ruthlessness to know that her approval alone would see the second part of the plan accepted.

And we will need her favor even more urgently if anything goes wrong.

The man who had invested Lucia as a saint, Arch-Prelate Wurther, sat opposite Gyle, swirling his wine and looking about contentedly. He met Gyle's eyes and smiled amiably. The prelate looked harmless enough, like a parish priest promoted past his capability, but he was a wily old hog. The Church of Kore was no place for fools.

Next to the prelate, the Imperial Treasurer Calan Dubrayle was leaning back in his chair, eyes unfocused; mentally counting money, perhaps. He was a slim, dapper man with careful eyes. He'd been appointed Treasurer following the ascension of the emperor; his analytical mind and head for the gold that flowed through the coffers of Urte's mightiest state made him perfect for the job.

Gyle had no love for either of the two men talking in the corner. When his homeland had revolted against the empire eighteen years ago, he and Belonius Vult had been part of that rebellion. Kaltus Korion and Tomas Betillon had been the generals who'd eventually crushed the uprising—and now here they all were, part of a fresh conspiracy, the Noros Revolt forgotten. Except it wasn't, not really. You didn't forget things like that, no matter how many years had passed.

Kaltus Korion looked like a hero, and was, to the man on the street. His pale hair was swept back from a strong face, framing steely eyes and a jutting jaw. His combative manner only heightened the heroic illusion. The man with him—burly, uncouth Tomas Betillon—swilled wine as he tapped Korion on the chest, making some point.

Neither will like the next part of the plan, Gyle thought.

He rubbed his thumb and forefinger together, invoked his gnosis and bled a little heat into his red wine to combat the chill in the room. All eyes went to him as he did it: everyone else was a pure-blood mage and highly sensitive to any use of the gnosis. He opened his hand palm-up, to indicate that what he'd done was no threat.

Mater-Imperia Lucia inclined her head to him gracefully, then called to the two military men, "Kaltus, Tomas . . . I believe Master Vult is ready. We await your attention."

Korion and Betillon stalked back to their seats. Korion's low grumbling quieted only when Lucia narrowed her eyes. The Living Saint glanced down at her papers, then around the table. "Gentlemen, in twelve months the Third Crusade begins, giving us the chance to achieve certain of our objectives. Among them, the destruction of the merchant-magi cabal; the death of Duke Echor of Argundy—the only real rival to my son; the destruction of the Ordo Costruo and Antonin Meiros; the plunder of northern Antiopia and subsequent enrichment of our treasury, and the recapture of Javon. Magister Vult and Magister Gyle have invested much time and thought and we've already covered the Javon problem." She turned to the two Noromen. "That aspect of your plans already has our approval." She looked at Vult. "So, with my son's permission, Governor, please continue."

The emperor inclined his head distractedly, not that anyone really noticed.

Belonius stood and thanked her and then began, his clear voice easily filling the room, "Your Majesties, gentlemen. According to our plans, Javon will be paralyzed and unable to support the shihad by the time the Moontide arrives and the Leviathan Bridge rises from the sea, thus securing the northern flank—and our supply lines—for the armies of the Crusade. This leaves us free to turn our attention to other things, namely the destruction of the enemies of the empire. As Mater-Imperia Lucia has outlined, many of those are internal enemies. You've all seen the documents Gurvon provided before the meeting. They prove not only that Duke Echor Borodium, the emperor's own uncle—and outwardly a strong supporter—has been in contact with the emperor's disgraced sister Natia, but that he has made approaches to the governors and domestic rulers of all of the empire's vassal-states on her behalf, canvassing their support.

These are treasonous acts worthy of death. But the fact remains that Argundy is the second-largest kingdom in the empire. When Echor's brother conspired with the emperor's sister and was executed, Echor was not in a position then to prevent that, or take the field in her name, but his resentment remains strong, and now he is in control of Argundy—"

"We should have killed him when we had the chance," the emperor grumbled, making a face. "When he was kneeling before me, kissing my signet, and pleading for his brother's life, I should have seized an ax: *chop chop!*" He sniggered at the mental image.

Gyle saw Lucia's eyes tighten just a little: impatience, tempered with a mother's indulgence. "Darling, you remember that was impossible," she chided him gently. "Echor has married into the Argundian kings. Beheading him would have guaranteed revolt at an inopportune moment. Buying him off bought us time to deal with him. That time is now."

Constant's nostrils flared at her tone, but he ducked his head and fell silent.

Belonius breezed past the interruption. "To weaken Echor's standing, we need to lure his vassal-state allies to destruction. We need them to join the Crusade. The Second Crusade yielded inadequate plunder and all but destroyed trade. The vassal-states claimed they had emptied their treasuries to fund it and got nothing back, and because of that, they would not support any more Crusades in the future."

Betillon scowled contemptuously. "If they'd committed more troops, they might have—"

Unexpectedly, Calan Dubrayle broke in. "No, actually, Magister Vult is quite right: the Second Crusade was a waste of money. The Sultan of Kesh is not stupid. In the preceding years he and anyone with wealth shipped their gold and riches eastward, far from our reach. They also poisoned waterholes and burned their own crops for hundreds of miles inland. We spent millions marching our armies all the way to Istabad and recovered—what, a third of our outlay? By the time I'd taken the emperor's share and the Church's, the vassal-states were left with nothing."

You might have added another group, Treasurer: the noble magi who robbed their soldiers to enhance their own coffers. They took as much as the Imperial Treasury and more.

"You say that as if it were a bad thing," Betillon chuckled. "Keeping the provinces weak is half the battle."

"Maybe," Dubrayle noted, "but it doesn't leave much enthusiasm for more Crusades."

Vult coughed to regain the floor, and went on, "Argundy, Bricia, Noros, Estellayne, and Hollenia have all said they will not join this Crusade."

"Noros," Korion snarled, jabbing a finger at Vult. "If your people don't join the Crusade in their thousands, I'll give them another crackdown that will make Knebb look like a holiday."

Betillon laughed harshly: he'd been the Rondian general to order the slaughter at Knebb during the Revolt. He was still known as "The Butcher of Knebb."

Gyle still remembered entering the smoking ruins of the town and seeing the carnage for the first time. Something inside him had changed forever that day. For now, he worked hard to keep his expression carefully blank.

"I will *demand* their participation," whined Emperor Constant. "They're *my* subjects."

"Darling," Lucia chimed in, smiling sweetly, "even dogs have to be fed or they become unmanageable."

"Our Beloved Mater-Imperia is wisdom itself," Vult put in quickly. "The Crusade needs the manpower of the vassal-states. Every province of the empire *must* participate."

"Why?" Korion demanded. "Rondelmar must control the action in Antiopia when the time comes, and that means dominating the military. We're only one third of the empire's population: if every state sends every eligible soldier, we will be outnumbered. If Echor were to unite them, we would be overwhelmed."

"But my lord," Vult countered, "during the Second Crusade, the armies of the vassal-states were in Kesh and therefore, they were not *here*. They were grubbing around for loot as desperately as we were. The circumstances have changed now: they don't want to go. If they hold back and Rondelmar sends all its troops into Antiopia for two years, who will stand up to Echor?"

"He wouldn't dare," Constant said, outraged. "He *bowed* to me! He kissed my ring!"

Kissing your ass doesn't mean he loves you, Gyle thought.

Silence greeted the emperor's declaration, but Gyle saw Mater-Imperia Lucia's eyes narrow again.

"Magister Vult," said Arch-Prelate Wurther, "you say that getting the vassal-states to commit to the Crusade is vital, but if we do that, how will we control them? More important, how will we ensure that the plunder finds its way to the proper places? Your notes on this matter were frustratingly vague." The prelate wagged a finger admonishingly.

"Their commitment is paramount," Vult replied. "If Echor and his allies are not in the vanguard of this Crusade, then a domestic coup while the Crusade is in progress is inevitable."

"Rondelmar has all the strongest magi," Korion countered. "A Pallas battle-legion is worth at least three from the provinces. They would not dare."

"Actually, that is not entirely true," Calan Dubrayle put in mildly, again taking Vult's side, making Gyle wonder what was in it for Dubrayle. *Maybe he just likes annoying Korion?* "The most recent census revealed that more than half of all magi live outside of Rondelmar. Most of the strongest are here, it is true, but numbers matter. And the loyalty of those within is not to be taken for granted," he added.

Emperor Constant's mouth fell open and his eyes went to his mother's face as if for reassurance. "My people love me," he squeaked. "All of them."

Yes, yes, they kissed your rukking ring. But some love Echor and others love your poor, tragic, imprisoned elder sister and they all wonder whether your ass on the throne really does represent the will of Kore.

"Carry on, Magister Vult," Lucia instructed, silencing her son with a warning look.

"The Treasurer is correct: a ruler must always be vigilant. Our emperor is a paragon of all the virtues; lesser men have baser morals." Vult made a subservient gesture to Emperor Constant, then to Lucia. "I therefore propose that we make a public concession, one that will ensure that we get all of the zealous manpower we could want from the vassal-states and at the same time put the heads of our enemies firmly in the noose: we offer Echor command of the Crusade."

"What?" Kaltus Korion leaped to his feet, exploding with fury. "That isn't in your notes! *Who* the Hel do you think you are? It is my *right* to command the Crusade!"

"General Korion!" Lucia's voice cracked like a whip. "Sit down!"

"But—" Korion looked set to shout at her, and then abruptly swallowed his words. "Your Majesty, I apologize," he said, trying to calm himself. "But I don't understand; I am the Supreme General of the Rondian Empire, I *must* lead the Crusade." He struck his own chest, over the heart. "It is my due."

Gyle watched Korion thoughtfully. *Plunder the East, return with all the loot, with a massive adoring army at your beck and call . . . Perhaps you're eyeing the Sacred Throne yourself, General?*

"You're still standing in our presence," Lucia reminded the general in a voice that dripped acid. "Sit down, Kaltus, and let us debate this like adults."

Korion stared at her for half a second and then sat, abashed.

Gyle looked at Vult. *Interesting.*

Emperor Constant looked puzzled. He obviously didn't understand what was going on. Betillon looked as outraged as Korion. Dubrayle and Wurther were expressionless, which seemed exceedingly wise.

Mater-Imperia Lucia tilted her head to Vult. "Continue, Magister."

Vult took a breath. "Thank you, Mater-Imperia," he said, emphasizing her title as if that might deflect some of the fury that was radiating from Kaltus Korion. The two men had hated each other since the day Vult had betrayed the Noros Revolt by tending his surrender to Korion.

"It is my command, turncoat," Korion told him in a low voice.

Vult flushed angrily. "The future of this empire is at stake. This is not a time to think of one's *personal* standing. This is a time to reflect on how one can contribute to the greater good." His eyes focused on some imaginary point halfway between Korion and Mater-Imperia Lucia. "This is a time to put the well-being of our emperor first."

"Hear, hear," said Wurther, sipping wine with a twinkle in his eye, earning him a belligerent glare from Betillon, which troubled the Churchman not at all.

"The common people, the merchant-magi, and even many of the loyal magi spread throughout the empire do not wish to see another Crusade like the last. They were promised the world, my lords. They were told to expect plunder beyond all dreams, that the East was awash with gold. And I believed that too, as firmly as any."

Gyle knew Vult's financial situation. The Governor had invested heavily in the Crusades and lost.

Vult continued, "Argundy, Bricia, and Noros are from the same stock as Rondelmar, yet they balk. The people of Schlessen, Verelon, Estellayne, Sydia . . . they refuse involvement outright. Last time they invested men, money, and stores, and they lost all but the men. They slaughtered heathens by the thousand, but what did they gain? Nothing—Pallas took it all. Why would we march again? Why?"

We? Gyle smiled to himself, then caught Lucia watching him. She raised an eyebrow but said nothing.

Vult tapped his papers. "Only one thing will bring the provinces into this Crusade: the belief that this time will be different. And only one thing can send that signal: the leadership of this venture being given to the man they associate with balancing the power of Pallas with that of the provinces: Duke Echor of Argundy. Appoint him, and the provinces will join. Fail to do so, and you may as well prepare to man the entire Crusade on your own." He didn't say "if you can," but those words hung in the air.

The room fell silent. Korion and Betillon exchanged a glance as if daring each other to protest. Constant still looked childishly confused, but the others were catching on: *Lucia wants this. It will happen.*

Korion stood, and Gyle watched the man swallow his pride as he addressed himself to Lucia. "Mater-Imperia, I apologize. This plan is wise. A military commission is nothing when compared with the perpetuation of the might and majesty of the House of Sacrecour."

No one had ever called Kaltus Korion stupid.

The same could not be said for Tomas Betillon. "I don't under-stand," he grumbled. "Let the proclamations go out, see how many sign up first, before we commit to something we don't need to."

"And be seen to back down?" Dubrayle asked caustically. "I think not. An emperor states a path and does not deviate. He does not negotiate with his subjects: he just makes sure his proclamations are realistic and enforceable."

"There's another thing," Gyle threw in, as if it had just occurred to him. "You have the battle-standards of the Noros legions in your hands, and many from previous rebellions in Argundy and other provinces. Give them back."

Korion's jaw dropped. "Fuck you, Noroman. I keep my trophies."

"If the battle-standards are returned, men will flock to enlist," Vult chimed in. "They will see themselves as forgiven. It will give them back their pride, and give them a reason to forgive the empire."

"Forgive?" sneered Constant. "I taught them a lesson in the for-giveness of the empire: there is none!"

You taught us, did you, your Majesty? Gyle thought. *Was that how it was? I understood you spent most of the Noros Revolt cowering in fear of assassins like me.*

"It is but the misguided perception of the common man," Vult replied smoothly, "but these feelings persist."

The emperor's mother stroked her son's arm and whispered something in his ear. The emperor nodded slowly. "My mother reminds me that the people of Noros are yokels. We are fortunate to have two such rarities as yourselves able to attend upon us without chewing grass and stinking of cow shit."

Betillon smirked. No one else moved a muscle. The moment stretched on.

Well, that shows us the true extent of our welcome. Gyle turned slightly. Out of the corner of his eye he watched Belonius, appar-ently impervious to the insult. *But then, he probably shares Con-stant's assessment of his own people.*

"The suggestion is an excellent one," Mater-Imperia Lucia told the room. "The provinces know who their masters are. Rubbing their noses in it is counterproductive. Give them Echor in charge and their battle-standards back, and they will enlist in droves."

"They'll outnumber us in Kesh," Korion reminded her.

"Not significantly. And once there, I am quite sure you will turn it to our advantage."

"How?" sniffed Korion. "There's no one to fight. We hear the Amteh priests have declared some sort of holy war but, realistically, they've got no magi, no constructs, and no discipline. Crusades aren't wars, they're two-year treasure-hunts."

Lucia permitted herself a small smile. "To which Magister Gyle has a response." She made a welcoming gesture. "Our guest awaits."

"Our guest?" chorused Korion and Betillon in mutual exasperation.

"This is the Closed Council," Constant whined, "not the tap-room of a tavern."

Gyle ignored him, rose and walked to the door. He tapped, and the guard opened it. He breathed deeply as he went into the ante-chamber, inhaling fresher air. *They're like squabbling children, not leaders of men. They've no vision, no plan. It's all just pettiness, self-interest and boasting.*

Except Lucia. Her, I could follow.

The man waiting in the antechamber was robed in black with heavy furs draped about his shoulders, despite the summer heat. He dropped his hood and stood as Gyle entered the room. With his dark coppery skin, jet-black hair pulled tightly back from his face, and a neatly trimmed beard and mustache, he was both striking and alien. His eyes glinted like emerald chips. Rubies adorned his ears, and a diamond periapt hung about his neck.

"Emir," Gyle said, striding forward. "I trust you are well?"

"Magister," Emir Rashid Mubarak of Halli'kut purred in welcome. He embraced Gyle courteously, kissing both his cheeks and patting his back in the space between the shoulder blades. In Kesh that was a gesture of reassurance—*see, I could kill you, but I do not.* Rashid was officially the fourth-ranked mage of Antonin Meiros's Ordo Costruo, a three-quarter-blood descended from a pure-blood and a half-blood mage. His half-blood mother had been the child of a pure-blood who had married into a Keshi royal line before

Meiros's Leviathan Bridge was even completed. Her son was the result: a polished gemstone of a man, finely cut and glittering. "I am deathly cold. How do you stand it?"

"This is summer, my lord. I advise you to depart before it snows."

"I shall be leaving immediately afterward. How goes the meeting?"

"Well enough," Gyle said. "Constant is in a sour mood. Address yourself to Lucia and ignore the idiocy from Korion and Betillon."

"Tomas Betillon is well known to me. I am practiced in dealing with him." Rashid shrugged. "What is that word you use for us: barbarian? He is that, I am thinking."

Gyle glanced at the guard, who was staring at Rashid as if he were a construct beast of unusual strangeness, and suppressed a smile. "He surely is." He gestured toward the door. "Shall we go in?"

Vult met them at the door. "Ah, there you are." He inclined his head toward Rashid.

The Emir bowed. "It is my great pleasure to meet you at last. Magister Gyle has told me so much of you."

Vult's mouth twitched with humor. "Nothing bad, I trust, Gurvon?"

"Only the truth, Bel."

"Oh dear. Well, Emir, you came despite that. We are about to discuss your role in our plans. Come in, my friend."

Rashid paused. "Do not mistake me for a *friend*, Magister Vult. I am far from that."

Belonius Vult smiled smoothly. "We have enemies in common, Emir. That is the strongest form of friendship I've ever known."

1

How You Meet Your End

The Rune of the Chain

The ability to lock up a mage's powers is unfortunately required. Though we are all descendants of the Blessed Three Hundred, some among us are unworthy of that lineage. To cut off a mage from their great gift is a drastic step, not easily or lightly done. The sad truth, however, is that villainy does manifest among us, and is magnified by our capacity for harm.

MARTEN ROBINIUS, ARCANUM MAGISTER, BRES

Norostein, Noros, on the continent of Yuros
Julsep 928
1st month of the Moontide

Jeris Muhren, Watch Captain of Norostein, descended the clockwise-curving stairs. The darkened stairwell was narrow, damp, and treacherous. A dank, stale smell rose from below, along with the clank and clatter of stone and steel. It was early morning on a summer's day outside, but winter's cold still lurked in the dungeons of Norostein's Governor's Palace. There were no guards down here, unusually. Their absence made him wary, and he loosened his sword as he strode on.

He pushed open the door at the bottom of the stair and entered a small chamber, where he was surprised to find another before him: a youngish-looking man with a weak chin partially hidden by a wispy blond beard. His thin body was draped in heavy velvet robes and a gold band encircled his worry-creased brow.

Muhren hastily dropped to his knee. "Your Majesty," he murmured. *What's he doing here?*

"Captain Muhren," King Phyllios III of Noros responded formally. "Please, stand."

Muhren rose, puzzled. Phyllios III was a puppet ruler, with the governor's hand firmly up his ass—at least, that was the word on the street. The failed Revolt had broken the Noros monarchy, leaving the king a powerless sideshow in a decrepit palace. The Governor ruled Noros now, in the name of the emperor—but right now that same Governor was a prisoner in his own dungeons.

"My King, you should not be here."

Phyllios shrugged lightly. "The guards were ordered away an hour ago, Captain, and no one saw me arrive. I am not so confined to my palace as you might think."

Muhren blinked. *Last day on the job and I'm still learning.*

"How is our prisoner, Captain?" the king asked. His voice was tentative, but there was a certain vengeful cunning Muhren had not heard before. Phyllios had been a young man during the Revolt, when he had seen his people crushed. The Rondians made an example of him, forcing him to become a parade attraction: he had been flogged naked before his people before being forced to crawl before the emperor and beg forgiveness. That had broken whatever manner of man he might have become and turned him into a powerless cringer—at least, so Muhren had once thought. Appointing the watch captain was one of the very few prerogatives left to the king and Muhren had been Phyllios's choice. That pact had revealed a stronger man than most knew, but he was still very cautious, even timid.

"He is deeply unhappy, my liege. Cold, uncomfortable, and very much afraid."

"Of whom? Surely not you or me." Phyllios's tone was self-mocking, but not self-pitying.

"Of the Inquisition, my liege."

"Inquisitors are coming here?" Phyllios's calm wavered.

"Inevitably, my liege. He's an Imperial Governor, arrested for treason. They will most certainly be here in days, and they will take him away and break him in the process of deciding whether he is guilty of anything. The emperor cannot afford to permit any governor to appear to be acting beyond his authority."

Phyllios nodded gravely. "What will they learn from him, Captain?"

Ah, now that is the question. I don't care about anything else they might learn, but they will inevitably find out about Alaron, Cym, and the Scytale, and my own role in those events. And then all Hel will burst free.

But for your own safety, I can't tell you this, my King. Muhren had ransacked the governor's offices, to give himself a legitimate reason to arrest and imprison Vult in the aftermath of the struggle to reach the Scytale. Now he lied to his king. "There was nothing altogether startling in what we found, my liege, just evidence of the usual corrupt games men like Vult play. Cronyism. Backhanders. Illegal interests. Nothing that will rebound against the throne."

"How many people know he is here, Captain?" the king asked.

"Too many, my liege." Vult's arrest had been carried out with the help of a squad of soldiers on the outskirts of the city; that had been unavoidable. Muhren wasn't naïve enough to believe they would stay silent on the matter, especially as they had brought back two more bodies, Vult's accomplices, and buried Jarius Langstrit in a secret grave.

"Do you wish him to be questioned, Captain? By the Inquisitors, that is." Phyllios's eyes narrowed with a shrewdness he seldom displayed in public. "Is there aught he might say that would imperil you?"

Muhren hesitated. *That's the thing, isn't it?* "A trained Inquisitor can learn anything there is to learn, my liege. From anyone. If they decided there was something to be learned, they would question *anyone* connected." He met his king's eyes.

Phyllios nodded slowly, hinting at an astuteness few would have credited him. "I will miss you, Muhren. You've served Norostein well. I'll not find another like you."

Muhren bowed his head, suddenly feeling emotional. He'd put his heart and soul into the Norostein Watch, but the king was right: he had to be gone before the Inquisitors arrived. "I will ensure no trail leads back to you, my liege. And I will be gone by sunset."

"Farewell, Captain." Phyllios reached out and patted Muhren's arm, the closest to an affectionate gesture that Muhren had ever seen from the withdrawn, lonely man.

"Farewell sire. May you live forever."

Phyllios shook his head slightly. "No one cheats death, my friend. It is only a question of what we achieve in life, and of how we meet our end. These are the things that matter." He sighed heavily. "I will pray for you, and for the soul of our prisoner." Then he was gone.

It's how we meet our end . . .

Muhren composed himself for a few moments, then he turned to the opposite door and descended further into the dungeon. The king was right: the guards were gone. His boots echoed down the silent corridor.

Belonius Vult did not turn immediately when Muhren unlocked the door to his cell and entered. He shut the door behind him before appraising the governor coldly.

Vult was a pure-blood mage, twice Muhren's blood-rank and roughly four times as powerful. That was how things worked with the gnosis. *We are literally a different breed to other men—and to each other.* Some magi bore that difference with humility, placing their skills at the service of the whole, but most were like Vult: arrogant beyond belief. The deserving Blessed, unchallengeable, and utterly self-serving.

Vult turned at last, and his eyes blazed with fury as he recognized his visitor. His shoulders hunched as he drew in a deep breath and his hands unfurled in whatever gesture would accompany the devastating spell he ached to unleash. But he was imprisoned in a dungeon and bound by a Chain-rune, rendering him impotent. A Chain-rune usually only constrained one weaker than oneself, and Vult was far stronger than Muhren in gnostic abilities—but it also prevented gnostic energies from replenishing, and Vult had been utterly exhausted when he had been captured. For perhaps the first time in his adult life, Belonius Vult was helpless.

Despite his plight, he retained a certain majesty. His robes might be soiled, his face dirty, and his hair and beard tangled, but his bearing was more regal than the king's. If he was afraid, it didn't show; Muhren could see only anger and vengefulness. He was obviously plotting exactly how he would visit retribution when someone inevitably intervened on his behalf.

"So, do you have the Scytale? Not that you would have the wit to understand it," Vult asked spitefully. "You sword-swinging oaf: do you not realize that the Inquisition is coming? They'll take it from you and pluck out your eyes for merely looking at it."

"Yours too, Vult."

"Langstrit died groveling," Vult jeered. "Eighteen years spent as an imbecile and he regained sanity just long enough to die at my hands. I wonder if he thought it worth it?"

"To keep the Scytale from you? I'm sure he did."

Vult scowled, and belatedly changed tactics. "Muhren, it's not too late for you. I've read treatises on the Scytale. I can unravel it and together we could use it. We're both men of Noros—veterans of the same war. Together, we could use the Scytale to make Noros great—the equal of Pallas."

Muhren had been expecting the offer, but he would not have trusted Belonius Vult with a single fiber of his being, not if he were the last man alive. "We don't need your help, Vult."

Vult's eyes flashed. "We? *We*, is it? Think what you're saying, man! Alaron Mercer is a green-bud—*a failed mage*. And that Rimoni bitch has barely a trickle of gnostic-blood. The little quim has no value at all. It's hardly a cabal to inspire fear in your enemies, is it? Let alone to make Mater-Imperia tremble. You need me, Muhren, if you're going to survive, let alone Ascend. You should be begging for my aid."

Muhren looked at him levelly. Vult might be considered devious and cunning, but he was entirely predictable in his lust for gain and glory, dangling dreams as bait, and always with himself at the center of the universe. "Where is Darius Fyrell?" he asked, the only question he had come to ask. In the battle for the Scytale, only Fyrell had escaped. He couldn't afford loose ends.

Vult sneered. "Fyrell? Out there, planning my rescue, of course. Seeking the opportunity to strike back."

"What did he know?"

"Everything," Vult told him, gloating.

Muhren considered that. Darius Fyrell had been Vult's man for a long time, so it was highly probable that he had known exactly what they hunted. He may even have been among those who had questioned General Jarius Langstrit during his secret incarceration. Fyrell was a formidable mage—a necromancer, primarily—and a total blackguard. His loyalty to Vult was not blind, but it was strong. Tesla Anborn had burned him badly, but necromancers were death-mages: they could survive dreadful injuries. He did not doubt that Fyrell was out there somewhere, and quite capable of launching a one-man assault on these dungeons.

"Where was your rendezvous point?"

"There was none," Vult replied with a satisfied smile. "We were in constant communication—arranging a meeting point was needless." He looked down his nose at Muhren, taking in the bandages, the dented armor, and bruised face. "He's probably in better shape than you are."

"Who else knew?"

Vult considered the question like a lord contemplating the request of a vassal. "Besko. He's dead now; Langstrit burned his face off. Koll . . . I know not, nor care. The little shit had his uses, but his role was—well, shall we say *temporary.*"

"No others?"

Vult rubbed his chin. "None."

Muhren exhaled heavily. "Good." He drew his dagger.

Vult's face changed utterly as the realization struck him that he was not immortal after all. His cheeks went ashen and his eyes bulged in their sockets. Beads of sweat erupted like boils on his brow. "No—Muhren, think—! The riches—"

He tried to dodge away, but he was no warrior, and without the gnosis he was no stronger than any other man. Muhren grabbed his collar and pinned him to the wall with his left hand. His right brought the dagger to Vult's left breast.

"Jeris—no! Please—" Vult's legs gave way and the front of his robes darkened as his bladder emptied. His panicked eyes locked on Muhren's, pleading desperately.

He drove the wide blade in, punching through cloth and flesh until it skewered the madly pumping muscle beneath. Scarlet soaked the robes around the wound. With his gnosis powers exhausted, the governor was unable to call on whatever powers he would normally have invoked. His eyes emptied slowly, and Muhren let the dead weight slide down the wall. The smell of feces filled the room as the dying mage voided his bowels. His last breath bubbled out, and a trickle of blood spilled from the corner of his mouth as his legs quivered and kicked once, then he lay there, lifeless to the naked eye.

Using his gnosis, Muhren saw a faint mist forming at the man's lips and nostrils. He focused his will and spoke a single word: "Dissipate." Nothing dramatic happened, nothing more than an unseen wind, a breeze, that blew the mist away before it could form an entity that might linger. This spell could only be cast at the point of death, and it meant no ghost would haunt the body of the governor; there would be nothing for an Inquisitor to summon back and question. Vult was utterly dead. Not even his necromancer friend Fyrell could restore him now.

Muhren pulled the dagger out and wiped it clean on Vult's sleeve. He'd killed before, many times, with blade and gnosis: he'd been a soldier in the Revolt, and there'd been the odd criminal resisting arrest since. But he'd never been involved in anything so cold-blooded as this. He felt soiled, as if Vult's blood were staining his soul.

He sheathed the dagger and walked away. He left his badge of office in the upper chamber, to be returned to the king. His house was already emptied of anything that held meaning to him. A pair of packs were strapped to the horse waiting in the courtyard above. There was a funeral to attend, and then the road awaited.

Alaron Mercer stood and watched his mother burn.

It was customary to burn the bodies of magi before they were interred. No mage wanted to be bound after death to serve some necromancer or wizard as a slave-familiar; burning the body helped dissipate the soul, allowing it to move on rather than leaving it vulnerable to summoning and control. But watching his mother's cremation, knowing that she'd loved him in her harsh way, was horrible. He could feel tears etching his cheeks.

Alaron was a young man of middling height and light build, though he was gradually filling out. Thick reddish hair framed a face that was slowly losing its boyish uncertainty, a firm jaw and cheekbones emerging from beneath the puppy-fat. He was clad in traveling gear, with a sword at his side. He had been failed as a mage, banned from practicing the gnosis, but an amber periapt was tucked inside his shirt nevertheless. He hadn't failed through incompetence but because of corruption, and this would no longer deter him. He would be what he was meant to be; let the authorities stop him if they could.

To his left stood Pars Logan, a veteran of the Revolt; he'd organized the funeral. His shoulders were stooped now, and his spine curved, and the wind lifted what was left of his fine gray hair, but he stood as straight as he could. He'd known Tesla Anborn since the First Crusade, when she'd lost her eyes and a little of her sanity, but loyalty was everything to men like him.

On Alaron's right was Ramon Sensini. His small, thin frame was planted solidly, his lean, dark features and stoic expression older than his eighteen years. Ramon was Silacian, his mage-blood the result of his tavern-girl mother's rape. Despite his ignoble birth he was richly dressed. After graduating from the Arcanum, he had returned to his home village, and as the only mage there, he had prospered. His graduation had been conditional on his serving in the Crusade and now he was dressed in the scarlet and black of a Rondian battle-mage. He was off to join his legion that very day.

The only other man present was a Kore priest, a non-mage cleric barely older than Alaron. He looked bored as he ran through the rites, but he was watching every movement hawkishly. No doubt he had someone to report to; the death of a mage was always noteworthy news to someone.

The burning grounds of Lower Town were on the shores of Lake Tucerle, where most of the poor spread their ashes, but Tesla's would be interred in the Anborn family vault, behind the family manor out in the countryside. Alaron could not stay, but Pars had promised to lay her to rest there himself.

As the sun came up, the pyre collapsed in on itself and the skeleton that was emerging from the raging flames fell into the midst of the blaze, sending heat rolling off in waves.

As Alaron choked back a sob, his shoulders shaking, Ramon put a hand on his shoulder. "Amici, my windship leaves in an hour. I need to be on it," he said in a gentle voice, devoid of the lively wit that normally colored his words.

Alaron nodded. He felt hollowed out, but at the same time, he felt readier than he ever had to face whatever life threw at him next. His mother was dead and his father was hundreds of miles away. The girl he'd loved had broken his heart, then stolen the greatest treasure in the world. His best friend was about to go to war, and the Inquisition was on its way—and yet, despite all this, he felt oddly prepared. "I understand. I just need a moment longer." He faced Ramon and hugged him to him. "Thank you," he whispered as tears continued to roll from his eyes.

"Take care of yourself, amici. And give Cym a good spanking when you catch up with her," Ramon added with a twitch of his mouth. "Who knows, she might enjoy it."

"I wish you were coming with me."

"Me too, amici, but I'll be dead if I don't go to the legion." Not only was Ramon's adopted paterfamilias the head of a dreaded Silacian familioso; he also had Ramon's mother in his hands. He had insisted Ramon go on Crusade, and Ramon had no choice but to obey.

They hugged a final time, made promises about contacting each other, and then the Silacian hurried away, leaving Alaron to stare glassily into the cremation fire as the wind rolled across the lake, flattening the waves.

The glow was dying down and the sun rising above the mountains surrounding the wide sloping valley when Jeris Muhren joined him. The Watch Captain cut a heroic figure, even dressed for the road. His stallion snorted impatiently as he dismounted and strode to Alaron's side and the other horse tethered to the rails sidled nervously. Alaron's horse was smaller, thinner and far less impressive; they were a mirror of their masters.

Muhren made a Kore-genuflection to the pyre, his face solemn. "She was a good woman," he observed. "A true-hearted daughter of Noros."

"Da mostly brought me up on his own," Alaron replied. "Ma was just this . . . scary thing." He wiped at his eyes. "She found it hard to love." His throat caught. "So did I," he admitted.

"What she endured would have marred anyone. That she retained her dignity and morality is a tribute to her, and to Vann. Few men would have given her the love and support he did, for so little in return." Muhren put a hand on his shoulder. "They both had my utmost respect. I thought of Vann as a brother. He was immense during the Revolt, despite worrying constantly for you and Tesla at home." He gave a rueful smile. "Indeed, I hoped to be his brother in truth by marrying Tesla's sister, your Aunt Elena. However, my feelings were not returned."

Alaron wanted to ask more, but for now it could wait. "We should go," he said. "If you've done all you have to?" They both knew what he meant.

Muhren nodded grimly. "It's done. The alarm won't be raised until we've left the city, provided we leave within the hour."

Belonius Vult is dead. Alaron thought about that. *The Traitor of Lukhazan, finally given what he deserved.* He couldn't help a hard smile forming at the thought. *Let the bells ring out.*

After one final silent farewell he turned his back on the pyre, hugged the old soldier and then went to his horse. The stallion was nipping at it belligerently, but Muhren curbed its aggression with a word. They swung easily into the saddles and the warm westerly wind tousled their hair as they turned to face it.

"We'll leave by Hurring Gate," Muhren said, fixing his cloak-clasp.

Alaron nodded, but his mind was already questing ahead, returning to the question that had been plaguing him for the last three days. *Where are you, Cym?*

They were well into the countryside, trotting through woodland fringing the golden wheat fields that sprawled beneath the foothills of the Alps, when behind them arose a distant clamor: the bells of the city greeting the death of its most hated son.

Two days later, a windship rode the air currents toward Bekontor Hill, Norostein's windport. Dozens of windships of all shapes and sizes were tethered among the forest of platforms and towers, while beneath them hundreds of porters serviced the mass of wagons and carts hauling goods and people to and fro.

The vessel that swept up the valley that afternoon was a rare visitor. Its timbers were shaped as much for artistry as functionality and decorated with ornamental carvings; the sails were tasseled, and emblazoned banners displayed the Sacred Heart, bright sigil of the Church's darkest sons. The Inquisition had arrived.

The windshipmen were common sailors, and they were careful to avoid disturbing their white-robed passengers, who were gathered in the forecastle. The three-decker had lavish quarters below, but today everyone was on deck to see Norostein reveal itself below. Beyond the city the eternal snow of the Alpine peaks glistened in the afternoon sun.

The ten Inquisitors were all magi of Pallas: eight men and two women armored in steel chain mail beneath fur-lined cloaks. The Sacred Heart glowed in red and gold on their chests. Straight swords hung from their left hips. Their leather gauntlets and boots gleamed. Collectively they were a Fist: one Commandant and nine Acolytes.

This Fist had an additional member, appointed to advise this particular mission. The Kore Crozier was an effeminate-looking man with a mane of curling black hair and full lips. As the vessel approached its landing site, he deigned to speak to one of the Acolytes. "This must be a kind of homecoming for you, Brother Malevorn."

"Yes, my lord Crozier," Malevorn Andevarion replied respect-fully. "I spent seven years in this pit."

The other man snorted softly. "You did not come to love it then?" He was known as Adamus; though he had forsaken his family name on taking the title, the tradition that was observed to the letter was also subtly ignored. Everyone knew Adamus Crozier was related to the Sacrecours.

"I am Palacian," Malevorn said proudly. "My family is pure-blood. Even the nobility of this dung-heap are only half-bloods. If it wasn't for my uncle's posting to the occupation force, I'd have been edu-cated in Pallas, as I'd expected." The fall of the Andevarions, whose patriarch, Malevorn's father, had committed suicide in disgrace after his legions had been annihilated by Noros rebels during the Revolt, was a humiliation that drove Malevorn every second of every day.

The Crozier nodded sympathetically. "You had some company, I understand? Kaltus Korion's son, and the Dorobon heir?"

"My lord is well informed," Malevorn replied. He could feel the way the Crozier watched him, and had been regarding him ever since he'd been assigned to his squad. He knew his own looks: he was handsome in a way that made him seem older, with a fine-chiseled, rakish face and voluminous dark hair. He knew the way his sensuous smile could make a girl wet. Some men were just as susceptible, and rumor had it this Crozier was one such.

The Crozier smiled indulgently. "I like to take an interest in the most promising of our brethren."

Malevorn gave a small bow of acknowledgment, and saw his fel-low Acolytes glaring enviously. None of them had yet managed to exchange pleasantries with the Crozier. He saw their eyes flicker from the Crozier to himself, saw conclusions drawn.

The first of you to suggest what you're thinking is going to regret it, he promised them all.

"Did you meet Governor Vult?" Adamus Crozier asked.

"I did, my lord. At my graduation—and socially, from time to time."

"Society?" The Fist Commandant, Inquisitor Lanfyr Vordan, sniffed. "Is there such a thing here?"

"I was asking Acolyte Malevorn about the governor," Adamus Crozier observed mildly. Inquisitor Vordan flushed and fell silent, but Malevorn kept his amusement hidden. When this mission was over, the Crozier would go home and Vordan would still be there.

"The governor was not popular with his people, my lord," Malevorn told Adamus.

"Traitors seldom are," Adamus replied, a lilt of humor in his voice. "I too have met him, in Pallas last year. He has a high opinion of himself."

Malevorn smiled dutifully. "So it is said, my lord."

He knew little of their mission, but there was plenty of gossip among the Fist. He glanced at them, neatly arrayed in their little factions: Brothers Jonas and Seldon stood with dark and sour Sister Raine. All three were half-bloods, illegitimate children of pure-bloods with a talent for theology and connivance. Raine was screwing Vordan, a sound career move, or so she seemed to imagine.

The older men were above all that: Brothers Dranid and Alain were gray-haired veterans whose youthful urges had been purged by years of self-flagellation and prayer. Malevorn envied their skill, but found them utterly boring company.

Then there was Brother Dominic, who was born to follow. He'd latched onto Malevorn immediately, like a puppy seeking a master. He was a competent enough mage and warrior, but he had no head for conspiracy and he knew that made him vulnerable, so he invariably sought a protector, the most alpha of the group. Malevorn, despite his youth, was that person.

Finally, his eye strayed to Brother Filius and Sister Virgina, the fanatics. Every Fist seemed to have them: people who believed utterly in the Kore and its right to dismember, torture and pillage for its own good. Filius was a dull, balding young man with snake eyes and Malevorn couldn't stand him, but Virgina was another matter. She'd taken that name when she'd joined the Inquisition, ostentatiously vowing to remain chaste in the service of Kore. Such vows were rare—magi bloodlines were valuable—but it was her right. She was a pure-blood like Filius, Dranid, and Malevorn, and used her gnosis with vicious efficiency, and she knew her way around a sword. Her face was that of an angel; her hair was a halo of gold, but her single-minded devotion drained all femininity from her. Something perverse in Malevorn wished to ruin her vow, though not from desire. He just resented perfection that wasn't his own.

Inquisitor Vordan made an abrupt gesture with his thumb, dismissing Malevorn peremptorily. "We must discuss the mission, my lord," he said to Adamus, who made a small, almost apologetic duck of the head and allowed Vordan to draw him away.

Dominic accosted Malevorn immediately. "What did he say, Mal? Did he say why we're here?" Dominic was from the country, near the Hollenia border, and it colored his speech, his slow way of talking, and his rolling gait, not to mention his simplistic worldview. Sometimes it made Malevorn want to slap him, but he put up with it. It was good to have someone at his back, because there were plenty here who'd stick the knife in, given half a chance. Inquisitorial Fists were supposed to be bands of brothers, but he'd quickly learned that they were as vicious as any gang of thieves.

"We spoke of the governor."

"Belonius Vult," Dominic exclaimed. The whole Fist was listening, hanging on every word. They knew that they were being sent to question someone, and that their Fist had been specifically chosen; anything else was pure conjecture.

"Vult's only a half-blood," Filius sneered. "I'm amazed he has the wit for the role." Filius judged people's worth purely by their bloodlines and devotion to Kore; Malevorn, pure-blood though he was, knew there was much, much more to furthering oneself than that. *Thank Kore!*

The windship descended upon the mooring towers like a great bird of prey. Ropes snaked through the air and bound the vessel and it quivered and jerked to a halt like some insect snared in a web. As they gathered their belongings and prepared to disembark, Brother Jonas, who resented him most, made a cocksucker gesture at him, flicking his eyes between him and the Crozier.

Malevorn eyeballed him back stonily.

<Hope you like the taste of semen,> Jonas sent.

<Why, do you?>

Jonas made a gobbling face, and he and Raine convulsed in silent mockery. No matter: they'd regret their little jokes when next they trained.

An officious little man who gave his name as Clement met them off the landing platform. Wringing his hands, he drew Inquisitor Vordan and Adamus Crozier aside. Malevorn let his eyes trail over the city basking in the cool sunshine. This high up, even the summer days were chilly if the wind was blowing off the mountains.

Norostein . . . Names and faces came back to him, the boys of Turm Zauberin mostly: *Francis Dorobon and Seth Korion. Gron Koll. Boron Funt. That imbecile Alaron Mercer and his lowlife friend Ramon Sensini. And the teachers: Fyrell and Yune and the rest. Principal Gavius.* Then his mind roved on to the tavern girls he'd screwed, and the Arcanum girls he'd had too. The two guardsmen he'd almost killed in a tavern fight. There'd been a few fun times, but mostly it'd been dourness, rain, and boredom. He'd hoped to never see it again.

They descended to the ground by a pulley-elevator and Brother Alain, a poor flyer, touched the ground reverently. The rest eyed Vordan, who was looking grim. There was no affection for their Commandant, but there was a certain justified fear: Lanfyr Vordan was known for executing Acolytes who failed him in the field.

"Gather," Vordan growled, before making a grudging gesture toward Adamus Crozier. "The Crozier will address you." Clearly having a churchman installed above him for this mission rankled.

Adamus inclined his head in acknowledgment. "Hearken. This is the situation: last month, Governor Vult was on a diplomatic mission in Hebusalim when he sensed an attack on the security wards of his offices here in Norostein. He immediately returned here to hunt the perpetrators."

Malevorn raised an eyebrow, wondering how the governor's domestic security outweighed his ambassadorial duties.

"When he returned, he sought the thieves," Adamus went on, "but he did not discuss the theft widely. Master Clement here tells us that only three others knew fully what was going on. The Watch were not involved in the hunt."

The Acolytes looked at each other, all wondering the same thing: what had been stolen that the governor would not use the full resources of his office to recover? *Something illegal, obviously.* Malevorn glanced about him, saw Filius and Raine draw the same conclusion. The rest just looked puzzled. Conspiracy required a certain type of mind.

"Subsequently," Adamus continued, "a midnight skirmish began in the mercantile quarter, which split into two separate chases: one south to the mountains and the other north to Lake Tucerle. There was fighting at the lake and the Watch got involved, but the only bodies found were several construct creatures, and one young Council aide." Adamus looked at Malevorn. "The aide was one Gron Koll."

Malevorn blinked. *Gron Koll? Dead?* An acne-ridden face flashed before his eyes. Gron Koll had been a loathsome toad, but his cruel imagination had been amusing. That someone might murder him was not entirely unexpected. *Is this why I'm here: because I knew Koll?*

"The other pursuit involved the governor himself. Clement only learned of it the next morning, when the watch captain took a detachment south into the foothills and returned with the governor as his captive. He also brought back two more bodies: a councilman called Eli Besko and a pilot-mage named Olyd Krussyn. Whoever they were pursuing appears to have escaped."

Malevorn recalled Grand-Magister Besko—he'd been senior in the council. Fat, obsequious, ambitious—and one of Vult's. He'd never heard of Krussyn.

"This brings us to the crucial point: we were assigned this mission three days ago, when word finally reached Pallas of these events. At that time, the governor was in prison, awaiting our arrival and questioning. But two days ago, while we were still in the air, someone went into his cell and murdered him."

Kore's Blood! Vult's dead?

Everyone stiffened, and their focus intensified. Virgina and Filius ostentatiously crossed their Sacred Heart badges.

"The last man believed to have seen Belonius Vult alive was Jeris Muhren, the Watch Captain. He has since left the city." Adamus glanced at Vordan. "He is our chief suspect."

Malevorn recalled Muhren: a highhanded prick he'd clashed with sometimes while out drinking. Muhren was a Revolt veteran who'd probably hated Vult's guts since Lukhazan.

"There is another man missing who is also probably involved," Adamus continued. This time his look at Malevorn was even more pointed. "His name is Darius Fyrell. You know him also, Brother Malevorn?"

Fyrell too? Incredible! "I do, my lord Crozier," he said aloud. "He was a teacher at Turm Zauberin."

"And a young man Vult had been observing is also missing. Clement knows the name, but not the reason. Alaron Mercer."

Alaron Mercer. Malevorn almost choked. Earnest, naïve, obstreperous, self-righteous, pig-ignorant Alaron fucking Mercer, the boy he'd relentlessly pummeled and pounded through seven years of the Arcanum. A quarter-blood scum who'd never known his place. The last he'd seen of him was being dragged screaming from the graduation hall, condemned as a failed mage: a fate Mercer so richly deserved that Malevorn'd felt like celebrating for days afterward.

"Mercer is an imbecile, my lord. This type of intrigue is beyond his ken." *Tying his own laces is beyond Mercer's ken.* "It must be coincidence."

"Keep an open mind," Vordan admonished him. "We have no preconceptions here." Malevorn ducked his head. Vordan looked about the circle. "We will commence our questioning of those involved. Firstly, to the Governor's Palace. After that, we shall see." He glanced at Adamus. "With your permission, my lord?"

"Proceed." Adamus Crozier licked his lips, and raised a finger. "There is something important at stake here. A man like Jeris Muhren does not commit murder for anything as petty as revenge. He was Watch Captain for almost a decade."

Horses were waiting, saddled and ready. Malevorn shouldered Seldon away from a fiery-looking chestnut stallion, quelled its disquiet with animism-gnosis, and swung himself onto it. As Vordan pushed his own mount into a trot, the Fist fell in behind him, jostling for position.

The Governor's Palace dominated the central plaza of the city, the focal point from which the upper town radiated. Once it had been the dwelling of the King of Noros, but he now resided in a far smaller manor two blocks away. The Fist rode into the plaza and fanned out, driving frightened citizens from their path. Clement led them to where the other officials waited on the stairs, their faces apprehensive. Inquisitors had rights to question that even lords did not, and license to punish heresy wherever they found it. And as the Acolytes were discovering, heresy was wherever you wanted it to be.

Malevorn had graduated from Turm Zauberin last November as a gold-star trance-mage. He could have chosen any career at all, and he had been courted by absolutely everyone, from the Pallas Guard to the Kirkegarde, from the Legions to private mercenary companies. One middle-aged pure-blood heiress topped the military bid, offering a life of indolence and debauchery, provided he married her and got her with child. But she could not give him what he wanted above all: a way to restore his family to the uttermost heights of the empire. His father had been Supreme General of Rondelmar until the Noros general Leroi Robler had humbled him, humiliated him, and driven him to suicide.

While the military might eventually have given Malevorn some prominent role, that would take decades. Only one institution could get him to the top fast enough to suit his ambition: the Inquisition. They only took the best, at *everything*—fighting, gnosis . . . and intrigue. They needed minds cruel and cold enough to cut through lies and blasphemies and skewer heretics before their venom spread. In the courts of law, the Inquisition outranked the Crown. He might have to go without some status and creature comforts for a few years, but should he excel, in a few years he would be supping with governors and kings.

And should I not excel, I'll have a knife in my back, put there by one of my so-called "Brothers." He glanced at the angel face of Virgina, climbing the stairs alongside him. *Or one of my "Sisters".*

The cloud of officials hovered about the Inquisitor and the Crozier, fluttering like anxious butterflies. As they entered the foyer, Vordan beckoned his seniors, Alain and Dranid, to follow him to the dungeons, along with the Crozier. Apparently the governor's body still lay as it had been found. Malevorn would have liked to see it, but Vordan abruptly turned on him. "You know people here, Brother Malevorn? Speak to them." He was left alone with Dominic and a suddenly deflated crowd of minor functionaries. *Humans: why would I know them?* All the magi had gone east to Pontus. He glanced about, already bored, until he saw Gina Weber.

Ah, now then . . .

He put a hand on Dominic's shoulder. "Stay with this lot," he whispered in his friend's ear. "Ask about Koll's death. And Fyrell."

"But—" Dominic followed his gaze to the blond girl in the corner who was obviously already transfixed by Malevorn's face. "Oh." His face fell.

Poor Dom: you want me to be perfect, but I'm not.

"Miss Weber," he said, striding through the irritating fug of officials, letting his smile transfix her. Her face swelled with apprehension and pleasure.

He'd fucked her once, three years ago, when he'd found out she was betrothed to Alaron Mercer. He'd only done it to spite Mercer; there was little about her that excited him. She was slightly dumpy, too pallid, overly prim. But she'd genuinely believed his lines—she really thought he'd loved her. She'd cried as he penetrated her, and bled like a good virgin. She probably still dreamed of it.

"Malevorn?" Her hand went to her mouth. Her eyes took in his Inquisition badge. "You're here," she said lamely.

"I am indeed. And delighted to see a familiar face." He bent over her hand, noticing the engagement ring. Betrothed, but not yet wed. And Mercer was missing. This might be more amusing than he'd thought. "Is there somewhere we can talk?" He didn't let go of her hand.

"But . . ." She looked about uncertainly. Every pair of eyes in the room seemed to be on them both.

"Clearly I can't question you in front of everyone."

Her jaw dropped. "But . . . *question*?" She visibly gulped.

"You're engaged to a fugitive," he reminded her. The bovine bitch actually looked puzzled. "Your fiancé is missing . . ."

"He is?"

She's even dimmer than I remember. "I'm told Alaron Mercer is involved in this case, and that he's missing." He took her arm, and guided her firmly toward the nearest office. "Where has he gone?"

"But—" She looked up at him, her lower lip trembling. "I'm not engaged to him anymore. Father broke it off after . . . you know."

Malevorn felt himself smiling. Of course they would sever any connection to a failed mage. Mercer must've just *died* inside. *Magnificent.* He seized the door handle, jerked it open. A secretary of some sort looked up, his mouth falling open. An ornate door lay beyond: obviously the office of someone important. He pulled Gina Weber toward it. "You," he told the secretary, "out!"

He had the girl inside the next office before she could squeak again. It was empty. He locked the door behind him with a gesture. "A lucky escape for you," he told her. "Mercer's in trouble now."

"I know," she said, still apprehensive. He stroked her shoulder, and the stupid bitch took it as a sign that she was safe and sagged a little. "Someone broke into the governor's offices. I saw Alaron the day before, but I'm sure he couldn't have done it."

Mercer was here the day before the break-in? Great Kore, is he involved after all? "Tell me about it," he told her, touching her reassuringly, nonthreateningly, all the while working at her gnostic defense with Mesmeric gnosis, allaying her wariness and breaking down her resistance to what was to come.

Gina looked up at him. "Your friend Gron Koll was here. He had a job as an aide to the governor. The night of the break-in the house staff found him drunk in a downstairs lounge." Her face was pale. "The weird thing is, they said that they'd thought he was with *me*." Her voice rose with indignation. "I was never here that night."

Someone disguised themselves as you to get in and to nail Koll. Fancy. He smiled down at her, stroked her arm gently. She was a little fleshy for his tastes, but her bosom was generous. He looked into her eyes, fishing for that return spark. *Remember, Gina? I wrote you secret poems and letters, then climbed in your window and took your precious virginity. Do you remember how I sank into your soft arms?*

She did.

He worked her slowly backward toward the desk as he talked, talking to distract her from his sly movement. "This is so valuable," he told her. "The Inquisitor will be delighted. You must tell me all you know. There will certainly be a reward." *Oh yes, there will.*

Her breath was coming in rapid, shallow bursts. Her pupils were huge as he stroked her cheek. "It is a shame circumstances have kept us apart," he said, interrupting her blathering about her fiancé. She was one of those woman magi whose skills and temperament did not suit the frontline, or anywhere close to it. She was only good for one thing: breeding. He gently turned her so he'd not have to look at her. Even she realized what he was doing now, and surrendered to it. Pathetic . . . but his cock hardened.

She looked backward and up at him. "I didn't think I pleased you," she said, her voice tremulous. "You stopped writing, after that one night . . ." He could feel her whole body quivering to her heartbeat.

"The Principal found out," he lied. He leaned over and kissed her nape. She tasted of fear, but she was utterly passive, already capitulating. As he slowly unbuttoned the back of her dress, she sighed needily. He let the shift slide down her body while he cupped her ample breasts and began to massage them, pinching her engorged nipples, working them hard. She gasped, somewhere between pleasure and pain and need. He could smell her wetness.

He pushed her dress and petticoat over her hips, baring her white buttocks. She tried to turn and face him, but he kept her turned away. While his left hand toyed with her breasts, his right slid down her back and stroked her, sliding his fingers down the crack of her buttocks, teasing her anus, then sliding them into the wet depths of her quim. She emitted a soft, surrendering sigh, then moaned, trying to squirm about and seat herself on the desk, but he kept her turned away. *Your face is the least pleasing part of you.* He worked her with his fingers, increasingly roughly, while unfastening his own belt and wrenching his pants down over his rigid tool. His scabbard clattered to the floor as he stepped out of his clothes and bent her over the desk.

"Let me face you," she pleaded. He tightened the grip of his hands on her breast, pinned her and then pushed her down, face flat to the desk. "Mal, I don't like—"

Someone knocked at the door. "Malevorn?" Dominic called.

"Two minutes," he called, positioning his full, rigid cock in the cleft of her buttocks, right against her puckered anus. She twisted her neck, her face pleading, and it excited him in a way her willingness never could have. He shoved himself all the way in as she howled silently, her body going rigid. He gripped her hips and without gentleness began to pump himself into her. Skin slapped skin as she gasped in agony. He felt the animal inside him, let it give voice, grunting exultantly as he rammed himself deeper and deeper. He came with a bellow, a molten lava-flow of his seed spurting into her as she cried in pain, then he held her there, transfixed on his shaft, his whole body caught up in the rapture of the moment, rigid and shaking. It felt like aeons of sheer bliss.

Eventually the sound of knocking intruded again.

"Fuck off, Dom," he shouted.

"Vordan's back. He's looking for you!"

He heard himself growl, then sanity returned. He braced himself, felt his legs shaking at the exquisite release, and pulled himself out of her. Her legs gave way and she slid to the floor.

"Well, it has been lovely to see you, Gina," he smirked. *Insipid cow. You got what you deserved.*

He dressed quickly and left her coiled in a fetal huddle on the office floor, her face hidden, her shoulders heaving.

Dominic glanced past him when he opened the door, then looked at him in consternation. "Is she all right?"

"Sure. She's just recovering from her big moment." He winked, and pulled the door shut behind him. "Let's go and find our beloved leader."

The questioning of the council people was initially fruitless. A servant had glimpsed Muhren coming and going, but though Vordan entered the man's mind and ripped it apart, leaving him a semi-sane wreck, there was nothing further to learn. It seemed clear that Jeris Muhren was the murderer.

Malevorn reported his little findings concerning the break-in directly to Adamus Crozier. He'd be damned if he'd let Vordan take what he'd learned without giving credit. The Crozier was pleased, and quashed half-hearted complaints by Clement about an "alleged incident with the Weber girl."

See, Gina? I'm untouchable now.

The breakthrough came the next day. Malevorn and Dominic were in Lower Town, on the shores of the lake, seeking the site of the conflict that had happened there a week or so before. They found more than expected.

A roped-off piece of grass and stonework contained the burned and mutilated remains of five construct creatures, ghastly things the size of ponies that were part-scorpion, part-wolf. Malevorn recognized them at once: Darius Fyrell had once shown them off to his pupils.

Where are you, Fyrell?

Perhaps he projected the thought; perhaps it was just coincidence, but whatever it was, it triggered something unexpected. A shape rose from the water, fifty feet away. The onlookers gasped, and someone screamed. He felt a thrill of fear before a rasping mental voice shouted into his skull, *<Andevarion? Help me!>*

It was Darius Fyrell, or what was left of him. He collapsed at the water's edge as the crowd backed away.

The Magister looked like an animated corpse. His hair and half the skin on his face were burned away. Nothing of his clothes remained except for a scorched undergarment about his groin. His right arm was a stump that finished at the elbow; his biceps had been burned or carved away to the bone. His left leg was so twisted he could barely stand.

Malevorn ran toward him. "Magister!"

<The Scytale!> Fyrell shouted into his mind. *<Tesla Anborn has the Scytale!>* Then he collapsed.

Malevorn barely noticed. His mind was still reeling. *Does he mean the Scytale of Corineus?*

Adamus Crozier and Inquisitor Vordan shut themselves in a dark room with Fyrell's remains for a full night while the Acolytes waited outside, sleeping if they could. Dominic, blithe and complacent under Malevorn's protection, was one of the sleepers. He hadn't heard the words Fyrell had blared into Malevorn's mind. But Malevorn never slept a wink.

Tesla Anborn has the Scytale of Corineus . . .

He thought through every scenario he could imagine but still he could find no way that the greatest treasure of the magi could ever be in the hands of Alaron Mercer's blind wreck of a mother. It was simply not possible.

Yet when Vordan and Adamus emerged from the cell, their faces were hollow-eyed and disbelieving. They called the Fist together, excluding any locals. "Hearken," Vordan croaked, and then he fell mute, shaking his head. That in itself told Malevorn that he'd not misheard Fyrell.

"Jeris Muhren. Tesla Anborn. Alaron Mercer. Cymbellea di Regia." Adamus reeled off the short list of names in a tired voice. "There may be others but they are not identified." He looked around the circle of Acolytes. "They must be found."

Malevorn added two more names. *Ramon Sensini. Vann Mercer.* He wondered if Fyrell had told Adamus that Malevorn now knew what it was they sought. He raised a tentative hand. "My lord, is Magister Fyrell . . . ?" He let his voice trail away.

"Unfortunately, Magister Fyrell died under questioning," Vordan said. "Several times."

Jonas laughed aloud, then shut up fast as Vordan ran his eye over him.

It took another day to determine that Tesla Anborn had been cremated four days prior, not far from where Fyrell had been found. They ransacked the Mercer household, but Vannaton, the father, had allegedly left months before, and no one had seen Alaron since before the night of the incident. Next day, responding to a town crier promising rewards, a beggar claimed to have seen two men ride east from Hurring Gate five days ago. Adamus probed the man's recollections deeper, pulling an image from his mind that removed any doubt: it had been Jeris Muhren and Alaron Mercer. The process left the beggar with the intellect of a vegetable, saving them any need to pay the reward.

Adamus Crozier sought out Malevorn as they left the city next morning. "Brother Malevorn, you know these people. What is your affinity to Clairvoyance?"

Malevorn hung his head. "My lord, Clairvoyance is not a Study I have any affinity for."

Adamus looked disappointed, but accepted this philosophically. "Brother Dranid has met Jeris Muhren, so he can lead the scrying. But we cannot afford to let them know we are hunting them, lest they go to earth. First we will hunt them by other means." He smiled with some relish. "Your venators await us outside the city."

Malevorn's spirits lifted. The day he joined the Inquisition, he'd been assigned his own construct: a venator created by Animagi. The reptile had huge featherless wings and was large enough to take a saddled rider and intelligent enough to be tamed. The constructs had been bred by the Pallas magi for the Church and the legions. Riding them was a supreme joy. "I cannot wait," he admitted, enthusiasm getting the better of his normal poise. The Crozier smiled at that.

That afternoon, as the Inquisitor Fist erupted from the forests north of Norostein on winged beasts, Malevorn roared with exhilaration. The hunt was on, and the Scytale of Corineus was the prize!

2

IDENTITY AND POSSESSION

Scarabs

There is a technique I have developed, which involves transference of the intellect from the initial body to another host. It is not a pleasant technique, but it is one that can save the soul when all is lost for the body. I have found after much testing that a large carapaced insect is the ideal vehicle for this transfer, being robust enough to survive the demise of the body and escape, and with a neatly compartmented mind able to hold the memories and self of the mage for a short time, until a new host is found. The Dhassan scarab is ideal, though the Pontic dung-beetle is a useful equivalent in Yuros.

EDIS HULDIN, NECROMANCER,
ORDO COSTRUO COLLEGIATE, PONTUS

One of the reasons necromancers are as hard to kill as cockroaches is that they turn into one when they die.

BRYDI TEESDOTTER,
ARCANUM OF SAINT TERASSA, HOLLENIA

Brochena, Javon, on the continent of Antiopia
Rajab (Julsep) 928
1st month of the Moontide

I'm only dreaming, Cera Nesti told herself. *This is not real. I will wake from this.*

But it felt real: an endless maze of corridors, dank stone walls dripping with a pus-like sticky fluid, and everywhere the stench of decay. Massive cobwebs wafted in the chill breeze, constantly shifting as she sought a way out. Spiders as big as hands crawled along the ceiling above her, their bulbous clusters of eyes following her every move—and they were just the babies. Their mother was somewhere, just out of sight, a massive thing, larger than a horse, that barely managed to squeeze through the narrow passages.

There was light ahead, and something chittering behind her. Cera had to keep moving; if she stopped, the spiders would drop and spin a web about her, and then she'd be nothing but meat for Mother Spider.

She hurried forward, seeking the light, praying it was the way out, but it was just another chamber, the center of the earthen floor dug up like a waiting grave. With shaking hands, her legs trembling, she approached the hole, her hand going to her mouth as its contents were gradually revealed.

Elena Anborn lay there, her throat cut, blood staining her white shift. Her eyes were empty, her skin like alabaster. There was something big and black crawling from her mouth.

Cera stared, swallowing a sob. *I did this. I killed her. I loved her and I killed her.*

Then Elena's eyes suddenly flickered into life. They bore through Cera's skull, accusing her, condemning her. *Betrayer!*

Her hand came up and she pointed—not at Cera, though it felt to the young woman as if a finger speared her chest. Elena's finger pointed straight up, and her eyes were mute with horror and vindication.

Cera looked up, and then she really did scream. Timori, her precious little Timori, hung bound in spider-silk, crying, struggling, helpless. She reached for him instinctively, though he was far from her reach.

Then the darkness of the ceiling above him moved and light glistened on dark, mottled carapaces. Spindly black legs waved and myriad eyes stared down at her. Digestive fluids poured from a maw full of toothy hooks. Mother Spider filled the ceiling.

Cera jerked left and right, but the doors were gone. Something gripped her arm, she screamed again, and—

—*woke.*

"My lady! My lady! Please, wake up!"

Cera stared blankly into Tarita's frightened eyes. The tiny Jhafi girl clutched her arm, right there, but still Cera could half-see that hideous chamber. When she registered the pewter cup her maid was holding out, she snatched it and tipped it over her own face. Water splashed down her neck and chest, wetting her sheets and pillow, though they were already sweat-soaked and tangled about her like thick cords of spider web.

She dropped the cup, seized Tarita, and hugged her.

Two weeks ago she had sacrificed Elena to save Timori and herself. Two weeks of this: the living world and the dream world blending and blurring until sometimes she couldn't tell which was real. Both were nightmares; both were surreal.

I betrayed my people to save them—to save Timi.

To save them, I had to sacrifice Elena. She was supposed to die, but she's still alive, walking around this palace as if nothing happened. Except it's not her at all: Gyle says that Rutt Sordell now inhabits Elena's body.

These magi are monsters.

"What time is it, Tarita?"

"The first bell just chimed," the little maid replied. She was only fifteen, though she'd seen much—more than Cera, of certain things. "Shall I open the curtains?"

"Please." Perhaps the sunshine would burn away the afterimages of Mother Spider that kept invading her vision. She sniffed, wrinkled her nose. Her bedclothes smelled of sweat. "I need a bath." *I am Queen-Regent. I have to get up. I have to face the day.*

Tarita pulled open the curtains, then went to order the bath. Cera sat up slowly, plucking at the nightdress that clung to her skin. The mirror on the far wall reflected her: tangled black hair falling past her shoulders. A long, strong face, serious and severe, more handsome than pretty. Normally olive-brown skin growing pale from too much time spent in shadows. She'd ventured outside the palace only once these past two weeks, since *it* happened, and that was to bury her sister in a private ceremony. There had been no mourning period, no public funeral, for Solinde had been branded a traitor for aiding the Gorgio family in their attempted coup last year. Cera knew the accusation to be false, but she also knew that the real Solinde had been slain during the coup and replaced with a magi-shapeshifter called Coin. It was Coin they had buried, and of course she could tell no one. Who knew where the real Solinde lay?

She froze suddenly at a tiny telltale sound and her eyes flashed to the interior wall where a panel began to slide open and black spider legs waggled through. Her hand went to her mouth as the legs became fingers, fingers in a black leather glove that slid the panel fully open.

A man stepped through.

Her hands went protectively to her breasts as she flinched.

"Get up," the man told her in his flat, terse voice. "You have work to do." He locked her bedroom door, then walked to the window.

She cringed. "Yes, Magister Gyle." She pulled a sheet about her and got out of bed.

Gurvon Gyle's eyes roamed the room as they always did, noticing changes, anything different, out of place. Then his eyes came back to her and he exhaled impatiently. "Girl, I have no interest in your body. Dress, and listen."

She dressed behind a screen nevertheless, pulling on undergarments, then a plain shift, enough to preserve some decorum until she bathed.

Gyle's eyes weighed her as she stood silent before him. "You're not sleeping," he said eventually. "I send you sleeping drafts and you do not take them: why?"

"I don't like them." *Because if I take your potions, I can't wake and Mother Spider catches me.*

His eyes rolled. "That's up to you, but you look awful. People are talking."

She hung her head. *If I can't sleep it's because of you, and what you persuaded me to do.*

Over and over she asked herself: *could I have done differently?* And the answer was always: *of course.* But what she had done, faced with hidden enemies whose reach and power seemed immeasurable, was to betray her own protector, Elena, in return for the promise that she and more importantly, her younger brother Timori, the rightful king, be allowed to live. It had been hard to agree to such a thing, after all Elena had done for her. To then have to watch it unfold had been utterly ghastly.

Gyle reached out, and though she flinched from his touch, he lifted her chin and looked into her eyes. "Listen, Cera, we've pretended you're ill long enough. The world rolls on, and there are things that must now happen to preserve what you have gained."

Gained? What have I gained?

"You've saved your life," Gyle reminded her, in that creepy way he had of answering her unspoken thoughts if she didn't guard them. "You've saved Timori's life. You've saved House Nesti from extinction. You have the pledge of Francis Dorobon that your family's soldiery will be permitted to live; there will be no purge. You've saved Javon from being a target for the Crusader armies. You have gained much."

She jerked her chin from his grip and stepped back a pace, out of his reach. "Those aren't gains, just controlled losses."

He smiled wryly. "Call it what you will. Cera, today your Inner Council meets. You must be there to ensure the next steps take place."

"Where will you be?"

"Watching. Listening. Rutt Sordell will be beside you. He will steer the conversation as needed."

She shuddered. *Rutt Sordell:* Gyle's right-hand man, now in possession of Elena Anborn's body by some evil of the gnosis. When

Gyle had first proposed his bargain, he'd said that Elena would die, quickly and mercifully, but he'd lied. Instead, Gyle's former lover and then enemy had been battered half to death before having her throat cut, only to then be saved and *inhabited* by Sordell. How or why, Cera could not comprehend. She knew only that it was an atrocity.

"Cera," Gyle said, in the tones a tired parent might use with a stupid child, "our bargain is far from fulfilled. House Nesti has clung to power here in Javon through aligning itself with the majority Jhafi and their desire to join the shihad. But that is madness: the shihad will be destroyed. Rondian legions are invincible, and there are two legions—ten thousand men—coming here inside a month. Each legion will have fifteen magi and several units of construct cavalry—have you ever seen a construct, girl?" He shook his head. "Well, you will, very soon."

"My people will fight," she whispered.

"No, they must not, not unless you wish to see them exterminated. You must arrange capitulation. Only then, when you've handed over this kingdom intact to Francis Dorobon, will you have fulfilled what we agreed."

"But I . . . you—"

"You agreed, girl, to step aside and let me save your people. That does not mean that you no longer have a role. Last year, when you were forced to pick up the crown, you became a beacon for your people: for both Rimoni and Jhafi. If you show them a direction, they will take it."

"You don't understand. It's not like that, I don't have that influence, I'm just a girl," she responded, aware she was babbling like a child but unable to stop.

"You underestimate yourself, Cera. By defeating the Gorgio last year, you have become Javon's banner. Only you can unite them right now."

She glared at him. "I am nothing anymore."

He stepped closer, moving too fast, and caught her shoulders. "Cera, listen to me: you need to stay calm, and see this through. There is no room for dissent anymore. If you cannot convince your

Inner Council that all is well, I'm going to take a hand, and I will not be gentle." His gray eyes measured her, his face hard, matter-of-fact. She felt helpless in his grip.

The Jhafi are right: these magi are demons. They are afreet, pale-skinned maggots from Shaitan's living corpse. There was only ever one good mage: and I had her killed—no, worse: possessed.

She cringed as Gyle reached out and brushed a tear from her right eye. "Courage, girl. The lives of your royal counselors and your entire people depend on you holding your nerve."

Brochena Palace was a maze of passages. There were many more than most knew of, tiny walkways behind false walls, hidden niches and crawl spaces, where someone with skill and knowledge could creep unseen and learn all that was hidden.

Gurvon Gyle slipped along the passage that ran parallel to the Council Chamber, to the section of the wall with the observation hole. He'd enhanced it, removing a brick, then creating the illusion that it was still there. No childish false eyes or easily detectable holes for him. The only risk was a cleaner poking their broom through, but he stopped it up with a real brick when he wasn't using it.

Now he pulled the brick aside and peered through, just as God-speaker Acmed finished the Mantra of Family, which enabled the women to forsake their bekira-shrouds and speak openly. Cera and Elena pulled off the shapeless black cloaks and the meeting came to order. Gyle's view was from behind one row of counselors, with Cera seated to his left, furthest from the door. Elena Anborn sat on her right hand—except it wasn't Elena, of course: it was Rutt Sordell. Elena's face was hard for him to look at: she seemed subtly *wrong*, to one who knew her so well. But no one else noticed. The counselors had been told of a failed attempt on Cera's life. Solinde had died, and Lorenzo di Kestria, but Cera and Elena had survived and slain the attacker. That was all they needed to know

The others about the table were familiar faces: the faithful Nesti retainers, promoted by Olfuss to the royal bureaucracy when he became king: jovial Master of the Purse Pita Rosco, his bald pate gleaming in the sunlight that was pouring through the high windows. His spiritual opposite, sour old Luigi Ginovisi, the Master of Revenues. Comte Piero Inveglio, the merchant nobleman whose voice tended to carry the most weight. Conservative, bitter Seir Luca Conti, the grizzled knight who led the Nesti soldiery and, by extension, the armies of Javon.

Opposite the Nesti loyalists were the Brochena faction: Don Francesco Perdonello, the tall, high-browed Chancellor, head of the bureaucracy, and two of his departmental heads who seldom spoke except to confirm Perdonello's utterances. Signor Ivan Prato, the young Sollan drui whom Cera preferred to the older, more highly ranked clergy, and of course the pricklish Godspeaker Acmed al-Istan, representing the Amteh Faith, completed the roster.

There was no Lorenzo di Kestria, who was dead, and his role as head of the Queen's Guard had not yet been filled. Also missing was the urbane Harshal ali-Assam, who had been sent out some months ago to negotiate a deal with the Harkun nomads infesting the southeastern deserts of Javon.

"My lords, welcome. I apologize for the illness which has incapacitated me these past two weeks. But I am well again, and there is much to do." Cera's voice carried clearly to him. Over the past year she'd learned how to run a meeting, dominating rooms of men many years her senior—an unexpected development, thrust upon her when Gyle had murdered her father and mother. *And yet here we are, working together.*

"Thank you for your condolences for the death of Solinde. I know that she shamed the family name last year, but she was my sister, and Timori and I loved her." Cera paused, swallowing. "I see from the minutes of the last meeting that you voted a message of condolence to the di Kestria family for the loss of Lorenzo, their youngest son. He was Commander of my guards, and much loved. I endorse that message of sorrow."

She barely sounds like a girl of almost nineteen, Gyle reflected. *She is more queenly than Mater-Imperia herself, in truth.* He could sense Elena's hand in her development. Elena and Cera had grown close, especially after the Gorgio coup and the death of Olfuss. *She must become my tool now.*

"What happened that night, Princessa?" Pita Rosco asked gently. "There are so many rumors, but you and Elena were right there, and you have said little. Did Gurvon Gyle come? Who was the Rondian you slew?"

Elena spoke up—or rather, Rutt Sordell did. Gyle winced inwardly: Rutt Sordell was a powerful magus, but he was no actor, no mimic. The voice patterns sounded wrong to him, and it wasn't just the recent throat wound that had left Elena's voice deeper and rasping. "Gyle wasn't there. The man was an Inquisitor of Pallas. We were questioning Solinde when he appeared. He slew di Kestria and Solinde before I could neutralize him."

Elena doesn't speak like that. She doesn't use words like "neutralize." And she doesn't call Lorenzo "di Kestria": they were lovers, *for Kore's sake!* Gyle ground his teeth. *Rutt and I need to talk again.*

Cera stepped into the ensuing silence as the men around the table shared uncomfortable glances. "Really, gentlemen, I don't want to talk about this, and there is much else we must focus on."

Well done, girl.

Cera led them away into less sensitive topics: the treasury (depleted but improving), the Harkun issue (awaiting word from Harshal ali-Assam), and the military (drilling, recruiting, morale and numbers up as they prepared to march on Hytel). Rutt-Elena kept his mouth shut, thankfully.

Inevitably the talk turned to the shihad. "There is massive movement of refugees from Dhassa and the Hebb Valley," Comte Inveglio reported. "Our traders report that the roads are choked. The common people are trying to run to wherever they think the Crusaders will not go. Rich men are carrying all they own in huge caravans while the poor walk empty-handed from the fields. Whole families are displaced, and it will get worse. Many are seeking refuge here in Javon. The gates of the Krak are under siege."

"We should open those gates," Godspeaker Acmed interjected. "It is our duty to the shihad."

"Our duty is to our own people," Seir Luca Conti growled. "Besides, we can't feed a million Dhassans."

"The treasury could not afford it," chorused Pita Rosco and Luigi Ginovisi, in rare agreement.

"We have a duty as human beings to aid them," Acmed maintained, sticking out his bearded chin belligerently.

To Gyle's surprise the drui Prato weighed in on the Godspeaker's side. "They are desperate, my lady," he said, addressing Cera directly. "Homeless, penniless, lambs to the slaughter unless we aid them. How can we look away and call ourselves children of God? Of any God," he added with a nod to the Godspeaker.

Gyle listened impatiently as the discussion was sidetracked onto this question, one he'd not anticipated. *I don't give a fuck whether you feed the damn refugees or not. You'd be crazy to let them in, and Francis Dorobon will let them starve once he gains power anyway: Move on!*

Eventually Cera decided that she would send a messenger to Sultan Salim of Kesh—her prospective husband—and ask for advice. *May as well play that card while you still hold it*, Gyle thought wryly. *Anyway, get to the real issue . . .*

Cera guided the discussion to the matter he was waiting for: the march on Hytel. "As you know, gentlemen, earlier this year we came to agreement that we would join the shihad, on our own terms. Salim agreed. In return for my hand in marriage once the Moontide is over, he allowed us to choose our actions, rather than place our armies at his disposal to fight the Rondians." The men all nodded, mostly unhappily, for only Acmed was Amteh, and the rest profoundly disliked the idea of their Princessa marrying the Sultan of Kesh, for any number of reasons. "We agreed that the target of our shihad will initially be Hytel. It is the home of the Rondian sympathizers: our enemies, the Gorgio."

Gyle nodded to himself. The remnants of the Gorgio were now shut in Hytel under siege, their once powerful army severely reduced by the attrition of Jhafi raiders during a disastrous retreat north last year after Elena had turned the tables on them. Gyle had been among the Gorgio recently. The only reason Alfredo Gorgio hadn't surrendered was that the Dorobon were expected to accompany the Third Crusade and attempt to seize Javon once more.

"Our intelligence tells us that the Gorgio are preparing for the Dorobon to return," Cera told the meeting. "We have some detail of where and in what strength."

"What is your source?" Piero Inveglio asked.

"A good spymaster doesn't reveal their source," responded Cera quickly, a glance at Elena hinting it was her.

Good girl, well deflected. Gyle was the real source of that *false* intelligence.

"They are expecting a fleet of windships to land a single legion west of Hytel in the desert at the end of this month and march immediately to Hytel," Cera went on.

"Why only one legion?" Luca Conti wondered.

"Windships have a small capacity. The Empire cannot divert more from the main invasion force going into Hebusalim," Cera replied smoothly, just as Gyle had ordered her. "Only a third of a legion are expected in the first wave: less than two thousand men, and only half-a-dozen battle-magi at most. Those magi will be exhausted from the flight and their landing site has insufficient water."

Seir Luca frowned. "It seems foolish of them. Are they so stupid? Why would they not fly all the way to Hytel and land where they are secure?"

Silence him, Gyle urged silently.

"The Dorobon never bothered to learn about this kingdom," Rutt-Elena interrupted in a snarky voice. "They think all they have to do is arrive." Sordell had never learned to deal with debate civilly. Gyle winced again. *Can they sense that this is not Elena?* He thanked Kore that this was only a temporary situation. By month's end, the Dorobon would be here and he'd be able to move openly and finally find Rutt a new body to inhabit.

Seir Luca scowled, glanced sideways at Piero Inveglio and closed his mouth. No one else spoke.

"They will be vulnerable," Cera said, repeating what he'd told her to say. "Trapped in the desert, newly landed, their magi drained—we could field ten thousand Nesti, that's five to one odds, and crush the invasion before it's begun."

"What of the Gorgio?" Seir Luca asked. "They have as many men as us."

"Trapped in Hytel by the northern Jhafi tribes," Piero Inveglio replied briskly.

Acmed visibly brightened at this mention of his people's military prowess. "The northern tribes stand ready to aid you. Twenty thousand riders to ensure the victory," he growled.

It took time, but the men slowly began to nod. Gyle listened in silence as they first accepted the concept, and then moved on to the detail: logistics, supplies, transport, which units to field and who to put in charge. By then the deal was done, with just one thing left to throw in . . .

"I will accompany the army north," Cera told them in a firm voice.

"No!" protested the whole table.

"A battlefield is no place for a woman!" Seir Luca added. The rest exclaimed agreement. "You cannot, Princessa. Your place is here. We cannot afford to lose you if anything goes wrong."

"If I am to be seen as fit to fulfill the regency through this time of war, then I must be there. This is not a debating point, gentlemen," she said, slapping the table. "It is a decision." She glared about her, as if daring them to disagree. "Timori will be here, safe from danger." Gyle could sense the pang of guilt that accompanied those words: she knew Timori was anything but safe, and longed to say so. But she didn't.

The men grumbled and mumbled, but she got her way.

Well done, girl. You've put your head into the trap, just as instructed.

The meeting wrapped up, the men dispersing with much low conversation and no little shaking of the head. He strained to listen, heard the way they made excuses for her: "She's been unwell," "She's just lost her sister," "That night must have been awful for her." They had learned to love her during the past year; they could forgive a little erratic behavior.

Soon the room was empty except for Rutt-Elena. Gyle stared at "her" as she turned slowly, her eyes penetrating his illusion and focusing on the spy-hole. "She" pouted sullenly. "Well?"

Gyle inhaled, pulled a lever, shoved the panel of false wall aside and stepped into the chamber. Being so close to this woman made his stomach churn. Elena had been his lover for too much of his adult life for it not to feel profoundly wrong that she was now Rutt Sordell's meat-puppet.

"We got what we needed," he told Sordell, pulling up a chair and sitting, indicating that Sordell should do the same. He did, gracelessly. "Cera did well," Gyle observed, "but you were a damned liability."

Sordell made a sour face. "What do you mean?"

Gyle slapped the table. "Listen to yourself, Rutt. Does Elena ever speak as you do? No, is the answer. She's dry, but she's positive. And she doesn't slouch, she sits up straight. You walk like a man: Elena was like a cat. Whenever I see you move I'm amazed no one else realizes. Any trained mage could spot what's going on."

Sordell glowered at him. "Go to Hel, Gurvon. I'm a *man*, not a goddamn woman. You think I like this? It's driving me insane."

"You've got a body capable of the gnosis, Rutt," Gyle reminded him. "Would you rather be in a non-mage's body with no access to your powers? Or back as a scarab beetle, crawling around my pocket while your memory slowly fades away?"

"*No, of course I wouldn't, damn it!*" Sordell shouted, sounding nothing at all like Elena for all that it was her voice. Elena didn't raise her voice, she sharpened it, then cut you to ribbons. "But being in this body—in *her* Kore-bedamned body—is killing me. I'm going mad." He clutched his skull. "*She's inside my head!*"

"Then silence her," Gyle snapped. He clenched his fists. "You control her, not the other way around."

"I don't know how to confine her without harming myself," Sordell moaned. "You don't know what it's like, Gurv. She's inside me, day and night. She's inside my dreams. She's whispering to me wherever I go. She's like a parasite inside my skull."

Gyle looked heavenward. "For Kore's sake, Rutt, take control! It's just for another month, and then the Dorobon will be here. I've asked for a naïve young battle-mage to be assigned to us, a new host for you. Someone you'll fit like a glove. You can change bodies then, I promise you."

"You better deliver on that promise, Gurv," Sordell snarled. His eyes turned inward. "What will you do with her then?"

"Mater-Imperia wants her," Gyle replied. "But it will be my call, not hers." He was surprised by a sudden longing. *Perhaps, restored to herself . . . No.* He shook his head. *No, she'd never . . .*

Sordell's mouth rolled into a sneer, as if he'd read his thoughts. "Listen to you, the big man who thinks he can ignore what the Living Saint wants. Send her to Saint Lucia and move on, Gurvon. Elena was a bitch and you're better off without her."

Gyle inhaled, exhaled. He nodded slowly. "You're right, Rutt." He tried to ignore Elena's face and see through it to the soul of his trusted lieutenant. "One month, no more. Then you'll be free."

"I'll be counting the seconds," Sordell replied, his voice hollow. "I can't take much more of this."

Sometimes Elena dreamed of fleeing down pulsing corridors pursued by a chitinous sound, of scrabbling legs, too damned many legs, and a horrid, alien intellect that wanted to devour her: a scarab, called Rutt Sordell.

Mostly, though, she was awake—and the nightmare went on.

She watched from inside her own skull as Rutt Sordell walked *her* body up the stairs, toward the room where once she'd practiced her fighting skills. Bastido waited in the corner, but Sordell didn't use the fighting machine. Sordell never exercised. He just read, and drank, cast divination spells, and drank more, ate and drank and pissed away the hours.

One of the worst things was still being able to sense all that he did, but because of the fog that she dwelled in, each sensation was unexpected. Everything happened to her by surprise: tastes, smells, sounds, touch. They continuously shocked her, made her shriek inside. Though her sight felt impaired, as if everything and everyone were seen down a long tunnel of light, every sensation jabbed at her, as if she'd been skinned alive, then lowered into a nest of scorpions.

But the very worst thing was the simple truth that he, and not she, determined absolutely everything her body did. She could feel his presence, that ghastly scarab beetle, nested in a burrow in the roof of her mouth, behind her eyes, its feelers rooted deep in her brain, controlling everything. Its mere presence nauseated her, made her want to flee screaming into the darkness. It was not an option, however: this maze she ran through had no exit.

Only one thing kept her going: *knowing Sordell can hear me.* The Argundian had been a lazy, arrogant prick and she was damned if he was going to dwell in her body unchallenged.

Sordell walked her body past a guard, whose head turned to follow her as she passed.

<He's looking at you, Rutt,> she told him malevolently. She felt Sordell flinch and quicken his stride. *<He knows Lorenzo's dead and he's wondering if he's got a chance of filling his shoes.>*

<Shut up, Elena.>

<He's watching your tail right now, wondering how you'd like him to bend you over and—>

<Shut the fuck up!>

<He's wondering why you look like a woman but walk like a man. You can't act for shit, you know that?>

<Be silent!> They turned a corner and Sordell redoubled his pace, panting.

<Listen to you, you slob. Listen to your wheezing.> Sordell tried to blank her, but she wouldn't let him. *<You're ruining my body, Rutt. Why don't you try Bastido, eh?>* They reached the door to the practice room. She saw her fighting machine as Sordell glanced guiltily that way. *<Scared, are you? I used to fight Bastido on the fourth setting. You couldn't manage the second.>*

Sordell grasped a bottle from the table and swigged. Bad red wine. She gagged, he belched.

<Argundian pig.>

He drank some more.

<You're a coward, Rutt. You always were and you always will be.> He guzzled more wine. *<Shut your mouth, you bitch.>*

<I wish I could. But it's your mouth now. Your soft womanly mouth. Your womanly face. Your womanly body. Think you're going to come out of this experience unchanged? I doubt it.>

He bellowed aloud, "BE SILENT, DAMN YOU!" and downed more wine. Sordell groaned, rubbing his temple furiously. He finished the bottle and flung it against the wall, where it shattered and cascaded into the shards of glass already there. This scene had become an evening ritual. He clutched another bottle.

<*Did you see how Gurvon looks at you now?*>

<*He doesn't.*> Swig. Guzzle. Almost vomit. Groan and clutch the belly.

<*Sure he does. He was screwing me for most of our lives, Rutt. When he looks at you now, he doesn't even see your clothes. He's looking at my tits and wondering if you'd consent to a quick fuck for old time's sake.*>

"ARGHH!" Swallow, hurl. Sordell threw the bottle against a wall, watched it crash into tiny pieces, spraying wine everywhere. He wobbled to his feet, then everything swung and dropped. They both mewled in pain as their knees hit the stone floor. Sordell scrabbled beneath the table for the half-full bottle of Brician brandy he'd left there. Swallow: syrupy sweetness with a resounding punch. One shot, another, another. "SHUT UP, WOMAN!"

<*You're killing yourself, Rutt. Slow down. You're killing us both.*>

He vomited, then drank again, trying to wall her out with alcohol and blind Argundian stubbornness. She laughed at him, the bitter derision of a prisoner laughing at their captor, and kept jeering at him right up until the moment he slid sideways and hit the floor.

Everything went black.

But she was still conscious. Still *present*.

And free to think.

3

DOMUS COSTRUO

Souldrinkers (1)

Word came out of the East, that one of our brethren had found a way to unlock the potential within us. A woman called Sabele had inhaled the soul of a dying mage and gained the gnosis. So I tried it. I had nothing to lose: sooner or later someone was going to hand me over to you, for the "crime" of not gaining the gnosis when you did. Do I regret it? Not at all. At least I took a few of you bastards down with me.

NOTES FROM THE TRIAL OF JORGI HARLE,
DARK PATH MAGUS, PALACIA 488

The Souldrinkers—Dokken, Shadowmancers, Dark Path, whatever you call them—they are the secret evil that blights these lands. Harle was just one of many. We must root them out, every last one.

ARCH-PRELATE GEOVANNI, AT THE FIRST
INQUISITIONAL MOOT, PALLAS 491

Hebusalim, Dhassa, Antiopia
Rajab (Julsep) 928
1st month of the Moontide

Kazim Makani cut the air into a thousand slices, his blade a blur, his bare chest corded with taut muscle as he spun and twisted. Jamil liked to tell him that he was a *beast*, primal, a wild thing. But he felt more caged than free.

It was dusk in Hebusalim and he was in an abandoned dog-fighting pit, near an old Dom-al'Ahm. The Godsingers were chanting, summoning the faithful to their knees, but Kazim ignored the entreaty. His place of worship was here, his spiritual icon the scimitar in his hand.

Panting, he finished another sequence. His skin was soaked in sweat. He'd been pushing himself hard, trying to drive all other thoughts away. Memories of Ramita and Antonin Meiros; thoughts of his secret heritage. He could feel that hideous strength, the gnosis, coiled and waiting inside him, pleading to be used, but he ignored it. He shunned it, trying to pretend it wasn't there.

Someone called, "Kazim?" and he glanced up and saw Jamil had entered the tiered seating above the pit, his scarred and lined face cracking into a rare smile. "Get cleaned up," he called down. "We're wanted."

"Who by?" Kazim asked suspiciously. Jamil was his friend, but he was also Hadishah, and that loyalty came first.

"Rashid."

Kazim cursed softly. He had no wish to see Rashid, but despite this he hurried to obey, for Rashid Mubarak was head of this chapter of the Hadishah and his word was law.

"What's happening?" he asked Jamil after he'd poured water over his head and dried it with the cloth Jamil had handed him.

The Hadishah warrior shook his head. "I don't know, but something big. Very big."

Kazim grimaced. "As long as that hag Sabele isn't there."

Jamil looked at him steadily. "You must learn to accept who you are, brother."

They both knew he was afraid to see the Souldrinker jadugara Sabele and his sister Huriya; unlike himself, Huriya had embraced the revelation of their shared Souldrinker heritage and followed Sabele willingly—but then, she'd always been a conniving minx.

"How can I?" He looked at Jamil. "Have you seen Huriya?"

Jamil shook his head. He'd had hopes of a relationship with his friend's beautiful sister, but those were gone now. "My kind and yours—the union is forbidden. Unknown, even."

That gave him pause. *Ramita is magi now . . . The world conspires against us.*

"Can you tell what I am, just by looking at me?"

Jamil said hesitantly, "Now that you are training, and depleting your powers, it becomes evident. Your aura is different. It is . . . hungrier." He looked profoundly uncomfortable about it all. "Come, my friend. We must not keep Rashid waiting."

They hurried to the Dom-al'Ahm, removed their sandals and entered, barely noticed as they hurried past the ranks of worshippers prostrating themselves to Ahm and praying in echo to the words of the Godspeaker at the front. They took stairs leading below the dome, to a chamber lit by a single torch. The door closed behind them, cutting off the sound of the prayers.

"Thank you for coming." Rashid's melodious voice filled the small room. He was seated cross-legged on an intricately woven carpet beneath the torch.

Kazim and Jamil sank to their haunches on another larger carpet opposite him.

"The time has come for the next stage of our plans."

"We are ready," Jamil said, and Kazim nodded in reluctant agreement.

"Good," Rashid responded. "For in a few weeks' time, we're going to destroy the Ordo Costruo."

Huriya Makani stared through the stone latticework of the remains of the zenana, the women's wing of the broken palace, overlooking a ruined garden. The abandoned fortress northeast of Hebusalim had never been repaired after falling during the Second Crusade. Now it stank of stale piss and rot.

She turned as her mentor Sabele hobbled around the curve of the narrow balcony. Sabele was a crone while Huriya was in the full bloom of youth; despite her deeply tanned skin, Sabele was actually a white woman, born in Yuros centuries ago, while Huriya was a dark-skinned, black-haired Keshi of barely sixteen years. But they were both Souldrinkers, magi who had triggered their gnosis by inhaling the soul of a dying mage. Huriya had never suspected she had the trait until Sabele had revealed it to her, but nerve and greed were things she had always had in abundance, just like Sabele. The hag, herself a Souldrinker for centuries, had been visiting Huriya secretly most of her life, promising great rewards for patience—predictions that were finally coming true.

"Are we alone?" Sabele croaked.

Huriya clasped both hands together and bowed. "We are." She'd been scanning the area carefully with her newfound gnosis.

Sabele smiled her aggravating smile, the one that said she'd out-witted her protégée. "Look again, girl." She peered through the stonework. "Don't look just for men."

Ah. Huriya swallowed her irritation, closed her eyes and reopened her mind. She reached out to the sentinels she'd placed about the old fortress. Under Sabele's supervision she'd been capturing weak demons and placing them into the bodies of birds, mostly crows. She now had a flock a dozen strong that followed her everywhere.

A moment's communion told her what she needed to know.

"There are jackals outside the walls," she reported, a little afraid. "And something else."

Sabele smiled. "Better, child." She touched Huriya's shoulder and sent a tingle of pleasure through her nerve system, an exquisite combination of mental and sexual bliss that left her panting slightly, her nipples stiffening, her groin tingling. She exhaled heavily. Sabele knew her too well; she knew how to keep her enslaved. The ancient Souldrinker could reduce Huriya to a quivering lump of flesh with just a touch on the arm, giving pain or pleasure, whichever suited her whim. Huriya hated and craved such moments.

One day I will have learned all you can teach me, hag. Then beware . . .

"Come," the crone said, and led her through the maze of half-wrecked passages, dead vines clinging to the stonework and snakes slithering through the shadows, toward the gates. Huriya could feel the jackals entering; she glimpsed them though her demon-birds' eyes.

When they reached the courtyard they paused at the top of the stairs. The beasts below turned and silently regarded them. They were larger than common jackals, with at least twice the body mass, and they rumbled and growled and ducked their heads as if bowing. Then as one they fell to the ground, writhing through the agonies of mutation. Limbs began to form, arms and legs; jaws shortened and narrowed as fur came away in flakes and became dust. Some pissed or shat as they changed, losing control of their bodies in the moment, but then their torsos reformed into lean, muscle-laden flesh. They were men and women of many races, many colors, blond hair and dark, copper skin and white, and all young to middle-aged, strong and well-made. She watched breathlessly as they changed before her, their faces contorted by pain or pleasure, as if experiencing some ultimate orgasm.

"Are they all shape changers?" Huriya breathed.

Sabele arched an eyebrow. "Our kind have tended to band according to prime affinity. It is both a strength and a weakness. This group have been a pack for centuries. They are like insects of the same hive."

"Then there are others like me?"

"You are my apprentice, girl. You will stand above them all."

Huriya smiled inwardly at this as her eyes were drawn back to the bodies writhing—*like beasts*—beneath her.

Just as the shape changers were climbing to their feet, a mountain lion entered the courtyard. He did not waste time with any messy transfiguration; he simply reared upright, shedding his shape as he came on. He strode through the strewn bodies as they rose, a godlike body appearing from beneath the fur he shed. His mane became tawny hair that fell past his broad shoulders, and his corded belly flexed as he moved. His manhood was semi-erect amidst the golden thatch of hair at his loins. His thighs were like tree trunks. His face shone in the late sun, and Huriya's breath—and her scorn—caught in her throat.

Mine, she growled inwardly, drinking him in with her eyes. One of the female shape changers, a hard-faced creature all sinew and sun-blackened skin, seemed to hear her thought. She glared at Huriya threateningly.

"Pack leader Zaqri," Sabele greeted him as he went down on one knee.

"My Queen," the golden man replied in Rondian. His words were echoed by the rest of his pack—and it was *his*, Huriya could see that clearly.

"Thank you for coming, Zaqri my child," Sabele croaked in the same tongue. Huriya knew enough of it by now, through mind-to-mind learning, that she could follow the conversation. "I have a mission for you."

"You have only to command us," Zaqri told her.

"I know." Sabele smiled. She was standing a little taller and her skin looked less lined, almost as if she were growing younger.

Huriya wondered if it was illusion; perhaps it was pride.

"Come, there is food and clothing in the dormitories. How long have you been on the road?"

"Three weeks in beast-form, my Queen," Zaqri replied. His eyes went to Huriya, measuring her, and she looked back steadily. He had a wild beard and tangled hair, and a thick pelt on his chest. The beast clearly still lurked within.

"This is your new student?"

Sabele inclined her head. "Huriya Makani."

"Daughter of Razir?"

"The same."

He knew my father? Huriya's skin prickled.

Zaqri nodded appraisingly. "It is good that his line returns to our tribe. She has awakened?"

Sabele stroked Huriya's arm, sending a pleasant shiver through her. "She fed on a half-blood."

Zaqri bared his teeth. "A good start."

A good start. Huriya almost forgot to breathe, barely masking her excitement. *Does he mean that I could be stronger?* The rest was easy to work out. *I have to kill someone stronger than me and drink their soul.*

Sabele had not told her that—had perhaps not intended to tell her, not when she was the obvious next meal.

But Sabele was still talking, and the mission that she outlined soon erased all other thoughts. "We go to Krak di Condotiori, to visit destruction on the Ordo Costruo."

A whole order of magi to devour . . . Whose soul might I not consume then?

4

INTO CAPTIVITY

Pregnancy manifestation

A great wonder came to pass: Agnes, a mere human who had been taken to wife by Sertain, Magus Primus, became herself Magi of the Second Rank by virtue of bearing his progeny in her womb.

THE ANNALS OF PALLAS

Gestational manifestation was once common place, as the Ascendants were young and virile. Now it is a rarity as the original Ascendants reach their old age and pass on. At times the human wife of a pure-blood might experience a temporary gnostic awakening, or a very weak permanent effect, but the last human woman we know of who has experienced full awakening through carrying an Ascendant's child has long since died. New Ascendants created by the Scytale of Corineus have exclusively married pure-bloods, and any liaisons with human women have to my knowledge been fruitless.

ASA CENIUS, BRES ARCANUM SCHOLAR, 911

Kesh, Antiopia
Rajab (Julsep) 928
1st month of the Moontide

<Namaste!>

Ramita Ankesharan watched as the unknown woman she'd been staring at suddenly jolted as if struck by a thrown stone and looked wildly about her. She pulled the curtain across so their eyes would not meet and smiled to herself in satisfaction. In the other corner of the carriage's pokey cabin her maid dozed, oblivious. More importantly, so did the armed man beside her.

Third one today, she reflected, glowing inwardly. She had been trying to hone her fledgling gnostic skills, using the very least energy she could—any error might alert those with her, and she couldn't afford that. It was like creeping past a slumbering snake: to misstep would be death. But so far she was treading soft and sure. She rubbed at the bulge at her belly. *I will protect you, my little ones. I will see you safe.*

She had very little idea where in the world she was: Dhassa and Kesh were foreign lands to her, and she'd never paid much attention to maps—not that they'd had any when she was growing up in the marketplace of Baranasi. Now her world was limited to this carriage, rolling slowly eastward on roads choked with all of humanity. Bench seats faced forward and backward, with barely room for feet between. The tiny windows were curtained to keep the dust out, but the air inside the cabin was hot and smelled. Sweat soaked the bodice of her salwar kameez and dripped from her face into her gauzy dupatta scarf. Her belly churned with each lurch. It was already visibly distended, though this was only the third month of her pregnancy. Her hands cradled the bulge protectively.

Prune-faced Arda slumbered in the opposite corner. She was Keshi, and the most close-mouthed woman Ramita had ever met. Not that conversation was easy in the nauseating bump-and-sway of the carriage. She found herself missing Huriya, until she remembered the way her lifetime friend had betrayed her, by her part in the murder of her husband, and she forcibly evicted the girl from her thoughts. At least Arda was a known enemy.

An armed man slept beside Arda. Mostly he rode above with the driver, where the air could at least pretend to freshness, but he liked to sleep in the afternoon. His name was Hamid and he looked all Keshi, but he had the Rondian magic, the gnosis—he sometimes made little flames dance on his fingertips to show off. He was maybe twenty, with a cocky manner. He liked to leer at the female refugees they passed, calling out lewd offers, but he did not pester Ramita, to her relief. Of course she was a valued prisoner, so maybe he was frightened to tease her. Or perhaps being pregnant and a Lakh, he found her repulsive.

The journey was an ordeal. All of Dhassa and Kesh were on the move, fleeing the coming Crusade. The rich had left long ago, but the poor, with no incomes if they fled their businesses and farms, had hung on as late as they could before joining the flood of refugees. If she were to pull open the curtains she would see them up close: their handcarts weighed down with massive burdens, all their lives and property bundled up and lashed down. She would see barefoot people trudging through the dust and stones, faces set in hard-eyed, blank stares: mothers carrying their children on their shoulders, others breastfeeding as they walked. Men who were already little more than skin stretched over frames of bone scavenged the refuse for anything they could feed to their starving wives and children. Occasionally horsemen galloped by, careless of those they scattered before them as they rampaged through, intent on their missions. Dhassa was emptying. In the last Crusade, the Rondians had plundered eastward all the way to Istabad. This time would be worse, the people were saying.

She glanced furtively at her sleeping companions, then opened the curtain once more. The last person she'd thrown her mental stone at was out of sight, somewhere behind them. She found her eyes drawn to two young girls, walking hand in hand, heads bowed, featureless forms in bekira-shrouds, utterly anonymous. <*Namaste,*> she called to the one on the right. Nothing. She tried again, a little harder, and both girls flinched, their heads whipping about, the narrow eye-slits both drawn straight to the carriage rolling past.

Chod! Ramita dropped the curtain aside. She knew instinctively what she'd done wrong: by not focusing enough on one, she'd called both. She scolded herself. If her plans to escape were to come to fruition, she had to do better than that.

She'd been working hard, like a good Lakh woman, but she'd been subtle too, lest Hamid sense her activities. No one alive yet knew that she could do these things. To escape, she needed to perfect her call, to make it narrow, strong and focused. The people outside the window, changing by the moment, were the perfect subjects for practice, so she waited a minute, until the two girls were somewhere behind, and tried again on someone else.

Often, though, she could not bear to watch them. Even Arda's blank scowl was better than the suffering she saw everywhere, especially when her eyes strayed to the sides of the road and she saw the remains of those who had just given up, women and children, mostly. Their skin was burning black in the sun but their souls had long gone. Sometimes a wailing child still clung to a fallen mother, ignored by the rest of the passersby. Hamid and Arda would not let her stop and help them, and she hated them even more for that, though she could also see that if they tried to save them all, this carriage would soon be stacked high with infants and she would have to sit on the roof.

I have two of my own coming. They must be my only concern.

So for now, she concentrated on self-learning these strange skills her pregnancy by Antonin Meiros had bequeathed her: the last gift of her dead husband, and the proof that it was he and not Kazim who had fathered her children.

I will escape somehow. I will bear my children into freedom.

Arda woke, which ended her secret training session. The woman stared at her with contemptuous eyes, as she had throughout the journey. *To her I am a whore who sold myself to an old jadugara and let him impregnate me. But I don't care what she thinks of me.*

"Where are we?" she asked. Huriya and Kazim had taught her Keshi as they grew up together, and she spoke Rondian now as well, thanks to her husband's tutelage, though she was not terribly fluent in that awkward language.

Arda considered her with her raisin eyes. She seldom responded even to direct questions, but for whatever reason, she answered this one. "Near Sagostabad."

"Is that our destination?" Ramita asked, while Arda was in the mood to speak.

The old woman blinked slowly. "Halli'kut."

Halli'kut. Where Rashid Mubarak is Emir. Ramita felt an invisible cord tighten about her throat. She was pretty sure Rashid was the leader of the Hadishah; he'd certainly been the puppet master who'd contrived her husband's death. The last time he'd spoken to her, he had laid out her fate very clearly: if the babies in her womb were Antonin's, then her blood rank would be strong and Rashid himself would take her to wife. If they were not, she would be given back to Kazim.

Ramita could not decide which fate was worse.

She found she'd lost her appetite for questions.

Sometimes they slept in abandoned houses, small, crude shelters of mudbrick. Other nights, they simply stopped, and Hamid and the driver shared the roof while Ramita and Arda each took a bench-seat. Neither woman was even five feet tall, but still the benches were too short and hard for comfort. The air was not much cooler than during the day, but at least the pitiless sun was gone. And all about them refugees suffered, rubbing blistered, aching feet and road-sore backs, sipping rancid water when their bellies cried out to be flooded. There was never enough of the lentils and grain, the only foodstuffs left, and Ramita dozed uneasily, the constant wail of hungry children permeating her dreams.

That night, though, the wagon turned off the main road sometime before dusk and rolled along a dirt track away from the tide of people flowing east. As they wound their way up a slope, her eyes pierced the deepening shadow and she saw a gleam of smooth white stone higher up the rise.

Once through the single gate in a low dun-colored wall guarded by a whole squad of soldiers, the road became steeper, but it was now paved, and lined with sturdy trees. Water that would have saved scores of lives on the road was being poured about the roots of the trees and over the manicured lawns by bent old men with shoulder harnesses for the buckets. The soldiers looked plump and self-satisfied.

Hamid was on the roof with the driver, but he dropped to the foot-step outside the carriage door and pushed the curtains aside. "Tonight, we dwell in paradise," he declared cheerily. "Hot spicy meats and gravies. White man's beer. Real beds. Young maids with juicy yonis." He was almost dancing with delight as he clung to the side of the carriage. It was the most he'd said to either woman the whole journey. He leaped to the paved road and trotted alongside, grinning broadly.

The carriage rolled into a courtyard flanked by white marble pillars and pink sandstone walls. There were people everywhere, guards and servants, milling about in apparent chaos. Ramita stared, taking in the Keshi patterns of the men's checkered head-scarves as well as the heavy black bekira-shrouds the women wore. None of the women looked to be of rank; they scuttled about with straw brooms, their backs permanently bent by their labors. Amidst them, the men, servants and soldiers alike, strode straight and tall.

The carriage made one last turn and they lurched to a halt, the horses neighing irritably. She glimpsed a welcoming group, a cluster of brightly colored figures on the steps, and looked down at herself. Her sweat-soaked bodice was sticking to her breasts and droplets were running down to her distended belly and pooling in her navel. Even when she was a market-girl in Baranasi she would not have let herself be seen like this. She hastily pulled her bekira-shroud over her head. Arda, who always wore one despite the heat, covered her nose and mouth with her scarf and raised the cowl. Ramita followed suit, for once grateful for the all-enveloping garment.

The doors opened, and hands reached in to offer aid. Arda pushed ahead peremptorily and Ramita caught her thought: *The whore does not precede me.* She smiled to herself. She'd heard Arda's thoughts as clearly as if she'd spoken aloud. Her self-taught fumblings with the gnosis had not been in vain. *Newly hatched birds eventually learn to fly*, she told herself. But when she left the carriage, blinking in the light, her legs wobbly for disuse, she saw who awaited her and shut her mind down completely, as her husband had taught her.

"Hello, Ramita," Alyssa Dulayne purred. "Welcome to the Haveli Khayyam."

Ramita's fright at seeing the woman did not prevent her from noting the name: *Haveli Khayyam*.

Alyssa Dulayne's honey-colored hair tumbled about her bare shoulders, a shocking display in this setting—but pure-blood jadugara always did what they liked. She wore a Rondian gown with a deep cleavage, showing her pale skin in flagrant disregard to the rules of the Keshi Amteh. Once Ramita had thought Alyssa a friend, but she knew better now.

Behind her were two others, probably also magi. The paler-than-normal Keshi men with lordly demeanors had gems at their throats. One was middle-aged, with a worldly air; the other was bright-eyed and puppyish. Ramita thought she recognized them from her one foray into Ordo Costruo society. The rest were Keshi nobles and their soldiers.

Alyssa stepped forward and stroked Ramita's cheek as if she were a child. "How was your journey, my dear? You look dreadful." She spoke in Rondian. Her voice was smooth and playful.

Ramita jerked away. "I am a prisoner, and have been treated as one."

"A guest, my girl—a very *special* guest. The unborn are well?"

Ramita's hands went to her belly reflexively. "They are well."

"But no manifestation?" Alyssa inquired, reaching out, her periapt suddenly pulsing beneath her chin, lighting her skin with a flickering blue-green glow.

Ramita felt as if the air about her had turned solid, as if she were frozen in glass, held immobile effortlessly. Alyssa herself was unimpeded. Her fingers caressed Ramita's brow, and she winced a little at the sweat. <*Nothing at all, child? Let's see . . .*> The penetration came next, the mage-woman's needle-like mind enveloping hers, making her tremble. She didn't try to hide the fear; that would be expected. She thought about the journey, the discomfort, the loneliness, the fear of what had gone, and what would be: a mask of memories, held up for the Rondian jadugara to see. *<No, still nothing . . . What a shame. I did hope that old goat had knocked you up, not young Kazim Makani.>* Alyssa paused thoughtfully. *<Though his blood is not without value.>*

Ramita refused to rise to the bait. She let her mental mask speak for her, a narrow emotion-palette of loneliness, resentment, and fear. It wasn't hard—even a non-mage could do it, and she'd learned from Antonin Meiros himself. She smiled inwardly as Alyssa lost interest. Another little victory.

"Poor girl," the jadugara said. "Life is so uncertain for you. But fear not. You will rest here a time, until you're ready to push on. I myself will take you to Halli'kut." She smiled smugly. "The journey will be much faster, and much more comfortable."

They took her inside, to a room on the ground floor with barred windows. There was a wide bed, many pillows, a smooth tiled floor, cut flowers and pretty linen. And a bath. *A bath!*

Arda came in with her, directing a pair of maids with peremptory gestures and monosyllabic commands to fill the bath, bring in Ramita's few bags, lay out fresh clothes. Ramita sank onto the mattress, which was harder than she wanted but still a thousand times better than the carriage bench. Her whole body ached and her bones felt like they were still vibrating to the movement of the carriage. The smell of her own body when she removed the bekira-shroud was pungent and unpleasant, but at least the bath was filling fast.

Mercifully, they let her wash alone. She sank into lukewarm water, rose-scented and clean, glorying in the luxuriant touch of it. There were jasmine and lavender soaps and rich argan oil to moisturize the skin afterward: luxuries she'd never known in Baranasi but had become accustomed to at Casa Meiros. She wondered if her mother now bathed like this every day. Were her younger brothers and sisters growing like pampered princes now? Had Jai returned to them? Were they all safe? How would they cope when the money stopped, now that her husband was dead? Had anyone even sent them word? She so seldom thought of her family these days, for their world was so far removed from hers, but just now she longed to see them.

With the gnosis, perhaps I could do it? But her native caution reasserted itself and she put the idea aside. She could not risk it, not with Alyssa so near. She knew so little. She had no training, only instinct to guide her, and that instinct was saying "no." She sighed unhappily and returned to cleansing herself.

Her breasts were growing larger, her nipples more prominent, and her belly was stretching all the time. She was carrying twins, and would become big quickly, the way her own mother always had. For generation after generation, her mother's line had begat twins and triplets, with never a singular birth—they spent half their lives waddling about like ducks.

She emptied a small vial of oil into the water, then arched backward and immersed her whole body to let the oil soak into her skin. Then she closed her eyes and tried to think.

She had maybe three or four days here, in this place that was far from Hebusalim, but not so far as Halli'kut. It might be her last chance.

And if Alyssa detects what I'm doing, so what? They'll learn the truth soon enough anyway.

She closed her eyes and pretended she was looking out the carriage window at a specific woman, picturing the face she needed, remembering the brittle nature of its owner, the sharp voice and piercing eyes. She started on as narrow a focus as she could and called softly to the only person left she knew she could trust.

<Justina!>

<Ramita?> Justina Meiros's mental voice was utterly incredulous. *<Ramita? Sol et Lune! Is that you? I can barely hear you—>*

Ramita daren't call louder. *<Please help me.>*

Justina instantly knew what she meant. *<Here, let me do the work. Just focus on the sound of my voice in your head and I'll cloak us . . . Great Sol, you're alive! And you've manifested the gnosis! Sol*

et Lune . . . I thought you were dead! Rashid said you were murdered alongside Father!>

Ramita choked back sudden tears. This was not her first attempt to call the daughter of her late husband, and she'd began to fear she'd never manage it. *<Rashid's men killed my husband. Alyssa has me prisoner.>*

<Rashid—? Alyssa—? But—Sol et Lune!> She felt Justina's astonishment and they almost lost contact, but when Justina gripped her mind again, it was filled with intensity. Justina's touch was brutally blunt, like a dagger-hilt, and she felt it probing deeper inside her; she could almost feel her harsh breath on her skin.

<Rashid told me he knew nothing of this! He swore! *And I believed him! And Alyssa . . . it can't be!>* She sounded stricken.

<Alyssa is evil,> Ramita fired back. *<She went through my mind when she was "teaching me." You should not have trusted her.>*

<She what?> Justina raged. *<Why didn't you tell me?>*

<Because she was your friend. And you were so rude to me.>

<Rukka mio!> Justina's mental touch blazed like fire and then ice. *<Where are you?>*

<It is called Haveli Khayyam, near Sagostabad.>

Justina's voice was somewhat stunned. *<You can reach me from there? My God, that's the edge of* my *limits . . .>* It felt to Ramita like she stopped for a moment, then swallowed her disbelief. *<I know it.>* Her mental voice became anguished. *<Alyssa was with me only days ago . . . She said there'd been an attack, and she would shelter me . . . Rukka-rukka-rukka . . . They've played me for an utter fool. I am* an utter fool. *Damn her!>*

<Alyssa may hear us,> Ramita put in, praying Justina's mental anguish had not drawn attention already. *<Please, help me. For the children's sake.>*

Justina's mind immediately refocused. The chill of her mental touch was forbidding. *<I know the Haveli Khayyam. Rashid and Alyssa took me there one spring. How long will you be there?>*

<Three days, perhaps. I do not know.>

<Remain there—delay leaving. Feign illness if you must. I'm coming for you, I swear, but it's a long way and I'm being watched. Do not risk contacting me again.>

Abruptly, she was gone from Ramita's mind. Ramita lay back in the water, panting slightly. Her belly trembled with the sudden movement, a slithering inside she didn't at first comprehend, and then she realized her children had moved inside her. She gave a small cry, and clutched her belly tight. *I'll protect you, little ones. I will save you. Just hold on . . .*

All next day Ramita lay abed, frightened to draw attention to herself. She worried that Alyssa might unmask the gnosis inside her, or read her mind and realize that Justina was coming, but the Rondian jadugara never came near her. She heard her once, her laughter carrying down from an upstairs balcony; the flirtatious laugh was answered by a huskier male voice. *That woman is a slut*, she thought to herself. *The lowliest Untouchable has more self-respect.* The vindictive thought made her feel better.

Inside her, the unborn babies squirmed, a sensation that was both alarming and comforting. Godsingers could be heard in the distance, calling the Amteh faithful to prayer, but as she lay forgotten in her bed, she was content. Justina Meiros was coming and nothing else mattered.

They let her eat in bed, and finally Alyssa visited, at dusk. Ramita had started coughing, laying the groundwork for feigning illness if required, though if Alyssa had the healing-gnosis that would be risky. She wished she knew more of the gnosis, and that she'd tried harder to get to know Justina, though Antonin Meiros's daughter had been aloof and unfriendly. But Alyssa barely looked at her.

The next day dragged past, as featureless as the last, and Ramita alternately prayed to Parvasi for strength and wept in memory of her husband, only three weeks dead. She longed to reach out again to Justina, for reassurance, but she dared not. The only people she saw were Arda and the maids, when they came to clean her room.

She was fading toward sleep, well after the third night-bell, when Hamid swaggered in, posturing like a street tough. "What do you want?" she asked him warily.

"I'm just locking down the wards," he told her, whatever that meant. "You were asleep the last two nights and missed it."

Go away . . . she said groggily, only then realizing that she'd not spoken aloud but with her mind. She froze, praying he'd felt nothing, but no such luck.

The young man stared at her curiously, his eyes coming alive. "Did you do that?"

"Do what?" she answered, feigning ignorance.

He leaned toward her. "I'm sure I—"

She felt his quicksilver, ferreting mind inside her, an invasion she cringed from, then he squealed in triumph. "You have it! You have the gnosis!" He stood, his eyes filled with greedy wonder. "Lady Alyssa said this could happen. This is glorious, lady. You are blessed with a child of Meiros, a new magus to serve Ahm!" He bent and kissed her swollen stomach, to her utter revulsion. "Ahm be praised! This is glorious news!" *And I am the one who will deliver it,* she heard him think.

"Please, I—"

Hamid seized her hand. "We must give thanks to Ahm! A child of Meiros! And you, you are now one of us! A magus, another magus to serve the Hadishah—do you understand, lady? You are one of the magi now! Oh, this is a night of miracles!" He prayed fervently over her while she watched him with fear and bemusement. He reminded her a little of Kazim, boyish and excitable. But dread of Alyssa sent her into desperation.

I can't just lie here. I have to do something! If she had a weapon she would have used it, but he was a warrior. How could she best him? She cast about, and her eyes fell on the heaviest thing in reach.

I have to try . . .

She clutched at her belly. "Please, Hamid, help me get up. It isn't right to just lie here to receive guests. Especially at this moment."

She saw his mind flurry, desperation to run and tell the world warring with his sense of propriety. She saw questions form in his mind: How did women receive women anyway, especially pregnant women? Should he call a maid? What was the right thing to do?

"Hamid, please?" She thrust a hand at him, demanding his assistance, and he reacted instinctively, helping her to her feet. She pretended to sway, then stood, feigning dizziness. "Thank you," she panted, edging closer to the thing she wanted: the chamber pot beside the bed.

He saw her reach for the heavy basin and immediately turned his back. "Er, I should go . . ."

"Wait!" she said quickly, which at least stopped him, though he didn't look back, in case he saw something a young man shouldn't. *Oma bless you for your manners*, she thought with a strange sort of fondness as she picked up the chamber pot. She'd used it an hour ago, so keeping it from sloshing as she raised it over her head was tricky.

"My lady?" he asked, half-turning his head anxiously.

"I'm sorry," she said, and smashed the chamber pot over his head, wincing as he crashed to the ground in a spray of broken pottery and piss. He twitched, quivered and went still.

Now what do I do?

Alyssa Dulayne let the last of the evening light kiss her shoulders as she tossed her head lightly and laughed at Taldin's latest tale. He was ex–Ordo Costruo, like her, a part-Keshi lady's man with an amusing imagination. He liked to conjure illusions to embroider his tales, making them play out before the eyes of the company. And when they were alone together, his imagination and body were pleasingly versatile. She was currently viewing the world through a pleasant alcoholic glow and her body was aglow with the languid heaviness of arousal.

"More wine, Alyssa?" Taldin purred in her ear, his breath and beard tickling.

She giggled and thrust the glass at him. "Fill me," she replied, her voice emphasizing the double meaning.

"To the brim," he said, raising the bottle. Below the balcony spread the gardens, a vivid green patch on a darkening brown quilt that stretched away toward the jagged skyline of Sagostabad, the largest city in Kesh. It was home to millions and the smoke of the evening cooking fires and hearths was billowing into the sky as if the city were ablaze.

"I'll hold you to that," she replied gaily. She leaned against the balcony and looked out at the view, and then turned back to Taldin.

The handsome quarter-blood was not just adept in illusion, but also at animism and morphing, a quicksilver blend of skills reflective of his fluid mind. He knew that this was just a temporary liaison, and she found his attitude refreshing in this world full of desperate clingers-on.

She nuzzled his face, giggling throatily, opening her lips to receive his tongue. She liked his dark skin, the attractive contrast against her pallor. They licked each other's lips, making hot promises with their eyes. *I like this one*, she thought, and wondered for a brief moment what the servants were making of them.

Somewhere below, she heard a faint, vivid flaring of the gnosis: Hamid, stupid naïve Hamid, crying aloud, and as quickly silenced. She froze, instantly wary.

Taldin heard it too and wordlessly they stepped apart, shields flaring. Taldin moved toward the stairs—but no shields Taldin was capable of raising would have saved his life that night.

A woman in midnight-blue robes appeared in the far corner of the balcony, floating out of the twilight gloom: a white face in a cloud of black hair. She gestured with her right hand and stone tiles peeled from the balcony floor and flew at Alyssa: a torrent of lethal stone.

Alyssa gave a small shriek and flew to one side, gathering her shields in time to deflect the stones, but Taldin was neither swift enough nor strong enough to do the same and she saw a square stone slab the width of his torso slam into his chest corner-first. He rebounded off the balcony, his ribcage already shattered, then a further torrent of stone pulverized his skull, turning the face she'd been kissing three seconds before to meat jelly and broken bone, nothing more than a dark smear in the rubble.

Justina Meiros turned to Alyssa. "So, my darling." Her hard, acerbic voice throbbed. "Shall we dance?"

The whole house shook, and above Ramita's head the very stones cracked and boomed as dust fell from the ceiling and poured in through the barred window. There was a momentary pause, as if the world did not quite know how to react, and then the screaming began.

Ramita grinned suddenly, quickly stuffed her belongings back into her two bags, then sat back down on the bed and waited. A minute later, Justina Meiros opened her door with a blast of gnosis and stepped through.

"Ramita?"

"Hello, daughter," Ramita greeted her, knowing how much the term irritated her husband's child and unable to refrain from using it despite the situation.

"I've told you not to call me that, bitch." Justina scowled as she bent over the fallen Hamid. "He's not dead," she added, turning Hamid's head over with her foot and studying his face. "Best I remedy that."

Ramita shivered. "Spare him," she blurted. "He was kind to me." He hadn't been, not really. But she didn't want to see a death.

Justina scowled, but acquiesced. "We must go."

Ramita clutched her shawl about her. "I am ready."

"Do you have any possessions here?" Justina asked her.

"Only these," Ramita replied, showing her the two bags. "Everything else was at home."

"Father's house has been pillaged," Justina said angrily. "Everything is stolen or ruined."

Ramita felt the same way. She hadn't owned much; now she had nearly nothing.

Justina's eyes bored into her. "I'm doing this for the children, not for you. You are nothing to me but an annoying Indranian bitch. But Father seemed to like you, and you have conceived of him, so I will see you and your children safe, for his sake."

Ramita was reminded of just how many secrets she held that she could not afford this woman to know, especially her own perfidy in betraying her husband—secrets her enemies knew.

I pray she will never learn such things . . .

Justina gripped her shoulders and shouted aloud. Ramita lost all coherent thought as they flew upward, the fabric of the building exploding around them. They erupted through the balcony, where the very stone was scorched, in places partially liquefied. One battered body slumped against the broken balustrade; the lawn below was littered in corpses. Ramita felt her limbs trembling in shock, but Justina placed her on a solid patch of stone, ignoring the destruction as if it were commonplace. She gestured, and a huge bundle flew toward them, then unrolled itself: a flying carpet, the very one Antonin had once used to show her the Leviathan Bridge. She knew what was expected; she walked as steadily as she could to the center of it, then sat cross-legged. Justina barely gave her time to settle before sending them soaring upward toward the rising half-moon.

"What happened to Alyssa? Is she dead?" Ramita asked hopefully.

"Alyssa? Huh! She wouldn't stand and fight someone like me. She's a manipulator, a parlor witch. You can't fight with divinations and scryings. She ran for her life." Justina gave a small, bitter laugh. "And I let her go. For old time's sake." Her mouth curled into a little grimace of self-mockery.

"Where are we going?"

"To the Isle of Glass," Justina told her, as though this explained everything. "Shut up and let me concentrate. Someone is already trying to scry us." The carpet picked up speed, thrumming northward through the darkening sky, and Sagostabad fell away behind them in the night. Ahead lay only darkness.

5

MERCELLUS DI REGIA

Rimoni Gypsies

The Ascendants and the allied armies invaded Rimoni, and there was no revenge they would not contemplate to destroy the power of their former Imperial masters forever. Thousands of people, sometimes whole communities, were exterminated, particularly around Rym, the capital. Soil was systematically salted and forests burned to the ground. Immigrant colonies were brought in to displace the locals, leaving many landless and forced into nomadic, poverty-stricken lives. The covered wagon of the Rimoni gypsy is now a common sight across the continent, and while some welcome them grudgingly for the trade they bring, others do not, for the Rimoni themselves never forget that they were once the masters.

ARNO RUFIUS, LANTRIS 752

Eastern Noros & Northern Rimoni, Yuros
Julsep 928
1st month of the Moontide

The road east from Norostein took Alaron and Muhren from the high slopes, where towns had been hewn into the rock, down into the lush farms and vineyards on the valley floor. With so many men away, marching with the Crusaders or selling goods and produce in Pontus, it was left to the women to work the fields.

The journey felt surreal. Every night he fell asleep fully expecting to wake up in his bed, having dreamed all this danger and intrigue. People like him did not find themselves on quests for the Scytale of Corineus. The presence of Jeris Muhren beside him gave proceedings a certain grounding, however: the former watch captain was nothing if not solidly real, and he was firmly in control. *Hel, he's a genuine living legend,* Alaron admitted, *and I'd be screwed without him.*

Muhren knew people—literally, at first: they'd enter a tavern and half the men in the room would erupt with greetings. Anonymity was initially so difficult they took to sleeping in the woods. After a few days they'd left behind all that immediate recognition, but Muhren still *knew* people: he knew if they were honest or not, and if the information they were passing on was genuine or rumor only. It wasn't gnosis; Alaron thought he'd have sensed that. It was just that Muhren seemed to know what made a person tick.

He also knew how to cinch a saddle and clean a horse's hooves without getting kicked, and where best to site the fire, how to bring down game and cook it, how to prepare a campsite, when it was going to rain and when that rain would stop. He could even tell when the water in the stream was safe.

But he didn't know Cym at all.

"She said she'd go to her mother in Hebusalim. That's where she's going," Alaron repeated, tired of the debate already.

"But her family summer in Silacia, picking grapes for the familioso," Muhren said stubbornly.

The man could not conceive of being wrong, or so Alaron thought.

"And you've told me they purchased a windskiff."

"To *sell*. They sell everything—that's what the Rimoni do."

"No, Alaron. She will want to use it to fly east."

"I piloted it. She just helped me build it."

"She's a smart girl; she'd learn quickly enough."

"They live hand-to-mouth. Her father would have sold it."

"They're not so poor as that," Muhren replied. "Mercellus is as shrewd a man as I've met. And he wears gold earrings."

"They wear their wealth—Cym says some nights they have to eat boot-leather."

"That old story?" Muhren laughed aloud. "Come, we'll take the pass on the coast road south to Silacia."

"North, then east to Pontus."

Muhren just shook his head, kicked the flanks of his horse and surged ahead.

Alaron cursed, and bounced along in his wake. He called his horse Mallet because every night as he dismounted it felt like someone had taken a mallet to his backside. *I'm going to have an ass like tooled leather after a few days more of this*, he thought grumpily. Muhren's mount was called Prancer. *Bastard.*

It wasn't that Alaron couldn't ride, but he'd never ridden for days on end, and such long distances—the farmlands and forests of Noros were boxed in by mountains, and he'd never ridden further from Norostein than the journey from his parents' town house to the family manor house, which had been sold in the spring.

The road they were on ran east to the coastal ranges, then south into Silacia. The farmlands and villages soon gave way to wilder countryside, the road winding through woods and alongside mountain streams. The weather was pleasant enough—the summer temperatures were mild and the air humid enough to raise a sweat in direct sunlight. But mostly the clouds high overhead drifted along under cooling breezes. Alaron estimated they were covering about thirty miles a day.

The land became more rugged and undulating, with steep, rocky hills devoted mostly to sheep-farming, and pinewoods where logging gangs chopped down the great pines, then hauled the logs away on oxen-carts. Many of the rivers and streams were strung with fishing weirs.

The wildlife grew larger as they traveled east. Otters frolicked in pools and foxes haunted the margins of the farms. They heard the distant howls of timber wolves, and Alaron saw his first wild bear, gorging on the fish from a weir it had destroyed.

As the road became more overgrown, Muhren grew more cautious. At his insistence they both wore shield-wardings, though they were draining and distorted distance-vision. "There are bandits here," he warned. "If we display wards, they'll leave us alone."

On the fifth night, the stream they were following fell down a waterfall into an icy, crystal-clear pool. A platform of rock jutted a little from the woods, affording them a view back the way they had come, and Alaron was surprised to find they were so high. The valley westward was all trees, the pastures hidden by the folds of land. The Alps were lost in the clouds, but to the north, the opposing hills were clear and massive. He'd studied maps; he knew Noros was small compared with other provinces of the empire, but to him it seemed vast and untamed.

"Do you think we're being followed?" he asked.

Muhren was shielding his eyes from the westering sun as he peered back the way they had come. "We've not been scryed—my wardings haven't been tested, at least, not that I'm aware of. Even a pure-blood Inquisitor with the right affinities would struggle to scry me undetected." He sounded calm about that possibility.

"Then what are you looking for?"

"Dust clouds on the road. It's dry enough that we've been kicking up a faint trail." He glanced at Alaron. "I also started leaving some minor ward-spells on the path: little cantrips that are dissipated if trodden on. I can sense if they are broken. It doesn't tell me who, but it might indicate if we're being followed."

"Have they been triggered?" Alaron asked with a little trepidation.

Muhren shook his head. "Not yet." He patted Alaron's shoulder. "Let's make camp. Make sure the wood you use is dead; it smokes less. Use Air-gnosis to break up the smoke if you have to. I'm going hunting."

Alaron got a fire going, and made a wooden rack for the billy and by the time Muhren returned with a dead hare over his shoulder he had a broth cooking. Muhren was perspiring from the climb back to their camp, but butchered his catch and added the pieces to the pot before pulling off his clothes and wading into the pool.

"Isn't it freezing?" Alaron called.

"We're magi, Alaron."

"Oh yeah." There were ways to insulate the body from hot and cold if you didn't mind tiring yourself, but Alaron had never been strong or skilled enough to routinely resort to them.

After a minute or two splashing about, Muhren waded from the water. "I swear there's an eel the size of my leg under that big rock," he laughed. "If we had time I'd spit and smoke him." He looked more relaxed than Alaron had seen him before, with no cares beyond food and sleep. The Jeris Muhren he'd grown up knowing, the Watch Captain of Norostein, was terse, wary and always poised on the edge of action. Naked, he was an impressive figure, strong and lithe, with no lack of athleticism despite his bulk. His torso was already brown, as if he took every opportunity to enjoy the sun. "I'll watch the fire, lad," he said. "Have a splash yourself."

Alaron felt reluctant but after a quick sniff under his arms he stripped self-consciously, feeling skinny and pale beside the muscular watchman. The water was so cold he nearly choked, until he remembered to use the gnosis to regulate his temperature. Just a few minutes was enough to exhaust him, but at least he was able to get clean. He found a place on the rock platform where the stone was still warm from the sun and let the wind dry him. He was still panting from the exertion, but he felt fresh and strangely alive.

Muhren threw him a blanket, wrapped another about his own waist and went to tend the horses, which were whickering peacefully as they grazed on the tussocky grass. Alaron stared out across the trees, listening to the wind rustling the leaves. It was hard to understand why people would choose to live in tiny houses in piss-rank alleys in stinking cities where the air was smoke-laden and the water polluted, when you could live out here. There was probably a reason, but right now it didn't feel good enough.

"Where is your father?" Muhren asked. He and Vann Mercer were old friends.

"He went east a few months ago, to try his luck trading in Dhassa. He says you can still find traders east of Hebusalim where the Crusade doesn't usually go—he says lots of traders do it."

"He'd better take care. I've a feeling this Crusade is going to be a lot worse than the last."

Alaron sighed. It was another thing that was gnawing at him.

Then he felt it: the questing eye, like a orb in the sky that was beating down on him, tendrils snaking about it, ripping at the wards he'd clothed himself in. It wasn't aimed at him; he could tell that instantly. He just happened to be close to the person it was aimed at. "A scrying!" he called urgently, leaping to his feet.

Muhren ran toward him. "I can shield you within my ambit if you're close enough, and your presence will disrupt the attempt to find me." He pulled out his dagger and began to gouge the earth. "Counter-wards, quickly."

Alaron joined him, putting his gnosis into boosting Muhren's ward. A shape began to appear in his inner vision, a masklike visage with eyes that were seeking—

Muhren grasped a handful of earth and tossed it into the air above him: Earth to counter Air-gnosis. Alaron felt two things click into place around him: the earth fanned out like a shield, hanging around them in an immobile cloud, and Muhren's wards merged with his. The shape he'd sensed—a product of his imagination, not truly visible—vanished. He trembled, rubbing at his temples.

Muhren squeezed his shoulder encouragingly. "We've repelled them for now. They won't try again soon: scrying takes more effort than hiding." He gazed toward the west. "It came from the direction of Norostein. I didn't recognize the mental signature."

"Inquisitors?"

"Most likely."

"It was targeting you, not me," Alaron noted, frightened by the realization that pursuit was no longer just an abstract thought; it was real.

"They've linked me to Vult's death. Perhaps they've even found Fyrell."

"Will they try again?"

"Almost certainly. But defense is stronger than attack in the gnosis. I can set up wards to cover us while we sleep. And the more distance we can put between us and them, the better." He smiled reassuringly. "Don't worry, lad. They won't find us."

They settled in for the night, wrapped in blankets on either side of the fire, eating the stew and sipping from a flask of whisky Muhren produced from his saddlebag. One sip was enough for Alaron; it was potent stuff. The scrying came again, but Alaron scarcely felt it this time. Muhren grinned as the attack fell apart. "See, lad? If they're going to find us, it'll be with leg-work, not scrying."

"What else could they do to find us?"

"Sorcery—necromancy or wizardry, using spirits of one sort or another to find us. Animism, setting creatures on our trail. But those methods all take time, and they're erratic. If we keep moving, eventually we'll outrun their resources." He stared into space, measuring with his mind. "Once we cross the pass south into Silacia, I dare say they'll have lost us in terms of scrying."

"Will they give up then?" Alaron asked hopefully.

"With the Scytale of Corineus at stake? No—but they'll have to use less direct methods. The longer we can avoid them, the safer we'll become."

They fell silent for a while, wrapped up in their own thoughts. Alaron wrestled with a bleak future of constantly running, drifting rootless with no place to call home, never finding Cym, and never losing the Inquisitors. It was a dismal prospect.

"Tell me about you and Aunt Elena," he said eventually, as the last of the daylight left the sky. The moon was waxing, and he could see its cratered face. *Are there woods and trees up there too?* he wondered. *Or is it all a desert?*

Muhren sighed ruefully. "Elena Anborn." He ran his fingers through his hair as if trying to make himself more presentable to the memory. "Now there was a woman in a million." He poked at the fire with a stick. Somewhere, miles away, wolves howled, and they listened for a few seconds until the noise died down before he went on, "I first met Elena in 908, when the Noros king was defying Pallas and open revolt was brewing. I was twenty-seven, she was twenty-one. There were a lot of meetings among the magi in Norostein then. She already had quite a reputation—she was the first woman in Noros to win honors in swordsmanship, so most of the men wanted to try her out. More particularly, they wanted to demonstrate that her honors were undeserved, because surely no woman could be the equal of a man." Muhren chuckled softly. "Lad, she could fight like a hellion and curse like a windshipman. She broke a few skulls and made no friends at all."

Alaron smiled. He'd only met his Aunty Elena a few times, but he knew exactly what Muhren meant. "Did you challenge her too?"

"I did. I had a fair reputation myself, but I pretty much got bullied into going a bout with her. 'For the honor of Men,' or so it was put to me. Not that I felt her unworthy—I knew the blademaster who'd assessed her was honest and a hard taskmaster. If she'd impressed him, she was good enough. I was curious, though, and by then, I was something of an admirer."

"What happened?"

"I let my admiration weaken my sword arm, and she broke it."

"The arm?"

Muhren chuckled. "Yes, the arm, not my admiration. She sent me flowers while I was with the healers. It was the tradition then for an unwanted suitor to be sent white flowers, and that's what she sent." He grinned. "Though she tucked one red rose into the bunch. Perhaps to tease me, perhaps to convey some measure of respect, but I never found out which. The Revolt began and she joined the Gray Foxes and disappeared."

Alaron had been born during the Revolt, while his father was away fighting, but his earliest memories were post-Revolt: country life at Anborn Manor, with his father always with him, teaching, instructing, playing, and laughing. His mother had been a frightening figure even then, moody and withdrawn, cowering in shadows, too volatile and unpredictable ever to love.

"I saw Elena again from time to time. The Gray Foxes started off as a scouting unit, before they became a guerrilla force later in the war. She always handed me a flower if there was one at hand, just to remind me that she'd beaten me. They started out pink, which I took to mean that she was still considering me, then in the second year, when the war turned ugly, they became white. She was sleeping with Gurvon Gyle by then."

Alaron thought he had heard that name before, but he'd not met the man. "Who was he?"

"You're asking me about the man who stole the girl I wanted?" Muhren said with a faint smile. "I didn't like him. He was cold, ruthless, and mercenary—though to be fair, he never sold out, despite being one of Belonius Vult's confidants. He fought to the end and then went into hiding rather than surrender—all the Foxes did. They were the last unit to be given amnesty after the Revolt, and only then because the Rondians wanted Gyle as an adviser for the Second Crusade."

"Aunty Elena would visit us sometimes, when she was on the run," Alaron told him. "I was very young, but I remember her turning up out of the blue some nights. She'd bring me sweets."

Muhren grunted. "I've not seen her since the Revolt. The Foxes went on the Second Crusade, but I stayed in Norostein with the Watch. I don't know where she ended up."

"In the East," Alaron replied. "She used to send money, to help Mother. She visited twice, but never for long."

"She had the body of a dancer," Muhren mused. "Not an ounce of fat on her."

"Still none, last I saw her." Alaron grinned. "I watched her practice, that last time. She moved like lightning."

Muhren nodded slowly. "Is she still with Gyle?"

Alaron shrugged. "I've never met him—I've heard of him, of course; everyone knows the Gray Foxes. They were heroes."

"They were killers," Muhren replied, and his voice sounded haunted. "They'd kill enemy soldiers in their sleep, murder informants, burn buildings with people inside them. They destroyed bridges and burned windships. I'm not saying we didn't need them, and it was war, but they did some evil things. And word is now they've turned to crime."

Alaron found himself wanting to protest, *Not my Aunty Elena!* But he could hear how that sounded, like the naïve protestations of a child. "I wish she was here anyway," he said eventually. "She'd kick those Inquisitors back to Pallas."

Muhren smiled wryly. "Likely she would, lad."

Next morning they moved at a faster pace, heading for an Alpine pass into Silacia Muhren knew of. Alaron still thought they should have gone northeast to the Brekaellen and on to Pontus, but he'd never be able to resist the scryings of their pursuers without the Watch Captain, so he had to acquiesce. *And maybe he's right*, he told himself.

It took four days more to reach and traverse the pass, mostly at walking pace as the steepness of the hills precluded the horses moving any faster. There were clear wheel-ruts marking the road south; traders and the Rimoni caravans came this way. Occasionally they came upon an inn or a small village, but they avoided them all. "What they don't know, the Inquisitors can't learn," Muhren grunted. Game was plentiful, supplementing their hardtack and grain, and as far as they could tell, they passed unseen.

On the tenth day they began to see larger-scale cultivated land again. Goat herders waved out to them, lonely men surrounded by flocks perched high on the rocky slopes. Olive groves started to appear, clothing the land. It was hotter here, and the sea winds carried more salt and rime than moisture. Muhren told him that the gulf-winds were mostly southeasterlies that tore up the Verelon coast and watered Norostein: Silacia got much less rain, and almost none in summer.

Flocks and fields meant villages, and more eyes to see them, but if they were to learn where the di Regia caravan was this summer they were going to have to chance meeting people. Muhren's affinities, Theurgy and Fire, meant he was poor at Clairvoyance. Alaron had a little affinity for it, but he didn't know Mercellus and trying to scry Cym had yielded nothing.

They knew Cym's family tended to work the vineyards near the coast, so that was where they started. Muhren had a smattering of Silacian, so he went into the villages and estates, cloaking himself in illusion to disguise his appearance. Alaron stayed with the horses, waiting anxiously.

The second afternoon, the twelfth of their flight, they finally got the information they needed: the di Regia caravan had passed that way, going south.

Three days later, they found them.

Silacian houses were built of stone or clay bricks, painted pale cream, with baked red clay roof-tiles. The vines, now heavy with fruit, fanned out in neat rows about the residence. They had court-yards to the rear, with long trestle tables set under trees and screens to shade from the blazing sunlight. In the summertime meals were always served outdoors and the scents of cooking flowed down the road to greet them, the succulent smell of roasting meat setting their mouths watering. They could hear laughing children and women singing. The sun was still high in the sky, beating down on the wide-brimmed straw hats they'd purchased at the last town to shield their eyes.

In a field below the house, a dozen wagons had been drawn up in a circle. The horses were grazing placidly, ignoring the gypsy children buzzing about them like a swarm of insects and shrieking with laughter and energy. The older ones were busy with chores, hauling water and chopping wood. The men all had curling black hair and wore white or dun shirts. The women wore white blouses and colorful patchwork skirts, and headscarves confined their hair to long cascades down their backs. They had dark, lean faces with big noses, and heavy brows above hard, wary eyes.

"Are they working for the vintner?"

Muhren nodded. "Rimoni are forbidden to own or rent land, so they travel, mostly doing seasonal work."

"Do we go to the house or the caravan?"

"The house first," Muhren replied. "Politeness dictates that the landowner is made aware of any newcomers." He pointed toward the house, and Alaron could see a tall man with long gray hair and a heavy mustache waiting on the stairs at the front. "And in fact the owner awaits us."

Muhren dismounted and went to talk to the landowner. The conversation was brief, and entirely in the local tongue. Muhren turned and translated for Alaron, while the landowner, who had a scar across his left cheek and a distant air, waved a boy over and sent him pelting toward the caravan. "His name is Torrini. He has sent for Mercellus." Muhren smiled. "We've found them."

Alaron looked about him with renewed interest. Was Cym here? He saw eyes and faces at the windows of the house: the family and servants perhaps. A young boy waved at him when their eyes met and he waved back. Then a voice called aloud in Rondian and he turned to see a man striding up the slope toward them, a big smile on his face.

"Jeris, my friend!" called Mercellus di Regia, as Muhren hurried to greet him. As he embraced Cym's father, Alaron remembered that Mercellus had been involved in the Revolt somehow; that was how he knew Muhren. They certainly looked like old friends. Master Torrini visibly relaxed when he saw Muhren's welcome.

Introductions were made, and Alaron found himself summoned forward to shake hands with Mercellus. Cym's father was a big man, almost as tall as Muhren, but a little stouter, with a massive sweeping mustache and a mane of hair shot through with veins of silver. His hands were powerful as they gripped Alaron's.

"Welcome, young Mercer! I know you, si? You and my daughter made the windskiff last year!" He laughed aloud at the memory, and Alaron did too, a little less wholeheartedly—he had after all made a total fool of himself by colliding with Anborn Manor during the test flight. Once they'd managed to repair everything, they'd sold the skiff to Mercellus. He didn't see it here though. And Cym hadn't appeared.

He began to put two and two together. "Is Cym—?"

Mercellus cut him off with a finger to the lips, a friendly smile still on his lips, but his eyes were harder. The gypsy clan leader turned back to the landowner and gushed a torrent of Rimoni, to which the owner gave a crooked nod of assent.

"Signor Torrini gives us permission to accommodate you with us," Mercellus explained, and Muhren shook hands again with the vineyard owner before following Mercellus toward the circle of caravans in the field below.

The children flocked toward them like sparrows as they entered the field, and the youths and adults all paused in their work, no less curious. Alaron thought he recognized some of the faces from the windskiff tests, when the boys had all glared at him in mute warning, that if he overstepped with Cym he was dogmeat. They looked no friendlier now.

But one of the girls surprised him by smiling right at him. She had a wide, almost moonlike face, and daring eyes. When she tossed her head and thrust her chest out a little he found himself coloring. Mercellus noticed and barked at the girl, "Anise!," and she lowered her gaze in a flutter of eyelids.

Mercellus paused in midstride and faced Muhren. "I can guess why you are here, my friends," he said in Rondian, including Alaron in the conversation. "Cymbellea has gone. She left for the East six days ago."

Muhren groaned softly. "How is she traveling?"

"Now? By skiff."

Alaron felt the tiny hope he'd had quickly fade away.

Mercellus put a hand on Muhren's shoulder. "I am sorry you missed her. I would have felt better if she had been traveling with others. But my daughter is a law unto herself." There was a certain rueful pride in his voice as he said this. "Tonight, though, you will be our guests." He made a gesture toward the wagons. "You will experience true Rimoni hospitality."

"Then it was worth the trip for that alone," Muhren replied warmly.

Rimoni food was like nothing Alaron had ever experienced, full of tastes that made his mouth sizzle. The meat and vegetables were rubbed with dry seeds and pastes, then barbecued. Fruit filled the baskets on the tables. There was even Silacian white wine, gifted by Signor Torrini for the occasion. The first tiny glass tasted a little sweet to Alaron, but he soon got accustomed to the taste, and by the third glass his head was floating.

Mercellus sat with them at the head of a long bench-table in the middle of the circle of wagons. Several of the men had musical instruments that they played with verve and incredible skill, and Alaron found his feet tapping in anticipation. His eyes strayed to a cluster of giggling young women and he realized with a shock that they were all staring at him, passing whispered comments behind their hands. The moon-faced girl smiled coyly at him.

Anise . . .

"So, Jeris-amici," said Mercellus di Regia with an ironic smile, "how much trouble is my daughter in?"

Muhren puffed out his cheeks and made a face.

Mercellus winced. "That bad, my friend?"

"Worse," Muhren admitted. "She has something very valuable, and some dangerous people want it back."

"She was being very mysterious," Mercellus replied, sipping his wine. He sounded calm, but Alaron could see worry-lines appearing as he spoke. "She was carrying something she wouldn't show me. I did not press the issue. She was anxious to take the skiff and go." His eyes shifted to Alaron: "She has been learning how to pilot the craft you and she created."

"Where is she going, Mercellus?" Muhren asked.

"To Pontus, and then to Hebusalim," Mercellus replied in a low voice. "I could not dissuade her, nor could I stop her."

Alaron didn't think there was much Mercellus di Regia couldn't do if he set his mind to it. But he also knew Cym. *And if she really is Meiros's granddaughter, that makes her—what? A half-blood? No wonder she was always better at the gnosis than Ramon and me.*

"Is there anything I can do to aid your search?" Mercellus asked, after a few moments of reflection.

Muhren frowned. "Something of hers that she wore or used constantly, perhaps?"

Mercellus tilted his head thoughtfully. "I know just the thing." He waved a woman over and whispered to her, and Alaron watched her walk to the largest wagon. She returned holding a small wooden doll, an ugly thing with tattered clothing and chewed legs. The thatch of hair was almost all gone and the face-paint had been scuffed away. "This doll is named Aggi," Mercellus told them. "She loved Aggi when she was a child; she slept with her, played with her, talked to her, took her everywhere." He smiled to himself and placed the doll in front of Muhren, who pushed it toward Alaron.

"We'll find her," Alaron said earnestly, pocketing the doll reverently.

"It's a big world, lad," Mercellus replied. "Don't make promises you cannot be sure of." His eyes held all the worry a father could have over a wayward daughter.

"She left a note for us, Mercellus. In it she claimed a rather special woman as her mother . . ."

Mercellus's eyes narrowed a little, then he exhaled. "Justina Meiros," he admitted. "She told me she'd left such a letter—I thought it unwise at the time." He looked from Muhren to Alaron and back again. "But if it has set you on her trail and you can see her safe, then perhaps not so unwise."

"Did she tell you anything else of why she wished to go east?"

Mercellus was clearly loath to admit not knowing what Cym was doing, and Alaron guessed he must be galled to have a daughter he could not control. "She is a good girl, but she goes her own way," he repeated. He didn't mention the Scytale.

"How did you come to have such a child, Mercellus?" Muhren asked.

Mercellus sighed wistfully. "How does a poor Rimoni trader come to woo the daughter of Antonin Meiros?" His eyes glazed over. "How indeed?" He looked at Muhren, a smile playing about his lips. "I have told few this tale, my friend—not for shame but for respect of others' privacy. But I feel you should know this. It may help you, if you follow my daughter into the East."

Alaron took a hasty sip of wine and leaned forward. He wondered if his ears were flapping. He even managed to put aside noticing Anise and the way her hips swayed when she walked.

For now, at least.

A fond smile stole over Mercellus's face. "It was 911, after the Noros Revolt. My role in that conflict had brought the attention of the Inquisition, so I thought it wise to leave for places the empire would not look. For a time, my caravan dispersed into Metia and Lantris and I myself took to the road alone. I went east. I wanted to see the great Bridge, and the land called Javon, where thousands of Rimoni had settled during the early Moontides.

"The Bridge was far below the ocean that year, of course, but there were windships, and I managed to gain passage as a windship-man. The work was hard, working the sails in twelve-hour shifts, as even the largest windcraft have small capacity and cannot bear many crewmen. But it got me to Hebusalim. I had little money, but I was a young man and I had the dances and music of my people." He grinned. "Later, you will see our dances. We will even teach you, if you are willing. I was a fine dancer and a fair singer, though I say so myself. I met Simos, who was very good on the jitar, and together we played the taverns, trying to make enough money to buy passage to Javon. We were good, Simos and I—very good. Very popular, especially with the ladies, si?" He winked broadly.

Muhren chuckled and the Rimoni grinned toothily. "We had a reputation, and it got us into fights sometimes. Other times it got us into the bedrooms of well-to-do women. Most were unwed; some were not so."

Muhren shook his head knowingly and Alaron found his eyes straying back to Anise. She had a faint pout on her lips that vanished the moment their eyes met. She began to rock her shoulders a little, as if a slow dance were spreading through her limbs. One sleeve fell off her shoulder and she pulled it back up while pretending not to notice him.

Some dancing later, huh . . .

"Eventually we attracted some unexpected attention," Mercellus went on, interrupting Alaron's thoughts. "A servant in finer clothes than most masters wear came to call. He offered us a soirée at a private residence, for more than we'd earn in three months, so of course we accepted." He shook his head as if in disbelief, even after all these years. "The next evening we were taken to a fine house where the walls were entirely of marble. In Hebusalim, the women and men live in different parts of the house: the women tend the kitchens and have their own bedrooms. When the master desires—*ahem*—congress with his wife, she is summoned to his private rooms. The women's quarters are known as the zenana. To our surprise it was to the zenana that we were summoned." He laughed throatily. "At that point we knew we were in for a memorable night."

Alaron felt his cheeks go red. He glanced at Anise again, telling himself it was to distract him from this story, which was clearly going to become distinctly risqué, but it didn't work. In fact, the way she was swaying across the grass with the other girls made it worse.

"The house belonged to a Rondian woman named Alyssa Dulayne, a pure-blood mage, very beautiful, with hair like clear honey and skin like milk. She greeted us in a dress of blue gauze, almost completely see-through. I was three-legged, my friends—we both were. Simos was all eyes, and she didn't care." He took a sip of wine to moisten his tongue. "I should tell you that magnificent specimen though I am, Simos was an Adonis. He couldn't dance for shit, but he had curling hair and puppy eyes, and a horn the size of a horse. The girls all went for Simos first and I got the leftovers, but they were no less pretty. It is no bad thing to have a handsome best friend!"

The musicians struck up a slow rhythmic strumming on their jitars, and the girls began to move about them, hands together, gracefully reaching skywards, their chests curving outward tantalizingly. Alaron hastily looked away and took another sip himself.

"Well, this Alyssa clearly was going to eat Simos alive—but she did have a friend. If Alyssa was the golden Sol, this woman was the moon: her hair was like the curtain of night, glittering with stars, her face as white as snow, with blood-red lips and dark eyes. We were not told her name, but I named her *Moonchild* in my mind. Unlike Alyssa, she was not dressed as a wanton, but in a demure velvet dress that concealed her body entirely, yet hinted at the curves beneath. But she was little interested in the pleasures Alyssa planned. She was sucking on a hookah and her eyes were glazed. I began to think that maybe only Simos would be fortunate that night."

Anise was looking at him over her shoulder, Alaron realized, her eyes flashing. *I'm dancing for you,* her look said, and he couldn't look away, even as he became aware that the Rimoni boys were beginning to notice. They were all wearing knives. Something in the wine or the music or something else entirely made him feel bold. *I'm a mage*, he reminded myself. *Think you scare me?* Then he frowned. The thought tasted ugly, like something Malevorn Andevarion or Francis Dorobon might think.

He looked away from the girls and concentrated on the story.

"To cut to the chase, Simos played and I danced, and because I knew Alyssa wanted Simos, I danced as if the other woman, my Moonchild, were the only one in the room. I leapt, I strutted and pirouetted like one possessed, all for her. We played our whole repertoire, and then suddenly the jitar stopped, midsong, and when I looked back I found that Alyssa had pulled it from Simos's hands and placed herself in his lap. I looked away, at a loss what to do, but when I turned back my Moonchild was standing right before me. I almost jumped from my skin, she moved so swiftly and silently. Right at that moment, she frightened me. Her pupils were so large I could see no whites in her eyes. Her mouth was slightly open and her teeth were as vividly white as her lips were red. I remembered legends from Sydia of blood-drinking corpses. Then the dress slipped from her body and she stepped into my arms and kissed me."

Mercellus stopped speaking, and stared at his hands. "I need tell you little more. She kept me with her for one night only. She was not a virgin, but she was nervous and awkward. I never found out her name until much later. Simos and I traveled on to Javon and stayed there together for a year, then he met a local girl and married her. He lives there still, if he lives at all. I returned, not liking the place—there was too much hostility between Rimoni and Jhafi—but no sooner had I arrived back in Hebusalim than that same servant sought me out, for quite a different errand."

"A child?" Alaron blurted.

"You are a bad audience, boy," Mercellus chided him wryly. "Yes, a bambina. I had got Justina Meiros with child and in the year I was away, she had given birth. But she was an indifferent mother; she did not want the little bambina, so when she was told I had returned to Hebusalim, I was summoned and given the child. She had not even named her." He shook his head. "Justina was utterly indifferent to me throughout the interview. I was told I was the only man she'd lain with before conception so there was no doubt whose child she carried. I would have taken the girl for nothing, to get her away from her cold-hearted mother, but in fact they paid me generously." He blinked slowly, as if to banish the memories back to the back of his mind. "And so that is my tale, and now I have a daughter like no other."

Alaron swallowed. "I was in love with her," he blurted out before his brain could intervene.

"Clearly," Mercellus said, his voice both fondly amused and warning.

"She doesn't love me though," Alaron added quickly. "We are just friends."

"I know. I cannot *control* my daughter, but I *know* her."

These past weeks Alaron had been carefully taking all the feelings he'd had for Cym and packing them away. He could feel them, rattling in the trunk, demanding release, but quite deliberately, he ignored the temptation. Instead, he turned to watch the dancers again.

At a small gesture from Mercellus, the rhythm changed. While he had been talking, the middle of the circle had been gradually cleared of tables and more and more of the women, the older ones who had been cooking, now entered the space. They brought a different feel to the dance: wider hips, bigger bosoms and knowing faces. Wives made eye contact with husbands as the men formed a loose cordon around the dancers, clapping and swaying in time to the music. There were no nervous looks or giggles from the married women, just hot looks at the circling men. One of the matrons of the clan made a loud whooping cry and spun toward a man who wore a sash of the same material as her skirt; she planted her feet and jiggled her breasts while fluttering her hands provocatively. Her husband ululated wildly and began to dance around her, thrusting with his hips.

Alaron gaped, and nearly dropped his wine cup.

Muhren clapped him on the shoulders. "Go on lad, join them."

"No way!" Alaron spluttered.

Mercellus laughed. "This boy is eighteen?" he asked Muhren, as if Muhren was Alaron's father.

"Nearly nineteen," Alaron growled. His birthday was in Noveleve.

"And he is not already married?" Mercellus raised his eyebrows.

"No takers," Muhren said dryly. "He's an argumentative little cuss. But he's mellowing a little."

Alaron glowered at him.

"But a mage, si?"

"Quarter-blood."

Alaron took in the calculating look on the gypsy chief's face and his face burned hotter than he had thought possible. A sixteenth-blood mage could not breed more magi with a human, but a quarter-blood could, with better odds of conception than a purer-blooded mage. He began to feel like a horse being assessed for stud. "Ah, look, I'm quite tired. It's probably time I found my bedroll and—"

Muhren stood up and gripped his shoulder. "Boy, it's time you learned how to dance."

Rimoni dancing was like fencing, Alaron decided sometime after his fourth glass of wine. There were set movements that flowed into each other, leading from the shoulder or the hip: thrust and give ground, let the other person counter as you spin away. It was sparring, with eyes for blades. The melody was a trick, a feint to deceive, but if you followed the beat tapped out on the wooden box of the jitar, you stayed in step.

One thing ten years of waving a practice-sword around had taught him was how to move, balanced, precise, and poised. He'd seen the way the gypsy men were looking at him, prepared to jeer, but he managed to keep them quiet, for all their dismissive gestures and smirking. He struck another pose, akin to a bow, and moved on to the next girl.

Anise.

She was definitely following him, positioning herself in the same eight as him each time, and whenever their eyes met, she smiled. The other girls remained aloof and retreated to their mothers after one song. But it didn't look like Anise's mother was present. Whenever the dances paused, she would retreat to sit with a younger boy with the same big eyes. This time, though, she backed away from Alaron, her look both bold and coy. He felt like everyone here was watching them, but he couldn't help staring back. It was as if his brains had floated south as he danced.

"Who is she?" he asked Muhren when the watch captain appeared at his side.

"Anise? She's an orphan. She and her brother were raised by their grandparents, but they both died a few years ago." He poked Alaron in the shoulder. "Rimoni girls who are not virgins when they wed lose their dowry," he said pointedly. "So do those who wed outside the clans."

Alaron's cheeks burned. "We're only dancing."

"I know. I'm just making conversation. Furthering your education."

Alaron glared at him. "She keeps chasing me."

"To her, you're a rich Rondian mage. She may think you're worth losing a dowry over."

His eyes strayed back to her, trying to work out if her flirting was based on money or attraction. All this talk of virgins and dowry was doing nothing for his composure. "Ah, I should probably go and get some rest," he muttered.

Muhren nodded sympathetically. "That's probably wise." He glanced at Mercellus, who was laying down the law over something with one of his men. "Our packs and bedrolls were supposed to be put in the lee of one of the caravans. We'll set up beside the stream. I'll join you after I've had a chat with Mercellus."

Alaron fumbled his way through the twilight to get his and Muhren's packs and bedrolls into place. An older Rimoni man with a gray ponytail had helped him find them, and though neither spoke each other's tongue, after much gesturing and smiling he'd been shown a good camping spot, set amidst a stand of willow beside the small stream. The old man shuffled off, and Alaron lit a small gnosis-light and erected the two small tents. He'd become practiced at the task over the past weeks and now he did it without having to concentrate.

Then he extinguished the gnosis-light and sat on the banks, bathing his feet in the cool water, listening to the gentle rippling of the stream. Overhead, the giant half-moon told him that the month of Julsep was racing toward its end. He pictured Cym in the skiff, high in the skies.

We made that skiff together, he reminded himself, smiling at the memory.

Music still flowed from the Rimoni camp, less frenetic now, the melody more intricate. There was singing, men on the verses and women on the choruses, and it sounded sad and lovely, reminding him of the ruined villas they'd passed over the past few days: the bleached bones of Empire.

He let his mind drift through a pleasant "what-if?" fantasy of staying here, where no one knew he was a failed mage, with the Scytale safely in the hands of someone who'd know just what to do with it, someone like Antonin Meiros. He could stay here and maybe rescue sweetly alluring Anise from being an unwed orphan girl. They could dance under the moonlight every night, far from blood and war.

It's not what I used to dream, but those dreams will never work out now . . .

"Alron di Meersa?" a girl's voice called from beside his tent. He was momentarily startled, and his heart jumped a little. *It's her.* He turned as Anise swayed between the willow fronds and then tiptoed to where he sat. Before he could rise, she'd swept her skirts beneath her and sat down. She put a hand on his shoulder. "Alron, si?"

"Al-a-ron," he said, his heart thudding. He was glad it was dark so she couldn't see him blushing.

She repeated his name in a sing-song voice that made little bubbles dance inside him, then tapped her own chest. "Ah-neesa."

"Anise," he repeated, making her beam with pleasure. She moved away from him, leaning back on her right arm, looking at him first with her left eye, then her right, and giggling as she did. She had a wide mouth and full lips, dark skin and a tangled profusion of black hair, not a beauty but pretty, and totally unlike Cym. Alaron couldn't help smiling—and trembling, to be so close. "Uh, do you speak Rondian?"

She giggled, understanding enough to shake her head. "Rimoni," she tinkled, then cocked her head, her eyes catching the moonlight. "Magi?" she asked him.

He nodded tensely. *These people were slaughtered by magi five hundred years ago—*

But she didn't seem to care. She said something like, "Ora mi mostra!" He liked her voice.

"You want to see?" he guessed. He summoned the gnosis, just a tiny blue flame, and made it dance on his fingertips. She gasped, then giggled as he made it vanish, then reappear. She tried to cup it, then pulled away at the heat of it. Her laugh made his head feel like it might detach from his neck and float away.

"È bello!" she laughed, then she seized his hand and closed it on the flame, looked up into his eyes, waiting.

I'm going to get a knife in the back for this . . .

He kissed her. Seductively warm, moist lips covered his and pulled him in as her arms wrapped about him, sliding over the fabric on his shoulders and back. He seemed to fall into her, onto her, as she laughed throatily. It felt like a dream, like something that really ought to be happening to someone else. *Where's this going?* he thought with both fear and exhilaration. It was very odd: he'd only just met her, couldn't even hold a conversation with her, but he knew that he liked her—more than liked her. *Isn't that strange?* He could imagine the teasing Ramon would give him for this, but that made him kiss her harder. That Muhren might appear at any moment apparently made it all the more imperative that he not stop.

Above them the moon limned the water with mercury and the stream gurgled with pleasure. He stroked her shoulders, as that seemed a safe place to touch her, only to find the dress falling away, leaving her warm, bare skin, soft and smooth and more wonderful than the richest fabric. She sighed softly into his mouth, pulling him onto her.

"Anise!" a young male voice called from somewhere amidst the trees. He broke off from kissing her as she hissed vexedly. She pressed a finger against his lips, shook her head.

"Anise!" The boy's voice came from around the tents now. "Anise!"

She giggled in Alaron's ear, making his skin tingle all over. "Ferdi," she whispered. "Mio fratello." *My brother*, Alaron surmised. She wrapped her arms about him, held him to her. "Shhh." The boy moved about noisily, disturbing the horses a little, without coming near them.

After a minute or so, Ferdi stomped away, back toward the wagons. Alaron decided that Muhren must have stayed for another drink with Mercellus di Regia, and as Anise pulled his face back to hers, he found himself hoping he'd take his time.

Then she stiffened beneath him and her breath caught in her throat. He looked at her eyes, saw them widening at something above him and he went rigid, then looked up slowly, half-expecting to see someone standing over them, one of the quick-bladed Rimoni boys come to protect her honor.

It wasn't a boy.

A cloud of massive shapes like giant bats was gliding across Luna's face in a spiral formation, and it was bearing down toward the Rimoni camp. Even at this distance he could see they were giant, impossible creatures—*constructs*. And that meant Pallas, for only the Pallas animagi could breed such creatures in any number. And Pallas meant Inquisitors.

They've found us!

Anise pushed him away, a look of fear on her face, and Alaron was no less afraid. His heart was pounding as the beasts glided right over them.

There was no challenge, no threats, no warning; there was only lightning, blazing from above into the circle of wagons.

6

Legion Service

The Wandering Star

For centuries we have known of the heavenly body the Hebb call "Simutu," the so-called Wandering Star. We now believe it to be a lesser moon, one with a highly elliptical orbit. That it draws most closely to Urte every twelve years, during the Moontide, is of course no coincidence. Simutu's name is drawn from the Hebb word for copper, due to the moon's coloration. The Hebb say that those born beneath Simutu are prone to madness and capable of prophecy.

ORDO COSTRUO COLLEGIATE

Northpoint, Pontic Peninsula, Yuros
Julsep 928
1st month of the Moontide

As the windship swung low over the mass of humanity clustered on the edge of the continent, Ramon Sensini felt his excitement rise. Two weeks of constant motion were coming to an end. That day they had broken through clouds about the Pontic Hills, where the ground fell away in a long sweeping slope toward the East and the glittering ocean and the clouds boiling on the horizon. All the traveling magi had gathered in the bow, pushing Ramon aside, and started cheering and pointing. The panorama was spectacular. The land ran toward a great rim where huge cliffs towered over the rushing waters hundreds of feet below. Even at this distance they could hear the roar of the waves pounding upon the cliffs. White clouds of sea-spray shrouded the coast, and the tang of saltwater hung in the air.

One of the travelers pointed southwest, where a dirty stain spread over the green swathe. In the middle of it rose a huge spear of white, topped by a brilliant light. "The Tower!" he shouted, and others took up the call.

Ramon squinted until he could make out a pale needle with a glowing blue light at its zenith. He felt his own sense of wonder stir. This was the legendary Northpoint, the prosaically named northernmost anchor of the Leviathan Bridge—Antonin Meiros's continent-joining, epoch-changing Bridge. He tried to see further, but the distance defeated him. Even now, though, men were crossing to the eastern continent, bringing war and death, and soon he would join them.

Their windship landed west of the camp, amidst a forest of masts and spars looking like the aftermath of a forest storm. There were at least four dozen windcraft here, ranging from tiny skiffs to massive warbirds, more than he'd ever seen in one place, and it was only one of several landing fields he'd glimpsed from above. The stench of the camp rose to greet them as they touched down.

Wind raked the plains, whistling through the city of tents, setting the canvas slapping and the guy-ropes whistling in a scattered rhythm. Fields full of tents, boxes, barrels, and mountains of grain were infested by swarms of dockers, worker ants dumping, shifting, carrying, loading, and unloading thousands of tons of supplies for the war. The soldiers were the smallest part of this temporary nest of humanity. This place was Portage XXVI, three hundred acres of land plowed and flattened for the windships to land on, and the same again for a camp swarming with the men of the legions. Outside the soldiers' camp were twice as many more people: merchants and traders, wives and fiancées and children, whores of both genders, beggars and opportunists. Forty legions—roughly 200,000 men, were marching over the Bridge into Dhassa to join the eight legions already there, and two others in Dorobon colors were preparing to be shipped to Javon: a scarlet tide was bearing down upon Antiopia. The Crusade had begun. Already the vanguard was marching onto the Bridge, and every day two or three more legions joined them as the bottleneck of soldiery resolved itself.

The last two weeks had been a blur of motion for Ramon, starting with a windship journey from Norostein to the Brekaellen Valley. From there he'd taken further ships, cramped little vessels filled with a dozen fellow magi, mostly by-blows of magi promiscuity, with the odd disgraced high-blood horrified to be sharing the journey with such riffraff. He was the only southerner, and the Argundians, Hollenians, Andressans, and Metians onboard had been delighted to have someone to practice their bigotry upon. He could barely wait to lose them all. He shouldered his pack and scuttled away before anyone could manage a parting shot, verbal or otherwise.

The camp was a bewildering mess, the normal rigorously applied legion camp layout falling apart under the pressure of so many noncombatants and so much equipment and supplies. The livestock enclosures alone were larger than most of the legion camps. They were filled with either horses or hulkas, the massive bullock-constructs bred to move supply trains. The hulkas stood twice the height of a man, weighed eight to ten tons, and were bred by animism-gnosis, combining aspects of oxen and giant Antiopian beasts called elephants. They had neither horns nor tusks, and were bred to be placid and endlessly patient. Thanks to a radical recent gnostic advance, they now understood simple verbal commands and needed no driver. Some cavalry units had been similarly blessed with intelligent steeds; khurnes were horses bred for strength and speed, with a single vicious horn on their foreheads, and like the hulkas they had the intelligence to understand verbal commands.

Gazing up at the watchful eyes of a hulka, Ramon was reminded of his old college classmate Boron Funt, who was similarly massive, and similarly dour. "What do you want?" he demanded grumpily. The hulka blinked slowly and looked away, as if its thoughts were too profound to share. *Creepy damned things.*

He found a ragged child who agreed, for a copper, to guide him to the tent flying the legion flag with the number XIII emblazoned upon it. He flipped the kid his coin, then pushed his way tentatively inside.

A man looked up, squinted and scowled. "Sensini?"

"Yes."

"That's 'Yes sir,'" the man growled. "And salute when I address you."

"Yes, sir, sorry, sir." Ramon saluted like he'd seen other men do and that seemed to suffice.

The man before him—his new commanding officer—was as ugly a mage as he'd ever seen, broken-nosed and belligerent-looking, with a receding hairline and the blotched skin of a drinker. Most magi took some care of their appearance, encouraged by the Church's desire for magi to at least try to look semi-divine, but this man clearly didn't care. His uniform was tatty, his boots scuffed, but he exuded tough competence.

"I am Legate Jonti Duprey, Commander of the Thirteenth." Duprey looked over Ramon disapprovingly. "And you're a sixteenth-blood mage? I asked for a damned half-blood!" Duprey ran his fingers through his remaining hair. "What kept you?"

"Delays in Norostein, sir," Ramon replied. He wondered how Alaron was. Had he found Cym yet? Leaving Alaron to cope on his own felt like sending a lamb into the desert, but if he hadn't shown up for this legion posting, his paterfamilias would have turned nasty.

Duprey tapped the paper on his desk. "We march in two days, Sensini." Then the tent-flap opened and a hulking blond youth came in. Duprey peered at him. "Kippenegger?"

"Yar, ycha bie Fridryk Kippenegger." The newcomer was clearly Schlessen. He had a pale complexion, his blond hair fell past his shoulders and he was built like a bull. He was clad in a tooled leather breastplate and wore his arms bare with copper armbands shaped like snakes coiled about them. His biceps were as big as any other man's thighs. He wore two throwing axes and a sword as long as Ramon's body.

Duprey rolled his eyes. "Sir. You call me 'Sir.'"

"Yar."

Duprey waited, stony-faced. Ramon suppressed a smile.

Eventually the Schlessen twigged to what was expected. "Yar, sir." Kippenegger glanced at Ramon. "Rimoni?"

"Silacian."

The Schlessen grunted. "Stay away from my things." But he said it with a little smirk, perhaps a flash of the alleged Schlessen sense of humor.

"You're here to report to me, not chat," Duprey snapped. He sighed heavily. "It's like this every fucking time: I have experienced, disciplined troops, but every Crusade I get new magi who know nothing about the legions. Why we can't begin the conscriptions a year in advance of the march I don't know. Actually I do: money." He hawked as if to spit, then decided against it—it was his own tent, after all. "So, welcome. Our full complement of magi will be allotted tomorrow."

"Allotted, sir?" Ramon asked.

"There's a ballot for those magi not already commissioned to a specific legion. Most legions have a peacetime core of six magi, and then add the rest from the volunteers by allotment. You were assigned to us on graduation. You'll be battle-magi, assigned to a specific maniple, understood?"

"Yes, sir."

Kippenegger blinked. "Yar." He frowned at the silence. "Er . . . sir."

Duprey sighed heavily. "Right. Sensini, you'll be assigned to the Tenth Maniple—I presume your papers mentioned this?" He waited with a look of tired expectancy on his face. Legions were roughly five thousand men, divided into ten maniples. The Tenth Maniple was the noncombat unit: scouts, engineers, clerks, cooks and logistics, plus a contingent of archers: they were considered the lowest of the low. Most magi thought themselves above such an assignment.

"That will be fine, sir," Ramon replied, trying to keep his voice neutral. In truth, his paterfamilias had practically skipped for joy when he'd read Ramon's assignment letter: in his view, whoever controlled supplies and wages controlled the legion.

Duprey blinked, then looked relieved. "I suppose as a sixteenth-blood you had no higher aspirations, eh? Kippenegger, you'll be battle-mage of the Ninth Maniple. I can't imagine I'll get anyone else as low-blooded as you two. The rest will be assigned from the allotment." He grimaced. "Bloody latecomers, thinking they can wander in at the last minute and get the pick of the legions. Cretins."

Ramon winked at Kippenegger. "Yes sir." The Schlessen stifled a grin.

"Did I ask for an opinion?" Duprey glowered sourly. "Forty-odd legions are crossing into Antiopia, four by windship, and the rest marching. Thank your lucky stars you're magi; you'll get a horse. Go and unpack and take the weight off your feet. We've added a new Secundus earlier this month, and we'll get six more magi tomorrow so if you want the best beds, you'd better choose smartly." He jabbed a finger at the studious-looking aide-de-camp in the corner. "Nyvus, see these two to the mage-barracks, please."

The aide was probably a non-mage, but he had an air of authority beyond his years. He led Ramon and Kippenegger from the command tent toward a larger pavilion. Not far off, Ramon could see a crowd of a hundred or more magi, obviously all recent unassigned arrivals, clustered about a big white pavilion near the command tent. He recognized faces from his own windship voyage and hoped none would be assigned to the Thirteenth. *But let's face it, whoever we get are going to be pricks.*

Inside the mage-tent, fourteen beds had been set out, each half-screened from the others. All were empty but three, which had sleeping men sprawled on them. The nearest woke the moment they entered.

"Wha—? Oh." The man rubbed his eyes. Evidently some kind of security ward had jolted him awake. He waved a hand at Duprey's aide. "Thank you, Nyvus, I'll look after them from here." The aide left with a smart salute. "Nyvus is the most military man we've got," the mage commented, looking Ramon up and down. "Let me guess: Sensini?"

"Si."

"And Kippenegger?"

"Yar."

The man stood up. He was wrapped in the crumpled blue cloak that denoted a pilot-mage. Ramon blinked at the geometrically patterned skirt beneath it. "Baltus Prenton, Windmaster of the Thirteenth, at your service." He was clearly from Brevin, a cold, wet northern province bordering Schlessen that had been "civilized" by the Rondians, which had resulted in Brevians being held in contempt by both peoples.

"You dress like a woman," Kippenegger observed grumpily. Ramon suppressed a smile. It appeared that thoughts made their way from the Schlessen's brain to his tongue fairly unchecked, which promised to be amusing. Ramon wondered if he was trying to pick a fight with Prenton for some obscure reason, or whether there was some requirement among the Schlessens for chest-beating when dealing with other northerners.

The Brevian just smiled. "Why so I do. 'Brevin, where men wear skirts and women wear pants,' so the old jest goes. We call it a 'kilt,' old boy."

"The men of Brevin are just hairier women," Kippenegger told Ramon with heavy contempt.

"Can we dispense with the whole 'my tribe's better than your tribe' thing?" Baltus Prenton replied mildly. "It's rather tiresome and it serves no purpose, don't you think?"

Ramon said quickly, "Fine by me. No one has anything good to say about my people anyway."

"That is because you are rodents," Kippenegger informed him. Then he frowned. "Ach, I suppose you are right. We're going to have a bunch of Rondian *shizen* assigned to us so best we 'vassals' are friends, yar?" He extended his left hand. "Call me Kip."

Ramon and Prenton shook hands right-handed with each other, then left-handed with Kip, and the Brevian gestured toward the two other men, still sleeping obliviously. "Coulder and Fenn: my countrymen, both battle-magi—Duprey's not assigned the upper maniples yet; he's waiting to see who he gets from the allotment." He nudged a bottle on the small table. "There is Brician red, if you want it."

"No beer?" Kip grumped.

"I was lucky to get the wine," Prenton told them. "The stores have practically everything except what you want, the traders are all thieves and everything's being shipped east, so no one knows where anything is anyway."

"Is that normal?" Ramon asked. He smiled internally: when officers had no idea what was going on, there were profits to be made.

Prenton harrumphed good-naturedly. "Normal? What is normal? Listen, this is the second Crusade I've been on. Did you hear about last time? Damned nightmare, I tell you. The Thirteenth was assigned to a region in West Dhassa where nothing was supposed to happen. The men went crazy stuck in the desert with nothing to do while the villagers crept around at night slitting throats and poisoning the wells. Finally the legate snapped and loosed us on the town—total rampage, but against orders, you understand. We got decimated for mutiny—you know what that means?"

Ramon and Kip both nodded: one man in ten executed, by lottery.

Prenton shuddered in horror at the memory. "The survivors had all amassed pay and pensions canceled. The rankers had to start from scratch."

Ramon and Kip looked at each other. "So the men of this legion are all mutineers?"

"Most. Some have left, new men have come in, but we're a punishment legion now, so the recruits are no better. The officers were all disgraced, of course, so me, Duprey, Coulder, Fenn, even poor Tyron and Lanna who spoke against the rampage, we were all bound over to serve another twelve years in the Thirteenth. The taint remains, you know. The rest of the army think we're rabble." He shook his head grimly. "Anyone with connections avoids us like lepers. Kore knows where we'll be assigned this time. Anyway, pleased to have you with us, lads."

"The legate said we'd have more magi allotted to us."

Prenton laughed. "Indeed. Right now all those who were too lazy or badly connected to get themselves assigned earlier are pleading, begging, offering their virginity, or selling their firstborn to get into one of the glamour legions. What they don't know is that those positions went months, even years ago. The only places left are in the workhorse legions."

"How do they decide who goes where?"

Prenton smiled wryly. "Bribery and cocksucking, the usual." He waved a hand. "Pick a bunk and settle in. Each legion gets fifteen magi: five command positions and ten battle-magi. We've got Legate Duprey, Secundus Marle—he's a nut, so watch him—Coulder and Fenn, we three, plus the chaplain and healer, so six more to reach full complement. They'll whine like buggered nuns when they're allotted to us—it'll be as tedious as all Hel."

They spent the afternoon settling in and washing their things while Nyvus came and went, officious and efficient. At dusk they sat outside with Prenton on fold-up chairs, watching the blood-red sunset which promised good weather to come.

Many of the legions had already gone, and more marched every day. In two days it would be them, stepping out onto three hundred miles of stone, trusting in the engineering and gnosis of Antonin Meiros and his Ordo Costruo. It was a daunting thought, despite the numbers who'd already done it and survived. Tales of freak storms in the ocean swamping the Bridge and washing away swathes of men ran riot through the ranks, though no one could say exactly which legions had supposedly perished.

They met Coulder and Fenn briefly, though neither was interested in speaking of anything but dicing, but Baltus Prenton was more than happy to chat, mostly about the low quality of recruits this year: petty criminals with no respect for authority, bankruptees trying to work off debt, and minor dissidents punished for saying and doing the wrong things—crimes not serious enough to warrant incarceration or execution. "It means the bastards question every order," Prenton grumbled good-naturedly. "At first, anyway. Then the centurions lash a few; that knocks the rebellion out of them."

"Can we count on them in a fight?" Ramon asked.

Prenton snorted amiably. "A fight? Dear Kore, this is a *Crusade*, lad, not a war. There'll be no *fighting*, only endless days of marching around from ruin to empty ruin. There may be a bit of looting and pillaging thrown in, if we're lucky. The Keshi don't fight back. They run and hide." He made a face. "The biggest risk is their God-awful food."

Ramon thought the camp food unpalatable enough. They ate slowly, trying to savor a mush that definitely contained potato and beans, but little else that was identifiable. There was wine—of sorts: a Brician chardo that was almost certainly off. But Prenton was pleasant enough, and gradually Kip and Ramon relaxed.

"So who is Duprey?" Ramon asked Prenton.

"The legate? He's a bankrupt merchant. Well, that's how he ended up in the legion, but he's been army for fourteen years," Prenton replied. "He was a battle-mage during the mutiny and was put in charge afterward when the previous bastard used his political connections to get a pardon. Like us all, he's hoping he'll get enough plunder from this Crusade to get out."

"Is there really plunder to be had?"

Prenton's nose twitched. "Last time the Kirkegarde and the Imperial Guard got it all. They confiscated whatever they could get, even from their own men."

"But you're all back for more," Kip commented.

"What choice is there? Anyway, Pallas have put Echor in charge this time. That lifted the musters: Echor will look after the provinces."

"Will he?" Ramon asked doubtfully.

"Perhaps. If he thinks it'll give him a chance to bully Constant. You know the story, right? Duke Echor is Constant's uncle, but only by marriage. Emperor Hiltius made him Duke of Argundy when he married Hiltius's sister. But then Hiltius died—"

"Was murdered," Ramon put in.

Prenton put a finger to his lips. "We never say that, even among friends." He wiped his mouth, then lowered his voice even further. "Magnus took the throne and led the First Crusade before he too 'died.' His eldest child was Princess Natia, by his first wife Alitia, who died in childbirth. By then he had a son by his second wife, Lucia: Constant, whom he despised. Natia and her husband, Echor's brother, had been groomed for the throne by Magnus, but when

Magnus died, Lucia turned the tables on them. She had the husband executed and Natia imprisoned and Constant's ass on the throne in time for the Second Crusade, and the rest, as they say, is history."

Ramon knew all this, but Kip clearly had been only vaguely aware. "Is Natia still alive?" the Schlessen asked.

"Reportedly, but no one has seen her for years. She was imprisoned when she was fifteen—she'd be in her thirties by now. She's probably gone mad, if she's even still alive." Prenton raised two fingers. "Constant has two young children, Cordan and Coramore, so Echor has been bumped down the succession. He favored Natia, obviously, but when Constant came to the throne, Echor was too powerful in Argundy to dismiss. So they've been treading very softly around each other."

"How did Echor get the command?" Ramon asked.

"I imagine he flexed some muscle or made some trade-off behind the scenes," Prenton replied. "Some are saying he could come back from this Crusade with money and glory enough to seize the throne. That's the real struggle going on, not fighting the Keshi."

Next morning, Ramon took Kip aside and explained his role—*look tough but keep your periapt hidden, and if anyone gives trouble, hit them hard*—then went out into the rainstorm looking for the man his paterfamilias had ordered him to find.

At the fringes of Portage XXVI were hundreds of huts, tents, awnings, and shelters of all descriptions. The wind whipped through them, water poured through the gaps and every face was an etching of avarice and misery. This was where the deals were cut, for the goods the army didn't officially want but couldn't do without.

"I'm looking for Giordano," Ramon told a perfumed boy in a woman's silk dress who sashayed toward them through the tangle of guy-ropes.

"Giordano's no fun," the boy purred, batting long lashes and stroking his chest. "I'm fun."

Ramon kindled his periapt. "Giordano," he repeated more firmly.

The boy's eyes went round and he shot backward. "Red Snake sign, that way."

"Filth," Kip growled in Ramon's ear. "Should be castrated for going about like that."

"He probably already has been. Come on."

They found a tent, larger than most, with a red snake painted on a board. There was a sour-looking young man with olive skin and dark hair sheltering beneath the awning. Ramon greeted him in Rimoni, asked for Giordano, gave his name, then, more important, he gave his master's name. The youth took their weapons, which was expected, but he missed the periapts, for he wasn't expecting them. Then he led them inside.

Giordano was a big man of middling years, running to fat but still visibly strong. A young Rimoni girl was shaving his chin with a straight-edge razor, her strokes carefully avoiding his impressive mustache, which sat like twin black rats on his upper lip, long twisted tails jutting sideways.

"Master, he says he's Ramon Sensini, of the Familioso Retiari," the youth said, bowing as he spoke.

Giordano waggled a finger: "wait" in the Silent Tongue. The youth bowed again and left. Ramon and Kip watched the girl finish her shaving. She washed the man's cheeks with scented water, kissed his cheek, and went to a wine decanter and began pouring. "My daughter, Regina," Giordano told them, smiling while his eyes measured them. He extended a hand, with a signet ring. "Welcome, Sensini. Pater Retiari has written to me of you."

Ramon kissed the signet ring. "My friend is Fridryk Kippenegger. He will stand by the entrance." He took a seat while the Schlessen slouched back to the entrance and flexed his muscles idly.

Ramon accepted the glass of wine Regina offered but didn't drink. He took her in with a glance: she had her father's plumpness and looks, including a hairy upper lip and careful eyes, but she was paler than her father, and there were flecks of gold in her deep brown hair.

"My Pater sends his greetings," he said to Giordano, switching to Rimoni.

"Pater Retiari is well?"

"He prospers by day and sleeps well at night," Ramon said, words that signified security and strength. His paterfamilias controlled large tracts of countryside about the town of Retia, using his influence over the supply of the largesse of the land to hold the town to ransom. In Rimoni and Silacia the agrarian populace far outweighed the urban, and though the lands were owned by hated Rondians, it was beholden upon all good Rimoni to steal from them. The real wealth of Silacia was controlled by familioso heads like Pater Retiari.

"That brings me great joy," Giordano rumbled dourly. "Though his proposals are not so easy as he may think."

Ramon spread his hands. "What could be easier? You control much of the flow of poppy into Yuros. Pater merely wishes to remind you that such of these goods that enter his lands must also be subject to his tariffs."

Giordano looked mournful. "The sad truth is that they do not pass through his lands, amici. They pass *over* his lands." He made an expansive gesture to the skies, mimicking the flight of a windship. "So no tariff."

"The sadder truth," Ramon replied, "is that my Pater has intercepted two consignments passing by land through Retia this year. Both shipments were sourced from Pontus, and bore your sigil."

Giordano made a disappointed face. "These must have been resold shipments. I do not convey by land through Retia. I have given my word to your Pater." He glanced at his daughter. "Bring more wine, Regina. The Brician."

If that wasn't a code-phrase, I'm losing my touch. "She will stay." Ramon raised a hand. "She has a sweet face," he lied. He looked at Kip. *<On alert,>* he sent. The girl glanced at her father and back to Ramon, her jaw tensing.

Giordano narrowed his eyes. "Signor Sensini, I honor my agreements. A businessman must do this or all trust is lost, and without trust what do we have?"

"What indeed?" Ramon replied. "Pater Retiari feels that his honor has been impugned by this disregard for his territorial rights. He feels that the only way he may be reconciled is to take a share in your enterprise." He showed Giordano his palm, tapped it. "Pater Retiari feels that delivery to him directly would allow greater volume and more profit for both you and him."

Giordano grimaced. "There is no margin."

Ramon laughed. "This is the *poppy*: there is plenty of margin." He eyeballed Giordano with all his impudence. Even Kip, who couldn't understand the words, could feel the tension rise.

"Pater, I will handle this," Regina said suddenly, turning on Ramon and reaching out, clenching her fist with an abrupt gesture. For an instant, Ramon felt a tightening in his chest, his throat constricting and his eyes blurring. Behind him he heard a sudden grunt, the rasp of steel on steel, and a body thudding to the ground.

Then his eyes cleared as he exerted his own powers to destroy the attack. With one hand he reached out toward the girl, and with the other toward Giordano. He stole the breath from their mouths with Air-gnosis. Giordano's face went purple and the girl's eyes went round as her father fell to his knees. Her shields wavered, Ramon hammered a bolt of light through them and she shrieked and collapsed. Giordano gave a choking cry, tried to crawl toward her, then fell onto his face.

Ramon released the gnosis and glanced behind him. Kip was standing over Giordano's guard, who was flat on his back. His eyes were glassy. Kip was rubbing his knuckles and examining a rent in his shirt. Steel glinted beneath. "Little bastard tried to knife me," the Schlessen complained.

"You didn't kill him, I hope?"

"Neyn," Kip grumped. "He can't take a punch for shit." He peered outside. "All clear."

Ramon grinned. "If he wakes up, hit him again." He bent over Giordano and revived him with a flow of Air-gnosis. "Get up," he told Giordano as he blinked to life.

Giordano went to curse, then saw the knife Ramon was holding to Regina's throat. "Stregone?" Giordano asked, stating the obvious.

"Si," Ramon replied, "I am stregone, like your daughter. You are not the only one with a mage at your disposal. Pater Retiari has me." He nudged the unconscious girl. "She is your flesh and blood, though. You must value her."

"Do not harm her, please."

"Of course not." Ramon broke the cord about Regina's neck and dangled her periapt. "Listen, Giordano, I will make this offer only once. You will direct all of your poppy to Retia, and my Pater will give you a fair price—or else I will chain-rune your mage-daughter. You understand what I mean? She will be unable to use her gnosis, leaving you helpless against all the people you've pissed off." He raised his hand over the girl. "Choose."

Giordano's gaze flashed from him to his daughter. "If I go down, others will rise. I'm the only one who ships to Rimoni: all my rivals ship to Bricia."

"I know this," Ramon replied. "My Pater wants a partnership with a countryman. My visit here demonstrates that he is in earnest, and has the power to back up his plans."

A bead of sweat ran down Giordano's face. "What plans?"

Ramon smiled. "We do not reveal such things to men who are not partners of my paterfamilias." He met Giordano's eyes. "Are you a partner?"

Regina groaned and opened her eyes. She stiffened as she registered the knife at her jugular. "Pater?"

Giordano bowed his head. "Please, release her. I grant you Liberta: no one of my family will assail you again, I swear." He swallowed. "She is my life."

Ramon assessed the man. In a world of lies, vows had to be honored or no business could be transacted. A man who reneged on a pledge of Liberta demonstrated that no one could ever trust him, and all of his partnerships and business contracts would be void. He dropped Regina's periapt into her cleavage, winked at her, and stood. "I accept your pledge of Liberta."

He helped the girl to her feet and offered her his wine. She glared sourly at him, took a sip, and spat. "Pater, you are unharmed?"

Giordano nodded, patting his chest. "I am whole." He indicated the seats. "Please, Stregone, sit once more, in friendship."

Regina eyed Ramon with considerable wariness. He guessed that she'd had little or no formal gnostic training. "I trained at Turm Zauberin," he said, to mollify her.

Her eyes became intent. "Could you teach me?"

"I leave tomorrow."

"Are you married?" she asked in a businesslike voice.

He grinned. "I am not. But Pater Retiari will choose my bride."

She smiled slyly. "You have one night left here in Pontus?" She straightened, and pushed out her ample bosom.

"Daughter," Giordano admonished.

"He is stregone, Papa," Regina pouted, "and of our people." She swayed to a seat, crossed her legs and looked Ramon in the face. "I like him. Later we will do business of our own."

Ramon colored and looked at Giordano, who raised his cup. "To business, Signor Sensini."

The following evening, Ramon, Kip, and Prenton were sipping the brandy they'd been gifted by Giordano while Kip gave Prenton a lurid account of Regina's looks, deportment, and bust size. Ramon neither confirmed nor denied a thing. The idea that he might have just fathered a child was vaguely troubling, especially when he'd been half-afraid the girl was only using their "transaction" as an opportunity to turn the tables on him for humiliating her. But the encounter had been fun in the end, and far more equal than the odd relationship he had had with his maid in Retia. The girl had appeared to regard sharing his bed as part of her duties, and after several weeks of refusing her, he'd finally just got on with it. There was some chance he'd sired a child on her too, no doubt as Pater Retiari intended. *Some magi have dozens of bastards*, he reminded himself.

"So assault is a Rimoni seduction technique," Prenton observed drily, finishing his brandy. Then they all stiffened as Duprey's voice carried to them. "The legate is back from the allotments," Prenton exclaimed, swiftly secreting the bottle. Ramon and Kip finished their thimbles and were hiding them in their pockets just as Duprey strode in, gesticulating toward them.

"These are your fellow magi," he called over his shoulder to the six figures following in his wake. All were clad in embroidered velvet cloaks of scarlet and black. "Where are Coulder and Fenn? Dicing, no doubt. Prenton, Sensini, Kippenegger: on your feet!"

Prenton swept to his feet with an immaculate bow, a movement well beyond Kip, who didn't even try. Ramon improvised: Rimoni and Silacia had been civilized longer even than the Rondians. Duprey turned back to the newcomers, who were all huddling into their hoods as if they'd really rather not be identified. The legate looked pleased, as if he'd had a good day's fishing. "These are our new magi from the allotments," he said grandly. He indicated the tallest. "This is Renn Bondeau."

Ramon stifled a groan as a surly, baby-faced young mage who'd been on his flight to Pontus emerged from beneath a hood, scowling as he took in Ramon and Kip. He flicked a half-bow, without extending a hand, but Prenton didn't allow him to get away with this.

He seized Bondeau's hand and pumping it enthusiastically, crying, "Welcome to the Thirteenth, old chap."

Bondeau forced a smile.

Duprey turned to the second figure. "Our new Farseer: Severine Tiseme." A pretty, curvy young woman was revealed when she reluctantly lowered her hood. She too ran her eyes disdainfully over Ramon and Kip.

Baltus Prenton made a courtly bow. "Milady Tiseme, we are honored."

Severine looked at him with faint surprise and smiled. "Thank you," she said with sudden brightness. "Magister—?"

"Baltus Prenton, Windmaster," Prenton said, with a most winning smile.

Duprey swept a hand over three figures clustered together: "These are Hugh Gerant, Evan Hale, and Rhys Lewen of Andressea," he announced, not bothering to hide a slight twinge of annoyance; Andressans were notoriously fickle and troublesome. All wore their hair in long curls down their backs and affected trim mustaches and goatees and each had a bow slung over one shoulder; on the plus side, Andressans were also renowned archers. The tallest, Gerant, grunted something unintelligible. "Unfortunately, none of them speak Rondian," Duprey noted in a resigned voice.

Prenton promptly greeted them in Andressan, eliciting a little surprise but no friendliness from the trio.

"And finally, some excellent news," Duprey said, sounding utterly disbelieving of his own negotiating skills or good fortune. "I've managed to secure a *pure-blood* mage for the legion—I believe this is a sign that the Thirteenth is finally going to be given some respect." He raised a hand and the final mage lowered his hood slowly, revealing a pale, good-looking young man with a weak chin, swept-back blond hair and an uncertain expression. "Gentlemen— and lady—meet Seth Korion, the son of General Kaltus Korion himself."

Ramon clapped a hand over his mouth to keep his laughter in. *Sol et Lune, it's the Lesser Son!* Memories of years of bullying and abuse leaped to the fore, escaping from where he'd buried them. Malevorn Andevarion, Francis Dorobon, and Seth Korion, per- petrators of his worst experiences growing up: their names were branded on his soul. *Seth Korion in a punishment legion—what the rukking Hel is going on?* Then he thought about Duke Echor being in charge of the Crusade, and he had to stop himself laughing out loud again. *Rukka mio! Has he got Kaltus digging latrines?*

Seth Korion's eyes went straight to Ramon and then away, as if he could not decide whether to pretend he didn't know him or not. *After seven years at Turm Zauberin, you better rukking well acknowl- edge me.* Ramon licked his lips and found his composure. "Seth Korion," he drawled with absolute relish. "Fancy seeing you here."

7

THE KRAK

Hadishah

I would name them animals, but they are less than that; if they are dogs, they are rabid dogs. Your precious jackals have destroyed another hospice of the Ordo Justinia, this one in Falukhabad. These are women trained in medicine and mid-wifery, Sultan! Every day they save the lives of your subjects, yet they are preyed upon by these killers! Why will you not protect my sisters?

SOURCE: JUSTINA MEIROS,
LETTER TO SULTAN SALIM
KABARAKHI I OF KESH, 907

It is the jackal that cleans the carrion from the desert. Think of these Rondians as carrion. Only the strongest in faith have the will to do what is required by nature. It is easy to mouth platitudes and make promises of shihad, but where was the sultan when Betillon was raping children in Hebusalim?

SOURCE: HADISHAH PAMPHLET, 907

Galataz, Kesh, Antiopia
Shaban (Augeite) 928
2nd month of the Moontide

"Kazim Makani, my young pilot!" exclaimed a vaguely familiar voice.

Kazim turned, and then his face split into his first genuine smile in months. A roughly dressed man in desert garb strode toward him, his scarred and whiskery face alight with welcome.

"Molmar!" He embraced the man, kissed both his cheeks. "Sal'Ahm!"

"Sal'Ahm," Molmar responded, his eyes bright, though he frowned a little as he looked at Kazim more closely.

He can see what I am, Kazim thought sadly.

But the Hadishah skiff-pilot hid the moment quickly. "Are you ready for some flying, my friend?"

Kazim found himself nodding enthusiastically. "I can't wait."

When he'd first learned that there were Keshi magi, he'd been shocked, and the breeding-houses of the Hadishah magi still sounded hideous to him. But flying in Molmar's windskiff earlier that year had been wonderful. Soaring above the desert, seeing for miles, he'd felt free and all-powerful. It gave him hope that his own gnosis might not be a demonic power of Shaitan, but something that could be turned to good.

They were in Galataz. He, Jamil, and Haroun had ridden nearly four hundred miles in the two weeks since they'd been given their assignment. Jamil was his friend, but Haroun was another matter; there was now a history of mistrust between them, but Rashid had assigned him as translator.

Jamil and Molmar greeted each other as old friends, and Haroun too: they'd all crossed Kesh together with Kazim. Then the door of the Dom al'Ahm opened again and more men entered, armed and booted, despite the strictures against weapons and shoes, that neither should be worn in a place of worship. The newcomers were led by a big scar-faced brute introduced as Gatoz. Jamil kissed Gatoz's cheeks formally, then Gatoz turned to Kazim. No embrace was offered. "Kazim Makani," Gatoz said in a gravelly voice. "The emir bids me accept your presence."

And evidently you don't want it. Kazim bowed stonily.

"I pray you accept my leadership and give your all for Ahm," Gatoz stated.

"Kazim is a good lad," Molmar stated defensively.

Gatoz met Jamil's eyes and Kazim sensed silent communication passing between them; afterward, Gatoz looked somewhat appeased. More introductions were made; two more magi, Talid and Yadri, both part Dhassan. They looked like boys, younger even than Kazim himself, with fluffy little beards and fervent eyes. There were also half a dozen Hadishah, ordinary men trained to kill. They were clearly overawed by the magi; they gave reverential bows, murmuring names Kazim quickly forgot.

The final man was a bulky, puff-cheeked Rondian in Keshi garb. He had deep green eyes, a pale, curling beard halfway down his chest and a shaven, sunburned skull. "This is Magister Stivor Sindon, formerly of the Ordo Costruo," Gatoz told them. "He gave allegiance to Emir Rashid years ago, when Antonin Meiros broke faith and allowed the Crusade."

Magister Sindon ran his eyes over Kazim. "You're the Souldrinker," he stated, his expression deeply distrustful. "What are your affinities, boy?"

Kazim had not gotten far enough into his training before he'd rebelled and refused to learn any more from Sabele. "I don't know," he admitted sullenly.

Magister Sindon raised one eyebrow, as if his impressions of the training afforded Hadishah magi had been confirmed. "No doubt all will be revealed in time," he said coolly.

Kazim felt his instant dislike deepen. *Just once I'd like to know more about what is going on than the people around me.*

Molmar plucked at his sleeve. "Come, brother. Let's prepare for the journey."

The windskiff rose at Molmar's gesture, topping the walls of the Dom-al'Ahm as Kazim stared about him, feeling that same rush of excitement he'd felt when he'd first flown. *Whatever my "affinities" are, flying must surely be involved*, he thought.

His first flight might have been just a few months ago, but it felt like a lifetime. He'd been an occasionally devout Amteh worshipper who believed himself human, not magi, and all he'd cared about was to rescue Ramita Ankesharan and take her home. Now he had blood on his hands; he'd lost his love and gained monstrous powers instead. But as Molmar hauled on the sails and the skiff caught the winds with a thrum that shivered through his core, he felt his spirits rise.

Jamil and Haroun and two other Hadishah were aboard too. Below them rose a second skiff bearing Gatoz, Talid, and Yadri and piloted by Sindon, who flew with casual effortlessness. The city of Galataz spread beneath them, barely visible through the smoky miasma that covered it. Many had fled, seeking safety from the oncoming Crusade, but as many more remained, apparently hoping not just to survive the advent of the Rondians, but to actually profit, Jamil had told him darkly.

The second skiff rose on a summoned wind and gracefully darted past them, Gatoz waving ironically. The gesture irked Kazim. He looked about him, opening himself up slightly to the new senses the gnosis brought. He had to fight the urge to be ill, but he did it nevertheless. There was a piece of wood at the base that ran the length of the hull; it thrummed with energy. Remembering Molmar's past lessons, he retrieved the word "keel." The single mast was fixed to it, and there was a spur of wood behind the mast, which Molmar held onto. Unfocusing his eyes and extending his senses, he could see a faint blue light that ran from Molmar's palm into the spur and down into the keel. He reached out slowly and touched the spur himself, below Molmar's hand. He could feel the tingling power of the pilot's gnosis and he closed his eyes and tried to share in it—to add to it.

The windskiff shuddered and their elevator wavered.

<*No, like this,*> Molmar said into his mind. <*Feel the winds on your skin and send them through you into the wood. You are not the source, just the translator of that energy.*>

It came instinctively. His skin dimpled at the cool air rushing past and he breathed it in and tried to envisage himself as something that this energy would pass through. The keel shuddered again, but this time it did not falter but gained in strength. He felt them lift higher and grinned.

<Very good. Now, my friend, call the winds from behind. Think of yourself as inhaling, sucking it toward you, through your skin.>

This was harder, for the wind was elusive and ever-changing, but Molmar clasped a hand over his and he felt the other man's presence inside his head. In fright he tried to block him out, scared Molmar would see right into his black heart.

<Hush, lad. I'm not going beyond your surface thoughts.>

<You swear?>

<Of course. Your secrets are your own, Kazim.>

He flinched. *Can I believe that?* Though he felt a kinship with Molmar, he barely knew the man. All he had ever known of the gnosis had been evil, except this one thing: flight. But Molmar had been the only one of his new "friends" who'd never lied to him, never tried to manipulate him—that he knew of.

<All right.> He opened himself up—though he couldn't say exactly how, as he had little idea how the gnosis worked, except that it appeared to follow his will and his emotions. But that looked to have sufficed.

<Well done, lad.>

Kazim met Molmar's gaze and they shared a moment of understanding. Something he'd never got from his poor blind father shone in the other man's face and he realized that Molmar, born in some secret Hadishah breeding-house, had no more connection to family than he did.

We are kin, he and I, he thought, and smiled.

Then Molmar pointed to the other skiff far ahead, silhouetted against the face of the moon. "Let's catch them," he said gleefully.

Kazim remembered that mocking wave and his competitive streak rose. "Let's do it," he cried, and the winds surged behind them, the skiff's sail bulged and they soared faster and higher.

They didn't quite catch Gatoz's skiff that night, but it was fun trying, and when they landed just before dawn in a valley a few miles from the Krak di Condotiori, Kazim felt tired but more fully alive than in months.

He peered around him with interest as they were led below ground, into a series of caves, the size of which he couldn't even begin to guess at. There were more than one hundred men within already, and rumor had it that the tunnels led all the way into the Krak itself. The network had apparently been formed in secret by magi loyal to Rashid; they had taken more than a decade to complete.

The following day, Jamil took him to a lookout point where they could gaze at the Krak, only a few miles away. Even at this distance, its walls looked massive, the great sandstone ramparts towering above the valley beneath. Two sharp-peaked, snow-capped mountains known as The Tusks rose on either side of the mouth that was the gorge that rose toward the keep. Kazim could see a man-made lake behind the walls, with canals and a white waterfall that disgorged a torrent into the valley below. There were no houses in the valley—building there had long been forbidden by the defenders—but it was filled with refugees.

Jamil told him that the legendary fortress which guarded the pass into Javon was the wartime retreat of the Ordo Costruo. After the Javon Settlement the Bridge-Builders had decided to take an open hand in politics; they had occupied and enlarged the fortress using the gnosis until the edifice, which could already break most human assailants, became utterly impregnable to anyone without magical means. During the first two Crusades, even the Rondians had left it alone. Right now its main function appeared to be to keep refugees out of Javon. The valley below its walls was awash with tents and campfires, and the most the Ordo Costruo was prepared to do for them was to send out food, though never enough.

"How can anyone bring down such a place?" Kazim wondered.

Jamil smiled grimly. "The way all strong places fall," he replied. "By treachery."

By the end of the week, even more men had funneled into the caves, turning the hot air thick with the smell of sweat and bodily wastes and making it hard to breathe. Most were soldiers of the sultan, there to overwhelm the enemy once the defenses had been breached. Their captains all looked similar, like Jamil, with paler faces than most Keshi or Hebb. They were from a limited gene-pool, the children of Rondian magi captured and forced to breed over the past century.

Gatoz was in charge, and on the designated night he led the long column through torchlit passages deep below the ground toward the Krak. Kazim, hovering nearby, heard him saying to Jamil, "This was an old escape route, sealed off when the Ordo Costruo took possession of the fortress. The emir's magi have secretly reopened the tunnels. The pro-Rondian faction remains ignorant." He licked his lips. "The nefari bastards think they are invincible. We'll show them that there is no such thing."

"What is happening inside?" Jamil asked.

"Rashid placates them, twists them about his fingers. Tonight he will seek leadership by the vote, and if he is successful, he will gain control of the Order *bloodlessly*." Gatoz sounded almost offended by the word. "But if they resist, then he will strike, and we will strike with him."

Kazim closed his eyes, searching his feelings. Antonin Meiros had been head of this order, and he'd been thought of by all of Antiopia as the most evil man alive. But Kazim had consumed the man's soul, and now he knew him better than any. Meiros had not been an evil man at all. Were his Ordo Costruo any worse?

"Do we have enough men for this?" Jamil asked tersely.

Gatoz grunted. "Rashid leads the pro-shihad faction. Half the order—all the half-bloods and weaker—already follow him. The pure-blood whiteskins all follow Rene Cardien. They are stronger in power." He smiled sourly. "There will be blood, and lots of it." He looked straight at Kazim. "You are quiet, boy: do you have the stomach for this?"

Kazim felt his face color. His courage challenged, his resolve to not use the gnosis wavered—exactly as Gatoz clearly intended. "Of course I do."

The march underground was slow, tense and oppressive. Torches were thinly spread and they tramped in semidarkness, the weight of the stone bowing their shoulders. Outside, it was daylight, but in here the night was eternal, and though it was barely a mile, it seemed to take forever. Then whispered orders passed ear to ear down the line, ordering silence and readiness, and most fell to their knees to pray wordlessly.

Kazim stretched his shoulders. Most of the sweating soldiers around him were poorly equipped; helms of some sort or other were prevalent, but few had armor and most held only poorly made scimitars. There were lots of them, though, so if they could be fully deployed, the magi might be overwhelmed. But if they were bottle-necked and confronted piecemeal . . . it didn't bear thinking about.

"Stay close, brother," Jamil muttered in his ear. "We have invested much time and energy into your training. I know you do not wish to use your new powers and I respect that. But you owe the Had-ishah for all we have done for you. Repay us with obedience, and swiftness of action."

The wait was interminable. Food was passed along the lines, tiny leaf-bowls of spiced rice and chicken, which some managed to keep down, but others with nervous stomachs couldn't, adding the stench of vomit to the fetid air. It was a huge relief when the signal came and they trooped silently into corridors lined first with stor-age chambers and then habitable quarters. A dead Dhassan servant lay in a pool of blood just inside a side-corridor, and Kazim heard others locked behind closed doors they passed.

The attackers mustered in a large underground chamber that had huge doors in each wall. It was completely empty, except for the tapestries and banners of the Ordo Costruo. Gatoz ordered groups before each door, organizing multiple launching points for the assault. "The magi are above us in the great hall," he told Jamil. "The fools elected Rene Cardien over Rashid." Kazim heard the satisfac-tion in his voice. "Tonight we sup on magi's blood." Kazim didn't think he was speaking metaphorically. "We move in two minutes."

All eyes went to the door ahead as Gatoz went through it, only to return seconds later; he put a finger to his lips and waved them forward. Kazim wished he'd taken the time to pee. A thousand fears surfaced—that this was a trap, that the magi were completely aware of their incursion and waiting to strike. He prayed as he had that night in Meiros's house, for the courage to strike when he must. *These are magi, they can incinerate armies. If Rashid has miscalculated we are dead.*

They found themselves at the base of a wide spiral staircase and Gatoz waved them up. He briefly caught Kazim's eye, but there was little hint of recognition. *The bastard would rather I died in this,* Kazim thought. He gripped his scimitar tighter. *Well, I won't die.* They padded onwards, upward, then someone shouted aloud in Rondian and there came a faint roaring sound.

Jamil caught his arm. "Stay with me brother!" Their eyes met, and Kazim could read all the decades of hatred there. Jamil was normally a coldly dispassionate fighter, but today was different: today he was being given the chance to strike directly at the enemy he hated and feared most: the magi. "Ahm is great!" he cried. "Tonight we dine with magi or with God!"

"Forward! Ma'sha Ahm!" Gatoz roared from below. "Ma'sha Ahm!"

God's will be done.

The tramp of feet became a roll of thunder, battle-cries boiled through the air and a vivid blast of light flashed within the rooms above.

"Onward," called Jamil, his arms raised as they topped the stairs and found a courtyard. A thin line of Rondian soldiers formed before them, their faces white with fear. The invaders surged forward, but before they reached the enemy line all of the windows above blew out with a tremendous crack, showering the defenders with glass. Kazim saw one go down shrieking, speared by a foot-long shard of window; another was taking aim at him with a crossbow when he jerked and fell as something like lightning flew from Jamil's hand. Almost subconsciously he opened his gnosis-sight. If he willed, it he could probably do just as Jamil had done—but he shied from using his stolen power, despite the energies crackling inside.

It's what Sabele and Rashid want me to do: surrender to the power. I refuse.

He reached the thin enemy line almost before he was ready, carried forward by the momentum of the charge. He battered aside a spear with his shield-rim and thrust his scimitar into a soldier's neck, sent him writhing to the ground with blood spurting skyward in a scarlet spray. Another loomed behind and launched a clumsy overhand blow. He blocked it easily, counter-slashing across the man's face, and watched him drop before leaping through a gap after Jamil, then spinning to smash his shield into the back of a Rondian crossbowman's neck. He heard bones crack as the man arched his back and he went down. Kazim's blood was up now. Weapons flashed on all sides, grazing his arms, his side. A helm flew free, revealing a boy not even twenty who looked at Kazim numbly as his blade punctured his chest, then his eyes emptied as he sagged to the stone.

Just a kid . . .

There was no time to dwell on it. Jamil blasted open a door and Kazim leaped through, his curved blade crashing against the straight sword of an officer, a portly man with a shaggy mustache. He was out of shape, foolish-looking, and Kazim flicked through the man's defenses in a moment, slashing open his throat then spinning away even as his enemy fell choking, only to almost die transfixed on two spears determinedly wielded by two men working in concert.

But Jamil fired a bolt of light into the nearest of them, his shriek echoing in the marble hall, and a Keshi man leaped ahead of them both, a howling dervish singing a hymn to Ahm. He almost beheaded the first spearman, the one Jamil had burned, then the second buried his spear in the Keshi's chest. The Rondian released the spear and drew his sword. He looked at Jamil, his eyes terrified.

"Magus?" he croaked, backing up. On the ground the dervish choked his life away like a spitted fowl.

"Mine," Kazim shouted. He leaped and swung, forcing the man to block high, then low. To his credit, the Rondian swiftly countered, a blow Kazim barely parried, and went for him again with a bloodcurdling yell. Kazim feinted a slash, then resolved into a straight thrust, his weight half-forward, and the Rondian took the scimitar in his thigh. He stumbled, and the rest was butchery. Jamil surged past and Kazim was borne along in a crowd of Keshi fighting men.

The far door revealed stairs, and a roar like thunder carrying from above, together with the screams of men and women, magi fighting magi.

The thought of wading into that maelstrom made Kazim waver, but Jamil pulled him aside. "We follow the first wave, brother. Don't get caught in the front!" Then he raised his voice and bellowed, "Up the stairs! Kill them all! God is great!"

The Keshi flooded upward, whipped on by Jamil's shouts. For maybe half a minute they ran unimpeded, then they recoiled and stopped. "On! On!" Jamil shouted, searing the air over his men's heads. "On!"

The mass of men lurched slowly forward again as the clash of steel reverberated above.

Kazim found himself pushed upward in a sweating, heaving press as they stumbled into a cloudy miasma of heat and burned meat. Something rumbled, and the whole building shook. He shoved the man in front of him, frightened to be so enclosed, while he in turn was pushed by a fat Keshi warrior with a spear and no helm.

Suddenly a flying shape swooped down the stairwell, a white-skinned woman in an apricot ball gown, her pale hair unbound. Gems glistened on her fingers and throat, and the air about her crackled with light. A wash of fire jetted from her hands and charred a group of Keshi on the stairs. A male magus joined her, holding a crossbow that spat bolts every few seconds. The Keshi hurled spears that clattered harmlessly against unseen shields, then the man in front of Kazim took a crossbow bolt in his chest that punched straight through him and pinned him to Kazim's shield. He lost the shield as the man fell. The magus was looking right at him as he fired again, but he dropped, and the fat man behind him took the bolt through his right eye. A recoil of fear ran through the press of men, who started tumbling down the stairs, tripping those who came behind.

Kazim looked up as the magus alighted on the balustrade and backhanded a man across the throat; his bare hand severed the

Keshi man's spine. Behind him, the woman poured flames down the stairwell, and then gaped in surprise as Jamil threw a bolt back at her. It rebounded against her shields and she cried, "Another traitor magus!" Her voice was outraged.

Kazim saw the man had heard her, but his attention was on him and a steely grip fastened onto his mind. <Die, Keshi scum,> he heard the man command him, an attack that should have frozen him in place, helpless. But he'd had just enough training; it sufficed to repel the blow, then he countered, leaping forward and slamming into the unseen shielding. The force of his blow knocked the man from his perch and he floated away and hovered a few feet from the balustrade, eyeing Kazim warily. "Here's another!" he shouted to the woman as he kindled blue fire at his fingertips and readied another strike.

Suddenly someone below shouted "Charge!" and men pelted up the stairs, renewing the assault and sweeping Kazim along with them. While he was trying to keep his feet, the mage flowed alongside, pouring bolts of energy toward him that struck the oncoming soldiers instead, dropping them to be pounded by the feet of those behind. For a nightmarish few seconds Kazim dodged and ducked and watched others die in his stead—then the female mage below screamed, and the man was gone, bellowing in rage.

Kazim shoved through the crowd of men and looked down the stairwell to see the pale-haired girl twisting in desperation on the shaft of a spear that entered her belly and emerged from her back. Even as he watched she went limp, and plummeted. The other mage wailed and swatted spears and Jamil's energy bolts aside as he tried to reach her. He wasn't looking up.

Kazim didn't think it through; he just leapt.

Luckily, the mage's shield was too depleted to repulse Kazim's full weight; he was leading with his blade, and thrust through the man's back, his blade piercing the ornate evening coat and emerging through the middle of his chest. His full body impacted a split-second later. The mage grunted and dropped like a stone, and Kazim shouted in triumph. They struck, and his blade snapped as he rolled clear—straight into a pillar. His head cracked the stone in a single blaze of white light, then blackness enveloped him.

He woke to the sound of rejoicing. The very earth shook as men jumped and shouted, and pummeled the ground with sword-hilts and spear-butts.

"RASHID! RASHID! RASHID!"

He tried to rise, and then abruptly rolled over and vomited instead. He was lying beside the stairwell, amidst a pile of wounded Keshi. *We must have won*, he thought, though his head felt like nails of bone were jabbing his brain. He tried twice before he could stand, then clambered painfully up the stairs looking for Jamil. Men he didn't know thumped him on the back excitedly as they passed him, and cheers rained down from the next floor in torrents. "RASHID! RASHID! RASHID!" he heard as he climbed over still-warm bodies, past dying men. The steps were too slippery to walk on, and he found himself climbing. Every wall was blackened, every window shattered. Torn bodies lay everywhere, and blood smeared every inch of the floor. Most of the dead were Keshi, but some still lived, moaning, crying, screaming for help, though no one heeded.

"RASHID! RASHID! RASHID!"

Inside the great hall, men danced, and wept and hugged each other.

Kazim staggered inside, and all of a sudden heard, "Kazim! Kazim!" Jamil staggered to his side, grimed in ash and blood, but very much alive. Kazim felt an intense surge of relief. Jamil held a half-full decanter of amber fluid. "Brandy!" he yelled, as if it were some nectar of the gods. Perhaps it was. They embraced like brothers.

Jamil looked him over concernedly, and then tipped brandy straight onto the cut where he'd struck the pillar, making him squeal in sudden pain. Jamil gave a gleeful laugh as Kazim seized the decanter and swigged. He had never tasted anything so potent, so delicious.

"I'll take you to a healer, brother." Jamil patted his shoulder.

Kazim looked about him, at the dying Keshi warriors with wounds far more severe. "It's nothing," he grunted. "These men need help more."

Jamil blinked. "They are not magi. You are more important."

"Since when do Amteh revere magi?"

Jamil snorted. "Relax, brother: we have won! The power of Shai-tan is broken and Antonin Meiros's Ordo Costruo is no more!"

"How did it happen, in the *real* fight?"

Jamil rolled his eyes. "You're determined to be miserable about this, aren't you, boy? How? Through the hidden blow! Over the years Rashid won over nearly half of them, and they were ready. Cardien's pure-bloods still believed that peace would prevail, so they were unprepared. A sudden strike turned the balance our way, though we still faced many of the mightiest. Alone, Rashid and his faction would have perished, but then we good soldiers of Ahm joined the fray." Jamil's face became sober. "We threw men at them by the hundred: martyrs to Ahm, drawing their fire, soaking up their strength. I myself slew the fire-witch in the stairs, and then you, may Ahm bless and keep you, leaped upon that maniac air-mage. Many more such deeds were needed, but we broke them. The remnant were captured." He pointed to a cluster of Rondians, mostly women, surrounded by Keshi brandishing naked blades. There were perhaps two dozen of them.

"How many died?"

Jamil cocked his head. "Eh? We killed twenty-seven magi. *Twenty-seven!* And captured twenty-three for our breeding-pens! We slew fifty of their soldiers. Such a victory is unheard of."

"And our losses?"

Jamil shrugged. "Around three hundred dead, brother, including thirty of my kindred. Nineteen of Rashid's Ordo Costruo adherents perished—a lot of death." Then he grinned fiercely. "But it is a victory, brother."

Kazim stared at the prisoners, sitting terrified amidst the carnage and the savage celebrations. Their periapts had been taken, and most bore wounds. *We killed twenty-seven and they slew more than three hundred of us, yet this is victory?* They were magi, though—and no longer invincible.

He studied the captives, most of whom were female, seeing their hollow-eyed disbelief, the absolute dread and despair. One terrified girl, maybe fifteen years old, clung to the arm of an older woman who met his gaze with cold fearlessness. For some reason he felt a sense of loss wash over him. He was surprised to realize not all were white—several were of olive hue, including one stunning woman with dark skin and pale hair who was the subject of a bidding war between several Hadishah magi. He drew on the remnants of Meiros's memories . . . Odessa d'Ark. She glared about her like a dethroned queen.

These were Meiros's people, the Bridge-Builders. They created the palace, the aqueducts . . . He could name them, thanks to Meiros's own memories that still haunted him. He turned away.

But suddenly he was the center of attention as Emir Rashid Mubarak caught sight of him. "Kazim Makani! One of the heroes of the hour—come, brother!" The emir pulled him into an embrace and his mouth curled into a smile, though his eyes were measuring. A beautiful blond white woman with a wide mouth and sleepy eyes walked beside him. "The slayer of Francois Vertros, I am told, by dint of leaping on him from fifty feet up! Magnificent! Come, you must join us." Rashid turned to the blond woman. "Alyssa, this is the youth I told you of, the slayer of Antonin Meiros—a true hero of the shihad."

Rashid spoke loudly for the whole hall to hear, and more cheers resounded about him, his name passing from mouth to ear. The blond woman purred something and Kazim found himself being led to a chair at the front of the queue, ahead of the dying and crippled, to have his bloody, throbbing head attended by her personally, while men came up and bowed, and touched his clothing to their lips.

It felt heady . . . and yet sickening, too. The heavy, metallic scent of blood was everywhere, clogging the air, cloying every inhalation. But it was also exhilarating, to be fêted, to have his courage proclaimed by the emir before all his men. The blond woman smiled tightly at him, her fingers deft as she prodded and teased his nose back into shape, numbing the pain as she worked.

<My name is Alyssa Dulayne,> she told him silently. *<I know who you are, Kazim. I've heard all about you from your little Lakh girl.>*

Kazim jolted, looking up at the woman. Her face was radiantly beautiful, but her eyes were reptilian. *<Where is Ramita? Is she well?>*

She masked the briefest scowl. *<She is well.>* She cocked her head, looked at him intently. *<She has not contacted you, then?>*

He shook his head.

<If she does, do tell me. She and I are good friends.> Alyssa smiled. *<What a handsome young man you are.>*

Kazim shut his emotions down, abruptly scared of this angel-bitch. The idea that she could be a friend of Ramita's was utterly inconceivable. He wished he could leave, but she pulled him to his feet and showed him to the watching men as if displaying a pet tiger. Their cheers enveloped him.

So this is glory, he thought uneasily.

After a minute or so he was allowed to rejoin the press, but men continued to slap his back and shout his name. He began to shove his way through the crowd, seeking solitude, but the next room was a ballroom, where several dozen people of many races milled about, naked, washing the blood and gore from their bodies. Some were in half-beast form, jackal and lion-headed men and women drenched in gore. He had begun to back away when he saw Huriya.

My Lord Ahm . . . He clutched his chest as she sashayed out of the press of what he now realized were his kin—Souldrinkers. Her eyes were glazed over, as if she were high on opium—or death.

"Brother!" she called, holding her arms out to him. She was clad in a kameez of embroidered silk as if this were a lavish party, and was one of the few not stained by battle. But the scent of death clung to her as she pulled him into an embrace. She was tiny in his arms. "I hear you are a hero once more, brother."

He pushed her away and dared to look with his gnostic sight. The whole room changed: imprinted over the bodies of the Souldrinkers were their auras, streaked with scarlet and alive with tendrils that reached out and plunged into each other. It was as if they were all one many-bodied being, feral, bloodthirsty and monstrous.

Huriya's aura was not quite a part of it, not yet, but her soul-tendrils were reaching for him.

He backed away. "What's happening to you?" he asked hoarsely.

She giggled. "Why, brother, I'm embracing what I am. Isn't it time you did the same?"

He continued to retreat. "What happened to you, sister? You weren't like this . . ." He spread his hands helplessly. "I hardly know you."

Huriya's face changed a little. A kind of mocking nostalgia. "Sabele made me, brother." A sneer crept over her face. "Do you remember how proud you were, telling me about the fortune teller who'd told you that you would marry Ramita one day? How happy you were, and how you babbled it to anyone who would listen, though she expressly forbade you to speak of it?"

He nodded mutely, his face flushing.

"Sabele came to me as well, *every year*—I am a child of Razir Makani also! The same blood flows in my veins! I have the same potential—and Sabele read a far greater destiny for me: to become a seeress, her apprentice, and then a queen." She stabbed a finger at Kazim. "The difference between us, brother, is that I can keep a secret."

He gaped at her. "You told no one?"

"No one! Not even poor stupid Ramita, though I shared her room all my life!" Her face contorted with malicious glee. "When Meiros came for her she was terrified, but I knew that this was the moment I had been born for—you also, brother, for Sabele has seen you, sitting on a throne."

The thought made him ill. "She said nothing to me."

"She knew you did not have the stomach for it. All you wanted to do was play kalikiti and moon after Ramita. She knew you would need to be led by the nose. But I will be her successor, and then I will exceed her!" She posed as if at the end of an elaborate dance. "Isn't it magnificent?"

He shook his head. He could see the tendrils of her aura reaching out again. For a moment his vision swam, then he instinctively slapped them away.

She recoiled as if he'd slapped her. and every Souldrinker in the room turned and stared at him with those same sated, venomous eyes.

He backed away, hurried from the room and ran straight into Jamil, waiting outside. His friend was staring into the room, his face pale and eyes afraid.

"These are your kindred?" he asked hoarsely.

"They're no kin of mine," Kazim snapped, storming past. His friend followed him, and though they only walked, inside they fled as if for their lives.

"I saw Huriya," Jamil said, watching him carefully.

He turned and gripped Jamil's shoulder. "If you value your soul, my friend, stay away from her."

"They fought with us—they slew many magi."

The image of the Souldrinkers feeding on members of the Ordo Costruo filled his mind: repugnant scenes of mouths inhaling the smoky discharge of death. "Then they did it for themselves, not for Ahm." He licked his suddenly dry lips and redoubled his pace. "Let's get out of here."

But there was no escape. Rashid had ordered the surviving kitchen staff back to their ovens, and the servants started delivering brandy and wine. Even the most devout Amteh men followed Rashid's example and began drinking as food began to arrive on silver platters. A sense of unreality filled the ballroom. The prisoners were gone and the tables had been set. Kazim and Jamil had been assigned places of honor, and stumbled disbelievingly to their seats as the first courses arrived.

For Kazim, the meal passed in a dream. So this was how the jadugara lived! The food was like nothing he'd ever tasted, so far removed from the plain dishes he'd eaten all his life that they scarcely seemed to be food at all, more like the sustenance of gods. And the drink was divine. He felt like they'd stolen their way into paradise and now they were feasting while heaven slept. But what he'd seen while with Huriya tainted the tastes.

Among the victors were around forty of the Ordo Costruo. Though most of them were half-breeds, with dark features, there were a few whiteskins, like the blond beauty Alyssa Dulayne, and Stivor Sindon. They dominated the high table, toasting each other extravagantly, only occasionally glancing with disdain at the Hadishah part-bloods like Jamil and Gatoz; they might be half- and quarter-bloods themselves, but they'd not been bred in captivity like cattle. He could feel their suspicions whenever they looked at him, knew they saw him as a threat, for what he was. But at least the other Souldrinkers did not join the feast.

Alyssa seemed to be going out of her way to keep near him, though her relationship with Rashid clearly went deeper than politeness. The scent of her perfumed skin, the touch of her soft fingers brushing his arm, the lowered lashes and sideways glances, they were all a slow tease, but Kazim felt no attraction to her. There was something corrupt about her, and not just in the way she sashayed about the hall earlier, careless of the gore and the cries for help, as if it were some kind of exotic hashish bar, not a place where such slaughter had occurred.

"Rashid is welcome to her," he told Jamil as they made their excuses and left.

Jamil sniffed. "They say she lies with women as eagerly as with men, and spends most of her days in a hashish dream with Justina Meiros." He spat disgustedly.

Justina Meiros, Antonin's daughter: he had seen her face in the outpouring of Meiros's soul. "Is she here?" he asked.

"I have no idea, brother," Jamil said, unconcerned.

Rashid intercepted them when he saw them leaving. With a firm gesture he stopped his coterie of admirers from joining them. "Jamil, Kazim, I need a word," he started as he led the way to a curtained recess. From the window they could see the vast Zhassi Valley below, washed silver by the rising moon and dotted with orange lights, the glow of the refugees' meager cooking fires.

We did it, Kazim thought. *We've actually ended the Ordo Costruo.* He could not muster anything but sorrow.

Rashid laid a hand on his shoulder, another on Jamil's. "My brothers, I wanted to thank you both, alone and away from the others." He glanced toward the curtain. "The Ordo Costruo is broken and now my Hadishah can fight openly. For the first time the armies of Salim will have mage-support. Power is shifting, brothers. Until now, the Rondians have never known fear. That is about to change."

Jamil's scarred face glowed with satisfaction. "All because of you, my lord Emir."

Rashid acknowledged the praise as his due, and as Kazim inclined his head to show agreement, the emir turned to him, his eyes searching. "I know you did not use your powers, Kazim. You fought only as a common soldier would—and still you shone! Think how much greater your impact will be when you allow yourself to fight with all that you truly are."

Kazim kept his face still, though it took effort. All his life he'd lived with his heart on his sleeve, but the games Rashid played were changing him into someone more wary and secretive.

Rashid looked him in the eye. "Many have given their all for our cause, brother. It harms us all that you do less." When Kazim didn't respond, he added, "Sabele asks to see you."

When Kazim swallowed and shook his head, the emir said with an air of satisfaction, "Good. I would rather you were with us than her."

That gave Kazim something to think about, but Rashid swiftly moved on. "My friends, for now we will tell the world I was elected head of the Ordo Costruo. If we maintain this fiction well enough, we can hold this fortress for a time, and still aid Salim. But I have a new mission for you two, with Gatoz's team."

"Anything, my lord," Jamil said eagerly.

"This fortress is on the southern border of Javon. Do you know the situation in Javon? The Queen-Regent declared for the shihad; she is betrothed to Salim himself. But recently there have been signs that she is wavering. A very dangerous Rondian spy has been seen at the royal court." Rashid drew them closer to him, his voice dropping. "You will go to Brochena, the capital of Javon. I want you to find and kill a man named Gurvon Gyle."

Jamil led Kazim to a room, a fine one with two soft beds, which had been reserved for them. But before they had even undressed, Gatoz walked in, and gestured curtly at Kazim to follow. He threw an anxious look at Jamil, and with some trepidation he went with Gatoz. His friend shook his head, and didn't follow.

Gatoz led him down a winding stair into the bowels of the rock. Dampness and the smell of stale air thickened about him, cloying his lungs. The Hadishah mage said nothing until they arrived in a small room where a guardsman stood beside a bolted door. He bowed, and at Gatoz's gesture, immediately unlocked the door, revealing a corridor lined with more barred doors. It was clearly a dungeon.

Gatoz flicked his fingers and the door on the right unlocked and fell open. Bewildered noises came from within, and a tentative inquiry in a strange tongue, a young woman's voice. It was quickly echoed by others.

Kazim followed as Gatoz walked into the cell.

There were four prisoners, all female, all Keshi, chained to the walls by the hands; the manacles forcing them to stand. All had sun-blackened skin and poor clothing. The room stank of urine and feces, the floor filthy and wet. Their eyes were hollow with fear, the presumption of suffering and death to come.

"These maids tended the Ordo Costruo magi loyal to Meiros," Gatoz said in a cold voice. "They are collaborators with the enemy." He drew a curved dagger.

Kazim's skin immediately formed a sheen of sweat. "How can a maid be a collaborator?"

Gatoz watched him warily. "They would not spy on their masters. Those not with us are against us."

One of the maids, an older woman, raised her hand. "But we—"

Gatoz bellowed, "Silence!" and backhanded her across the face. Her head cracked back against the stone wall and she whimpered weakly.

Gatoz jabbed a finger at Kazim. "You refuse to utilize all that you are for the shihad."

"I would die for the shihad," Kazim replied defensively.

"Die, maybe, but you will not use the gnosis," Gatoz retorted. "You're too squeamish to do what must be done for the glory of

Ahm." He raised his blade to the throat of the woman he'd struck. "On the journey here you aided Molmar in flying. That is double-standards, boy. We must clarify your thinking." The woman shrank from his knife as he caressed her skin with it, ignoring her pleading eyes. "You need to replenish yourself."

"No." The word was out before he could stop it.

Gatoz's eyes narrowed. "I see through you, Kazim Makani. You think with your gnosis depleted, you will not be tempted to use it. You wish to be the Souldrinker who does not drink, an empty vessel, freed from the option of using the power you fear."

It was as if Gatoz was seeing into his soul—*or Molmar did, and told him.* Kazim felt himself go cold.

"It doesn't work that way. Hunger will grip you—not for food but for the energy that sustains the gnosis. You depleted yourself flying: that usage is already gnawing inside you, a thirst that increases as your reservoir of power runs dry." He looked hard at Kazim. "You are feeling it now."

Kazim stared. It was true that despite the feast, a strange emptiness filled him, a need for more than the meal could give. He swallowed uneasily.

"I will make a bargain with you," Gatoz said. "Drink this woman's soul and these others can go free." He sounded utterly indifferent either way.

"No—you cannot—" He tried to look Gatoz in the eye. "Ahm would never give his blessing to such a thing."

"Shall I call Haroun and ask him what Ahm would command? Your Scriptualist friend thinks as I do."

That this was probably true only deepened Kazim's horror.

"You are running away from your true nature," Gatoz went on. "You have a strong body, but a weak mind. You suffer fear and call it conscience." He turned to the older maid, his eyes pitiless. "Decide."

"I cannot," he pleaded.

The knife slashed and blood fountained. The woman convulsed, but with her hands fastened tightly to the wall, she could do nothing. The other three women howled as her lifeblood gushed from her.

Kazim stared helplessly, then, without conscious thought, he moved.

Get away from her, his mind screamed, and he flung his hand up. Gatoz was pushed bodily backward, striking the door hard enough to concuss a man, and though his shields flared about him, softening the blow, still he fell awkwardly. The blade clattered from his hand and he shook his head, dazed.

Kazim went to the dying woman, meaning to try and save her— but he had no idea how; just *wanting* was of no use this time. Unlike flying or throwing people about, healing required skill and knowledge, neither of which he had.

He lifted the woman's chin and tried to pump energy into the cut, but the blood only flowed harder and his hands became slick with the scarlet fluid. "Please, heal!" he shouted at her as her eyes went dim. "*Please!*"

But the woman went limp; her face lost all focus and as she sagged she exhaled and a diaphanous mist oozed from her mouth and nostrils. He could almost taste it; he knew what it would be like to take it in. He could inhale all this poor woman's life, all the memories, her loves and passions, the suffering and fear; they were his to consume, and they would make him strong.

The three women watched him, their hearts in their eyes, their lives at stake.

"You were stronger today," Molmar told him at the end of the next night's flight north into Javon. Perhaps it was meant only as a compliment; perhaps the pilot-mage truly knew nothing of what Gatoz had done. Kazim couldn't tell, but he could no longer trust anyone. He shut Molmar entirely from his mind.

I saved three lives, he reminded himself, but it was the life he'd taken that filled his mind. Her name had been Wimla. She was a mother of two, a good woman, blameless. Her children would now grow up without a mother, as he and Huriya had. And to him, her name would always mean one thing: *capitulation.*

8

THE TIDE LANDS

The Tides of Urte

The tides of Urte are an extremely important factor in understanding the lives of the people and the flow of cultures and civilizations. Coastal living is precarious and sea-travel impossible, such is the magnitude of the tides. The distance between high and low tidal marks is never measured in less than hundreds of feet, and the force of the waves on even the gentlest day would demolish a castle wall in minutes. The lakes and rivers have tidal influences that can imperil the unwary; the largest lakes in Yuros, like Lac Siberne in Andressea, have tidal shifts of more than thirty vertical feet in the cycle, and building within a mile of shore is perilous. Despite this, the sea remains important to the coastal villagers, who will scavenge the tide pools daily, and literally reap a harvest of fish, though freak waves and sudden squalls often take a deadly toll.

ORDO COSTRUO COLLEGIATE,
PONTUS

Eastern Silacia, Yuros
Julsep and Augeite 928
1st and 2nd months of the Moontide

Alaron clapped a hand over Anise's mouth just as she opened it to scream. He wanted to cry out himself at the torrent of fire and dazzling white lightning pouring from at least half a dozen magi above. The Rimoni wagons were ablaze and the people caught in the circle were crying out. Then dark shapes began to drop from the winged beasts. They floated downward, their armor and swords gleaming in the flames. Their tabards bore the Sacred Heart of the Inquisition.

"*Niy-niy-niy!*" Anise shrieked, the sound muffled by his palm. "Ferdi!" Her eyes pleaded at him to go out there, to perform miracles and save her people.

All his inadequacies hit him at once. *These are Inquisitors. I wouldn't last three seconds!*

It felt like cowardice, but he wrapped his arms around her as she thrashed against him. His eyes flew back to the wagons, though his mind pleaded with him to run. Then he saw Ferdi, Anise's little brother, outside the wagons, beaten back by the flames. Above him, the constructs circled lower, squealing malevolently. Two Inquisitors landed right behind the little boy: one was a woman, her golden hair curling about her beautiful, cold face. But it was the sight of the other that stopped him dead. *Malevorn Andevarion.*

While Alaron's brain froze at the sight of his college nemesis, Ferdi panicked and tried to run.

The golden-haired woman barely moved; she leaned forward, then back, her face showing complete indifference as her sword-tip plunged through the middle of Ferdi's back.

Alaron cradled Anise to him as her brother slid off the woman's blade. Her teeth closed on his hand and he felt them tearing his skin until they grated against bone, but he hung on and sent a pulse of mesmeric-gnosis into her, an unsubtle blast of darkness that overwhelmed her and shut her mind down. Her limbs were suddenly jelly and her face fell slack. Together, they slumped to the ground.

The Inquisitors' constructs landed behind them, filling the night with their huge wings, and he thought surely someone would see him, kneeling on the edge of the light, holding the girl in the white blouse. But then a crowd of men burst from within the circle of wagons, waving weapons. Only one wasn't burning already: Jeris Muhren.

Alaron leaped to his feet as the Inquisitors swung to meet the onrush. He opened his mouth to bellow a charge and join the fray when Muhren's voice rang through his mind. <*Run, you fool, run!*>

Drink had killed Jeris Muhren's father when he was still young. Now the damned stuff was going to kill him too.

Not that he was drunk, but he'd had just enough, and that combined with the conversation and celebration swirling about him had blinded him to what should have been obvious: a scrying. Watching the dancers, wrapped up in an intense discussion with Mercellus, he had failed to realize the danger.

As he blinked in the aftermath of the scrying, Mercellus looking at him worriedly, he suddenly realized that this time the spell had not come from miles away but from directly overhead. But it was already too late; the moment he saw the winged giants descend in their close-ordered flight, he knew what they were facing.

We should never have stayed here, he railed against himself.

He'd faced death many times in the Noros Revolt, and no few times since, policing the backstreets of Norostein. But Inquisitors were a different matter from footpads and muggers, or even legion battle-magi. "Run!" he shouted at Mercellus as the Rimoni headman drew steel and rose. Mercellus roared in his own tongue and his people scattered, mothers scooping up children and the menfolk seeking weapons. Muhren sought Alaron, then remembered the boy had already gone to their campsite. *As I must. We have to escape.* But before he could move, the circle of wagons went up in an all-engulfing ring of flame, heat washing over the Rimoni as they ran like rabbits, seeking a way out. Dark shapes swooped overhead, randomly spewing fire and lightning.

He glanced sideways, mentally farewelled Mercellus, comrade of countless scrapes in the Revolt and so many wonderful evenings since, drinking and laughing about things that would otherwise make him weep. Then his mind went to Alaron and the Scytale.

Don't try to help us, Alaron. Just run.

He summoned his gnosis and hurled one of the blazing wagons aside, risking revealing himself to carve a path out of this blazing circle for the Rimoni. "This way!" he shouted to the trapped gypsies, and though they didn't understand the words they got the meaning and poured after him.

"Attenzione!" one of the Rimoni men yelled, pointing skyward as the dark shapes of the Inquisitors started dropping from their mounts in a leisurely fashion. Their cloaks flared about them like wings; their armor glinted orange in the flames. A mage-bolt transfixed a woman in front of him and fire washed overhead. The air was filled with swirling smoke. Somewhere in front of him someone screamed a Rimoni war-cry that became a choked cough. He stumbled over a fallen child and rolled to his feet in time to see a young golden-haired beauty in an ermine-lined Inquisitor cloak bury her broadsword in the back of a young boy. Her cold, perfect face seared itself in his mind. Then his eyes flew past her and he saw Alaron on his knees at the edge of the fields, cradling Anise.

<Run, you fool, run!> he sent as a heavyset, bearded Inquisitor ran at him, thrusting his blade at his face. He nudged the blow aside and kept coming, struck shielding, shorted his foe's wards to one point by slamming a gnosis-lit fist at the man's face, then swung low, where the shields frayed. His blow hacked apart the man's left ankle and as he went down Muhren leaped over him and slammed his heel down, breaking the man's neck. Then he reached the golden girl who'd stabbed the boy and crossed blades with her. She moved with almost blinding speed, but he read her blows and instinctively blocked and shoved. Though she was considerably smaller than him, Earth-gnosis anchored her stance and she didn't budge.

<He's here, he's here!> she crowed.

Answering minds clamored, <Hem him in, take him alive!>

He blocked another blow and leaped for the sky. The young woman's blade slashed past his feet as he left her earthbound—then a massive winged shape roared and flew at him.

Up, spin and slash. He rolled past the point of a lance that was spewing gnosis-fire and swung two-handed at the figure holding the weapon as the snapping jaws of the construct creature crunched by his ear. He struck the lancer's shield-wards square on, their opposing speeds lending the blow superhuman power. The Inquisitor's shields failed and Muhren's blade cleaved right through his nose-guard and smashed his face to pulp. The force of the impact spun him away as the construct plowed on, its rider slumped in the harness.

<*Jonas!*> a woman's voice screeched from his right, warning him in time to turn and see a ball of fire coming at him; he blasted it away with a mixture of his own Air- and Fire-gnosis. Jaws opened in the flames and he had to lurch away from the construct's maw, barely escaping having his leg ripped off. The sallow-faced young woman riding the beast peppered his shields with mage-bolts as he dropped beneath her mount and hacked brutally at the leading edge of its wing. Bone crunched, blood sprayed and the thing yowled and spun toward the ground. He dropped free of the falling beast and whirled on, bursting into the open—and was suddenly exposed to attack.

Lightning struck him from both sides at once. The air filled with vivid white light and he was held motionless in the sky, absolute agony eclipsing all other sensation. He dimly heard the shrieks of the constructs, glimpsed their snapping jaws, then a lance-shaft burst through the stars all about him and punched through his belly. He lost his sword as both hands grabbed the shaft. He coughed up blood as numbness that was worse than the pain spread through him.

"Alive!" someone bellowed. "Take him alive!"

Never.

There was a spell, one of the few necromancy spells he knew, that they'd all learned during the Revolt. *Soul's End*, they called it: the spell to obliterate your own soul at the point of death, so that other necromancers couldn't bring you back and question you. The only thing was, it destroyed your soul utterly. If there truly was a paradise beyond the skies, you would never know.

Paradise. He'd never really believed in it anyway. It was just another lie the Kore told.

He spoke the spell before the spreading numbness took his one chance from him. Darkness became light, became fire, became smoke . . .

Then the wind blew the smoke away.

Alaron ran, Anise's limp body in his arms. He felt completely overwhelmed by everything he'd seen, from Ferdi pierced by the golden woman's sword to the human torches that had been dancing Rimoni men and women only moments before, to Jeris Muhren, transfixed on a lance. All the while he fled he was never more than a heartbeat from collapsing to the ground, sobbing; or turning and running back into the midst of the enemy, waving his sword like a drunk.

Instead, he followed Jeris's last order: *Run, you fool, run!*

He lurched into the campsite. The trees hid the flames and dulled the noise, but still images from the attack kept assailing him. He forced them away; right now he had to get away from that place. Prancer was edgy, but he used his animagery-gnosis to calm the animal, then put Anise into the saddle and tied her in place so she wouldn't slip off. He re-saddled Mallet, then bundled up his bedroll and attached it to the saddlebag. The horse was puzzled, but he quieted him. His mind was still bursting with the horrors of the attack, but there was solace in movement, in action.

Malevorn was there . . . he knows *me . . . Stay calm,* he scolded himself. *He's not God, and he never could do Clairvoyance.* It had been Malevorn's lance that slew Muhren. He added it to the list of things for which he wanted vengeance.

I have to go east. Cym went that way. He walked both horses forward, using animagery as well as the reins, and even remembered to use Earth-gnosis to erase the traces of his passage. Malevorn was the only one of his pursuers who knew him, and maybe they didn't know he was there. Maybe he could get away.

Darkness swallowed them, but he exerted his gnosis for some night-sight and soon found the road. He dared not gallop for fear of the sound of the hooves, so he walked the horses instead. Every now and then he glanced behind, and caught glimpses of flames: Signor Torrini's villa was on fire too now. Guilt at his helplessness warred with absolute hatred for those who had perpetrated this obscenity.

Finally the flames fell from sight as he rounded a hill a mile to the east, back the way they'd come. He checked Anise, found her merry face deathlike, but she still breathed. He left her tied there, then returned to Mallet.

The horse looked at him resentfully. "Yes, I know we rode all day," he whispered brokenly. "But we've got to go on." He kicked his heels to Mallet's flanks and with Prancer following, they trotted through the moonlight into the eastern darkness.

He rested at dawn, finding the thickest copse he could to conceal them from the air. He picketed the horses on a short rope. Anise was stirring, so he laid her down, fighting to quell his stinging tears as he helped her mind throw off the spell he'd used to stop her screaming.

Her eyes opened and for a second she blinked up at him blearily and smiled, as if imagining that they'd dozed off together beside the stream. Then she looked about her and sat up fearfully. "Alron—?"

He gripped her arm. "Anise, it's okay," he said, though he knew she didn't speak his language. He sent reassurance; he was accomplished enough at mesmerism to use the gnostic art of manipulating other minds to take the edge off her panic, though their lack of a common language hindered him. "You're safe," he lied as convincingly as he could.

"Alron?" she repeated, looking about her, and as a torrent of memories struck her she began to shake and unleashed a babble of Rimoni. "Alron? Dove sono il mio popolo?"

Where are my people?

But he didn't have the language to respond. He found the odd word he'd learned from Ramon, wishing he knew more, trying to soften the message, but there was no way. "They are dead—morto, si? Morto," he tried.

At first she was puzzled, then she swallowed a sob. "Mio fratello? Ferdi?" Then she remembered; he saw the look of horror crawl across her face.

He shook his head, feeling utterly awful. "Morto," he whispered.

Her whole face dissolved. She began to shake her head from side to side and a wail began in the back of her throat. It tore at him and he pulled her to him, holding her close though she beat at him, ripping his shirt and his skin with her flailing fingernails, until she realized that he was neither going to hurt her, nor let her go. Then she burst into agonized tears and he wept with her, finally, for Muhren, and Mercellus, and Ferdi . . . and then it was for Langstrit, and for his mother, and for all the hateful things people like Belonius Vult and Malevorn Andevarion would do to gain power over others.

When he next became aware of anything beyond the weeping girl, the sun was rising over the valley and he could see a Silacian farm not far away, built on a rise. He climbed unsteadily to his feet, pulling Anise with him, catching her as her legs wobbled. Her moon-face was a picture of misery. "I need to find you somewhere safe," he told her, knowing she wasn't understanding. "Come with me."

He put her on Mallet's back and walked the two horses toward the farm. A group of men stood by a wooden gate, peering westward to where two columns of black smoke rose. They had pitchforks and machetes in their hands. When they saw him they fanned out, calling challenges.

"Please, do you speak Rondian?" he called nervously. "Can you help us?"

The men were swarthy and weather-beaten, and they looked at each other with dark eyes. They noted his Noros garb, his dirty, sweating face and tired eyes. They peered at Anise and made threatening noises. His hand went to his sword, a gesture that made them all pause.

The eldest of the Silacian farmers stepped forward. He spoke Rondian with a heavy accent, but his words were understandable. "My name is Alfonso. Who are you?"

"My name is . . ." He paused. "Not important. This girl—she is one of Mercellus di Regia's people. There was an attack at Torrini's. Will you take her in?"

The Silacian looked at the other men, then spat. "Inquisitio," he growled. "Murdering bastidos."

Damned right they are. "This girl needs a home," he said, throwing in Rimoni words as they occurred in the hope they stuck. "Per favore? Prego? *Please!*"

He watched Alfonso carefully as he considered, looking at those about him and conferring in a low stream of Rimoni. Then he turned back to him. "Others have come. I show." He waved a hand brusquely. "Follow."

Alaron led Mallet and Prancer behind the farmers to a stable with a corral where a pair of donkeys and several oxen chewed placidly. An array of Rimoni men and women were there, and they stared mutely at him and Anise. He recognized some of the faces—they were di Regia people. Then someone screamed, a sound pitched somewhere between joy and sadness, and a girl erupted from a doorway and ran toward him.

Mallet and Prancer danced backward in alarm and he had to fight to keep them calm as the girl threw herself at Anise, pulling her from the saddle and wrapping herself around her. Both burst into fresh tears as he stood there helplessly, staring about him. More women came forward, moving cautiously, and he realized that most of them were Rimoni, not Silacian, seeing the differences only in their dress, not their faces.

One of the matrons stared at him, firing a burst of questions he completely failed to understand. "She asks, how is this girl with you?" Alfonso translated.

The woman didn't wait for an answer but reached for Alaron and grasped his periapt, pulling it into view, then dropping her hand away as if afraid it would burn off. "Stregone!" she cried, "Stregone!"

The whole yard went silent as they all looked at him. "You are magi, si?" Alfonso asked warily.

When Alaron nodded, the men gripped their pitchforks tighter, their knuckles white. He wondered if he would have to fight his way out. Then Anise pulled herself from her girlfriend's hands and stepped to his side as if shielding him. "Egli è il mio uomo," she said, pressing herself to his side. He thought he understood: *This is my man.* There was more, and he picked out words for "fire" and "brother" and "horse" as the girl, her chin high, defiantly laid claim to him. It was the strangest feeling, like a wedding proposal at a funeral.

"She says you saved her," Alfonso said eventually while the ring of suspicious eyes looked on.

"I tried," Alaron replied, holding Anise against him. "I couldn't save her brother," he added, unable to keep the guilt and pain away. "I should have done more."

"You are . . . what is word . . . ? Pure-blood?"

He shook his head, blinking away tears. *I wish I fucking was.* "Quarter-blood."

"Quattro-sangue? Then you could have done nothing," Alfonso said softly. "Niy contro Inquisitio."

"Did many people escape?" Alaron asked hopefully.

"A dozen here. Maybe others, si? I think we learn more as the day passes."

Alaron bit his lower lip. "They will be hunting for me," he told the man. "I can't stay." He didn't know that for certain, but it was likely. "Please, will you look after Anise? And all these people?"

"We will do what we can. It is hard," Alfonso added apologetically.

Alaron thought quickly; he grabbed Prancer's reins. "Take this horse—use it to pay for Anise's lodging."

Alfonso frowned, and another round of intense conversation followed. Then he looked the two horses up and down. "Is a war-horse," he said firmly. "No good for farm work." He looked at Mallet. "This one."

Alaron pursed his lips. He was dreading a flight of winged beasts and their riders swooping from the sky at any moment. "All right—but you will treat Anise as your own daughter, yes?"

Alfonso frowned, his eyes going from the horse to the girl to the circle of listening Rimoni. "Si," he said heavily, glancing at a woman in an apron beside the door. He fired a string of words at her. "I tell my wife. Is good horse. Good bargain."

They shook hands. "Thank you," Alaron said gratefully.

Anise looked up at him, but as she realized what he was doing, she clung to him. "Niy, niy," she whispered, adding in awkward Rondian, "You stay."

He shook his head and pushed her gently to arm's length. "I have to go."

She blinked fearfully, stamped her feet. "Niy." She fired a volley of words at him, ending with a question.

"She asks to go with you," the man said, while the matrons of the di Regia people shook their heads.

I wish she could . . . It was crazy; he barely knew her, could hardly even communicate, but right now, she felt as important to him as Cym, as vital as the Scytale. There was no logic to it—but then, there had never been any sense to the crushes he'd had before. Things didn't work like that. And who knew what fantasies she'd harbored all her life, what future she'd imagined that somehow could be fulfilled by him? If Malevorn Andevarion and the Inquisition weren't in the next valley, he might even have agreed to stay with her. Right now a life of rural obscurity was a wonderful fantasy.

"It's too dangerous," he said sadly. "I can't stay, and she can't come with me. Please, explain to her—"

He wrenched himself from Anise, unable to block out her wailing as he began to unbuckle Mallet's saddle. The women gathered around her, glaring resentfully at him as he checked Prancer's saddle and transferred all his gear. When he was ready, she stepped from the cloud of women, her face soaked in tears but her head high. She said something to the old man, who blinked. "She asks if you will return?"

He swallowed. "I hope so. If I can."

Anise said something else.

"She asks, 'Should I wait for you?'"

O Kore! He felt his heart pause midbeat. Breathing was suddenly impossible. A future appeared to him: a long journey away, rescuing Cym—who never loved him and never would—and then returning here, with Anise beside the door, waiting. She would see him and run down the lane toward him, her face alive with joy.

But there was another future, trapped in a circle of steel and fire and spitted like Jeris Muhren on the lances of the Inquisitors. And a young woman, growing old alone, waiting for someone who would never come back.

He could say yes and give her something to hope for, if that was what she wanted.

Or he could say no and have her hate him, but at least she would be free.

He met her eyes, wondering what sort of dreamer she could be to place her hopes in such tenuous things. In the face of such a look, he couldn't give a simple answer. "Tell her . . . tell her I'm going to die. No one escapes the Inquisition."

He watched her as the words were translated. She walked up to him with a grace and dignity well beyond her years, and tilted her head up. He didn't need this translated.

Tears stung his eyes as they kissed gently.

The moment was all too brief. She stepped away. "Buona fortuna," she whispered.

"And you," he said hoarsely.

"Che sarà sarà," she said.

"What will be, will be," Alfonso translated.

Anise turned and slowly walked back into the crowd of women as Alaron's throat seized up. He exhaled heavily, turned to Alfonso. "Is there a path I can take east?" he asked quietly. "Not the main road."

"I show you."

Alaron rode all day, fighting the fatigue that at times saw him nodding off in the saddle. Alfonso had set him on a hilly path leading through groves of wild olives, but there was enough foliage to mask him from the air, provided he had enough warning. The Silacian farmer planned to hide the survivors in his granary silos if the Inquisitors came. "We have been hiding things from Rondians for centuries, Noros boy," he said calmly. He gave Alaron a bag of feed for Prancer and some baked sweetcakes from his kitchen.

He stayed well away from inhabited areas, terrified of bringing death to more innocents. Instead he followed the game trails, keeping one eye on the skies, and near sunset he saw a shape too big to be a bird circling high above. He immediately headed for the deeper woods and stayed there until after dark. Then he found the road again, and trotted east all night, running on adrenalin and fear, the half-moon bright enough to light his way. Prancer grumped, but did as he was bid.

Near dawn he found himself at a crossroads he vaguely remembered on the journey south—just a couple of days ago, though it felt like a lifetime. They'd approached it from the north, so he turned Prancer in that direction—and then he froze.

A dark silhouette was sitting atop the hill above him, barely two hundred yards away. At first he'd thought it was just a large bush, then massive wings unfurled. He shuddered and stopped dead, sending gnostic calm to Prancer. The horse trusted him now, and though his nostrils flared, he stayed silent.

If they'd waited at the crossroads I'd have walked straight into them . . . But the greenery around the crossroads was overgrown so perhaps there was nowhere for the beast to land, or maybe they didn't even know it was there. Perhaps this particular hunter was just sloppy, or lazy. Whatever, he was deeply grateful for the stroke of luck. *<Come boy,>* he sent to Prancer, and guided him toward the western trail. It was smaller than the northern road, and not much used, according to Muhren; it was Alaron's only option now.

He rode for as long as he dared, but all too soon the sun rose again. He walked Prancer up a little stream into a tiny gully where fresh water trickled, then managed to find an overgrown glade out of sight of the path. Though he was exhausted, he rubbed Prancer down first, then tied the horse to a fallen log, leaving the tether long enough that the beast could reach the stream and drink. He huddled into his cloak as the day brightened and kept watch as he ate, chewing dried meat and sipping water. He was quite sure that at any moment winged shapes would swoop overhead, screeching in triumph, but the air remained empty of all but birdsong and wind and at last the weight of his eyelids dragged him down into slumber.

It was after dusk when he woke, and his stomach was rebelling. He realized he'd not eaten properly in a day and a half, and Prancer was nuzzling the half-empty feedbags and looked severely disgruntled too. But he had only the vaguest idea where they were, and no idea when they might get more supplies, so he was loath to let the warhorse have more.

Stop running blind, he ordered himself. *Stop thinking about what happened to Muhren and the rest and try to* think.

He'd seen only two Inquisitors since he'd been on the road. Presumably they were searching for him, but they must have fanned out—maybe they thought he would continue going south? Perhaps he could slip outside their search perimeter. He decided to try the coast road and to keep moving at night, relying on the moon to light the way.

He fed the warhorse as much as he dared, then walked him along the westward-winding wooded trail. The track ended in a clearing shortly after passing a group of woodsmen's huts, maybe the only reason for the track in the first place. There were plenty of fallen logs, some partially sawed, many concealed by the long grass. Crossing the clearing was nerve-racking, and the ground beyond was uneven and treacherous, a wall of trees tumbling down toward another stream. He couldn't immediately see any obvious way down, but circling to the south brought him to another track, rutted by hooves and dragged logs. He walked Prancer down the path into the deeper darkness, and as the trees crowded about him, shutting out the open sky, he risked a little gnosis-light. The sudden glow made the fingers of the branches seem to recoil in shock, so he dimmed the light to a tiny glow.

Then he froze as something shrieked in the sky above. He instantly extinguished the gnosis-light and his gaze flew upward, but utter darkness reigned. Then came the patter of rain on leaves. Straining his ears, he thought he heard the flap of giant wings, but he couldn't be certain. Beyond that he could hear a dim roaring sound, one that came and went rhythmically. He puzzled over it until the rising wind and heavier rain obliterated the noise. Something was in the skies above him, he was sure of it, but he had to move. Trembling with apprehension, he lit his gnosis-light again, then he and Prancer descended the track.

At the bottom of the track was a gully and another stream flowing eastward, or so he thought. He let the horse drink, but not too much, then they began the arduous slog downstream.

Onwards, he thought.

Dawn seeped into the sky, a barely discernible lift in the shades of gray. The rain had stopped about an hour before and from beneath its curtain of sound came that distant booming, rushing sound that had so puzzled Alaron. By now he was so tired he was glassy-eyed, not thinking straight. The stream had met another and had steadily grown; it was a muddy brown river now, a wide bed of shingle over which the water unhurriedly twisted its way along. The banks were overgrown, so he walked Prancer in the dry parts of the riverbed, constantly crossing and recrossing the river as it wandered along.

It dimly occurred to him that he should be stopping to rest; they were both soaked to the skin, and he was ravenous. He'd let Prancer forage grass on the banks, but he was frightened the horse might eat something he shouldn't. The hills on either side of the river were thick with stunted trees and undergrowth, but he caught sight of a stand of willows on a flat patch of ground on a bend and gratefully stumbled toward it. The sky grew lighter, revealing mist patches clinging to the slopes higher up. That distant sound like rolling thunder rose louder as the wind shifted.

"Come on, lad, let's rest here," he said, and Prancer whinnied moodily. There was a large pile of dung drying there, obviously from something equally big, and it was making the horse distinctly nervy, so Alaron buried it. Once he'd rubbed Prancer down, he finished the remains of his hardtack, softening it with river water. The day looked set for more rain, but for now the only sounds were birdsong, the wind in the leaves and the distant roar of what he finally realized must be the sea.

The sea . . . He'd never seen it for real before, only illustrations in textbooks, pictures of massive cliffs and crashing waves hundreds of feet high. *Will the coast road—if there truly is one—take me right to the edge?* He hoped so. His father had spoken of the sea—and of course, crossing the great Bridge—and he'd always wanted to see it for himself.

He finished his desultory meal, and settled himself to try and sleep. He felt bone-weary, not just from the traveling, but from the loss of Jeris Muhren and the horror of what he'd seen at the Rimoni camp. Ferdi's face kept haunting him, his casual, brutal slaying replaying over and over in his head. His killer had been utterly indifferent, as if she were just brushing off an insect.

There has to be a Hel. There has to be a place for such people.

He went to close his eyes when from above a shrill cry like a giant eagle filled the gully. A great black shape swooped down and flew along the river, only yards above the water. It was like a featherless bird with a wingspan of thirty feet at least, the musculature and veins clearly visible as it soared past him, close enough that its passing stirred the leaves. Its body was hues of gray and cream, and a long serpentine neck was topped by a bulbous head. A word dropped into his mind from his father's tales of the Revolt: this was a venator, a winged reptile bred for hunting. There was a rider on its back, mounted just behind the neck on a complicated-looking saddle, with straps binding the rider to his seat. *A male Inquisitor,* he thought, peering at the young, sour-looking rider with his fur-lined cloak streaming out behind him.

Alaron felt Prancer take fright and reached out delicately with his gnosis to quell the horse's fear. It was a delicate balance to strike, needing to be strong enough to override Prancer's fear and yet delicate enough that the sudden flaring of gnosis would not draw the Inquisitor's attention . . .

But he failed. Erring on the side of caution, he didn't do enough and Prancer reared, dragging at his picket. The rider heard the noise and he jerked on his reins, pulling the venator's head around so he could scan the ground—and saw Alaron.

He ran to Prancer, sending calm, making the horse wait for him as he wrenched the picket cord free and hurled himself into the saddle. From the corner of his eye he saw the venator bank and soar, already more than a hundred yards away. The dim light glinted on the Inquisitor's helmet and the tip of his lance.

He had no great plan in mind; he just faced his frightened horse downstream and jammed his heels into his flanks. Prancer whinnied and burst into a gallop. For now there was only flight.

The Inquisitor was on him in a few seconds. His venator shrilled, making Prancer veer wildly through the shingle, slewing left, then right, trying to keep his balance. The rider's lance was clamped into a holder that formed part of the saddle, which left the rider's hands free to deal with the reins and keep the beast under control. One gauntleted hand lifted and sent a vivid blue mage-bolt searing at him. He barely managed to get his shields up in time, and he clearly caught the Inquisitor's smug smile.

<I've found him,> the Inquisitor broadcast. *<He's running for the coast.>*

Damn! Alaron fired a bolt back, aiming for the venator's head, but the rider's own shields easily encompassed his massive steed and the bolt sizzled into nothing. He wrenched Prancer to one side as the venator swerved toward him and massive claws tried to snatch him from the saddle, then he fired a mage-bolt at the creature's pallid belly, putting in enough energy that it shrieked and veered away. He heard the Inquisitor curse as he fought for control.

Then Prancer thundered into the river and all Alaron's concentration had to go into holding on as water fountained about them. The venator swooped again, the Inquisitor gestured and a wall of shingle and earth erupted at the horse's feet. Alaron retaliated instantly, thanking Kore that Earth-gnosis was something he was proficient in, and succeeded in quelling the effect enough that they galloped through without falling—but the venator was on them again, the backdraft from its huge wings battering them as a lance stabbed downward. Alaron snatched out his sword and hacked at the shaft while Prancer weaved away from the raking claws. He blazed gnosis-fire at the venator again, but he was so off balance that he missed entirely. Then overhanging trees near the bank forced the venator away and he took the opportunity to desperately suck in air.

How far away is this bastard's support? he wondered. *How much time do I have?*

Abruptly the Inquisitor changed tactics and urged his winged steed ahead. As massive wing-sweeps sent it climbing, Alaron felt him calling again, and this time he sensed distant replies. He hauled on Prancer's head, trying to slow him, seeking more control and less blind haste, and as he did, he heard the rolling thunder of the sea somewhere ahead. All about him, the hills were closing in, and there were no paths into the thicket. There was nowhere to go but onward.

Do I leave Prancer and take to my chances in the forest? But that seemed futile, unless he could somehow kill the venator or its rider and get away from this place.

Yeah, quarter-blood against Inquisitor, he thought sardonically. *How's that going to work out?*

The Inquisitor was well ahead of him now, and turning to come back. He'd hauled his venator almost upright and it was hovering in place as if to say, *You can't go this way.* Beyond the fearsome beast and its rider the landscape seemed to be opening out, as if lowlands lay beyond. The thunder of the waves was even louder.

Well, if that's where he doesn't *want me to go . . .*

Alaron stroked Prancer's flanks as he strengthened his controls, binding the horse to trust beyond reason. The horse was trembling and sweating, terrified and near exhausted. This chase could not go on much longer. Something had to give.

All or nothing. He dug in his heels to Prancer's flanks, urging him forward, his sword held aloft. In response, the venator flapped its wings and the Inquisitor lowered his lance.

Here goes . . .

He kicked Prancer into a canter, sending loose shingle in all directions as he bounced forward, readying his gnosis for whatever opportunity came his way.

Take the Inquisitor down—or the venator . . . Live through this . . .

Eighty yards, seventy, sixty, fifty . . . Prancer kicked into a gallop, then the Inquisitor commanded the venator to lower its head and they careered together at an insane velocity. The lance-tip blossomed fire and bolt after bolt of blue flame began to sear toward them. Most flew wide, but some hammered his shields, blurring his vision as they closed. The speed of impact was going to make his shields almost useless. He heard himself bellow in defiance as they drove into each other.

The moment was on him almost before he realized. He repelled another mage-bolt, then he saw a glowing lance-tip and a beaked maw coming straight at him. He blazed energy at the rider and wrenched Prancer's reins sideways.

He didn't attack but threw himself flat on Prancer's back as they pounded *under* the venator's path, as he sent coruscating light into the flight path of his foe. The massive creature careened past; the lance tip ripped the air inches from his shoulder and a venator claw buffeted his shoulder, but they passed unscathed.

<On!> he sent to Prancer as the Inquisitor bellowed in frustration and sent his winged beast soaring skyward. Then the land vanished from beneath his feet and he understood why the Inquisitor had been trying to block his path.

He and Prancer had just run off the edge of the world.

The reason he'd thought the land was opening out was because he'd reached the cliffs, and there'd been no warning roar of waves because it was low tide. The river ended in a waterfall that plummeted fully six hundred feet, straight down to a huge expanse of bare rock strewn with tide pools. Far, far in the distance he glimpsed a line of spray and a distant blue-gray-green expanse, then his attention was wholly given over to the fact that he was plummeting to certain death.

He summoned Air-gnosis, one of his weakest affinities, let go of Prancer with a despairing cry and managed to halve his falling speed as the horse plummeted onward and hammered into the sea-smoothed rocks with a sickening crunch. The body bounced once, and Alaron threw all he had left into avoiding the same fate, desperately trying to at least soften the impact. The wall of rock flew at him, but with one last almighty surge of power he landed no harder than if he'd fallen from a tree. His knees cracked against the stone, but his splayed hands caught his upper body and then he rolled to absorb the rest of his fall. He came up battered but breathing and looked around at the bleak, featureless cliffs that spread north and south. The shelf he was standing on was completely bare. Water had carved channels and worn the rock smooth by the tides, and he started to remember geography lessons where he'd studied such places. Tidelands could be a few hundred yards wide to a dozen or more miles, and they were usually only bare for about four hours a day . . . and the incoming waves could cover them in minutes.

There was nowhere to hide and nowhere to run. He'd landed near a narrow channel that wound from the waterfall above toward the ocean miles to the east, but it was only a few feet deep. He'd dropped his sword as he fell and couldn't see it anywhere. *Brilliant . . .*

Fatalism filled him. There was no way a lowly quarter-blood like him could get out of this. He tried to summon mental images of the people he loved: his parents, Cym, Ramon . . . Anise—*thank Kore I didn't tell her to wait*—and that was about it, really. Not so many to farewell.

The venator topped the cliffs and spiraled toward him. He watched it land heavily above Prancer's body. Its beak dipped and ripped, tearing still-warm flesh from the corpse. The Inquisitor unstrapped his harness, left his lance in its cup and slid to ground. "Alaron Mercer, I presume," he said ironically. He looked like he might be in his midtwenties—a half-blood, Alaron guessed, on the basis that he'd not already been overwhelmed. He'd not last much longer though. He had nothing left now, not even a weapon.

He backed away, and the Inquisitor followed him at a leisurely pace. "The Crozier wants a word with you," he said conversationally, drawing his sword.

"Malevorn," Alaron croaked.

The Inquisitor grinned evilly. "Andevarion said he knew you. We have a wager going over who will find you. I thought I'd run out of luck when I got sent east, but it appears fortune is on my side."

Alaron stumbled backward through the small stream and fell onto his backside on the far side. The Inquisitor gracefully leaped the stream and landed above Alaron with his feet planted wide and his sword pointed at his chest.

"Kore's blood, you've been a nuisance," the Inquisitor said, "but I've got you now." Mage-fire blossomed from his left hand

and blasted into Alaron's midriff. His shields failed and his wet clothing sizzled as the energy jolted through him. He curled up, stricken, trying to breathe. The Inquisitor put the sword point to his throat. Alaron looked along the straight steel blade and wished only to die.

"I, Acolyte Seldon of the Eighteenth Fist, arrest you in the name of the Inquisition."

<I've found him!> Seldon's call resounded through the ether and Malevorn rolled his eyes as he followed the call back to the east. *Damn.* Muttered curses echoed dimly through the ether as the Fist's mental links conveyed the mix of relief at the finding of their quarry and annoyance at losing the wager.

The torture and lingering death of Mercellus di Regia, the Rimoni caravan-master whose people they'd butchered, had confirmed that Alaron Mercer had been with Jeris Muhren when he arrived at the camp. A search of the wreckage had revealed no sign of the Scytale—of course, Malevorn officially didn't know what they were seeking, so he kept his mouth shut. But Commandant Vordan had been visibly frustrated as he'd ordered the venator riders to fan out, hunting his former classmate.

It still seemed ridiculous that Alaron Mercer could be involved: obstinate, stupid merchant-spawn that he was. But it appeared he really was. Malevorn reported what he knew of him before the Fist fanned out to seek their quarry, then he'd been sent south, to a pass that led into Rimoni. He'd thought it a reasonable chance, but it looked like Seldon had won the bet.

He swung his venator northeast, using Air-gnosis to help it gain altitude. The mental voices of the others—nine voices now, no longer eleven—came from all points. Jeris Muhren had fought like a beast, killing Brother Alain on the ground and then Brother Jonas in the air. He'd fought well, for a half-blood.

Until I spitted him. Malevorn smirked inwardly. That had gained him praise from Adamus Crozier—but not Commandant Vordan, who'd wanted Muhren alive. *How was I to know he knew the Soul's End spell?*

Below him the land skimmed by, featureless at this height. He flew swiftly, thrilling to the sheer speed of his beast. He could sense his fellow Acolytes converging, and their excitement as they anticipated the end of the hunt.

Never thought I'd be pleased to see you again, Mercer. But it won't be a long reunion.

As Alaron stared along Seldon's blade, watching gnosis-energy crackle along the steel, a dark shape rose behind the Inquisitor.

At the last instant, Seldon felt it coming, half-turning as his shields were touched, but the attack came like a striking snake. The figure had arisen from the rivulet, holding a forked trident, and it propelled itself across ten yards like a released spring. Seldon hacked the trident in half with his gnosis-limned blade, but the other hand lashed out, carving a gouge of light in the Inquisitor's shield before a huge snake-like tube of flesh encased in mottled scales whipped around and encircled him. The Inquisitor shouted as coils of snake-flesh engulfed him and the human-like upper torso of the attacker stabbed down again with a knife. At first Alaron thought that the attacker was riding a serpent, but then he realized in utter disbelief that he *was* the snake. The creature was naked to the waist, with a muscular pale green torso and a hairless skull with a leathery comb. Its face combined savagery with cold intelligence. But it was below the waist that this thing was truly alien: its hips flowed directly into a massive snake body, at least two foot in diameter and two dozen feet long, which was currently wrapped around Acolyte Seldon's upper torso, pinning his sword arm. The Inquisitor tried to break out, roaring out a blast of mage-fire from his mouth, but the creature swayed aside even as it twisted the Inquisitor in its grip, causing the blast to shoot harmlessly into the air. Then it pushed its knife through Seldon's shields and buried it in his right eye. The Inquisitor went rigid, then limp, while Alaron gasped and tried to back away.

A coil of snake skin encircled him from behind and he was forcibly spun around until he found himself facing a female. She was towering over him, her mouth open and filled with barb-like teeth.

Her torso was also bare, with pale breasts tipped with black nipples. Unlike the male she had two thinner snake limbs, and her crest was multiple hairs as thick as fingers, black and waving as if they were blind serpents.

He was dimly aware that the venator was trying to lift off, but at least half a dozen more of these creatures were wrapped about it, pulling it down, their weapons rising and falling. He almost fainted in shock when the female opened her mouth and said in perfectly understandable Rondian, "You will come with us."

"Wha—?"

She silenced him by jerking him toward her with her horribly powerful snake limbs and kissing him on the mouth.

He was too stunned to react at all; could only gape helplessly as his mouth filled with water. He coughed, choked, then began to black out as she dragged him rapidly back to the channel and pulled him under.

They all heard Seldon's death-scream. It wasn't a warrior's cry, more the shriek of a terrified child, and it confirmed Malevorn's impression of him as weak and unworthy. *But how the hell had Mercer killed him?*

Brother Filius got to the scene first, just as the tides raced in. He'd seen the venator initially, splayed out on the rocks, its blood drenching the stone. Great chunks of it had been hacked off, almost as if the creature had been butchered. Seldon was lying not far from it, and Filius had recovered his body—or what was left of it. The young Acolyte had been butchered too. Though it was impossible to be certain, it looked like he'd been killed by being stabbed through the eye socket. Then the rest of his flesh from the chest, thighs and shoulders—the choicest cuts, as Dranid had muttered—had been carefully cut away. What was left looked horribly like the waste after butchery.

There was a dead horse there, too, with no saddle, only a rope halter, and that had been butchered too. But whoever had done it was gone, leaving no clue as to *where*. There was no sign at all of Alaron Mercer.

The tide had turned before all the Fist arrived; they took Seldon's corpse to the top of the cliff before it was engulfed and gathered around the remains, which were covered by a cloak to spare their eyes. Vordan was chanting in old Yothic, the runic tongue. Malevorn, watching impatiently, found his eyes straying to the Crozier. Adamus looked more curious than shocked. His curly hair fluttered in the sea breeze and Malevorn found himself wondering if the bishop's wide lips and olive skin hinted at Rimoni blood. Purebloods descended from the Blessed Three Hundred were mostly Rondian, but not all of them; there had been men and women of many races in Corineus's flock. The Crozier met Malevorn's eyes and he bowed his head. He wasn't permitted to return such familiarity and he wasn't sure just what Adamus might want of him—but really, if it helped his career, who gave a shit?

Beside him Dominic looked shocked; in his world, Inquisitors were indestructible. For three to die in as many days was in truth alarming. They were all beginning to wonder what they were up against. Something was clearly going on. Malevorn recalled that Alaron Mercer's exam thesis had been about the Scytale of Corineus being lost. He'd thought it ridiculous then; now he was beginning to wonder.

His eyes went around the depleted circle: Vordan looked grim, and why not? Fist Commandants were not supposed to lose men. Vordan and Adamus were the only people (apart from himself) who knew what they were seeking—unless Raine did? She was sleeping with Vordan and men did talk to their women sometimes. But the sullen, ugly girl looked as confused as anyone. Jonas and Seldon had been her friends so she was isolated now, though of course she still had Vordan to look out for her.

Brother Dranid looked stolidly uncaring, and Filius was bursting with anger at the desecration of Seldon's body, loudly vowing revenge. Malevorn had always thought that those who ranted loudest were hiding their weakness. Filius didn't frighten him.

Finally he let his eyes go to Virgina, the golden girl, standing aloof, praying devoutly with her mouth while her eyes strayed, watching the circle just as he did. Their eyes met and just like always, she closed up and looked away with a toss of her hair. *What a good Daughter of Kore. And a child-killer, lest we forget.*

Finally the chanting was done and cold winds whipped in. Vordan had not been praying for Seldon's soul; he'd been summoning it. The Acolyte's misty form came as commanded, wailing at his predicament.

"Who killed you?" Vordan demanded in a voice that resonated with the gnosis.

Seldon's ghost's answer stunned them all.

Alaron huddled naked in the cave-mouth, high above the thunder of the ocean below. Racing waters boiled and roared like a thousand serpents as they engulfed the flats and battered the cliffs. It was high tide, and the armies of the ocean were launching a mighty assault upon the land.

He heard a loud sliding sound, his face whipped about and he saw the male creature coming toward him, a stick of barbecued meat in his hand.

Horse meat? Venator? Or human—

For a moment he thought he would be sick. Then the smell hit him: roasted meat, tangy and rich with blood and heat. His mouth filled with drool.

Kore forgive me, but I need to eat.

It tasted like spit-roasted chicken, and he hoped that meant it was venator flesh.

The creature stayed with him, regarding him cautiously, and Alaron studied him in turn.

First the female had dragged him along the channel, then they plunged over the lip of the tidal-shelf and into the depths—by then he'd realized that her kiss had bestowed a water-breathing spell on him—how or why, he had no idea. Snakemen existed in Lantric legends, not in reality.

They'd swum—he had no idea for how long as he'd blocked out the nightmare by fainting—until at last the snake-creature had brought him ashore at a narrow part of the tidelands. She'd kissed him again, returning his air-breathing, then with a snake-man carrying him like a child in his arms, they'd made their way up an impossible cliff to a cave near the top.

There were nine adults, horrific enough, with their human-snake bodies, but then two of the females had disgorged smaller versions of themselves from distended bellies and Alaron had stared until he realized that they had not just given birth but had been carrying their offspring in belly-pouches. *Incredible.*

He stared at the male who'd fed him. He was typical of these creatures: apart from his coloring and comb, his upper torso was almost human—*almost,* but not. His eyes were fishlike, and there were no earlobes. His nose had a membrane that covered the nostrils when beneath the water, but they were open now. His neck was thick, bull-like. His chest muscles were massive, and clearly visible beneath his almost transparent skin, which only darkened about his waist as it merged with the snake skin. Alaron risked a glance lower and noted there was no penis or scrotum, though there was a bulge that suggested it might house such appendages. He'd glimpsed a similar mound covered by a membrane between the female's two snake-limbs. They could obviously breed—and they could speak. Their voices were low and melodious, a fluid, almost hypnotic sound, far more cultured than their wild appearance suggested.

"You wish for more?" the male inquired. His tongue was thick and purple, his teeth rows of hooks. Up close, one could never mistake him for human, especially not when you saw the thin, slitted black pupils of his amber-colored, reptilian eyes.

"No, thank you," he replied tentatively. He tried to clear his thoughts. "Who are you?" he asked.

"I, or my people?" the creature responded. Then it made a wet gurgling sound that it took Alaron a few seconds to realize was soft laughter. "My name is Kekropius, my mate's name is Kessa, and we are lamiae."

"I never knew you were real," he exclaimed weakly. A lamia was one of the mythic creatures of Lantric tales—to think they actually existed . . .

"It is good that we are not known. We must be secret to evade the hunters."

"What hunters?"

Kekropius scowled, a fearsome sight. "Those who hunt you also. The Inquisition."

Alaron gaped. "Is that why . . . you saved me?" He stopped abruptly. "I haven't thanked you. They would have . . ." He trailed away, feeling ill at the thought.

"We know what they do," Kekropius replied darkly. He glanced back at his people, coiling about each other before the roasting fire, never getting too close to the flames. "I could not stand aside and let them take you."

They fell silent while Alaron plucked up his courage. "How is it you even exist?" he finally dared to ask.

Kekropius slithered closer. "Ah, now that is a tale. But not one we tell outsiders." He looked Alaron over with piercing eyes. "You wear a periapt. You are a mage?" The question seemed to have dangerous overtones.

"Yes," Alaron replied carefully, "but I hate the Inquisition."

"And they you, it seems. He was arresting you, that one I slew?"

"They've been chasing me for days."

Kekropius leaned in closer until his face was inches from Alaron's. "Why?"

Alaron had his answer prepared. "I am a failed mage and they wouldn't let me practice my skills, so I ran away to Silacia. I thought I'd be safe." It made more sense than the truth.

"We have heard of failed magi before," Kekropius said, apparently accepting his story. He cocked his head. "This is too large a matter for me alone. It must go before our council. Until then, you must remain with us, as our guest." His tones were conciliatory, almost apologetic, but there was a threat there too.

Alaron thought of running, but he didn't. For one thing, he was still weak. Any attempt to run and he'd be easily hunted down. Secondly, if these strange creatures didn't find him, the Inquisition would. In truth, he was intrigued, and not a little afraid, but they treated him well, neither binding him with ropes nor spells, though he was sure they could if they wished to.

He had thought they would return to the sea, but the next night they went inland, following a river flowing between thickly wooded slopes. The lamiae slithered on their massive snake limbs faster than he could walk, but Kekropius and Kessa stayed with Alaron. Though they didn't tell him much about themselves, he soon worked out they were air-breathers, with a rudimentary, instinctual version of Water-gnosis; all the water-based affinities appeared to be at their disposal, in a limited way. Healing came easily to them, cuts and scratches vanishing in minutes, and some lamiae could heal others; he saw that when one of the young gouged an arm on a broken tree-branch. And he could detect mental communication constantly flickering among them, hinting at Mysticism, but they projected emotions and images rather than words. Whether any could Divine, the other water-based Study, he couldn't say.

Beyond the gnosis and the ability to speak, they were as much beast as man. It looked like they were driven by appetite and little more. They ate meat both raw and cooked, and roughly thrice what a man would eat—they could stuff themselves enough to last for days at a time. Close up they had an animal smell. Rescuers or not, Alaron was quite simply terrified of them.

Kekropius told him they would reach their destination in three days. They watched the skies warily, but saw no sign of pursuit. There was always someone watching over Alaron, even during the day when they slept, the meat cooking in cunning food pits that emitted no telltale smoke until opened at dusk.

On the third night, just before dawn, they reached the top of the small river they'd been following. They stopped before the cave-mouth from which the water issued and Kekropius turned to Alaron. "This is our home. We call it Sanctum Lucator."

The Haven of Lizards, Alaron translated. The words were old Runic, which he'd learned at the Arcanum, and seemed to confirm that the lamiae were more reptile than mammal; he'd noticed it in the way they moved, the way they were sluggish at night; it was in their alien eyes and the way their skin changed in different lights.

Kekropius touched his arm. "Our laws forbid contact with men. Though we have rescued you, we are compelled to bring you here. Our council must see you, and debate what to do with you."

"But I've got to find—"

Kekropius interrupted. "I am sorry to put you in this position, but you cannot leave without the permission of our council."

Alaron's temper rose, but he drove it back down. "That's just a formality, right?"

Kekropius shrugged enigmatically. "It is a serious matter. We have no greater secret than that of our existence. Though you are the enemy of our enemy, we cannot risk this place becoming known to the Inquisition." He ducked his head. "It may be that you will not be permitted to leave."

Before Alaron could react, another lamia, larger even than Kekropius, blocked their path forward. Fire flared above its left hand and lit its features. The newcomer had a reptilian face with amber eyes and looked even less human than Kekropius. In a deep rumble he said, "Kekropius? You were not expected for days."

"Naugri, I greet you. We ran into trouble and had to return." Kekropius waved a hand toward the sacks of cooked meat. "We found fresh meat, but ran into an old enemy."

"You were not seen?" Alaron realized that Naugri was not actually carrying a torch and his mind churned. *Fire-gnosis—what are these creatures?*

"Our secret is safe," Kekropius started, but Naugri jabbed a finger at Alaron.

"Then what is this? A prisoner?"

Kekropius laid a hand on Alaron's shoulder. "He is my guest, rescued from the enemy."

Naugri slithered forward and Alaron saw that he wore a huge sword on a belt just above where his waist became snake trunk. "We take no guests. All of the First People are our enemies." He drew his sword; fire ran along the blade.

"Naugri, sheath your weapon!" Kekropius snapped. "The Council of Elders will decide this matter."

The two faced each other for several long fraught seconds while Alaron held his breath and wondered whether he ought not to be trying to blast his way out of this—if he could. He could feel Kessa's cold presence behind him; she could probably move much faster than he could. He wondered what she would do if Naugri attacked her mate.

Then abruptly the flames on Naugri's blade winked out and he stalked away. "The Elders will decide," he rasped over his shoulder as he went. "But either way, the human will never leave the valley alive."

Alaron looked at Kekropius. "What's he saying?"

The lamia's amber eyes blinked apologetically. "I am sorry. Naugri is just speaking his mind. He is very . . . blunt."

"But you can't keep me here!" He clutched the wall for strength. "You might as well have just let the Inquisitors kill me!"

Kekropius looked back at Kessa. "My mate told me to intervene. Sometimes she sees things that may be."

Alaron's eyes shot to Kessa, whose face remained impassive. *Divination.* They have Water-gnosis, and some of them have other affinities. "What did she see?"

Kekropius shared a glance with his mate, and something passed between them. "Safety," he said softly. "She saw you lead us to safety."

They took a long passage deeper into the hills. The rocks here were limestone, porous, and easily shaped, and someone had been using Earth-gnosis to do so: the cave had been smoothed and widened, the water-channel widened and deepened and a path cut alongside. They crossed over a narrow stone bridge and followed dim natural light to another cave. The air was cold and damp, but it smelled clean and fragrant and Alaron inhaled heavily, trying to steady himself. He felt like he'd stepped into a dream.

They emerged into a narrow tree-lined gully just as the sun rose, turning the slit of sky far above pale blue. He stared about him in awe: a low, man-made dam ensured the bottom of the gully was filled with water. He glanced at Kekropius and corrected himself: not *man*-made. There were other cave-mouths scattered around the pool, subtly concealed by the topography of the land. Naugri was waiting beside the pool, watching three lamiae young swimming, laughing gaily as they rippled gracefully above and below the surface. Naugri snapped at them and their laughter faded, their eyes going round as they saw Alaron.

A dark shape detached from the walls and slithered to Naugri's side. His mate: he stroked her head fondly. She turned to face the newcomers, then ducked behind Naugri fearfully as she saw Alaron. "Man," she said fearfully.

More and more lamiae appeared, their skin hues changing from green to gray as they left the foliage. They bared pointed teeth and hissed menacingly.

"Kekropius, what have you brought us?" called a cold, creaky voice from the mouth of the nearest cave, and the entire gathering stopped and bobbed their heads.

"Mesuda-Eldest," Kekropius said reverently. "We have a guest."

The newcomer was the first of this gathering that Alaron saw to show any obvious signs of age. She was hunched and moved awkwardly, and her skin did not change readily. Her comb was dry and shriveled, as was her face, like wrinkled leather; there were flaking patches on her snake-skinned limbs and her breasts were barely discernible. Only her twin snake-legs and a certain caste to her face marked her as female. She glided to Kekropius's side and peered at Alaron, swaying gently.

These creatures are impossible . . . He felt as if he'd stepped out of the real world and into Lantric mythology. *They have to be constructs . . .*

The old female smiled. "He guesses the truth." She slithered up to him and stared; though her body was stooped, her eyes were level with his. For a second Alaron was unsure whether his instincts had lied and he was in immediate danger, so deep and complex were the emotions he saw in the old woman's eyes: loss, awful grief, and lingering fury all vied for mastery in her complex gaze, overlaid with sad tranquility. They both exhaled together and he felt their minds touch. She had a strange fluid style, but it was recognizably the gnosis. He hurriedly shielded his thoughts.

"Yes, boy," she said softly. "We are constructs."

Naugri snorted grimly. "Must we tell our secrets so swiftly, Eldest?"

"One way or the other, our secrets will be safe, Naugri," Mesuda replied evenly. "Take him to the high chamber." She reached out and lifted Alaron's periapt from about his neck. "For safe-keeping, child," she said softly, then, to Kekropius, "Feed him, and send him to the meeting within the hour." She glanced at Kessa. "You may attend and report."

Constructs were not common on Noros, but they were part of life in Pallas and the north. The Imperial Beastarium in Pallas was renowned for breeding constructs, for the military and for commerce—mostly that meant beasts of burden, but they also created the venators for the Inquisitorial Fists. Many of the beasts had been inspired by Lantric mythology—Rimoni might have been the first great Empire of Yuros, but Lantris was undoubtedly the first great culture, and its gods and goddesses the first widespread religion, suppressed by the Kore but never quite eradicated. Children grew up with the fairy tales of the Lantric Pantheon and their debauched ways, and they provided inspiration for some of the output of the Beastarium. But two things were forbidden: constructs could have neither human components, nor human intelligence. If these were truly constructs, they were very, *very* illegal. *And these lamiae have the gnosis . . .* That was something he'd never heard of.

"What is your name, child?" the old woman, Mesuda, asked him.

"Alaron."

She stroked his cheek with her big, brutal-looking hands, and it took all his strength not to flinch. "I hope we have the chance to know each other better," she said gently, then turned and slithered away.

Alaron was taken to a small chamber inside the caves. Without the periapt his use of the gnosis would be weaker, less efficient. He thought about the numerous opportunities he'd had to run over the past three nights that he had passed up; they felt like mistakes now.

I have to trust that Kekropius means me well, and that Kessa's divination was right.

After a brief meal of dried meat, Kekropius and Kessa led him to another passageway, a steep smooth trail spiraling upward. He got the impression that Kessa had something at stake here, and guessed that her precognitive skills were as much on trial as he was. "What did you see?" he asked her, but she ignored him.

The hills were honeycombed with passages and chambers, though they seldom saw others. In one dim cavern he saw two young-looking lamiae, one male, one female, clasping each other. He was powerful, she slim and lissom, with big slanted eyes, and their hands were slender and graceful as they stroked each other's bare shoulders. They were kissing, their arms and snaky hair entwined, and they both started guiltily and jerked apart when they sensed his gaze. If he hadn't been so nervous he would have laughed aloud. Kessa hissed at them and they fled.

The cave-mouth opened onto a small dell open to the sky and bathed in evening sun. Four creatures were seated on subtly shaped boulders set at each corner of the compass. Kessa led him into the middle, and stood behind him. "These are the Elders," she hissed. "Give respect."

One of those Elders was Mesuda, who bobbed her head, as if to reassure them. "Welcome Kessa, mate of Kekropius and trusted child of the lamiae," she started, and a rumbled greeting ran about the circle. "With her, as her guest, is Alaron-mage, a human."

To Alaron's right sat a hulking being who looked like an older version of Naugri, with scarlet mottling on his snake limb. His breath smoked in the cool dawn air. "I say again, why is he not already cooked?" he rumbled.

Opposite him, a female lamia with a wizened face and a tangle of gray hair cackled merrily. She didn't appear to be able to straighten her shriveled body, but her yellow eyes were bird-bright. "No, Hypollo, we should torture him first. Pain gives the meat more flavor."

"My wife has seen him provide a greater value, Reku." Kekropius's voice cut across her laughter and Alaron turned in surprise. *He's an Elder too?* His rescuer gave no sign of familiarity. "Kessa has that gift."

"An unreliable gift," sniffed the ragged female, Reku. "I do not want her shifty dreams to cheat me of a fine meal."

Kessa rose slightly on her powerful snake-limbs and her shoulders went back slightly. A threat-gesture, perhaps. Alaron could feel her conferring mentally with her mate, after which she subsided again, a chastened look on her face.

The four Elders went silent, and he could feel information flowing through mental linkages. He had some proficiency in Mysticism and it wouldn't have been hard for him to tap into that link, but he knew better than to try; these creatures were used to being intimate with each other, and his presence in that link would be impossible to conceal. Instead, he concentrated on what he might do if this went badly: he wasn't much of an Air-mage at the best of times, and they still had his periapt. Running would futile, but he was damned if he'd let them eat him.

Their mystic communion ended as suddenly as it had begun. Mesuda raised her hand. "Speak, Hypollo. What is your verdict?"

Hypollo studied Alaron, his giant reptile head cradled on one fist. "Eat him. He is a danger to the people."

If I go right, and jump, I might stand a chance . . .

Mesuda bobbed her head. "Kekropius?"

"I believe in my wife's visions," he said, as Alaron had hoped—no, *prayed.*

"Reku?"

Reku clasped her hands together, measuring Alaron with beady eyes. "Gut him slowly, to bring out the juices, then strangle him with his intestines to seal in the flavor. Cook him with apple and cloves."

Kore's blood! He glanced over his left shoulder. There was a cleft there too, but he suspected it went straight down to the pool. *No, I should go right.*

All eyes went to Mesuda. The crone bowed her head. "Then my vote is the casting one. Hear me! The first rule of we lamiae is that no outsiders shall ever know of us and live. In times of doubt we must revert to the core tenets of our people." She looked sadly at Alaron. "I am sorry child, but I concur with my fellow elders. You must die."

Alaron stared in disbelief. These people had rescued him from certain capture, torture, and death. That they now would dismiss him with so little consideration, and decide to eat him—*to eat him*—was more than he could take in. His senses were flooded with stunned, meaningless detail, even as his reflexes bade him move, to flee or to fight.

"No!" he shouted, "*no*, you can't! I've got to find Cym!" He threw his head about wildly, seeking an escape. "I've got to help her make it to—"

A heavy hand fell on his shoulder and bent him over backward. Kessa's mouth opened above him, twin fangs erupting from her upper mouth. She wrenched him to her and bit, her teeth puncturing his throat like knives of ice. He stared up at her as she released him, looking down at him with softly dilating eyes. He slid down her body, his cheeks brushing her breasts and belly as if he were spending his last moments of life in some idiot attempt to seduce her. Then the ground rose up and smacked him in the face—and all the while, his mouth tried inanely to finish his last sentence—

"—*Hebu . . . salim . . . !*"

His hearing and sight faded until the world dissolved softly into a vague blur of nothing.

9

A DREAM OF ESCAPE

Magi Longevity

One of the benefits of the gnosis is longevity. Partly this is derived from active and conscious exercise of the gnosis: use of Healing and Shape-mastery are particularly efficacious, as is the darker art of Necromancy. Just being magi seems to impart greater resistance to illness and harm. The Ascendants lived four or five times the normal span. Pure-bloods can expect to live two centuries, and notable benefits are also enjoyed by lesser magi. Of course, they are also in the front line of the military, so the perils are often great also.

ORDO COSTRUO COLLEGIATE, PONTUS

Brochena, Javon, Antiopia
Shaban (Augeite) 928
2nd month of the Moontide

Molmar put the skiff down several miles southwest of Brochena in an uninhabited bit of desert where empty ditches and mounded earth spoke of failed irrigation programs. By dawn they were installed in a safe house in the slums of Brochena. Kazim and Jamil sat with their fellow assassins on a verandah before a paved court-yard where Gatoz and Magister Sindon were talking to a man with a smoothly shaven skull and an urbane manner. He was Jhafi, but apparently known to the Hadishah; he was introduced as "Zan," and he welcomed them to the city.

"It will take days to arrange the attack," Gatoz told the group. "Magister Sindon and Zan-saheeb will arrange this, while we keep to ourselves. We must stay hidden." He glanced at Zan, gesturing for him to speak.

"The information we have," Zan said, "is that there are secret passages in the central keep. A sharp-eyed agent of mine detected Gurvon Gyle emerging from such a passage, thinking himself unseen. He appears to be in contact with Cera Nesti, the Javon Queen." The man sounded pained by this revelation, as though he had something invested in this queen, an attachment that had been betrayed. "My people have not made any move, knowing such a mage to be beyond us. Instead, we contacted your masters."

"Tell us about Gurvon Gyle," Gatoz said.

Zan licked his lips. "He is a Rondian mage who was hired by King Olfuss to protect him and his family. He betrayed that trust and the king died. However, one of Gyle's agents, a woman named Elena Anborn, apparently betrayed Gyle, protected the king's children, Cera and Timori Nesti, and helped restore Nesti rule. I say 'apparently' as it now appears that Gyle, though hidden, is again working with Elena Anborn."

"Is this Anborn woman a target also?" Jamil asked.

Gatoz broke in, "Certainly. She is a Rondian mage. But Gyle is the main target."

"What about the Nesti queen?" Molmar asked, his voice indifferent.

Zan responded, "Cera Nesti was fervently in favor of the shihad. I believe Gyle has used his gnosis to gain a hold over her. If we kill the snake, his venom will drain away." He looked about him for more questions, and when there were none, went on, "The Nesti in Brochena are mustering for war, and many Jhafi are joining them, for love of the queen. They are due to march north in a week or so. Their target is Hytel, a northern city."

"If we can find Gyle, we will kill him before they march," Gatoz put in.

"How will we find him?" Jamil asked.

"I will find him," Magister Sindon put in, his usually mild voice vehement. "I know Gyle, believe me. I have used his services before, and he trusts me."

There was more, but it was mostly detail. Kazim neither knew nor cared about Gurvon Gyle or Cera Nesti; he found his attention wandering and wondered instead where Ramita was. It hurt to be estranged from her, but increasingly he could see no future for them. The world was pulling them apart.

If the children belong to Meiros, then she will hate me doubly—but if they are mine, they too will be Souldrinkers. Better that they drown at birth.

Slowly, the light that was his love for Ramita was going out, the taint of what he had done, and what he was, tarnishing all that had once been so bright. It was so wrong, to have loved her for so long, only to have it all come down to this numbness. For the first time he asked himself: *if you were offered her back, would you take her, knowing the distress it would cause her?*

To his shock, the answer was—he really didn't know. And that hurt.

Brochena, what little they saw, was a strange place to Kazim. It reminded him a little of Hebusalim, the way the architecture had traces of both East and West, but here it was the Rimoni influences he noted most, in the straight lines and columns, and the sun and moon faces adorning the largest buildings. He saw no Rimoni in person, though. Master Zan told them that the Yuros immigrants mostly dwelled closer to the palace. "They have the money," he said simply, his tone more neutral than Kazim might have expected. Zan looked rich himself, or at least the child of privilege.

The next three days were a strange, surreal dreamscape of boredom and nervous tension. They could not go out, nor could they train, in case the noise drew attention. They were shown no plans, given no briefings; the only order was a terse, "Not today," from Gatoz every midday. The Nesti soldiers were mustering and drilling west of the city, and many Jhafi were going to march as well, in support of this mini-shihad to Hytel.

"Why is Gyle here?" Kazim emerged from his misery enough to ask Jamil.

"I've no idea," was all Jamil could answer.

What Kazim couldn't bring himself to ask was whether Jamil knew what Gatoz had done at the Krak. He felt himself sinking further into a kind of despair, in which innocents would be slain until he turned into precisely the sort of monster Rashid and Sabele wanted him to be. His only consolation was that as he'd not used the gnosis since that incident, his well was full, and he did not suffer from that gnawing hunger. Time dragged by in iron chains while he bottled his fury. The noise of the city outside barely penetrated their walls; inside, hours were frittered away on dice, cards, and sleep.

Finally the day came, though there was nothing about it to distinguish it from any other. Kazim woke late, having lain on his pallet wondering where Jai was. And Keita, the girl his brother—if Jai could still be called that—had taken south. She was pregnant too, like his Ramita. *Plump, needy Keita, who snared my soft Lakh brother.* He hoped they were faring well.

They were all mooching around the courtyard when Gatoz walked in and clapped his hands, calling them to attention. They expected to be stood down again, but instead he said simply, "Tonight."

That one word shook their minds awake.

After that, all was preparation: oiling bowstrings and sharpening blades, daubing their faces with wet soot so they would better blend with the shadows, festooning themselves with weapons, then limbering up gently, in readiness for action. Jamil tried once again to tell him how to enhance his blade or his arrows so that they could better penetrate a gnosis-shield. Though he barely listened, the words were seeping into his subconscious; he could feel them there, churning around, as he tried to determine which made him more guilty: to use his power or to not use it.

Just before dusk, Haroun led the whole group in prayer, choosing verses from the Kalistham that reminded them that the greatest goal of every warrior of Ahm had to be to give his life for his brothers. "Only you, Ahm, are constant, in this shifting, changing world. Only you are real. We are but the dream you dream. How can a man know what is truth without you, for you are the only truth."

"There is only Ahm," the men responded, over and again.

Haroun finished and blessed them, his palms held high to heaven. "Ahm be with you."

Then the Hadishah blended with the night and went seeking their prey.

Cera and Timori Nesti looked out over the city as it heaved with activity. Even up here on the balcony she could hear the clang of the hammers in the smithies, the calls of the traders, the rattle of the wagons, and the tramp of the soldiers. The balcony faced north, overlooking parade grounds where ten thousand Nesti soldiers were readying for the march north. *Two days*, she thought, frightened and strangely empty. She clutched Timi's shoulder as her eyes became wet and unfocused.

It was all coming to an end, the odyssey that had begun when Elena Anborn had saved Timori and her from Gurvon Gyle. For a time she'd held her courage and with Elena had reclaimed the kingdom. But that had been just an illusion. Look how quickly Gyle had stolen back into her palace, unseen and untouchable, and shown her just how easily he could destroy them if he wished. She, Timi, and everyone they loved would be killed unless she did as he demanded. All she had to do to end this, he'd told her, was to betray Elena.

But he'd lied: that was just the beginning.

A ruler must make hard choices, without loyalty or malice. Elena herself had taught her this lesson when tutoring her on politics, so she'd done just that. But she couldn't live with that choice now. It ate at her guts and accused her every time she looked in the mirror. Now only one betrayal remained. Gyle had promised it would be bloodless: an encounter with the Dorobon, an honorable surrender, and after that, her brother could live in peace, subservient to the Dorobon but still alive.

"When do you march?" Timi asked eagerly. Like everyone else, he believed that they were marching to an easy victory.

"In two days, darling," she told her little brother—not so little anymore; he was eight now, and thought himself a warrior. They'd even made him a sword, and armor, with a helmet to fit his little head, to keep it safe. He thought he was so grown up.

"We're going to *win*," the boy-king said fiercely.

"Of course," she said, trying not to cry.

She turned her eyes to the east, where Mount Tigrat shone in eternal snow, high above the deserts. The peak was far away, on the edge of sight, a white gleam amidst the shadowy line of the mountains. The distances were deceptive: it looked near, walking distance perhaps, but in truth it was almost fifty miles away across the plains. One of the old tales of Javon was that the old pagan gods, predating the coming of Ahm, dwelled on the peak. Another story had the mountain hollow, housing a city of afreet. She wished she were a mage and could conjure a host of afreet to fight for her, like in the fairy tales. But only Shaitan-spawned Rondians had such powers in this world: evil white men and women with devious minds and cruel hearts.

"Majesty?" a voice called. Tarita, her maid. The young Jhafi girl had been Elena's maid, but now Elena didn't have one. *Because she's not really Elena anymore.* Cera had taken Tarita in so that she would not be thrown onto the streets, or worse. "Majesty, it is time for the king's bath." She had Timi's nanny, Borsa, with her.

Timi made a face. "I don't need a bath," he declared. He looked up at Cera and noticed her tears. "Cera, why are you crying?"

Cera wiped her eyes. "I was just thinking of Mother and Father," she lied. *I should have been: I think of them too little.* "Go and bathe, dearest."

Borsa led the boy-king away, promising him a treat afterward, and the banal conversation filled Cera with longing for simpler times. *But they never were so simple. There were always enemies and plots and dangers; I was just too young and blind to see them.*

"Madam?" Tarita still waited on her.

"Go on ahead, Tarita. I shan't need you until I change for dinner." She waited until the maid had gone, then stood, waiting for the inevitable sound behind her.

"Cera," Gurvon Gyle said softly from the shadows, impossibly close.

She tried not to show that he could still frighten her by mere stealth. "What do you want?"

"To see you," Gyle responded.

She screwed up her nose. He'd taken to teasing her like this, telling her that she was intelligent and comely, as if kind words from him meant anything. He was trying to give her confidence for what was to come, she knew, but praise means nothing when you know it for lies. "You've seen me. Go away."

Gyle clucked softly. "Be calm, Cera. We've not far to go now. A march north, a parley, and it will all be over." He stepped to her side, still partly in shadow. "You've done well. Your counselors suspect nothing."

"I don't want your praise."

"You've earned it."

"Deception is not praiseworthy."

He snorted softly, gazing across the desert as the westering sun carved long shadows across the sands, and the alleys of the city filled up with darkness. "I need Elena this evening," he told her.

"She is no longer Elena," Cera said automatically. *Because of my betrayal.*

"No, she is not," Gyle agreed. "But I need her, nevertheless."

"Why?" she asked, not expecting a reply.

"A meeting. Nothing more." He touched her arm. "Another will be watching you," he said. "Someone who can reach out and touch you as easily as I do now."

She shuddered from his touch on her skin but didn't move. He stroked her upper arm and stared at her profile. His eyes and fingers gave her a creepy sensation, as if she was a bird and he a cat. "Please, I need to be alone," she said at last.

He stroked her cheek. "You're going to need a protector, Cera," he told her. "Someone to remind Francis Dorobon that you cooperated in all ways and are no longer a threat."

She swallowed, while her skin prickled and her blood ran cold.

"I admire you, Cera," he said in a low voice. "You rallied your people at the moment of need. You fooled Elena, which I seldom managed.

You know how to lead, and you understand the power of knowledge. You made a fine queen—you would have made a fine mage."

"The last thing I would want is to be one of you," she said bitterly, knowing she was lying.

"I could get you into Dorobon's bed—he's an arrogant boy who thinks himself cultured and sophisticated, but he has no depth. Not like us. Work with me on this and you will still be Queen in the end. You can still have all you dream of."

"You don't know what I dream," she whispered hoarsely.

"I think I do," he replied. "You dream of power. I, and only I, can give it to you."

You murdered my father, you bastard . . .

"Gurvon," said a rasping female voice from within the room behind. Not-Elena—Rutt Sordell—was there, glowering sourly. "It's time to go."

Gyle nodded, his eyes still on Cera. "Think on it, Princessa," he said softly. "You need a protector. You need me."

She turned away in stony silence so that he wouldn't see her face.

Gurvon Gyle strode confidently along the secret passage, the gnosis-light from his sapphire ring illuminating the way. Elena-Rutt came after him. Elena would have kept up easily, but in these few weeks of possession, Sordell had been destroying his host's physical fitness; Elena looked puff-faced and pudgy about her belly and hips. Her hair was greasy and unwashed, another lapse the real Elena would never have allowed. The real Elena exuded health and energy. Sordell was ruining her.

Elena must be hating that . . .

"Keep up, we're late," he growled.

"You're the one who wanted to see the little princessa," Sordell reminded him. "Are you fucking her?"

"It was necessary to see her," Gyle replied tersely. He bounded down more stairs, feeling a grim satisfaction when Sordell struggled to catch up. "And no, I'm not."

"You should," Sordell rasped. His throat wound was still agonizingly painful, or so he said. Sordell had always been a whiner. "It would utterly piss Elena off."

"Giving you shit, is she?" Gyle asked unsympathetically.

"You've no idea," Sordell panted. "Damn it, Gurvon, this has gone on too long. Find me another body. A *male* one."

Gyle sped up. Having Elena's possessed body so close to him was deeply unpleasant. "Just a few more days, Rutt. Show some Kore-bedamned backbone."

"She's whispering to me all the time," Sordell said, his voice catching like a frightened child's. "I can't *stand* it."

"Live with it." He forced himself to meet Sordell's haunted eyes, making himself confront the fact that Elena was still in there. *I loved her*, part of him insisted. *Love?* another part responded. *You're not capable.* Gyle ground his teeth. "I need you in there, Rutt. Do your damned job."

"I mean it. I'm going *insane*." Sordell raised his hands as if about to tear his own eyes out.

Gyle sniffed, wrinkled his nose. "You've been drinking, haven't you? I told you not to, not today! Damn you, Rutt! You're endangering us all!" He whirled and stormed onward.

<*He wants me, Rutt. Can't you see it in his eyes?*>

<*Shut up, Elena.*>

<*Me, Rutt, not you—though he might settle for my body and your soul.*>

<*I mean it! Shut up!*> Sordell tried to hurry, but the dimensions of this damned woman's body were all wrong, and he stumbled again.

<*C'mon, Rutt, you've always wanted him to favor you. Didn't you think there'd be a price?*>

He wished—*prayed*—for something to drink. "Dear Kore . . ."

<*Oh, please! Rutt Sordell, the great unbeliever, the arch-cynic, is praying?*> She laughed and laughed inside his head and he couldn't make her stop.

The tunnel had become some kind of nightmare made real, and he staggered about, lost and alone, stalked by things too frightening to confront. Some said that all men were born with one of two reactions to threat: retaliate or run—but against the ghost inside his head he could do neither.

His evil dream only ended as he burst from that womb of darkness into a courtyard, barely lit by the red-streaked sky above. Dusk had come while they were underground. He blinked in the dim light, and looked about him warily. Those of the team who could be spared from other duties elsewhere were waiting: dapper little Mathis Drumm, an illusionist and dabbler in Morphic-gnosis, Mara Secordin, a bloated, ugly psychopath with billowing red hair coiled in thick tresses about her huge breasts, and the serious-faced Brevian Earth-mage Glynn Nevis, who'd been recruited barely a month ago. He loathed all of them. None were fit to lace his boots.

<Or your bodice,> Elena chimed in caustically.

He flinched, as if an insect had flown at his face. Mara caught the gesture, and her teeth glinted. Those teeth weren't human: Mara had taken the shape of a shark too often and she seldom managed to change fully back these days. It was part of her dangerous madness.

"Why are we here?" Mathis Drumm asked. "We have our orders already."

"You have," Gyle agreed. "This is about something else." He turned to Sordell. "Something has happened that you all need to know about."

"What would that be?" Glynn Nevis asked diffidently. The Brevian didn't like to look terribly interested in anything: he thought animation was childish. Bored, aloof poise was fashionable in the northern parlors these days.

And you're just a parlor mage, Nevis, Sordell sneered silently. Inside him, he felt Elena agree.

"Our enemies have made a play—a major change to the game— and I have an eyewitness," Gyle told them. He raised a hand as if greeting the shadows. "Magister Sindon?"

Sordell flinched as the darkness disgorged a robed man. The newcomer wore the badge and colors of the Ordo Costruo, Sordell noted with some surprise. He flicked back his hood to reveal a placid, sensible face. The baldness of his head was offset by his thick beard. He looked more like a baker than a mage.

"Magister Gyle," the man responded in a voice as gray as his beard.

Sordell looked about him, not liking this place. There were too many shuttered windows, too many blind spots; though the building appeared to be empty, he couldn't be sure. Night was falling, but the street noises were distant.

He returned his attention to Sindon. The name was familiar; Stivor Sindon was one of Rene Cardien's, a pro-Yuros faction of the Ordo Costruo. But no saint, apparently, not if he knew Gurvon.

Gyle half-turned so that he faced them all. "Magister Sindon and I are old acquaintances. He has news that has great bearing on the Crusade." Sordell heard something in Gyle's voice that was seldom there: surprise. He noted that even Elena inside him was straining to hear what was being said.

Sindon looked about him, his face grave. "Thank you, Magister Gyle. I do indeed come with important tidings." He hung his head, and something like shock entered his voice. "The Ordo Costruo has been usurped by Rashid Mubarak. He has been elected Antonin Meiros's successor."

"What?" Sordell felt the words tumble from his mouth as his jaw dropped, and saw similarly stunned looks on all their faces, even Gurvon's, and he had clearly already been told this news.

"How?" demanded Mathis Drumm, his orderly Brician world turned upside down. Not even Glynn Nevis looked bored at this news.

Sindon put his hands to his head as if struggling to speak. "Rashid Mubarak bought the votes of the majority, playing on the murder of Meiros as a Rondian plot. He now holds the Krak di Condotiori. Those of us who refused his leadership have fled."

"The man's a serpent," Drumm declared.

Mara Secordin glared at that; she didn't like people speaking impolitely of serpents. Of all those present, she seemed least affected by this surprise, but then she really had only one major emotion nowadays: hunger.

Sindon exhaled, shaking his head. "It sounds incomprehensible, but it is so. For myself, I refuse to accept his leadership, as do many others." He looked appealingly to Gyle. "Will you take us in?"

Gyle looked around at the other magi. "Magister Sindon, I think I speak for us all when I say that you are most welcome among us."

"How did Sindon know you were here?" Mara asked suspiciously, twisting a thick tress of her scab-colored hair.

"He contacted me using a relay-stave, hoping I was still here in Antiopia," Gyle responded, and Sindon nodded in confirmation. "He felt I would be better able to provide sanctuary for his people than Betillon."

"Constant has no love for the Ordo Costruo," Nevis mused in his affectedly casual voice.

"Quite," Sindon agreed. He turned to Gyle. "Might I bring in the others?"

"Please do, Magister." Gyle was playing the benevolent host, the pitying healer offering succor in the man's hour of need. Sordell had to suppress a smile of derision, then had a pleasing thought.

I wonder if there are any who have a suitable body for me . . .

Sindon turned and made a sign, and the door from which he'd emerged opened again, allowing more hooded figures to enter the courtyard, fanning out as they came. "Magister Gyle, we're so grateful," Sindon said, offering his hand.

Sordell saw Gyle go to take the offered hand, when he abruptly froze.

At the very last moment, something didn't ring true. Gurvon Gyle was in the very act of reaching out to clasp the hand of this man who'd hired him before and paid well, then he paused. It wasn't Sindon so much as these newcomers: their robes were too bulky; they concealed too much.

Sindon's pupils went wider. *The game is up*, those eyes said.

It is. Gyle swore softly. *And I have too few pieces on the board.*

"Watch out—" he began, then Sindon's hand flashed vivid blue and a searing mage-bolt slammed into his shields—shields that hadn't been there an instant before. His whole vision flashed in dazzling rainbow colors as an unseen force smashed him head over heels. All around him people started moving, but all he saw was the sky arc over his head, then he and his shields smashed into a pillar. They cushioned the impact some, but not entirely, and pain hammered through him as he felt his left collarbone crack.

As one, the six newcomers opened their cloaks and discharged concealed crossbows; the bolts ablaze with gnosis-fire and aimed straight at Gyle's team. Drumm went sideways as one bolt missed, but another impaled his shoulder and spun him around like a top. Two bolts exploded in Nevis's chest and his rib cage ignited, the bones lit from within. He flew backward like a thrown toy, already dead.

Mara Secordin didn't appear to move, but her hand *shifted* and then she was holding the bolt directed her way in her fingers; it flared, then disintegrated.

Sordell shouted loudly in denial, and the bolt directed his way froze in the air before clattering harmlessly to the tiles.

The attackers dropped their crossbows and advanced with swords and gnosis. Nevis was down and Drumm wobbling, so Gyle tried to concentrate on Sindon, who fired another gnosis-bolt at him. He blocked it, though not comfortably. *He's a half-blood, like me*, he thought as he whipped out his own blade, seeking a wall to put his back to. One of the attackers, a young man, darted to his flank and threw a mage-bolt at him that he barely managed to deflect. *Kore's Blood, is that kid a pure-blood?*

Then Sindon blasted at him again and as the rest of the attackers charged, their faces emerged from their hoods: Keshi, all of them, and screaming for Ahm to bless them. *Rashid's renegade Ordo Costruo*, he thought frantically, then that hyper-powered boy flanking him stabbed like a striking snake and all he could do was parry and blast and parry, and try to survive.

Kazim roared and struck again, but the gray-clad Rondian was fast, faster than any man he'd fought, Rashid included. *Gurvon Gyle.* He'd not intended to use the gnosis, but he hadn't been able to help himself. He could almost hear Rashid and Sabele cackling. But Gyle's blade was flickering faster than sight, flinging up a net of steel that Kazim could not penetrate. He could feel Gyle countering with more than a sword, too: the mage's gnosis was attacking him with seen and unseen blows. So far his simple gnostic lessons were sufficing, but he didn't know how long he could last, and still he couldn't land a blow.

Out of the corner of his eye, he saw a second Rondian go down: Gatoz cut a small bearded mage almost in half and blood gushed across the stone floor, slippery and treacherous. He sought better footing, though that left Gyle free to attack Sindon. Gyle's steel flashed and battered against unseen shields and purple sparks lit the air around the Ordo Costruo mage.

Then the obese woman with the damn red hair bellowed with rage, and her whole face changed. In a blur, her chin became an undershot jaw which opened wide as a man's head. Her arms flashed out and she seized Yadri by the shoulders and pulled him to her. The young Hadishah mage barely had time to scream before she bit his throat out. Blood gushed over her chest as she flung the body away; the flesh missile bowled Jamil over.

Talid tried to strike at the other woman—*Elena Anborn?*—when purple light beamed from her hands into the young assassin's face. For an instant the dark shape of his skull was visible, then Talid collapsed, his face withered away.

Their attack was coming apart, Kazim suddenly realized. The two women were still on their feet, and they were turning the tide. The fat woman had a look of mindless savagery on her face as she waddled toward Jamil. Kazim could see his friend was not badly hurt, but he was dazed, and that would be fatal. He had to get between them—but the other woman, Elena Anborn, was in his way . . . He gathered his courage, though the power that had destroyed Talid terrified him, and charged.

Sordell felt his blood rise as the tide turned. He wasn't a warrior, but he enjoyed killing, and using the necromantic-blast to destroy the young Keshi was the best thing that had happened to him since he'd been put in Elena's damned body. The problem was, Necromancy wasn't Elena's thing, so the effort had been costly. Suddenly the hours of drinking instead of learning how to use Elena's body began to feel fatally stupid. Elena would have been dancing about, blade in hand, by now, but he'd not even drawn his weapon. At least he could rectify that. He gracelessly yanked out his sword as Mara, beside him, yowled.

The shutters surrounding the courtyard flew open and a torrent of bolts filled the air—all of them directed at her, Sordell realized. *Kore be thanked.* She slapped them away, then her hand whipped around and her gnosis battered Sindon across the courtyard, away from Gyle. Sindon's body made a dent four feet wide in the brickwork, but he barely flinched. Then Sordell was forced to defend himself again as another attacker came at him.

This Keshi was a towering young man with athletic grace and a fanatic's ferocity. Sordell threw up his hands and blocked the youth's sword with shields alone, but the effort staggered him. He bought himself time by shoving the young assassin away with telekinesis, but somehow the youth resisted that too, though he was knocked off balance. *He's magi too*, Sordell realized with shock, and suddenly galvanized by the fear that he was burning too much power, he hacked at the youth. But he missed, and was forced to block another thrust . . .

Too. Fucking. Slow.

He stared stupidly at the foot of steel in his right shoulder, the curved blade like a half-moon. Icy numbness blossomed about the wound even as he tried to muster some kind of response.

The young man twisted the blade, and he screamed as the world tilted.

Stupid damned body, never worked for me anyway . . .

Kazim spun from his falling foe, yanked out his scimitar and slashed at the back of the monstrous red-haired woman. Unseen wards smacked his sword away, and then the steel itself warped in his hand. He gaped, uncomprehending, as the blade twisted, smoking hot in his hand. From the corner of his eyes he saw Sindon fling Gurvon Gyle all the way onto the roof, then leap after him, but it was the fat woman who filled his vision. They'd been briefed about her—*Mara Secordin*—but before he could remember if they'd said anything useful, she was on him like some Lakh demoness, an extra pair of arms—no, *snakes!*—erupting from her shoulder blades just above her arms and snapping at him. He lopped the head from one with his ruined scimitar, but the other one's jaws clamped onto his shoulder. Fangs punched through the leather and punctured the muscle. He slashed again and managed to slice the snake-arm in half, but it evaporated as if it had never been and Mara barely winced.

Kazim staggered away from the demoness, the ruined blade falling from his hand as his shoulder went numb.

He lived through the next instant only because of Jamil, who shouted in defiance and thrust his sword at Mara. He didn't kill her, but he did puncture her shields and cut her arm. Red blood spattered about her and she shrieked and turned toward Jamil.

Kazim saw his chance. *I'll just—*

His legs wobbled as numbing pain shot down his shoulder and his right arm went limp. The blood on the tiles did the rest, and he slipped and fell beside the fallen Anborn woman as Mara Secordin drove Jamil back.

Suddenly he was struggling to manage even small things. Sight and sound became a confusing vortex behind his eyes. The world was receding, or he was. *Is this death? Am I dying?* He felt numb, and yet moving was all pain. He tried to stand, managed, but barely.

There was no one but dead people around him. Yadri and Talid, torn and blasted, motionless. The two Rondians, lifeless mannequins. Sindon and Gyle were gone. Mara was pursuing Jamil through a door. Then he realized that Elena Anborn still lived . . .

I should finish her off, before she does the same to me—

He fumbled for a dagger as the woman stirred and her mouth fell open.

A black chitinous body like some obscene bloated beetle crawled from the woman's mouth. It seemed to peer up at him, and purple light formed in its eyes. In a flash he recalled how Talid had died and so he backed away, fear overtaking all other emotions.

Without shame, he ran, on legs that wavered like a newborn colt's.

Elena came up like a drowning man from beneath the surface of the ocean, fighting through the tumult, following the bubbles of light. She tasted a ghastly oily film as the cavity in her upper mouth where the scarab had nested burst, followed by the iron-sugar sweetness of her own blood. Then everything, *everything*, came back and she was ALIVE and the body she dwelled in was HERS.

She rolled and slashed, but too slow. The scarab scuttled from her reach. She went after it, *needing* to *killthefuckingfilthything . . .*

Her blade struck sparks from the cobbles inches behind it, but the scarab reached the shadows and was gone before it even occurred to her to summon the gnosis. She howled in silent rage until sheer relief overtook her frustration.

I'm alive. I'm free. I'm ME . . .

She flooded her mouth and shoulder wound with healing-gnosis, clean, beautiful energy that was HERS ALONE. She spat pus and blood and then vomited out the sheer horror of the nightmare she'd escaped. *Sordell was gone.* She almost wept.

The courtyard had fallen into silence. She could taste the crisp metallic feel of gnosis on the air as light flashed outside. Mara Secordin was screaming blue murder, the beast in her let loose. Gurvon was out there, fighting Sindon; she didn't know the traitor mage but she knew Gurvon, and she expected the Ordo Costruo man was in deep shit by now. Bodies lay all about her, unmoving. The last attacker had fled the scarab emerging from her mouth, and no blame for that. She rose, reeling at the effort. She'd closed the wound, but the blood-loss had been real, and thanks to that bastard Rutt Sordell, she was horribly out of condition.

I've got to run before Gurvon comes back.

She went out through a side window, blown open by Mara's fury, and into the road. She knew roughly where she was, and where she had to get to. The streets were empty, in that way violence empties a place; she could sense folk cowering in dread behind their closed doors.

She ran, not fast—her wounds and blood-loss prevented that—and she didn't look back. But she didn't run blindly either.

Ahead of her, the young man who'd wounded Sordell was also running on unsteady feet. One of Mara's snakes had bitten him. *Dead man*, part of her thought, but she followed him nevertheless, hoping to learn who these people were. *The enemies of my enemies might be friends. Or not.*

She came up on him quickly, and he barely saw her. He tried to parry, but she was more or less back in control of herself, and he was reeling dizzily. She battered his blade aside with her blade, then slammed her hilt into his temple, and he dropped like a sack of wheat and sprawled at her feet.

Now what? She stared down at him. Young, handsome, really, with a half-grown beard and thick, dark lips. He was big, much bigger than her. He'd moved like a panther until Mara got him. His shoulder where she'd struck was swollen, the flesh mottled and greenish. He'd probably be dead by dawn. She placed her blade against his throat, then relented: she might be able to keep him alive long enough to question him, perhaps learn who he was; who his friends were, maybe even verify Sindon's story.

Then a low voice called to her from the shadows, "Mistress Elena—?"

She looked up warily as a plump Jhafi man emerged from the darkness, flanked by smaller, more agile shapes.

"Mustaq al'Madhi? Is that you?"

10

THE ISLE OF GLASS

Religion: Omali

You will smile, brother, when I say that every morning we pray to Agni the Sun and bathe in water to cleanse ourselves of nightly sin. We touch the earth and pray to Bhumasi for fertility of harvest and womb. We go to the temples of whichever deity pleases us that day, sometimes to many, and stay as long or short a time as we wish. We pray to Gann the Elephant for luck, and to Hanu the monkey for strength of body and mind. Soldiers revere Ram, and lovers the divine couple Krishu and Radhika. And we never forget the Trimurthi and their consorts. In truth, this must be the holiest of lands, for the gods are never out of our thoughts. Yes, brother, your Lori, who hated every second of Sollan worship, is drowning in faith!

LORENZO DI KESTRIA, WRITTEN WHILE
TRAVELING IN LAKH, 924

Isle of Glass, Gulf of Dhassa, Antiopia
Shaban (Augeite) to Rami (Septinon) 928
2nd and 3rd months of the Moontide

The flying carpet took them far to the north of Haveli Khayyam, flying through the night at a torrid pace. From time to time Justina waved her hand, almost as if flapping at midges, which puzzled Ramita until she realized that the jadugara was warding off supernatural attacks. She was frightened that Justina might succumb, and then they would fall from the skies.

"What is happening?" she called anxiously in Rondian.

Justina glanced behind her. "Nothing. Go back to sleep."

I haven't slept yet, Ramita thought ruefully. She was tired but not remotely sleepy, not when they were shrieking through the air thousands of feet above the dark earth. The eastern skies were glowing behind them and to the right, which meant they must be traveling northwest. Beyond that, she had no idea where they were.

As the sun rose, staining the vast scarred face of the setting moon pink, she realized in shock that they were flying over water— and not just a lake, but the ocean itself. She had once flown over the sea with Antonin Meiros, but still gave a small shriek of fear, though from so high up the great waves were just ripples in a rain-swept pond. When Justina had said they were going to the Isle of Glass, she'd envisaged an island in a river. She should have known better.

The rising sun revealed how drained and haggard Justina Meiros looked. Normally her face was flawless as white silk, but in the new dawn crow's-feet were revealed about her eyes and the corners of her mouth. Her eyes were bloodshot, and thin colorless mucus was streaming from her nose.

"What are you staring at?" she snapped when she felt Ramita's eyes on her.

"You look tired. When will we return to land? You need to rest."

"I'll rest when we arrive," Justina replied tersely.

Ramita shut her mouth. There was no communicating with her daughter when she was like this. She smiled at the thought that aloof, arrogant Justina was her daughter-in-law; it was endlessly amusing.

But I am magi too now. There was so much she didn't know, so much she burned to ask—there was so much to learn, not just about this Rondian magic, but about the world—and how to have children. She'd always ignored the details, for of course her mother would be present. But now her family was who knew how many hundreds of miles away. *I should have asked to be taken home. Ha! As if Justina would heed anything I say.*

Steadily they flew on, the enchantments woven into the carpet keeping the winds from plucking them off the rug and the rain at bay. They were flying lower, and slower, and the waves were greater now: mighty troughs and peaks in constant motion, each one dozens of feet high. The Leviathan Bridge was out of sight, away to the west, Justina told her when she asked, but she could see massive cliffs in the distance, far to the north and east: the coast of Javon, apparently. More information was not forthcoming.

Gradually their destination came clear. A series of huge jet-black pillars of stone jutted above the waves where the land to the east ended, a jagged range of hills running into the sea. Waves crashed about them, massive white explosions of spume and spray, but never covered them. It was only when she got closer that Ramita realized the peaks were hundreds of feet above the surface, and as wide as they were tall. They gleamed like glass.

"They are called the Pillars of the Gods," Justina told her. Her harsh, clipped voice held grudging resignation, as if she'd decided that she would have to communicate with Ramita at least a little. "They're the cores of old volcanoes, eroded by the sea. There is no stronger stone, for it is fused in heat that melts metal like butter. They will stand for all time."

Ramita stared in wonder. They did indeed look as if Sivraman and Vishnarayan had made them, or perhaps Agni had forged them in his smithy. They looked utterly inhospitable.

As they swooped toward one of the larger of these great pillars, Ramita realized that it wasn't really flat; in fact it was hollow, like a cylinder. Justina guided the carpet in closer, fighting the winds ripping at them; they pitched and steadied as she fought the aircurrents until she'd brought them directly over the opening at the top—then she dropped them within. and they fell into shadow until the carpet struck stone some forty feet down. Ramita squealed in relief and fright at the same time. The winds howled above them like a pack of jackals, but beneath the rim they did little more than whip at her hair and clothing. She crawled to the edge of the rug, feeling weak-limbed and ill. Inside her belly her babies were squirming. She kissed the smooth glassy stone, pressed her forehead to it, and let it steady her.

Beside her, Justina moaned and flopped onto her back, panting as if she'd run all day—in a way she had. Ramita had only seen her mask slip once or twice before, and she found it oddly comforting to see her spent and frail. It reminded her that Justina really was a person, not some animated statue.

"Come on!" Justina scolded herself, sitting up and glowering at Ramita. "Feel that?" She held up her long white fingers, like sun-bleached bones. The air was frigid, Ramita realized as the wards about the carpet faded. "The temperature here is barely above freezing. We must get below."

Below? Ramita looked about, and saw a small door in the stone walls. She groaned, but stood up and hefted her bags. Justina went to the door and pressed her hand to the single knob. Gnosis-light flared from it, seeping between her fingers, then the door opened of its own volition. The jadugara turned. "Hurry. It's starting to rain."

Ramita staggered past her as raindrops began to splatter about them, the water mixed with chips of ice. She'd never seen such a thing before. The frigid cold was going straight to her bones.

With a gesture, Justina caused the carpet to roll itself up, then she drew it through the air with one hand while opening another unseen door in the wall opposite with her other hand, her kinetic-gnosis doing all the work. In a trice the carpet was sealed away in the storage compartment. Then she closed the doors, leaving them momentarily in darkness, until lights like little stars flared on the walls, revealing a rough-hewn chamber. Justina gestured imperiously toward stairs spiraling down into the pillar of stone. "Follow me."

They descended many flights, and as they did, Ramita felt the air becoming steadily warmer. At the base of the long stairs, Justina spoke aloud in a strange tongue, and doors so cunningly made they were invisible in the wall slid open, revealing a warm darkness. She called again and light flared inside, brighter than those that had lit the stairs. Ramita blinked hesitantly, but Justina pulled her inside quickly and spoke again, and the doors slammed shut with a frightening boom.

"What is this place?"

Justina scowled. "Father created it as a secret refuge. We have stores kept on ice, enough for more than a year. The earth supplies heat. Air is taken from outside and constantly circulated. There are books and musical instruments, anything one could need." She looked down at Ramita in that way she had of emphasizing that she was almost two feet taller. "And the only rukking company I have in this damned place is you."

Ramita smiled sweetly. "Think how much worse it is for me. I've only got you." She looked around curiously. There was a fire-place surrounded by couches, and rugs on the floor. A tabula game-board. Another stair going further down. "Are there more rooms?"

"Below," Justina answered shortly. She strode to a cabinet shaped from stone and pulled out a bottle and a glass. "Father's room is off-limits. Mine is the larger one with the red wall-rugs. Pick any other." She poured a drink and turned away.

"Thank you for coming for me," Ramita said to her back.

"I did it for the children."

Ramita screwed up her courage. "Where were you, the night my husband was murdered?"

Justina's voice cracked a little and her rigid demeanor sagged. "Alyssa hosted a party to celebrate Odessa's birthday. They had new wines from Bricia. There was no reason to believe that anything was going to happen . . ." She turned her face away.

"And since then?"

Justina made a half-sobbing sound. "I've been with Alyssa and my other friends. They told me you were dead. That your body and Father's were torn apart by a mob. There was nothing to go home for." Her voice broke and her shoulders heaved. "Alyssa was so *kind* to me . . ." She fell into a chair and cradled the wine bottle as if it were a newborn child.

Ramita took a few steps toward her, reaching out.

Justina's head snapped around and her eyes blazed. *"Do not presume to give me your sympathy, you dung-skinned parasite! You're the reason he's dead!"*

Ramita went rigid in shock. *Does she know about Kazim?* Then she realized that Meiros's daughter was only lashing out blindly from the pain inside. She swallowed her fright, backed away quietly and picked up her bags. As she left, Justina rocked soundlessly in her chair.

She found a room below, disentangled herself from her clothing, and crawled between the sheets. She didn't know how to make the light stop shining so she pulled the blankets over her head and let all the fear and the ache of the long weeks of captivity gather behind her eyes, pressing her down, until she was nothing but darkness herself.

It was amazing to her how quickly wonders could become commonplace, ever since Antonin Meiros had chosen her, of all people, to wed. The devil-magic of the Rondians had once been just a legend, like the old Amteh tales of pale-skinned afreet, the servants of Shaitan. Then, suddenly, she was married to one, and frightening magic became ever-present, buildings that were like dream palaces compared with her own humble family home in Baranasi were a daily part of her life. She scarcely noticed marble and gold now; flying carpets were just another way to travel . . .

But even by the standards she was now used to, this place was strange and uncanny.

There should have been no natural light, this far below the surface, but Meiros had created massive transparent skylights high in the walls of the top-floor lounge. Elsewhere, he had set pale glowing lights like tiny candles, each little filament that glowed bright as the sun controlled only by a touch to the glass bubble that protected it: one touch to light it, another to brighten, a third to extinguish: simple, wonderful. The first day she played with one for hours, turning it on and off over and again, feeling each touch draw a little from her reservoirs of energy. By the second day the lights were just another fact of life; likewise the fire that consumed no fuel, the heat that flowed through the ventilation holes, and the fresh water that poured from taps set cunningly over marble basins. There was always hot water for her bath without any need to build a fire.

These everyday miracles did not mean there was no work. She still had to prepare their meals from the icy-cold chamber below filled with row upon row of animal carcasses and bins of frozen vegetables of all kinds. She fell into the role of maid for the two of them without complaint; she'd been brought up to labor and had never expected anything else—and Justina seemed incapable of anything useful.

However, doing the maid's work was one thing; being treated as such was quite another. When Justina ordered her about, Ramita snapped that she should do it herself; if asked respectfully, she would acquiesce. Not that Justina asked for much, rudely or otherwise; her protector spent most of her days in her room, with opium smoke seeping through the cracks of the door. She knew that her husband would not have stocked his sanctuary with such a thing, so Justina must have brought her supply with her.

There were five levels to the living quarters of the Isle of Glass and it wasn't long before Ramita knew them all. The top floor with its high ceiling and daylight shafting through the rock was the lounge, and she lived according to its rhythms, sleeping when the skylights were dark, working when they were lit by sunlight. Next level down were functional rooms: the kitchen and laundry, and a separate stair that went into the food-storage area on the next level down. Below that, accessed by the main stair, were the sleeping rooms, seven of them. She'd never entered Justina's, or her late husband's, but the other five, including her own, were spartan and cold. She hung some of the blankets on the walls of her room, as much to make them more welcoming as to bring a bit of warmth to the chamber.

The next flight down were a large library and office, where two desks were well stocked with writing implements and stacks of unused parchment. The final floor housed the ice-room and storerooms and a large chamber with bathing pools, which had huge doors to the outside. The pools could be heated, but Ramita didn't bother; she was quite happy with the one-person bath in her room.

She had quickly decided the library was the nicest room in the Isle of Glass sanctuary. The rounded outer wall was filled with books, mostly histories of Urte written by the Ordo Costruo.

Ramita nosed through them with difficulty; she'd learned how to read only recently, and was not yet proficient. But she started reading the observations of the Bridge-Builder magi about their world, and found that she agreed with some while others made her wrinkle her nose. Some threatened her, contradicting things she regarded as true—she didn't enjoy reading those passages but she made herself do so anyway.

She spent hours staring at a massive map of Ahmedhassa, or Antiopia as the Rondians called it, and Yuros that covered one wall of the library. It had been rendered in plaster stucco, with the mountains and valleys shown in relief; she'd never seen such a thing before. Cities and major towns were marked in both Rondian and Keshi alphabets. First she found Baranasi and stroked the name longingly, then she traced her journey north, through the deserts and southern Kesh to Hebusalim. She eventually found the Pillars, where she was now, jutting from a peninsula west of Javon. They were depressingly far from anywhere else, which made her feel all the lonelier.

It was even more frightening looking at Yuros, she decided, where such a vast expanse had been rendered in greens depicting the forests and lush plains. They had so much water—there were lakes and rivers *everywhere*—while Antiopia was depicted as brown and dry.

The most puzzling thing was the line of the Bridge. The mapmaker—her husband, she presumed—had shown it as a thin red line, but he had also molded an underwater landscape of ridges and highlands, and it was these the Bridge followed. On one of the rare occasions she found Justina in the library she gathered up her courage and asked her about it.

"Do you not know?" Justina replied loftily, then, "no, I suppose not. Yuros and Antiopia were once one continent, linked through the Pontic peninsula by a mountain range to Dhassa. The Ordo Costruo believe we were linked as recently as fifteen hundred years ago." She poked a finger at the map. "Father believed men began to farm and settle in villages about three thousand years ago—before that they were all nomads, constantly traveling around."

Ramita frowned. She'd been taught that the gods had created men and women in Lakh, thirty thousand years ago; non-Lakh people were the spawn of the Rakas demons who stalked the edges of the civilized lands. She could almost hear her husband chuckling quietly as she explained this to him. "Why is there no mountain range now?" she said out loud.

"Father thought a meteor strike took it out." At Ramita's blank expression she explained, "A massive rock, fallen from the heavens. Father said there were strange rock types found when they built the bridge."

"Guru Dev says the Gods cursed the Rakas, and Agni hurled a huge boulder down to destroy their king."

Justina snorted softly. "Primitives," she muttered to herself, just loudly enough.

Ramita kept her temper. "Perhaps the gods wished to divide East and West," she observed.

"There are no gods, only us."

Ramita made the sign against blasphemy, but having Justina actually talk to her was a rarity, so she let it pass. "How can our peoples be so different if once we were all in one land?"

Justina raised her eyebrows, almost as if the question had impressed her. "Well . . . we believe that groups of people *evolve*—successive generations take on characteristics after long periods in certain terrains or climates, things like fairer or darker skin, or they're taller, or smaller and quicker—things which help them to survive. We used to debate why, after being divided so long, the peoples of our two continents are so *similar.*"

"Similar?"

"Monarchies, religions, male dominance . . . we're not so different really."

Ramita opened her mouth to reply and shut it again. Guru Dev had always said that if you knew little about something you should use your ears, not your tongue.

Justina thoughtfully traced the line of the Bridge on the map, her eyes distant. "Father thought that when men spread across the land they changed to suit their terrain and climate, but many other things are inherent, part of humankind's nature. He said that when the two continents were divided, Yuros and Antiopian culture diverged, but only gradually. When we Ordo Costruo first flew to Antiopia 200 years ago, we found Dhassa and Kesh were ruled by priests of Ahm. Our coming triggered a massive change in society. From the arrival of the first windships to the building of the Bridge, we Ordo Costruo changed Dhassa and Kesh utterly."

Her voice held a note of pride Ramita had not heard before. *Ah, so this is something you care about.* "What happened?" she asked, genuinely interested.

"Because we had the gnosis and superior learning, and because we had no gods and dealt in rationality and reason, we undermined the powers of the Godspeakers. We built buildings and roads and aqueducts that no non-magi could have managed. We changed the landscape. Those traders and landowners who dealt with us became hugely rich and influential, and they seized secular power from the Godspeakers, who were left with just religious power. This change had already happened in Yuros centuries before, under the Rimoni Emperors, and just like then, it triggered unrest and open bloodshed. My father was horrified, but unrepentant—the Godspeakers had ruled like tyrants, and it was our coming that broke them. The Sultans of Dhassa and Kesh owe their rule to my father and his followers."

This was history Ramita had never heard and it made her feel queasy, to hear something so alien. "Did your people ever come to Lakh?" she asked timorously.

"A few," she admitted, "but after the violent upheavals in Kesh, Father forbade us from going south, not just to live but even to openly use the gnosis. He wanted to let other societies evolve at their own pace. He wanted us to be a distant example, not a present threat." She tapped the map thoughtfully. "Though in reality, we did meddle. My older brother spent time in Khotri. And Father took me to Teshwallabad in secret, once." She screwed up her nose. "Smelly place."

Ramita barely managed to suppress her smile. "You'd have hated Baranasi."

But such conversations were rare; for the most part Justina remained aloof. Ramita was never precisely bored, but she ached with loneliness as the days passed by, dreamlike. She'd never been alone before, or not been surrounded by a continual babble of speech. Here there was no conversation, no other faces; instead, she spoke to her babies, the little beings growing inside her. They wouldn't burst into the world for months, but she wanted them to always feel loved.

Sometimes she spoke with her husband's memory, telling him what she thought of something she'd read, or complaining of Justina's inattention. She told him she missed him, which she did. He'd been kind and patient with her; though he'd purchased her with money—a lot of money—he'd treated her with dignity and respect. She wished he was here now, to see the way her stomach was swelling with his children.

She didn't use her gnosis, though she wanted to; instead, she waited for Justina to run out of opium and come back to herself, and teach her, as she had promised. But as days turned to weeks, her daughter-in-law remained locked in her opium dreams.

Eventually, Ramita lost all patience. She kicked open the door to Justina's room and tipped a bucket of cold water over her head. "Enough!" she cried.

"What—!"

The jadugara was lying half-clad across her low bed, a hookah on the floor beside her, the air hazy and thick with smoke. Ramita waved it away, nauseated. "Get up, you useless cow!" She looked around at the packages of dun-colored powder spread haphazardly across the floor, then bent and gathered them up. Justina was still staring blankly as she tipped them onto the fire. "You're pathetic," she told the drooling woman. "What would your father say?"

Justina blinked and stared stupidly as her opium went up the chimney.

Ramita stormed out, slammed the door and fled to her room. *How am I to do anything? I'm stuck in the middle of the ocean with no place to go to, twins in my belly and a useless addict as my only companion.*

She burst into tears.

Three days later Justina tottered up the stairs to the lounge and collapsed onto a sofa.

For those three days she had oscillated between screaming fits, weeping storms, and snoring like a pig.

Ramita didn't turn her face toward her.

"You missed some," Justina whispered. "I threw it down the privy." She groaned. "I'm sorry. I've always been weak." She seemed to expect sympathy for this.

Ramita pointedly studied her book. She'd been reading a passage about a barbaric place in Yuros: *The forests of Schlessen are primarily pines, firs, and other evergreens. Some stands are hundreds of feet tall, and the sunlight cannot penetrate all the way to the forest floor. There are legends of tree-spirits that guard the deep woods. Schlessen tribesmen still make sacrifices to placate them before every hunt.* She could not imagine such a place. She'd never seen more than six trees in one place in her life.

"You don't know what that stuff is like," Justina whined. "It makes everything so beautiful and warm; every sense you have is filled with goodness—you feel so *complete*. It's better than sex, because you don't have to deal with another person. It's better than drink and food, better than dreaming. It's a perfect place, and you can go whenever you wish—"

Chief among these Schlessen tree-gods is Minaus, a bull-headed man who is their war-god. At the winter and summer equinox the tribes burn effigies to ask his blessing on the coming season. Sollan drui give blood and semen to the roots, to feed them. They maintain that the trees are sentient, and in touch with each other. They say that the great forests are one organism, and that one day they will once again cover the lands, destroying the transient labors of man.

Ramita sipped her tea. She looked up at the skylight and guessed it was about midmorning.

"People hurt you. The opium never does." Justina burst into a coughing fit that made her shake like an old woman.

"It is more than hurting you," Ramita pointed out calmly. "It is killing you."

A long pause. "I know." The admission was whispered, barely audible.

In Southern Schlessen the chief woodland spirit is an antlered bear named Ursus, who eats children. Stillborn babies are sacrificed to him, buried beneath the roots of sacred trees to placate him. Sometimes even living children are given, if there is great need of his blessing.

It is this sort of ignorance that we of the Ordo Costruo must fight.

She turned to face Justina, staring at her as if she were the elder. "You must teach me the gnosis."

Justina bowed her head.

"What is this for?"

They sat cross-legged, facing each other, which reminded Ramita uncomfortably of her time with Alyssa Dulayne at Casa Meiros, being taught the Rondian language directly, mind-to-mind. But much to her relief, Justina made no effort to link minds. She'd arranged four saucers in front of Ramita: one contained water, another dirt, the third a lit candle and in the fourth was an oil that she'd also set alight, though it did not flame but gave off a heavy, slow-moving smoke.

Justina passed her hands over the saucers. "These represent the prime elements. Each mage has an affinity to one of these more than the others. It's not something you choose: it is in you, part of who you are. Some have two affinities, and very occasionally there are those with none—that's all right; it's just a way to reach for the gnosis and understand it."

Ramita contemplated them. "What do I do?"

"Touch them. Play with them. Study them. Engage your gnosis and see which one feels most comfortable. Don't think about it too much, just follow your instincts."

"And what is that?" She pointed to the wooden board in front of Justina, which had strange little symbols etched onto it. A pile of red glass stones was heaped alongside.

"I will be using this to get an understanding of where your strengths lie."

Ramita made a face. She didn't like the sound of this. "Where do I start?"

"Why not start with the earth? Take a pinch of it, poke it around. Rub some into your palm. Sniff it. Put a pinch on your tongue. Most of all, try to touch it with your gnosis."

Ramita wrinkled her nose. *Taste it? Ugh!* She reached out reluctantly and did as she was bid. The soil was from one of the potted plants positioned under the skylights by dripping taps; she'd been tending them as part of her routine. Now she let her mind drift to her mother Tanuva's rooftop herb garden. She had always loved working there with her mother, tending the herbs, learning their mysteries. They were happy memories.

"Now engage the gnosis," Justina ordered, "while still thinking about the soil."

It came easily as she thought about her mother and the way she sang as she worked. There was a seed in the soil, she realized. Perhaps Justina had put it there deliberately. She felt a tingling in her fingertips and opened her eyes to see a greenish glow coming from beneath her skin and bleeding into the seed. Suddenly it sprouted, a single tiny unfurling stalk that reached out blindly, but Ramita took fright and it withered, to her disappointment.

Justina pursed her lips then picked up eight stones and placed them in a line down one side of the wooden board.

"I'm sorry," Ramita said sorrowfully, "I killed it."

"That doesn't matter. Try the water."

She wasn't sure how long it all took, but the shifting shafts of light moved across the room while her mind filled with sensations both familiar and strange. Water could be moved around by gnosis alone; she even made some more drip from her fingers, though afterward she felt parched and sickly.

The flame at the end of the candle was another matter. As a child she had been fascinated by fire, and she'd often angered her parents by letting their precious candles burn down just so she could watch the flame. She was able to move the flame to her fingertips, which thrilled her, but it made her nervous too. She never forgot that fire was dangerous, but trying to tame it made the time fly by.

"And the air?" Justina asked. Her voice sounded a bit strained, Ramita thought, but she became engrossed in her final task.

The smoke from the oil was the hardest: it was intangible, insubstantial, and she could see no way to impose any pattern. When she sighed and opened her eyes, Justina was sitting studying the stones she'd piled onto the wooden board. "Well?" she asked, suddenly tired. She reached out and scooped up her cup of green tea, a little surprised to find it had gone stone-cold. She looked around and realized the skylights were graying as night fell.

Sweet Parvasi, where did the day go?

Justina's mouth twitched. "So, Ramita, tell me a few things." She then proceeded to bombard her with the strangest and hardest questions Ramita had ever had to answer. None of them appeared to have a right answer, and none of them related to magic: what did she dream about? (Baranasi, even when people from Hebusalim were in the dream.) What colors did she prefer? (Natural hues, with a splash of brightness.) What was more important, a deed or an intention? (A deed, of course!) There were many others, often variations on a theme, and some embarrassingly personal. All the while Justina shifted the red glass stones around, adding some here, removing them from there.

Finally she stopped as if she too had just discovered how tired she was.

"So, Ramita Ankesharan," she started, "this is not definitive, but by my reckoning, your prime affinities are Earth- and Hermetic-gnosis." She sounded engaged, more than Ramita had ever heard her—almost likable, or maybe, more that for the first time Ramita could begin to see why someone might like her, if they were so inclined and hadn't already been thoroughly alienated . . .

Ramita blinked. "I thought the Fire—?"

Justina shook her head. "That's your secondary elemental affinity. You did well with it, but you were wary. Your weakness is Air. I'm not surprised, you were scared shitless during our flight here."

"Oh." Ramita reappraised herself. "What is 'Hermetic'?"

"It is a physical branch of the gnosis, concerned with the makeup of the world—plants, animals, the human form. I imagine you are a very tactile person, someone who likes working with your hands, and with animals. You're not terribly imaginative," she added, a little disdainfully. "You only believe in what is proven. You have no interest in concepts or philosophy."

"Why should I? It's just a load of dung spouted by underemployed priests."

Justina smiled wryly. "My point exactly." She tapped the board. "This will guide us. Most magi have years of training, so you've a lot to make up, and who knows how little time in which to do it. We may have only a few days to teach you how to defend yourself."

It was a frightening thought. Ramita leaned forward. "What do these stones show?"

Justina quickly ran her fingers over the board. "Down this side are arrayed the elemental symbols: this one here represents Fire. This is Water, these Earth and Air. Now, down this side are the symbols for Hermetic, Thaumaturgy, Sorcery, and Theurgy. See where the stones are piled highest? Those are your strengths. Where there are no stones at all, you are weak."

Ramita looked at the stones, read the words in each square. There were sixteen of them. "Sylvanic? Animagery?"

Justina nodded. "You are strongest as a plant and nature mage: what you did with that seed was impressive, especially for a first attempt. Wood and plant material are everywhere, and they are highly versatile. And as I said before: you'll learn how to make animals do whatever you want. You'll even be able to take their shape."

Ramita swallowed. *Me? Take animal shape? Impossible!* The mere idea belonged in fables, not reality. But then: *Why not?* She found herself smiling. "What else?"

"Fire and Earth obviously, especially Earth. You'll be able to shape stone like it was clay, once I've shown you how. I've seen strong Earth-magi walk through walls—and punch like the kick of a mule."

Ramita felt giddy at all these possibilities. "What am I weak at?" she asked, to sober herself up.

Justina pointed at the empty squares. "See? Nothing in Clairvoyance or Divination—in fact, there's little in the Sorcery Studies at all. They'll be a closed book to you—although Necromancy is linked to Earth-gnosis so you might be able to conjure a dead man's spirit."

Ramita screwed up her nose.

"And see here," Justina went on, "Theurgy—mind-work—will also elude you. You'll have a profound weakness to Illusion—that means you'll basically believe whatever illusion is conjured is real, unless you're especially vigilant. And you'll not be able to leave your body."

"Ugh. Why would I want to?"

"Exactly: your mind rebels at the thought. The gnosis is an extension of who we are. Think about it: none of this is a surprise to you, is it? You're a self-aware young woman, well grounded in your reality. The mage you will be is an extension of who you are." Justina's voice had none of her usual sarcasm, just honest assessment.

"What about you?"

Justina grunted diffidently. "Me? I am an Air-mage with a little Sorcery. You and I are very different, girl—in fact, we're almost diametrically opposite."

That's no surprise. "What happens next?"

Justina yawned. "Next? I teach you the basics: how to use the raw gnosis." She yawned again. "Starting tomorrow. I'm hungry." She looked at Ramita meaningfully.

"Perhaps it is your turn to cook," Ramita grumped. "I'm the one who has been working, not you."

"Girl, you don't want my cooking."

"You do nothing here. I cook, I clean, I wash, I dust. You sleep and drink."

Her mouth twitched in amused bitterness. "It's good that we stick to what we're best at."

Ramita stood up so that she could have the rare opportunity to look down on this stuck-up jadugara, who might not be without hope, based on this day's glimpses of a nicer self, but was still an irritating and pricklish cow. "Perhaps I will now look after only myself."

Justina's eyes took on a dangerous light. "We are not equals, girl."

Ramita sniffed. "No. Apparently we are 'diametrically opposed.' You can still do your own cooking."

The pack gathered in the old palace throne room for a cooked dinner Huriya was made to prepare. Many of Zaqri's pack still walked naked. Huriya could see the animal inside still reigned over some of them, who tore at the meat with claws and teeth, then mated in the corners. All exuded that primeval hunger she was beginning to see as the defining mark of a Souldrinker. The constant need to replenish consumed gnosis was beginning to change her too. *It frightened Kazim, but I'm not afraid . . .*

The older ones had more control of their desires however; after eating they gathered about Sabele. There were four such seniors, Zaqri and another male named Perno, and their women, dark-skinned sisters from Lokistan called Ghila and Hessaz. They had a fierce, primal vitality. All wore loose kirtas and nothing else. The two women were jackal-lean and smelled strongly of musk and heat. Neither spoke Rondian, so the conversation switched to Keshi.

"Join us," Sabele told Huriya when she'd served the others. The Lokistani sisters grudgingly made a place for her, possessively stroking their mates' arms. Their eyes were still amber and black, the eyes of beasts. She glared back defiantly and pushed out her chest, far more bountiful than the skinny bosoms of either beastwoman.

Perno grinned. "She has some fire, this Makani girl."

Hessaz growled something in his ear and as he whispered something back, they were all openly measuring Huriya. Their eyes made her quiver. "Did you know my father?" she asked Zaqri in a bid to conceal the flush building about her neck.

"I did," Zaqri replied. He glanced questioningly at Sabele, who nodded. "He rejected our ways. It hurt us all."

"After he was burned by the Crusaders he went south to Lakh. My mother was already pregnant." Huriya stopped then, deciding all of a sudden to wait and see before revealing Kazim's existence. She saw Sabele nod appreciatively.

"So you are twenty-two?" mused Zaqri, accepting her words at face value. "You look younger." Then he frowned. "You spoke of your father in the past tense. Is he dead, then?"

"Last year, in Baranasi."

Zaqri looked surprised. "How did you come north then?"

"I found her," Sabele put in, her lie sounding like truth. "I brought her north." Clearly some secrets were not for telling, however much respect she might give these others. Her voice made it clear that the subject of Huriya's past was now closed.

"What new task do you have for us?" Perno asked.

Sabele glanced at Huriya. "I seek a former companion of Huriya. She too has the gnosis, but she is hiding from us. We need a different set of eyes. Her name is Ramita Ankesharan. Huriya will show her to you, mind to mind. Then we must find her. There is much at stake."

Huriya presumed that it was Ramita's unborn children that Sabele wanted. Well, whatever it was, she looked forward to communicating with Zaqri, mind-to-mind, and in other ways . . .

Zaqri bowed his head. "We will find her for you, Seeress."

"I have every confidence in you, dearest grandchild," Sabele purred, glancing about at the room, settling upon an energetic couple a few yards away. "I wish I had the vigor of youth still," she cackled lasciviously.

"You are young where it matters," Perno told her.

"Flatterer," Sabele replied dismissively. "Go and play, all of you. I need to think."

She made a disgruntled Huriya clear away the food and plates while the Dokken pack drank and fought and mated on the rugs scattered about the floor. After she'd finished her tasks, Huriya slunk away. She feared the pack when they were in this mood; it was almost as if they were one organism, sharing their minds and bodies, and outsiders were detested. As she returned to her room, she glimpsed Ghila and Zaqri together. The Lokistani woman was skeletal, her ribs clearly visible beneath her black skin, but Zaqri looked lost in her eyes as he tangled his limbs with hers. Huriya stopped, hungering for him as he took one of Ghila's small but engorged nipples in his mouth; his majestic body was coiled above his woman, his immense prong engorged, and Huriya felt her mouth go dry as she watched. Then he looked up and saw her, and Ghila turned her head too. Zaqri growled, and Huriya fled.

11

FISHIL WADI

The Dorobon Monarchy

One powerful Rimoni clan in Javon, the Gorgio, refused to be a party to the Javon Settlement, as they wouldn't intermarry with the Jhafi. They retained voting privileges, but were constitutionally ineligible for the succession. Consequently, despite the hatred most Rimoni harbor for both Rondians and magi, the Gorgio supported the Rondian invasion, and that aid was vital in securing the kingship of Javon for the Dorobon family, kin to Emperor Constant.

The Dorobon reign lasted until after the Second Crusade when, weakened by insurrection and rebellion, they succumbed to the Nesti-led Javonesi. Neither the Dorobon nor the Gorgio have ever recovered.

SOURCE: ORDO COSTRUO COLLEGIATE, PONTUS.

You do not graft a sick branch onto a healthy tree

PROVERBS, THE KALISTHAM

Brochena, Javon, Antiopia
Shaban (Augeite) 928
2nd month of the Moontide

Gurvon Gyle stole into the tiny whitewashed cell and sat beside the bed. Mercifully, the sole occupant, a thin shape with fire-blackened skin, was asleep. There was almost no flesh on the face of the burn victim at all, and the entire front of the body was charred, but the gnosis—and sheer damn-it-to-hell tenacity—had kept the victim clinging to life.

<*Yvette,*> Gyle whispered into her mind—he thought of Coin as "she," though "she" had no fixed gender. Her given name seemed to calm her, to remind her who she used to be, though her body stank of burned meat and bodily waste and the bedclothes were wet and soiled around her buttocks. He stared—it was hard not to—at the flaccid penis lying sideways, with no scrotum beneath but a vagina instead. The physical abomination fascinated him in a queasy kind of way.

Her body didn't stir, but Coin's mind woke. <*Gyle? What do you want?*> Her mental voice was high, sexless—and pained. <*I hurt so much. The burning never stops.*>

It was cruel to keep the burned shapeshifter alive, but he didn't care, nor did he care whether she was suffering or not, unless it impaired her recovery. Coin was an asset, and when he'd discovered that she was still clinging to life he'd contrived to save her. In truth, though, it was Coin's own tenacity that had preserved her; Gyle had mostly just hidden her away while he tended her, then, once she was out of immediate danger, buried another in her place. Coin had been caught in a fire-blast—Gyle still didn't know why; she must have moved in the wrong direction when Inquisitor Targon had attacked Elena. He couldn't work out how Elena had killed Targon, either—but he'd taken credit for it when reporting to Mater-Imperia Lucia, Coin's mother.

<*I see much evidence of healing,*> he told her, truthfully. The clean flesh at the edges of the burns was fighting a slow war of attrition against the burned tissue. Any normal person would be dead,

and most magi too, but whatever else she was, Coin was a pure-blood magi with power to burn. *<The hand you tried to shape-shift last week has shed most of the burned skin.>*

<Is it ugly?> she asked. Her eyes had been burned away.

<It looks almost normal,> he lied, eyeing the clawed appendage, its shiny pink scar tissue stretched across the tendons and bones like canvas over a tent-frame. *<You must try to do more shifting.>*

<But it hurts,> she protested. *<Everything hurts. It is too much.>*

<Nothing is too much for you,> he told her, appealing to her determined side. The Imperial line could never admit such a taint as hers, so she'd been hidden from public view all her life, treated as a monster. Her mother had declared her a stillborn, so her name had not been entered into the records—but she'd grown, and become a player nevertheless. That was down to her willpower. *<Nothing is too much for you. You are a Princess of the imperial line.>*

<I'm a freak,> she replied morosely.

He touched her hand and sent her empathy. He really did admire her courage in going on. That she'd risen above her state to become the most feared shapeshifter in the underworld of the magi was to her immense credit. She was a strange thing: a malformed personality with an utterly malleable body, like a child in many ways. *An abused child.*

<Does Mother know I'm alive?> she asked.

<Oh course. She sends her love,> he lied. In fact, he'd told Lucia that her child was dead, and the Living Saint had not been displeased. He peeled a banana from the bowl beside her bed. Coin protested she was not hungry, but she let him feed it to her through the remnants of her lips. He gave her sips of water afterward, slowly and patiently. One didn't waste an asset like Coin, someone who could turn herself into anyone, and maintain the disguise under duress that would break most magi. He'd gone to some lengths to conceal the fact that she still lived, even from his own team.

Not that I've much of a team left right now. Sindon's attack had cost him three: Drumm and Nevis were dead, and Elena had vanished. Rutt Sordell had come scuttling back to him and the scarab was currently in his pocket, trying to persuade him to let him have Coin's body once it was healed. Mara was unharmed, and he'd summoned others from their assignments in Hebusalim to replace Nevis and Drumm, but their position felt precarious. The thought of Elena, alive and in control of her own body again, made him more nervous than he had been for months. His resources here were spread dangerously thin, and at such a crucial time. Tomorrow, the Nesti marched north.

<What is the matter?> Coin asked, surprising him with her perception.

<Nothing,> he lied. *<You must try more shifting, using all of your body. Shapeshifting is only one step away from healing. You must alter your flesh to prevent the scar tissue from becoming permanent.>*

<I will never recover,> she groaned.

<You will,> he told her, instilling certainty into his voice. *<I have something for you,>* he added. He fished out a jar of liquid in which floated two human eyes, trailing white tissue. They looked like the thin tentacles of the freshwater jellyfish found up in Lantris. He hooked one out and slowly fed it into her eye socket.

<Eyes!> Coin's mouth fell open and a gurgle emerged from around her blackened stump of tongue. *<Real eyes!>*

He put the other in place and could immediately feel her gnosis working the connections of the eyes, fitting them to her own burned-out sockets. It wasn't going to be easy, and it would take days, but if she got it right, it would be a giant step toward her rehabilitation. *<Anything for you, Princess.>*

<Thank you,> she sent fervently. *<Thankyouthankyouthankyou.>* She didn't ask where the eyes had come from.

He touched her hand, the half-healed one. *<I will remake you, Yvette,>* he promised, and she flooded him with gratitude, with *worship.*

<I'll wash you now. Concentrate on the eyes,> he whispered, squeezing her hand gently. She twisted her blackened, peeling lips into a semblance of a smile, then sank into a trance, already engrossed with assimilating the new eyes. Mara was even now devouring the beggar-girl who had donated them; after all, waste not, want not. There was never any shortage of beggars.

He busied himself with cleaning Coin's tortured body, applying what little healing-gnosis he had. For the hundredth time he missed Elena, who would have had Coin halfway to recovery by now.

Afterward, he climbed the stairs and, after checking for silence, pulled a catch and slid open an opening into a cobwebby cellar filled with debris. Another stair took him into the web of tiny passages that riddled Brochena Palace. It was late evening and the upper levels were quiet. Finally he wriggled into the secret space adjoining Cera's room.

A gray shape huddled beside a small candle turned to face him as he approached. The watcher was a bony woman with an enormous nose pierced by a large gold ring that hung down to her upper lip. Her gray-black hair was pulled away from her face. Her name was Hesta Mafagliou; she was a Lantric quarter-blood about fifty years old. He didn't know if he could fully trust her, even though he'd known her for a decade or more, but she'd been posing credibly as a Rimoni in the city since she'd arrived a few weeks ago, and her primarily Sorcery-based affinities were useful.

"How is our princessa?" he whispered in Hesta's ear. She smelled stale and bookish, as if she spent most of her time in abandoned libraries.

"Writing at her desk," Hesta whispered back. Her breath was laced with coffee and tobacco. Her big eyes loomed like moons in the dim hidey-hole. "She's a homely thing," she added cattily. Hesta's desire for other women was the weakness that had driven her from society and into Gyle's circle of agents. She might have been attractive when she was younger, but these days her sagging breasts and paunch meant she'd have to use her strong Mesmerism affinity if she wanted to seduce anyone.

"Fancy her, do you?" he asked.

Hesta shrugged. "There are prettier women here."

"You're here undercover," he reminded her. "You will touch no one until I allow it."

"There will never be anyone for me again," Hesta said softly, her eyes briefly distant. Her safian lover had reneged on their relationship when it became public and had somehow managed to escape the total ruin that had enveloped Hesta's family, all because of her "unnatural" desires. *There is only ever one true love in anyone's lives,* she'd told him once. *All the others dwell in its shadow.* It had made him think uncomfortably of Elena.

He nudged Hesta aside and stared into the room. Cera was visible in profile, her long, serious face mostly hidden behind her curtain of black hair. She wore a heavy velvet robe over her nightgown and was signing sheet after sheet of paper, all minor orders and authorizations. The bureaucrats had overloaded her with last-minute matters.

"Has she had any visitors?" he asked.

Hesta shook her head. "Only the little maid."

"Tarita? What do you make of her?"

"Observant. Spirited. Loyal to Cera."

"Is she an informant?"

"Possibly. She has the nerve for it, I deem." Hesta glanced sideways at him. "Would you like me to find out?" Her tone suggested exactly how she'd "investigate" Tarita.

He shook his head. "She will go north with Cera and you will not. I want you here to secure Timori. You'll have Mathieu Fillon with you."

Hesta sniffed. "Fillon is just a boy."

"He is a Fire-mage of some talent."

"He refuses to take orders from women."

"He will do as I tell him, and I will tell him that you are in charge."

"What about Sordell?"

Gyle's mouth twitched. "Without a body he is useless for now."

"Put him into Fillon's body."

"Rutt let me down. He does not deserve another chance so swiftly. And you would find him even less biddable than Fillon." He patted the woman's shoulder. "I'm relying on you and Fillon to secure Timori. Do not fail me." He could feel Sordell's anger at his words but didn't care. *Learn, Rutt.*

Hesta's yellowed teeth glinted between parted lips. "I'll do my part, boss."

He stared through the spy-hole and decided Cera needed a little reminder of who controlled her. He touched a latch, opened the panel and slipped into the room, masking the noise with gnosis. He was within a few feet of Cera when she looked up abruptly and almost screamed.

"Hush, Princessa," he told her. "It is only me."

"Wh-what do you want?" Her eyes flew about the room, then came back to him.

He reached down and caught her chin, watching how she flinched at the contact. *They say she is passionless, but I don't believe that. They just mistake her passions: her drives are led by the mind. As are mine.* He was surprised to realize that she stirred him, but he shook off that urge. Francis Dorobon would expect her to be a virgin. But he did wonder if one day she might, despite everything, become a true ally. He liked her rational manner; he saw elements of himself in her.

"Cera, during the march my people will be near you at all times. Nothing you do will be unknown to me." It wasn't quite true, thanks to the loss of Elena, but he needed her to be afraid.

She looked away. "You've told me this."

"Breathe a word of doubt to anyone and I will have their throats cut. Then the Dorobon forces will be unleashed upon your people, and your family and all their retainers will simply cease to exist."

She swallowed visibly.

"You must exude confidence at all times. You must project *belief* that your forces will crush the Dorobon."

She nodded mutely.

"And remember: my people here will have Timori at their mercy."

"I know," she whispered.

He seized her shoulders, his hands gentle, and pulled her upright, tilted his head, and made her meet his eyes. Again, he was surprised by the urge to have her—then he realized why: *she is the closest thing to Elena I have.* The thought quelled his latent desire.

"Cera," he said, "I . . ." For a moment he lost track of what he'd meant to say, then recalled himself. "Cera, you remember our earlier conversation? I have suggested to Francis Dorobon that he keep you as a hostage. He is young and lusty and I will urge him to bed you, to show himself your master. You could gain a mage-child and introduce the gnosis into your family, if you are willing."

Her eyes filled, but he could feel the desire for power warring with revulsion, not just at the thought of Francis Dorobon, but also at the idea of doing something that he, Gurvon Gyle, wanted her to do. He watched dispassionately as a tear rolled down her cheek.

"Yes," she whispered huskily, and he pulled her close, as if offering comfort, though he could tell his closeness revolted her.

Perhaps that was why he did it.

Cera's only previous military march had been when she'd led the Nesti in reclaiming Brochena last year. Of course, they'd known before they left that the Gorgio had fled and that there was no likelihood of battle, so it had been more like a parade. Every village had greeted them with cheers and songs, and waving cloths dyed violet, the Nesti color.

This time was different. This time they were marching north to certain battle against a terrifying enemy. Conventional wisdom was that to have any chance you had to outnumber the Rondians five to one, and be willing to endure almost fifty percent casualties. She tried to imagine every second man dead; it was a hideous thought.

It's down to me to ensure it does not come to that, she reminded herself grimly.

Some nights she slept in the main suite of whichever noble's house lay in the army's path. Tarita looked after her every need, and was quick to administer a tongue-lashing to anyone who did not instantly supply whatever Cera required. Other nights, when there was no convenient place to stay, she and the little Jhafi maid shared a tent, and her presence helped to keep her despair at bay.

She'd not seen Elena—Rutt Sordell—for days. He'd apparently been sent on a mission, and she'd been obliged to repeat that to her counselors. It was a relief not to have Not-Elena close by, but it puzzled her too; that hadn't been the original plan. She allowed herself the faint hope that somehow Gyle's schemes might be unraveling.

Each night she ate with her commanders. Paolo Castellini, the tallest man in Javon, sat at her left hand. Seir Luca Conti was at her right. Both were grim men with little conversation. Opposite sat Emir Ilan Tamadhi, commander of the Jhafi forces that comprised four-fifths of her army. They were anticipating encountering a third of a legion, less than two thousand Dorobon, newly landed in the desert and exhausted, their Air-magi drained from the crossing. The Nesti and Jhafi army combined numbered almost thirty thousand, fifteen times the forces of their enemy, which should be plenty. Except it wouldn't be; the Dorobon forces would in fact be two fully rested legions. The Rondians had sent most of their wind-fleet to Javon, despite the loss of impetus this would give to the Crusade in Kesh, and the Gorgio would be with them. Cera, faced with this unexpected might, was instructed to capitulate to save the lives of her army. With their queen-regent and boy-king held captive, the Nesti would have no choice but to sue for terms, and the new Dorobon reign would begin.

And I will be given to Francis Dorobon.

"The men are in good spirits," Luca Conti said, interrupting her bitter thoughts. He took another mouthful of curried chicken and potato. "In two days we will meet the enemy. Our scouts report that they have landed less than a thousand men so far, and they have no idea we are coming." His voice held just a touch of satisfaction.

I'm so sorry, Luca. This loss will break you. "And the Gorgio?" she asked, trying to sound positive.

"Still in Hytel, immobile," Paolo Castellini responded, his morose eyes doubtful. "Their inactivity is puzzling. I would that Donna Elena were here," he admitted, quite a concession for a man who'd never been comfortable around her, even before she became Not-Elena. "Is she near?" he asked.

Cera gave a small shrug. *Be confident.* "She is aware of all that is happening," she said, hating herself, but her words satisfied the two men, neither of whom was an intriguer.

Ilan Tamadhi was more inquisitive. "It makes me uncomfortable that all we might say may be heard by the enemy without her presence. The original reason Olfuss hired the magi in the first place was to ward our councils from eavesdropping Gorgio magi."

"I know," Cera said, "but she will be back before the battle, I am sure."

The emir still looked troubled. He had liked her bodyguard, won over by Elena's heroics and dry humor; he had been the most openly puzzled by the aberrant behavior of Not-Elena.

She pushed her food away. Lying and eating was too hard. She felt like she'd choke if she had to say another word. "I need to walk," she said apologetically, and the three men rose, making noises about her lack of appetite and her pallor. She knew this confirmed their fears; they'd rather she'd stayed in Brochena. She wished with all her heart she could tell them the truth, but that would trigger the very slaughter she was trying to prevent.

She said her goodnights and fled to her tent. Standing guard was Maxi, one of Lord Stefan di Aranio of Riban's younger sons. He saluted briskly, eager to impress. The Aranios had dozens of sons, all stolid and all a little dim, in her view, but they were loyal, and that was what counted. "Maxi, would you like to walk with me?"

The young knight's face lit up. "At your service, Majesty." Maxi was a simple soul. Solinde would have broken his heart without even realizing she was doing it.

She bit her lip, sad to be thinking of poor dead Solinde at a time like this.

They wrapped themselves in cloaks against the cooling air before walking through the Nesti camp. The sun was barely below the horizon and the hills were dusted with lavender, the violet hue washing into the evening sky. All about them, campfires fueled by dried dung glowed. The stench of the ditch-latrines wafted on a swirling wind, mixing unpleasantly with the smoke; the miasma of military camps that she had been enduring the whole march. Tonight especially it made her stomach turn.

"What is this place?" she asked.

"Fishil Wadi, Majesty," Maxi replied. "A dried riverbed runs through the valley." The young knight was cheery, waving to the men who lined up to call out greetings, eager to show their willingness and readiness to fight, and Cera found herself wishing she'd stayed in her tent so she need not see all these optimistic faces. If there was fear, no one was showing it, and that tore at her soul.

I am so sorry for what is going to happen. Please forgive me, but I'm doing it to save you. It just won't look that way.

They walked on, heading for the horse-pens, where the Nesti knights' giant stallions were kept. These heavy-hoofed beasts were of Yuros stock, much larger creatures than the Antiopian steeds. They might be slower, but they were terrifying when massed for the charge. Their highborn riders were confident and assured as they came to pay their respects, the same young men she'd seen peacocking around the court, preening as they strained to catch her eye.

A handsome man with familiar features called out, "Majesty, are the enemy near?"

She bit her lip. Rico was one of Lorenzo di Kestria's older brothers. He'd only just arrived, replacing Lorenzo as the Kestrian son attending the throne, and she hadn't yet found a role for him. She forced a smile and shook her head just as a sudden gust of wind from the west made every tent flap wildly.

A cloud of dust rose and rolled over the valley and they watched it swallow the horizon. "Majesty, is it a dust-storm?" Maxi asked, his face perplexed.

"I don't know," she said. It wasn't the season, and there had been no wind a few seconds ago.

Then she realized it was all going to happen *tonight*, not tomorrow or the day after. *The Dorobon are here, now.* "Seir Rico," she called to the Kestrian knight, "have your brethren see to their horses. There must be a storm coming." She felt tears stinging the backs of her eyes.

It's all going to happen right now . . .

A stinging gust of wind slapped them all, dust lashing their skin, and all around her the men pulled up kerchiefs to cover their mouths and covered their eyes. She did the same. The wind blast through the camp, causing the tents to flap wildly, uprooting the poorly secured as a high wail rose about them, like a funeral lament. Visibility collapsed, and the world turned a dirty brown.

Maxi seized Cera's arm. "I'll take us back to the tent," he shouted, the words snatched from his mouth, and she let him pull her along. Horses squealed and men shouted, the sounds like the voices of afreet, wisps of sound darting about at the edge of hearing. And all the while the certainty grew within her that this was just the prelude. They clambered back up the hill to the command tents as men staggered blindly across their path, trying to shield their eyes, even as her own filled with stinging grit, bringing tears that soaked into the scarf over her head.

Abruptly the winds dropped, but the dust cloud still enveloped them, destroying all visibility—then a dull orange light flashed vividly from down the valley where the Jhafi were camped, followed by another flash, and another. Distant shouting reached her ears, and screams. The air had gone almost still and as the dust began to settle the sky started to emerge, still pale despite the onset of night.

The sky was full of windships—forty or more, including twelve massive warbirds that were pouring fire down from the heavens while skiffs went swooping low over the Jhafi camp, spraying lightning and death.

She dropped Maxi's hand and fell to her knees. The trap was tonight, and it would not be bloodless at all.

I love a plan that works. Gurvon Gyle's windskiff skimmed the Nesti camp, leaving the Dorobon fleet pounding the huge mass of Jhafi warriors lower down the valley. Mara Secordin stood before him in the bow, her bloated form a strain on the craft, but it was worth the extra effort to keep it airborne, for the lightning that crackled from her fingertips and flashed into the clumps of men below was devastating. The Nesti knights were being tossed around like toys. He preserved his own powers, waiting for when he would need them most.

Behind him were four more skiffs bearing the magi and crossbowmen placed at his command by the Dorobon leadership. He sent a mental command for them to close up as he bore down on the low knoll where the Nesti banners hung. It was like a nest of ants, but he could see his quarry immobile below him, staring out at the gradually revealing battlefield. To the north, the Dorobon cavalry were beginning to sweep into the valley, a steel onslaught that would wash over the top of the Jhafi footmen like a blue and white avalanche. Dorobon footmen were circling behind the Jhafi, already east, the anvil upon which the cavalry hammer would smash the Jhafi. And all the while the fleet would roll on, pinning the Nesti in place and forcing them to watch the destruction of their native allies.

Afterward, the Jhafi survivors will say the Dorobon did not assault the Nesti. They'll whisper of collaboration. Divide and conquer.

He swept lower, targeting the command tent. Light flashed across the battlefield, Dorobon magi illuminating the field so that their men could see to massacre the natives. As he watched, the cavalry plowed through the Jhafi, whose lines had already been so destroyed by repeated fire and lightning that they struck not a blow in return. People spoke of outnumbering and wearing down a Rondian legion, but when that legion held the initiative and commanded the air, they were nigh-on invincible.

Arrows began to fly at them, some striking the hull, but Mara blasted apart a clutch of archers in retaliation while he strengthened his shielding. Behind them, the skiffs in his train returned fire, before the Nesti scattered in confusion—all apart from one group who clustered grimly around the royal tents. He saw the royal carriage being readied and glimpsed a womanly shape being bundled inside. He set course directly for Cera.

<*Close up!*> he shouted into the minds of the pilot-magi with him. <*There!*> He showed them the target with his mind and the skiffs formed a flying wedge as they descended upon the carriage.

They simply flew into the lines of men being thrown into a cordon before the carriage. Mara had opened the way, growling savagely as she poured raw energy before her, her dead eyes the only part of her that wasn't incandescent. The Nesti line buckled as the royal guardsmen were enveloped in blue fire. Arrows ripped through his sails, but any that might have hit him were flipped aside by his shields. Then the hull slammed through the walls of bodies and he glimpsed a soldier speared on the bowsprit before his weight snapped it off.

Mara rose up, roaring like a beast, and the flying wedge of the skiffs struck a second later on either side of him as he launched himself from the hull, blade already drawn.

A young man threw himself bodily at him, but he blocked with the gnosis and held the youth in place by telekinesis, then punched his blade through the youth's breastplate. As he crumpled another man closed in: old Seir Luca Conti, waving his heavy Rondian broadsword. Beside him, Mara lumbered forward, drenching men with water before blasting lightning into the quagmire she'd created. A swathe of men collapsed, their limbs crackling and jerking, thrashing about.

"Gyle!" Seir Luca snarled, and his blade hammered down at him. He blocked calmly and threw the man backward with the gnosis, then flung a bolt of lightning at the man's breastplate and watched him dance too. He paused to flash light into the eyes of a young man foolish enough to think he might be a hero, then skewered him calmly through the belly as he fumbled about blindly. As he kicked the fallen guard off his blade, Seir Luca steadied himself. He ignored the sparks crackling about his armor, and screamed, "Die, Rondian diablo!"

Talk is cheap, Conti. He caught the next blow, steel belling as the impact jarred his grip, but he held on and countered, a move Conti barely managed to block. His big blade wasn't as nimble as Gyle's, so he darted forward and sideways, slammed a man on Conti's left away with a push of gnosis, then cut down, straight into the back of Conti's knee. The old knight with whom he'd shared many relaxed evenings of wine and tabula in former times choked back a cry. His heavy blade arched around savagely in reflex even as he went down, but Gyle leaped the blow and drove his narrow blade in under the knight's armpit and split his heart. Blood erupted from the grizzled warrior's mouth as he shuddered and fell to the ground.

Gyle saw Mara take the head off another man with a sweep of a taloned hand when a shout arose from his right. Paolo Castellini, his sad face towering above the press, swept his two-handed falchion through the neck of a Dorobon mage. Then a blast of air picked up the knight and flung him head-over-heels backward. He slammed against the carriage.

The carriage! Gyle strode forward as the lines in front of him reeled from another fire-strike, then fell apart as Mara waded forward, using telekinetic energy to tear apart the men before her. He parried the one man left standing, then jabbed with his blade, thrusting his point over his foe's guard and into his eye. Then he was through.

The carriage door opened and Cera was there, her face white as she took in the destruction of her guards. Mara snarled happily, hungrily, and started forward, her teeth growing and her face changing to something that was in no way human.

"NO!" Cera shrieked, her eyes going to his. "NO!" Her eyes said: *You promised no blood!*

<Shut your mouth, girl!> he sent, shutting her down with a savage mental blast and she reeled, struck dumb, while he blocked a blow from one of Stefan di Aranio's sons, then casually stabbed him through the throat.

"Cera Nesti," he called aloud, using the gnosis to amplify the sound. "Command your men to surrender and they will be spared!"

There were hundreds of yards of chains. Each Nesti man had been manacled and the long lines sent marching toward Hytel. The Gorgio's iron and coal mines were about to receive a generous consignment of slave-miners. Cera wished she were among them.

Better to die beneath the earth than let Pater-Sol see what I let happen.

She could just make out Paolo Castellini, his birth not noble enough for the Gorgio and Dorobon to single him out for ransom. He was bent over, though he still loomed above the rest of the soldiers as he trudged away. She felt her eyes fill up again. All she did now was cry.

If she turned around, she would be able to see self-satisfied Alfredo Gorgio fingering his neat goatee, his pink pig eyes gloating happily. The soldiers of the Nesti, his oldest enemies, were now prisoners destined to work his mines until they dropped dead. Better yet, the Jhafi, the despised mudskins, had been slaughtered by the tens of thousands. Their surrender had not been accepted, and Emir Ilan Tamadhi was dead; captured and hung ignominiously.

If I had any honor I'd kill myself.

She looked sideways at Gurvon Gyle, who was hovering protectively beside her. His narrow eyes took in everything, but in spite of his great triumph he seemed restless, tired—somehow dissatisfied. She wondered why, then guessed. "Where is Elena?"

"Do not speak unless addressed," he told her, avoiding her question. "Francis Dorobon will expect to be called 'Your Majesty' though he is not yet crowned. He is a boy and his moods are changeable." Gyle didn't sound like he thought much of his new master.

But he still expects me to bed him.

She felt like a used rag. Her evening dress was coated in grime, like her skin. Her armpits were soaked and she could not cry all the grit from her eyelids. Her tangled hair was coated in dust.

Gyle made a huffing noise. "Go and wash your face, Princessa," he ordered in a low voice. "You're about to meet your husband-to-be."

I don't want him. I hate him. I hate you. But she bowed her head and went into her tent. Someone had come in already and removed all the weapons, even the eating knives. Now only Mara Secordin and Tarita were in here, and the obese mage-woman was eyeing Tarita as if she were a dish at a feast. The little maid looked petrified. "Majesty," she gasped, falling to her knees when she caught sight of Cera.

"Get up, Tarita." She pulled her up and hugged her, tried to impart comfort she didn't feel. "I need to wash, so that I do not look a disgrace before them."

"Do not wear violet," Mara Secordin rasped, her jowls wobbling as she stepped closer. There was blood on her hands and face and she looked immensely satisfied. "Wear blue or white. Dorobon colors."

"No," said Gyle behind her. "Stay in violet: it will amuse Francis Dorobon to humiliate you while in your family colors."

Cera looked back at him, hatred in her eyes and heart.

"Get out," Tarita snapped bravely, lifting her chin. "This is a lady's tent,"

Mara Secordin chuckled wetly. "The girl has spirit," she noted with amusement. She licked her lips, her eyes going cold. "I like that."

"Tarita is my ward," Cera said, clutching the little Jhafi to her.

Gurvon Gyle considered them both. "She is your ward," he agreed eventually, to Mara's visible disappointment. "But she will keep a civil tongue in her head."

"She will," she agreed, looking pointedly at Tarita. *Please don't upset them, Tarita. I couldn't bear to lose you too.*

Tarita said nothing, as if she felt she'd made her point. "I'll bring water, my queen," she whispered.

"No," Gyle interjected. He indicated the washing basin. "Mara."

The fat Rondian witch waddled to the basin and then gestured. Water spewed from her fingertips and filled the basin. Cera felt her stomach clench. "I'm not washing in that," she choked.

Mara turned to her, an ugly smile on her face. "It's perfectly clean, girl. I am a Water-mage."

"No."

"Wash," Gyle hissed. "Francis Dorobon is outside waiting."

Sol et Lune! She shuddered, then abruptly stepped around Mara, taking care not to touch her. She plunged her face into the basin. The water was body-temperature, but it felt intrinsically tainted to her. She grabbed soap and washed furiously.

When she was able to look about her again, Gyle was gone and Mara Secordin was watching her with flat eyes. She had thought Rutt Sordell and Samir Taguine vile, but this woman was worse. She had eyes like an crocodile. Then trumpets blared outside and Mara grabbed her upper arm with pudgy fingers. "Go out alone, girl. Look frightened. Beg and grovel for your life."

I won't.

"And for your brother's life too, of course," Mara added maliciously.

Her defiance collapsed. She would do anything to keep Timi alive.

Outside the tent, a circle of armed men were fanned about her, facing inward. Her eyes went first to Gurvon Gyle, whose face was tense. *<Be calm, girl. Be proud. Do not resist, but do not lash out. Impress him with your demeanor: you have nothing else.>*

I have nothing else. I have just led the soldiers of my family into slavery and my Jhafi allies into a death-trap. What remains?

"This is her?" A high-pitched, arrogant voice rang across the little glade. "I say, Gyle, I rather think you oversold her, don't you?"

Her eyes went to Francis Dorobon.

He was clad in quartered blue and white, a golden lion rampant in the center of the pattern. He had one of those faces she loathed: handsome, but clearly on the verge of running to fat as soon as he decided exercise was beneath him. Perhaps being a mage he would be immune to that, but somehow she doubted it. His big chest and proud head loomed over her. Blue eyes, flaxen hair, and a cruel mouth. The beginning of whiskers, cut to some elaborate Rondian fashion.

She didn't curtsey as Francis Dorobon walked toward her but stood stiffly, her eyes going past him. There was a stout, matronly woman she recalled from when she was young, during the brief earlier reign of the Dorobon family: Octa Dorobon, the matriarch of that line. Cera's father had killed her husband. Her florid face held a look of grim satisfaction. A younger and female version of Francis stood beside him, his sister Olivia, already plump from good living. Beyond them hovered Alfredo Gorgio, his face unable to stop smiling. With him was his eldest niece and female heir, Portia Tolidi, a pale beauty with a thick tangle of curling auburn hair. She'd been hovering close to Francis Dorobon.

Looks like she's already got her claws into him, she thought grimly. Portia was accounted one of the beauties of the realm. But she had also helped Tarita survive the massacre in Brochena last year, she remembered. The thought gave her hope, though right now there was nothing but disdain on every face except Gyle's. His was unreadable.

"Kneel, Nesti," Francis snapped as he circled her, his eyes appraising her.

She remained standing. "It is not right for a queen to kneel."

He nodded thoughtfully, as if considering her words, then he lashed her across the face with the back of his hand. She staggered as the world tilted, but somehow she kept her balance. Her cheek throbbed and the inside of her mouth began to bleed, the flesh gashed on her own teeth. *I won't cry. And I won't rukking kneel.*

"She may have some spirit," Francis remarked, as if appraising a horse he might mount.

Isn't that the plan?

She blinked away tears and met his gaze, refusing to cower, even when he raised his hand again. He dropped it, smirking. "She is not badly made, I concede," he said. "But she is no beauty." He glanced at Portia Tolidi with lusty eyes. The redhead looked away coyly.

"As a wife, she has great value," Gyle chimed in. "Kings are permitted mistresses; we all know that."

"The Nesti are broken. A Gorgio alliance is worth much more, and Portia is pure Rimoni," Alfredo Gorgio protested, bartering his kin as if she were nothing but a clause on a treaty. Which she probably was, to him. Francis's hot eyes said something different.

"The Nesti are far from broken. This force was but a third of their strength," Gyle countered, but then Octa Dorobon's voice boomed out over the gathering, silencing everyone. Cera saw Francis cringe at the sound of her voice, his shoulders hunching.

"Rimoni are little better than these mongrelized Javonesi polluted by mudskin blood," Octa stated. "My son will marry a Rondian pure-blood. You overstep yourselves, gentlemen," she told Alfredo and Gyle together. She waddled forward and grabbed Cera's chin roughly. "This mudskin bitch is not worthy of my son. But she will make a useful hostage." Her eyes went back to Portia Tolidi. "Do what you like with that creature."

Eyes flashed from stony faces as the allies reconsidered their friendships anew.

I am already consigned to yesterday. Cera looked at Gyle and then away. *Now what?* she wondered.

<Now we are patient,> Gyle's voice filled her mind. *<We bide our time until opportunity presents.>*

12

THE ZAIN MONASTERY

Mount Tigrat

The southernmost mountain of the central range stands serene above the desert plains, its peak crowned in snow throughout the year. The Jhafi say that the old gods, the pagan deities supplanted by the Amteh Faith, dwell on the peak of Mount Tigrat still, forgotten by men but unable to die. Others say it was the earthly throne of Markud, the King of Heaven. The afreet are the maggots that burst from his corpse, left behind when he ascended to the sky.

ORDO COSTRUO COLLEGIATE, PONTUS

Brochena and Mount Tigrat, Javon, Antiopia
Shaban (Augeite) to Rami (Septinon) 928
2nd and 3rd months of the Moontide

The first couple of days after the attack by Magister Sindon and his Keshi mages had been spent recuperating under the protection of Mustaq al'Madhi: days and nights of sleep and healing, punctuated by intense conversation. Elena had told the Jhafi crime-lord all she dared: that Cera was under the control of Gurvon Gyle and the palace was a nest of Rondian mage-spies, and the march north might be more dangerous than anyone suspected. Unfortunately, Gurvon

had not shared any details with Sordell—perhaps he'd been subconsciously wary, knowing Elena might be a prisoner inside her own
body, but she was cognizant of whatever Sordell knew. The problem
was that Mustaq himself was now isolated from the Jhafi leadership.
Gyle had sniffed out and slain all of Mustaq's agents in the palace
except for one. Tarita had been the one to reveal Gyle's presence
and set in train the assassination attempt by Sindon's men. Elena
shivered in fear for the little maid if she were caught.

She'd managed to stabilize the young assassin she'd captured,
though he'd not yet regained consciousness, even after two weeks.
The venom Mara had set in his veins was horribly virulent, a
gnosis-augmented poison that would have killed most people in
seconds, but the young man had the gnosis himself, so perhaps
unconsciously his body fought back. She'd laid a Chain-rune on
him however, unwilling to risk him waking early and uncontained.
She intended to question him before determining his fate.

The danger of Gyle tracking her down meant she could not linger in Brochena. Fortunately, she'd left her windskiff, the *Grayhawk*,
hidden in one of Mustaq's safe houses, so when she was ready to
move, she provisioned it with gear and lentils, grain, some spices,
coffee, and tea, then laid her captive in it. It was Darkmoon, the
brief time when Luna hid her face. Stars dusted the skies like a
diamond-encrusted coif about a woman's face. She kissed Mustaq's
cheeks, thanked him again, and took to the air, flying east toward
the mountains.

One thing Gurvon had always encouraged his agents to do when
on assignment was to find and develop a refuge, a place to flee to
if things went bad. *Don't tell each other where it is, in case they are
forced to reveal it,* he'd tell them. *Don't even tell me.*

It was good advice, and it had saved her life before. Her refuge
here in Javon was perched high on the slopes of Mount Tigrat. It
had once been a Zain monastery, abandoned when Amteh fanatics
among the Jhafi had butchered the holy men, who preached that
physical and spiritual perfection was as important as love of God,
and promulgated an extreme form of asceticism. Such teachings
pleased neither the Sollan drui nor the Amteh Godspeakers, but

the Zains were accomplished healers and learned in other useful skills—especially engineering and architecture—and that was usually enough to persuade rulers to let them be, though occasional atrocities took place from time to time, as had happened here. Such was the lot of a pacifist sect in hostile lands.

Over the past four years, she'd periodically taken the *Grayhawk* to the monastery and worked there for a day or two, storing food and fuel, repairing the inner walls and the old well. It was below the snow-line in summer, but not winter. The exterior walls still looked decrepit, and a pair of mountain lions dwelled there at times, but it was perfect for her. The old communal baths were fed by a stream that ran through fire-heated stone hypocausts: the chimneys were vented back beneath a waterfall to conceal any trace of smoke. Hundreds of monks had once dwelled there, living mostly in a maze of underground chambers, but there were higher rooms too, well lit by sunlight. The silence was as chilling as the air, but it spoke to her.

She reached it well before dawn. The young man had not moved during the flight, but his breathing was strong and regular. The venom was almost gone from his system, but she had kept his awareness suppressed, maintaining the coma until she was ready to have him wake. She knew that she would probably have to kill him, and that troubled her. They shared enemies, but she suspected he was Hadishah-trained, and to those fanatics any white person was a devil.

Grayhawk caught the winds gracefully, banking and swooping on the monastery like a bird of prey. Elena steered toward the lower courtyard, which had a carved entrance leading to the underground caverns. Bats and night-birds squeaked and scattered as she landed the skiff delicately.

The wind moaned softly in the broken battlements like a contented lover. The air was cool but not yet cold, warmed by the last of the late summer heat. She heard one of the mountain lions cough and looked around; there she was, atop a wall, staring down with undisguised hostility. She sent a warning. The first time she'd encountered the pair, she'd given them a nonlethal beating; now they knew to give her a wide berth. The female yowled softly, discontented, but padded away. She heard the male growl and sensed them climbing up to the eastern slopes. She was master here, and even the great cats knew it.

The first few hours were filled with housekeeping as she settled in: wheeling the skiff into the cavern and re-covering the entrance with debris; adding her cargo to the stores, all the while taking a mental inventory. There was enough food for three to four months, if she was to feed two people for the entire period, though that wasn't her intention. She'd revive the boy and question him, then either kill him, or maybe leave him somewhere faraway to fend for himself.

She moved the young man last, using telekinesis to float his stretcher through the corridors and into one of the monastic sleeping cells, his gnosis locked away. There was something odd about his aura she'd not seen before, though the realization that the Hadishah now had magi didn't surprise her, once she'd thought it through. Magi were the ultimate weapon; it was only natural that the Hadishah would seek to recruit gnosis-users somehow. She laid him on the sleeping cot she'd readied and left him there, locking the door behind him. *I'll deal with him later*, she told herself. As she left, she removed the blocks to his mind that were keeping him in the coma, allowing him to awaken in his own time.

As the sun rose, she felt both energized and also conscious of exhaustion. The rays shot through the gaps in the land and kissed the slopes of the mountain with gold. She watched the lavender light burst across the darkling skies and a wave of illumination broke across the shadowed land. Her perch high on the mountain looked southeast, over the arid plains where the Jhafi herders eked out their existence. The nearest city was Riban, more than forty miles away, well out of sight. She chose a room in the highest remaining tower, despite the windows overhung with dead vines and the dry stench of bird droppings. She would deal with those tomorrow. The vines were sultana-grapes, but the fruit had already been devoured by the birds. She set her bedroll against one wall, unbuckled her weapons and lay down.

It took about a minute, and then it hit her:

The months of being a prisoner in her own body; the loathsome feeling of having another use her flesh. Sordell had spoken with *her* tongue, walked with *her* legs, shat from *her* bowels, pissed from *her* bladder. Once he'd even pleasured himself experimentally, taunting her as he did so. Their vicious mental duel had been harrowing, as she'd staved off the necromancer's attempts to destroy the last vestiges of her consciousness. Equally galling had been the knowledge of her own failure, not just to penetrate Gurvon's schemes, but to see the change in Cera. She'd blindly walked into that final betrayal, at the hands of the girl she'd thought of as a daughter.

First she shook and then she started retching before it all turned to tears, a flood of tears such as she'd never cried in all her life. Water was her element, and she let it run from her eyes, purging the pain and terror with the waters of her body. *Never again*, she swore.

She could not sleep, not yet. She longed for alcohol—a residue of Sordell's addiction—but refused to succumb, going instead to the baths. She didn't bother to heat them, though the mountain water was stagnant, and frigidly cold. She stripped, waded in and immersed herself, then she took the soap and scoured herself. Her shoulder was scarred where Sordell had allowed her to be wounded, but it was just another scar. She scrubbed at her flesh until she almost bled, trying to cleanse away every last trace of the presence of Sordell. It was futile, she knew that. Mysticism, the gnostic art associated with healing the mind, was what she needed, but self-healing one's own mind was not possible, and there was no one else she could trust to do it for her. Sordell's possession of her was just something she would have to live with, until time smoothed it away. If even time could do that.

When the cold finally hit her, she emerged and dried herself, then wrapped herself in a blanket, returned to the tower room and lay down. Despite the frenzied cleansing, she still felt awash in Sordell's filth.

I'm going to make them all pay: Sordell, if he's still alive. Gurvon: oh yes, absolutely. It's been far too long, my lover. And you too, Cera Nesti. I pity you, that Gurvon found your weak spots and turned you against me, but I won't forgive you . . .

She closed her eyes, and called on all the internal discipline and dispassion that had once carried her through all the horrors of the Noros Revolt and used it to ease the immediacy of her fear and hatred. She let her passions go still, stared into nothing, trying to anchor herself again.

Here in Javon, during the years spent protecting the Nesti children, she had changed from killer to protector. It had taken those four years to relearn how to laugh without sarcasm or malice, to care without calculation. Olfuss Nesti had shown her how a ruler could be honest and uncompromised. Fadah his wife had shown her that motherhood was a gift, not a burden. Solinde reminded her that life could be fun, and Timori had shown her the beauty of innocence. But of them all, it was Cera she cared most for, the one she loved. And it was Cera who had betrayed that love.

And then there was Lorenzo, her all-too-brief romance. The man who had been guide and gatekeeper on her road back to being a fully-formed human being. She'd begun to fantasize where their relationship might go . . . and now she'd never know.

Her imagination conjured a crossroads in the desert. To her left, she saw her old self, clad in a cloak the color of clotted blood: the Elena who'd been Gurvon's lover, ruthless and withdrawn, sarcastic and hard. That Elena could survive this war and do what had to be done. She would snuff out her conscience again and take to the underworld. She'd kill and torture and maim until every enemy was dead, or she was caught and hanged. She'd fight until the end.

But I don't want to be her again . . .

She turned slowly at that crossroads and looked the other way. Another Elena stood to her right. She was walking away, wrapped in a shadowy cloak. She didn't know where she was going, only that it was *away*. Life was hard, too hard, and it meant nothing in the end. All ended in dust.

No. I cannot walk away from this mess. What we do must mean something, even if only to those who follow us.

She opened her eyes and was back in her chamber, staring into space.

I'll find another way. I'll not lose myself in hatred or despair. I'll become the person Lorenzo was teaching me to be. I'll fight, but I'll not cut out my own heart to do so.

The first thing Kazim remembered was that ghastly beetle emerging from the mouth of Elena Anborn. And running. Maybe he shouldn't have, but he'd never seen such a thing, and the sudden horror had overcome him. He still shuddered at the image. More memories returned: the realization of pursuit while venom turned his limbs to jelly. He'd been too slow. Elena Anborn's blow had smashed the world away.

He cautiously closed his eyes, but found only darkness. For a few sickening moments he thought he was blind, until his sight recovered enough to make out a dim line of pale illumination. Eventually he realized that it was light from beneath a closed door.

He groaned and clutched at his shoulder, the one the snake-arm of Mara Secordin had bitten. It was bandaged and it ached, but it felt functional. There was no other wound, but he felt stiff as an old man. He sat up slowly, realizing that his bladder was full to bursting. He pushed a blanket aside, them fumbled about until he found a bucket and relieved himself. The stink of piss filled the tiny room.

Cautiously, he tried the door. It was locked. Then, recalling his reluctant lessons from Sabele, he tried to use the gnosis to unlock it. *Nothing.*

He felt both terror and relief. *Have I lost it? Am I no longer a mage?*

Then he reached deeper and realized that it was still there—but it was barely discernible, tremendously weak. And he couldn't reach it. Something forbade it—another's spell?

For some reason he thought of Gatoz, blackmailing him into swallowing the maid Wimla's life, and took a perverse pleasure in being denied the gnosis. *I'll not take another life into my own*, he vowed.

He hammered his fist against the strong, iron-bound door. "Hey? Hey?" Anyone there?" There was a slot, but only someone outside could open it. He fell silent, waiting, until he heard soft footfalls approaching. Then the slot slid open and he confronted steely gray eyes that bored into his. They were surrounded by pale skin, sun-burnished. *Elena Anborn.* When she spoke, her voice had a rough burr to it, as if her throat was lined with sandpaper. He glimpsed an ugly scar across her throat as she stepped away, where someone had slit her throat, a wound she'd somehow survived. He stared, remembering the hideous beetle that had crawled from her mouth. Part of him expected her mouth to open and the insect to emerge again.

She spoke, questioning him in an unknown tongue. Then he realized he knew the words, though her accent and her dialect— the Jhafi version of Keshi—rendered it alien. Her barbarian mouth framed the words strangely and it took him a few seconds to interpret: "Step away from the door."

Numbly he obeyed, wondering if he was about to be slain. He was healed, though; he could no longer feel the poison.

Did she heal me?

She unlocked the door as he bunched his muscles, wondering if he could knock her down and take her prisoner before her fellows came. But something flashed in her eyes and his limbs locked up. She stepped inside, wrinkling her nose at the smell from the piss-bucket. "Come," she said briskly, then backed out again. "Bring that," she added, pointing at the bucket. His limbs loosened again.

I'll smash it over her head and kill her and run . . .

He picked it up and followed her out the door. She walked ahead of him, too fast to keep up, and he felt like a newborn kitten as he tottered after her. She walked with a predator's grace, balanced at all times, her hand on her sword-hilt. She was wearing a dun-colored tunic and short leggings that left her knees and calves bare. Her legs were as well-muscled as any man's. The part of him that was devout Amteh was offended at her state of undress. Even Lakh women did not bare their legs. It was obscene.

"Empty the bucket in there," she said, jabbing her thumb toward a door, and he did as bid, finding himself in a privy-chamber with a long shaft dropping into darkness. He tipped the piss down the hole, wondering where he was. He'd seen no natural light as yet, and the walls were hewn, not bricked, so they were underground.

He steadied himself, then walked out still holding the bucket, weighing it in his hand. It was heavy enough that he could crack a skull if he swung forcefully. He measured the distances. The Anborn woman was some ten feet away, watching him carefully.

Not yet. He walked toward her, but she backed and half-turned, outpacing him with her masculine stride.

"What is your name?" she asked, her voice rattling, perhaps from her throat scar.

Let her think I'm cooperating. "Kazim," he replied, his voice emerging sounding thick and odd from his throat, making him wonder how long he'd been out cold.

"Do you know who I am?"

He sensed that lies would be swiftly detected. "Elena."

"El-en-ah. Not Al-ha-nah," she corrected. "Do you know where you are?" Her Keshi was impressively fluent.

He shook his head, tried to get closer, but she turned and bounded up some stairs to a higher level. He followed, his eyes drawn to the blasphemy of her legs, the way her calves bunched and extended, the strong thighs and the taut shape of her bottom. He jerked his eyes away, annoyed at himself for staring, and clambered after her. The effort was costly. He found himself sweating as he reached the top. *Why am I so weak? Has she bewitched me?*

The Rondian jadugara led him to a kitchen. "Eat," she said, pointing to a table so old the wood was gray—but it had been dusted clean, and there was food; a dry spiced lentil dish, rice and some flatbread, newly cooked, judging by the steam, and the smell of cooking in the air. A fire blazed gently in an open stove in the corner. There was a glass bottle half-filled with red wine. She looked at it with longing in her eyes, but she didn't take any.

There were pokers and tongs of wrought iron, he noted as he put down the bucket and sat. *Better weapons.* He dropped some rice onto the bread, added the cooked lentils, rolled it all up and wolfed it down. His stomach felt utterly empty; his limbs were hollow. The food vanished in seconds and he looked around hungrily.

"There is more," the woman offered, walking toward him with a pot containing more lentils. She stopped within touching distance, apparently unwary.

He rose in one movement, swept up a poker and swung it at the side of her head.

She gestured, and he flew backward, slid along the dirty floor and bashed his hip against the wall. He grunted painfully and tried to rise, but it was as if his legs contained no bones. He lay there, looking up, expecting to see her bearing down on him with bared sword.

She looked down at him as if nothing had happened. "Is there enough chili in it for you?"

He tried to stand, but couldn't. His hip throbbed, but that wasn't enough to cause this debilitation. It was *her*: something she'd done to him. With magic . . .

He tried to reach his own powers again, even though he hated them, but still he could feel nothing. His gnosis was there, he could feel it, but it felt like it was wrapped in a gauze that he couldn't tear. It was beginning to frighten him. Even those vile energies would be preferable to this helplessness.

She cocked her head, gazing at him like a bird. "You're a mage, aren't you?"

He shook his head sullenly.

She laughed. "I can tell, boy."

He found enough strength to sit up. "I'm not a boy."

She looked at him appraisingly. "I suppose not. How old are you?"

It was none of her business, but he didn't want to be thought a child. "Twenty-one years old."

"Are you Ordo Costruo?"

He thought about lying, but answered truthfully, "No." He stuck his chin out. "I am Hadishah."

She sighed, as if a suspicion had been confirmed. "I suppose it was inevitable some would take that path."

"We're going to kill you all, Shaitan-whore."

She grunted again, a graceless sound that deepened his dislike. She was all wrong to his eyes: not masculine, but certainly not feminine either: not in the way a good Keshi or Lakh woman was. Her body was too muscular, and she lacked the curves he felt a woman should have. Her bust was small, her waist too muscled to be narrow. Her shoulders were wider than a woman her build should have. She wasn't big, maybe five foot six, but she was strong and athletic-looking. There was no jewelry apart from one gem at her throat that pulsed faintly beneath the ugly scar that ran right across her jugular. That she'd survived such a wound was frightening in its way. She was the embodiment of all that the Godspeakers said of white women: graceless and godless.

Are they all like this? Then he remembered Alyssa Dulayne, and guessed this Elena Anborn might be unusual even among her own kind.

"Listen, Kazim," she said in her sandpaper voice, "you're hundreds of miles from Brochena, and from your friends if they're still alive. I've blocked your gnosis, and you're still weak as a child from that poison. Stop being a fool and let me help you recover."

"Why should you help me?" he asked truculently, though his fears mounted. *Where am I? Why does she want me alive?*

She sighed wearily. "Kazim, I could have killed you at any time. I could have gone through your mind to learn all I need to know from you. I didn't, because doing so would have left you a drooling imbecile. We don't need to be enemies. I suspect we have the same goals."

He dismissed this obvious lie. "You fought for Gyle," he growled. But he tentatively got to his feet and teetered back to the table. She put more lentils into his bowl and handed him another flatbread. He wolfed it down while she poured him water, which he drained in one swallow.

"Do you know the story of Inshil and the Afreet?" she asked.

It was an old story from the Kalistham, about an afreet tempting a sainted Godspeaker. He was surprised she knew it. "Yes," he replied cautiously, wary of word-games with this she-demon.

"Do you remember how the afreet entered the body of Inshil's brother and tried to tempt him to do evil?" Elena asked him. He nodded cautiously. "And do you remember that scarab you saw come out of my mouth?" She gave an involuntary shudder that he found unexpectedly affecting. "That was the earthly form of an afreet who had possessed me."

He looked at her, trying to work out if she was possible. *All magi are liars*, he remembered Haroun telling him once. "You were unconscious when it happened," he retorted.

"No, I was aware. You saw it and ran."

He bowed his head, ashamed. Afreet were real, he believed that firmly. Perhaps she was telling the truth. "Is the afreet still inside you?"

A look of loathing crossed her face. "No," she whispered, suddenly vulnerable. She covered the moment quickly. "It's gone now. I'm *free*." She said the last word with such relish that his doubts lessened.

Can this be? "Are all Rondian magi possessed by devils?" he asked her.

She surprised him by laughing, a shrill squawk that was undignified, though comfortingly human. "No, we're not all possessed by afreet! But there are some among us who are evil all by themselves." She sipped her water, looking at him curiously. "How many magi serve the Hadishah?"

He shook his head: she was still an enemy. She didn't question his response, or press further. But she did ask him of his parentage. The name of Razir Makani meant nothing to her. Sabele had told him that magi persecuted Souldrinkers, he remembered, so that was another secret he had to conceal from her.

"How did you come to attack Gurvon Gyle?" she wanted to know.

That felt like safe enough ground. "A spy alerted our leaders to his presence." He scowled, remembering the botched attack. "We did not think to encounter more than him and one or two others," he admitted.

She smiled grimly. "You still managed to surprise him, and that's no mean feat. He trusted Sindon, of course. I always knew that bastard was two-faced." She leaned forward, her eyes intent. "Was what Sindon said true: are the Ordo Costruo now controlled by Rashid Mubarak?"

He knew he shouldn't talk to her, but he was angry at being her prisoner and wanted to upset her. "He more than controls them—there was a purge! We killed dozens of them. Only those loyal to Rashid are left."

"Rashid Mubarak," she exclaimed. "I presume it was he who murdered Meiros?"

His mouth went dry. *No*, he thought, keeping the thought well hidden, *I did that*. He managed to shrug.

She got up and started pacing while he finished his food. "Listen, Kazim, your people are probably dead. Gurvon and Mara are . . . *thorough*." She exhaled, putting her hands on her hips. "You're still weak. I can help you recover, so you can go home."

He considered that. *Home*. He had no home now, not really. In Baranasi his father was dead, and his adopted family were living on the wealth they'd won for selling Ramita to Meiros. In Hebusalim, Rashid and Sabele waited for his will to bend and break, delivering him into their clutches like a brand-new weapon.

And this jadugara is right: Jamil and the rest, they're probably dead too. He would miss Jamil and Molmar, perhaps even Haroun. But he hoped Gatoz was already in Shaitan's fire-pit.

"I must complete my mission," he replied, not out of duty or fervor, just playing for time.

"I can respect that," she said slowly, "though you haven't got a chance." She walked back to the table and sat again. "Not without me."

He studied her face. Crow's feet at the eyes, and a tan that didn't disguise her Yuros-pallor. She had eyes like polished steel and a thin-lipped mouth set in grim determination. "What do you mean?" he asked.

"I mean that now that I have escaped the afreet, I have the same purpose as you: to kill Gurvon Gyle."

He dropped his eyes. Staring at a woman was impolite, even if this one was barely female. "You are a Rondian. Why would you wish to kill your own?"

She looked away. "So many reasons I can barely count them," she whispered huskily.

Silence reigned for a few moments while somewhere above, winds whispered over stone.

"You would not arm me," he said dismissively.

"I would, if I could trust you not to turn on me," she replied.

He wiped his mouth with his left hand, then wiped the hand on his pants. *You can't trust me, jadugara.*

"Would you swear on the Kalistham?" she asked levelly.

He stiffened. *If I swore on the Holy Book, then I would be bound.* Some oaths could not be broken. He got up, paced the room, trying to think. "Would you swear not to turn on me also?" he asked, buying time.

Her eyes narrowed, then she rose. "I would. Come with me."

She led him upstairs into a large room filled with broken furniture and wind-blown dirt, half swept up. "I've not finished in here," she said, almost apologetically.

He wasn't really listening; there was a window and he wanted to see outside. The view revealed that they were high on a hill, a mountain even, overlooking lower hills that fell away to the plains. Judging by the fall of shadows, it faced southeast. "Where are we?"

"Hundreds of miles from Brochena; dozens from the nearest village." She tapped the table and he flinched as a book flew from a shelf and landed beside her hand. "This is a Kalistham," she told him.

He left the window, still blinking in the light. It must be late morning, maybe midday. He felt wobbly from being upright so long. He made it to the table and surreptitiously supported himself on it. The book was indeed the Amteh holy book. It offended him that she'd used her gnosis to move it. "What do you want me to say?"

"Swear that I am blood-brother to you and that together we will slay Gurvon Gyle and his agents," she replied.

He wrinkled his nose. *Blood-brother? With a woman?* "That cannot be. You will never be my brother."

"Then blood-sister," she rasped irritably.

"Blood-sister? The Amteh doesn't allow—"

"Yes it does," she interrupted, sounding like an exasperated parent. "The tale of the Third Caliph."

He scowled, realizing she was right: the Third Caliph had been a girl who pretended to be male and succeeded in slaying her father's murderer where her brothers had failed. "It is so," he admitted.

She drew a knife and ran the blade across her palm, wincing. Blood welled from the wound, and she offered it to him, and the knife.

If I stabbed quickly . . . He met her eyes, saw them turn bleak. *If I even tried, she'd tear me apart . . .*

He ran the blade over his hand and blood flowed, more than he'd intended. The cut stung, and the sight of the blood made his knees wobble. He said the words, and she repeated them.

They clasped hands, then each kissed their own palm, wetting their lips with shared blood. She stepped close. She was much shorter than him, more than six inches. "You're a big bastard, aren't you, 'brother'?" she remarked ironically. She went up on tiptoes. "Bend down, damn it."

This was the last chance to strike at her. He let it pass, kissed her cheek, leaving a bloody imprint. She returned the gesture.

"Sealed," she said, with grim satisfaction. "Sal'Ahm, Kazim Makani."

"Sal'Ahm alaykum, Elena Anborn."

He means it, Elena decided. *Not happily, but he'll hold to it.* She watched the young Keshi from the corner of her eyes as he finished his water. Her bloody lip-print was vivid on his cheek and she remembered similar marks on her own cheeks, left there by Cera Nesti.

I was true to my vow, Cera, but you weren't.

"There are baths below," she told the young Hadishah. "They're clean, and I've had the furnaces going for an hour or two: the water should have warmed somewhat." He was an impressive specimen, she decided. He'd moved well during the fight in Brochena, so he was well trained, though not in the nuances that experience brings. And though he'd shown nothing of his gnosis, she'd gotten the impression of considerable raw energy.

Badly trained, but potent: bastard of a half-blood, maybe?

"Please don't leave the complex," she said to his back as he stood.

He turned and faced her. "The name of Makani is one of honor," he said with offended dignity. "I have sworn. I will honor the spirit, not just the letter." He looked away, wincing as if remembering something that he took no pride in. She wondered about his background. The temptation to rummage through his brain while he'd been in a coma had been immense, but in the end a combination of decency and pragmatism had decided the issue: alive and sane he might be useful, and if not, she could always change her mind.

"As will I, Brother," she said gravely. She studied his face: thick black hair, and a beard and mustache that gave him a dangerous air. His face combined strength and natural beauty. *I bet the girls sigh over you, Kazim Makani.* She knew his physique from nursing him: a beast of a body, with muscles cording his stomach, biceps too big to encompass with both hands, and a deep, powerful chest. There was something dark inside him, though, something that was eating at him. It emerged whenever he looked reflective.

I guess you grew up being told the magi were spawn of Shaitan, and then found you're one of us. That'd screw with anyone's head. She could tell she offended his all sensibilities. *Hel, I'm a woman, I'm white, I'm a warrior, and I'm magi. Take your pick!*

"It's midday," she told him. "I'm going to do some exercise." She indicated the stove. "It's your turn to cook."

"Men do not cook, *Sister*," he said, wrinkling his nose with distaste.

Amteh men: bless 'em. "Sure you do, *Brother*. Better learn fast."

The old garden was now overgrown with vines and wild camellia, all brown and dead at this time of the year. Here in Antiopia most things bloomed in winter. Stone bridges crossed empty ponds, the water pipes having been destroyed. The garden was open to the sky, but had no views over the plains below. She'd cleaned enough space in it that there was room to practice. She'd been both dreading and looking forward to this moment.

Okay, let's see just how badly Sordell treated my body.

The answer, she soon learned, was not well. It was appalling how much condition she'd lost. Within minutes she was perspiring in bucket-loads. Her tunic and pants were soon soaked in sweat as first she jogged what should have been gentle circuits before commencing a basic weapons-drill on the central bridge.

Inside ten minutes she was almost dizzy. After fifteen she had to stop to immerse her head in the one pond that still had some water in it. Ten minutes more and she was almost prostrate, but still she forced herself to go on: cut, thrust, spin, block. Dance forward, give ground. She'd brought practice blades here on a previous visit, but today she used her steel; she still wasn't sure that she trusted Kazim entirely. *I'm a Shaitan-spawned jadugara. He'll rationalize easily enough that an oath to me need not be honored.*

After an hour she stopped, utterly exhausted, and looked up. Kazim was watching her from a window above the courtyard, his face a mix of fascination and revulsion. As soon as he saw her staring, he vanished. She looked down at herself, picturing what he'd seen.

A white witch, with her clothes so wet and sticky he can practically see my nipples. Not to mention bare calves and wet ass-crack. Charming. She shrugged. *Well, rukk him, anyway. He'll just have to get used to me.*

Kazim slapped the plate of boiled roots in front of the jadugara woman, and poured water. She raised a mocking eyebrow and he glared at her. He put the other plate in front of himself, spooned a mouthful between his lips, chewed.

Chod! He spat. The roots were half-cooked and the spices he'd chosen utterly wrong. He gulped water to rinse his mouth out. He caught a half-smile on Elena's thin lips. "Women cook," he snapped. "Not men."

At least she'd bathed and now wore decent clothing—a proper salwar kameez—though the smock-dress was low-cut at the front, finishing just above her breasts. He colored as he remembered the way Elena's sweat-drenched clothes had clung to her body as she practiced. *Not that it stirred me*, he told himself.

Elena waggled her fingers, radiating a slow wave of wet heat into the vegetables on her plate and they visibly cooked before her. Then she ate them, wincing at each mouthful but clearly too hungry to pass up even his meager efforts. She washed it down with water and stood. "Luckily for both of us, it's my turn tomorrow, Brother." She took her plate to the basin beside the stove and rinsed it, then left without another word.

He went without; the undercooked food tasted dreadful. *She's the woman, she should damn well cook.* He went to bed hungry.

That night he lay awake most of the night, daring himself to run away, oath or not. Jamil and Gatoz might be looking for him. He could go to the nearest village, get his bearings, then make for Brochena. He was sure he could remember how to find the house they'd been kept in. Perhaps Sindon was still alive too. Haroun hadn't even been with the attackers; surely he was alive somewhere in the city.

But I swore on the Kalistham . . .

It crossed his mind that she was a Rondian jadugara, that her own oath was worthless. But his was not. She might be a born liar, but he was not. The fact that if he ran she could probably find him in seconds also ran through his mind.

He rolled over and went to sleep, and by the time he woke up, the debate was over. He would stay.

Next morning she made Yuros-food: an oat dish with heated milk that she called "porrij." It was not as bad as it looked, once sweetened with fruit. "Where is the milk from?" he asked curiously.

"There is a vat of goat-milk, preserved by spells," she replied as if this were commonplace.

After they ate she went back to her training, ignoring him completely. To avoid having to watch, he went off to seek somewhere away from her eyes where he could do the same. He was a Souldrinker and the killer of Antonin Meiros, so staying away from her seemed like a wise thing to do. All morning long he drove himself to train hard, and harder before collapsing into the baths.

That night he bowed to the inevitable. As she prepared the meal, he swallowed his pride and joined her beside the stove. "Show me, Blood-sister."

She surprised him with a warm smile of approval.

13

THE CROSSING

Pontus

Rondians brag of Pallas, and Argundians of Delph. The ruins of Rym still take the breath away. The Hebb chant prayers to Hebusalim and think her a deity in her own right, though this angers the Godspeakers. But no city contains a wonder greater than Pontus, where all the world comes to stare in awe at the Leviathan Bridge rising from the sea.

ORDO COSTRUO COLLEGIATE,
PONTUS

The damned Bridge is open only two years in twelve. For the remainder of the time Pontus is as dull and forsaken as a tavern after closing time, frequented by the odd drunken customer lolling in the spillage the rest of the patrons left before buggering off home.

MYRON JEMSON, ARGUNDIAN,
IN JOURNEYS EASTWARD, 901

The Leviathan Bridge
Shaban (Augeite) 928
2nd month of the Moontide

Ramon stared down the ramp which curved elegantly between two huge, open sluice gates and onto the Bridge. He sent calming emotions to his new mount, a mare he'd named Lucia, Lu for short. *<Easy, Lu, it'll be fine, I promise.>* Of course he didn't believe his own bullshit: this damned Bridge was going to collapse the moment he set foot on it.

He'd been totally unprepared for how frightening it was to actually step from the earth onto manmade stone over the ravenous seas. The cliffs stood two hundred feet or more above the pounding waves, that shattered against the land in massive clouds of spume. The ocean below was relatively calm, they were telling him, but still it pitched and heaved in troughs that could swallow a Silacian village whole. Everything was in motion except the ribbon of stone that extended from where he stood for as far as the eye could see.

Antonin Meiros's Bridge. A few days ago they'd learned that the old mage had been murdered, his body torn limb from limb in his own home by a vengeful mob of Hebb poor. He wouldn't have cared, except that he knew Cym was searching for her mother, Justina Meiros, his daughter. Cym had likely been counting on Antonin Meiros to receive and use the Scytale of Corineus—so what would she do now? Was Justina even still alive?

Not my problem, he told himself. *I can't afford to get drawn back into that. I've got my own war to fight.*

He glanced at Kip, who looked ridiculous on a gelding no bigger than Lu. The Schlessen had never ridden in his life before five days ago, and his attempts to learn had not gone well. If it had not been for the legion healer he'd probably be on a stretcher heading back to Pontus already.

"You ready?" he asked cheerily.

Kip looked at him with mute dread and slowly shook his head.

Ramon's eyes went to Seth Korion. The general's son was sitting on the back of a roan khurne; its sharp, faintly curved horn erupted from its forehead. Alone of the horses it was standing placidly. It had arrived the previous day, sent by Korion's illustrious father, apparently, and the other horses were skittish around it. Most of the other magi were green with envy, but Ramon found the creature's intelligence unnerving.

"Well, lads, here we are," Baltus Prenton exclaimed, trotting up to join them. "What a spectacle, eh?"

It certainly is that. Five thousand men moved about them, bawled on by their unit commanders, as Pallacios XIII prepared to join the exodus. They would need to cover twenty-five miles a day; it was a two-week journey to the far shore. Hulkas-drawn wagons would haul most of the baggage, and they would camp on the bridge. Most of the soldiers looked as nervy as he felt, even the veterans. Crossing the Bridge had become a rite of passage for Yuros legionaries. Today they would all join that brotherhood.

About him the other magi of the Thirteenth waited. Their Legate, Jonti Duprey, was conferring with his tribunes, who commanded the ten maniples. The tribunes were all veterans, and in the case of the Thirteenth, that meant ex-mutineers, bitter men who visibly resented the magi. The rankers didn't show much in the way of reverence for their gnosis-wielding "protectors" either, apart from their clear respect and affection for the Healer, a solemn, middle-aged Rondian woman named Lanna Jureigh. She'd been responsible for putting Kip back together after each fall. Right now she was riding alongside the chaplain, a bland mage-priest named Tyron Frand who only came alive when talking about poetry and books.

The magi had established their little cliques by now, except for the commanders, who stayed aloof. Tyron Frand and Lanna Jureigh could usually be found together, and Prenton, Ramon, and Kip had teamed up, though the affable Prenton had the enviable ability to get on with anyone. Seth Korion, Renn Bondeau, and Severine Tiseme clearly felt themselves above the rest; Renn and Severine were openly flirting by now. The three Andressans, Gerant, Hale, and Lewen, remained taciturn and inseparable, while Coulder and Fenn spoke to no one on any topic other than gambling. At least no one was isolated. Ramon was pleased to have a friend in Kip: the Schlessen might be a gnostic lightweight, but he had a warm nature once you got past the chest-beating and posturing.

The legion's Secundus, Rufus Marle, commander of the First Maniple as well as Duprey's second in command, had a palpable scent of violence about him, and was perpetually on the verge of lashing out. He and Duprey were close, and the other magi, even Bondeau, were frightened of him. He'd been taking the magi through riding and fighting drills all week; only Lanna, Tyron, and Severine, their Farseer, had been spared.

Now Duprey raised a hand, the drums rolled, the tribunes saluted and hurried to the head of their columns. Marle glared about him. "All right, you fannies," he roared, "let's get moving."

The trumpets blew, and a ragged cheer went up.

"Forwaaaard . . . MARCH!"

Ramon lifted his eyes skyward. "Papa Sol, Mater Luna, watch over us." He dug his heels into Lu's flanks and trotted down onto the Leviathan Bridge.

The first thing that struck him was how hollow the sound of his horse's hoofbeats were. Then came the sense of exposure: there were no trees, no overhanging hills, nothing but the Bridge and the sea beneath him and the sky above. Within a few hundred yards it was as if the land had ceased to be. The spray from the waves beating against the cliffs cast up such a mist that the land had vanished behind them into a shapeless darkness, and the only thing clearly visible was Northpoint Tower's beacon—and that was already frighteningly distant. When he reached down and brushed his fingers against the parapet he realized the Bridge itself was vibrating. Lu, like the other horses, was skittish, but they seemed to take comfort from the mindless plodding of the hulkas and that calm gradually spread among the men too.

The Bridge was surprisingly narrow at only forty yards wide, and once off the ramp, the shell- and mica-flecked stone was dead flat. They had studied the Bridge at the Arcanum, of course. Even though it was maintained by Earth-gnosis augmented by the giant sun-soaking crystals on the five towers, it could only withstand the pressures of the seas because it was anchored to an underwater ridge that ran from Pontus to Dhassa—and even then it could be no more than nine hundred feet from the sea floor. That was why the Bridge was above sea level for only two years in twelve, when the tides were at their lowest. That was a damn good thing, in Ramon's opinion, or there would be one permanent Crusade.

Overhead, gulls dipped and shrieked, and even higher, windships followed the line of the Bridge southeast. No doubt there were Pallas Air-mages manipulating the weather to aid the crossing. *Better filthy weather elsewhere than storms here*, Ramon thought thankfully.

At night, they slept in bedrolls under the vast moon that gleamed almost bright as day. The legionaries were carefully respectful in their interactions with the magi, but Ramon felt nothing but suspicion emanating from them, especially toward those like him and Kip, from outside the empire.

On the third evening, Korion, Bondeau, and Frand, the serious-faced chaplain, gathered at the parapet, peering down at the waves and occasionally firing mage-bolts at passing birds. Dozens had already been sent plummeting into the waves. Severine was laughing gaily and applauding the best shots. The rankers ignored them.

"She is pretty, yar?" Kip observed from his bedroll, where he was sitting uncomfortably, massaging his buttocks.

Ramon ran his eye over the young woman. She was short and curvy, with a narrow waist and a cloud of curly brown hair artfully piled about her cherubic face. She had a squealing laugh and a way of clapping her hands excitedly that looked profoundly affected to Ramon. "Repulsively cute."

"Oh, bravo!" she exclaimed as Bondeau blasted a gull into charred feather and bone. The three men crowed and slapped each other's back. "Come on, Master Frand, your turn! You've not hit one yet!"

"Too much drink!" Korion laughed, his face flushed. The high-bloods had gotten hold of some wine and were drinking eagerly, bored already by the endless Bridge. "Tyron's drunk as a shepherd!"

Frand bowed in a wobbly way, swigged again, then took aim at a passing gull. He missed by at least ten yards, causing another gale of laughter. The chaplain abruptly reeled away from the group and sauntered in their direction. "Hey, you two?" he cried, his voice slurred. "Do you braff?"

Ramon raised an eyebrow. "Do we what?"

"Braff: shoot birds, you know?" The chaplain raised the bottle again. "I'm completely lammy, you know," he added unnecessarily. He leaned against the rails. "I wonder, if we all leaned against this side, would we tip the Bridge over?"

"Hey, Frand, don't talk to those foreign shits," Korion called.

Bondeau swaggered toward them. "No, we should get to know our fellow magi," he said, a cruel smile lighting his face, and in a few seconds, Ramon and Kip found themselves ringed by cold-eyed Rondians. It reminded Ramon horribly of college; he and Alaron had been in the same situation dozens of times, when Korion had been joined by Malevorn Andevarion, Francis Dorobon, Boron Funt, and Gron Koll. It had invariably ended in pain and humiliation. The little area about them fell silent, the soldiers nearby eying them warily while pretending not to have noticed anything.

Bondeau stepped forward, almost within touching distance. He was nowhere near as tall as Kip, but still he eyed him disdainfully. "I am descended of Hanicius of the Blessed Three Hundred. What is your lineage, fellow magi? Do you even know?"

"They probably don't even know their fathers' names," Korion put in. His bravado felt forced, as if he'd just as soon not interact with Ramon at all.

We all knew who your daddy is, Seth—but where was he when you got this job?

"Provincial sluts don't ask about lineage when they see a mage," Bondeau snickered. "They just spread their legs and pray for children—like that Turniphead in Coldany on the way south," he chortled. "Remember her?"

Ramon felt Kip begin to smolder. "Turniphead" was slang for Schlessen.

While Bondeau postured, Ramon carefully did nothing. He'd had his fill of bullying high-bloods. Kip was clearly finding restraint harder. *Keep calm*, he silently urged his friend.

"Seth says you were at Turm Zauberin, runt. How could you afford that?" Bondeau asked Ramon abruptly.

"My familioso sent money," Ramon replied levelly. The word "familioso"—the Rimoni family clans whose specialty was smuggling and murder—brought a slight pause to the proceedings, and Ramon began to hope they might get out of it.

Then Bondeau spat at his feet. "You think I give a fuck about your criminal family?" he sneered. "I could wipe out your whole damned village if I wished and not take a scratch." He made a small gesture and the front of Ramon's shirt bunched, as if held by an invisible fist. Slowly he lifted him into the air. Kip grabbed his shoulder, then found himself also lifted effortlessly by the collar.

"Shall I toss them over the edge?" Bondeau asked Severine, whose pretty face was now tense with worry. Her eyes were on the commanders who were distracted some fifty yards away.

"Renn, put them down," she said.

Instead Bondeau gestured, and Ramon found himself hurled out into empty air, the parapet now yards away and the roaring sea far below. A gasp went up among the soldiery as Kip followed him, the gnosis holding him fast by the front of his shirt. He was struggling uselessly.

"Put us down," Ramon choked.

"Down? You want to go swimming?" Bondeau feigned dropping them both, then caught them again effortlessly.

"Back on the bridge," Ramon gritted. *One day I'm going to be above all this, I swear it . . .*

"Say 'please,' familioso scum," Bondeau called.

Kip swore, but Ramon had been bullied enough not to argue. "Please."

With a flick of the finger, he found himself flung back over the rail and dropped sprawling in a heap before a line of hard-faced rankers. Bondeau didn't even look at him. "Now you, Turniphead."

Kip glowered. "Neyn."

Bondeau smiled. "Well then . . . perhaps your Air-gnosis will save you? Though I rather got the impression you're an Earth-mage, so I doubt being out there will agree with you." He twisted his hand, turning Kip upside down.

The girl, Severine, quickly plucked at his sleeve. "Renn, don't." She was looking increasingly worried, although more about causing a scene than Kip's safety.

"He's learned his lesson," Frand slurred.

"He hasn't begged," Bondeau said stubbornly.

Suddenly Rufus Marle was there, cantering into their midst. He gestured, and Kip flew through the air and landed beside Ramon, who barely rolled aside in time. The Schlessen cracked his knee and rolled about, wincing. Bondeau laughed gaily, then shut up as he saw the livid expression on Marle's face.

"I was only playing, sir—it was just a jest—"

Marle scowled. "Do it again and you'll be the one going over the edge, Bondeau. Show some respect for your station, man: you are blood of the Blessed." He turned and glowered down at Ramon and Kip. "As are you two. Pick yourselves up." His eyes smoldered. "We're marching to war. The next sign of division in our ranks will be rewarded with a thrashing." He spurred his horse away and clattered back to Legate Duprey's side. The watching legionaries looked carefully away.

Bondeau smirked as Ramon and Kip climbed to their feet. Severine put an arm about his shoulders and whispered something, making him laugh throatily, and without a backward glance they swayed away.

Ramon and Kip glowered at their backs.

Later that evening Tyron Frand sidled up sheepishly as they heated a tin pot of stew over the fire. "I'm sorry about that," he muttered. "It was foolish and unkind."

Kip and Ramon looked at each other. The Schlessen was still nauseous from being hung over the void. Ramon could have flown—Air-gnosis was an affinity—but Kip would have gone straight down.

"Nice friends you've got," Ramon observed.

Frand looked uncomfortable. His bland face was basically pleasant, with a sensitive mouth and thinning, straight hair. He was in his midtwenties, Ramon thought—although he was a mage, of course, so he could have been a lot older than he looked. "Beginnings are awkward times. When we've all fought together, we will bond as brothers in Kore," Frand said hopefully.

Ramon eyed him doubtfully, and came to some unexpected conclusions; that Frand wasn't really all that drunk, and that he'd been deliberately missing the birds. "How did you end up in the Thirteenth?"

"Every legion is assigned a chaplain—but I'm primarily a healer," Frand added, which explained a little; the Rondian elite considered healer-magi unmanly. "I help Mistress Lanna, though I'm also expected to fight if needed."

"How come Renn Bondeau and Severine Tiseme aren't in a better legion?" Ramon asked.

Frand glanced over his shoulder then said softly, "Bondeau is heavily in debt. And young Miss Tiseme is . . . *indiscreet*. She wrote a song last year mocking Mater-Imperia's sanctification; this is her punishment."

There might be hope for her, Ramon thought. He leaned forward. "What about Korion?"

Frand shrugged. "Of that, I have no idea."

Kip grunted. "And what's your problem, Master Frand?"

Frand looked rueful. "A foolish relationship." Ramon and Kip waited for more, but nothing was forthcoming. "I don't think less of you provincials, you know," he said, as if this were a great virtue. "It's just the way of things, isn't it? Everyone wants the mage-blood. It isn't your fault your mother got lucky. So did mine, eh?" He walked off without waiting for a reply.

Days passed, each the same as the last: they rose, ate, packed up, mounted, and plodded onwards, the men marching behind them, all in time to the rattle of the drums. They couldn't train, they couldn't even gallop, and the initial wonder had long since been replaced by boredom. Occasionally they overtook merchant caravans hauling goods backward and forward over the Bridge—trade still went on despite the coming conflict—and Ramon looked out for Vann Mercer, Alaron's father, but he never saw him. Kip and Ramon practiced their Rondian on each other, and occasionally chatted to Prenton or Frand, who was going out of his way to be conciliatory to them. Bondeau and Tiseme had become the chief topic of gossip: they'd begun slipping into the wagons late at night seeking privacy. Frand said Tiseme was desperate to get pregnant so she'd be sent home. "Though getting knocked up by a bankrupt bastard seems counterproductive to me."

"Yar," laughed Kip. "I am a much better catch: I have a herd of seventeen cattle in my village."

"Then I'm even better," Ramon announced. "My familioso Pater basically owns my village and the countryside around it, and he gives me pretty much anything I want." *So long as I do exactly what he wants. And so long as he still has my mother . . .*

"I thought she would go after the general's son," Kip observed.

Ramon scoffed. "Seth's such a limp-dick I doubt he could do the deed." He told them about Korion's disgrace during the exams, then said quickly, "Keep that to yourself, Chaplain. And try not to end up relying on him to protect your back."

Frand looked across to the campfire of the young noble-magi, who were singing along with the lute Prenton was playing. "I think young Seth is a lost soul," he said softly. "I'll go and join them: I know that song," he added, waving farewell.

As the chaplain went and joined the circle of singers Ramon nudged Kip. "Come on, there's another little 'chat' I need to have with someone."

Kip brightened. "Can I hit them?"

"Only if I say so," Ramon warned.

Kip made a sulky face, then winked.

He found the man he wanted sitting in a circle of ten grizzled veterans drinking beer and staring into the embers. They were the legion's ten tribunes, the senior non-magi officer of each maniple—and the ones who did the real commanding. None was under forty, and all had the studied irreverence of the career sol-dier toward interlopers. They all grudgingly rose and gave the imperial salute as the two magi approached though. "Magisters," the nearest drawled. "How may we serve?"

Ramon focused upon the smallest of them, a balding fellow with a face like a ferret. "I need to confer with my tribune."

The circle of men frowned in surprise. Though battle-magi out-ranked the tribunes who commanded each maniple, they expected their tribunes to do all the actual soldiering.

"Storn, isn't it?"

"Yes sir. Everything is under control, sir," Storn replied, trying to hide his instinctive look of consternation.

Don't like people taking an interest, then? "Nevertheless, Tribune Storn," he replied evenly, gesturing for him to follow. *<Keep the rest here,>* he told Kip.

The Schlessen grinned around the circle. "You have beer," he noted. The nearest man grudgingly poured him a mug. He downed it in one swallow. "Yar, not bad." He proffered his mug again. "I might have some."

Ramon led Tribune Storn away to the rim of the bridge. He noted the man didn't look down at the dark waves crashing below. "So, Storn, how are things progressing?"

"There is nothing you need trouble yourself with," the tribune said, speaking quickly. "Water is sufficient and the food adequate. Healer Lanna has the men with cock-pox under quarantine and—"

"Si, si," Ramon interrupted impatiently. He met the man's eyes. "Tribune, I have spoken to men who have served in the legions." It was true: his paterfamilias had taken some trouble to ensure that Ramon knew how a legion worked. "I am young but I am not igno-rant. I know what the Tenth Maniple is."

Storn made a show of flinching as if in shame. "We are the hum-blest of the legion's units, Magister Sensini. We serve the rest. Some look down on the tenth, but we are essential."

It was the rote answer; Ramon waved it away. "Storn, don't give me that *merda*. All of the food, drink, supplies, equipment, live-stock, and pay flow through the Tenth Maniple, and the man con-trolling it all is you."

Storn blanched. "My lord, I am just a humble tribune—I have no great aspirations—"

Ramon chuckled. "You know, I made a good friend in Pontus. You might know him. The name's Giordano."

A sickly expression crawled across Storn's face. "Uh . . ."

"Signor Giordano deals with many tribunes, and they are all are from the Tenth Maniple of their legion. He supplies them with all manner of items that the legion stores cannot source. He claims to know you very well."

Storn floundered momentarily, then made an apologetic gesture. "The army storemasters are useless, Magister. Sometimes we must deal with locals."

"The goods Giordano supplies aren't exactly standard issue, Storn. Some would call them illegal. And yet he has a thriving business."

Storn chewed his upper lip. "Magister, where is this conversation going?"

Ramon leaned against the parapet, looking out to the fading horizon. He'd had only one evening to cement the deal with Giordano, but it had gone well. He had a list of contacts for Hebusalim, and the names of the tribunes the Rimoni businessman dealt with; he'd been delighted to find his own tribune was one of them. "Tribune, how would you like to be ridiculously rich?"

Pallacios XIII reached Midpoint Tower on schedule, a week after leaving Yuros. Midpoint was the largest of the five towers supporting the Bridge, the nexus for the solar energy, and the light it radiated was so bright that the night was banished for a mile around it. Similar beacons of light could be discerned far to the northeast and southwest: Dawn and Sunset Isles respectively. Being close to one of the legendary towers was debilitating, so the legion pressed on as quickly as the men could manage. Only lesser magi were posted here, so the weather control was not as efficient, and occasional rainstorms broke through to lash the marchers. Visibility was down to a few hundred yards at best, and they were constantly wet and miserable. Bondeau used his gnosis to shelter Severine and himself, and Ramon hated him even more—he could have done the same, but it would have exhausted him within a few minutes. He longed to feel the sun on his face.

Then the storms faded and the heat started rising, growing fiercer with every step closer to Antiopia. Desiccating winds blew from the south, turning faces first pink, then red, until the burned skin started peeling. Olive-complexioned Ramon was one of the few unaffected; everyone else became irritable, and it felt like he was spending all his time breaking up fights. The soldiers were like rabid dogs, biting and snapping at anything in reach unless they were lashed into submission. While the other young magi were oblivious to their maniples, he and Kip had decided that protecting and championing their men would win their loyalty. Rankers generally liked to kick around men from the tenth. Ramon used his position to ensure his maniple got the best of everything, but Kip was more direct. Eschewing his weak gnosis, he meted out justice with his fists, and the Schlessen was soon the best-loved mage in the legion. To Ramon's mild disgust, the soldiers respected capacity for violence above any amount of fairness and consideration. Any illusions he might have had about the legendary discipline of the Rondian soldier gradually eroded as he realized it was violence and fear that kept the rankers in check, not patriotism and a sense of duty.

The journey felt like forever, the days dragging on as they left Midpoint behind them, but it was only a week later that the advance guard caught sight of the beacon of Southpoint, visible a few hours before the Dhassan coast appeared. The stupendous cliffs filled the southern horizon, and beyond the cliffs, brown hills shimmered in the haze. The churning waters below roared louder as the cliffs grew closer, and gulls dive-bombed the column, their clamor deafening.

By now they were all longing for solid ground, and the Bridge resounded to the tramp of five thousand men as the tempo of the drums lifted them and they raced the sun to the land. Ramon had to restrain Lu from galloping, but he grinned at Kip, whose sweating face was a mess of pink, peeling skin. "Almost there!"

Progress slowed when they reached the coast. All conversation was rendered impossible by the thunder of the waters below. Ramon had to restrain himself from throwing himself to the ground and kissing it. Duprey had assembled his magi and marched them to the front so they could be first ashore, then the legate made them line up to welcome their soldiers as they trooped from the Bridge into Antiopia. Relief at arriving had the rankers cheering Seth Korion as if he was his father Kaltus, and they acclaimed Duprey as if he'd built the Bridge himself.

The landing site was at the foot of Southpoint, but their camp was a mile inland: the hardest mile of the journey. Three other legions were in the staging camp before them, preparing to march onward. The word was passed from man to man: two days' rest, then it was two hundred miles of dirt roads to Hebusalim—and all the water-holes were already running dry. The exultation of arrival was soon replaced with the grim reality to come.

"Please, not Dhassa again," Legate Duprey prayed aloud. "Let us see true action this time."

Ramon shrugged; he couldn't be happier if the Thirteenth was held behind the lines with nothing for him to do but shake down the local traders. Pater-Retiari had plans for him, he had his own agenda, and the real war would only get in the way.

14

THE GUIDE

Constructs

The most controversial of all aspects of the gnosis is surely the question of constructs. Once we discovered that the gnosis could be used to fuse one life-form with another, giving us the power to create hybrids, we magi had truly become as gods. Naturally, this had to be legislated before madmen ran amok, creating nightmares that would consume us all.

ORDO COSTRUO COLLEGIATE, PONTUS

Restrict, restrict! It's all you blinkered fools know! We have the power to do whatever we please! Why shouldn't we?

NOTES FROM THE TRIAL OF ALDUS GANNON, BRES, 665

Coastal Yuros
Septinon 928
3rd month of the Moontide

Waking again was utterly unexpected. It felt more like being born. Alaron was enveloped in warm arms, cradled in someone's lap and suckling on a teat. His mouth was filled with warm milky fluids, and a woman grunted painfully as he suckled hard.

I'm a child again . . .
Or this is just death, final memories . . .
Or rebirth . . . Ha!
Kore was wrong, we are reborn, like the Sollan drui say . . .
. . . So why am I still wearing my clothes?

His eyes flew open, and he gagged. A wall of pain hit him, especially his throat, which was utterly throbbing where he'd been bitten. He looked up, at the faces of the Elders staring down at him.

He was still on the top of the peak, and he was being nursed in Kessa's arms—it was her breast he'd been suckling. He felt his face go burning scarlet, and tried to thrash free of her, but her coils wrapped about him. *<Be still,>* she sent, thrusting her engorged nipple at him again. *<Drink, if you wish to live.>*

It was very possibly the most humiliating thing he'd ever done: to suckle a virtual stranger's breast-milk before these strangers who'd just passed a sentence of death upon him. And she wasn't even human—but that didn't stop him from doing it. Embarrassment was one thing; death was quite another. He had no idea why they were now apparently intent on saving him, but if they'd changed their mind, all well and good.

After another minute of gulping down the milky discharge, she pushed him away. Her face was almost purple and she looked utterly disgusted. Kekropius put an arm on her shoulder and she shoved him away. *<Revolting creature,>* she spat into all of their minds. *<Don't ever make me do that again.>*

Alaron just lay there on the stony ground, his limbs completely numb. He didn't think he could move them to save himself. He was paralyzed—but he was alive.

Movement gradually returned as the Elders came and went. He was never alone; Kekropius stayed with him, a comforting presence sending reassurances that he would recover. The minutes crawled past, and then suddenly he could twitch his toes and fingers. He wept with relief.

After that, full recovery came swiftly and within ten minutes he was sitting up. Soon after he was able to keep down the water they brought him, washing the milky taste in his mouth away with utter relief. It wasn't that he wasn't grateful, but . . . *yuck!*

"So, Alaron," Kekropius said, a faint smile on his face. "You have traumatized my mate, but her milk contains an antidote to her venom. You are also now her son, and therefore mine. Whatever will we do with you?"

Alaron couldn't even begin to comprehend all of that. "Why?" he croaked.

"For the word you spoke as you fell. *Hebusalim.* The Promised Land."

His mouth fell open, but he couldn't think of anything to actually say.

Kekropius smiled with all the warmth his reptilian face could muster, and Alaron recognized what passed for hysterical mirth among the lamiae in his almost impassive face. "Kessa has some divination. She saw you leading us to the promised land: *Hebusalim.* When you spoke that word as you fell, we Elders realized immediately that her foresight might be true." He paused. "Well, in truth, Mesuda recognized this and changed her vote. As Eldest, she has the casting vote. Reku and Hypollo still wish to eat you."

"Yeah, well, I'm sure Reku would be delicious in a casserole too," Alaron growled.

Kekropius hissed with laughter again as Alaron gingerly rubbed his neck. He could feel scabs, but the healing was well advanced. It still felt like there was one Hel of a bruise. "So, you're all constructs, reptiles fused with humans, and you have some gnosis." He met Kekropius's eyes. "You know what I'm saying?"

The lamia Elder nodded. "We have no training, but the gnosis fuels all we do. It even sustains our lives: without it we would die."

"How did they give you the gnosis? That's impossible, surely—"

"None of us know. It is just how we are."

Alaron rolled his eyes. "Great Kore! You know, I studied Animagery at the Arcanum. They even taught us how to fuse a mouse and a bird in my final year. Mine lived about ten minutes before its heart burst. But constructs with human intelligence are illegal . . . so some renegade Animagus made you, then the Inquisitors found out?"

"No," Kekropius corrected him, "we were bred by the empire."

Alaron's mouth fell open again. It was a day for shocks, like dying and being reborn. "The empire?"

"There is a secret beastarium in Hollenia," Kekropius told him. "It was founded to research things the Kore forbade, in case the empire found them useful." He flexed his fingers thoughtfully. "You are right, though: we are essentially reptiles. They wanted to breed a race of warriors to serve the empire in warm lands. It was an experiment, grafting human souls into reptile-human hybrids, then infusing us with gnosis, breaking all their own laws."

Alaron rubbed his eyes, scarcely believing what he was hearing. "Whose souls?" he asked sickly.

"Slaves," Kekropius said softly. "From Hebusalim."

"Kore's Blood! You're from Hebusalim?"

"The first—indeed, the only batch—were my parents' generation. They are all dead now." He cocked his head, looking down at Alaron. "How old do you think I am?"

Alaron considered. Kekropius was clearly an adult of his kind, and an elder. If he had Water-gnosis, which gave access to healing and could be used to preserve youth, he could be even older than he looked. And the slave trade had begun well before the First Crusade thirty-six years ago. "Fifty?" he guessed.

Kekropius shook his combed head. "I am seventeen."

Alaron stared. "No way . . ."

"We have a short lifespan. I will die of old age in three to five years." Kekropius looked wistful. "We have short gestations, and attain full size inside three years. But we live to only twenty-five at most, and we go down fast in our last years."

Alaron thought about Mesuda and Reku, hunched over and shriveled up. Right now he didn't feel terribly sorry for either of them, but Kekropius's calm acceptance of his fate was different. He'd stuck up for him, and of course, he'd saved his life by killing Seldon. He liked Kekropius, found him strangely good company; it was almost impossible to believe that he was barely three years from dying of old age, let alone that he was younger than Alaron himself.

"Can't you do anything about it?"

Kekropius shook his head. "Short lives suited the empire's purpose for us—we had no time to learn anything but obedience." He shook his head. "We grow swiftly and learn voraciously. Our days then were spent in weapons-drilling and lessons in obedience."

"And you escaped?"

Kekropius frowned, and spoke as if reciting from memory, "We were being readied for what they called the Holy Crusade—the First Crusade, by your reckoning. My parents' souls were harvested from slaves and placed within the bodies the magi had made. But they were too few, so they were held back for the Second Crusade in 916. I was born in 911, between the Crusades. Our generation were taught Dhassan by our parents and Rondian by our tutors. We were trained to fight."

"Did you?" Alaron asked breathlessly.

"Yes, but not for the empire. In 914 one of the magi at the beastarium took pity on us. He informed a faction at court, hoping to have the breeding program closed and us released. He was naïve; when the emperor realized that our existence could be used to discredit his regime, he moved quickly, intending to have us all killed. Luckily, our patron got wind of the decision and released us into the wild before the Inquisitors came."

"How many?"

"We numbered in the thousands—there were many types, not just we lamiae. But the Inquisitors pursued us relentlessly and now there are fewer than seventy in our group. There may be other enclaves, but we've never found any of them."

"How did you get here?" Alaron was having a hard time taking this in; it felt almost like a fairy story.

"While most of the constructs took to the forests, our group headed for the coast. We'd been following the edge of the land, moving on every few months, until we found these caves. This has been our home for two years now. We had more or less decided to settle here permanently."

Alaron marveled that all this could be happening and yet people knew nothing of it: imperial Animagi creating abominations—yet that hardly seemed the word, not for Kekropius, anyway. "And the 'Promised Land'?" he asked.

Kekropius looked at him sadly. "Alaron, my generation is dying out. The younger generation do not even speak Dhassan; they remember only that the Crusades were to their homeland, a place promised them by their elders. My father told me that our people are so short-lived that we are like children. We don't have time to fully mature here"—he tapped his head—"or here." He touched his heart. "We are fast losing our heritage."

"Write it all down," Alaron said reflexively.

"We've never learned how."

Alaron looked up at him. "I could teach you."

Kekropius blinked slowly. Alaron had learned to recognize this as a sign of intense cogitation. "We would be in your debt." He cocked his head. "Do you truly know the way to Hebusalim? We have traveled this coast for fourteen years. We don't know our way home."

Alaron met his eyes, heart pounding. "I do know the way, and I can show it to you."

The lamia's face betrayed a hopelessness he'd not shown before. "We are dying out, Milkson. Our breeding pool is too small, and the world too perilous. Sometimes I wonder if there is any point."

"There's always a reason to go on," Alaron replied. "I don't know much, but I know that." *It's about the only thing life has taught me.*

The Eighteenth Fist gathered in a circle about Commandant Vordan and Adamus Crozier. It was dawn and the venators were hissing impatiently, awaiting the command to take to the air. Wind whipped at their cloaks, a cool dry southern breeze that cleared the cobwebs of sleep.

The tale the ghost of Seldon had told them had been almost unbelievable: some kind of snake-man creature, clearly a construct, had killed him. Vordan had admitted that some years ago there had been a breakout from a secret beastarium; the distorted creations of a renegade mage had escaped. It had been left to the Inquisition to clean up the mess; they had believed all the illegal constructs had been found and slaughtered, but it appeared that was not the case. He would report the find, he said, but tracking down Alaron Mercer remained the priority.

Malevorn nodded to himself. *That was logical, if Mercer really does have the Scytale of Corineus.*

Of course, these creatures might well have slain Mercer and taken the Scytale—but if so, surely the remains of Mercer's body would also have been found. They could only pray these things hadn't simply lost the Scytale, let it wash into the sea.

They'd been searching the coastline for days, flying fifty miles in either direction, but they'd found nothing. This region was barely inhabited; a few communities lived on the cliff tops, subsisting by combing the tidelands when the waves receded, but that was it. Adamus Crozier turned to Malevorn. They'd been working together late into the night, the bishop using a Mysticism-link to try to scry Alaron via Malevorn's memories of him. Such things could work, but only at short range, and there had been no tangible results. Being with the bishop alone had been uncomfortable at times— Adamus had made it clear that he wished to know Malevorn carnally, but he had refused. It might be a bad career move, but he was an Andevarion and had his pride. To his surprise, the bishop appeared to respect him more for that refusal.

"Master Andevarion," the Crozier said now, "you were not this boy Mercer's only classmate. Surely there are others we might summon to our aid?"

"We were a small class, my lord Crozier," Malevorn replied. "Just seven: Mercer and Sensini, his only friend." He cast his mind back. "Gron Koll is dead." *And unmissed.* "Francis Dorobon is a strong scryer."

"Dorobon?" Adamus glanced at Vordan. "I think not. Anyway, he is in Javon."

Ah, so you're off chasing that kingdom of yours, Francis? Good for you. "Seth Korion, though I don't remember him as being proficient." *At anything.*

"Not a Korion," Adamus responded firmly. "Who was the seventh?"

Malevorn had almost forgotten him: fat, blathering, pompous ... "Boron Funt." *Not a name I thought I'd ever be saying again.*

The Crozier's eyes lit up. "He is one of ours. We recruited him on Gavius's say-so."

"He too is a strong scryer, my lord." *Or so he pretended.*

Vordan looked at Adamus. "Do we know where this Boron Funt was posted?"

Somewhere with a blazing log fire and roast pigs on the spit.

"Someone will know. I will send for him," Adamus said confidently. "In the meantime we will continue our search." He turned to Vordan. "Commandeer a villa and set up base. Mercer will be found, I assure you."

But Alaron Mercer continued to elude them as the days passed, and their frustration grew.

It took much persuasion, but the lamiae finally resolved to seek Hebusalim. It would be a slow process, as their scouts had seen Inquisitors searching the coastal cliffs. But night-travel through the woods was possible, for the lamiae used gnostic heat-sensing, a self-taught skill in which they were as proficient as any Arcanum-trained mage. They set out in small groups, initially covering only a few miles each night, but once they had left the heavily choked undergrowth of the Silacian hills and entered the pine forests of eastern Noros it was easier. Alaron mostly rode on Kekropius's back. They were managing more than fifteen miles a night, but it wasn't fast enough: by his reckoning the Bridge was two thousand miles away; at their current rate it would take six months to reach Pontus. And how in Hel they were going to make it over the Bridge he had no idea.

But there were moments of inspiration: a rare sea-view at dawn revealed a dim shape on the horizon that he realized could only be the volcanic island of Phaestos. At last all those geography lessons were useful: he knew it to be uninhabited, after the last eruptions in 886, and it offered a way to cut hundreds of miles from their journey. Mesuda sent scouts swimming toward it while the main group rested for a few days.

Alaron felt as if he'd stepped into a very strange dream. Despite the lamiae's human characteristics, they were very much an alien species. They ate fish primarily, wolfing it down whole to a main stomach below the hips, at the top of the snake body. Kekropius told him the males had two hearts to power their long bodies; they could move at dazzling speeds, and could climb anything. They were terrifying in their strength and anger, but though they quickly reached physical maturity, they were like capricious children, swiftly fascinated or bored. The Elders' role was somewhere between older sibling and parent.

While contemplating the alien nature of his companions, Alaron had an idea. Kekropius sent him to talk to Reku. The ancient lamia woman—at twenty-two, she was declining fast—was perched on her own on a low bluff, beneath which the refugees were camping. Most of the males were hunting while the females were preparing cooking pits or tending the young. More had been born on the journey, and he watched with awe as the whelps matured at incredible speed.

Reku turned her craggy head as he approached. She was losing her sight and was even more hunched over. When he compared her with the majestically built younger lamiae, it was almost pitiable to see her decline. Though she was no more likable. "Come to offer yourself as my last meal, boy? Roasted with garlic would be nice."

"I've brought some worms for your dinner," he snapped back, tired from the journey and irritable with loneliness. Though he was now their guide, only Kekropius would actually converse with him and it was wearing him down.

To his surprise she cackled gleefully. "Are they juicy fat ones, like human fingers? Drown them in wine, boy, then I'll suck them down whole." She mimed a swallowing gesture and smacked her lips with a show of great pleasure.

"Better yet, they are actual human fingers. See, I've cut off my fingers to feed you," he told her, joining in the game. He hid his hand in his sleeve and waved it at her.

"Fingers," she purred. "I hope you didn't fillet them, I love to crunch on the bones and suck out the marrow."

Yeuck. That sounds too much like experience. "Aunty Reku," he said, using the lamiae address form, "may I ask a question?"

She regarded him with a birdlike cocking of the head, a half-mad-looking one-eyed stare of appraisal. "Of course, child of Kessa." She made a teat-sucking sound, her eyes teasing.

He flushed; that memory still rankled. "Aunty, do any of your people have the ability to see things that are far away?"

Reku blinked several times and licked her lips: a sign of great interest. She leaned toward him. "Some." She cocked her head. "We have the gnosis, and it answers our personalities, just like you magi. Some of us can wield fire and others can fly."

Ha: thought so! "Might I be able to talk to one of those who can see far away?"

Reku turned her head and changed eyes. Her pupils were narrowing and dilating. *Appraisal.* "What for?"

"To find someone."

"Will it put my people at risk?"

He hesitated. "Not if done properly," he answered honestly.

She exhaled thoughtfully. *Acceptance.* "Talk to Ildena, but only after her mate Fydro returns from hunting. Tell him I approve." She seized his left hand before he could react, then slowly drew it to her mouth.

"Uh, what—?"

"I have given you something—you owe me something in return." She opened her mouth and jerked forward, pinned his forefinger and bit down, drawing blood with her tiny pin-prick teeth. "Mmmm," she purred, rolling her eyes.

He didn't move, perspiration beading on his brow as he tried to work out if this was a game or some kind of bargain sealer for securing her agreement. Her thick purple tongue coiled about each finger in turn, its surface both rough and slick. Then she pushed his hand away and roared with laughter. "Your face, boy, you should see it!" She hunched over and wept, shaking with hilarity.

Eeeyeurgh. He wiped his saliva-coated hand on his shirt, and hurried away.

The next night, as the lamiae awaited the returning scouts, he took Kekropius with him as his chaperone. Fydro was a burly lamia with a surly face. Kekropius did most of the talking, explaining that Fydro's wife might be of great aid to the clan, but that she would need to learn from the human mage to enable this. Fydro was reluctant, as they were newly mated; Ildena was a delicate beauty and he was exceedingly possessive of her. Eventually he agreed, but only if he was present. He appeared to regard Alaron as some kind of devil who would use his gnosis to seduce his wife. Alaron thought this bizarre. The lamiae were so alien he couldn't even conceive of wanting to seduce one—even though in Lantric myths lamiae were sometimes lovers of this or that demigod or hero. He'd even stopped noticing breasts while with them; to the snake-people they were just another body part of no great importance, and he was so surrounded by personal body parts he'd practically stopped seeing them.

However, when he actually met Ildena for the first time, he began to understand Fydro's feelings. Ildena's face and human torso were lovely. She was small by lamia standards, slim and delicate, and her big golden eyes were shot through with seams of violet. Her hesitant, spooky smile was bewitching. Her narrow waist swayed as she entered the room, and her bosom was so high and shapely it kind of hooked his eyes.

Fydro draped a blanket about his wife's shoulders and Kekropius shot Alaron a warning look. *Okay. I'm not even tempted.* He averted his eyes. *Not really.* "Uh, can she speak Rondian?" he asked. Not all the lamiae could.

"I understand," Ildena replied, her voice deeper than he expected, with a musical lilt.

It took a lot of negotiation, every step contested by Fydro, who kept erupting into fits of anger, but eventually Alaron managed to get Ildena to sit opposite him—albeit with a table between them. He clasped her hands to channel a link and took her through the most basic lessons of Clairvoyance, although he'd never been much good at it himself. But he could do Mysticism, and that meant the mental link he forged was strong and efficient. He showed her how to seek the whereabouts of other lamiae. She had been using the gnosis since birth, and this new skill was really just a more systematic approach to something that had previously only manifested by accident. She found the scouts, swimming safely home, then she scryed their former haven, the Sanctum Lucator, and found it still undisturbed. He showed her how to make what she scryed appear in water or smoke, so that others could see what she saw. The night flew by and at the end of it, they were both exhausted and exhilarated. She slumped, weeping with happiness, into her husband's arms.

"Enough," she sobbed, while Fydro stroked her shoulders and stared at Alaron with smoldering eyes.

He probably thinks I've corrupted her. He rose and bowed formally. "Thank you," he managed, before lurching toward the door. Kekropius caught him, and the rest was a blur. He slept away the day, and they began again that night. This time they used Aggi, the little wooden doll Cym had once played with as a child, to search for her, but still they found no trace.

His life changed. Other lamiae came to him, wanting him to teach them the way he'd taught Ildena, and his training at Turm Zauberin meant he was able to help all of them, even those for whose skills he had no affinity. The lamiae had the potential for every aspect of the gnosis; they might be self-taught but they were instinctive users. He worked out they were all roughly quarter-blood in power, and eager to learn.

Between teaching them and scrying for Cym, he barely had time to sleep, but he found he actually began to enjoy his time with the lamiae.

Sometimes he even dreamed that he'd grown a snake body instead of legs.

"Boron, welcome." Malevorn greeted the plump young priest, putting all the fondness he could muster into his voice. He offered his hand, but Funt staggered from the newly arrived windship and vomited on the grass instead. Most magi with any kind of air affinity were immune to flight-sickness, but Boron Funt was an exception—*probably because he eats constantly*, Malevorn thought. "A bad flight, my friend?" In the two weeks since Adamus Crozier had sent out the summons for Funt, they'd made no progress at all in their hunt. The trail was going cold.

Boron looked up at him with green jowls and miserable eyes. "Mal? Thank Kore!" He lurched upright, and seized him in a giant bear hug. "Ghastly, simply ghastly." Then he looked around, and realized that he'd stumbled right past a Crozier and an Inquisition Commandant. His face went from green to white. "My lords!" He fell to his knees and prostrated himself.

"Rise, young priest," Adamus said with a smirk. "We are all brothers in Kore here."

The windship had landed on the lawn before the villa the Fist had commandeered. Malevorn made the introductions, cringing somewhat to be associated with this buffoon. The Inquisitors looked upon Boron with utter contempt, and he completely agreed with them; it did his own standing no good at all to be associated in any way with this rolling piece of blubber. But he was appointed Funt's guide and told to room with him. Unless Funt had been miraculously cured of snoring and flatulence, the coming nights promised to be Hel.

Vordan and Adamus took Malevorn and Funt off to brief Funt on who he was to seek.

"Alaron Mercer?" Funt laughed uncertainly. "Is this some kind of jest?"

"No joke, Boron," Malevorn told him with utter sincerity. <*This is deadly* fucking *serious.*>

Funt straightened. "I remember Mercer," he told Adamus and Vordan. "Do you wish me to start now?"

"As soon as you're settled," Vordan told him. "He must not detect your scrying. He has eluded us thus far, so I suspect he may be more skilled than you credit him. Of course, he may be dead, but I think not. So proceed with caution. Am I understood?" His iron gaze transfixed the plump young priest.

"Absolutely, perfectly, completely!" Boron blathered. "You can rely on me, Commandant."

"Excellent. Then proceed."

When they were alone in their suite, Boron plucked at Malevorn's shoulder. "*Kore's codpiece! Alaron Mercer?*"

"The same."

Boron's eyes narrowed. "What's going on? Your Fist was pulled from the Crusade for this. I heard gossip that Governor Vult is dead. Gron Koll too," he added, unable to resist a smirk. "What's happening?"

Malevorn considered. Boron might be a glutton and a coward, but he had always had a nose for secrets. "I don't know, my friend," he lied. "But I'm sure you'll sniff it out."

Boron laughed, his first sign of genuine pleasure. "Oh, I shall, Mal. You can't keep a good plot from me."

"Cym? Cym?" Alaron shouted, heedless of danger, but no one replied. The empty island mocked him, echoing his cries back as if teasing him. He looked about him wildly, but no one answered. He bent over the wreckage, gripping it with shaking hands, and fought to hold back his tears.

Ildena touched his shoulder tentatively, which made the watching Fydro hiss. "Alaron?" the lamia asked softly. "This was hers?" She was wrapped in a blanket, at Fydro's insistence, despite the heat of the sun.

The lamiae had taken his advice to travel to Phaestos to shorten the journey, though for Alaron it meant swimming under a water-breathing spell again, clinging to Kekropius's back for dear life as they fought the deadly waters. But the lamiae were strong swimmers, and he managed.

They'd made their base in the ruins of the mining town, a ghostly place that looked like the aftermath of a young god's temper tantrum. The peaks of the triple volcanoes at the core of the island smoked menacingly. The vegetation was stunted and there were no animals, only birds by the thousand, though the seas were alive with seals, thriving in the warm waters.

They'd found the wreckage of Cym's skiff on a rocky plain.

"She and I built it," Alaron said hoarsely. It had been such a wonderful time, just the two of them alone, working together in harmony. Of course, he'd been in constant torment from his longing to kiss her, but apart from that, it had been bliss.

"Is it repairable?" Kekropius asked, slithering about the broken hull.

Alaron's first impulse was to scoff, but he made himself look more closely. "The keel is cracked, and so is the mast—look, she's tried to repair it, but couldn't. She's probably better at sylvan-gnosis than me, but neither Ramon or I knew enough to teach her."

"Some of our people can perform these feats," Kekropius mused aloud. "We could rebuild this for you."

"Would you be willing?"

"You are leading us to Hebusalim, the Promised Land," Kekropius replied. "We will do anything for you."

Apart from letting me go off alone, Alaron noted to himself, and immediately felt ashamed. The lamiae had saved his life; to criticize their protectiveness was unworthy.

"It'll take time," he warned.

"But it will be worth it, I deem," Kekropius replied. "We are all tired. This is a good place to rest and regain our strength."

So Alaron and the lamiae spent Septinon on Phaestos, hunting, fishing, and repairing the skiff. It was a community project; to Alaron's amazement, everyone wanted to contribute, and show off their burgeoning skills. The more Arcanum training he passed on, the more they learned, and they used his skiff as a means to compete, as well as to give something back. Raw materials were plentiful, and so was their enthusiasm. Wards of all sorts were worked into the timber. They added a bowsprit with a snake-haired head that could twist and turn like a real snake and spat fire or lightning at the pilot's command, using the gnosis reservoir in the hull. They made new sails with animal hides, and bound them with spells he taught them to prevent them from shredding, and to catch the air better.

The repairs all hinged on the keel though: unless it could be re-bonded as good as new, the Air-gnosis needed to lift the craft would not be trapped, and it would be unable to stay aloft. Anyone with sylvan-gnosis worked on it constantly, regrowing the broken timber into a whole. Alaron watched the snake-creatures chant over it day and night for weeks, and it gradually fused again.

Those who didn't aid the repairs scoured the island, but there were few other signs of Cym's passing; just a couple of camping sites that might have been hers near the northern coast. It was tempting to stay here—indeed, some suggested it—but it wasn't safe; wind-ships passed overhead most days, and Imperial couriers riding winged constructs too. So they worked and rested and readied themselves for the journey onward.

All Alaron had to do was direct their efforts. It was strange to be in charge of something, to have these people taking his orders and listening attentively to his advice, but he was the only trained mage, so he had to step forward. Though his knowledge of many Studies was limited, he soon found that if he could explain the theory of a spell to them, they could invariably work out how to make it real.

When his skiff was finally ready, the lamiae celebrated with a feast of fish and birds held in the lee of the volcano slopes. They danced their eerie, snaky dances and played alien, strangely haunt-ing flute music. Alaron flew the skiff about the glade to demon-strate, and they all shrilled out cries of triumph. He managed to avoid crashing into any buildings too, he noted wryly to himself.

"What is its name?" Kekropius asked him after he landed.

Alaron blinked. He'd never named the craft, as it had been built to sell. His first instinct was to call it after Cym, but he suspected that would annoy her. "Seeker," he said, eventually.

"A good name," he said. Next morning, the name was embla-zoned on the stern.

They left Phaestos near the end of Septinon, as the moon waned. Alaron flew and his companions swam. He sensed some worry among the lamiae, that he might fly off on his own, but he owed them. They hit the coast of Verelon near the falls of the powerful Maeglin River, west of Cypinos during the Darkmoon. Sometimes they saw scavenger folk, but not many; the cliffs on this side of the Gulf of Silium did not have the same tidelands as the western shore. The greater risk was the Imperial road, which at times passed within a few miles of the coast, but they were careful.

Alaron stayed close to the lamiae and flew only at night. During the day, when not sleeping, he would continue scrying. Ildena grew more and more proficient and more confident. Fydro lost some of his wariness after he got her with child, and as her belly bulged, it took away some of her delicate grace. The lamiae's gestation was rapid, and he was vaguely horrified to realize that they gave birth to proto-eggs, though the eggs remained outside the body for only a few days, allowing the newborn to form properly outside the confines of the womb before breaking free.

But that was all still to come for Ildena, who continued to scry with him. They made some progress, beginning to pick up vague traces that teased him back to a conviction that Cym was alive after all, just out of reach. Scrying the Scytale gave him nothing: he'd barely seen it, and it was probably heavily warded. But as hope grew, his main war was with loneliness. He missed Ramon and Cym and sometimes daydreamed of Anise, the way her lips had tasted, but she was a vague memory and he struggled to recollect her face.

The new moon of Octen rose as they skirted the islands east of Thantis, the last major city in Verelon before the South Sydian plains. Without Alaron to slow them down the lamiae moved swiftly, and they had traversed Verelon swiftly, covering more than a thousand miles in two months. *Seeker* proved fast and resilient; with its armory of spells woven into it, it felt like he was flying a tiny warbird. Ramon would have drooled over it.

The breakthrough came as the full moon rose on what was becoming an increasingly rare clear night. The days were shortening, autumn hues were tinting the leaves and the wind was increasingly from the colder North. Alaron was scrying with three lamiae while the clan breakfasted at sunset, before the day's travel. Ildena was glowing with pride: she had reached the point where she could scry the ways ahead and help them avoid danger. Two other females, fierce Nia and sharp-tongued Vyressa, jealous of Ildena, had demanded the same training. No one questioned why he was seeking this girl, but "Cymbellea and Alaron" had become a romantic tale for the fireside and they were willing helpers.

Working together, holding Aggi between them, their scrying range was enhanced. They sent their mind's eyes out, seeking the spirits and ghosts, the myriad eyes of the otherness that saw so much more than human eyes ever could. They noted the windships and wagon-trains and cavalry patrols that were near, and guided the clan by ways unseen. They mapped paths to pass the coastal farms and scavenger villages. They saw the campfires of the Sydian horse clans, bringing the new yearlings to the cavalry buyers near the Imperial Road.

And one night they found her.

Black hair framed a finely chiseled face. Dancing eyes were wistful as she sat beside a fire, whittling at a piece of wood, carving it into a doll just like the one they held. Alaron's heart almost burst with wonder, and his eyes welled up. The lamiae women shrieked, "It is her!"

Alaron's eyes were still upon the tiny image in the water. She was wrapped in wards, but they were not well-set. He found a gap and sent a single word into her mind. <*Cym?*>

Her eyes jerked about, her expression going from panic to hope. <*Alaron?*>

The connection snapped. But it didn't matter. She was alive, and he knew where she was.

"*Got her,*" Boron Funt beamed. He reached for a sweetbread.

Malevorn stared. It had been weeks, and he'd almost given up. Their room was strewn with food and drink. The rest of the Fist were dining in the main hall, and outside the venators were swarming about two steer carcasses like a flock of gulls. "You've found the gypsy girl?"

Boron stabbed a greasy finger at the map. "Somewhere here, northeast of Thantis, near the coast." He swallowed noisily. "Mercer has found her: it was his scrying that led me to her. I was able to lock onto his scrying and follow what he saw."

"Kore's Blood, we're hundreds of miles away! Do you have a fix on Mercer?"

Boron shook his head. "I don't know, exactly. You can't follow a competent scryer back to their position, and it appears he's somehow become vaguely proficient. She was shielded too, but the spell locking her down was poor, otherwise neither Mercer nor I would have found her." He frowned. "Mercer's search was surprisingly strong. There were other presences, with strange mental signatures. He has help."

"I have to hand it to you, my friend," Malevorn said with grudging respect. It was easy to forget that beneath the gross exterior, Boron Funt was no fool. "We couldn't have done it without you."

It was true. Boron might not be able to walk one hundred paces without losing his breath, but he could work with his mind for hours on end. He'd been hunting the ether for weeks. A skilled mage could follow the mental traces of any other magi in his range, and Funt was undoubtedly skilled. Most magi in the empire had gone east, so if someone was out here scrying, Funt reasoned it was probably Mercer. It'd taken time, but he'd come through.

Malevorn peered at the map. "She's more than a thousand miles away," he breathed. The windship could make around twenty miles an hour with good winds, so two days' travel to where Boron had made the connection. Malevorn patted Funt on the shoulder. "Well done, my friend. I'll go and tell the Crozier."

He found Adamus in his office, speaking in a low voice to beautiful Virgina. When he went to leave again, Adamus waved him inside. "Later," he told Virgina. She wouldn't meet Malevorn's eyes as she left, leaving Malevorn wondering exactly what he'd interrupted.

The Crozier regarded him with hooded eyes. "So, my young Acolyte," he said into the ensuing silence.

Malevorn found his voice. "Your Worship, Boron has found the girl Mercer is hunting."

Adamus came alive. "He has? Excellent! Tell me."

Malevorn reported as swiftly as he could, his words running together as the eagerness took over. When he was done, Adamus stared into space, then stabbed a finger at the chair on the other side of his desk. "Sit."

Malevorn sat warily. "Your Worship?"

"Master Andevarion, I like you. I think we share a dedication to the empire and an unwillingness to tolerate fools." He poured two cups of wine and offered one to Malevorn. "We must find an understanding."

Malevorn took the cup, his mind racing. "What understanding, my lord?"

Adamus Crozier cocked his head. "Do you know what it is we seek, Malevorn?"

"Alaron Mercer, lord."

"You are a warrior. Your skills do not lend themselves to conspiracy." The Crozier looked at him with reptilian eyes. "Do not lie to me again."

Malevorn swallowed and decided that honesty was the only policy here. "There is an artifact involved."

"Do not name it." Adamus sipped his wine, then smiled. "Good, we understand each other. He who finds this thing has the opportunity to become great, but that requires knowledge. The artifact is a key; it is not the treasure. Those able to make full use of this thing are few, and clearly Mercer does not have access to such a person, for all he does is run and hide."

Mercer is a cretin. I'm going to roast him alive.

"Vordan knows about the artifact, but he and I do not see eye to eye. He wishes this thing to be returned to the Church, when his loyalty should be to the emperor."

"Commandant Vordan is a renowned warrior," Malevorn commented cautiously.

"He is. But I chose the Eighteenth Fist for this mission because you and Elath Dranid know Norostein, not because I wanted to work with Lanfyr Vordan. And your Fist was selected before we realized that this Mercer boy might be crucial. It feels like fate: I sense Kore's hand upon us. So it is important that we are allies in this matter. In my eyes you are a future Commandant, perhaps even more."

The Crozier needs my help. He felt a surge of pride. *But who says I couldn't work the Scytale out myself? I can swing a sword and use the gnosis, yes; but I can also think.* "Dranid and Vordan are skilled swordsmen and more senior than me."

"Indeed—Elath Dranid is the best swordsman in the Fist, I'm led to believe." His voice left a trailing question. "But I think they have peaked. You are still on the rise." The Crozier toasted him with his goblet. "When the time comes, this artifact will lead to conflict.

Vordan will want it for his faction and I for mine. Already they see you as being aligned to me."

No doubt why you've been sliming around me in the first place. "I see." *Sometimes you just have to pick a side.* "In this, my lord Crozier, I'm your man." He took a first sip of the wine. Brician chardo, like nectar. He smiled slowly.

Adamus lifted his wine cup. "Excellent. See that your friends Funt and Brother Dominic know which way the wind is blowing." He frowned. "We must get to this Alaron Mercer first."

15

DISSENT

Theurgy: Illusion

Men surround themselves with illusions. Most find reality just too hard. Only the great are prepared to deal with what truly is.

SERTAIN, ASCENDANT MAGE AND FIRST
EMPEROR OF RONDELMAR, PALLAS 421

North Javon, Antiopia
Rami (Septinon) 928
3rd month of the Moontide

"Come in, Magister," boomed Octa Dorobon, and Gurvon Gyle winced at the sheer loudness of the woman. *How does she keep any secrets at all, when she is audible across half a city?* But he kept his expression composed as he entered the Dorobon suite at this latest palace on the road to Brochena. Apparently Cera had stayed here on her way north. Now she was locked in a dungeon below. Instead, Octa, her son Francis, and daughter Olivia shared the main suite. All three were arrayed before him now. But they were not to whom he bowed first.

In the center of the darkened room, the transparent image of a woman's head and shoulders floated above a bowl of scented bubbling water, the image formed of steam, light, and the gnosis. Lucia Fasterius, Mater-Imperia of Rondelmar. "Your Holiness," he greeted his patron, while his mind leaped through the implications of her gnostic presence.

"Magister Gyle, welcome." Lucia greeted him with a warm smile, her image rotating to face him. Her voice echoed from the relay-staves. "My favorite Noroman. Again you have come through for us." Kind words, but at the back of her eyes lingered the memory of their last conversation, when he had brazenly demanded more money, having supposedly slain Fraxis Targon.

"The plan worked perfectly, Holiness," he responded cautiously. He sat in an empty seat beside Francis Dorobon. Both son and daughter looked awestruck to be in Lucia's ethereal presence.

"A pleasing change," Lucia replied with the faint hint of sarcasm. "My good friends the Dorobon are now free to occupy Brochena and bring Javon to heel. You may return to Pallas and collect your many rewards."

Ah, so that's what this is about.

"Would that I could in good conscience, Holiness," he replied, feigning regret. "But the job is only half done."

Octa Dorobon's florid face colored, a puce color that in most people would signify fury but in her meant only mild irritation. "My people can take this from here," she rumbled.

Gyle leaned forward, splitting his words between Octa and the phantasm of Lucia. "Mater-Imperia, Milady Dorobon, with utmost respect, you have ten thousand men and twenty-five magi or there-abouts. The windship flotilla has already left for Hebusalim. This is a nation of at least six million souls, and that's not counting the Harkun nomads. Only Hytel sympathizes with your cause, and mil-itarily they are broken."

"So are the Nesti," Francis Dorobon boasted. "And the Jhafi."

"That Nesti contingent was less than half their strength. Forensa is still fortified and on its own outnumbers you. As for the Jhafi, twenty thousand men slain or scattered is but a drop in the ocean. Without windships, your men will not have the freedom of the bat-tlefield. You cannot expect another Fishil Wadi next time you fight."

Francis listened, pouting a little, but he didn't interrupt or contradict.

Perhaps he isn't entirely stupid.

Lucia frowned. "I would have thought you eager to return home, Magister Gyle."

And face your anger, with nothing to hold over you? I think not. "I never leave a job half done, Holiness."

"I see no need for your services any longer," Octa belched.

He didn't flinch as he met her gaze. "Then you have the logistical problems of how to bivouac your troops in Brochena managed, milady? You know where to deploy them, to deter reprisals, and whom to contact among the provincial nobility to secure truces while you settle in? You know the state of the finances and the familial ties that can be used to manipulate the noble families? You already have your agents deployed in the field, and are aware of the Harkun concentration below the Rift? And you have hostages secured to paralyze your chief rivals?"

Octa glowered at him while Francis blinked owlishly and his sister licked her lips in surprise. He saw the siblings exchange a look. *Never seen Mommy spoken back to? Welcome to the new world.*

Lucia's voice cut across the silence. "Are you angling for more money, Gyle?" she asked, the hint of whimsy in her voice making the inquiry a jest, which it most certainly wasn't.

"Not at all, Holiness. I merely wish to ensure that all that we have worked toward is not lost through a hasty transition." He faced her fully. "Though the delay will give you time to ship the agreed amounts to my bankers at Jusst and Holsen."

Mater-Imperia tilted her head curiously, a half-smile brushing her lips. Once the bullion was with his bankers they would issue promissory notes redeemable by the Dorobon themselves, and he would not need to return to Pallas at all. "You have no official status, Gyle. It will be up to Octa whether she listens to you or not."

"Actually your Holiness, it will be up to the king, technically," Gyle reminded the room. He watched Francis blink at this thought. *Yes, boy: you're going to be given higher rank than Mommy . . .*

"My son is not king yet," Octa bellowed. "You'll do what I—"

"You said I was," Francis interrupted her, his voice caught between indignation, fear, and daring. "You said so last night. 'My little king,' you called me. And I'm of age." His sister looked like she'd just wet herself with excitement.

"It was a term of endearment, child," Octa replied. "And you are not king until crowned."

"Octa darling," Lucia put in smoothly, her expression thoughtful, "in the end, we all have to let go. It is painful, but eventually our sons become men."

"But he is still so young," Octa wobbled, her knuckles white on the arms of her throne, clinging on fixedly. "He is barely out of the Arcanum."

"Transitions are painful, my dear," Lucia told her, "but nothing lasts forever. We must emerge from periods of change still bound together in love."

Gyle wondered why this conversation was happening in front of him. Lucia did nothing on a whim. *Perhaps she's disciplining Octa, reminding her that she might have a new kingdom to play in, but she remains her servant. Perhaps she already has her claws into Francis? Kore knows he's more tractable than Octa.*

Octa Dorobon bowed her head. "My son will be crowned as soon as it is practical."

"Excellent. And he must also be wed," Lucia told her.

"I have several brides in mind among the young women of Pallas," Octa replied, fixing her eye on her son.

"And do you have a favorite?" Lucia asked, her image spinning to face Francis.

Francis ducked his head. His sister Olivia leaned forward, her eyes bright. "Franny's been meeting the locals," she chortled, then remembered herself. "Erm, your Holiness."

The faint warmth on Lucia's face drained a little. "Who?" Her image floated toward Francis. "Who, boy?"

"Portia Tolidi," Francis mumbled.

"I see," Lucia said, musingly. Octa went to make an angry comment, but she cut her off. "Tell me of her, young Francis. Is she pretty?"

Francis glanced at Octa. "She is the most beautiful woman in the world," he replied earnestly.

"How lovely. She is Rimoni, yes?"

"Pure Rimoni, Ma'am," Francis replied eagerly, his face lit by young lust. "She is of old senatorial stock among the Rimoni, and so fair-skinned she is almost white. Her hair is red-brown, like a rippling waterfall of bronze, flecked by gold as it catches the light."

Lucia laughed. "You are a poet, young Francis." Gyle could see the brittle anger behind her amiable façade. "Is she willing?"

Francis blinked, his eyes going to his mother's face. Octa scowled, as if to say, *This is your problem.* "Your Holiness?"

"I asked: is she willing? Does the degenerate slut spread herself for you willingly, or do you prefer rape?"

Francis went scarlet. "Uh . . . uh . . . I *love* her, your Holiness."

Olivia dissolved into giggles. Octa all but spat.

"Of what value is this Rimoni whore?" Lucia asked coldly. "Her family are broken, and I am told she is the last survivor of one of Alfredo's cousin's lines, with little or no influence. And far from a virgin even before you began rutting with her, I've no doubt."

Francis went the same puce as his mother. "She is a vision of loveliness."

"Of course she is," Lucia sneered. "We've all felt that way once, boy. But your mother knows what you need, and it isn't some Rimoni quim latching on to you. You are a Dorobon, descended of the Blessed Three Hundred. Father bastards all you like, but you will marry pure."

Francis hung his head resentfully.

"I thought you versed in politics, Francis," Lucia scolded, while Octa glowed. "You think to be king, but to me you are behaving like any callow boy who's just discovered what the tool between his legs is for."

That's pretty much the sum of it, Gyle thought. But it was time to rescue the young man, and win a friend. "With respect, Mater-Imperia, I believe that Francis has been playing his hand very well indeed."

Lucia's image turned to him, her face measuring. "How so, Magister?"

Gyle bowed to acknowledge that she had allowed him to voice a contrary opinion. "Holiness, Francis has known all his life that he is to rule Javon. He has studied the land from afar." His eyes strayed to Francis; he was listening intently, nodding to himself as if to say, "Yes, this is so." "Francis knows that to win hearts, he must show manliness and mastery. What better way to do so than to take the most beautiful woman in Javon to his bed? In doing so, he shows that he is willing to be a part of this land, but also that he will rule it, as he rules her. And though the Gorgio are reduced, they will recover. They have mining wealth and many new slaves. They will rise again, and they will remember that Francis favors one of their own."

Lucia regarded him steadily. "Go on."

"Francis knows that his love for the girl is transitory." He met the young man's eyes, fixed them firmly. *Yes, boy: all love passes.* "But what better way to learn the arts of love than with as magnificent a creature as the Tolidi girl? He will take others to his bed also, to show mastery and favor. Great kings have many mistresses."

"My son will marry a Rondian mage," bellowed Octa.

He ignored her. "Francis has studied Javonesi law. He knows already that as King of Javon he may take as many wives as he likes." *Well, he knows now.*

Octa's eyes bulged. So did Francis's, but in a different way. Olivia's jaw flopped open.

"It is true, Holiness," Gyle told Lucia. "This is a Rimoni and Jhafi land: under al-Shaar, the law of the Prophet, a man may take many wives. This is enshrined in the throne of Javon, as under their constitution the king is of both faiths. There are even Rimoni kings who have taken both a Rimoni and Jhafi wife."

"My son is here to overthrow the Javon kingship, not adopt it," Octa shouted, half-rising before the effort of supporting her own weight became too much and she sagged back into her throne.

"My dear Octa is quite correct," Lucia said, her eyes glittering dangerously. "We are not going to perpetuate their pagan vices."

"Holiness, I would contend that were Francis to take wives from among the Javonesi as well as contenders of his mother's choice, it would strengthen his hold on power."

"How so?" Lucia asked, before the purple-faced Octa could vent her invective.

"As I have already said, our forces here are badly outnumbered. Once the Crusade is over, Imperial ability to support this monarchy reduces even further. To establish the Dorobon here with any chance of longevity, some degree of assimilation is required. Hostages are needed to pacify the great families, and wives make excellent hostages. So do young sons as pages. Men whose heirs are hostages, but have hope of some title and influence when they are grown, are less inclined to rebel. Show a willingness to meet the ways of the people and you blunt their blades."

He glanced sideways at Francis. He was gazing into space, his mind clearly taking in the thought of having as many wives as he wanted. *Bait taken.* He smiled inwardly.

"To compromise is to show weakness," Octa snarled.

"Not so. Compromise is a show of strength," Gyle countered. "The brittle blade breaks. Good steel bends and springs back."

Lucia studied him, while her tongue slid about her lips. "You have the Nesti girl in your custody, do you not?" she said, turning to Octa.

Octa scowled. "She will be executed publicly when we reach Brochena."

"I also hold her younger brother, the previous king-elect, Timori," Gyle put in.

"And refuses to hand him over," Octa snarled.

Lucia released a small chuckle, showing her perfect teeth. "Regard this man, Octa dear. He is a snake, but a most useful one. Do you remember the old Sollan fable of Empress Delfa and her viper? The one who killed all her husband's enemies, then turned on her when she would not give it her only child to eat? I sometimes wonder when I shall have to deal with him as Delfa dealt with her pet."

Gyle went to one knee. "You know I am your servant, Holiness."

"Give the young king to Octa."

"I will surrender him," Gyle agreed. "When Francis is crowned . . . and has married Cera Nesti."

"Vermin," Octa snarled. "Lucia, allow me to have him beheaded."

Gyle stayed on one knee, watching Lucia's image.

The Emperor's mother considered. "And no doubt have this Timori slip through our fingers and the kingdom also?" Her face loomed larger and floated toward Gyle. "Magister, I do not appreciate your manipulations."

"Holiness, a viper has no legs. His belly is always to the ground. He can move only by coiling and twisting. It is his nature. But he has his uses." He met her eyes. "I assure you that unless Francis can bind the Javonesi to him, with hostages and marriages, this kingdom will rise against him en masse, and he will need ten legions, not two, if his head is not to end up on a spike."

Lucia stared. She clearly wished to contact him directly, but this mode of communication restricted that option. She was compelled to speak aloud, before witnesses. He of course had the same restriction. But there were other ways to communicate.

He pulled out a gold coin, showed it to her, then pocketed it again.

Her eyes went round.

Message received: I have your precious, utterly embarrassing daughter.

"Magister," Lucia said slowly. "You may have a point."

Octa looked as if she'd just been forced to drink urine. "Lucia, I . . ." Her voice trailed away as the image of the Living Saint turned to her, her very serenity of visage a threat. "We are always happy to receive Magister Gyle's advice. We shall consider it."

"Do," Lucia told her. "He is usually worth listening to." She glanced sideways at him. "And watching."

Gyle became aware that Olivia and Francis were staring at him with something like hero worship in their eyes. But their mother's eyes could have immolated him. He pressed home his advantage. "Holiness, it is normal in any allied kingdom to appoint an Imperial Envoy until more formal arrangements are in place. Though I am not of the Imperial bureaucracy, I have experience of local conditions. I believe that I would make an excellent Imperial Envoy until Francis is crowned."

Octa swallowed and her cheeks went scarlet, but when Lucia nodded shortly, she was forced to swallow her rage. She swept up her goblet and drained it furiously, then crushed it and dropped it to the floor.

"Magister, there is none better placed, *at present*," Lucia said slowly. "And I will consider the marriage question further. There may be something in what you say."

Francis and Olivia's mouth flopped open. Gyle could scarcely contain his own amusement at their expressions. *Yes, I won. Take note, children.* "I hear and understand, Holiness."

"Do you? Listen to me, Gurvon Gyle. I will appoint you as Imperial Envoy until Francis is crowned. I will then allow him to give you whatever title he sees fit. And I will send you the gold you crave." Her face flashed malevolently. "You will send me two persons, one who was yours, and one who was mine. Meet my expectations, and all will be well between us. Fail to deliver, and frankly, I will tear down Hel to find you."

He bowed his head. *Elena and Coin.* So be it.

The meeting ended without formalities. Lucia snapped "Octa," at the Dorobon matriarch and vanished. The silence she left was a living, palpable thing. Francis and his sister were staring back and forth between Octa, the tyrant who ruled their existence, and him.

Yes, I just faced down the most powerful person on Urte. No one is as almighty as they like you to think.

He bowed to Octa, to Francis. "My lady Dorobon, my lord: I bid you good night."

Brochena, Javon, Antiopia
(Rami) Septinon 928
3rd month of the Moontide

Something had changed on the journey south. At first Cera had been treated as a prisoner, but a few days north of Brochena, her status changed and she suddenly became something more like a guest. She could not go anywhere, but she and Tarita were given a better pavilion, and improved food and wine.

Entering the city was an awful experience. The populace were cowed by the Rondian legions led by magi on horned construct-steeds or hovering above in skiffs. The Nesti Counselors had already fled to Forensa, together with their remaining allies and troops, but the common people were tied to their homes and workplaces. They came out onto the streets to watch the hated Dorobon enter. The womenfolk who'd lost men in the slaughter of the Jhafi at Fishil Wadi wailed and tore at their hair, wrenching out whole tresses in their grief. Public mourning was a tradition here, a collective madness that could easily get out of hand. Tarita told Cera about mourning women setting themselves alight with lamp-oil, or publicly slashing their own wrists. Cera dreaded what they might do if they stormed her carriage, so she kept her windows closed as they wound through the sullen, disbelieving crowds, peering through the cracks in the shutters.

To her further surprise, she was given rooms in the palace, the lesser quarters she'd occupied as a child. Francis Dorobon now had the royal suite, of course, and his mother and sister the one next door. Her nearest neighbor in the palace was Portia Tolidi. They let her keep Tarita, through Gyle's intervention. Gyle had evidently been rewarded: everyone was calling him "Imperial Envoy" now, and he was ordering the stiff-backed Dorobon nobles around with sardonic condescension. New battle lines were being drawn in an elaborate game she couldn't grasp.

The defeat at Fishil Wadi was now a month ago, and she feared that she'd sold her soul for nothing. The days passed and only Gyle had any time for her. They made her eat at the high table, but no one spoke to her. She clung to small hopes: Gyle had intimated that he held Timori, not the Dorobon. He still spoke of her becoming Francis Dorobon's bride to stave off any thought of a mass uprising, but it felt increasingly unlikely. She could not go out, and Gyle had used his gnosis to seal the secret passages shut. Meanwhile Francis bedded Portia, and boasted of it at the table.

That night was yet another feast. Tarita had put her into a pleasing enough dress, and now she sat alone, watching the room. It was a celebration: Francis Dorobon had received the pledges of the leading citizens of Brochena: mostly merchants, and of course the bureaucracy led by Don Francesco Perdonello. The aristocratic face of the chief civil servant showed no emotion as he renounced fealty to the Nesti and swore to the Dorobon. He'd not looked at her. She knew he was doing what anyone would do, just trying to survive, but right then, she hated him.

Now all was laughter and gorging on good food and wine. She toyed with her meal, sickened beyond eating.

"Princessa, may I join you?" asked a cool voice in Rimoni.

She turned her head find Portia Tolidi standing over her. *Come to gloat, have you?* Her mood blackened, but she could not risk a scene when so many here despised her. "I cannot prevent it."

Portia tilted her head, causing a ripple of gorgeous red-gold hair to catch the torchlight. "Of course you can. With a word. I have no desire to torment you." Her voice was deeper than most women and sounded very sophisticated to Cera. She bit her lip in jealousy.

She helped Tarita survive the massacre last year, she reminded herself. *She may not be all bad.* "Then sit, for the sake of my maid."

Portia's mouth softened a fraction. She sat gracefully. "Grazie, Princessa. How is Tarita?"

Tarita, who was your brother's lover. "She is as well as can be." She met Portia's eyes cautiously. "She has great anger and sorrow."

"And so do I."

"Excuse me if I do not see that. All I see is one doing well for herself by her collaboration with an invader."

Portia didn't grow angry and leave as she'd hoped she might. Instead she flinched, as though ashamed. "Do not think that all the Gorgio wanted the Dorobon to return," she said in a soft voice. "And anyway, is not 'collaboration' also your intention?"

"It was never *my* intention."

"Then Magister Gyle's," Portia responded. "He praises you to Francis. It angers Octa."

That made her heart go cold. Octa Dorobon frightened her. "Then he must stop speaking well of me."

"He should, if he values you," Portia agreed. She leaned forward. "Have you heard his latest proposal? He has told Francis that under the constitution of Javon, a king may take multiple wives—a harem, like the Amteh do." She made the Sol-sign against blasphemy. "The constitution allows it, he says, for in theory, a Javon king must be Amteh as well."

Cera swallowed. *A harem? Gyle is insane.* "Is this true?"

"Don Perdonello's lawyers say it is. Gyle tells Francis that taking a wife from each of the important families will tie them to him, especially once he fathers children on them."

Cera tried to see if Portia felt threatened by this, but she couldn't tell. Her perfect heart-shaped face was devoid of emotion, so much so that it suddenly occurred to her that Portia might be no more willing to bed Francis Dorobon than she was. Though in Portia's case, he was already rukking her nightly. "How do you feel about it?"

Portia's eye's narrowed faintly and flickered about the hall. They were tired, those eyes, as if she slept poorly. Tarita said Francis rode her for hours at a time. Cera also scanned the room; no one was watching them that she could see. Octa and her daughter were staring sourly at Gyle, who was in the midst of some anecdote that had the knights about Francis howling with laughter. Even Alfredo Gorgio was laughing despite himself. "Francis is an overgrown child with a cruel mind," Portia murmured. "You are lucky that your Jhafi looks repel him."

Perhaps I am. But Gyle wants me to marry him . . . And Portia's attitude of sympathy puzzled her; the Gorgio were noted for their disdain of the native Jhafi. But Portia sounded compassionate. *And she aided Tarita*, she reminded herself again: a little Jhafi maid whom her beloved brother was bedding. "Francis seems besotted by you," she noted.

"He likes sticking his dildus in me, that is all," Portia replied crudely. "Apart from that he has no regard for anything I say or do." She looked at Cera sideways. "So, Cera Nesti: do you think that it is possible for us to be friends?"

Friends? "I will be dead soon. One way or the other. What is the point?"

"If you were truly going to kill yourself, you'd have found a way by now. Me too. I think we are both survivors."

Cera studied the other woman. Portia was almost five years older than she was, and far more beautiful. Her pale skin was radiant, her nose small and delicate, faintly freckled by the sun, her mouth a rosebud. She had hazel eyes and bewitching hair. She was dauntingly lovely. If Portia was a survivor, it could not have been an arduous task. But she respected the offer. "We shall have to see, I think."

"Who knows, we may end up as sister-wives," Portia said softly. "Don't tell anyone I told you." She winked, then rose and glided back to Francis's side. He stood and wrapped his arm around her, which forced all the other guests to stand also. Cera reluctantly joined them.

"It's to bed!" Francis shouted, showing off his lovely consort. "May you all have as lively a time of it as I!"

She looked for reluctance, for a sign of distress, on the face of Portia, but saw none. Only desire filled her beautiful face as she clung to the young ruler.

One way or the other, she is a fine actress.

Gurvon Gyle pulled his eye from the spy-hole, tiring of the sight of Francis Dorobon's ample buttocks as they humped up and down between Portia Tolidi's perfectly formed, spread-eagled legs. There would be no more conversation worth overhearing tonight. But the idea he'd set in motion had hooked the young man, that was clear. He'd spoken of it to Portia again; he was smugly taken with the idea of a harem dedicated entirely to his own gratification. What Portia Tolidi thought, he couldn't tell. She appeared to have no personality at all.

He nudged Hesta, who was using the other spy-hole a foot away. *<Stay with them until they are done. Report to me in the morning.>*

The Lantric witch half-smiled. *<What, not stirred by young Dorobon's efforts?>*

He closed his spy-hole. *<I've never seen such an unimaginative young man. I almost pity the girl.>*

Hesta tutted softly. *<A waste of a true beauty. The things I would do to her.>*

<Stay away from her, you old prune. The last thing I need is trouble between us and the Dorobon.>

Hesta licked her lips with a wry grin. *<As you command, O great leader.>*

He looked at her sternly. <*Who are you seeing at the moment, Hesta?*>

The Lantric witch grinned slyly. <*No one. I'm doing as I'm told, and celibate as an Anchorite.*> She made a reflective face. <*Now there's a thought: a pretty young nun . . . Did the Dorobon bring any?*>

<*No,*> he chuckled. <*Mind on the job.*> He slipped away into the darkened passages, emerging a minute later into his own room on the lower floor. He went to the one lamp and lengthened the wick so that the room brightened. He could almost feel the palace settling in for the night. The Matriarch would be in the chapel, praying to Kore. Olivia would be eating supper. Cera was under the eye of a female Dorobon mage he'd co-opted, an arrogant but capable young quarter-blood called Madeline Parlow.

He pulled out a relay-stave from his wardrobe, gripped it and sent his mind questing out into the night, calling cautiously into the ether. A darkly beautiful male face appeared in his vision almost immediately: Rashid Mubarak, Emir of Halli'kut. His mental touch was like perfumed silk.

<*Sal'Ahm, Magister Gyle. I was not expecting to hear from you.*>

<*Save the pleasantries, emir. Why was I assailed by Stivor Sindon and men of your Ordo Costruo faction?*>

Rashid sounded amused. <*Nothing to do with me, my friend. A regional commander of the Hadishah must have authorized the strike. I trust you are unharmed?*> His concern sounded anything but genuine.

<*Call them off.*>

Rashid gave him a crooked smile that promised nothing. <*I have news that Brochena has fallen to the Dorobon.*>

<*It has. Rashid, get Sindon off my back or you will lose him.*>

The emir's mental demeanor changed subtly. <*Magister Gyle, our agreement covers certain aspects of the theater of war, not all of it. No amnesty was ever agreed between us. We remain enemies, Magister. You would do well to remember that.*>

<*And you would do well to remember that I can nullify your agreement with the emperor with a single word.*>

Rashid paused, frowning. He bared his teeth momentarily, then nodded. <*So you can, Magister. I will call Magister Sindon off. I suspect that with the advantage of surprise gone his chances of success are limited anyway.*>

They broke the connection without pleasantries. The relay-stave was almost burned out anyway. He poured himself a nip of whisky, savoring the smoky taste on his tongue before swallowing. The one perk of dealing with the Dorobon was that their lands in Rondelmar were famous for the potent spirit. Then there was a knock at the door, and he reflected that there were other benefits was well.

Olivia Dorobon slid her ample body through the door when he opened it and fell eagerly into his arms. She was voluptuous, bordering on plump, but eager—definitely that. And there was much to be said for eager.

"Tell me more of yourself, Yvette." Gyle could speak aloud to her now. Her eardrums had rebuilt themselves sufficiently, and the lobes he'd severed from a freshly dead young man had now integrated with the rest of her mutable flesh. The new eyes were almost functional too, but they were too newly settled to be used; there was still a bandage over them.

"Why should I do that?" Coin's voice was still barely comprehensible, but he listened with his mind as well as his ears.

"I like to know the people I work with," he replied reasonably.

"The people you use," Coin corrected.

"Being a captain of magi is all about knowing the people around you," he said softly. "I care about all those I work with." It was an utter lie, but Coin was a child, intellectually.

"No one cares about me, not even Mother."

Your mother is the coldest being on this planet. He touched her hand gently. "Yvette, for someone to care about you, you need to share something of yourself."

Coin's head lolled sideways toward him, the bandaged eyes giving it a blank strangeness that was unsettling. But at least it was easier to look at than the skinless mess of flesh slowly regrowing over her torso and arms, the naked sinew and organs pulsing wetly with every heartbeat, every shuddering breath.

"What would you like me to share?" she asked contemptuously. "My beauty? My merry nature?"

"How old are you?" he asked her, his voice dispassionate.

"Twenty-seven. Mother sent me away. I was raised by priests of the Kore."

"When did you discover the gnosis?"

"When I was ten—it came early for me, they said."

"How did it manifest?"

"I changed shape—I made my cleft close, because I was ashamed of it. I wanted to be a boy, like the young priests. They were my friends."

Gyle raised his eyebrows. A mage's first expression of the gnosis was almost always elemental, not one of the more difficult Studies. For her to go straight to morphic-gnosis spoke volumes of her affinity. "Then what happened?"

"One of my friends, one of the novices, wanted me to be a girl so that he could lie with me. The older priests saw what was happening and I was taken away from the monastery and sent back to Pallas. To Mother."

Gyle squeezed her half-formed hand gently. It felt wet and raw, and left a smear of blood on his fingers. "And then?"

"I was given a tutor: Renata, an Arcanum woman:. She was Palacian, one of my cousins. She trained me."

Gyle knew the name. "She's dead now, isn't she?"

The lack of lips made it look like Coin was grinning. "I killed her. She lost her temper with me, so I made her heart stop." Her mental voice was hollow but satisfied. "I hated her."

Gyle felt his complacency evaporate. Willing another's heart to stop was not easy at all. *She's a pure-blood, Gurvon, four times more powerful than you are. Never forget that.* "What came after that?" he asked carefully.

"Mother taught me how to become other people: I had to learn their shape and their mind, and use mesmerism to get inside their heads. Mysticism would work better, but I have no affinity for it. So I'm better at impersonating a person's shape than their behaviors."

Gyle had already noted that trait in her. "Who is your father, Yvette?"

"Wanting to know if it's my mother's brother, are you?" she said with tired bitterness. "That was a lie: one that my *father*—the Emperor Hiltius, my mother's husband—allowed to be spread, to explain why I was a freak. I hated him for that. I was glad when he died."

When your mother killed him, you mean? Or do you even guess at that?

"I've never believed that piece of gossip," he told her, not entirely truthfully. "It must have been hard for you to grow up this way."

Coin turned her head away. "It was Hel."

"But you helped the family by killing the Duke of Argundy?"

Coin's voice turned reflective. "Mother said he was plotting against the empire and she wanted Echor to take over as Duke." She giggled faintly. "I bet she regrets that now."

I'm sure she does. "Do you have any friends?"

Coin went still, and then slowly shook her head. "How can I? I am never me."

I am never me. He thought about that. "I know what you mean, Yvette. I too have to spend much time pretending to be someone else. Being 'me' is a luxury. We're not so unalike."

"It's not the same," Coin rasped. "I've never been me, not since the monastery. I don't even know who 'me' is." Her hideously grinning flayed skull turned to him, her voice going from empty to suddenly full. "I can be *anyone else* you want me to be. *Anyone at all.* But I don't know how to be me."

"I'll help you find your true self," he promised, because it was what she wanted to hear.

16

COMMON GROUND

The nature of God

I say this, that there is one God, and that God is known by the Amteh as Ahm and the Omali as Aum, and the Sollan as Sol. One God, with many faces. If we can reconcile ourselves to this fact, then there will be peace in all of Ahmedhassa. You will note I exclude the God of the Kore, for this Corineus is merely a fabrication of Shaitan to justify the powers of these afreet they call Magi.

IMAM ALI-ZAYIN, HERETICAL GODSPEAKER,
AT HIS TRIAL AT SAGOSTABAD, KESH, 698

All gods are equal. Equally imaginary.

ANTONIN MEIROS, 791

Mount Tigrat, Javon, Antiopia
Shawwal (Octen) 928
4th month of the Moontide

Kazim pictured an attacker, a spearman, lunging at his back; he spun, blocked high and then thrust, driving him backward, before finishing with a lateral sweep of the blade. Decapitation. He froze,

examining the positioning of his feet. *Too close together.* He practiced the move again and again, until he was regularly finishing
with a stronger stance. He exhaled slowly, then straightened as the
dust he'd kicked up swirled all around the little courtyard.

A surreal rhythm had settled over the old monastery as the days
turned to weeks, the hours emptied of everything but the blade in
his hand and the enemies in his head. Each day he pushed himself
a little harder, a little longer. The time it was taking to regain his
strength told him how close he'd come to dying of Mara Secordin's
venom, and reminded him again that he owed Elena Anborn his life.

That thought led his mind to the garden on the other side of the
monastery. It had better air, better sun, more room—but he refused
to go there, because that was where Elena trained. He was still
struggling to deal with her as a person and as a woman. In Lakh,
men and women lived shared lives, but the distinctions between
roles and duties was been well-defined: men led and protected and
women provided and obeyed. In Kesh, the divisions were even
more pronounced; men and women lived almost entirely separate
lives from childhood until marriage, and even then everywhere was
segregated, from the Dom al'Ahms to the public baths. They even
lived in separate parts of their homes.

But Elena acknowledged no such rules.

There were a few women in the Kalistham. They were of two
sorts: dutiful wives and deceitful harlots. Elena was neither. She was
like no one he'd ever imagined existing. She was *only* a woman, but
she was as fast as any man he'd seen. Part of him longed to cross
blades with her, to test her—*no, to put her in her place.* He knew
how Haroun would see her: as a deceitful harlot. But she'd not lied
to him, so far as he could tell. He avoided her as much as he could
for she had no sense of propriety. When he told her that the way
she dressed offended him she'd just laughed—but then she'd taken
to covering herself more modestly in front of him, an unexpected
concession. And she spoke of interesting things: magi, and wars in
Yuros. Her manner affronted him, but she had a strange fascination
too. Though she did not conform to his idea of femininity, he could
not deny her grace of movement.

He took a swallow of water and tried to put her from his mind. She too was training hard. She claimed that the afreet that had possessed her had neglected her body, something he shied from thinking about. The idea of someone inhabiting another's body was nauseating, and of course it made her doubly nefara.

"What does nefara even mean?" she'd asked him over breakfast a week ago when he'd used the term to describe one of the deceitful harlots from the Kalistham.

"Nefara women are impure and unholy. They have polluted themselves. They corrupt any man who—" He broke off and coughed, suddenly embarrassed. "Anyone who has congress with a nefara woman must purify themselves or Shaitan will reap their soul."

She'd raised her eyebrows in that quizzical way she had. She had little respect for holy things, even the teachings of her own heathen religion. "How does a woman become nefara, then?"

"Many ways." He frowned, trying to remember what Haroun had taught him on the journey north through the desert. "Any major sin pollutes them—lying, theft, murder, adultery. Unnatural acts with a man or a beast. Performing witchcraft. Failure to attend prayer . . . There are so many." He faltered a little as his memory faded. "Wearing red clothing," he added hesitantly. "And drinking urine."

She'd laughed. "Drinking piss!"

"It is a sin."

"But who the hell would drink piss?" she demanded, slapping her thighs with mirth. "Or do you mean alcohol?"

"Do not mock. You are nefara yourself."

That stopped her, though not out of respect or anguish at the state of her soul. She'd choked on her water and fled for the privy, still snorting with laughter. He liked to think that Ahm would chastise her for that.

He sighed heavily and decided that enough was enough. He went to his new sleeping chamber. It was bigger, and on a higher level than the tiny cell he'd first slept in—it had probably belonged to one of the more senior monks. Elena had the other similarly sized room down the corridor. It had a better mattress too, one she'd brought from Brochena months ago. He'd swept his cell, even though such work was beneath a warrior—but who else was going to do it? It had a view of her training garden and he tried not to look down there, although sometimes when she was down there performing her deadly dervish dance it was difficult not to stare.

I'm learning where her weaknesses are, he told himself. So far he hadn't spotted any.

Elena pulled on a clean salwar kameez and smoothed it down, then wrapped her hair in a towel. Then she gathered her soaked training clothes and headed for the laundry. On the way past Kazim's room she knocked on the door. "Hey Brother, I'm going to do some women's work. Throw out your laundry." They'd each been doing their own, mostly to teach him that she wasn't his servant, but she decided the point had been made and she could afford to be generous.

No reply. "Hey!" She poked her nose through the door, wincing at the sound of her own voice. That damned throat wound had left it deeper and she hated it.

Kazim appeared wearing nothing but a towel, and she stopped, struck by his physique. His hair was longer now, tied back in a loose ponytail, and he was freshly washed. His still-damp bronze skin glowed in the half-light and any Pallas sculptor would have paid good coin to use his body, a study in lean musculature, as a model.

She forgot what she was going to say.

"What do you want?" he asked coldly, his voice a bucket of cold water.

Grow up, Ella! She sobered quickly. "Would you like me to wash your dirty clothes?"

He frowned. "So long as I don't have to do yours."

She half smiled. "No."

He indicated a mound of clothing lying around his bed, then walked back into the niche he was using as a dressing-room.

She picked up his clothes, then after a moment, took his sheets as well. They had a stale musk that was both unpleasant and enticing. She felt enveloped in his scent as she hefted the pile and took it down to the laundry room. It set off an unexpected reaction inside her, the musky tang of fresh male sweat bringing Lorenzo back to her, reminding her of what she was missing. She remembered all over again that he was dead, but now she thought of the good things too: the way he smiled, the way he kissed, the way he laughed. She hurried to the laundry, thrust the clothing into the great stone trough and set the taps running. *Get over it, girl.* But a gnawing hunger had been set off, as if a starving man had smelled cooking food, and she couldn't stop salivating inside.

That night, sitting alone after her meal, she gave in and opened a bottle of red wine. It went straight to her head. She was wise enough to stop after two glasses, and she took herself to bed before she decided to wake Kazim up and get into some stupid argument over his idiotic ideas about the world. She lay awake in the warm night, her stomach churning as she tried not to think about the way Sordell had poked and prodded at her body in full knowledge that what he was doing disgusted her.

But he's gone now. This body is my own.

She stroked her breasts slowly, fighting the urge to be sick. *It's mine. My own.* She shuddered, felt her gorge rise, and swallowed a mouthful of acidic bile. *No, Rutt. I won't let you keep this hold over me. I'm going to forget you, even if I have to erase my own mind.*

She pushed her hands down the flat plain of her belly. Her body was returning to its peak: strong, lean, and toned. After all the indignities Sordell had put it through, she finally felt like herself again. To prove it, she combed her fingers through the soft, fine hair of her mound, then pushed her forefinger into her cleft. It was dry, but only for a few seconds. She swirled the slick fluids over her nub and sighed as a shiver stole over her.

This is my body. I reclaim it.

Turn. Lunge, retract, spin, and duck. Kazim felt a flash of panic as a movement caught the corner of his eye, throwing him off balance. Elena was watching from the doorway. He stopped, panting, and glared at her. "What do you want?"

"We should train together," she replied bluntly.

He went stock-still. "Why?"

"Because men move differently to training routines. Because your technique is flawed and will get you killed."

He scowled. "My technique is perfect."

She lifted her eyebrows. "Come prove it. If you're up to it." She vanished from the opening.

He glared after her, furious. *How dare she?* He'd been taught by some of the Hadishah's best. *Who did this bitch think she was?* But he was following her up the stairs before he'd even thought it through.

She waited for him in the garden, on the central bridge; a curved stone arch with a knee-high wall either side above a dry pond. She held a wooden stave the size of a sword. She tossed him another. "Basic movements."

He caught the staff, took its balance and measure, then swished it about. She was almost a foot shorter and maybe two-thirds his weight, so she had a far shorter reach. But she was also a mage, with full access to her gnosis.

"No magic, jadugara," he growled. She'd not freed his gnosis, despite their agreement, and he'd not complained, for he loathed the very thought of it most of the time. But right now the fact that she could use her magic against him made his skin crawl.

"I won't need it," she answered blithely, making his hackles rise.

All right, you. He stalked toward her. *Basic moves—ha!* He went high, left-right, then low, right-left. Cross blow, right to left, then back again. She parried each casually, her movements economical.

"*Hyar!*" he cried as he lashed out at her face, bucked forward, and hacked at her legs with his right foot.

Except she'd already wafted away. She went under his high thrust and lunged. The tip of her stave took him in the groin, all the air went out of him in one painful gust and he collapsed, moaning, on the bridge.

"Just the basic moves, Brother," she said flatly.

He gasped for breath and slowly clambered to his feet. Part of him was utterly furious, desperate to launch himself at her, but the other part, the one that connected his balls to his brain, probably, was screaming at him to slow down and go easy.

He'd never been good at listening to that part of himself.

He roared, and launched a series of overhead blows culminating in a charge that she sidestepped with almost contemptuous ease before pirouetting and kicking him off the bridge. He grazed his knees and palms as he landed, but didn't pause; instead, he erupted in a leap that took him back onto the rim of the bridge, all the while swearing belligerently, until she swiped him across the throat and left him choking and fearing a broken windpipe. He went again, though, until she smacked her stave across both shoulders, then thrust it into his belly, leaving him winded on the ground once again.

"Are you ready to play nicely yet?" she asked drily.

He tried to look up at her, to let her know just how much he hated her at that instant, but his eyes were watering too much to see if she noticed. *All right, bitch. Point made, and taken.*

Thus began a new phase, like a new moon rising. He put aside his pride and went back to basics, and as he listened to her, he found she had much to say that he could value. To his surprise she made him start each day with yoga, the slow exercise technique developed in Lakh. He'd always disdained it as womanly—a man's exercise should be vigorous—but to his chagrin, he found the positions harder than he had thought. He still couldn't see the point, until she challenged him to skewer a specific knot on a wooden post with his blade. Most times he missed, though only by inches, but she could do it every time. "Control," she kept saying. "Every blow must count."

It wasn't just yoga. She made him run and skip, and drill for hours. She ruthlessly eviscerated his fencing technique, showing him all the bad habits he'd never suspected. It was a painful experience, his ego taking as many blows as his body. She was a Rondian, and a woman—and not even a big one. There was no visible sign that she was using the gnosis, but she could block every move, match him blow for blow and anticipate all he did.

She taught him how to anticipate, how to read movements, how this thrust leads to that riposte, and how to use that knowledge to deceive an opponent. Their sparring gradually evolved to an almost ritualized dance.

But he couldn't lay a blade on her. It was galling—freakish; he'd sparred with enough people in the past year or so to know that even a badly outmatched fighter occasionally got lucky. But it was as if she saw all he did before it happened, and she was able to evade everything he tried, which made him mutter darkly to himself that she was cheating, using the gnosis after all. But when he accused her, she just laughed. *And chod, she could move!* She was like liquid, like air, flowing from place to place in an eye-blink. His blows were always a split-second too slow. She made him feel clumsy as a baby elephant.

There was a beauty in it, in her—not in her weathered face or her spare form but in the perfection of her balance and poise, her elegant motion. She danced through his dreams as she did through his days, humiliating him, both awake and asleep. He hated her. He envied her. He even admired her, grudgingly.

The bout began like any other: him scrabbling in the dust at her feet clutching a knee she'd rapped forcefully when he'd parried too slowly. It ended with a ridiculous fall backward from the bridge's parapet into the dry pond, winding himself horribly.

But in between—he struck her shoulder.

Their blades had locked, just for an instant, and for once he'd been able to use his superior size and strength. He'd shoved, forcing her weapon away, then he'd whipped his own back before she could line up the parry. *Thwack!*

He went down on his knees, screaming his triumph as if he'd just hit the winning run in a kalikiti match back at Aruna Nagar. She stumbled, then straightened and almost smacked him about the head, and he'd have deserved it for dropping his guard, but right then he didn't care.

Instead, she gave a rueful laugh.

Their eyes met and he found himself sharing a smile. *Sharing.*

It made him uncomfortable, such familiarity with the nefara bitch.

She proceeded to thrash him for the rest of the afternoon, but that didn't matter; the breakthrough had been made, and there were more as the days passed until somehow they'd been here for three months. The rest of the world had ceased to exist; there was only her and him.

It wasn't a harmonious relationship, however: she was openly blasphemous, with no fear of any god, not even her Rondian Kore. That angered him, as Ahm was all he had left to cling to after so much had been stripped from him. He found himself parroting Haroun's teachings, trying to *educate* her—to *save* her—but she cared nothing for that, nor even acknowledged the risk he was putting his own soul in to be here with her. She was nefara and her state was contagious, but when he tried to explain, she just listened with a condescending smirk on her lips.

"Every sin blackens the soul," he started, one night over dinner. She'd brought out a bottle of wine—never a good sign; it made her rude, abusive, and intolerant. He'd taken to leaving the table early when she drank, but tonight he was too hungry. She'd offered him some but his refusal had offended and now she was drinking too much, too quickly, gulping it down like water. It made her truculent, which goaded him to argue. "Why should I drink with you? Even sharing food with you endangers me, nefara."

"Poor boy," she sneered.

"You should not drink, you've said so yourself."

She deliberately swigged more. Her pupils dilated. "Do you think it's easy for me, dealing every day with your utter contempt? I've met some pricks in my time, but you're up there with the worst. At least the men of Yuros acknowledge the skills I've got, even if they don't like me. You're just a self-serving hypocrite."

His own temper flared. "I've let you teach me—"

She laughed scornfully. "Oh ho: you 'let' me teach you—how rukking *noble* of you. You don't fool me, boy. You spout Scripture like a trained bird, but you don't believe half your own bullshit."

He balled his fists angrily. "I am a true believer!" he protested vehemently, though he was frightened she might be right.

"Sure you are. How many times do you pray, Amteh boy? Aren't you supposed to grovel on your prayer mat every three hours? I've not seen you do it once, and Kore knows I'm with you most of the rukking day."

"I pray alone," he retorted, his face coloring. In truth, he'd virtually forgotten prayer at all, without the bells and the call of the Godsingers to remind him. But he wasn't about to tell her that. "Do you?"

She scoffed. "Why bother? I'm already damned in your eyes. *Nefara*." She ticked them off with his fingers. "What were they? Lies. Theft. Murder. Adultery. I've done all that."

He stood up. "I don't want to hear this."

"I've even *worn red*, damn me forever to Hel." She scowled. "I've not knowingly drunk urine, but with Lantric wine, who can tell?"

He was shaking with rage, but he was also frightened. This wasn't like her. "Elena, stop this, please. It demeans you."

Her voice went up a register. "*Demeans* me? Listen, you bigoted baby: your nasty little rules mean nothing to me. If you don't think I'm good enough for you to learn from, then you can just rukk off."

"You are drunk."

"So what? Amteh men drink, despite their precious rules. I bet you've drunk plenty in your time."

His face went hot again. "That is between myself and Ahm."

"Oh sure: you can just ask for forgiveness because you're a man. But if a woman sins, she'd damned for all rukking eternity, right?"

"Men and women are different."

"Sure. I bet you've screwed a few whores too, right? They're nefara, right? What penance did you do for that?"

He flushed, remembered a woman in Baranasi, in the wake of losing Ramita. "None of your business, woman!"

"What *unnatural* acts did you do with them?"

He bunched his fists, his chest suddenly a furnace. "You have no right to judge me!"

"Ha! But you think you have the right to judge me?"

"Because you're a damned heathen!"

"Too right." She tipped up her cup, missed her mouth and emptied half the red wine down her front. "Unnatural acts, eh? Yeah, check, check, check." She cackled horridly. "On campaign you didn't want to end up pregnant but you still needed a fuck, so when you were fertile, you had to make your fun *unnaturally*." She went to fill her cup again, found the bottle empty and threw it into the fireplace. The dregs sizzled as shards flew. "And you know what? *I loved it.*"

He trembled on the edge of striking her, took half a step, his hand lifting.

She stuck out her chin. "Just try it, prick."

Somehow, he held back, spun on his heel and stormed away.

They didn't train the next morning. She spent the night vomiting and slept past midday. He was practicing alone in the tiny court-yard when she appeared at the entrance. Her face was downcast, her cheeks greenish and eyes bloodshot. "Kazim?"

He stopped and faced her, feeling something between pity and vindictive pleasure at seeing her like this. "What?"

"I'm sorry. I was drunk." Her voice was heavy with self-disgust. She ran her fingers through the tangled wreckage of her hair. He'd never seen it untied before, never seen her look so disheveled. "I said stupid things and I'm sorry."

"You don't mean it," he snapped, turning away. *Let her beg*, he thought, knowing she wouldn't.

She gripped the doorway unsteadily. "If you mean that I still believe what I said, you're right—but I shouldn't have said what I did. I gave unnecessary offense and I'm sorry for that."

He sensed that apologizing wasn't something she did easily. He could empathize with that, at least. He nodded brusquely. Maybe she was sincere after all.

"Sordell's drinking has messed my body up. He drank at least a bottle of wine a night and my body still craves the damned stuff. But I'm trying to fight it." She looked at him pleadingly. "Don't let me drink again."

"And how will I do that, jadugara? I can't *make* you do anything. Fight your own battles."

She flinched. "I deserve that." She turned to go, then paused. "If you are still willing to train with a nefara ferang, I still want to train with you."

He made a show of considering because he knew it would rankle with her. "I am permitted to associate with you if you do not transgress, nor seek to corrupt me," he said eventually. He wasn't actually sure on this point but it sounded right, and anyway, training with her was making a big difference. He was learning more from her than even Jamil and Rashid. He needed her, though he didn't like it. *Another damned compromise . . .*

"I'll keep my opinions to myself in the future," she said, although he doubted she was capable. She rubbed at her temple, wincing. "And I won't drink again."

"Shall I destroy the filthy stuff for you?" he asked, the jibe becoming serious even as he voiced it.

She swallowed, then said, "No. Put a bottle on the table every night. Let it be a test for me."

He blinked. *Interesting.* "I will do so tonight." He turned to face her. "So, are you ready for a tumble?"

To his surprise, she blushed furiously. "*What?*"

"A tumble." He made fencing gestures.

"You mean a 'bout,'" she said, snickering softly. "A tumble is . . . something different. No, I don't feel well today."

"I thought a healer-mage was immune to such things?"

"If only." She coughed, gagging slightly. "You reach a point where the drunkenness prevents you from functioning properly, gnosis included. Then you're just as screwed as anyone else." Her face turned a sickly color, her eyes went wide, and she fled.

She refused the call of the wine bottle on the table that night with stoic strength. And she was back training the next day.

"Kazim," she said one evening. "Hold still."

He looked at her, sitting across the dinner table from him. Her drunken episode a few weeks ago had left an uneasy peace, one they didn't prod at too hard. It felt comfortable between them again. *Almost.*

"What?" he asked warily. She was still a jadugara, and an enemy.

She reached out slowly and he forced himself to stay still as she touched his chest. Light and heat throbbed through him, a surge of energy that struck resistance, then something gave way inside him.

Energy flared around his fingertips. He quailed, and it vanished.

"What did you do?" he asked, quivering with trepidation.

"I freed your gnosis from the Chain-rune," she said. "It's time you learned how to use it."

17

A Message from the Grave

The Keepers

"Keepers" was the name taken by the first Ascendants, denoting their keeping of the secrets of the sacred ritual through which they had ascended. The name now refers to those original Ascendants still living, a shrinking group as time passes. However, a devoted mage is occasionally rewarded by being permitted to attempt Ascendancy. The last man known to have been permitted to seek Ascendancy was Fabian of Defonne in Andressea, in 907. He died in the attempt.

Ordo Costruo Collegiate,
Hebusalim Chapter, 920

Isle of Glass, Antiopia
Shawwal (Octen) 928
4th month of the Moontide

Ramita slapped the door of her husband's room. "I wish to go in here."

Justina stared at her like she'd just suggested they both pray together to Shaitan. "Of course you can't go in there, bitch. It's my father's room."

"Your father. My *husband*."

"I can't believe your presumption. He was one of the original Ascendant Magi—you're a street-girl."

"Market-girl."

"What's the difference?"

"All the difference in the world. One sells things, the other sells herself." Ramita colored furiously at the mere suggestion that she might be the latter. Her family was not rich—well, they hadn't been—but they were proud. They had *standards*. This arrogant cow needed to know this.

"Mmm. And how did you come to be my father's wife?" Justina made to brush past.

Ramita gripped the taller woman's arm, fully expecting to provoke a reaction, and true to form, Justina wrenched her arm away. "Don't touch me," she snarled.

At least she didn't fling Ramita across the room with a flick of her finger, though she could see her stepdaughter was visibly tempted.

"I'm not discussing this again."

"He was my husband. He cared for me."

"He *purchased* you."

"At least he *chose* me. He was stuck with you."

Justina's face contorted in anger. "How *dare* you?"

"And how dare you?" Ramita countered.

Justina bellowed in exasperation, "You just don't get it, do you? You were nothing to him but a convenient womb!"

"And you were nothing to him but a *disappointment*. He told me he loved me, at the end. When did he last say that to you?"

Justina went white, and her whole body trembled. "You push me right to the edge, girl. The very edge. If you weren't pregnant with his children—"

"But I am. And I demand to see his room!"

"You don't *demand* anything around here!" Justina stomped away and slammed her bedroom door.

Ramita stared after her, thinking, *I'm making progress with her.*

"Hit the damned thing!" Justina's voice went up another octave.

She should sing traditional Omali songs. She has the vocal range for it.

Ramita was standing in front of a sand-filled leather bag that hung from the ceiling of the big room by the pool. It was still swaying faintly, and her knuckles were sore from punching it. Her sari was not the best choice for combat training, but she was sick of her limited range of salwar kameez. "I *did* hit it."

"Kore's sake, it barely moved." Justina flounced away, as if to leave. She did this every few minutes; there was a rhythm to it. "Pretend it's me, if that helps."

I did.

Justina made for the door, as she always did when she was particularly frustrated, then turned and stalked back into the middle of the room again. "What's the angriest you've ever been? How about your precious market: who was your worst customer ever?"

"You don't lose your temper with a customer."

"Huh! What about your sister?"

"We were best friends. We were family." *For a while.*

"Kore above, I *hated* my brother." Justina said it like this was normal.

"I'm sure he felt the same way about you." Ramita balled her fist. *Right, let's try again . . . Summon the gnosis . . . think of stone . . . be strong . . .*

"How did it feel when you watched my father die?" Justina asked bleakly.

Smash.

Her fist ripped through the leather and sent the bag flailing wildly as it sprayed sand about the floor. A scream echoed about the chamber and Ramita stood blindly staring into space, panting like the air had been sucked away. She dazedly realized that she'd been the one who screamed.

Justina smiled grimly. "That's more like it. That's the place you go to when you want to really hurt someone."

Ramita turned and faced her, blinking back tears. "Rashid held me on my knees, and made me watch as"—*Kazim*—"as one of them stabbed him, here." She jabbed herself up under her chin. "*I hate them.*"

Justina said slowly, "Rashid . . . Did you get any other names?"

Ramita shook her head.

"Then I'll have to ask Rashid. Very firmly." Her face was like the snowy peaks of Ingashir. "And Alyssa. She'll know."

Ramita turned away and wiped her eyes, then looked back at Justina. "You were close to Alyssa."

"I don't want to talk about her." Justina flexed her fists. "She's none of your business."

"My blood sister Huriya helped them," Ramita said. "She murdered Jos Klein in her bed, then let them in." That was as close to the truth as she dared come with Justina.

"I remember her. Little Keshi minx with a smart tongue."

"She was my sister, all my life. But she put the shihad first."

"Alyssa was my friend for sixty years," Justina said grudgingly. "I thought we shared the same soul."

Ramita wrinkled her nose. "Alyssa Dulayne stole secrets from my head when she taught me your language."

Justina's eyes narrowed. "What secrets?"

"Little things. Just to hurt me." *Kazim.* "She told them to Rashid."

"Then think of her also when you want to hurt someone." Justina made a gesture and burned an image of Alyssa's face on the stone wall. "Target practice."

Ramita snorted softly and gathered blue mage-fire at her fingertips. She spent the next hour sending lances of light blasting into the image of Alyssa Dulayne's face until it was blackened and unrecognizable. She felt a lot better afterward.

"May I have some?" Ramita asked, picking up the almost empty bottle of red wine in front of Justina. It was late at night and the jadugara was drunk again. It did not happen as often as it had the first month here, but it was still more than once a week. It made training the next day particularly slow and bad-tempered.

"Father always said pregnant women should not drink."

"He and I drank together at Southpoint. And other times after he knew I was with child."

Justina sighed heavily. "Very well. In fact, what he said was no more than one glass every few nights. Another good reason not to fall pregnant. Not that that will ever happen again." She blinked, and colored slightly. "Go on, finish it, I've had too much."

Ramita took another glass from the tray and poured the few remaining mouthfuls into it, then sipped it cautiously. It tasted heavy and rich, filled with red Yuros fruits she'd been told of but never seen. "You said 'again.'"

Justina muttered something. "Yes. I really have drunk too much."

"You have a child?"

"Yes." Justina had a resigned look on her face. "I'm only telling you this now so you won't spend the next six weeks nagging me."

"Oddly, I am known for my cheery nature by everyone I've ever met except you. One child? Two? Boy or girl? How old? Who with?"

"A girl. She'd be almost nineteen now. Her name is Cymbellea."

"That's a pretty name."

"It's a Rimoni name. I didn't choose it. I gave her away as swiftly as I could and have not met her since."

Ramita cocked her head. "Never?" *The woman has no heart at all.*

"I didn't want her. It was an accident. I gave her to the father when he was next in Hebusalim and sent him on his way. Told him I never wanted to see or hear of him or her again. To date he has abided by this. Thankfully."

"Where is Rimoni?"

"In Yuros. He returned there. At least there she'll grow up regarded as a blessing, not the spawn of Shaitan."

"Were you and he married?"

Justina snorted. "Not fucking likely."

Ramita shook her own head. *Surely Justina's affinity should be stone: she's made of it.* Was there such a thing as an affinity to glass? She was also brittle, and cracked too easily. She dared another question, though, while Justina was feeling talkative. "Were you and Alyssa . . . what is the word?"

"Safian? No." Justina swore under her breath. "We did try it once, for the novelty. But she prefers men. And I . . . I don't really like anyone." She stretched awkwardly on the sofa. "Sex is . . . I could never really get interested . . . and I hated the afterward part, when you had to talk and pretend you'd liked it." She made a face. "I'd rather smoke opium." She rolled over. "Pathetic, aren't I?"

Yes. "No." Ramita tried to think of something nice to say. "You just haven't met the right person."

"There is no right person for me."

Ramita decided that this conversation, while fascinating, was going places she didn't want to. "I'm tired. Goodnight, Daughter." She went to rise.

Even the old jibe didn't get a rise tonight. "Uh uh." Justina waggled her finger slowly. "It's your turn to talk."

"What about?"

The white witch's face took on a gently yearning look that Ramita had not seen before. "You say my father said he loved you." She dipped her head defensively. "What was that like?"

Ramita felt a little bubble of tears form behind her eyes. She slowly sat down. "He loved you too," she said awkwardly. "Even if he never told you."

Eventually they opened another bottle of wine.

Ramita sat watching the ocean heave. There was a viewing platform at the pinnacle of the Isle of Glass, walled in for protection but open to the elements. On a still day with the sun beaming down it was the most beautiful place in the world. The view was west, high above the tumult of the ocean. You could feel the whole rock vibrate to the boom and crash of the waves. Watching the sun falling scarlet over the horizon, painting the clouds orange, pink, and gold, was like watching the gods at play.

She was learning constantly now, basic things that every mage should know: how to lock and unlock a door, even one with no handle or lock of its own. She could blast a target with raw magefire. She could move things by what Justina called "kinesis." She had learned how to hide herself from scrying. She could even shape hard stone as if it were wet clay.

And all the while, the babies were growing. Her belly was swelling swiftly, developing silvery stretch marks. Her breasts were painfully large. It was only her fourth month, but time was passing so quickly.

What is happening out in the world? Where is Kazim? Where is Jai? How is my family? She wished she could scry them, but her clairvoyance was virtually nonexistent. Mental communication might not rely on Air-gnosis, which was how she'd first contacted Justina, but she was warned not to seek to do the same with anyone else. Apart from her family in Baranasi there was no one she wanted to speak to anyway.

Then one day a voice whispered across the sky, both massive and intimate at the same moment, *calling her name.*

For an instant she was tempted, out of sheer loneliness, to answer, but it was a fleeting moment, and instead she hid behind the walls of solitude Justina had shown her how to build. Hiding-wards: she was inside a tower of shadow, and there was nothing here to be seen . . .

The presence lingered a second longer, and then was gone.

It tried again a minute later but she was ready this time. She bit her lip, wondering who it was. Rashid or Alyssa, most likely. Once the voice had faded, she hurried back into the tower, where stone and water would render her wards unnecessary.

"Justina," she cried, "Justina!"

Her stepdaughter was not in the lounge; Ramita found her emerging from Antonin's room and that fact alone almost drove the scrying attempt from her mind—as did the pallor on Justina's face.

She put those questions to one side and concentrated on the present danger. "Justina, I was watching the sunset when someone tried to scry me."

The jadugara's eyes widened. "They didn't succeed, did they?" she asked, her face becoming even more sickly.

Ramita shook her head firmly. "I blocked them."

Justina exhaled. "Thank Kore!" She reached out and fleetingly touched Ramita's arm. "Well done," she said, her first words of praise *ever.* "But . . ." She clutched at the wall.

Ramita stared at her pointedly. "Are you all right? What did you find in there?"

"There is something you need to see," Justina said reluctantly. "In Father's room."

Ramita's throat went desert-dry. "In there?"

"You may go in." Justina hesitantly stood to one side.

Now she was finally permitted to do so, Ramita was almost too frightened to go in. But she steeled herself, holding onto the stone doorframe and letting the earth—*her element*—steady her. The room before her was full, but orderly. There was a large bed, and a writing desk facing a transparent wall revealing a southeastward view, as clear as if it were a hole in the rock. She stared at it, trembling. The other walls were covered in hanging carpets in all hues, from Lokistan, Ingashir, Gatioch, and Mirobez. A tall dresser was topped by a pair of elaborate Lakh candlesticks, and the desk was covered with papers.

In one corner stood two life-size statues, carved of white marble. She felt tears sting: one was of her, the other of him. Hers stood just over half his height, wrapped in a sari, looking tiny and defiant. He wore robes, the hood cast back, his head shaven and beard trimmed in the manner she had cut it for him. She felt tears streaming down her cheeks as she walked to it and stroked his cold marble cheek. "Is this what you wanted me to see?"

Justina stepped into the room. "No. That." She pointed to a stone slate on the desk. "Touch the base, where the green gem is set."

Ramita reached out, then paused. "What is it?"

"A message."

"From my husband? Have you read it already?"

"Give me some credit, bitch," Justina replied indignantly. "Anyway, you don't read it; it will speak to you." She dropped her chin. "I was wrong: you should have been allowed in here from the start."

She's just admitted being wrong . . . unprecedented. Ramita decided not to comment, though. She stared at the slate before slowly reaching out to the green gem—then she stopped again, suddenly afraid of what it might reveal. "My husband has left a message? For me?"

"I've just said so, haven't I?" she said impatiently.

Ramita nibbled at her lower lip, scared that it might be some kind of repudiation. *I only pretended to care for you; You're only a market-girl.* Or worse: *I know about Kazim.*

She looked back at Justina. "I want to be alone."

Justina exhaled sharply. "He's my father."

"Then listen to it yourself later."

Justina wrung her hands in annoyance, then turned and stomped out, slamming the door behind her.

Alone, Ramita sat on the end of the bed, trying to build up her courage. At last she reached out and firmly touched the green gem. It tingled at her touch as imprisoned gnosis energy was released, energy that came with the mental impression of dry paper she had always associated with her husband. It made her feel both comforted and sad. Then a cloud of light shimmered above the plinth and her husband appeared, a tiny foot-tall version of her husband, seated in an armchair. He looked relaxed, and her pulse quickened to see him. Her throat went dry. No sound came, but his voice filled her head.

<Ramita, dear wife. I do not know when or if you will ever receive this message, but if you do, I hope it is soon enough that it will still have meaning. I have created it during Maicin 928, a few weeks after your pregnancy was confirmed. Do you remember that I had to travel away a lot that month? One of those journeys was a secret one, to my Isle of Glass, to create this message and ensure this place was well provendered.>

Ramita tried to send back: *<Husband, it is—>*, then realized as he continued speaking that it was futile: this was just an unchanging message, not her husband's ghost.

<I first left a message here three months ago, in case something happened to me before you fell pregnant. In it I urged you to return home and hide—but that plan has been overridden; that will no longer be possible for you, for your pregnancy changes everything.>

She felt her hands clasp her belly, the tight bulge pressing against the fabric of her salwar kameez.

<Ramita, if you are hearing this at all, it is because I am dead. I do not know how that might have come about: Divination is far from flawless. But I've known for some time that one or other faction will strike against me, and no man is immune to assassination by a determined enemy. I have always known that if I died after you became pregnant, you would need instruction, and so I told Justina that if

that happened, she was to bring you here. If you are hearing this, then she must have succeeded.>

Ramita wiped away the tears she'd barely been aware she was crying.

<Firstly, dear wife, I must tell you that I am immensely proud of you. And more than that: I care for you more than I have ever found the courage to say. I hope that I have managed to make what was an awful situation for you as tenable as possible. And although I know it is inconceivable that one as young and vibrant as you are could ever truly love an old "ferang," I hope that you will always remember me kindly.>

I do. I truly do.

<Secondly, let me tell you the reasons for seeking a wife like you— the Divinations that led me to you. As you know, my gnostic predictions led me to seek a wife who was neither of Yuros nor of northern Antiopia, and a woman who was likely to conceive a multiple birth. I told you at the time of our marriage that I had foreseen our children ruling a new age of peace and prosperity in Hebusalim.> He clenched his hands in his lap and bowed his head briefly, before looking up again. *<Ramita, this was not entirely true.>*

She found she was scarcely breathing. *Not true?*

<The whole truth is that I needed something far more immediate than that—twins born this year or next could scarcely take a hand in the conflicts of even the next Crusade, let alone this one. It is true that somewhere in the future my children by you may have some role to play, but they were not the reason I chose you and brought you north.>

It felt like the stone at her feet was turning to mud: unsteady, shifting, untrustworthy. *What is my husband saying? He always told me our children were the key . . .*

<My dear girl, dear wife, the real reason for seeking out a Lakh woman with a fruitful womb was for you yourself, not your children. You are the one who can end these shameful wars; you are the one who can bring peace to the world again.>

Her heart thudded. *Me?*

<I can only imagine the look on your face now, my good wife. You are so humble and modest that this will not sound real to you. You will think I am mad, or playing a cruel jest. But it is not so.>

That he could so easily predict her emotions made her almost forget that he was not truly there with her. "How can this be?" she whispered uselessly, looking at the image of her husband for answers, for reassurances.

<I have studied the phenomenon of Pregnancy Manifestation carefully, though I have always hidden my interest in the subject. I found only one previous instance where a mage has fathered a multiple birth. Normally we struggle to conceive at all, let alone father or give birth to twins or triplets. But I found one case, of a young Dhassan girl—sadly, she was a rape victim of the Second Crusades who conceived and was taken in by Justina's healing order. She gave birth to twins; the father was a quarter-blood Rondian who never knew of the children. The girl and the children all died when Rondians sacked the convent, so none survived, but records suggest her pregnancy manifestations were much stronger than they should have been. Despite having only birthed eighth-blood mage-children, she herself had the raw strength of a pure-blood.>

Ramita found she was holding her breath. Her arms crept back around her belly protectively as she started shaking her head in denial.

<However, this was just the beginning of my research, and once the Crusade was over and I had the time for a proper investigation, I looked deeper into her case, examining birth records on both continents. I traveled always in secret, keeping my true quest to myself alone. Unfortunately, magi are still relatively few, and records are poorly kept, but in spite of that I still found enough evidence that I was able to come to the conclusion that a woman who has a multiple conception by a mage develops significantly stronger gnosis even than the father. I began the hunt a year ago for someone just like you. I am an Ascendant, the strongest purity of mage-blood known—and I cannot begin to imagine what strength you will develop.>

Antonin Meiros's face softened and he rubbed at his close-cropped beard. <You know the rest: how I found you and brought you to Hebusalim. And now you are with child. I know you are anxious that there has been no sign of the manifestation, but it will come, and it will continue to develop throughout your gestation. I will do

all I can to protect and instruct you, but if you are here and listening to this, then I have failed and you will be alone, with Justina.> He smiled wryly. *<I know you and she do not get along—few people do get along with my daughter. But she will aid you for my sake, and for the sake of her little half-siblings.>*

Ramita glanced back at the closed door behind her. No, she and Justina certainly did not get along. But they were getting by, somehow.

<I should also tell you why I sought a wife in Lakh, not elsewhere. It is a vast, populous country, with great economic and military potential. When you give birth, Ramita, you will already be on a journey toward being the most naturally powerful mage in the world. Go home to Lakh and seek out Vizier Hanook. Do you remember I once told you that your name would be made known to him? It has been— and he knows that if I am dead, he should await your coming. You can trust him—he will look after you, and he will give you temporal power to match the power of your gnosis. Call the Ordo Costruo to you: you can trust Rene Cardien to support you. Use the power of the Ordo Costruo and Hanook's influence to lean on Salim of Kesh; use it to defy Emperor Constant of Rondelmar. You will have the chance to impose peace on them both when you are standing at the head of a Lakh army. Ramita, you can stop the Crusades once and for all.>

She gaped open-mouthed at the tiny image, her head shaking in denial. This was all insane.

<Please, my dear girl, learn well, and be brave. I know you will see and do extraordinary things, for I have divined some of the possibilities. Your success is far from ordained; some might say it is impossible, regardless of your power, but I believe in you.>

Her breath caught at the words: *I believe in you.*

<Do not be afraid to love again—perhaps even your Kazim, from whom I so rudely stole you. The whole world is waiting for you, Ramita Ankesharan, and you have the potential to change it forever. It is time for you to take that chance in both hands.> He raised his hand and placed them together. *<Namaste, my dear girl. And though I never had the courage to say so to your face: I love you, my dear wife, and I always will.>*

The image died away.

For long minutes she sat on the bed, trembling, as tears streamed down her face. *It's not the children. It is* me. *He expects me to save the world.*

She couldn't think about it. It was too big. Too much.

But after a time she raised her head, stretched out, and triggered the message again, to imprint it on her memory. And to hear his voice again.

She was sitting in the lounge, late in the evening, when Justina finally appeared from below. Ramita had saved her dinner, lamb curry. She was staring at the rose-gold skylight as it faded to gray. She'd spent the afternoon outside on the viewing platform, watching the waves shatter and thinking about her husband's message.

"He was insane," Justina said eventually.

Ramita turned her head to face her. Her husband's daughter was ashen-faced, and she moved shakily. "Was there anything else?"

"He left me a message too, about you and the gnosis." There had clearly been more to her message than that, but she obviously didn't want to discuss that. "He tells me I have to teach you all I know. I'm doing that anyway," she muttered, like a sulking teenager. "He says that you're going to outstrip us all."

I bet you don't like that. Ramita had to restrain a smile.

"He may be wrong, you know," Justina added waspishly. "He's not omniscient. That poor Dhassan girl he mentioned could be a one-off. This might all be a waste of time."

"I suppose we'll just have to see." Ramita observed. "Daughter."

Justina scowled. "Then tomorrow, be prepared to do some real work." She stalked to the kitchen bench, seized her plate of cold curry and stomped away.

18

ACROSS KESH

Windship Travel

One of the magi's first and most valuable discoveries was how to imbue wood with residual gnosis so that it could be made to support large weights. The next step, to build a hold around the enchanted timber and then add sails to capture the wind, came gradually, but by 420, forty years after the Ascendancy of the Blessed Three Hundred, air travel was a reality in Yuros, and it immediately proved its value both militarily and commercially. After observing sailing craft on Lac Siberne, more efficient sail and hull designs were designed, and superior airmanship followed. Rule of the air has been the cornerstone of the empire.

ANNALS OF PALLAS

Hebusalim, Dhassa, Antiopia
Rami (Septinon) to Shawwal (Octen) 928
3rd and 4th months of the Moontide

Pallacios XIII marched into the Hebb Valley under the full moon in the third week of Augeite. Mater-Lune's face was the same pock-marked expanse as in Yuros, but little else was the same. The lands were brown and arid, almost lifeless, or so it looked at first glance.

The few riverbeds were dry, not even muddy, and even the most spindly tree had been hacked down for fuel. The villages they marched through were empty, the local people long gone. The buildings were quite unlike those of Yuros; they were often entirely open on one side, to admit the air, and few windows or doorways had shutters or even doors. It made them look half finished, just dried-mud shelters with roofs of straw. It was five days before they saw a Dhassan, a black-skinned old man hobbling along the road with cloth-wrapped feet. Bondeau hurled the old man off the road with a hand gesture, making the column laugh. The old man just sat there and watched them tramp past, his eyes defiant.

At night the temperature plummeted, but it was still hotter than sultry summer in Silacia. Thankfully, the air was so dry it did not overwhelm the senses the way a heat wave in Yuros could; it was somehow a little more bearable, so long as you had enough water. Many of the wagons were massive water barrels on wheels, so heavy only a hulka could pull them.

"Look at them," Kip marveled. "How many steaks would you get from one of them?"

"We may find that out before the end of this journey," Baltus Prenton commented.

"I don't like them," Ramon said. "Animals that can understand verbal commands? That's creepy."

"I don't disagree." Baltus looked at Ramon. "You have some air-affinity, don't you? Ever flown a skiff?"

"Si, of course—at Turm Zauberin. It is fun."

"Excellent. You and Severine are going to be my backups. We're getting two skiffs when we arrive in Hebusalim. I need to know you can handle one if you have to."

Ramon grinned. "I'll be fine. It was my old friend Alaron you'd need to worry about. He flew a skiff into his own house once. Wish I'd been there." He grinned at the thought of his earnest friend, wondering as he did where he was, and if he'd found Cym yet, and the Scytale.

Just then, they topped a ridge. As the sun fell toward the west they found themselves looking down upon the holy city of

Hebusalim, where the Amteh prophet Aluq-Ahmed spent much of his life. The inner part was walled, but the vast expanse of the city lay outside the defenses, a sprawl of desolate-looking buildings from which hundreds of threads of smoke arose. The vast golden dome of the Bekira, the largest Dom-al'Ahm in the world, the resting place of the Prophet's wife, Bekira, and the Governor's Palace, a massive expanse of gleaming marble, its great rival, dominated the roofscape. Above it all stood the Domus Costruo on the westward hill, a stark, lifeless silhouette. Word was that Ordo Costruo had relocated to their wartime retreat, the Krak di Condotiori.

To the east was the distant line of the Gotan Heights, rimmed with legion fortresses, with a wall running along the ridgeline. The camp beneath was as large as the one they'd left at Northpoint. Legion encampments, with thousands of tents and pens for livestock, were dotted across the plain, and above and beyond shimmered the Dhassan mountains, looking so near but really far, far away across the desiccated plains.

Now at last there were local people: dark-skinned men who had set up row upon row of food stalls and were now busy roasting meat and nuts over tiny fires. A string of Rondian legionaries guarded them, making any who bought pay fair price. The legions had learned from two previous invasions that not paying the locals meant the stalls vanished, together with a good third of the food the men might otherwise have had to requisition. Protecting commerce helped the Crusades—and there were other incentives, too. Beyond the stalls were tents where slender figures in diaphanous cloth lounged under the awnings. The Dhassan prostitutes always had a male protector nearby, usually a husband or brother. The women had a dangerous-looking beauty, and the legionaries nudged each other, their heads drawn inexorably sideways as they marched past. The more brazen of the women paraded half-dressed, calling out to the men in broken Rondian.

"Eyes front, you slugs!" bawled the centurions. "Get your hands off your cocks and think about your shovels! You've got trenches to dig!"

Ramon glanced at Kip, who was staring at one dusky creature with golden skin and tangled hair that fell to her waist. "Shizen, look at her," he muttered.

"Not as pretty as a Silacian girl," Ramon remarked for form's sake. *And she's got dead eyes and she hates every one of us almost as much as she hates herself.* "She'll have more diseases than a leper colony. Don't go there, amici."

"Schlessen girls are the best," Kip proclaimed, though the way his eyes were roaming made it sound like he was speaking to reassure himself. "Blond hair and big—" He cupped his hands over his chest. "Boom, boom." Then the girl he was looking at slowly parted the front of her gown, and he shut his eyes and groaned.

Further up the line, Severine Tiseme was riding on her own because Renn Bondeau was gawping at the whores as lustily as any ranker. Seth Korion seemed to be trying to reassure her, but judging by his scarlet face and stammering, he wasn't managing so well. On impulse, Ramon spurred his horse and joined them, leaving Kip to pant over the next exotic beauty to bare her wares for him.

"Milady Severine, isn't it wonderful to have arrived," he said cheerily.

Seth Korion looked at him worriedly, and nudged his khurne away. Severine turned, her face wearing an expression of surprise, presumably at his effrontery in speaking to her. "What a ghastly place. It must remind you of home."

Nice. "It reminds me of Coiners' Alley in Norostein, but the girls are prettier."

"It's disgusting," Severine said loudly, her eyes on the back of Renn Bondeau's head.

"So is destroying the local economy so that women have no choice but to prostitute themselves or starve," Ramon replied evenly.

Severine tossed her head. "A woman of Yuros would not descend so low."

Ramon tilted his head. "You think not? They did in Noros during the Revolt. I have that on good authority."

Severine scowled. "Noromen are *provincials*. A woman of Rondelmar has greater moral fiber. Her virtue is her banner."

Rich, coming from the girl who's trying to get with child so she can go home. "I gather we will fly together," he commented, changing the subject.

"I think not. I will fly with Windmaster Prenton."

"Have you ever used a skiff?"

"The good colleges do not teach girls such menial tasks."

"So 'no,' then?"

She pouted. "I am a fast learner."

"You'll need to be. Prenton tells me that skiff-pilots who crash here end up as bones in the desert."

Severine tossed her head. "I will be fine. Look to yourself, Rimoni."

"Silacian," he corrected.

She faced him fully. "What do I care what breed of rodent you are?"

"Charming. Still, I suppose you hope to be with child and half-way home within a month or so, si?"

Severine flared. "I demand you retract that insinuation." Renn Bondeau's head spun and he began to rein back.

"Keep moving," snapped Rufus Marle from somewhere behind them, his voice edged with menace. Ramon saluted Severine ironically and edged back into line with Kip.

<What did you say to her, greaseball?> Bondeau demanded silently.

<Nothing at all.>

<You better not have.>

Ramon glanced at Kip, who had torn his eyes from the Dhassan women long enough to realize that there was tension in the air. "What is happening?" the Schlessen demanded.

"Just making new friends." Ramon winked.

Kip laughed. "Hey, you notice how Seth Korion runs away from you all the time? Did you push him around at your fancy college?"

"Hardly. Seth runs away from everything," Ramon replied.

"He is the big general's son, yar?"

"Sometimes big fathers have little sons."

"This is why you call him 'Lesser Son,' yar?"

"You're right on the mark. So, worked out how you're spending your hard-earned pay yet?"

Kip glanced back over his shoulder. "Broadly speaking, yar. Specifically, neyn. You?"

Ramon shook his head slowly. "I think I'll stay in camp. Five fingers are cheaper and carry less risk of pox."

Kip winced. "Most nights, I agree with you. But you have to do some things once, I think."

Ramon snorted. "No, you don't have to do everything, even once. But I can see I won't persuade you otherwise."

Kip laughed. "You are smart for a rat-faced Silacian sneak-thief."

That evening the camp emptied out. Ramon could see queues of men twenty-deep outside some tents, the three Andressan magi among them. Coulder and Fenn had found fellow gamblers among the Argundians and were off carousing. He wasn't tempted by either, though he found himself amused at how base the motivations of most men were. For himself, he had higher things on this mind. But only slightly higher. He pulled on civilian clothes and headed for the windship yards.

A trader had touched down an hour before and was unloading under the close watch of an imperial inspector. Ramon watched proceedings until the inspector left, then approached the captain, who was drinking from a flask while his men lounged on deck, looking longingly toward the whore-tents.

Ramon sauntered up. "Evening, Shipmaster," he called. He extended a hand. "Ramon Sensini of Retia."

The captain paused in his drinking and grudgingly accepted a handshake. "Faubert, of the *Fleur-Rouge*. What do you want, Silacian?"

"Oh, just seeing if you had anything for sale."

"Not me, lad."

Ramon raised an eyebrow, "Really? No sculf-hold?" He cocked his head knowingly.

Faubert frowned. "No sculf-hold here, lad." A sculf-hold was a hidden compartment used for smuggling. "I'm an honest trader."

"This windship is what, Andressan?" Ramon asked. "There's usually a crawl space behind the bowsprit, a false-bottomed hold and a shallow space the size of a mattress in the ceiling of the captain's cabin."

Faubert's eyes narrowed. "The inspector's been through us, lad. We're clean."

Ramon shook his head. "The inspectors don't know shit."

Faubert flicked his hand to his neck and tugged on a leather cord, revealing a glittering periapt. "You want to make a thing of this, boy?"

Ramon shrugged and revealed his own periapt. "No, but I could."

Faubert looked taken aback. "Not many of your people have those," he noted carefully. "What do you want?"

"Not much," Ramon smiled. "Just give me a good reason not to go and have a chat with that inspector and I'll be on my way. He'll confiscate all you have and clap you in irons. I'm much cheaper to get rid of." He pulled out his legion identity medallion. "Pallacios Thirteen, Tenth Maniple. I'm interested in trading."

Faubert frowned. "Perhaps. How come you know Andressan ships?"

"My familioso have dealings with Andressan smugglers."

"Huh, figures. All right, what do you want?"

"What have you got?"

Faubert pursed his lips. "Brevian whiskey. Very strong."

The whiskey he'd gotten from Giordano was long gone. Ramon grinned. "Sounds good. I'll take a keg. And some of whatever it is you're shipping back."

Faubert shook his head. "Going home empty, lad."

"Hogswill. With respect, no trader flies empty. What is it: poppy?"

Faubert clenched his jaw. "Look, I like you, boy, Silacian scum or not. Let's just acknowledge that if you turn me in to the inspectors I'll smash your legs so badly the healers will amputate out of pity."

Ramon grinned. "Would still be hassle for you, Captain Faubert. Whereas if you give me a few ounces of ground poppy and that keg of whiskey, you won't see me again." He offered a hand. "Deal?"

Faubert scowled, then spat on his hand and they shook.

Ramon was waiting when Kip returned from the tents, an awestruck look on his face. "These women . . . unbelievable, meyn freund. The way they move their hips . . ."

Ramon snorted, and slipped him a thimble of amber liquid. Kip sniffed it curiously and his eyes lit up. "This is . . . what I think it is, yar?"

"It certainly is." He showed the Schlessen the keg. "You can have one more thimble tonight, no more," he warned. "This might have to last us the entire Crusade." He patted Kip's shoulder. "I'll be back in a minute."

"Where are you going now?" Kip frowned.

Ramon winked. "Can't tell you. But stand by for some entertainment."

"*I AM AN ANGEL OF KORE!*" bellowed Renn Bondeau, his voice filling the camp.

"*I AM CORINEUS ALMIGHTY!*" Seth Korion cried.

They roused the camp with their clamor. Ramon, who was awake anyway, grabbed Kip and they hurried to the scene. They were among the first group of legionaries and officers, who were all staring up at the roof of a tall building, looking at Bondeau and Korion, who were perched there unsteadily.

Both of the young magi were naked. In their hands were bottles of red wine, and between them was a terrified-looking Keshi girl, wrapped in a sheet and wailing. An angry Dhassan man on the ground was shouting up at the two magi. Gold stars and flashes of blue light were pulsing from Bondeau's fingers and out of his mouth, and he was swaying impossibly at the apex of the roof. He had no balance, but somehow his gnosis was keeping him upright. "*I AM THE EMPEROR OF ALL THINGS!*"

"*I AM KORE HIMSELF,*" Seth slurred in reply.

More and more of the Thirteenth appeared, and their shock began to turn to amusement, especially when Bondeau leaned over the edge and vomited, then swilled more wine.

"*Renn? Seth?*" A shocked female voice rang out over the scene as Severine Tiseme stormed into the midst of the men. "*Get down from there!*"

The soldiers burst out laughing, then backed away as the female mage whirled on them.

"*Sevvie!*" Renn called, stumbling sideways, clinging to the arm of the Keshi girl. "*Sevvie! I wanted you to be first to know! This is . . .*" He looked at the girl in puzzlement. "*This is . . . who are you again?*"

The girl wailed and pulled herself free. They could all see her trying to get off the roof, but she was barefoot, and as naked beneath the sheet as Bondeau and Korion. "Help!" she called to the men below in heavily accented Rondian.

Baltus Prenton hurried forward and held out his arms to her. "Jump, girl. I'll catch you, eh."

"Be gentle with her," Bondeau slurred. "She's my wife!"

"*What?*" Severine shrieked.

"It's okay, Sevvie," Bondeau called. "Amteh girls can marry as many times as they like!" He staggered toward the Keshi girl. "I'm in love!"

The Keshi girl screamed and jumped, and Prenton deftly caught her with Air-gnosis and lowered her to the ground amidst applause from the troops. As soon as she was on her feet she fled as if every demon in Hel was after her. Her Dhassan man pelted after her.

The legionaries immediately backed away as Rufus Marle stormed onto the scene. The Secundus glared upward, his brittle façade of calm exploding. "Bondeau, Korion! You pair of drunken shits, *get down here now!*"

Seth Korion looked suddenly afraid and began stumbling around the roof as if his legs no longer worked properly. Bondeau looked at Marle belligerently. "Hey, you can't talk to me like that! I'm a . . ." His voice trailed off, then he noticed the bottle in his hand again. "Hey Secundus, you want a drink?" He waggled the bottle. "It's fuckin' good stuff."

Marle slammed a telekinetic punch into Bondeau's belly and the Rondian folded in half and slid from the roof. He hit the ground, barely saved from serious injury by Prenton's air-gnosis, but the bottle shattered, spraying porcelain fragments and red fluid everywhere. Marle hit him again, and he flew backward, struck the wall and slumped against it. Seth Korion stared down at them, then fainted. Prenton caught him too, then slumped to the ground, panting.

Marle roared at the watching rankers, "Get out of here, you slugs, or you'll be digging latrines for the rest of the fucking Moontide." The soldiers scattered as if from a cavalry charge. Ramon pulled Kip into the lee of a tent and stayed watching.

Severine Tiseme strode to stand over the fallen Bondeau. "Renn, you bastard, where have you been?"

Marle bent over him, and sniffed. He wrinkled his nose. "Opium," he spat. "There was poppy-juice in the wine. The fool."

Severine looked aghast. "He wouldn't."

"He did," Marle grunted. "Or someone did it to him." His eyes swept around.

Ramon ducked out of sight, pulling Kip with him. "Time to go."

Kip looked sideways. "But it's just starting to get good."

"No, it's over." He chuckled. "Damned potent stuff, that poppy-juice, eh?"

Kip's eyes widened. "Hey, did you—?"

Ramon winked. "Let's go." *Consider that payback, lads . . .*

The next four days crawled by. While Duprey went to a meeting of the legion commanders and generals in the Governor's Palace, Marle made the battle-magi drill and drill again, blasting away at targets at full gallop and sparring with each other. Prenton took Severine and Ramon, the only other magi in the Thirteenth with significant Air-gnosis, to requisition their skiffs from the main army equipment dump. They were well-used craft, battered from repeated sea journeys and by no mean the pick of what was there, but Prenton was pleased enough. "I'd rather a skiff that has proved herself than one some apprentice mage in Andressea has just chipped from a log," he observed wryly. He'd had Severine and Ramon doing solo drills since. Ramon had to admit Severine was much better at it than he was. But she was still a bitch.

Renn tried to pin the wine-and-poppy incident on everyone in camp before being forced to forget it, while everyone laughed at him behind his back. He dumped Severine.

Result, Ramon thought.

There was more important and less pleasing business to transact. Ramon took Kip with him into the city to find the men who supplied Giordano with poppy, and other goods. They were local traders, though their sources were not; the poppy grew plentifully in Lokistan, and the harvest found its way first to Falukhabad, then to Bassaz and into the Hebb Valley. The other crops they purveyed were more innocent—pepper, cinnamon, ginger, and turmeric. Pater-Retiari had no interest in spices, but Ramon had been pricing them anyway: they might be less profitable by weight, but they were entirely legal. Giordano's passwords eventually resulted in them being taken into a secret web of passages beneath a Dom-Al'Ahm, where, after a lengthy wait presumably designed to unnerve them, they were taken before a small circle of shadowy men.

"You currently sell a pound of poppy for one Rondian gilden and ten florin," Ramon stated, after curt greetings had been exchanged. He looked at the six in the circle, trying to pretend he had not spotted the others, watching from the shadows. He could almost feel the crossbows aimed at his back.

The spokesman spoke good Rondian. "You are well informed, Magister."

"But my friend Giordano must pay one and fifty," Ramon noted.

The trader shrugged. "He is a small buyer. It is less convenient for us to break down a shipment. A bulk buyer gets a better price."

"And he is Rimoni," another man noted, with a thicker accent. "We have less trust of your people."

"I'm Silacian, not Rimoni," Ramon replied, wondering if they even knew there was a difference. "Do Rimoni cheat you?"

"The Rondians claim that that Rimoni are untrustworthy," the spokesman replied.

"I would say the same of them," Ramon replied. He cocked his head. "You undersell your product. Giordano can take bulk, and will pay one and twenty."

"Signor Giordano cannot afford that," the spokesman stated.

"He can now." Ramon tapped his own chest. "Because of me."

"We do not know you," one of the other traders replied dismissively. "Do magi now create gold from thin air?"

"In a way," Ramon replied. "I have come to an arrangement with the Tribune of the Tenth Maniple of my legion. For the next three months he is hauling the legion's pay around with him. I have a promissory note against the full value—fifteen hundred gilden. That's only the beginning. I'd take your entire crop if I could."

He smiled as surprise rippled about the circle.

The spokesman snorted. "And what will you do when you cannot pay your soldiers?"

"They will be," Ramon replied calmly.

"You cannot come up with such money," the spokesman maintained.

"I already have," Ramon replied. He pulled out a sheet of paper, a promissory note for the full sum, bearing the seal of the Pallas Treasury. He passed it to the spokesman, who studied it skeptically.

"What is this phrase, 'Upon Mine'?" he frowned. "What does it mean?"

Ramon spread his hands. "It means that the liability falls upon the issuer of the note: Upon Mine. Such a clause is standard in Rimoni contracts. It tells us who we have to come after if there is a default."

"On this piece of paper the name is blank," the man noted diffidently. "And we only deal in cash."

"I will sign on behalf of backer," Ramon responded. "In Yuros, a man must by law provide for his sons. I am the illegitimate but acknowledged child of a very wealthy man." He pulled out a pouch from his waist and extracted a folded piece of paper with a broken seal still affixed. Only four other people had ever seen this particular piece of paper: Principal Gavius of Turm Zauberin, his mother, who could not read, his paterfamilias, and his father, who had signed it. "It is legally attested." *By Pater-Retiari's tame lawyers, on pain of losing their eyes.* He handed it over.

The man reading the paper looked at it doubtfully, then his eyes bulged. He looked up at Ramon with saucer-like eyes. "This is true? You are—"

Ramon put a finger to his lips. "I like to keep it quiet."

The man exhaled, and passed the paper around his circle of associates. "He will back you?"

He has no idea what sort of shit I'm about to land him in. Ramon smiled. "As a last resort—but he should not need to. Already my tribune is talking to the other tribunes who will be involved in transporting your produce into Yuros. He has promised them they will double their money. We have most of the funds for your first consignment raised already—in gold. All we need is for you to cancel all your other contracts—" He stopped and thought for a second. "No, on second thought, don't cancel them—just whittle them back by two-thirds. That way we won't drive Giordano's enemies to desperation."

The Hebb traders looked at each other. "Do you mind if we confer?" the spokesman asked. "We will need a little time, I think, for this is a big decision for us to make."

"Not at all, gentlemen. Take all the time you need."

They were ushered into a waiting room a short distance away, but the stout door had barely closed on them when Kip spun around and slammed him backward into the wall, leaving him winded, his head reeling. A massive hand grabbed a fistful of his tunic and he was lifted bodily, his feet dangling, and pressed against the wall. The giant Schlessen's face pressed to within an inch of his own. "What are you doing, Silacian?" he growled.

"Umphh—" he gasped, struggling for breath, then wheezed, "Put me down . . ."

"Not until I hear why meyn freund is importing that filthy poppy-scum." He loosened his hand a little so Ramon could draw breath properly.

After filling his lungs properly, he frowned. "I thought you knew. You were with me at Giordano's."

"You spoke Rimoni there." Kip tightened his grip again. "Have you ever seen what this shit does to people? There are whole towns on the fringes of the Rondian border where my people live like animals because of it." He raised a fist. "I'm not letting you get into this."

"Listen—it's not what you think, I swear," Ramon managed to get out. "I can explain—just put me down so I can breathe."

"Then explain," Kip growled, ignoring Ramon's pleas.

"Pater-Retiari has my mother—it's how he controls me. I can buy her freedom, but I have to do this."

Kip's lip curled. "Your mother's life—one woman's life—is worth all the death this slime will cause? Neyn, Ramon, not even Saint

Lucia's life is worth that." He shook Ramon like a doll. "Not good enough."

"Kip, I'm going to bring down Pater-Retiari with this deal. And my father, for what he did to my mother—she was *fourteen* when he raped her."

"How does trading opium achieve this?" The big Schlessen shoved two fingers up against Ramon's eyeballs. "Make me believe."

"Please, Kip, put me down first. I can't explain anything like this."

Kip glared at him, then opened his fist without warning and Ramon slid down the wall and landed on his tailbone. He spent the next few seconds writhing in pain and gasping for breath, unable to say a word.

Kip looked down at him without sympathy. "Talk."

Ramon pulled himself up until he was sitting against the wall, trying to ignore his pain and concentrate. He looked around—he was fairly sure they were alone, no one who might be listening in, but he wove an illusion about them to distort sound and sight, just in case they were being spied on.

"Allora!" he started. "Listen, if they accept those promissory notes, they start to circulate and become a legitimate item of exchange. Everyone sees the Treasury Seal, and they don't question who the backer is. They will multiply until they swallow up all the gold in Kesh."

Kip looked skeptically at him. "How did you get the seal?"

"It's a forgery, from Pater-Retiari. But it is entirely plausible when it's combined with this."

He handed Kip his letter of acknowledgment.

Kip grunted. "I can't read."

"Really? Oh . . ." Ramon paused. "Okay." He told the Schlessen his father's name, and at Kip's raised eyebrows, he held up his hands and said fervently, "It's true, I swear."

"Then you're not even—" Kip scowled. "You're one of *them*."

"I'll *never* be one of them," Ramon replied forcefully, "not in this life. But I'm going to shake their towers until they fall. I'm going to hit them where it really hurts—in their vaults. I'm going to destroy him, and Pater-Retiari, and those men in there too. But first I have to gain their trust, and that means I have to appear to play their game."

Kip's eyes narrowed. "Explain to me the difference between you *playing* their game and *appearing* to do so."

Ramon glanced about him again, then leaned in closer. His illusions looked like they were holding unchallenged, but he hated talking so openly of what should be secret. "We give them promissory notes, and they give us poppy. We stockpile it among the Thirteenth's stores, to drive up the price, all the while creating tensions along the supply chain. We stay solvent by buying and trading in spices, but we put the profits into paying our initial investors— Storn and his fellow tribunes—massive interest. That will create a tidal wave of new investment, and the promissory notes will start to proliferate until they are exposed as worthless and they destroy the market. All trust is lost, fortunes collapse, and panic spreads. Eventually everyone will come after me, but by that time, I'll have vanished, together with my mother. The debt collectors will not let it rest. They will come after Pater-Retiari and my real father—and that, my friend, is what will snap off their ivory towers at ground level."

Kip stared at him. "You can do all this?"

"Why not? Pater-Retiari's closest adviser is a former Treasury official. He's very smart—and very corrupt. It's really his plan—at least, the parts that enrich the Retiari familioso and gain control over the poppy trade are."

"But how do you expose the notes as worthless?" Kip said, his brow creasing, trying to follow the intricacies of Ramon's plan.

"By burning all the poppy, rendering two-thirds of all the opium stockpiled since the last Crusade worthless, and destroying the value of most of the money in the market."

Kip's eyes flashed. "You're going to buy it all, then burn it?"

"At the right moment, si."

"You swear?"

"On my honor."

Kip snorted. "I'm not sure that's good enough."

Ramon spread his hands. "On my mother's name."

Kip looked down at him, then rolled his shoulders and uncricked his neck. "Yar, very well then. We will try it. But I will be watching you." He poked a finger at Ramon. "Very closely."

"That's fair." Ramon climbed painfully to his feet and dusted himself off. "I guess I should have explained before."

"Yar, you should."

Ten minutes later the six Dhassan merchants sent someone to summon them back into the meeting chamber. Even before he was seated, Ramon could sense the change in the room.

"Magister Sensini," they greeted him. "One and thirty, and we have a deal."

Storn's eyes bulged. "All of it? But . . ." He swallowed. "I don't know that many other tribunes."

Ramon patted his arm. "You don't have to. When you double the money of the first investors, the rest will come forward. Their friends, and then their friends' friends. Do the sums: each wave of investors is bigger than the last, so we can use the deposits of the last in to pay a return to those who got in first."

Storn screwed up his face. "But . . . that only works when there are fresh investors," he said anxiously. "And what happens when we run out of product? Or if a shipment is seized?"

"Then the price will spike, and we promise them more. Eventually, the Upon Mine clauses are invoked, but not until all other options have been exhausted." Ramon grinned. "Then my backer becomes liable."

Storn looked sickly. "But he's—"

"Shhh," Ramon hushed him. "The breeze has ears." He patted Storn's arm. "Don't worry. By the time this Crusade is over, the only problem we'll have is getting our millions back across old Antonin's Bridge without the Inquisitors grabbing the lot."

"The penalty for poppy-trafficking is death."

"We won't be trafficking it. We're stockpiling it," Ramon reminded him. He rubbed his hands together. "I've already talked to a tribune in Korion's army. He's given me half their last pay consignment in exchange for promissory notes, and I've promised him ten percent interest per month on it. He thinks I'm mad, but he's read the name at the bottom. He's going to speak to the other tribunes on the quiet. We're going to be flooded in opium and gold. The hard thing will be keeping it quiet."

"I can hide it among the stores," Storn mused. "But what about the buyers we've cut out of this? Won't they come after us?"

"Undoubtedly—but Kip and I will deal with that. The suppliers stockpile in the years between Crusades because they get far more per pound during the months when the Bridge is open. They've already started sending me their stock." He tapped Storn on the chest. "You're going to need to buy more wagons."

Storn put his head in his hands. "You'll get me hanged." He peered at one of the promissory notes. "I still don't understand how we can get rich from buying opium then burning it," he added doubtfully.

Ramon grinned. "Look, it's simple. Let's say you give me a gilden. I give you back one and fifty—"

"How?"

"I borrow the fifty. Don't worry, I'll have paid back the creditor inside a week. So, I give you one and fifty, and I promise you that I'll do it again, so long as you tell your four best friends they can too, and I'll give them the same deal. So you and your friends give me a gilden each, and I give back one and fifty each. They tell their friends. More and more money comes in. I bank all the money, and give half back. So long as new investors come in, everyone is given a return, and all is well."

"And when we've found all the investors we can?" Storn asked anxiously.

"By then, amici, you and I have so much money that we can buy passage from anywhere to anywhere, and my backer is left carrying the can."

Storn looked again at the name on the bottom of the promissory note. "He'll back it?" he asked doubtfully. "Won't he just disown it?"

Ramon shook his head. "He might. But then no one would ever trust him again, and he'd be responsible for letting the whole banking and trust edifice collapse. He can't let that happen. Bankers like Jusst and Holsen *own* the Crown. It'll cost him everything, but he'll still pay up, and he'll bankrupt Pallas while doing so. Meanwhile we'll be living in villas in South Rimoni with wall-to-wall dancing girls and endless wine." He slapped Storn's shoulder confidently, watching greed and doubt war across the man's face. Storn had no family, no ties, and no assets, and no desire to see out another term of duty in the legions. Greed won easily.

"We're in this together," Storn growled.

Ramon clapped him on the shoulder. "Of course we are."

Camp life simmered as the legions camped in clusters about Hebusalim, awaiting the orders to march. Half the men who'd gone to the prostitutes had pustules on their groin within days, which—amusingly, for Ramon—included Kip and Renn Bondeau. Mistress Lanna and Chaplain Frand were working day and night to clear up the sores. Duprey told the entire legion that no one would be left behind. "You'll march, even if your cock is rotting off," he thundered from the front of the parade ground.

Severine was sulking. Bondeau had been well and truly banished from her affections, but she still craved a child. Any female mage who fell pregnant to another mage would be automatically sent home; mage-blood was too valuable to risk. Baltus Prenton regarded himself as next in line, and tensions between Bondeau and him were simmering. The trio of Andressan magi were also hovering, flexing their muscles, and posturing whenever Severine passed.

Meanwhile, the number and value of the promissory notes Ramon had issued had already increased tenfold, and the stores of the Thirteenth were bulging with false sacks of beans. Storn had local carpenters adding false bottoms to all their wagons to store the opium and ingots. The first investors had been paid their interest and had reinvested five times as much money, and every day brought more tribunes seeking a way in. It felt like a giddy stilt-walk across a crowded plaza, alarming and exhilarating both at once. But still the gold and opium poured in, and the price went up and up.

At the end of the week Duprey returned and assembled tribunes and magi in an empty house on the fringe of the city. "There will be two lines of march," he told them. Ramon had already heard this from dozens of sources; nothing stayed secret in the army. "General Korion will command the northern wing, who will take the pass into Zhassi Valley and drive Salim east, all the way to Halli'kut." He pointed to the map, tracing his finger along the intended route. This route had been largely picked over in the last Crusade, but only as far as Istabad. Halli'kut was reputed to be rich; it looked as if Korion had gotten himself the best route.

"Meanwhile, Duke Echor of Argundy is taking the southern routes, driving around the bottom of the mountains of Dhassa, through Medishar, Sagostabad, and Peroz." He jabbed a finger into the middle of the map, at a point in eastern Kesh, almost in Miro-bez. "Here is his goal: Shaliyah."

The tribunes and magi exchanged looks. Shaliyah, a major city, was some five hundred miles beyond the furthest extension of the last Crusade, through increasingly hostile lands. Though they'd crossed the Leviathan Bridge doing twenty-five miles a day, in unknown lands five to ten miles a day was more realistic. Any kind of resistance would see Echor's legions a long way from home—not that serious resistance was expected.

"What's out there?" Bondeau asked.

"Just one big rukking desert, that's what," Rufus Marle growled. "Not much else."

"Shaliyah is where the prophet was born," Duprey told the room. "A captured Godspeaker told us that the Dom-al'Ahm in Shaliyah has more gold than the whole of Pallas, and Duke Echor wants it. He's promised the loot will be shared equally among each legion that's with him."

"What did Uncle Kaltus think of that?" Ramon piped up, mak-ing a few of the tribunes smile.

Seth scowled.

"He looked like he'd just sat on a turd," Duprey chuckled. "Echor's got almost all the vassal-state legions with him. Everyone knows Salim will send Korion on a wild goose chase in the North. But no one's ever gone all the way to Shaliyah before."

There had been talk for months that this Crusade was Echor's big chance. If the Duke of Argundy came out of this with all the treasure of Shaliyah, then some kind of coup against Emperor Constant appeared likely.

I'd not mourn it . . . but I don't want to be on the frontline either.

"So which army are we in?" one of the tribunes asked, voicing the question on everyone's lips.

"We'd better not be left behind this time," Marle grumbled. "The men won't take it."

Duprey met his Secundus's eye and nodded slowly. "Fear not, my friend." He looked about the room as a smile spread across his face. "We're in Echor's column! We're going to Shaliyah!"

The room was silent for a few seconds as they took it in, then it rang with cheers.

"*Rukka*," Ramon swore quietly, his dreams of a cushy duty fleecing His Imperial Majesty's legions turning to dust.

And how the Hel am I going to hide all that damned opium?

19

THE VLK

Sydia

The history of Yuros is one of westward migration. The oral histories of all primitive peoples speak of long treks from the vast plains of Sydia into western Yuros. Where do all these people come from? Why do they leave? Why are they so diverse? Not even the magi have learned the full truth. The Sydians are the latest, but they arrived before Rimoni had developed sufficiently to record them, and the oral record is frustratingly unclear.

ORDO COSTRUO COLLEGIATE, PONTUS

Kore preserve me from Sydian men. And Sydian women. Most especially Sydian women.

MYRON JEMSON, ARGUNDIAN,
IN JOURNEYS EASTWARD, 901

South Sydia, Yuros
Octen 928
4th month of the Moontide

Alaron had been sitting in the midst of the circle of Elders for an hour. Reku and Mesuda were aging by the day; Mesuda looked even more hunched and frail, and Reku was almost totally blind now, but still stubbornly refusing to step down. Only Kekropius, curled next to Hypollo, looked supportive of his latest idea.

They sat in an old stone circle built by the Sollans in the centuries before this tiny, uninhabited island east of Thantis had been cut off from the mainland. Alaron found himself picturing the old sacrificial rites performed on this ancient site; it wasn't the most comforting place to present his plan to the Elders.

"No one would need to come with me," he concluded after outlining his intentions. "You all know where the Bridge is now—you don't need me anymore. What I'm doing might endanger you all."

"Listen to him," Hypollo growled, exasperated, thumping the ground with his tail. "You are the son of Kekropius and Kessa: they saved you and adopted you. You belong to the clan now."

Reku made a clucking noise of agreement. "You have proven your worth to us, Alaron Mercer. Hypollo is right: you may not just choose to leave us. You are family now. It is our decision, not yours."

Kekropius clicked his fingers loudly, asking the right to speak. "My son has given much to this clan. He has shared his Arcanum training and opened our eyes to many things. All of us have gained. The next time the Inquisition come for us, they will not find us such easy prey. He has earned the right to request this boon. I give my assent."

"I vote against," Reku snapped back. "He is too valuable. We still have much to learn from him. It is too soon."

"I concur with Reku," Hypollo rumbled. "We cannot risk his capture revealing our presence."

All eyes went to Mesuda. She blinked slowly, considering. As always her vote, as Eldest, carried the most weight. "Alaron Mercer, explain to us again why we should risk the safety of our clan for this girl. What you have said does not persuade me, but I sense there is more."

Alaron swallowed. He'd spoken previously to them only of Cym: a missing girl he'd pledged to find. Knowledge of the Scytale was dangerous, but it looked like he was going to have to tell the whole truth. Of course he could fly away without their permission if he had to, but that would be a betrayal of trust. They'd saved his life twice over; he owed them his honesty.

He took a deep breath. "You're right, there is more. Have you ever heard of the Scytale of Corineus?"

Cymbellea di Regia picked up the strange wicker and ribbon crown and carefully lowered it onto her head. She winced as the pins stabbed her scalp, hissing in frustration.

"Allow me," said Myrlla, the chief woman of the Sfera, the only tribeswoman who spoke Rondian. She waddled forward. Her swollen belly pressed against Cym's back as she carefully lowered the bridal crown onto her head and pinned it carefully before arranging the veil.

Too many pregnancies in too few years had stolen Myrlla's youth; she looked much older than her thirty years. Each of the dozen women of the Sfera, the tribe's magi circle, were either pregnant or had just given birth, except for Gilkira, the eldest, who was fifty but looked seventy. The women's tent was filled with squalling infants and toddlers. Cym hadn't been alone for months.

Stupid stupid stupid. How could I let these savages get hold of me?

She stared into the tribe's single mirror and scarcely recognized the girl it reflected. Her narrow face was losing all trace of baby fat, and the sun was darkening her skin. Her hair hung down her back in black waves, tied by a red scarf. The crown sitting above the scarf was a weird construction of wicker, finely knotted into intricate patterns and decorated with dangling ribbons of white. Even worse was the new tattoo on her forehead, a wolf's head set in a diamond, marking her new clan.

The Sydian women cooed and clapped and sang another of their jaunty songs that made Cym want to scream. She'd thought Rimoni caravans claustrophobic, but this was beyond horrendous: the brats never stopped screaming, and the women never stopped chattering.

This will be my life.

She shuddered; this was all because she never fully recovered her gnosis-energies after crashing the skiff on Phaestos Island in Julsep. Although she'd managed to fly herself to the mainland, it had depleted her badly. Augeite and Septinon had been a long, footsore nightmare as she tried to move unseen, skirting the towns and villages along the Imperial Road. She'd been reduced to stealing food from the occasional unwary traveler, and when there were none, hunting for eggs and setting traps for rabbits and pheasants. She'd gone for days without being able to wash. She'd been constantly under scrying attacks, which had become increasingly hard to block as her gnostic energy waned. At first it had been Alaron, much to her annoyance, though she'd never really believed he'd just stay in Norostein and forget her. More recently it was someone—or some*thing*—else: an alien mind that unnerved her; that was much harder to block.

The exhaustion got her in the end.

She'd successfully skirted the cities of Verelon and forded the massive rivers, and started across the Sydian plains, but on her fourth night in she'd jolted awake when her wards were triggered. Even stupefied and slow to react, when a tattooed face had loomed above her she'd managed to throw him off, and the next, but more came, and more, overwhelming her. The tattooed man had clamped a hand over her mouth and as searing pain racked her body he struck her head.

When she came around she couldn't touch her gnosis. Though she knew of Chain-runes only in principle—she'd never let Ramon and Alaron demonstrate it in case they couldn't undo it—she knew at once that was what had sealed her gnosis away.

After that she was helpless, a prisoner of a tribe of Sydians, one of the nomadic tribes that traveled the vast steppes of eastern Yuros. Men and women alike were short and stocky, and they aged quickly in these harsh lands. They dressed in leathers and furs from the beasts they hunted and herded, and tattooed their clan symbols onto their skins. This tribe's totem animal was the wolf, "Vlk" in their tongue. They'd claimed her that first day, etching her skin with their diamond-and-wolf symbol after subduing her by pressing a knife to her jugular. She'd feared worse, but they'd done nothing more than bind her wrists and hand her over to the women of their "Sfera"; the tribe's magi, all low-blood products of liaisons with Rondian magi. She hadn't immediately realized exactly how much trouble she was in.

They didn't remove her Chain-rune; very clearly, they just wanted her womb. But though she dreaded rape, no such thing had happened. Yet. Instead, she discovered she was to be married off, and then raped. *That will be tonight, after this sham of a ceremony.*

The Sydian mage who'd captured her spoke a little Rondian. His name was Drzkir, and he was a part-Brician quarter-blood, son of a legion mage his mother had lured to her bed forty years ago. It was a Sydian tradition, throwing their women at Rondian mages, deliberately seeking to become pregnant, and each new mage-child added to the clan's power. Drzkir was chief shaman of the Vlk, and he had seventeen children already—Sydian shamans, like the warriors, were allowed many wives. Though he considered himself educated, he couldn't read, and he obviously had no idea what the Scytale was. Cym told him it was a holy relic, and he'd accepted that, placing it among his collection of goat horns and necklaces of wolf teeth.

Drzkir had clearly intended to keep Cym himself but a higher power, in the shape of the clan chief, the Nacelnik, had intervened. After walking appraisingly around her, Gul-Vlk had declared that their new prize would marry one of his own sons.

This gave Cym an insight into clan politics: the Sydians might strive to breed magi, but they obviously did not want them becoming too powerful and overthrowing the traditional warrior rule. The Nacelnik feared Drzkir, so he wanted the fruit of Cym's womb to be of his own line. Drzkir was clearly furious—he'd been tracking Cym since she left Thantis, he'd told her proudly—but the Nacelnik was clan chief for a reason, so he controlled his anger.

It was an opportunity, and she had taken it. The Sydians spoke a polyglot tongue with enough Rondian and Rimoni words that she could just about make herself understood. She started to try and secure herself by charming Gul-Vlk, treading a careful line between sweetness and pride, praising, not groveling. He had seven adult sons, all potential suitors—and all were all brutal savages, even the most pleasing of them.

She asked Gul-Vlk for the right to choose her own groom as a way to delay the inevitable. The idea had amused him and he had declared a contest. For the last week, the sons of Gul-Vlk had been displaying their skills in riding, running, and fighting—and, to her utter mortification, their sexual prowess. She'd never believed the tales, that for Sydians, lovemaking in front of the entire tribe was part of the evening's entertainment, but it had turned out to be fact, not fiction. Some of the things she'd seen at Gul-Vlk's feasts had left her crimson with horror and embarrassment. She'd never thought herself a prude before now.

And tonight that's what one of these savages will be doing to me, right in front of everyone. She fought hard to stop the tears welling in her eyes. She would *not* show weakness, however scared she was.

Outside, the night was becoming wilder. As the drums began to roll, sounding like an oncoming storm, so the wind lifted the tent flaps, wafting in the all-pervasive stink of animal dung and unwashed humanity that constantly invaded her nostrils. The women treated her with elder-sister condescension. They tittered as they selected their most revealing dresses. They had a similar caste to their faces: long, narrow noses, long, pointy chins, and high, sharp cheekbones. Almond-shaped eyes were set in narrow faces, and their foreheads were all etched with the clan's diamond-and-wolf markings. Most had tattooed arms too, and some had designs over their backs and even breasts. *They have a wild kind of beauty,* she thought, understanding why Sydian women were considered a prize by the slave-takers—even though they had a reputation for murdering their owners in their sleep.

Despite herself, her eyes filled with tears. Of all the dreams she'd had, the plans for where her life would take her, it wasn't to here, to be a broodmare for some illiterate savage. *I'm Justina Meiros's* daughter. *Papa-Sol, Mater-Luna, please help me.*

The tent opened, revealing the hulking form of Gul-Vlk. He'd been delighted to make his seven sons—delivered of seven different wives—scrap it out for this Rimoni divka. It had been a good way to sort out the pecking order and see off any who might be wishing to take on the leadership at too young an age. Two had been crippled in the contest so far, and another was unfortunately dead; it was surely just coincidence that that son had been the most ambitious.

"Kybelya." He launched into what she thought must be a fulsome paean of praise as he walked around her, pinching her bottom and squeezing her breasts, all the while beaming at her. His rotting-meat stench was so overwhelming that she struggled to keep her gorge from rising. The victorious son, waiting outside to claim her, was just as bad, and the temptation to lash out was almost unbearable.

I will escape this, she told herself, forcing her lips into a smile. *I must, somehow.*

Myrlla kissed her formally on the cheek, then lowered the veil, enclosing her within a tiny lace tent. Then Gul-Vlk took her arm and led her out into the night. The women trailed behind, first giggling in low whispers, then, as the drums roared, wailing as if at a funeral while the men leered and made obscene-looking gestures with their fingers. Cym felt dizziness crawl over her, and she wondered if she was about to faint. Perhaps it would be better if she did.

Torches flared in the darkness beneath the silver moon. Gul-Vlk's arm was like a tree trunk and she clung to him, barely trusting her legs, thankful for the veil that turned the crowd into just a heaving blur. The thunderous sounds and fetid stench battered her senses even as the bilious taste rising from her throat got worse. Children reached out and patted her arms for luck, and warriors beat sword-hilts against leather shields.

The Nacelnik led her to a wooden stage hung about with cloth of red and white and pulled her up the stairs, growling warningly when her legs almost gave way. Her head swam and she thought again that she might faint, but pride took over. She had always been fiercely independent; she was not going to play the weak maiden now. She raised her head, and stiffened her spine.

I will not be broken by whatever humiliation comes. I am Rimoni. I am a Meiros. I am di Regia.

A towering figure robed in furs and masked by a wolf's head awaited them. His eyes, mouth and chin were all that were visible beneath the wolfskin. There was a priest too, of the strange variant of the Sollan Faith the clan followed. Then her eyes jerked unwillingly to her husband-to-be. Hyr-Vlk was clad only in breeches, with the skin of a wolf thrown over his shoulder. His naked torso was covered with a tangle of tattoos that culminated over his heart in a startlingly lifelike wolf-face. Its yellow eyes seemed to follow her, just as his did. She was ridiculously thankful for her lace veil, though she knew it would be gone all too soon, as would the thin cotton shift. She'd seen the public consummation of three weddings already; she knew exactly what was in store for her.

Gul-Vlk turned to the wolf-headed shaman and growled something in his own tongue. "Call the Gods," echoed Myrlla behind her in a quick whisper, startling her.

The shaman turned and held both arms aloft. He bellowed over the masses, "*Slunzi i mezich, slunzi i mezich!*"

"He calls the Sun and Moon to witness," Myrlla whispered as the gathered tribe repeated his words, over and over.

The voice, though oddly distorted by the wolf's head, wasn't Drzkir's, Cym realized dimly.

A bright golden light grew on the eastern hillside, and from the west a white light answered. The crowds hushed. "The Sfera create light to call Papa-Sol and Mater-Luna," Myrlla whispered reverently. "We Sfera are the hands of the gods."

The lights grew brighter and the clan began to sing a hymn in praise of the Sollan gods. Cym found she knew the tune, though not the words, and she sang along softly in Rimoni as tears began to run down her cheeks. Her hands clasped and unclasped almost of their own volition as an uncontrollable shiver ran down her spine.

I wonder if they will ever let me have my gnosis back? Maybe after the fifth child in five years, when she was too bloated and weak to run even if she wanted to. She stared into the orange glow of the nearest torch and seriously considered trying to reach it, to somehow immolate herself—

Suddenly the lights on both sides of the camp went out, accompanied by a chorus of distant screams that almost immediately fell ominously silent. An almost palpable uncertainty ran through the gathering as darkness closed in. The hymn faltered, and a murmur of fear rippled among the tribesfolk like wind through barley.

As one, they turned to the shaman, who stood with his arms still raised over them, but his voice was now silent. The torches began to wink out one by one and the darkness closed in. Even without her gnosis, Cym could feel that this was not natural. She reached up and wrenched off her headdress, and her husband-to-be flinched at the sight of her face, making a sign to ward off bad luck.

I think you might have more bad luck to worry about than just seeing your bride too soon, she thought with an exultant sense of anticipation.

Gul-Vlk hissed at the shaman, "What is the meaning of this?" Myrlla translated automatically, her voice fearful.

"THE GODS ARE NOT PLEASED!" the shaman roared aloud, and Cym went rigid in shock.

The words were in Rondian.

Suddenly dark shapes taller than any man had a right to be emerged from the surrounding night, shrieking unearthly cries and panicking the tribesfolk.

"Sudicki!" someone screamed.

"Demon!" Myrlla gasped.

Hyr-Vlk went to grab Cym, but the shaman thrust out a hand and the Sydian warrior flew backward off the stage and crashed to earth among his people.

Gul-Vlk started to shout for calm, but before he could finish he too was hurled into the crowd below.

The shaman's wolf-head loomed over Cym and an excited but familiar voice said, "Shall we go?"

Alaron had never had so much fun in his life. The Sydians had been caught totally unaware. Most were unarmed, for it was bad luck to bear weapons to a marriage ceremony, so no one was shooting arrows or waving swords. A few daggers flashed, but the warriors turned out to be almost superstitiously terrified of magi and did not come close.

The pregnant woman who'd been translating for Cym backed away, holding her belly protectively, and Alaron stood back and let her go.

All around him, the lamiae poured into the camp, baring teeth and wielding spears and the gnosis. Fire blossomed in the dark, and mage-bolts blazed at any warrior foolish enough to stand his ground, but there was little resistance. The Sydian magi were low-blooded and badly trained, with little control over their gnosis; they were no match for the lamiae. And the sheer inhuman aspect of the lamia warriors now pouring into the camp was enough to break the tribe's fighting men before they even raised their weapons. Naugri led the attack, crowing excitedly and followed by a rush of whooping serpentmen. After years of running and hiding, they were delighted to be able to strike openly.

Fydro and Hypollo had carried *Seeker* on their shoulders and now Alaron turned to Cym, who was still shaking with cold and shock and gaping wordlessly. He threw off the wolfskin and draped it about her shivering body, then ordered, "Naugri, help her."

The lamia swept Cym into his arms and slithered back to the skiff. He lowered her in gently while Alaron leaped to the tiller.

"Have you heard from Kekropius?" he asked.

Naugri licked his lips with his thick, reptilian tongue, then said, "He has your artifact." He looked Cym over, then bowed his head and rippled away.

Cym, still speechless, stared after him in stunned amazement.

Alaron kissed her forehead, drinking her in with his eyes. He hoped the tattoo was something that could be easily removed. His own arms and chin were merely inked, copied from a sha-man they had captured earlier. "I can't believe I've found you," he whispered.

She smiled bravely. "Neither can I—you, of all people." She peered at the lamiae as they crowded around, so alien a sight that she cowered against his chest, even guessing they meant her no harm. "Who are your new friends?" she asked timorously.

"Lamia—snake-people," he said with a grin.

She blinked. "Like in the Lantric myths?"

"Constructs, made to mirror the legends. I'll explain once we're in the air—but right now we'd better go." He waved the serpent-folk back, then powered up the keel. *Seeker* lifted willingly and he turned the bow toward the south. "We've got to get back to our caves before dawn."

They talked while they flew. Cym pressed against him as he worked the sails and tiller until she'd stopped shaking, then she edged away, to his regret, though she continued to listen avidly, intrigued, as he explained who the lamiae were and what he'd promised them. She was moved by their plight, and Alaron was reminded that the Rimoni themselves too often found themselves fugitives in the land they had once ruled.

She quickly told him her own tale—the crash on Phaestos, the long months on the road, and her ignominious capture—and he thought she sounded more vulnerable than he'd ever seen her. He couldn't believe they'd managed to reach her exactly at the moment of her enforced marriage—it felt like fate, not coincidence. It was almost enough to make him believe in a higher power again.

But then it was his turn again, and his awful duty to report not just the death of Jeris Muhren, but the probable death of her father and his caravan. At first she didn't seem to hear him, then she refused to believe him, until finally she howled in despair and collapsed in the bottom of the hull, screaming and wrenching at her hair, a harrowing sound that twisted Alaron's own gut. He couldn't leave the tiller, so all he could do was murmur weak sympathies as tears ran down his own cheeks.

Eventually she subsided, but when they landed, she stayed curled in a fetal position, refusing to speak or to move, until a group of young female lamiae crowded about her, murmuring and stroking her. To Alaron's surprise, Cym let them take her away. He guessed it was some kind of female thing, but whatever it was, he was grateful.

The lamia war party arrived back just before dawn. Kekropius came straight to him, his eyes shining. "I am proud, Milkson. Your plan was a success, and not a single one of our people was injured. You led us well."

Alaron felt himself blush. He'd not had a lot of praise in his life and he still found it hard to know how to react to it. "Thanks," he mumbled.

Kekropius pressed a cylindrical leather case into Alaron's hands. "This is what you sought?" he asked with a note of anxiety in his voice.

Alaron removed the cylinder cap and tipped the greatest treasure of the empire into his hands. He'd glimpsed it only briefly in Norostein, back in Junesse, a lifetime ago. It looked the same, as far as he could tell. "Yes, this it," he said, and Kekropius beamed proudly. He turned it over in his hands disbelievingly.

"It was right where the tattooed man said," Kekropius told him.

"Well done," Alaron praised, and the lamiae about him hollered triumphantly. At that moment it was easy to believe that they really were all so young in years.

They were currently based in a limestone hill riddled with tunnels south of the Imperial Road. Before resting, he and Kekropius went to find Cym, to make sure she was all right. They found her staring into space in the small chamber they'd prepared for her. Alaron wasn't sure whether she'd be in tears, but to his surprise she was sitting wrapped in a blanket, hugging her knees, pale, but otherwise calm. She looked Kekropius over curiously, but it looked like she had adapted to the reality of the lamiae with remarkable equanimity.

"I always believed the Lantric myths were real," she said simply. "I was right."

"But they're constru—"

She put a finger to his lips. "Real."

Kekropius took in her words with an odd look, then bowed from the waist. "Lady Cymbellea, all we have is yours."

Cym smiled slowly. "That, Alaron, is proper manners."

Alaron rolled his eyes. Then he pulled out the leather cylinder. It was about a foot long, a rod of wood plated with curved bone panels onto which were etched all manner of Runic symbols. Thanks to Turm Zauberin, Alaron was familiar with some of them. Attached to one end were eight two-foot-long leather straps, each tipped with a colored bead.

"This is the emperor's treasure?" Kekropius mused. "A strange thing. Do you understand it?"

"A little," Alaron said slowly. "A scytale is an encryption device—they were invented by the Rimoni legions to send coded messages. But no one uses them anymore. We only learned about them at college because of this one." He pointed. "Look: they used to wrap these cords about the rod in different configurations so you knew how to match certain letters with others. That way, so long as the sender and receiver knew the configuration, you could write a short note that would be nothing but nonsense to anyone else."

"Impressive," said Kekropius, wonderingly.

"Not really, not once you know the secret—they were already obsolete by the time Corineus came along. I guess they were too easy to decipher. I wonder why Baramitius used one at all? It seems an odd choice." He twisted one end thoughtfully, just to see if it would move, then gasped as it clicked and the runes on the shaft changed. "Look!" he cried, "these runes are only visible through holes in the outer bone shell—if you twist it, you get different runes." He whistled softly. "This isn't so simple after all."

Kessa slithered from a cavern and came up to him. She touched her left breast and then his lips. "Milkson," she said without any visible emotion.

Alaron's fingers went to his lips. By Kessa's standards, she'd practically danced a jig.

She peered at Cym curiously. "Your woman is well?"

"I'm not his woman," Cym said quickly, to Alaron's discomfort, but Kessa merely blinked and left again, moving with sinuous grace.

Kekropius patted Alaron's shoulder before following, leaving the young magi alone.

Cym looked at him. "So, oh mighty hero, what's a 'Milkson'?"

He went utterly scarlet, stammered a few incoherent words, and fled.

It was a long time until he got to sleep. He had to ward the Scytale in case someone tried to scry it, though he was fairly sure it had its own wards. Then he had to report to the Elders. Fortunately, there was no sign of pursuit. The last lamia to leave had reported that the unconscious Sydian magi had been tied up and left on the hillside above the camp. Order had eventually been restored among the tribesfolk and they had decamped before dawn and headed north. There had been some deaths when the tribesfolk had panicked— not many, but Alaron regretted even those who had died so he could rescue one woman from unwanted marriage. He wouldn't hesitate to do the same again tomorrow, but it was a good reminder that in any fight, there would always be losers.

"So, you now have your woman and this thing you sought," Mesuda creaked. "You will hold to your promise now and show us to the Promised Land?" The other Elders leaned in, watching him closely.

Alaron bowed. "It will be my honor."

I've got the Scytale back. I've rescued Cym. This is the most perfect moment of my life.

20

Tangled Webs

Noros

Argundians go to war for land and honor; Schlessens, for plunder and honor; Rondians, for power and honor; Rimoni, for passion and honor. Only a Noroman goes to war over contract law. They are a nation of shopkeepers and lawyers and they deserve all they will get when the Revolt is quashed.

Philippe l'Orlei, Pallas 906

We are men of principle, and a principle holds true whether writ large or scrawled in a margin. Our word is our bond. If a man cannot be trusted, he is no man.

General Leroi Robler, Norostein, 907

Brochena, Javon, Antiopia
Shawwal (Octen) 928
4th month of the Moontide

"How fare my king and his sister, Magister Gyle?" the shaven-headed Jhafi asked softly. Harshal ali-Assam was a Nesti man, here in Brochena in strictest secrecy: he wasn't talking about Francis and Olivia.

Gurvon Gyle, clad in a shapeless Jhafi kirta and wearing a loose turban, glanced about the little pipe-house. The beguiling smoke coiled about the ceiling, but he was close to the only window, and a lifeline of clean air. The other man seemed immune to the stuff; he'd probably grown up smoking it. They were sharing arak and a mezze of dried fruits and roasted nuts.

"They are both well," he said, equally softly. "She is in the keep. He is in a safe house."

"Where?"

Gyle smiled. "I'll need more from you before I divulge that, Harshal." He paused, then risked letting a secret slip. "Have you heard from Elena?"

Harshal's pupils narrowed as he took that in. *So, no then. Good.* He'd assumed Elena would go straight to the Nesti, but perhaps not—as they believed that she'd sold Cera out, not the other way around, that was understandable. Letting slip that he didn't know her whereabouts had been a shot in the dark. *And I missed.*

"We have heard she is no longer at the palace," Harshal admitted. "Have you and she fallen out again?"

Gyle shrugged. *Let him think that.* "If you find her, kill her swiftly, before she persuades you of anything," he advised. "The woman has a poison tongue."

Harshal showed no emotion. "Why did you ask to meet me?"

Gyle sipped his milky arak. "The Dorobon are better in theory than actuality," he remarked drily.

"Debtors rarely enjoy the company of their creditors," Harshal remarked, running a hand over his smooth skull. He was an urbane man in his thirties from old Jhafi nobility, well traveled, and with a considerable personal fortune. He was a connoisseur of wine and olive oil, and a practitioner of Ja'arathi, the milder form of Amteh. His ties to the Nesti were strong, he was well known among both Jhafi and Rimoni, and he walked easily among the Harkun nomads. He was a man of many talents, but his first loyalty was to the Jhafi.

"It looks like you Javonesi have been shocked into submission by the suddenness of the Dorobon strike. No one has retaliated. Are your leaders paralyzed by the threat to Cera and Timori?"

Harshal gestured noncommittally. "Wars take time to arrange," he noted. "But we are many, and the Dorobon remain shut in Brochena. The capital is not well blessed with resources. The people leave in their droves to avoid starving. Time is on our side."

This was all true. The Dorobon appeared to be blind to the possibilities. The refugee columns were growing by the day, and the Dorobon, not understanding that food in this land came from provincial strongholds like Lybis and Forensa, obviously thought letting the commoners go would weaken their enemies, burdening them with extra mouths to feed. But the refugees were no burden to the Aranio and the Nesti: they were fresh manpower.

"How long will this unofficial truce hold?"

"For a time," Harshal replied, "but not forever. You must remember that we *elect* our kings here in Javon. If one falls, we will unite behind another. It is a sad truth that very soon we will have elected a new king and Timori and Cera Nesti will no longer be so important. Already we note that the Dorobon are fewer than we feared. Our scouts report only two legions. Your windships have flown away. This truce will not hold for long."

Gyle nodded slowly, uncomfortably aware that the Javonesi understood the situation quite as well as he did. "Listen, Harshal, I am trying my damnedest to keep your prince and princessa alive."

"Why?"

"Because the Dorobon are a disaster waiting to happen. Cera understands this place. Give the situation time. It may all unravel without the need for open battle." Good lies should be plausible and contain as much truth as possible—though in truth, he wasn't sure it was a lie at all. "Give it time, Harshal. Tell your masters not to be hasty."

It was Harshal's turn to look noncommittal. "We hear rumors of some kind of marriage."

"They are true," Gyle confirmed. "I am working to arrange it, to secure Cera's safety."

Harshal's eyebrows shot up. "Why?"

"To secure peace. War is ruinous, man. Believe me, I've seen a few and I know."

"What does Cera say to this?"

"She is against it, of course, but she will go through with it for the sake of Javon."

"And Francis?"

"He is lukewarm, and his mother is vehemently opposed. She wants Cera and Timori executed."

"The people would be outraged. That would trigger the uprising."

Gyle spread his hands and assumed his most moderate, *reasonable* visage. "That's what I tell them."

Harshal steepled his fingers. "Are the Dorobon to be reinforced?"

Gyle smiled and shook his head. "Perhaps. How long can you give me before the Jhafi abandon Cera and Timori to their fates?"

"Maybe three months. Until year's-end."

Gyle contemplated that. "I can promise you the Dorobon will not be reinforced before then," he said carefully. *As far as I know they're not to be reinforced at all. But if I can stall any uprising until I can get reinforcements of my own, I can win this game. Me, not Octa Dorobon, nor anyone else.* "Hold off any action, please. Let me try to save your king and princessa."

"What's in it for you?" Harshal inquired. "You had King Olfuss murdered. The Nesti are not going to change their minds about you, Gurvon Gyle."

"Mater-Imperia Lucia ordered that strike, not me. Elena disobeyed my orders."

Harshal cocked his head at that. "That is not what Elena told me."

"She was under orders to reveal the truth to no one," Gyle replied smoothly. He couldn't tell if Harshal believed him or not; the man was too capable a player. "I want amnesty, not forgiveness. Lucia is looking for excuses to betray me. I'm richer than her son the emperor and I'll happily spread it round to escape her clutches."

He saw that Harshal remained unconvinced but attentive. The hint of money could achieve things that virtue and fidelity could not.

Octa Dorobon looked like a constipated toad, squatting on her throne with a look of concentrated agony on her face. Gathered about her were her adherents, the retinue of any great magi house:

cousins, nieces, and nephews; men and women who'd married in, seeking advancement; favored protégés: a gaggle of whining, complaining bitterness with the combined gnostic firepower to level a fortress.

That most of their hatred was focused at him did not trouble Gurvon Gyle, for now at least. It was not beyond possibility that Lucia had ordered his assassination, but he'd taken measures. And in the open light of day, he was careful to walk the line between ruling over them and consulting.

They were gathered in the Small Chamber, which had been Cera's council room. The Dorobon didn't do meetings; they sat on thrones and issued decrees they'd decided upon without consulting anyone, least of all him. But his new title meant nothing could happen without his approval. As the only way to relieve him of the title was to let Francis be crowned, and with her son becoming less controllable by the day, this was a cleft stick that was clearly driving Octa mad.

The room was now festooned with shields and busts and pennants of the Dorobon, and a cluster of thrones had been positioned at the far end. The central one was for Francis, once he'd been crowned; for now, it was Gyle's, seated between mother and son. There was one for Olivia, but it was never used; the daughter of the house had no interest in politics. The council table was gone and there were no other chairs, leaving the advisers standing around the walls, chipping into conversations if they dared.

"Mother, I have said that I agree with *Imperial Envoy* Gyle," Francis complained into the uncomfortable silence. "I want to be crowned under Javonesi protocols." So he could marry multiple wives. The boy was positively fixated with the idea of spending his nights surrounded by a bevy of beautiful, exotic women.

"You are a mage of the Kore, Francis. You will marry Leticia de Gallia or Felice d'Aruelle, or whichever royal pure-blood that I choose for you." Octa's piggy eyes went to Gyle. "Magister Gyle will renounce his obscene suggestion."

Her senior adviser, Fenys Rhodium, the widower of Octa's dead sister, stepped forward. "Only a priest of the Kore may marry your son, milady," he said. His pronouncement drew murmurs of agreement.

Gyle ignored him. His own position was strengthening as days passed. He'd made a deal with the Aranio family of Riban to bring in badly needed supplies of fresh food, making sure it was distributed in his name. Despite Octa's posturing, everyone here knew they needed him. Octa had used Rhodium to try to create her own spy network, but Gyle had quickly set his people onto them, killing a dozen of Octa's greenbuds in short order. She might suspect he was behind the slaughter of her new agents, but she could prove nothing. His people had long experience in foreign lands, and Rhodium's Pallas-bred intriguers were no match for experienced killers like himself or Mara Secordin, no matter how pure-blood they might be. And Rutt Sordell was back in a male body—a captured Dorobon agent—and was feeding them whatever misinformation Gyle thought might be *helpful*.

He turned his attention back to the matter at hand. "Milady, let me say it again: there are provisions in the local laws for the king to marry a multitude of women, if he so chooses. It is a way of tying an unsettled realm together. If your enemies have children in line for the throne, would they still be enemies?" Gyle saw Francis nodding at his words. The young king-to-be saw him as a true friend now, much to his mother's horror.

"Doubly so," Octa retorted. "I have seen brother kill brother for less."

"They would have a claim to legitimacy," Rhodium agreed, "which would make them doubly dangerous."

"But you would have those children as hostages," Gyle replied evenly.

"I will not legitimize any child born to my son outside of a Kore-sanctioned marriage," Octa boomed.

Francis pouted. "I don't want Leticia or Felice," he complained. "They're ugly and dull."

"You'll marry who I tell you to," Octa told him. They glared at each other, and Gyle could almost hear the mental conversation:

I'm king—I'm your mother—whine, complain—bellow, shriek. He suppressed a smile.

"Lord Francis," Sir Terus Grandienne, the Dorobon household's most senior knight, interrupted, "my men are chafing. When will you let us march on Riban?" The attempted change of subject was quite deliberate; Sir Terus was one of Octa's people. She despised the younger knights, Francis's playmates, who sided with him.

Francis refused to be diverted. "I am the king! I want a crown!" he pouted like a petulant twelve-year-old. The older men tried to hide their scorn while the younger clamored their agreement. Eyes were cast about, looking for someone to blame, and most went to those kneeling patiently at the far end of the room: Francesco Perdonello and a flock of his Gray Crows, the city's bureaucrats, laden with law texts for reference. Perdonello was the only remaining member of Cera's old Inner Council; most had fled to Forensa or died in the north.

Perdonello coughed discreetly. "Majesty, until the reconstruction of the constitution to legitimize—"

Francis whirled and flashed his hand as if slapping the air, and thirty feet away, Perdonello reeled at the unseen blow. His Gray Crows cringed behind him.

"*This* is my legitimacy!" Francis shouted, making his periapt glow. "I want a crown!"

Gyle watched Perdonello pick himself up. His face was expressionless, despite the fresh welt on his cheek. The head of the Gray Crows was not a man to show emotion, even in dire straits. Ironically, Perdonello had become even more influential since the dissolution of the Inner Council: it was supposed to have put all the power into Octa's hands, but what the Dorobon did not see, they could not control.

"The bills are almost completed, sire," Perdonello said gravely, as if nothing had happened. "Arrangements are being made apace. Next month, sire."

"It's taking too long," Francis complained. "Everything here takes too long."

"The Nesti burned your father's constitution, sire," Perdonello explained. "The traditional Javon constitution requires an elected monarch. We are altering the clauses as swiftly as we can, but thought must be given to so many contingencies, and then reviewed by lawmakers before being submitted for your warrant. The process—"

"Shut up, man! You go on and on! You bore me!" Francis glowered about him. "I'm bored with everything! Damned country: there's not even anything to hunt here!"

Octa's mouth pursed in irritation. "Francis, grow up. There is more to being a king than feasts and hunts."

Francis Dorobon clearly didn't agree. He jabbed a finger at Perdonello. "Finish writing your laws this week, man. Send them to me." He turned and looked defiantly at his mother. "And retain the clauses about polygamy if you want to keep your fingers."

Perdonello bowed awkwardly from his kneeling position as Francis flounced down from his throne.

"And Mother, what an excellent suggestion: I want a feast. And something to hunt!"

"There are mountain lions in the hills to the west," Gyle put in.

"Lions!" Francis spun toward him. "Excellent! I want to hunt lions." Gyle half-bowed in acknowledgment as he added, "Come, tell me of these great cats." He started walking toward the door, but his mother interrupted him.

"Magister Gyle will join you later," she said firmly. "We need his . . . wisdom . . . on a few more details."

Francis's mouth contorted. "Kings do not do details. Join me later, Gyle." He swaggered out of the room, taking his coterie with him to start the evening's carousing.

Once they were gone, Octa clapped her hands and barked, "Out!" at Perdonello and his Crows.

Gyle carefully did not meet Perdonello's eye as he watched them leave. He wanted to give no hint of the relationship they had been forging of late.

"Magister Gyle," Octa started, once the room was completely empty of all but her own people.

He turned to face her, carefully neutral in his stance. "Milady Dorobon."

The Nesti murdered her husband, he reminded himself, *and half her friends.*

"I do not like the way you seek to ingratiate yourself with my son. He is still naïve enough to believe that a man like you might actually wish him well."

What you're really worried about is that I might retain his friendship even after I have to give up my role as Envoy, he thought wryly. "I won him a throne, milady."

"Dorobon force of arms won the throne," Sir Terus Grandienne responded coldly. "We could have destroyed any army they sent against us."

"Well spoken, Sir Terus. We owe you nothing, Gyle."

"What use is he, then?" Rhodium sniffed rhetorically. "Apart from entertaining young Francis, that is. Perhaps we should make him the Court Jester?" A low laugh ran about the room.

"He knows how to speak with mudskins," snickered a niece of Octa's, a middle-aged battle-mage with double chins and a florid face. "Perhaps that's all he's good for."

"Yes, indeed," Octa agreed. "Let me state plainly: you are not welcome here, Gyle. The Crown may have made you Envoy, but you have outstayed your welcome. Even men of such importance as Imperial Envoys can have accidents. I think perhaps it best that you tender your resignation and leave, before something *unfortunate* happens."

Typical Octa: as subtle as an Estellayne bull. He stood and descended from his throne. "I will gladly relinquish my role: when your son is crowned, and not before." He looked about him, thinking about the three magi in his pay currently watching from spy holes around the room, as well as Rutt Sordell in the young mage right behind Rhodium. "I believe I have a hunt to arrange. This session of the court is over."

Sir Terus stepped in front of him. "You will give milady her due reverence," he ordered.

"I give what reverence is owed," Gyle replied coolly. "Excuse me," he added, stepping around Sir Terus.

Sir Terus gripped his shoulder and pulled him to a halt. "You are not excused." He pulled a glove from his pocket and slapped it across Gyle's cheek. "I challenge you to a duel, Gurvon Gyle, for your disrespect toward the matriarch of House Dorobon."

The room fell silent.

Oh, for Kore's sake. Gyle shook off the knight's hand off. Sir Terus Grandienne was a pure-blood, one of those who'd survived the Nesti poisons in 921, and he was a renowned fighter. To accept the challenge would be suicidal. Thankfully, dueling had long been identified as the leading killer of magi in Yuros, and with the need for gnosis-blood always rising, it had been forbidden. It still went on, though, for it was considered manly. "I think not, Sir Terus— although I shall be sure to mention the offer in my next report to Pallas."

"Coward."

The room hissed with the suppressed thrill of anticipated violence.

"A realist, Sir Terus. What was the last dictate issued by Emperor Constant about dueling between magi? I believe he called it an act of treachery and dishonor?"

"You can hide behind parchment if you like, Gyle. It won't protect you in the end."

"I'm not hiding, Terus."

"I believe you are a craven backstabber, Gyle."

Gyle glanced at Octa. There was nothing but amusement in her eyes. He turned back to Terus. "Well, Terus." He grinned suddenly and slapped the man's shoulder as if he were a friend. "Best you don't turn your back, then."

Terus's face drained of color. Dueling was one thing, but Gyle's reputation was deadly. Everyone here knew full well he would and could kill a man in his sleep if he wished to.

He turned and left before someone else got it into their head to make a name for themselves, but he couldn't quite suppress a smile. *Good luck sleeping now, Sir Terus.*

Cera folded the piece of paper and left it in the middle of her bed, then, her heart speeding, studied herself in the mirror. She hurriedly retied her ponytail and straightened her circlet, then left the room, ignoring the urge to glance back, and waited in the small antechamber. The adjoining room had been Timori's when they were younger—this had been the nursery suite, when she'd shared her room with Solinde—but she had no idea where he was being held. Portia Tolidi used it now, when she wasn't in Francis Dorobon's bed.

She would hear anyone coming up the hall, she decided, so she dropped to her knees and peered through the keyhole back into her own room. Her heart quickened as she saw the secret panel in the wall slide open.

She didn't know the heavily cloaked woman who entered the room, but she studied her carefully as she went to the unmade bed and picked up the folded piece of paper she'd left. She was middle-aged, and thin to the point of being gaunt, except for a pot belly. She had a huge nose, like the prow of a windship. Her coloring and the gold-looped nose-ring suggested that she was from Lantris. She read the brief note Cera had written, *I need to see Magister Gyle. Important*—and tucked it into her bodice. Cera prayed the Lantric woman would pass it on, though the intruder didn't leave immediately; instead, she bent over the sheets and started sniffing them.

Ugh! She's like a dog!

A door swung open behind her and she spun guiltily, too slow to conceal what she was doing. She looked up at Portia Tolidi, clad only in a robe, staring down at her. The Gorgio woman's mouth fell open and Cera put a finger to her lips, her face pleading.

The look on Portia's face turned to curiosity and she stepped forward silently, bent, and nudged Cera aside. She smelled of sex and stale sweat, and her hair was tangled. These little flaws in her porcelain perfection somehow made her more human. She put her eye to the keyhole herself, then whispered, "Who is she? What's she doing?"

Cera shook her head, fingers to her lips, thinking, *Maybe we're going to have to be friends after all.* She leaned in and breathed in Portia's ear, "Come away. We can't talk here. Come to the baths."

Portia nodded wordlessly, and they hurried away, not looking at each other. The stairwell led down five flights in a tight spiral and finished in an old Jhafi bowri that the royal family had used as their bath. No one else was there this early in the morning. Cera locked the heavy door behind them and joined Portia at the edge of the water as she was pulling off her gown, revealing her pale body. She descended the steps, her hips swaying gracefully.

It was hard to suppress her envy. Portia truly was perfect. Cera found herself staring at the narrow, flat waist and thatch of russet pubic hair, the narrow hips and long legs. The woman was even more beautiful than Solinde had been, and she'd always thought Solinde utterly lovely. She was horribly self-conscious of the pudginess of her own belly, not plump, but halfway there, and her unremarkable breasts, her unfashionably dark coloring. She half-turned to hide her face, and began talking to cover her sudden confusion. "I was going to bathe before dinner, but I wasn't sure what the day would bring and—"

"He bites me," Portia growled softly. "When he comes, he likes to bite my shoulder. Sometimes he draws blood. Look." She showed her shoulder, a mess of purple and yellow bruises and red scabbed welts.

The rest of Cera's meaningless babble died in her throat. "I'm sorry—"

"For what? Not stealing him from me? Just be thankful he only wants me."

Cera reached out, touched the other woman's upper arm, and then walked past her into the water. "We must get fully in." She pushed off into the dark waters. It was the lighting and the copper-colored tiles that made the water appear black, for in fact it was clear, fresh water from rain-tanks. She dived under the surface and swam to the far side, where there was a ledge to sit on.

She glanced back and saw Portia was still sitting on the steps. She had soap, and was furiously rubbing between her legs, grunting with disgust. Bubbles rose about her as she scoured herself, then washed her belly and breasts, and then did it all over again. When at last she was done, she glared about her, her teeth bared. She dived under the surface, then emerged halfway across the pool, her ringlets fanning out behind her long and straight, her body white beneath the surface. She went under again, then rose like a river fish and joined Cera on the ledge, carefully out of reach. Her hair hung straight, water streaming from the sleekly shining tresses.

The water had been warmed by the sunbaked earth before being piped into the bowri. It was gloriously tepid and all-enveloping. Cera felt her tension ease a little. She met Portia's bruised eyes. "Elena told me that water and earth can hide us from scrying."

Portia looked perplexed. "What is *scrying*?"

"It is a magic thing: some magi can see things that are far away, but they can be foiled by hiding in water or earth. This place is perfect for secret conversations; Elena told me so."

Portia's face took on an expression that Cera was startled to recognize as respect. "You know so much." She cocked her head, staring openly. "When I heard that you were ruling Brochena like a king, I was filled with admiration. That a woman could do so much—it made me proud."

Really? Cera felt herself coloring. "But in Hytel, people must have hated us."

Portia tittered softly. "Oh yes, Uncle Alfredo was in a fury. He cursed you, and utterly screamed blue murder about Elena Anborn." Her eyes flitted about. "Where is she? Is she hiding, waiting to rescue you?"

Cera shook her head, frightened to tell the truth, that she'd betrayed Elena and her own people. *It was to preserve them, I swear.* "Elena has vanished." *She's out there somewhere, and she must hate me so much . . .*

"Who was that woman in your room?" Portia whispered, leaning closer. Her breath smelled of cloves, sharp, but not unpleasant.

"I think she must be one of Gyle's magi. She had a nose-ring: that probably means she's from Lantris. Married women wear them there."

Portia wrinkled her nose. "That's demeaning." She flinched. "Like I can talk."

Portia was easy to read, or at least she seemed so to Cera. In public she had always exuded a kind of cultured sophistication, but here her mask was lifted and her emotions clear. *Portia isn't whoring herself—she's being pimped by her family*, Cera realized at last. *And she helped Tarita.*

She timidly reached out and seized Portia's hand. "I think maybe we can be friends," she whispered. She stared at Portia's shoulders, at the skin where Francis bit her. "Won't he even heal you afterward?"

Portia covered the marred skin with her hand. "He says he is branding me, to show that I am his." She lifted her chin angrily. "Every night is the same. I must undress, and then pleasure him with my mouth, to ready him. Then he takes me, always on top, for what feels like hours. And when he comes . . ." She bared her teeth and gnashed them ferociously. "He thinks I like it." She glared at Cera. "One day I will kill him."

Cera looked away, her mind working feverishly. *Is this real, or is it a trap? Is this something Gyle has devised to fool me, to make me betray myself? Or is this a real ally?* She wished longingly that she were a mage and could read the other woman's mind, and found herself missing Elena again. "When he sleeps . . ."

Portia scowled bitterly. "He does not sleep in my presence. And I can take nothing into his room, not even my clothes." She clenched her teeth again. "His mother strips me and then searches me outside his room. He sends me out before sleeping. They trust no one."

Cera closed her eyes bleakly. Everything seemed so hopeless. *But perhaps I really do have an ally.* She squeezed Portia's hand. "We will find a way. We still have our brains and our free will."

Portia squeezed back. "I meant what I said, you know. I do admire you. You have such dignity and courage."

"I'm just lucky I'm too ugly for Dorobon to want me."

Portia shook her head. "You are not ugly, amica. Not at all."

Oh, but I feel ugly, especially here beside you: flabby and shapeless and middle-aged before my time.

Portia put an arm around her shoulder, pulled Cera's hair back behind her ear and whispered, "You are a strong woman, Cera Nesti. You were a true queen, and one day you will be again." The feel of Portia's skin on hers made Cera squirm. She'd never been a hugging child. But this felt nice.

"But I don't know what to do. They're magi—we have no one to help us."

Portia shook her head. "We have friends, amica. Tarita knows people in the city, and word gets in and out, she told me. There are people on the outside who wish to aid us. Remember how your father defeated the Dorobon all those years ago? Like father, like daughter, amica!"

Cera swallowed. *Yes, there are people who might help . . . But we need access to the passageways again . . . we need to get the eyes off us. And we need time, to plan things . . .* She looked at Portia. "Have you ever been told how to shield your thoughts from the magi?"

Portia shook her head.

Cera smiled. "It's not hard. I can show you how."

"You would do this for me?" Portia's smile lit up her face. "In return, I can teach you also."

"What?"

"How to fascinate a man."

Cera snorted. "Me?"

Portia touched her lips with a finger. "Yes, you. Any woman can be fascinating if she wished to be. It's all in the way you carry yourself."

"But there is no man I wish to fascinate."

Portia snickered. "There is a whole court of men for you to twist about your fingers."

"But I'm ugly—"

"No! No, no, no—you are beautiful, as all women are. Beauty is more than looks, amica. Much more. You could entrance them all, if you wish to. It's all about self-confidence."

Cera's heart thumped. Suddenly the world seemed filled with possibilities again. Reluctantly she removed Portia's arm from her shoulders—it had been comforting—so she could face her. *She's what, twenty-three? Almost five years my senior . . .* She inhaled, let the responsibility settle on her shoulders. "I suppose . . . We can try it, but first you have to learn how to protect your mind . . ."

As she passed on what Elena had taught about concealing her thoughts, part of her mind raced on. *I need some kind of leverage over Gyle . . .* She smiled, remembering why she'd left that note in her room to be found in the first place.

Perhaps there is hope . . .

Gurvon Gyle waited in Cera's parlor, standing when he heard the door unlock. Hesta had found the note the day before, but he'd been tied up trying to confirm the coronation arrangements, an endless exercise in wrangling and nitpicking that was driving him crazy. If this was ruling, Francis truly deserved it.

The door swung open and Cera Nesti entered. Her Rimoni dress was damp in patches and her long black hair was hanging wet about her shoulders. It made her look oddly vulnerable, as if other things about her might also unravel. But her manner was focused, as if she was finally throwing off her despair. That gave him pause; she was suddenly interesting again.

"Cera," he greeted her, "you wished to see me?"

Cera started, then lifted her chin. "You may enter," she said ironically, in that way she had of acting way beyond her years. It reminded him of Elena, in a good way.

"Happy birthday, Princessa. You are nineteen today, yes? You should celebrate."

"There is nothing to celebrate," Cera replied, affecting carelessness.

He gave her a disarming smile. He liked her ongoing defiance, despite her helplessness. She was enduring, despite not having seen her little brother, despite having lost her people. But there was something about her today, something more confident. He wondered what it was.

"You left a note?" He sent tendrils of gnosis into her mind to try and discern her intent, but she barred them easily. Of course he could break into her mind, though not without causing damage. It annoyed him a little, but also intrigued him; it reminded him that she had been Elena's protégée.

And I turned her against you, Ella, he thought, *so mine the victory.*

"Magister Gyle, I heard something of interest two nights ago." At his raised eyebrows, she continued, "I was on my balcony, which is diagonally below Octa Dorobon's."

Interested despite himself, he looked toward the spy-hole with his gnostic sight to ensure Hesta wasn't there, then asked, "What did you see?"

Cera smiled unconsciously. "Octa was alone, waiting. She didn't notice me at all." *She still takes pleasure in stealth*, Gyle noted approvingly. "Then a glowing sphere appeared, about three feet in front of her. She was expecting it, I think."

Gyle leaned forward, itching inwardly. "Who was it?"

Cera smiled sweetly at him. "What do I get in return?"

"I do not take well to being toyed with, Cera," he warned, lifting his hand.

She offered her cheek defiantly. "Go ahead. Hit me. It's what I'd expect of you." She flared her nostrils. "But don't expect any further help against them."

Against—? He lowered his hand slowly. "All right, girl. What do you want?"

"To see my brother. And access to the passageways again. And for you to stop spying on me."

He shook his head. "The passageways are vital to me."

"And to me," Cera flashed back. "We can both use them, as we used to." She cocked her head coquettishly, a gesture so out of character it startled him, and set little alarm bells ringing. "I like sneaking about in the dark too, remember?"

Is she flirting *with me?* The thought of bedding her was . . . enticing. . . *if only to spit on your memory, Ella.* Since she'd betrayed Elena, he'd increasingly been thinking of Cera. Yes, she was somewhat plain, but still far more attractive than Olivia—and he was severely sick of that slug. And she had something Olivia would never have: an interesting mind. He found himself eyeing her speculatively. . . *Is the little girl growing up?*

No. It is better she go to Francis Dorobon a virgin. He expects that. But afterward, when Francis has tired of her . . . *Perhaps.* "Why would you help me?" he asked at last. "And don't even think of lying, girl."

She put her hands on her hips, which reminded him even more of Elena when she was in a defiant mood. "The Dorobon are worse than you, and they hate you. I think our interests are aligned, especially after what I heard Octa and the other mage say."

She does know how to play this game. "All right, I'm interested. But I cannot allow you access to the passageways. Not yet. Timori, possibly." He held up a finger. "Consider your news a down payment."

"Very well. But no one will spy on my rooms again. And you will let me see Timori next week."

He nodded impatiently. "Yes, all right." Cera offered a hand and he shook it crossly, unaccustomed to being outmaneuvered. "Well then?" he demanded.

"Octa greeted the other person as 'Mater-Imperia.'"

Gurvon froze. It wasn't unexpected; of course Octa and Lucia spoke out of his hearing. But about what? He reached out tentatively with his mind, but hers remained infuriatingly opaque. *Elena trained her too damned well.* "What did they speak of?"

Cera smiled. "They spoke of you, Magister."

His throat went dry. "Yes?"

"At first they just gossiped, like old women do." The disdain in her voice was clear. "But then the Mater-Imperia voice said, 'And what of the spymaster? When will you rid me of him?'" Cera studied his face as she spoke, measuring the impact of her words.

"And Octa replied?" he asked, forcing himself to look unmoved.

"Soon."

Soon. He clenched his fists and turned away to the window. *I shouldn't have renegotiated my deal after I caught Elena. I thought I was being so smart, doubling my fee, extending the contract, demanding to be temporary Envoy. You don't fuck with Lucia Fasterius . . .*

"What else?"

"Nothing else. Yet. But Octa is out there most nights."

It sounded plausible: being under the open sky did improve reception for Clairvoyance. He wondered how far advanced Lucia and Octa's plans toward him were. *I need to hear this for myself . . .*

He looked down at Cera, who stood before him, hands on hips, both wary and defiant. There was something different in the way she met his eyes, as if she too were seeing something new in him. She looked both regal and needy, a disturbingly attractive combination.

Something inside his empty core stirred. *She and I . . . is it possible?* He had an urge to seize her, to kiss her, to break her down. Since he and Elena had drifted apart, he missed having a true confidante, someone who was as intelligent as he was, as self-willed and ruthless. He suddenly realized what he might actually have in Cera Nesti: *A partner.*

And I swear she feels it too . . .

But Cera's virginity still had some currency, though he was suddenly loath to let Francis Dorobon have it. He regained control of himself and bowed slightly. "If this is so, I am indebted for the warning," he told her. "I owe you."

Cera met his eyes. "Why should the Dorobon rule this land? They have no ties here. They are just favorites of the emperor's mother. They have been given Javon as a present. They don't belong here."

"They have two legions," he reminded her softly.

"They have one," she corrected, "and one of mercenaries."

She keeps her eyes and ears open. And she was right: only one of the legions here had any particular loyalty to the Dorobon. He'd pulled strings to ensure that was so—as a contingency. He inhaled slowly, staring out the window at the city baking in the morning sun. The heat rolled off the stonework in rippling waves. The distant lake was half its normal size, the salt-gatherers dark ants against the gleaming plain of the shallower far side.

He turned from the view and studied Cera, who was still observing, still keeping her wits about her. He was impressed. "Very well, Princessa," he said. "We have a deal."

Cera's eyes narrowed. "Not 'Princessa'; I am Queen-Regent." She lifted her chin again. "Where is Timori being held? I need to see him."

"What of him? Without him you'd be Paterfamilias," he reminded her, "head of the Nesti in truth, not just as regent."

Her face swelled and she was abruptly a young woman again. "He's my brother!" she snapped indignantly.

She is smart, but she is not self-serving. She puts family first: a very Rimoni trait. He could respect that. Finding things to be loyal to was never easy. "I do not know where your brother is being held," he lied.

Her face changed, her expression becoming more measured. "Get him away from the Dorobon and I'll do whatever you want."

"Would you? And what do you imagine I might want, Princessa?"

She cocked her head, looked up at him with an expression of compromised innocence that was oddly stirring. There had always been something compelling about the notion of corrupting another. "I don't know or care," she replied, her voice resolute, but he could almost believe it contained traces of curiosity, even yearning. It was the shyness, the unwillingness combined with resignation that he found stirring. "I'll do whatever it takes," she said with a kind of desperate dignity.

It took considerable discipline to walk away.

"Well?" Portia whispered after she joined Cera in the crypt, walking between row upon row of tombs between the wall-niches into which the bodies of generations of Brochena's most royal former inhabitants were sealed.

They knelt before the sarcophagus of Fernando Tolidi, Portia's brother, buried here by the Nesti when they retook Brochena. After Portia had decided to let it remain here, a mason had carved his name in the stone and it had been properly sealed.

"It was just like you said it would be," Cera whispered hoarsely. "I stood straighter and imagined myself as desirable to him—it was astonishing! The way he looked at me totally changed." She remembered how potent that moment had felt, despite her loathing for him.

Portia smiled grimly. "I told you. He is the kind of man who likes to take a naïve girl and make her his." She looked away. "My Uncle Alfredo's like that."

Cera didn't want any details; she was already struggling to contain the morass of pride and shame inside her. "He didn't ask anything of me. I think he's still trying to get me into Francis's bed."

Portia made a face. "I can't wait to get out of it." She seized Cera's hand. "But I don't wish it upon you, amica."

"I don't know what I would have done if he'd demanded anything of me. I think I would have just thrown up."

Portia's eyes were pitying. "If it does come to that, pretend eagerness and ask him to teach you. That will make him feel masterful. Men like that," she added in tones of disgust.

Cera looked at her. "You really don't like men, do you?"

Portia's expression became stony. "Whatever I might have liked or disliked was ruined a long time ago. I just want to be free of them all. I think if I had the choice, I would become a Kore Acolyte—not because I believe in the Kore, but because their Acolytes swear to chastity."

"I wanted to be a Sollan priestess when I was younger," Cera confided. "But they aren't virgins. They do it with drui during the seasonal rites."

Portia smiled dourly. "I wanted to take the Sollan vows too, but my family wouldn't let me. They had other plans."

Cera squeezed her hands, wanting to comfort her, but not sure how. "I'm glad you're here with me," she whispered. "If I didn't have you to talk to, I think I'd kill myself."

Portia touched her lips in admonishment. "Hush. That would be a sin."

All day, Gurvon Gyle went from meeting to meeting in the city, face hidden by turban and scarf, clad in a leather-colored kirta. It was like wearing a thin cotton tent, but surprisingly good for moderating the heat. The air was desiccating as the lands awaited the late summer rains that would replenish the parched lands. Brochena was gasping like a dying beast in the desert.

His spies reported no sightings of Elena. He'd always told his agents to create secret refuges for themselves; she would be in one of those, secure from scrying. She'd be plotting something, of that he was sure—against him, and likely Cera too. Elena had been on the defensive when Cera was regent, unable to do anything except await the coming blow, but now she was out there with no ties to hamper her. No one was truly impervious to assassination, and few of the killers he'd known matched Elena's skills.

The hollow between his shoulder blades began to itch persistently.

The mood of the city was as dark as his thoughts. The widowed women of the Jhafi still lamented outside the Dom-al'Ahm, and Rimoni and Jhafi alike brooded sullenly from the city's few shady spots as the Dorobon soldiers marched past under the heat of the midday sun.

While the Dorobon family legion occupied the city, the merce- nary legion patrolled the outlands. Two legions might have been enough to win at Fishil Wadi, but they were too few to secure such a vast land as Javon, and Kaltus Korion had refused to send more men, for he thought to bring the Keshi to battle. Word was that Korion was marching on Halli'kut, and Duke Echor of Argundy somewhere further south, hunting for Salim.

He couldn't afford to think too much of that, though. He needed to secure himself, before Lucia sent her Inquisitors.

His final appointment that day was down a secluded alley near the lake, the smell of the salt water sharp and unpleasant. There was an old house there that had been commandeered by Endus Ryk- jard, the mercenary commander, a Hollenian half-blood mage. He knocked and entered quietly.

Rykjard was sitting on a shaded balcony overlooking the lake, his unruly hair bleached to straw by the sun. A little Jhafi woman clad only in a loincloth was kneeling at his feet. "Gurvon, my friend, this is the way to live, eh?" The commander cupped one of the girl's breasts and squeezed it, then said quickly in Keshi, "Run along, my sweet. Bring arak and water, and a mezze." As she scurried away, Rykjard's eyes followed her appreciably. "Tiny, the women here, but they have such juicy purses. Do you have one?" He grinned, his eyes and teeth startlingly white against his tanned skin; Hollenians tended to tan very darkly even as their hair bleached. Gyle had met him on the Second Crusade, during the sacking of a town some- where southwest of Hebusalim. They'd cut a deal over the plunder, and stayed in touch ever since.

"None I use regularly," Gyle said, sitting. He really didn't want to discuss women. "How does your legion fare, Endus?"

Rykjard grunted. "We're spread from the mountains south of Tigrat to the borders of Forensa, keeping up a screen against the Aranio and the Nesti." He spat. "Why doesn't the king let us attack?"

"He wants the plunder from Riban and Forensa for himself. And he won't leave the capital until he feels secure."

"So never, then," Rykjard grumbled. His girl returned with a flask and two glass tumblers of arak and a jug of iced water, and a platter of nibbles, then left. Gyle added water and sipped the milky-white drink and sighed, enjoying the cool aniseed sweetness.

Rykjard watered his own drink and swilled half of it in one gulp. "Ten thousand men to nail down a land this large is far too few, Gurvon."

"The emperor deemed it enough."

"The emperor . . ." Rykjard trailed off mockingly. "So, Gurvon, what did you want to see me about?"

Gyle lifted his arak, took another sip. This was the dangerous moment, the plunge into darker waters where the sharks lurked, the part of the conversation that could be used against him. "I wanted to run a hypothetical situation past you."

Rykjard knew the game as well as he did. "Say on," he invited. "What harm can speculation do, eh?"

"Imagine that at the end of this Crusade, the Inquisitors go from camp to camp, confiscating all the plunder in the name of Kore. They arrest any who try to withhold their loot, leaving nothing more than a paltry token to bribe the commanders. And here in Javon, the Dorobon send your legion home empty-handed."

Rykjard scowled. "In other words, much the same as what happened after the Second Crusade?"

Gyle nodded. "Exactly."

Rykjard pursed his lips and spat over the balcony. "They wouldn't dare."

"Wouldn't they?"

"Echor commands this Crusade, and he wants the vassal-states to support him. He'll make sure we're paid."

"Echor *thinks* he's commanding the Crusade. Do you suppose Lucia and Constant are just going to let him stroll back into Yuros in two years' time with all the gold and all the glory? And anyway, that's not going to help *you*, Endus, is it? You're stuck here on a three-year contract, no matter what happens."

Rykjard downed the rest of his glass and poured another. "I'm hearing you, Gurvon."

Gyle licked his lips. "How do you like it here, Endus?"

Rykjard's eyes narrowed speculatively. "This place? Too hot. Filthy. Seasons are all wrong. Surrounded by heathen bastards who'll knife you the second you turn your back." He chuckled. "Apart from that, what's not to like?"

"Lots of wet-pursed girls. And Rondian coin goes a long way here. The Rimoni have settled; why not your boys?"

Rykjard squinted at him. Clearly the idea had already occurred to him. "We're mercenaries. We've no ties. We bring our women with us, or we fuck the locals. None of us own land at home—we wouldn't know what to do if we had any." While retiring legionaries were traditionally supposed to be allotted land, most of it ended up in the hands of the magi-nobles. "But it's damned hot here."

"I'd rather be warmer than colder, my friend."

"There is something to be said for that." He took another sip of arak. "I could get used to this place. But the Dorobon intend to send us home at the end of our three years."

"They might not be in charge come the end of three years," Gyle suggested quietly.

"Might they not?" Rykjard mused. "You know, I've spent some time with their battle-magi. They're all pussies. My own magi may be lesser-bloods but they're hard as nails; they could take those high-blood cunts down easy. And my rankers are tough bastards too; they've been fighting border skirmishes in Argundy and Schlessen all their lives, not like these soft-cock Dorobon town boys. Though of course," Rykjard went on thoughtfully, "if the legions were to turn on each other, the Javonesi would be at our throats like a pack of jackals."

"You're right," Gyle agreed. "Any change in ruler would have to happen fast enough that it would be over and done before the Javonesi even glimpse an opportunity. Might need some outside help for that."

They were silent for a minute while Rykjard cogitated. "Adi Paavus would come if I asked," he said eventually. "Probably Hans

Frikter too. And the Estellayne woman, the one who runs the Free Swords—what's her name—?"

"Staria Canestos," Gyle supplied. "Toughest bitch I've ever met, and that includes Elena!"

"Staria, that's right—I swear she was the origin of the vagina-dentata legend!" Rykjard chuckled. "So with four legions—one here, and one each in Forensa, Hytel, and Riban—we could carve this place up and rule it." He topped up their drinks. "Where is Elena, anyway?"

There was a faint possibility that Elena might have run to Rykjard when she escaped Sindon's assassins, in which case Rykjard was toying with him—but he doubted it. In the circumstances, he opted for honesty. "I don't know. We've had a falling-out."

"A shame. I always liked Elena. She called a spade a spade."

No, you only thought she did. "If you see her, let me know. I've a few things to settle with her. There's money in it."

"Of course, my friend." Rykjard put the matter aside lightly. "So the way I see it is that the issue of the spoils won't come up until the Moontide is well past low tide, so, what—Junesse of next year?"

"Most likely. But there will be early signs: plunder caravans returning from the East toward the Bridge will be delayed, told they need more papers, et cetera. You know the drill: anything that ties up the goods somewhere the Imperial Guard can reach."

Rykjard spat sourly. "How will I even know, stuck up here?"

"I have eyes down there; I'll keep you informed." He slapped the table and rose to his feet. "It's always good to see you, Endus. Always good to talk."

Rykjard grinned broadly and waved a hand over the arak. "Stay, have another drink. Let's make a night of it."

"I'd love to, but sadly, I've got to be back in the palace for the evening banquet."

"Ha! Listen to the mighty Envoy." Rykjard stood and they shook hands. "Another time, Gurvon. You let me know if your hypothetical situation looks like becoming a reality, yes?"

"I certainly will."

As he left, he glanced down at the little bare-breasted Jhafi girl. She looked horribly young, but all the locals were short of stature and dark of skin, which made it hard to guess accurately. Her eyes were a lot older than her body, and without a hint of warmth. He wondered how her own people were treating her, now she was the property of a Rondian. Not well, he guessed.

Don't fall asleep after rukking her, Endus; I doubt you'll wake up.

Outside, the late afternoon heat closed in. He sighed at the thought of another endless evening of dining and acidic conversation, and then the fleshy pleasures of Olivia Dorobon's body. Or maybe not; he was boring of pasty white skin and rolls of fat. Cera Nesti had been flirting; he was sure of it . . . He wondered how amenable she might be if he knocked on her door—

No, not yet. Francis will cave in and make her his queen, I am sure of it. Best she remain untouched, for now.

Instead, he took himself to the hidden chamber within the secret part of the dungeons deep below the keep where Coin lay, regrowing her body.

Pale eyes rolled to face him, catching the light as he opened the door and Coin—*Yvette*—bared her teeth, a grimace or smile, her breath hissing. "Where have you been?" she asked painfully. "It's been *days*."

"Why, Yvette, I didn't know you cared," he said cheerily, lighting the lamp with a gesture, though he made sure to keep the light low. Coin's healing-gnosis worked best in the dark—she needed no distractions while she was trying to visualize what she needed herself to be. He pasted a welcoming smile on his face and hoped she would not notice as he swallowed the rising bile.

It had taken several weeks for her to make the eyes her own and fully functioning, but the skin about them had still not yet completely bonded, making her look goggle-eyed, like a fish. On his last visit he'd brought her the skin of a young Jhafi boy fresh from the morgue slab. The boy had been an orphan, with no family, but it had still cost plenty to persuade the mortician to commit such sacrilege. In the end, money had overcome religious scruples, as it usually did, and he'd collected the flesh flayed from the still-warm corpse and soaked it in brine to keep it supple before bringing it down here and laying it over Coin's skeletal body.

Today the sewn seams were still puckered and weeping and the new skin was mottled, almost translucent in places, revealing the musculature and sinews beneath like some horrific biology lesson. But there was no smell of rot, so the skin graft had obviously taken, fused by Coin's own gnosis.

"What do you think?" she asked coyly.

You look like a horror from a taxidermist's nightmares. "You've come a long way," he said diplomatically.

But he didn't fool her. "Revolted, aren't you?" she said, pulling her lips into a rictus grin. "But I'll be back to normal soon—maybe six weeks—and then you'll not even be able to tell it ever happened." She sounded excited for once.

"Does it still hurt?"

"A little. But look!" As he watched with bated breath a change crawled across her face. Painfully slowly her tangled hair lightened and her face widened until it hardened into a painfully familiar shape.

Elena. A mutilated scar-ravaged Elena.

"Don't do that," he rasped. His belly churned.

"I could be her for you," she said earnestly.

Every time he visited, Yvette offered a little more of herself, and it hadn't taken him long to realize that no one had ever paid her this much attention, not since childhood—and perhaps not even then. Yvette was becoming his—but she wanted something in return, and he was not willing to give that, especially not while she looked like a failed necromancy experiment.

"Not Elena, not ever." He backed away a step.

"Don't go!" she said quickly. "I'm sorry, I only meant to tease you."

He stopped and said kindly, "Yvette, I have told you: you don't have to be anyone else with me."

"But how will anyone like me if I'm not someone else?" she asked sadly. She sounded like she genuinely didn't understand.

"You are a person in your own right, Yvette," he said, wondering if the shapeshifter was capable of accepting what he was saying.

She didn't answer for a long while, and when she did, it was to change the subject. "I want to go outside. I'm bored here. It's not healthy, to be locked away from the sun."

"Not until you're fully recovered."

"Please, let me out." Her Elena-face melted away, revealing the plain, weak-chinned face she'd been born with. Tufty ginger hair sprouted from her scalp, and her new eyes had turned her own pale blue. She looked revolting, with the stolen skin of the orphaned Jhafi child weeping pus and blood where it had been stitched together.

"Not when you're like this, Yvette."

When she bared her teeth the insane child inside her was plain to see. Then she sagged morosely. "When?" she asked, her tone somewhere between slyness and desperation, and he could feel the question beneath the question, the one that had been building between them for the long hours they'd spent together as he'd cleaned her, fed her, and given her what she needed to heal herself, listening to her tale and giving her sympathy. All her life she'd been adrift, seen as repugnant by all who knew what she was.

She wants to be loved, or at least what she thinks love is, in all her naïve, innocent immaturity, and in return, she will give her very soul.

Playing with souls was part of the game. Though unreasoning devotion, whether to a king or a god or another human being, repelled him, it was ironic that he could engender such devotion so easily in so many.

<You saved my life,> she whispered into his mind. *<I'd do anything for you.>*

He had fooled wiser women than her. *<I value that, Yvette.>* He reached down and squeezed her fingers gently, knowing that in her imagination that simple gesture meant so much more. And all the while he thought about Cera Nesti, with her clever, seasoned mind and her virginal body.

"Should we steal the knives?" Portia whispered, making Cera suppress a giggle. They were seated alone at the noblewomen's table as usual; thankfully, Octa and Olivia generally ate in their rooms, except for important occasions.

The normal commotions of the high table went on around them. Cera stole a glance at Gyle, seated on the other side of the room. He noticed, raised his glass faintly, and she forced herself to return the gesture before looking away.

"He's fascinated by you," Portia said softly into her own glass. They hardly looked at each other, except for the occasional disdainful glances to maintain the fiction that they hated each other. "But there is another on his mind. He is torn."

"Is he? How do you tell?"

"His eyes stray to you often and linger, trying to meet your eyes, but when they do, he looks away, and he becomes unfocused. He wants you, but another has a claim on him."

"Elena?"

"Maybe." Portia slurped her wine. Another night in Francis Dorobon's bed loomed and she wanted to go there drunk.

Cera's belly churned at the thought of her father's murderer forcing himself on her. "I don't want him."

Portia ate some rice. "I know. You don't like looking at him. The pupils of your eyes grow smaller when you glance in his direction. Believe me, I know what desire looks like, and the opposite also. Gyle is screwing Olivia Dorobon, by the way."

"Her? She's—"

"Ugly as a cow's ass? Si! Nevertheless, she is not whom he is thinking of; she is just part of the game he plays. Some men have complicated lives." Portia flicked back a stray strand of gleaming red hair. Her porcelain face was immaculate. She was wearing an emerald-colored velvet dress that accentuated her coloring. Every man in the room had gazed longingly at her at some point that evening: every man, except Gurvon Gyle.

"You are so beautiful," Cera blurted, then blushed.

Portia licked her lips sourly. "Beauty is a curse. It draws the biggest bullies. They crowd about you, squabbling over you like dogs over a bone." Her eyes went to Francis Dorobon, laughing raucously with his friends.

"Whose attention do you want?" Cera asked, intrigued. She looked about the room, almost entirely full of handsome young men.

She wrinkled her nose. "None of them. I lost my virginity at thirteen and I'm sick and tired of it all. I get no peace."

Cera took a sip of the full-bodied red wine. "Portia, come to the bowri tonight. There is something you need to know."

"I will come after I leave the Pig's room. It would be good to wash again before I sleep. Wait for me at midnight, if you can."

They exchanged one swift glance, then by tacit agreement did not look at each other again.

Cera sat beside the water, half-dozing as she waited for Portia. A single torch lit the cavern, its flickering light glinting on the rippling surface of the water.

Then the grill-door creaked open and slippered feet glided down the corridor outside. Portia emerged from the darkness, once again clad only in a bathrobe. Cera got to her feet, the excitement of conspiracy making her flush. She went to hug her, then stopped. Portia did not look like she would welcome being touched.

"Cera, amica," Portia replied dourly, pushing past. She pulled off the robe and attacked herself with the soap, like that first morning when they'd met here.

Cera swallowed. "I'm sorry," she murmured, undressing and sliding into the waters. She sat on the stairs, just out of arm's reach.

Eventually Portia ceased her frenzied cleansing and dived beneath the surface before finally settling beside Cera on the steps, half-immersed. "There, we can talk now." She looked calmer, as if she had rinsed away her self-loathing.

Cera bit her lip, suddenly not so sure this conversation was a good idea. But she must have the courage of her convictions. After a few moments she pressed on regardless. "Portia, do you know what happened to your brother?"

Portia opened her mouth, then closed it again. "I know what I've been told," she answered eventually. "Your sister killed him." Her eyes darkened a little, then she said firmly, "I do not blame you for this."

"It wasn't Solinde who killed him."

Portia put a hand to her mouth. Her voice was tremulous. "You are sure?"

"I found out the truth, before Fishil Wadi," Cera whispered. "Elena and I learned that it was a shapeshifter in the pay of Gurvon Gyle."

"Sol et Lune!" Portia hissed. Her eyes went wide as saucers and she whispered, incredulous, "You *know* this?"

"Sol's Truth," Cera replied. "I saw the shapeshifter. Elena unmasked it, but that night an enemy attacked us and I never saw it again. I don't know what happened to it."

"Perhaps it is still at court," Portia whispered. "Perhaps it will take the place of someone we trust." Her eyes went wider. "Perhaps it will take the place of one of us."

Cera shook her head. "We would know." An idea occurred to her: "Perhaps it took Elena's place, because her behavior changed so much. Maybe she was not possessed, but entirely replaced!"

Portia shrugged. "I do not know about these things." She tilted her head and looked at Cera. "If I were a shapeshifter I would choose to be ugly, so that men would not look at me."

Cera laughed uneasily. "I would choose to be you." *You're so beautiful it hurts.*

"So you could be dragged to the Pig's bed every night? I don't think so." Portia scowled. "Thank you for telling me this. I believe you. And it is a relief that your sister did not kill my brother. That had been causing me a lot of distress." She smiled timidly.

Cera seized Portia's hand. "We teased Solinde for fancying your brother. But had we known him better, I'm sure we would have loved him."

Portia blinked. "You are kind," she whispered huskily. "It is good that we are friends, for their sakes. But Cera-amica, what are we going to do?"

Cera leaned in and breathed in her ear, "I have a plan starting to come together in my head. Did you know there are secret passageways all through the palace?"

Portia's eyebrows went up. "Really? Mater Luna!"

"I tell you, a spy can see into every room in the three upper stories."

Portia looked outraged. "That is horrible! And that woman we saw in your room has been spying on us?"

Cera nodded. "Gyle, too."

Portia bared her teeth. "Can we get into them? Can we use them to get out of here?" Her eyes blazed with intensity.

Cera was almost overwhelmed by the other girl's excitement. *She is so lovely when she looks like that.* "Maybe—but I expect Gyle will have sealed the passages leading outside."

"Then one night we will go from room to room with our knives." Portia's eyes glittered savagely. She pushed away from the steps and waded to the step below Cera's and knelt there, facing her directly. "We cut their throats!" She made a violent gesture across Cera's neck, making her flinch. "Then we run away!"

Cera swallowed. "Yes."

Portia's face was a bloodthirsty snarl, then, slowly, her expression changed to one that was very serious. Cera stared back at her, and it was as if gravity had let her go, as if she could float away. Every sense was overloaded: her nostrils filled with Portia's clove-breath and rosewater scent and her tongue tingled. Her eyes filled with Portia's mouth, her red lips and pink tongue. The constantly running water was a ripple of sound like a glissade of harp music. Her skin felt porous and the warm water caressed her whole body as Portia gently pushed her knees apart and knelt between them, pressed herself, breasts to breasts, belly to belly beneath the water, and kissed her tentatively.

O Mother Luna, she groaned, and revulsion for the sin she'd feared most of all warred with desire, but the war was brief and defeat was overwhelming. Her lips parted as her arms slid around Portia's shoulders and pulled her in. Their lips crushed softly against each other, and then Portia's tongue slid into her mouth and entwined hers, on and on in a perfect eternity . . .

"Please," she moaned, pulling away to breathe, "I'm not a safian—"

"Of course you are," Portia whispered. "I told you, I know what desire looks like, even if you don't."

"But—"

"Shhh." Portia's hands caressed her shoulders and back as her mouth sealed over Cera's again. The second kiss went on even longer while her terror and need grew in equal measure: *Someone will come . . . someone is watching . . .*

Portia gripped her around the waist and pulled her in, making her back arch, and took her left nipple in her mouth just above the water's surface and suckled on it while her auburn hair spread behind her, swaying like water-weed in the current. Cera gasped, clutched at the back of Portia's head and held her there while inside her, she felt heat and wetness go rushing to her loins. She opened her own mouth to protest, and instead found herself nuzzling Portia's crown.

"Come," Portia whispered. She rose like a naiad, water streaming from her skin, and took Cera's hands. Cera let herself be pulled upright, and kissed again. They floated to the top of the stairs, and Portia seized her bathrobe and spread it on the tiles. Then she lowered Cera onto the fabric.

That this could be happening seemed impossible, but Cera desperately didn't want it to stop, sin or no. The part of her that might have resisted was lost. She sank to the ground and rolled onto her back, her heart hammering, flesh trembling.

"Do not be ashamed," Portia whispered. "We are as the Sun and Moon made us."

Slim fingers stroked Cera's thighs and then entered the cleft between, sliding easily into her wet passage, and Cera lost her breath and never seemed to catch it again as Portia deftly stroked her, touching her right where she had not known she so badly needed to be touched. Her porcelain face shone in the torchlight, a look of amused concentration on her face as if she were studying Cera's every reaction.

I'm her puzzle-box, Cera groaned as the tempo and intensity rose, *and she's almost . . . figured . . . me out . . . ohhh—*

She orgasmed in a gush of fire and heat, the pleasure so intense it was almost painful, her hips bucking as she groaned and tried to push Portia's hand away, not recognizing the giggling sound coming from her own lips . . .

Portia grinned slyly down at her. "What's so funny?"

"Nothing." Cera's eyes stung, and she suddenly realized the burden of fear that had weighed her down for so long had lifted—maybe not forever; she could feel it waiting to settle back on her. But here, right here, everything was possible, and hope—cruel hope—now had her in her grasp, and she wanted to cry, and laugh. "Everything."

This changes everything . . .

Portia kissed her again. "There," she whispered, "that wasn't so bad, was it?"

Cera stared up at her, still not quite believing. *I'm not beautiful enough for you, even though you make me feel like I am.* "Solinde used to call me a safian because I wasn't interested in gossiping with her about boys," she whispered. "It was the one insult I could not face, so naturally, it was the one she used when she most wanted to hurt me."

"Sisters can be cruel," Portia said, kissing her throat.

"Are you—uh . . . also—?"

Portia looked at her a little helplessly. "I don't know," she admitted. "I have not done this before. I'm so tired of men demanding my body, but this—this is different . . . And you *need* me, Cera-amica—not *want*, but need, and that is different. I am here for you, to help you through." She touched the tip of Cera's nose. "I will see you through."

"I can't believe we . . . That what happened—"

"It did. And it will happen again, I promise."

Cera reached out, tentatively stroked Portia's perfect breast, reached down . . .

Portia caught her hand. "Not tonight—it is too soon after the Pig. I am still sore, down there. But another time." She guided Cera's hand back to her breast. "Just hold me. All I want is to be held."

The night bells chimed in the city below as Cera lay wide awake in her bed. After a parting that felt like being ripped in two, Portia was back in her own room.

Cera stared out of the window at the vast moon; the face of Luna, Goddess of Madness and Desire, lit the cityscape, basting it in silver, shining like Portia's skin, and it made Cera tremble to think of her so near . . . But the risks were so high: if the world even suspected they would be stoned, at the very least, and that would mean the end of all her ambitions. It was the stupidest of all stupidities, to surrender to a need she'd barely realized existed.

Liar: you've always known, and you've always run from it . . .

An old minstrel's song sprang to her mind, and she whispered it softly into the room:

Sweet Luna, watch over we lovers of your light,
Sweet Queen, hear my entreaty,
For I am mad with desire,
And I so desire your madness.

21

DEEPER UNDERSTANDING

Religion: Zainism

Zainists claim that all Gods (except Kore) are the same divine being. Their whole faith is built on such compromises. Do they not know that compromise has no place in religion? The imagination of men can be captured only by absolutes.

RASHID MUBARAK, EMIR OF HALLI'KUT, 901

Mount Tigrat, Javon, Antiopia
Shawwal (Octen) 928
4th month of the Moontide

"You don't understand. I don't want to do this." Kazim couldn't meet Elena's eyes. "We don't *need* to do this." He stared across the sunlight gardens from the balcony where she'd chosen to confront him.

They'd been having this running argument for days. Elena had thought he'd be grateful to her for removing her block on his gnosis, but he wasn't. For almost two months he'd been pretending to have forgotten these terrible powers, and the dreadful way in which he'd gained them, by swallowing the life of another man—and not just any old man, but Antonin Meiros, *the man who'd stolen Ramita.* All he had been, all his deeds and memories, hopes and dreams, his personality and emotions, all gone, turned to roiling energy inside

him. Some of that power had now been bled away, drained by the
fight against Gyle's people, but now that he could reach it again he
knew there was still enough to frighten him.

And the only way to replenish it is to take another life. Another
Wimla.

And there was the other part of his dilemma: since Elena had
removed the Chain-rune, he'd been beset by a hunger he couldn't
assuage. It was manageable, for now, but he'd come to realize that
the more he drained himself, the more that craving would grow.

Elena didn't understand, obviously. She'd said that his aura was
"odd," whatever that meant, but she clearly hadn't ever seen a Souldrinker before. Of course he couldn't explain that "oddness" to her,
not without her turning on him, so instead he fell back on the flash-
point of their many disputes: religious dogma.

"The power of the magi comes from Shaitan and I refuse to learn
it," he said self-righteously.

The look on her face was pure disgust. "Not this again. I am so
tired of your half-assed ignorance." Her face wrinkled up in indignation. "The gnosis is a tool, just like a sword is a tool. It's not inher-
ently evil in itself—"

My gnosis is. "It is unnatural."

"It's not—" She shut her mouth and slapped the stone railing. "If
it were *unnatural*, it would be *impossible*." This latest argument had
been going around in circles for an hour or more, and their delicate
peace was fraying. They'd survived any number of falling-outs, but
this threatened to be the worst. And clearly she felt just like Gatoz
or Sabele, that if he refused to use his powers, he was of little use.

He saw Elena almost visibly making an effort to put the matter to
one side. "Listen, we're running low on stores. We're going to have
to go to the nearest village and purchase more."

He frowned. "I thought we had plenty."

"At the rate you eat?" She wiped her palms on her thighs. "There's
a small village a few miles away. We'll take the skiff to the foot of the
mountains, then walk in. We can take a handcart to use in the village."

Perhaps in the village there will be someone I can contact . . . He
nodded his agreement. Then came the guilty thought: *There will*

be other souls I could replenish from . . . He buried the notion deep, scared by how easily it had come to him.

"You will do nothing to draw attention to us," she warned. There was little trust in her eyes. "Meet me at the skiff in ten minutes." She walked away, then paused. "The gnosis can be used defensively. You could learn that, surely?"

He rubbed his face, tired of the feuding. He felt his position was being eroded steadily. *Sooner or later she's going to lose patience with me. Then what?*

"I'll think about it," he said grudgingly.

Three hours later, wrapped in robes and with a turban about his head, Kazim stopped hauling the empty handcart up a rocky slope and turned to Elena. She was wrapped in a black bekira-shroud and only her eyes and hands were visible, the exposed skin dyed darker with tea-stain, her eyebrows blacked with charcoal. A red ribbon adorned her arm to signify that she was bleeding. He didn't know if she truly was bleeding, or whether it was part of her disguise, and he wasn't going to ask.

"You must take the cart now," he said, and at her quizzical look, patted the sword at his side. "You are a woman. You must pull this now. A warrior does not labor. In this disguise you are my woman and must do this. We will soon be in sight of the village."

She glared at him. "I presume there is some verse in your holy book about this."

"Alhana," he replied, using the Keshi equivalent of her name, "there are whole *chapters*. A warrior must stand ready to protect what is his; the woman labors at his side. It is our way. In the eyes of the villagers, you belong to me."

He studied her, then tucked a stray strand of her pale hair back into her cowl. "Do not speak to anyone but me. Your accent is atrocious."

Her nostrils flared, but she swallowed her retort and picked up the handcart's handle. Muttering curses under her breath, she followed him as they topped the rise and descended toward the village. He lengthened his stride to a casual swagger, deliberately leaving her ten yards in his wake.

The village was tiny, a few dozen mud-huts baked into the stony valley. Paddy fields had been hewn into the lower southern slopes, on the far side of the houses. Most of the villagers were working there, apart from a couple of goat-herders who were tending their flock on the nearer side of the mountain.

"Sal'Ahm," a voice called, and a small man in dun robes emerged from the nearest hut. Two women, one young and one old, were bundling roofing thatch in the shade of the verandah and two naked little boys were playing some game at their feet, using stones for pieces and lines drawn in the sand as the board.

"The light of Ahm be upon you," Kazim replied, putting his right hand to his sword-hilt and his left palm forward in the traditional greeting: *I bid you peace, but I am ready to fight.*

"Welcome to Shimdas," the man called, standing slowly. Another man, perhaps his son, emerged from the hut, holding a spear. "Are you alone?"

"There is just my woman and me. We are travelers, seeking the shihad."

The man made a dutiful reverence when the shihad was invoked, but his face did not become any more friendly. "The harvest has been poor, and Emir Tamadhi's soldiers took what little surplus we had." He pointed through the village to the south. "There is a larger town that way, not far. A major road goes through. There will be news of the shihad there."

"It is only food we need." Kazim produced a battered leather purse. "I have a little money." It was filled, but only with copper and a little silver; the trick was to look wealthy enough to buy, but not so wealthy as to be worth killing.

The man gave an oily smile. "Then welcome, my friend." He indicated the dirt road winding into the village. "Beside the well is a blue building; that is my brother-in-law's shop: his name is Dhani." He tapped the younger man's arm. "Hatim, my son, will show you."

Kazim nodded his thanks, then made a peremptory gesture at Elena, enjoying the livid glare he got in return. The two men watched them go past, their eyes curious. He supposed strangers were infrequent here. The son, Hatim, took the lead, walking in a strutting manner Kazim recognized: it was the way he'd walked back in Baranasi, before his life had been torn apart.

The buildings surrounded a small square, where a few trees in the middle shaded a well. There was a crank-pump to draw the water from below, and a clutch of women gathered in a small group, talking animatedly. The little blue-daubed shop had an awning out front and its window doubled as a shop-frontage, and most of the women were there. The villagers all fell silent as they became aware of Kazim, and Elena walking behind him.

Hatim grinned, revealing yellow teeth, half of which were missing. "This is the shop," he said, putting out a hand. Kazim scowled; their "guide" had led them down the only available road for fully sixty paces. He gave him a copper anyway. He was beginning to notice the men sitting in the shade. It wouldn't do to draw any more attention to themselves than they already had.

Do the Hadishah have anyone stationed here? Surely not. He exhaled heavily.

The villagers backed away as he went to the shop. He eyed Elena critically again; her nails were too clean and she was too straight-backed. He stepped closer. "Hunch over more," he whispered, then, aloud he said, "What do we need, woman?"

She joined him at the shop window where a man with gray stubble and an orange turban waited. They exchanged greetings while Elena examined the meager display. Behind the man she could see many sacks; the display was obviously just to show the range of goods available.

"Welcome, my friend," the shopkeeper rumbled. His eyes flickered over him with apparent disinterest, but if he was anything like a Baranasi shopkeeper, he could probably now describe Kazim and Elena in minute detail. "My name is Dhani. How may I help you?"

Kazim looked around him, checking that no one had come too near. A widow in a white bekira-shroud went past. She had big doe eyes framed with long lashes that she fluttered as she hauled two heavy buckets toward the well. No one else was close. "We are camped nearby, journeying from the north. We need food—plenty, for the road."

"Then you have come to the right place, my friend."

"My woman will choose." Kazim showed his purse. "But you negotiate with me, yes?" The shopkeeper smiled with apparent warmth. Perhaps he found men easier to bargain with than women. "What is the news from Brochena?" Kazim added casually, while Elena bent over the display and began picking out seeds, each representing a sack.

"Ah, Brochena," Dhani said. "It is not good. The traders say that the young Dorobon is harsh. He gives the soldiers license to do as they please."

Kazim stiffened, and so did Elena. *The Dorobon?*

"I have been out of touch for a long time," he said apologetically. "Why do you speak of the Dorobon?"

The shopkeeper looked at him curiously. "Where have you been hiding, my friend? How can you not know?"

<Tell him you're a mercenary recently in service of the Kestrians> Elena whispered in his mind as he floundered.

"Uh, I took hire with the Kestria." *My accent is wrong, too*, he realized. *These Jhafi speak strangely.*

The shopkeeper pursed his lips, then shrugged as if he didn't really care what Kazim might pretend. "The Nesti went to Hytel with many of their soldiers, and many Jhafi led by Ilan Tamadhi," Dhani told him. "But the Dorobon set a trap. They rule in Brochena once again."

Elena had frozen, her eyes wide. "Woman, attend," he said gruffly, and she winced, then went back to her work.

<Ask about Cera,> she whispered into his mind.

"What of the queen?"

Dhani looked like he might spit, but being surrounded by his own goods, he swallowed instead. "The Nesti whore is part of the Dorobon's harem."

<No!>

Kazim flinched at Elena's mental distress, but asked, "The Dorobon has a harem? Has he converted to the Amteh?"

Dhani sniggered sourly. "They say he plans to take a woman from every high family, both Rimoni and Jhafi, and plow each of them nightly. Even his own people are outraged." He shrugged at this lurid gossip. "So some say."

"He is magi." Kazim turned to one side and spat.

"He is. Brochena is awash with devils." The shopkeeper peered at the stores Elena had placed before him, and raised his eyebrows. "You are purchasing much, my friend. The next town is not so far away. Not that I am complaining, you understand."

"I prefer to avoid the larger towns," Kazim replied, in what he hoped was a mysterious way. What had felt like a simple enough lie when he started was proving a little complicated.

They haggled until, conscious of the many eyes on them, he settled on a price that felt fair to him. The widow was still struggling with the crank-pump, but no one had gone to help her. As he tried not to stare at her, he realized she was wearing little beneath the white garment.

The shopkeeper looked pleased and Elena somewhat disgusted at the bargain he had agreed, but he ignored her, paid the man, and thanked him.

"It is my pleasure," Dhani replied, pocketing the coins. He glanced at Elena. "Your woman has fine hands," he commented.

Kazim pretended annoyance as he sought a credible response. "She thinks herself a princess. She is lazy and good for nothing."

The shopkeeper laughed. "I have a daughter like that. Two years married and still my wife must help her cook."

"This one's cooking is barely fit for jackals," Kazim declared, and Elena deliberately trod on his toe.

"Is she at least pleasing when on her back?" Dhani inquired, winking lasciviously.

Kazim eyed Elena, who was looking at him with eyes like daggers. <Shut up and let's go,> she sniped crossly.

"She is flat-chested and bony," Kazim said dryly. A little revenge for all the beatings he'd taken.

<You're both pigs.> she sent irritably.

<It's just a joke,> he sent back. <Don't be so precious.>

<You might be joking: he's not. And it's not rukking funny.>

<You have no sense of humor, so how would you know?> He felt suddenly indignant at her, and thirsty. He left her to load the

handcart and strode to the well. About them, the villagers had apparently decided that the entertainment was over; some converged on the now-vacant shop window while the rest left, presumably for their homes.

The widow was still tugging ineffectually at the crank-pump. She was small, but even beneath the bekira-shroud he could see her breasts were ample. When he got closer he could see there were stains on the white fabric, and she smelled of babies and milk. Widows had no status, so he simply pushed past her. She shrank from him as he took the pump-handle and cranked it, then bent his head to the gush of water, cupping it in his hands and drinking deep.

When he had finished, he wiped his face and looked up to find the widow was staring at him curiously. She was young to be a widow; and from the light creeping through her shroud, he could see she was shapely. She twisted, coyly preening, and with her left hand, lifted her skirt a little, showing him her left ankle, which was narrow and graceful. Her foot was painted with swirls of henna and he felt a sudden stirring. The display of an ankle was an offer.

Widows in Amteh society had a precarious, vulnerable position. They were permitted to remarry, but any children under the age of ten were usually sold into slavery so no man would have to tolerate raising another man's child. The Kalistham were not explicit, but most interpretations agreed that a widow was nefara until purified by remarriage. They survived however they could.

He picked up one of her buckets, put it back beneath the pump and hauled on the handle. Water flowed strongly and the two buckets were filled in no time.

She reached out and touched his bunched bicep, making an admiring sound. She was barely five feet tall and maybe half his weight, but she had lovely eyes.

"These are heavy. Would you like me to carry them for you?" he asked in a low voice. Beneath the smells of motherhood she had an enticing musk; it reminded him of the way Elena smelled when they sparred. He felt his loins stir dangerously.

I've been cooped up with the Rondian bitch too long, he told himself. *I need a real woman, to purge these urges.*

Once he'd rationalized his actions to himself he didn't care what Elena might think. He glanced over his shoulder to where she was still loading the handcart, hunched over like a typical middle-aged woman.

Which is what she is.

He hefted the buckets, then called, "Wait for me here." He looked inquiringly at the widow, who shared an intimate smile with him and indicated an alley between two huts. He strode in front of her from the square.

<*Hey, what are you doing?*> Elena called furiously.

<*Wait here, and don't talk to anyone.*>

The widow led him to a hut, in poor repair and downwind of a midden. He wrinkled his nose, but when he carried the buckets inside, there was fresh lavender hanging from the ceiling in bunches, sweetening the air. There was one sleeping pallet, a tangle of sheets wound about a young boy of maybe seven, who was dozing; a newborn mewled softly beside him. The elder boy's eyes flickered open and he stared in fright at Kazim, his expression gradually changing to one of wordless disgust.

He is young, but he knows what is happening here. Kazim suddenly felt ashamed of himself.

The widow snapped at her son, who fled to a back room. Kazim felt his desire waver, but then he smelled her again, and his belly rumbled with that new, other desire. For an instant he pictured her dead, blood welling from her mouth, and a smoky, nourishing bubble of energy—

"Where do you want these buckets?" he mumbled, his face coloring.

The widow pointed to the stove and he placed the buckets beside it, then turned to face her. *It would be so easy . . .*

"Three or five," she said matter-of-factly: three to pleasure him, five for intercourse. A gross overcharging, most would say, but he pulled out six coppers and dropped them on her table. Her hand flashed out, swept them up and secreted them in a pouch hanging amidst the lavender. Then she turned to face him and started to disrobe.

The hole inside him where his gnosis sat was screaming to be filled, making him waver in his decision. She looked at him, puzzled, and then he saw fear blossom behind her eyes—that was enough to bring him back to sanity. He exhaled and released the hilt of his sword, which he had not even realized he'd been grasping, and sagged inside with relief and self-disgust.

Was this what my father went through every day after giving up the gnosis? he wondered. *Or did someone chain his power to ease the struggle?* The thought of his father strengthened him. He could be stronger than his need.

Every need. "No," he said, "this is wrong." Whoring was probably all she had left, but that did not make it right. "Why does your husband's family not take care of you? Or your own?"

She dropped her eyes. "We eloped. I have no one, and I cannot go back."

She is doubly nefara, he told himself, but the condemnation felt cruel. She had married for love. This could have been Ramita and him. He backed away. "Keep the money," he told her. "I will not do this to you."

She looked confused, troubled even, unsure if she were being condemned, pitied, or patronized. "You are a good man," she said carefully. "Where are you from?"

"Far away," he said softly.

"Will you visit Shimdas village again?" she asked. Her voice sounded needy. "We do not have many men here."

He studied her face, seeing the pox scars, her unhealthy eyes, and lank hair. But she had a quiet dignity that even the debasing life she was forced into had not broken. "Perhaps," he told her, surprised to find that he meant it. *But I could never stay . . .*

She read that final thought in his eyes and her face went imperceptibly flat: a tiny dream that he might perhaps be the man who made her a wife again, restoring her to decency, winked out. He wondered if she harbored that hope every time; wondered how she lived with what she did—how she went on.

Abruptly she was all business. "Thank you for the water," she said, as if that was the most profound thing that had taken place.

But six coppers would help her through, for a while at least. He turned and left.

Elena was sitting in the village square on her own, exuding hostility. No one was near her. The shopkeeper was staring at her intently, perhaps wondering if she was as free with her body as the widow was.

<*Good fuck?*> she sent, her mental voice nasty.

<*I didn't touch her,*> he retorted, and went back to Dhani the shopkeeper while she simmered, clearly disbelieving. An idea had occurred to him. "My friend," he said to the man in a soft voice. "A favor, please?"

The shopkeeper cocked his head warily.

Kazim dropped his voice to a whisper. "If any of the shihad come here, tell them that Kazim is near. That he has become a Zain." *That should lead them to the monastery.* He pressed two silvers into the man's palm. "Other than that, forget we came."

Dhani nodded, then bade him good day.

<*What was that about?*> Elena asked sourly as she climbed to her feet, moving like an old woman now. He didn't reply, just strode away, leaving her to bring the now-laden handcart.

She apologized on the way home, much to his surprise. "I'm sorry," she said, "I thought the worst of you, and you were only being kind to that widow."

He blinked. *Well, in truth, if her son had not looked at me like that, I'd have screwed her.* Did deeds or actions matter more? It was a question for the Scriptualists, not him. He met Elena's eyes and decided he too could do conciliatory gestures. "I am sorry also: you are right, about the gnosis."

Elena blinked back at him. "Really?"

"It is part of who I am now," he conceded. "I have to learn to control it." *Or at least control my desire to use it—or I am going to kill someone.*

She looked pleased, though it was too late for her to begin gnostic teaching once they'd stowed the new stores so instead they sparred for a little. He was conscious of a new tension between them, a physical tension. He'd not purged himself with the widow, and the desire he'd felt to hold someone and be held was still beating inside him. Watching her walk away set it off again. *Elena . . . I am wrong about her: she is not an old ferang jadugara. She is a woman.*

Ramita's father used to say that some people connected emotionally and others intellectually, but he and Elena had a physical connection. They were both athletes—competing athletes, yes, but there was mutual respect too, maybe even more than respect now. He sometimes saw a heat in her eyes as they fought, and now he knew it was in his also. But it was twisted around the need to kill and replenish the gnosis, and that frightened him.

Next morning, he spent a shaky few minutes in the privy, his bowels loosened by fear of what he was about to take on. *I must master this, or it will destroy me.* But he also slipped a dagger inside his tunic. They had a tacit agreement that no real weapons were to be worn while training, but he was suddenly afraid that he badly needed one. *If she learns what I really am, she may need to die—though I cannot imagine dealing that blow, especially after the vow we made . . .*

When he returned to the gardens she was dressed in a salwar kameez and sitting cross-legged on a stone bench. At her gesture he sat at the other end of the bench, in easy reach of her, cross-legged also. He blanked his mind as Jamil had taught him to steady himself. Only then did he meet her eyes. "I am ready."

"Okay. First, let's get an idea of what you can do," she replied. She reached out with her right hand, palm facing him. "Touch my hand," she told him, closing her eyes.

He blanked his mind utterly, dropping his purposes in behind a mask of compliance. His right hand he pressed to hers, palm to palm, and closed his eyes too. And sent his left hand to the hilt of his dagger.

She sighed softly as their auras touched. Her mental presence was much stronger through the touch-link, and it had a certain texture, a warm, astringent dampness that was distinctly her: herbal and fragrant, like a mint paste. Initially it felt unsettling, but it wasn't unpleasant.

"You're sensing my gnosis," she whispered aloud and in his mind. "My prime elemental affinity is to Water."

"How do I seem to you?" he asked, curious despite himself.

"Restless. Pricklish, like little jabs of lightning. Your touch is . . . unusual . . . draining, even." She reflected a moment. "Your prime affinity is to Air."

That made sense to him. He recalled the joy of soaring alongside Molmar through the night skies of Kesh and Javon, and the way he'd been able to help the pilot-mage by feeding energy into the keel of the skiff.

She must have followed his train of thought, because it felt like she was there in the memory, in the bow of the skiff, her hair unbound like a pennant. She turned to face him and grinned. *<The gnosis is an extension of who we are,>* she called above the roar of the winds. She laughed with pleasure. *<You're going to love it when I teach you how to fly.>*

His inner vision changed: suddenly the skiff was gone and there were just the two of them, arms spread like wings as they soared above the desert, the land spread beneath them like rumpled sheets. The sun and moon shared the sky and his sight went on forever. Elena's face was lit by the same joy he was feeling, the sheer unbridled pleasure of being weightless and free.

<Can something so lovely really be evil?> He wasn't sure whether he meant the gnosis or her.

<Come on!> she called merrily, suddenly diving toward the earth, and he went with her, plummeting, yet fully in control and reveling in the sudden speed. She rolled and he mimicked the maneuver, felt exhilarated as he roared past on a wind of his own summoning.

She looked across at him, smiling slyly. *<Having a good time, then?>* She was very different now; her usual closed-minded world-weariness had given way to enjoyment of the moment, and it shook him, made him thunderingly conscious of what he was risking. He felt giddy just looking at her and that scared him.

He fought for composure, forcing himself to calm.

<So, Wind-magus Kazim, what's your answer?> she said, smiling into his mind. *<Can something so lovely really be evil?>*

She'd caught that stray thought. What else had she heard? He hunched behind mental shields, closing her off a little, and the intensity of her mind's presence in his receded considerably. She looked a little hurt, as if she'd felt that the brief moment they'd shared meant something, then her face became businesslike again.

<Listen, Kazim, I need to know your class affinity—that's the way you use the gnosis. Together with the elemental affinity, it determines what you can do. Even though you're only wanting to use the gnosis nonaggressively, knowing your affinities will help you create stronger shields and wards.>

He gave reluctant acquiescence. His right hand was still entwined in hers. He wondered if she realized.

He slid the dagger out of its sheath and held the blade still inside his tunic.

The sensation of her changed as her liquid warmth washed over him with a tang like summer rain. Her face swam behind his eyes, her gaze penetrating as knives. *<Don't be alarmed, I'm just testing your responses,>* she told him. Then forked lightning jagged toward him. He yelped and caught it. She smiled then poked her tongue out, impish as a young girl. *<Catch me if you can,>* she called, and sped away, soaring like a bird across the skies of his inner vision.

He followed, shaping the crackling energies of the lightning in his hand, then sent it blazing after her. It was her turn to squawk as she corkscrewed away from the searing bolt.

He pursued, feeling like a bird of prey as he tore across the skies in pursuit. Then suddenly *she* was that bird: an eagle, shrieking in hunger and fury. He gained swiftly, calling his challenge across the heavens as he knifed through the air toward her. His claws raked at her, but an instant before he caught her, the vision winked out and suddenly he was facing her again, panting slightly.

<I can see where this is going,> she said, her voice light and animated. *<Air and Hermetic: did you see the way you instinctively changed shape to follow me? And you're so strong too! You shouldn't have been able to get near me.>* She shook her head, her mental voice slightly awed. *<Who was your mage-sire? They must have been strong.>*

He ignored the question. <*What is this "Hermetic"?*> he asked, interested despite his fears.

<*It's physical magic,*> she replied. <*Shapeshifting, animal magic . . . I bet you're good with animals. Healing even, if you applied yourself to it. You're so strong it's amazing.*> Her face flashed across his inner eye, intent, unwary. <*It's odd though. It's like there's a blockage. There should be energy flowing into you, the way it is into me, replenishing what we've lost. I don't understand why . . .*>

Her voice trailed off. A series of images flashed inside his head, a train of thought he couldn't seem to switch off. They ended with Ramita screaming, and Antonin Meiros collapsing at his feet.

And a soul like mist flowing into his own mouth.

Elena spoke aloud. "*Oh.*"

She opened her eyes as she let the link fall. His were already open.

She looked down at the knife he'd pressed to her left breast and went utterly still.

I am so blind. Elena stared at him, at his striking young face with its beautiful bone structure and haunted eyes.

Dokken. Souldrinker. Shadowmancer.

No wonder he hated his own power. What she'd seen inside his mind played out again in her memory as she tried to hope she might emerge from this moment alive. Vivid, harrowing images surfaced: the blind and burned father he'd never really known, and who'd never told Kazim what he was. An old woman, *Sabele*, manipulating him into becoming what she wanted: a weapon for her ambitions. Emir Rashid, enacting the crone's plan for his own gain. And his beloved sister Huriya, turning into a monster before his eyes.

And most of all, the girl he'd loved. *Ramita.* He'd crossed a continent to find her, only to lose her by the very act of killing the man who'd taken her from him. She saw the Lakh girl as he did: the personification of goodness and gentleness, too dutiful to ever think of herself, too virtuous to not return kindness with kindness, love with love—but also too judging to ever forgive him. Without her, he didn't know what to do.

He's a lost soul.

She wanted to hold him, to soothe him, but there was the point of a dagger gouging the flesh above her heart. She remained motionless.

He can't replenish because that's not how Dokken recover energy. He needs to kill. But he doesn't want to. She felt her regard for him deepen. *All the power in the world and he doesn't want it. It's burning him up, and he* hates *it.*

She'd grown up hearing the legends of the Dokken. *Kore's Rejects*, the Church called them. Every so often someone found and killed one. But she'd never encountered one herself before now.

She realized that her next words would either save her or kill her. He believed with all his heart that at this revelation, she would attack him, and yet he'd not fled her, because he knew she would have found him. So he'd confronted the matter head-on instead, with a secret edge that she'd never suspected until too late.

She clung to the fact of his remorse, his self-loathing at what he'd done and what he'd become, and gambled on the right words to say.

"Kazim," she said softly, opening up herself entirely to him, letting the truth of herself flow through her hand and into him, giving him back as much as she'd stolen. "It's okay. I believe in you."

I believe in you.

She might have been lying to him. *These magi lie.* But it didn't feel that way, not when he was suddenly drowning in her, and all that she was. It was as if he'd already killed her and this was her soul, flowing into him. The wild girl playing in the woods around the big house—*Anborn Manor*, the vision told him—and a brilliant and fiery elder sister, her best friend and most spiteful rival: *Tesla*. Tears and laughter, and then shock at her sister's horrific disfigurement. A new grimness of purpose: months and years of blade-work that made what she'd put him through look like child's play. The triumph of awards, and then the Revolt. A massacred city: Knebb. Gurvon Gyle . . . he reeled at the intimacy of her memories, leaped ahead, to Javon, to Cera . . . to betrayal.

She is sincere. She wants Gyle dead, even though he was her lover. She wants the Crusade to be destroyed, even though it might cost the lives of her people.

And she doesn't hate me, though I deserve to be hated.

He dropped the blade and fled to his room before he shamed himself in front of her.

22

FISHING

Opium

The wealth of the Sultans of Mirobez, Gatioch, and Lokistan is based upon one thing: the drug trade. From their high mountains, the poppy-seed flows westward, out into the plains of Kesh and even to northern Lakh, conquering all before it. Gold and riches beyond imagination flow the other way.

ORDO COSTRUO COLLEGIATE, HEBUSALIM

The seed of the poppy is the greatest curse to befall this land, worse than the Crusaders.

SULTAN SALIM OF KESH

Isle of Glass, Javon Coast, Antiopia
Shawwal (Octen) 928
4th month of the Moontide

Ramita clung to a slick outcropping barely five yards above the place the last wave had crashed. She was drenched in sea-spray, her salwar kameez clinging to her ungainly form as she clambered awkwardly down the face of stone. Beside her, Justina was walking as confidently as if this were a path through the gardens at Casa

Meiros, her feet apparently glued to the rocks—which they were, through the gnosis. Supposedly Ramita's were too, but she could not yet learn to trust them. They were here, according to Justina, to go "fishing," whatever that was.

Another massive valley of water opened up beneath them, revealing the depth of the pillar of volcanic rock, as smooth as the glass that had lent its name to the place. Then abruptly it boiled up again and another wave slammed down. All visibility was lost as spray engulfed them and Ramita shrieked in fright and locked herself to the rock. Justina laughed aloud, apparently purely at Ramita's discomfort.

As the spray fell about them like rain, the jadugara shouted through their mind-link, <*Now, cast out with your mind and seek something living!*>

Ramita tried, casting her mind into the alien depths of the water. Her mind's eye filled with darkness, and the water on her skin seemed to wrap itself about her. <*Can you feel anything?*> she called to Justina.

<*No, it's up to you: I'm not an animagus.*>

Ramita groaned. Part of her was still aware of her body, locked rigid to the walls of the pillar of stone. The rest of her was casting about, seeking . . . *seeking* . . .

There!

She felt something, another being, cold and utterly alien, but it had a heartbeat and it slid through the water as a bird flew through the air. Then abruptly she found another, and another, and then there were hundreds of them swarming about, made silver by the light gleaming from above, darting about her as she flitted from heartbeat to heartbeat, all kindred, each the same yet different, all a part of a whole that barely comprehended itself. The ocean was alive with calls, shrill squeaks, and whistles that she could almost comprehend. She felt as if she were dissolving into them, feeling every sensation in a dim palette of experiences: *hunger bite swallow better hunger hunger hunger* . . .

Justina touched her arm. <*You've found one? Bring it up, and I'll do the rest.*>

She chose one and with difficulty separated it from the others, and then began to pull, using the telekinetic gnosis, the mental muscle that Justina had been building in her these past weeks with her repetitive exercises. She felt the creature panic, heard the alarmed calls of its fellows as she wrenched it upward. The others scattered, alarmed by the frightened movements of the captive creature, scared its uncontrolled thrashing would bring a predator.

A minute of pulling slowly on the invisible cords of her gnosis saw a dark shape break the surface. She quailed a little as she saw it, almost letting it slip. It was massive, with great heavy-lipped jaws and a body that was as big as her own, with lantern-like eyes as large as her hand. Its greenish belly-scales gleamed but its upper body was dark.

Justina yelled triumphantly and a great bubble of water rose and wrapped itself about the fish. "It's a fish the Yuros men call a 'groper,'" she shouted above the waves. "I've got it now! Come on!"

Together they ascended the side of the pillar of stone, Earth gnosis enabling them to cling to it so it was as easy as if walking upstairs. *It is still tiring*, Ramita thought; *there are a great many "stairs."* Beside them, wrapped in water and gnosis, floated the great fish. Every so often it tried to break out of the bubble of water, and Ramita could feel its fear as the light of the sun shone brilliantly through into its clear prison. She sent soothing energies, tried to calm it, which perhaps worked, as its movement became less frantic.

<*Well done,*> Justina called, her voice unusually cheerful. <*Do keep him calm; it makes it easier for me.*>

Together they got the fish all the way back up the one hundred yards or so to the viewing platform. Getting it inside was harder, down all those flights of stairs, and they left a trail of seawater behind them as they moved it into the seldom-used communal bath, which Justina had filled with seawater through a special tap. As they released the groper into the water, it flashed about in fright seeking an exit, before gradually subsiding into watchful stillness.

Justina turned to Ramita. "Now, try and do what we've talked about."

Ramita looked down at the fish and back at Justina, and then cleared her mind of all things but the link she still shared with the fish. Trying to ignore her fear, she waded into the icy water, just down to the second stair, and sat, dangling a piece of defrosted raw fish from the ice-room. She lowered it into the water. *<Here, come to me.>*

It took a long time to coax the creature from where it hid, and when it did come it almost snapped off her fingers as it wrenched the chunk away. It gulped down the meat and shot away.

By the third piece of fish, she had managed to convince it to stay. She stroked its head, staring back into its huge eyes, not realizing that she'd submerged herself until she felt water in her throat and panicked, thrashing for the surface, spluttering, while Justina hooted derisively. The groper flashed away, and could not be lured back all day.

By the end of the week, she was swimming with it and had learned to change her skin to fish-scale, and breathing underwater no longer held any fear.

<Feel the way it feels,> Justina whispered into her mind from the side of the bath. *<Now, slowly, press your legs together, and then forget that they are legs . . .>* Her mental voice was trembling with suppressed tension. *<Shape is an illusion.>*

Ramita kicked awkwardly through the water, feeling the groper beside her, sensing its confusion at her ineptitude. She couldn't ignore his concerned bleatings: to him, her movements were distressed, and they might draw danger. There were other fish he feared, and the terror was ever-present: monsters that were little more than massive tubes of teeth and appetite. She cast its fears aside along with her own and decided to have faith.

My hands are fins. My legs are a tail. I have no fixed shape, only a form that I am moving from and one I move toward . . . I move like . . . this . . .

<Great Kore!> Justina's voice sounded stricken.

Shape is an illusion. She felt the change as it shivered and shimmered through her. The core of her remained the same: a womb, a heart, lungs, a spine, a brain, a skull . . . but the peripheries became fluid as she filled them with the gnosis and then persuaded them that they were something else. She thrashed her tail, jetted through the water, and smacked into the far wall. She shrieked in pain, sending her fishy companion into a paroxysm of anguish.

<*By all that's holy, you did it,*> Justina whispered into her mind, but Ramita barely comprehended the words in her current state. <*I've never seen anyone learn to shape-change so quickly.*> Meiros's daughter was shaken.

Ramita swam with the groper a while longer, before Justina persuaded her to retake her own form. For a moment she was scared she wouldn't be able to do it, but it flowed back to her as naturally as breathing. Justina had taken days to reassure her that it would not harm her unborn children, and she prayed the jadugara was right.

She climbed from the water and wrapped herself in a towel. She swallowed twice as she tried to recall how speech worked. "How is it that I have done this so quickly?" she asked eventually. "You told me it could take months."

Justina was awed. "Most animagi can learn to visualize the shape of a creature they have chosen long before they are capable of infusing enough gnosis into their flesh to make it mutable. But it's as if you are made of the gnosis." She bit her lip. "I think Father may have been right in his predictions. You are very strong."

Ramita exhaled, pleased but puzzled. "Strength is not skill. You've told me so yourself."

"I know. But part of that skill is learning to trust your own powers. Most people are afraid of what they are doing to themselves, and hold back—even Rondian magi who believe that their powers come from Kore. But you seem to have no fear."

"I trust my husband," Ramita said simply. For it was true: ever since seeing and hearing his message, she'd felt as if his hand were upon her. She felt safe, somehow, as if he were watching over her from the heavens. Which she prayed he was.

"Then you're a more trusting soul than I am," Justina said tartly.

Another day, another lesson. They were sitting cross-legged inside a circle of melted silver painstakingly painted onto the surface of the landing area at the top of the pillar of stone.

"This is a risk," Justina reminded her. "You do understand that?"

Ramita nodded, a little impatiently. Justina had said this twice already and it was beginning to get on her nerves. "I understand: I am opening myself up to the outside world. I need to keep that controlled, or I will lead others to our hiding place."

"If someone detects you, they may be able to follow you back. The circle we've drawn will make that harder, but not impossible. If anyone senses you, you have to stop the spell instantly."

They'd been practicing this for weeks. Clairvoyance was one of Justina's affinities, but not something Ramita could do at all—but she had to be able to defend against it. She needed to learn how to be open to the world, to receive messages from afar without giving anything away, and to do this, Justina would have to link minds with her and take her with her as she scryed into Kesh.

<Are you ready?> Justina sent, holding up her palms.

Ramita held up hers. *<I am ready.>* Perhaps.

They touched, and Justina's chilly steel-edged mind invaded hers. She was used to the feel of her daughter-in-law's mental identity by now, uncomfortable though it was. She was brittle and closed in, not the open and soothing presence her husband had exuded. But she wrapped herself about that sharp coolness and gave over control.

They flew—not bodily, and not even their souls, which remained locked inside their bodies, but their perceptions altered utterly as they soared instantly over the seas, past the cliffs and the deserts. Abruptly they were over a city: Hebusalim, which was lying in ruins, smoking and semidesolate.

<Kore's Blood.> Justina blanched. *<It's like a ghost city.>*

Ramita sought the white tower of Casa Meiros and felt an acid burn behind her eyes as she saw it broken and burned out, her husband's sanctuary, entirely smashed. She wished herself closer, but Justina's jagged presence seized her and held her fast.

<No, stay with me.>

<They've destroyed our home,> Ramita wailed.

<Inquisitors will have come there, men as powerful as Father. Who knows what they found?> Justina added in a worried voice, *<I hope there was nothing about our island.>*

They hovered above the city a while. Then Justina turned her mental eye eastward and they seemed to flow above the land-scape, mostly in a gray mist, before reappearing in odd places, like a wrecked room in a clay-brick house, or beside a badly churned watering hole.

<*Where are we?*> Ramita asked.

<*Just places I knew,*> Justina replied. <*Did you see that room? It was at Haveli Khayyam. Someone has ransacked it. That mud pool was an oasis I loved: I suppose the armies and refugees need so much water they leave nothing behind.*>

Ramita was awed: they were seeing the whole world, or so it seemed. <*Why do we sometimes move through a gray fog?*>

<*That is when we are traversing from place to place. You can only scry a place you know already, though if you are patient you can also work from a known place into the unknown. I'd show you more, but it is not an affinity for you, so there's no point.*> There was no derision in Justina's voice, just a statement of fact. It was frustrating to any mage, Ramita had come to realize, that they could not do everything. *It is good that there are limits,* she told herself. *It keeps them human.* She had to remind herself that "them" also now meant herself.

<*How can you do this?*>

<*I'm seeing through others' eyes,*> Justina replied. <*Humans mostly, but also spirits, ghosts, demons . . . they all have minds that are semi-open and a skilled magus can skim them to see what they are seeing. Let us say I want to see someone I know. I would seek their face in the minds of the spirits.*>

Ramita tried to take this in. A longing to see her parents filled her. <*Could you show me my mother?*>

Justina shook her head. <*I don't know her. I know her face, through my link to your mind, but that wouldn't be enough. And if she is in Lakh, that is too far for me.*> She paused, considered. <*Now, I will scry a person. A mage is too dangerous—they will sense us. Let's try a non-mage.*>

Justina sent her mind questing, and Ramita gasped as her inner eye was suddenly sent darting every direction at once. She felt as if she was being painlessly ripped apart as images flew about her, light and color and sound and tastes filling her senses. Then with a swirling like water going down a drain-hole, she was sucked toward one image in particular. She clutched onto Justina's mind like a limpet.

A face appeared, one that made her cry out in shock, with an immediate outpouring of emotions too strong and complex for her to deal with.

Huriya Makani. Justina had chosen to scry Huriya.

She gaped at her adopted sister. Huriya was sitting cross-legged, unknowingly in the same posture as Ramita, with something large and feathered in her lap. Ramita's nose wrinkled in revulsion as she realized what it was: a dead crow. Huriya was stroking it as if it were a pet.

The last time she'd seen Huriya had been the night Kazim murdered her husband. Huriya has welcomed the Hadishah into the house with the blood of Jos Klein, Antonin Meiros's bodyguard, all over her. She'd known what was coming. Something vile had been lurking behind her eyes.

She was just about the last person that Ramita wanted to see.

<Justina, I don't think this is a good idea . . .>

Then Huriya looked up.

She saw them.

"Ramita?"

Justina clutched Ramita's hands unconsciously, squeezing them painfully. She seemed utterly unnerved. "That's not possible. Huriya Makani isn't a mage. She's not pregnant, or at least not far gone enough to manifest . . . *It's impossible.*" Her white face looked more corpselike than ever.

"You should have told me," Ramita told her. "I didn't want to see her. Not ever."

"How was I to know? I just wanted to scry someone we both knew." Justina complained. "You and the little slut were thick as thieves."

Ramita shook with fury and guilt. "She aided those who killed your father—I've told you that before! Why would you even think I might want to see her?" She tried to conceal her own shock. *What had happened to Huriya? How could she too have the gnosis?*

Justina closed her eyes, rubbed her temples. "Well, I think we got away without being followed. The spirits don't like large bodies of water. This place is almost un-scryable. It makes it hard to scry from also, but even harder to view. That plus our protective circle should have thrown her off." She scowled ruefully.

Ramita felt the chill close about her beating heart. *Huriya-didi, what has happened to you?*

"What is it?" Sabele rasped.

Huriya sat up from her prostration and told her mentor, "Mistress, I was outside when I felt myself being scryed. They were surprised to see me, I think, because they revealed themselves."

Sabele's eyes narrowed to slits in her wizened face. "Who was it, child?"

Huriya could feel her chest thumping. "It was Justina Meiros, with Ramita."

Sabele's eyes lit up. "You are certain?"

Huriya nodded eagerly. "I saw their image in the ether—but they fled when they realized I'd seen them."

Crack!

She reeled as Sabele's hand smacked her viciously across the face.

"You fool! You let them realize they were seen? Empty-headed harlot!" Sabele shrieked in fury. "What have I been teaching you?"

Huriya hung her head, her cheek throbbing painfully, the skin burning. "I am sorry. It was the shock."

Sabele hissed in exasperation. "Damn you girl, you could have hooked into them then followed them home."

Huriya hung her head. "I am sorry, mistress," she murmured in a small voice. "It won't happen again."

"It better not." Sabele chewed at her lip, her face contorted into a caricature of disgruntlement. "Very well. If she tries to scry you again, you must be ready. Bring me my lamp. I must confer with Jahanasthami. This is an opportunity."

Justina would not let the scare with Huriya prevent them from pressing on with Ramita's training. Under her daughter's guidance,

Ramita lured in birds flitting above, mostly broad-winged gulls, and captured them. She didn't like them—they were as vicious as rats—and flying held more fear than yearning for her. But she learned their shape, though she refrained from taking it as it was dangerously different and she feared for her unborn children if she crashed. She released the groper and caught other fish, taking their shapes increasingly easily, ignoring her growing desire to dive from the pinnacle of the Isle of Glass and swim away.

She grew a tree from a seed, and a crop of wheat, replenishing their stores in a week of concentrated communion with the seedlings, enveloped in the tangle of roots and their slow pulse. Justina taught her a little healing. Meiros's daughter had not much affinity herself, even though she had founded a healing order—she'd just seen a need during a rare period of her life when she was willing to contribute to society. Where she was most animated in her instruction was Thaumaturgy, and especially Earth and Fire, where their talents overlapped. Though she was not an aggressive person, Ramita was taught how to use these elements, and protect herself from them. Soon she could douse a fireball in midflight if she was aware of it, and even if not, her wards could largely protect her. She collected bumps and burns along the way, but she also continually surprised Justina with her sheer strength, which pleased her enormously.

The most difficult lessons involved the gnosis studies she had little affinity for: like learning to hide from scrying by wards alone, or banishing a spirit or ghost. Justina would conjure them, making a dead bird rise and fly at her or a demon appear, a little spirit of limited potency but enough telekinetic power to pull hair and poke eyes. Ramita had to banish them, and that required fastening onto their nasty little minds and sending them away. It was difficult and unpleasant, but it was necessary, as Justina constantly reminded her.

"In a duel of magi, it is the gaps in your defenses that will kill you," Justina repeated over and again. "Think of it as a suit of armor we're building, piece by piece."

When Justina was not training her, she was showing her things, like maps of Antiopia and how the lands fit together. They took risks, scrying towns in Kesh to plot the progress of the Crusade. One wing of the Rondian armies was in the central area, driving a Keshi army back toward Halli'kut. Another was careening into the central deserts. There were refugees everywhere and their plight tore at her heart.

As she learned to open herself, she heard the whispers begin. One day while sitting in a yogic stance, her eyes closed and inner eye wide open, she heard half-perceived almost-sounds that became whispers, words spoken in Huriya Makani's voice.

<*Ramita-didi, where are you? I know you're out there somewhere. Didi, I'm sorry, I was wrong. I thought of my brother before I thought of you. I thought you wanted to be free. I thought the children were Kazim's. I only wanted you to be free again, my sister, my heart, my dearest.*>

There was much more: memories of happy times together in Baranasi, having fun together. The sights and smells of the great Imuna River at dawn, bathing and washing away their sins before the new day began. The market, alive with color and sound, people everywhere, the pulse of life beating strong and hard.

<*I need to see you, Ramita-didi. I need to put my hand to your belly and feel your babies move. I need to know that you forgive me.*>

But Ramita didn't forgive her. So she only listened, and did not reply.

23

THE BRANDED MAGE

Silacia

Situated in the northeast of Rimoni, the mountainous king-dom of Silacia, though racially akin to the Rimoni, was a thorn in the Rimoni Empire's foot throughout its existence. Ruled by criminal dynasties for as long as memory recalls, Silacia is still a byword for treachery. The familioso of Silacia rule through terror as effectively as any mage-lord.

MARCUS BENSIUS, BRES, 893

Silacia never sleeps. Nor should you.

PROVERB

Sagostabad, Kesh, Antiopia
Shawwal (Octen) 928
4th month of the Moontide

Ramon Sensini peered about, his eyes jaded, as a scouting detach-ment of the Tenth Maniple of Pallacios XIII trudged into yet another devastated village, scattering the ever-present crows. The horizon in every direction was flat, the earth brown and bare of all but for a clutch of spindly khetri trees. Most of the houses had

been torched, for no apparent reason. The well was dry. In the distance, the dust of the rest of the legion could be faintly discerned.
The air was still and silent and the sun was beating down pitilessly.
It was the fourth week of the march, Bassaz was well behind them,
and Medishar somewhere north of a crossroads they'd passed the
day before. So far they'd not seen a single enemy soldier, only a
thin trickle of hopeless and helpless refugees, stumbling from
their path.

Pallacios XIII marched in the rear guard of Echor's army, slogging through other men's dust and leavings. The trail of destruction
was worsening: burned-out buildings and charred fields, butchered
beasts, and everywhere they went, corpses piled beside the road.
Refugees stared at them with hollowed-out bellies and empty eyes
as they passed.

Of the twenty-one legions assigned to Duke Echor's wing, Pallacios XIII was the only Rondian one. Eight legions were from his
home duchy of Argundy, dour spade-bearded men fiercely loyal to
their duke. The next biggest contingent was from Estellayne, swarthy men with olive skin and fiery tempers akin to the Rimoni. There
was little love between the Argundians and the Estella, who shared a
border. The rest were two each from Noros and Bricia and one from
Andressea. The legions of the vassal states were all well drilled, but
Pallacios XIII was not the only punishment legion from the central
Empire; Andressea VI was too. Echor's army had no Kirkegarde;
few of the intelligent hulkas to ease the logistics, and no khurne
cavalry. There were no winged constructs to provide aerial support
either—all of those had ended up with Kaltus Korion's army. Apparently the duke was furious, but when he had tried to demand some,
he had been simply ignored by Korion.

The Crusade had shed any remaining glamour on the march
eastward. The Thirteenth were about two days behind the main
body of the army, and the trail of destruction left no room for any
false illusions about the romance of war. The magi began to be truly
inculcated into the grim business of the military. Ramon was compelled to lop off the hand of a ranker for theft from another soldier,
though far worse crimes against the natives went unpunished. He

became expert at finding hidden food stores, though keeping his maniple's wagons full meant leaving Keshi villages to starve. He loathed the headlong march more deeply with every day, but still they went on.

Ramon spent most of his days dealing with constant messages, with his tribune, Storn, routing and rerouting consignments both legitimate and illegal across the continent. Pallacios XIII had quietly taken over much of the opium supply and as they hoarded the drug among the supply wagons, they watched the prices rise. New promissory notes were issued daily, and Ramon soon began to make his monthly payments to investors with those same notes, hoarding the gold so that the legionaries were still paid in hard coinage. He received so many requests from would-be investors, greedy tribunes begging for more, that he had to stagger entry. It was beginning to look like every logistical tribune in the army was corrupt—but Ramon was also aware that many innocents were being sucked into his scheme. He paid in gold to those he thought decent men, and gave his notes to the rest. And even the spices he had bought up and sent west were escalating in price, keeping his operation nominally profitable.

By the end of Septinon, Pallacios XIII had managed to purchase twenty hulkas off other legions to transport the gold and the poppy in their baggage train—not that Duprey had noticed. The other tribunes had begun coming to Storn for loans to up their investment. On paper, Ramon and Storn were already worth more than one hundred thousand gilden of promised money.

Keeping it quiet was the hard part, though money helped. Gold siphoned from the pay-wagons kept those close to the action quiet, and having control of the supplies meant they could bribe key contacts into silence. The threat of Silacian familioso did the rest, even here, and the one man who did threaten to talk stopped his threats after Kip broke his jaw.

But Pater-Retiari was becoming impatient: the flood of opium he'd been expecting was not yet forthcoming, and he started sending messengers with demands, familioso thugs. Ramon gave them gold, always less than they wanted. Right now, Pater-Retiari did not dare threaten him or his mother. He was becoming, as he had hoped, too vital to displease.

Ramon had always been told the biggest danger with dealing in the poppy was becoming enslaved to it yourself, but he'd never touched it, not once in his life, and no matter the temptations, his personal discipline held. He didn't use the drug, and he made sure Storn and his aides didn't either.

I'm doing this for a reason, he reminded himself daily. *One day I'm going to bring down an avalanche of shit on both my "fathers." Then I can buy Mama's freedom and we'll be out of this at last.*

A call brought Ramon's attention back to the present: one of the Tenth Maniple scouts had come trotting in, his horse lathered about the mouth and gasping. Ramon reined in his own mount and waited; his beast could do with a rest too. The scout, Coll, was a rough-faced man with lank hair about a bald crown. His head was draped in cloth like a native Keshi, but his cheeks were still as red as his cloak. "Afternoon, Magister Ramon," he said tiredly. "Any idea how far ahead the legate is?"

Ramon tossed the man the flask of water he'd recently refilled, and Coll accepted gratefully, as Ramon reported, "Knuckles is up with the First. A mile, maybe more. Have you found something?"

Coll grinned; "Knuckles" was Duprey's nickname in the ranks. "Aye. An Inquisitor Fist, herding around forty refugees, all women and children. No men, but there's a whole mess of crows squabbling over something down a gully, and more jackals there than I've seen in one place before." He looked vaguely sickened. "I couldn't get close."

Ramon took his flask back and swallowed a mouthful himself. "It's not wise to mess with Inquisitors," he observed.

Coll looked away. "That's sure'n right, lad."

The groups of Inquisitors roaming the countryside were not attached to any legion; they had apparently been given a mandate by the Church to "seek out heresy"—any prisoners or large group of refugees or civilians were supposed to be reported to the nearest Inquisitor Fist, but Ramon had noticed that Duprey was particularly slack in doing so. Ugly rumors abounded: that those sent to the Inquisitors were not to be found afterward, but such accusations were always whispered. No one had ever stood up and asked the questions out loud.

It was yet another thing, eating away at them all. The march was taking its toll on Pallacios XIII's fifteen magi—or the new recruits, anyway; Duprey and Marle were experienced veterans with a job to do, and were all business. Baltus Prenton and Lanna Jureigh also appeared oblivious to the atrocities they encountered, like the bodies of two mutilated girls the scouts found on the outskirts of Bassaz, or the dead family near a watering spot outside a nameless village near the Medishar crossroads, all with cut throats apart from the father, who'd pushed a knife into his own heart. Or the twelve-year-old boy they'd had to hang after he'd managed to kill the ranker trying to rape him. Kip also displayed a practical stolidity in the face of horror, as if all this was familiar to him. The Schlessen were war-like people, most of their aggression directed toward each other, so perhaps this was truly nothing to him.

The Andressans grew more insular and pricklish, and Coulder and Fenn more obsessive in their gambling, shutting reality away. Seth Korion was perpetually throwing up, and the chaplain, Frand, was barely less sensitive, his voice always at the edge of breaking as he prayed each morning over the maniple standards. Renn Bond-eau seemed to deliberately court insensitivity, staring at each body, touching it, sniffing it, as if to make himself accustomed. Ramon found himself, if not exactly mimicking Bondeau's fixed purpose, at least striving for indifference. It wasn't easy.

The one who struggled most was Severine Tiseme. She'd become so highly strung that none of the men would bed her anymore, and each morning Lanna Jureigh had to coax her from her tent, calming her down after nightmares of fear and blood. During the day she became increasingly frivolous and girlish, as if reverting to childhood.

Ramon offered his flask to Coll again, and when he handed it back, they looked at each other meaningfully. "Forget what you saw," Ramon told the scout. "You saw nothing, right."

The scout sighed heavily. "Right you are, lad."

The matter would have rested there, if a windskiff had not scudded across the skies at that moment. The single figure at the tiller wasn't Baltus Prenton; the pilot's robes were pale blue and her brown curly hair flew like a banner.

Ramon stared after Severine, and then Duprey's voice rattled in his mind.

<Sensini, respond!>

<Sir?>

<Tiseme just took a skiff and headed back your way. Have you seen her?>

<Just now, sir.>

<Go after her. She's got a bee in her bonnet over something she's scryed and she's going to do something stupid. Kippenegger is already on his way to join you. I'm on my way back now. Track her if you can.>

<I understand, sir. I'm going after her now.>

He opened his eyes and saw Coll looking at him superstitiously. Ordinary men always found the way magi communicated unnerving. "You all right, Magister?"

"I'm fine, Coll. Stay here and wait for Knuckles." He jabbed a finger toward the skiff, already receding into the middle distance. "I've got to go after Her Ladyship." He heard the sound of hooves pounding back from the east, then Kip thundered through the middle of the wrecked village, hurtling after the now-distant skiff. He looked excited to be doing something other than marching. Ramon spurred Lu and took off after him.

It took them ten minutes to find the skiff, and they immediately wished they hadn't. Severine was standing alone, facing ten armored magi, each sporting the Sacred Heart on their tabards: an Inquisition Fist. Most were men, but there were women too. None were young, but all had the timeless youth of the pure-blooded. They were mounted on khurnes, the horns gleaming in the sun as they sat in a perfectly straight line behind their commander, who was listening silently as Severine railed at him.

Wonderful, Kip snorted, then his amusement died as he peered past the Fist Acolytes to where some forty Keshi refugees waited, their faces anxious. Most of them were female, but there were a handful of old men, and they all cowered silently under the spears of a detachment of soldiers. Ramon felt his throat tighten. *Sol et Lune, this is not good.* There was nothing he needed less than Inquisitorial attention.

He raised a placatory hand as he trotted toward the group. Two Acolytes immediately barred his path, their khurnes stepping before him and lowering horns. "Is this harpy yours?" one asked, a cold-eyed man with a perfectly formed square-jawed face, immaculate hair and a dueling scar worn like a trophy.

"We are from Pallacios Thirteen," Ramon replied steadily. "Mistress Tiseme is our farseer."

"She should turn her eyes elsewhere," the other Acolyte, a gray-haired woman with a smooth face, remarked irritably. "Before we pluck them out."

Severine's flow of invective faltered when she saw Ramon. "Get Duprey," she called.

"He's on his way." Ramon saluted the Fist Commandant. "Sir, is there a problem?"

"Is there a problem?" Severine echoed sarcastically. "These butchers are the problem." Her face had a nauseated expression. She stabbed a finger at the Fist Commandant. "I know what you've done."

The Inquisitor looked Ramon up and down. "You are?" His voice was chillingly deep.

"Sensini, Tenth Maniple, Pallacios Thirteen."

The Acolytes in front of them snorted and he saw them snickering among themselves. "*The tenth,*" the Fist Commandant said with heavy contempt. "You are not welcome here. Go back to your march."

Ramon looked at Kip. The Fist Commandant outranked them utterly, but they were answerable only to Duprey. "Legate Duprey ordered me here, Inquisitor," Ramon replied as steadily as he could. "We're obliged to await him."

The Inquisitor's stony face creased with displeasure. "Very well." He glanced sideways to the line of Acolytes, and then his eyes went beyond, to a tall robed figure who had emerged from one of the huts. A bald man, skeletally gaunt, with piercing eyes, and a livid brand burned into his forehead: the Lantric character *Delta*. There was something utterly desolate in the man's eyes. When he realized he was being watched, he flinched and shrank back into the hut.

Who in Hel was that?

Then he saw Severine's face: she'd seen the man and gone white. She hurried toward him. "Where's Duprey?" she demanded anxiously. "How far away?"

"You're the farseer," Kip growled unsympathetically.

Ramon felt much the same—she was a spoiled little brat, the sort he'd grown up loathing—but there was something going on here and he'd seen in his own land the result of what happened when Inquisitors were given a totally free hand.

<*What did you see?*> he asked her.

She met his eyes, for once neither sneering nor ignoring him, then turned back to the Inquisitor. "We'll wait beside my skiff," she told him, adding "sir," almost as an afterthought.

The Commandant narrowed his eyes, but nodded.

Ramon and Kip dismounted and walked their horses to the skiff. Severine's expression was torn between disdain and the need to speak of what she'd scryed.

"What did you see?" he asked her a low voice.

Severine said quietly, "I'll tell the legate when he arrives." She was sweating profusely, and shivering too, as if running a fever, but she sounded coherent, if distressed.

"Duprey's not going to tangle with Inquisitors on your behalf," Ramon told her. "What was it? Who was that bald man with the brand?"

She shuddered involuntarily. "I don't know . . ." Her voice trailed off.

Liar.

But she refused to say more, ignoring him stolidly until Duprey arrived, followed by Renn Bondeau, Bevyn Fenn, and the Andressan, Hugh Gerant. The scout Coll trailed behind them, barely noticed. Bondeau hurried to Severine and held out his arms, but she shoved him away and stalked toward the legate, leaving Bondeau glaring after her sullenly.

"Sir, you've got to make them stop," she demanded.

"Stop what?" Duprey asked, puzzled.

"They're killing people," Severine burst out, looking on the verge of tears.

"It's called 'war,'" the scar-faced Acolyte nearest Ramon sneered.

The legate made a gesture to silence Severine, then saluted the Fist Commandant. "I am Jonti Duprey, Legate of the Thirteenth. Is this a military matter?" he asked crisply.

The Commandant made the Imperial salute, thumping his right fist to his heart. "Ullyn Siburnius, Commandant of the Twenty-Third Fist," he named himself. "No, it is a religious matter, Legate. As such, it is out of your jurisdiction."

"They're going to kill them all, sir," Severine called in an anguished voice. "They've already slaughtered the men."

Bondeau's face clearly showed his view: *So what?*

"A Hadishah spy is among this group," Siburnius claimed. "If they turn her over to me, they are free to go."

Ramon glanced at the scar-faced Acolyte, watching the smile playing across the man's lips. *Sure they are.*

"There is an assassin among the women?" Duprey asked doubtfully.

"The Hadishah recruit women and children as readily as men," Siburnius replied.

"You're a murdering bastard," Severine snapped.

Ramon glanced at Renn Bondeau, who was watching her with growing anger, and at her outburst, he erupted, "Oh, grow up, Severine, you ignorant little bitch."

"Quiet, Bondeau," Duprey snapped. He clearly wished he was somewhere far away, enjoying a drink—a large one. But the central command had issued orders covering the jurisdiction of the Inquisition: Echor didn't like the Church and was seeking to limit its authority. He'd already decreed that they were forbidden to operate their own courts in the lands his army passed through; nor could they summarily execute suspects until their proofs had been checked by a legion commander.

Reluctantly, Duprey followed his orders. "How do you know there is a Hadishah among them?" he asked Siburnius calmly.

"Because I'm a pure-blood descendant of the Blessed Three Hundred anointed by Kore to hunt heretics."

"I need to see proofs, sir, not badges of rank."

"If it were so simple, I would furnish them," Siburnius replied, in tones that suggested otherwise.

"Ask him where the men are," Severine demanded.

"There are no men," Siburnius replied dismissively. Ramon thought back to Coll's words about the crows and jackals and met the scout's eyes.

Why should we care? These are enemies . . .

But the faces of the watching Keshi women told him that he did care.

Severine implored Duprey. "Ask him where the men are, please, sir?"

"Farseer Tiseme, the Commandant says there are no men," Duprey replied, his voice hollow.

"Severine," Renn Bondeau said in an exasperated voice, "they're just Keshi. This is achieving nothing."

That he's right only makes this worse. Ramon glanced at Kip, who was eyeballing the Acolyte opposite him, the gray-haired woman with flinty eyes. He was twice as big as her, yet they both knew who was the deadlier.

Severine gripped Duprey's reins. "Sir, about an hour ago, I heard the mental death cries of nearly thirty men," she said in a low, urgent voice. "They were slain near here. There was a man . . ." her voice faltered momentarily. "He has a branded scalp." She pointed at the hut. "He's in there: he's the one who was killing them. I saw his face in my scrying."

Ramon glanced at the man opposite him, memorizing his face, his dueling scar. Inquisitors had been unleashed in Rimoni and Silacia too many times. They were the demons of his people's nightmares. "What have you been doing?" he asked the Inquisitor.

"What do you care, Rimoni scum?" Scarface sneered.

"You could be next," the gray-haired woman Acolyte threw in. "Just keep talking, rodent."

Ramon felt Kip shoulder his horse alongside him. He knew that they wouldn't last three seconds against well-trained pure-bloods, but he appreciated the solidarity. *Severine's right. Something is going on here. Siburnius has broken Echor's orders.*

"Legate Duprey," Siburnius said in a bored voice, "my investigation will continue. If you wish to watch, that is your business." He ran his eye from Severine to Ramon and Kip. "Call these imbeciles off before they get hurt."

Duprey wavered, the conflicts of duty and fear clear on his face. Then he exhaled dejectedly. "Tiseme, fall in. That's an order." He looked pointedly at Ramon and Kip. "You two as well."

"They're going to kill all of these people, Legate," Ramon told him. "Severine is right. They do this in my homeland. It's their idea of fun. You can smell it on them." He could too, with a little air-gnosis. *Blood.*

Severine wavered, then gave a sob of defeat and ran back toward her skiff. Ramon pulled on his reins and cantered in her wake. He heard Duprey apologizing—*apologizing!*—behind him, and didn't turn lest his contempt show. He leaped to the ground and caught Severine's shoulder. "Meet me at the village a mile to the north," he muttered. "I'll show you where to look."

She stared at him then backed away, her face for once not filled with contempt. She looked as if she was on the verge of saying something, then she spun away.

First they heard the barking and snarling of the jackals, then the shrieking of the crows, as they trotted their mounts toward the edge of a small gully, hidden until they were almost upon it. Once Duprey had lectured them about interfering with Inquisitors and then left, Coll had taken Ramon and Kip three miles back to the west before leading them along a small trail heading south. After half a mile, the crows swirling above the gully were visible.

Severine arrived on a small mare, her eyes red, her face tearstained. *She's too sensitive for this,* Ramon decided, a little surprised to feel some concern.

Coll pointed down into the gully. "This is as close as I came," he reported. "As you said yourself, there's no wisdom in this."

"We'll see what we see, Coll. Those women back there weren't soldiers, were they?"

Over the past few weeks he and Coll been developing the beginnings of mutual respect: the scout knew his business, and once he saw that Ramon had common sense as well as the gnosis, he'd began to treat the Silacian as a genuine maniple commander, not just a figurehead—and he'd proven himself useful as a courier of messages and gold too. Like most of the rankers, Coll was a complex mix of brutality and humanity. Perhaps because they saw the people they'd invaded close up, the rankers had quickly realized there was very little difference between the poor of Antiopia and those of their homelands. It didn't stop the practical brutality of looking after themselves first, and others only if it suited, but it did mean they had little love for butchers, even Church-sanctioned ones.

Severine walked to the lip of the gully, her face shaky but determined. A waft of foul air from below made Ramon retch, but he clenched his stomach muscles and held down his rising gorge. Severine was not so strong; she went white, leaned sideways, and vomited over the edge. But her freckled face was still filled with purpose, a young woman inflamed by a cause. "I'm going down there," she said through gritted teeth.

Ramon glanced at Kip, then said, "Watch the horses, Coll."

Severine began to clamber unsteadily down into the gully, sending loose rocks and gravel sliding before her as she descended. The air was filled with the cacophony of crows, and the yapping of many, many jackals. The stink of rotting meat got worse, and Ramon had to call on his Air-gnosis to filter it just to breathe. Severine was clearly doing the same, but she was still sobbing as she led the way. Kip followed, panting heavily, but apparently of much stronger gut; he had no Air-gnosis at all, but he showed no sign of being about to vomit like the others.

They caught up with Severine at the edge of a blood-fouled pool, beside which was a mound partly covered with sandy earth, one end of a row some fifty yards long. There were more than two dozen jackals here, slavering menacingly as Severine faced them down. "Will they attack?" she asked fearfully.

Ramon shook his head, though he had no real idea what they would do: the jackals were hungry and frightened, and that was never a good combination. He exerted his animism-gnosis, sending a threat straight into the animals' brains, and the jackals whimpered and backed away twenty or thirty yards, running into each other as they fled. The crows rasped their own anger as they took to the air, revealing a bloodied mound of tangled flesh. Severine whimpered softly, while Kip swore in Schlessen.

What had been uncovered made the charnel yards behind Butchers' Row in Norostein look pristine. Tangled limbs and bloated bodies had been dragged out of the burial pits by the starved scavengers desperate to get to the meat. Ripped bellies spewed innards that had been dragged out, the tangled, chewed skeins now blackening in the heat.

"Those bastards," Severine panted, gagging.

Ramon found himself staring, speechless. The rational part of his brain estimated that the jackals had gotten to a dozen bodies, those in the first five yards of trench. He tried to do the numbers, came up with one that was horribly high, and stopped. Surely his math must be off . . .

"What did you scry?" he asked Severine softly.

Severine spoke in a hollow voice. "That bald man with the brand: he went from man to man. Every one of them he kissed on the mouth; and they dropped dead, screaming inside their minds as they did." Her voice fell to a whisper. "Then they fell completely silent." She closed her eyes. "This place is dead now; even the spirits have fled this place."

Kip surprised them by nodding. "Yar, it is as the frau says." His eyes gleamed with faint purple light: the color of necromantic gnosis, a common affinity for an Earth-mage. "There are no spirits here, no ghosts, not one. They are all gone." He frowned. "That is not usual."

"Every time he killed, the bald man's periapt flared up, a violet and green color," Severine whispered. She wrapped her arms about herself, hugging herself as if to give herself some comfort. "It lit up his face with a horrible light."

"A magister at our Arcanum told us there is a necromancy spell in which the soul is consumed," Kip commented, his voice hollow. "We were not taught it: the spell is *verboten*."

"Why was he branded?" Ramon wondered aloud. "Delta—I wonder what that means."

He looked at one of the jackals, the pack leader, which was edging closer. It barked furiously, and the others joined in, becoming bolder again. "Time to go, I think."

They fizzed some mage-bolts into the sand in front of the pack, clearing themselves a path out of the pit, and as they climbed, the jackals boiled back into the gully with a crescendo of satisfied canine growling, and returned to their gory feast. The crows spun about them like a dark tornado.

"We can't tell Duprey," Ramon reminded Severine and Kip as they remounted. "We're not supposed to have come here." He glanced at Coll and put a finger to his lips, but the scout was already tapping the side of his nose, winking solemnly.

Once they were close enough to the column but still out of sight, they parted company, Kip leaving first, hurrying back to his maniple. Severine lingered, looking at Ramon uncomfortably. "You stood up for me in front of the Inquisition Fist. That takes guts."

Ramon shrugged. "So does writing ditties about Saint Lucia."

Severine said ruefully, "No, that was just stupid. I'd be safe at home in Mouneville if I'd not been such a fool."

"Some truths should be told, especially about Her Holiness." He jerked a thumb in the rough direction of that hideous gully of death. "We'll talk about that back there too, one day. To the right person."

"You might. I just want to forget it now. Duprey is right. Those bastards would pull my lungs out through my mouth for the sheer fun of it." She bit her lower lip. "I'm going home, as soon as I quicken."

Ramon looked her up and down with his cheekiest expression. "You're aiming too high: all those high-bloods are nearly sterile. You need a nice low-blood if you want better odds of conception," he said, and winked mischievously; truth was, she wasn't so bad, not once she'd mislaid all her airs and graces.

Sadly she found them again. "Go screw yourself, rodent."

Severine's nightmares got worse, and now she awakened screaming, every third night or so, from visions of the branded mage. As she became increasingly erratic, she tried everyone's patience. Then she started getting struck by the visions in daylight too, and they increased in frequency as the column wound its way east and refugees became more and more common on the road.

Still the relentless march continued. Jonti Duprey came back from a legates' meeting and reported that Kaltus Korion's column had sacked Galataz and his men were now pouring toward Istabad. The duke was angry at being upstaged: so far the southern Keshi cities were like ghost towns, vast and virtually empty. The advance scouts had seen a few Keshi cavalry units, all of which fled when detected, but mostly all they found were refugees, walking eastward in endless lines. But refugees couldn't run forever, and the largest cities, like Sagostabad, Peroz, and Vida, were now overflowing with the homeless destitute. Disease was rampant, hundreds dying every day, and their bodies had to be burned because there was nowhere left to bury them. Echor left a legion outside each city to contain them, but he kept his soldiers away from the miasma of death, for their own protection. Inquisitorial Fists circled the stricken population like crows.

Still there was little or no fighting. In the towns of central Kesh there were no healthy young men, and the Keshi who remained, the women and children and the elderly, merely hid their stores and begged for mercy. The less disciplined of the legions stole and raped their way from settlement to settlement, and Pallacios XIII's mutineer rankers might well have done the same, but they were the last in the line and there was never anything left by the time they reached each town. Baltus Prenton's prediction that there would be no real battles for them was coming true.

Kip was disappointed. "This Crusade, it is like a holiday stroll," he commented morosely while wolfing down bread and gruel. His face was peeling badly from too much sun.

"And all the better for it," Ramon replied.

"It's not like a proper war."

Ramon glanced at his friend. Kip was a few years older than him and had been involved in tribal raiding among the forest Schlessen since his midteens. "What is a proper war like?"

Kip grunted uncomfortably. "Brutal. Dangerous. You feel . . . more alive than you've ever felt before, but you are surrounded by death. Every man you face, you must kill or be killed." His voice trailed off, his eyes faraway. "I've seen close friends butchered. I've lost control and done things . . ." He shook his head. "Maybe it is better that this is not a proper war, yar?"

"Si, much better. Let's just see it out, make some money, and get out alive."

At his regular officers' meeting, Duprey passed on news of isolated skirmishes: the windship-borne magi who'd destroyed an ambush near Peroz, and the storming of a fortress near Falukhabad that had been found to contain Keshi soldiers. By the time Echor's legion arrived, the Kirkegarde had already taken it and were busy rounding up every inhabitant to be taken as slaves.

<*Not slaves,*> Severine whispered into Ramon's mind. She'd stopped talking about her visions openly after Duprey had forbidden it. <*The Kirkegarde are taking them to the branded mage. I know it.*> Two weeks had passed since the incident with Siburnius's Fist, and she now associated anything and everything with that bald mage. She was obsessive. It didn't mean she was wrong.

Duprey had one last item on this morning's agenda. "The duke has demanded that we increase pace. The long-range scouts have found Salim's army—they're apparently retreating from Peroz toward Shaliyah. Echor wants to catch them and take Salim hostage."

The tribunes all groaned. The pace was already too fast. Echor was trying to get fifteen miles a day from the legions, but the sapping heat was taking its toll: heat stroke was rife, and they were losing too many of the draft animals. The mules and oxen were keeling over, exhausted and dehydrated, and there were no replacements to be had, even for gold. Ramon met Tribune Storn's eye. They were lower on food and water than was wise too, and the maps suggested that the lands between Peroz and Shaliyah were desolate.

"And some good news," Duprey added: "A captured Keshi revealed that Salim's treasury has been moved to Shaliyah." His eyes lit up. "He said the Keshi nobles have given all their wealth into Salim's hands to protect it—and all that gold is going to one place, lads: Shaliyah! Salim is planning to move the gold on to Mirobez after the rainy season, but the Duke's going to trap him in Shaliyah before that."

That cheered the commanders up and they strutted out into the sultry evening in better spirits, joking how they would spend their share of the spoils. There'd been few pickings so far, and the men were grumbling.

Ramon inhaled the fragrant evening air. The days and nights were growing a little cooler, and in the west, high clouds were forming.

Kip pointed them out. "What is these strange white puffy things in the skies? I seem to remember them from somewhere, but I can't recall." The giant Schlessen chuckled at his own wit.

Ramon half-smiled. "They are called 'clouds.' In some places they cover the skies entirely for months on end."

"Yar? Incredible!" He scowled. "Not here, yar?"

"The wet season is coming. Coll tells me it rains here in Decore and Janune—but that's two months away."

"It will still be dry as we cross the desert to Shaliyah then? Echor should delay. The soldiers are tired and weak. They need to rest."

Ramon agreed. "The food wagons are only half-full, and we've even less water. We've been burning through our stocks trying to keep up this pace. We should be waiting out the season in Peroz and pushing on in Martrois, fully stocked."

"Why don't we?" Kip asked.

"Greed. Echor wants the gold that prisoner claims is being moved east. If there really is any gold."

Kip grunted unhappily. "There better be."

Ramon looked around and nudged Kip. "On the bright side, Storn's got promissory notes from the rest of the column, and a clutch of them from Kaltus Korion's forces as well. We've got everyone's gold, everyone's promissory notes, and ten wagons full of opium."

"When will you destroy it?" Kip asked, looking at him intently.

"When we're out in the desert." Ramon caught Kip's skeptical look. "I swear it, on my mother's name!"

"You had better," was all Kip would say in reply.

A hand shook Ramon awake and he blinked his eyes groggily. He'd not even realized he'd fallen asleep. Storn was snoring softly a few yards away. He focused on the small shape wrapped in a blanket kneeling beside his cot. "Wha—?"

<Shh,> Severine whispered into his mind. He wrinkled his nose; she smelled of some rich perfume, days of sweat, and sex too, a heavy and unpleasant musk. She'd resumed her on-off thing with Baltus Prenton—and probably others, too, so desperate was she to escape this march.

Mind you, I probably don't smell too fresh either, Ramon admitted to himself. Bathing had long been a luxury they couldn't afford the water for.

She shook him again, as if to focus his attention.

*<What is it?>*he asked.

She tugged on his sleeve. *<Outside.>*

He wondered vaguely what she wanted. Stifling a yawn, he rose and followed her outside. "What?" he whispered irritably. "I'm trying to sleep."

She leaned into him. They were of equal height, and her breath teased his earlobe. Her voice came out filled with an almost despairing exhaustion. "I had another vision today—it's like I'm attuned to them: the more I think about them, the more they find me."

He felt his stomach clench. *She looks dead on her feet. She's not sleeping at all, is she?*

"The same thing?" he whispered.

"It was just three Keshi this time, all children. A branded mage bent over them and kissed them dead." Severine clutched his hand. "But it was a woman this time, with a shaven skull. Not Siburnius's bald man."

"You said she was branded too?"

"With an Epsilon," Severine breathed. "And just a few minutes ago, I had another vision, of a big half-Dhassan or Keshi: and he was branded with a Theta! He kissed a legion deserter dead. The deserter was chained to a wall somewhere northwest of here. There were Inquisitors watching." She grabbed him and pressed herself to him, trembling. "Ramon, you are the only one who's listening to me—"

He tentatively hugged her back, though the reek of sex repelled him. It had been many months since he'd slept with Regina, back in Pontus, and after having to help Healer Lanna cure the genital pox on hundreds of rankers, being anywhere near a woman was somehow not as appealing as it had been. "What do you want me to do?" he asked at last.

"I don't know. Maybe we can go to Duke Echor? He might listen."

I sincerely doubt that. But this was destroying Severine; he had to do something. He thought for a moment. "There's only one person in this legion the duke might listen to."

She looked up at him, the moonlight gleaming in her eyes. It was strange to be so close to someone he really didn't like. "Who do you mean?"

"The Lesser Son: Seth Korion."

"He won't help," she said despairingly. "He despises us both."

Didn't fall for your charms, huh?

"I heard that," she scowled, pulling away, and he let her go with a mixture of regret and relief.

"Sorry. Look, Seth Korion's got family in high places. I could ask him for you."

"Doesn't he hate you?"

"Si, but he's a little scared of me too."

She wrinkled her nose. "Why?"

"I know secrets about him."

"Like what?"

"If I told you, they wouldn't be secrets, would they?"

"I think secrets are despicable."

"The best ones are. Listen, I'll talk to the Lesser Son. We might need to show him more bodies, if you can find one."

"Duprey won't let me look. He keeps me busy all day, communicating with the other legions." She dropped her voice again. "One of the other legion farseers has been getting visions too. He's a Brician. His legate won't investigate either. He says the Kirkegarde are taking over the slave caravans too, and most aren't reaching the pens outside Hebusalim."

"What pens?"

"I thought you knew things? The legions are supposed to be sending all the able-bodied Keshi west to Hebusalim, to be slaves for the rich Palacian families. But the Brician says he's heard from a cousin in the Church that most aren't arriving."

"That sounds like a lot of people."

Severine nodded faintly. "Thousands."

"I'll talk to Korion."

Severine squeezed his forearm. "Thank you for helping. You're not so bad for a lying Silacian sneak."

"You're welcome. You're the nicest arrogant Rondian sow I know."

She curtseyed ironically. "To know me is to love me." A smile ghosted across her face like cloud across the moon, and then she was gone, leaving him awake and alone.

"I don't care," Seth said. "Echor hates my family. He wouldn't listen to me anyway." He sat uncomfortably on his khurne, the only one in the column, beside a charred farm building on the edge of a blackened field. The horned steed stood placidly, though Ramon and Severine's horses had been so distressed by the stink and the heat from the still smoking field that they'd had to be left hundreds of yards away. Crows swarmed and swirled over a clutch of half-burned bodies, eight Keshi dead lying on a barely smoldering pyre. Bodies took a lot of fuel and there was little here except for animal dung. The bodies had scarcely been touched by the flames, let alone consumed.

Ramon and Severine stood beside the pyre and looked up at Korion. Severine had found it three nights after her midnight conversation with Ramon, after another vision. Ramon hadn't actually seen her since then, but she was constantly inside his mind, telling him of new scryings, and conversations with her farseer friend in the Brician legion.

In her vision she'd seen the bald man, Delta, kill these people in front of Ullyn Siburnius's Fist, she told Seth and Ramon. "The Fist surrounded them and he killed them, one by one," she said plaintively.

Seth looked away.

"Delta has killed at least fifty people—that we're aware of," Ramon added. "And he's just one of several branded magi who're always aided by Inquisitors."

Seth stared off into the middle distance, to the dust clouds raised by rumbling wagons and marching feet. "So what? They're just Keshi." He sounded as if he would really rather not have known any of this.

"They're human beings," Severine snapped.

"They're enemies. And heathen."

"They're not even soldiers," she pleaded. "It's driving me mad."

Seth sniffed. "Then this is about you. If you can't take this, get out."

"I'm indentured," she reminded him sarcastically. "I'm stuck here."

"Until you can get yourself plumped," Seth sneered. His eyes flickered to Ramon. "You reduced to him, now?"

Severine opened her mouth then closed it furiously.

Ramon put a hand on her shoulder. *<I'll deal with this,>* he sent her. "Seth, can we have a private word?"

"I've nothing to say to you," Korion replied.

"Nevertheless."

He rolled his eyes. "Very well. But she can get out of my sight."

Severine stomped away and Ramon waited until Seth climbed down off his khurne. He whispered something to it, and the horned steed snorted and trotted obediently away.

"Well?" the general's son asked.

Ramon stared after the khurne. "There's something about those things . . . the hulkas too. Animals shouldn't be able to understand so much."

Seth shrugged. "Jealous? In my father's legions, all the magi have them. There is even a khurne cavalry century. And Father has war-hounds too, packs so intelligent they're more effective than human scouts."

"But here you are, in poor little Pallacios XIII," Ramon observed. "And I know why."

Seth stiffened. Ramon observed the inner turmoil with a little sympathy. There had never been much to like in Seth Korion, a spineless, gutless child of privilege. But the silver spoon had been snatched from his mouth. Though he'd been awarded a gold star by Turm Zauberin, Ramon knew as well as every other students who'd seen Seth blubbing in fear during the exams that he shouldn't have even been given a pass. And that was only one of the secrets Ramon knew of him.

If it was any other pure-blood but you, Lesser Son, I'd fear for my life to be alone and threatening you. But you're a coward, and we both know it.

"There's nothing you could tell anyone that they don't guess already," Seth said miserably.

Ramon cocked an eyebrow. "Really?" he said, looking Seth in the eye.

The general's son flushed. "But . . . you wouldn't—"

Ramon shrugged meaningfully. "Why wouldn't I?"

Seth hung his head. "Echor will never listen to me," he whined.

"He has enough interest in you to have had you assigned to one of his legions."

"I'm a hostage against my father," Seth complained bitterly.

Ramon shook his head. "No, if that were the case, you'd be a captive in his staff tent. He knows your father has all but disowned you. But you're still a Korion: the name has weight. And it will please his ego."

Seth said resignedly, "All right, I'll try. When the army reaches Peroz, there will be a muster. I'll ask then."

Ramon patted his shoulder, making the general's son flinch. "Thank you, classmate."

24

THE CUT

The Kirkegarde

When the worship of Corineus was instituted as the religion of the Rondian Empire, the next logical step was the formation of the Kirkegarde, a religious army, to safeguard and spread the word of Kore to a continent full of Sollan heathen. They were brutal, harsh and uncompromising. But they are as nuns compared with the Inquisition.

ORDO COSTRUO COLLEGIATE, PONTUS

Pontic Peninsula, Yuros
Noveleve 928
5th month of the Moontide

"What is it?" Virgina was staring, her composure for once awry. She wasn't the only one. The creature Dranid had captured looked like the ether-form of a demon, not something that *actually* lived and breathed—but breathe it did, in rasping swallows as it clutched its shattered right shoulder.

Have we left reality and fallen into a Lantric myth? Malevorn couldn't take his eyes from the . . . *thing.*

The entire Fist had come to examine their prize. Commandant Vordan's stern face was filled with righteous disgust, as was Filius's.

Malevorn wanted to shake Dominic, who looked like he was going to throw up. Raine was prodding at the thing's nethers with brutal dispassion, trying to determine its gender. The creature was naked. Its skin was human-soft on the chest, belly and inner thighs, but ridged and scaled on its back and the thick single snake-trunk that sprang from its hips. They'd had to chain the tail down to prevent it from lashing its way free. Its face was an abomination, somewhere half-way between human and the giant lizards that inhabited the coast of the Gulf of Lantris. There was a kind of hair on its scalp that moved like the tentacles of a river-squid. Its eyes were amber, with black-slitted pupils, currently fully dilated with pain.

"Vordan, you say you've hunted these things?" Adamus Crozier asked. His voice was as cool as usual, as if this creature didn't surprise him at all.

Perhaps it doesn't, Malevorn thought. *He's likely just pretending not to know.*

"Aye: it's a construct. This is one of those who took down Seldon, I'd swear to it. Just like those we hunted back in 917—and just as those Sydian savages described them."

It had been a frustrating month for Vordan's Inquisitors. Boron Funt's scrying might have pinned down where Alaron Mercer and Cymbellea di Regia were heading, but they'd arrived in South Sydia too late to apprehend them. It hadn't all been bad news, though: they'd found some Sydian tribesmen and managed to capture some of the stragglers who were apparently fleeing a "demon attack." Torturing the riders had elicited a garbled tale of demonic creatures who had snatched away a bride-to-be, on the girl's wedding night. Even with this progress, Funt had failed to make solid contact with Alaron Mercer again.

It was Elath Dranid's vigilance while hunting—he was the only one of them to think to continue to search behind themselves—that had revealed that in their haste, they might have overtaken their quarry. He had been patrolling their back-trail when he'd spotted the lone creature as it was scuttling for cover. He'd managed to take it alive after driving a lance through its shoulder. That made him the hero of the hour, though he was not the type to milk such moments. Even now he was remaining in the background, taking little part in the discussion. His role would come later: as well as being the best bladesman in the Fist, he was also the Fist's torturer.

"Does it speak any language we would understand?" Adamus asked.

"Those in the breeding reserve were taught Rondian," Vordan replied, "but this one looks too young to have been a part of that group." He bent over the creature. "Do you speak Rondian?"

It looked up at him mutely, its inhuman eyes ablaze with hate and pain.

"If it doesn't, teach it," Adamus suggested. "Force-teach it through mysticism and then we'll see what it has to say."

Raine raised a hand. "I'll do it." Her sour face had a nasty leer to it. Mysticism might not be much physical use in a fight, but you could destroy someone's mind with it. She licked her lips. "I've done this sort of thing before."

I bet you have, Malevorn thought. One could almost feel sorry for the wretched creature.

The process of force-learning took nearly a week, and the creature's cell was filled with hooting, sobbing, and pleading for hours on end, day and night. Malevorn couldn't begin to imagine what terrors Raine's imagination must have come up with to break down the creature's resistance.

Octen ended, and as the new moon's rise heralded the start of Noveleve, the room grew quieter. Whenever Malevorn was on dinner duty, he found Raine bent over the captive like a lover, whispering into its vacant eyes. There was something disturbing about her fervid gaze.

Meanwhile Vordan had the rest of the Fist flying wide patrols, to no avail. They'd been concentrating on the coastline, but no one had found any evidence of these creatures. The land was too vast, and they were too few. And evidently Pallas was becoming impatient; Malevorn had come across both Adamus and Vordan getting urgent messages via relay-stave from superiors anxious about the lack of progress.

One evening, Adamus confided that Mater-Imperia Lucia herself was taking an interest—she was threatening to send in more Inquisitors. "She's bluffing, of course," he told Malevorn confidently. "She can't afford this matter to spread any wider than it already is." Neither he nor Vordan had requested replacements for the three men they'd lost, for they couldn't be certain they'd be able to trust any newcomers.

Finally, during the week of the new moon, their fortunes changed. Raine emerged from the fetid little cell to announce that their captive now understood basic Rondian. She looked tired, but she was filled with a restless energy.

When she led Vordan to the cell, the captive creature shrieked at the sight of her face. It got so hysterical that Vordan sent her from the room. Its pleading was in Rondian.

With a quiet smile of satisfaction, Dranid brought out his blood-stained leather satchel and unwrapped the tools of his trade: the pincers and knives and cutters and hammers and graters. He rolled up his sleeves and set to work. One by one, the other Inquisitors left the room, until only Adamus, Vordan, and Dranid remained.

Malevorn lost interest quickly. Torture was something he dreaded. *Let me die fighting.*

He was alone in the cabin he shared with Dominic when Raine slipped in through the door. She didn't say anything, just pulled her shift over her head, revealing her naked, muscular body. It might be too blocky for his taste, but his cock stiffened anyway as she climbed onto him and pulled his clothes from his body, before spearing herself on his member, grinding against him until she came to a grunting, almost bestial orgasm.

Afterward, she lay on top of him, her squat face inches from his, sweating and panting until she caught her breath.

"What brought that on?" he asked curiously, studying her face. Up close, her skin was horribly unhealthy. She really was an ugly girl, but there was something in her eyes he recognized: ruthless ambition.

"All that mind-fuckery got me wet. I needed to work off some steam," she told him stroking the hair from his forehead. "Thanks for obliging." She kissed him tentatively, and he shut his eyes and let her. He swirled his tongue about hers, tasting her: *sour, tangy*. It had been months since he'd had Gina Weber in that office in Norostein. Life owed him a fuck, he decided, and ugly or not, she smelled good: of musk and blood.

"Did you finish?" she asked, and when he shook his head, she said, "Then lie back and let me sort that out." She pulled herself off him, slid down his body and took him in her mouth. He tangled his fingers in her hair, closed his eyes and let the rare indulgence sweep him away.

She knew her work and, slurping and grunting, she worked him to release.

Afterward she spat his semen onto his belly and climbed off the bed. As she picked up her clothing, she said, "Vordan would call you out if he knew what we'd just done—right after he gutted me." She pulled her shift back on. "You're in the wrong camp, Malevorn. Adamus is a pussy."

Then you know nothing about him.

"You're wrong—but thanks for the fuck."

"You're welcome. Let's do it again sometime." She slipped away, leaving him feeling soiled and sated.

Vordan called a meeting next morning. If he had any notion Raine had been unfaithful to him, he gave no sign.

"These creatures are called lamiae, after the Lantric legend," he reported. "They have this Alaron Mercer and the Rimoni girl, Cymbellea di Regia. They are traveling toward the Leviathan Bridge via Gydan's Cut." He looked at the bloody remnants of their captive. "They appear to be going to Antiopia—they regard it as their 'Promised Land.'"

Everyone snorted derisively at this heresy, then waited for Vordan to finish.

"We'll fly to Gydan's Cut. The hunt is on again, Acolytes."

Immediately after the meeting, Malevorn was summoned to Adamus's cabin. Their windship was sailing eastward through a strong northerly gale and driving rain.

"Was there word of—well, you-know-what?" he asked the Crozier.

Adamus smiled grimly. "The creature confirmed that they really are being guided by Alaron Mercer, and that they recovered a leather scroll-case from the Sydian tribe." He poured Malevorn a glass of wine. "The pieces are beginning to fall together and come clearer. This girl must have been the one with the prize all along. She went first to her people, with Muhren and Mercer in tow, but somehow she later became separated from them. Now she and Mercer are together with the prize, and these lamiae."

He stopped and frowned. "This Alaron Mercer seems to be far more capable than either you or Funt have suggested."

Malevorn flinched at the implied criticism. "Mercer is a buffoon, my lord, pure and simple. I cannot believe he has been anything other than lucky. The girl will be the real leader: Rimoni are known for their cunning."

Adamus looked unconvinced. "Perhaps. Regardless, this matter will soon come to a head. I have sounded out all of the Acolytes. You are with me, as is your friend Dominic."

Actually Dominic is with me, not you, my lord. "Any others?"

"Virgina understands that I will outmaneuver Vordan."

Since his encounter with Raine, Malevorn had started to find Virginia's porcelain beauty curiously uninteresting. Virginity was an unappealing trait when combined with fanaticism, he decided. But she was capable, and that counted for something. "She's more than just a pretty face, my lord," he said helpfully. "She can fight as well as any mage."

"I'm aware of her skills, my friend. And her weaknesses." Adamus considered him. "Raine currently cleaves to Vordan, as do Filius and Dranid, so we are split four against four."

"Dranid and Vordan go back a long way, my lord. But Filius is like Virgina."

"I'm working on him," Adamus told him smugly. "He too has his weaknesses. I don't think it will take long to make him see the error of his ways." He sipped his wine. "In the meantime, why don't you work on Raine? I think perhaps you've already made a start on that." He arched an eyebrow knowingly.

Outside, the venators shrilled miserably as the windship plowed on through the rain.

In the three weeks since Alaron had rescued Cym she'd adapted remarkably quickly to the reality of the lamiae and their situation. The Sollan faith acknowledged the creatures of Lantric myth as real, so Cym had no problem with their actual existence—if she found anything difficult, it was the fact that the lamiae were constructs. Even so, she had quickly charmed Kekropius with her open-eyed acceptance of his people.

Alaron had managed to remove the Chain-rune—it hadn't been easy, for the Sydian shaman had also been a quarter-blood, but in the end, his superior training had triumphed. She still bore the Vlk tattoo on her forehead, though. They'd not worked out how to remove it without leaving scars.

He made no attempt to dissuade her from taking the Scytale east—handing it over to Justina Meiros and her godlike father was obviously the logical thing to do now that Langstrit and Muhren were dead. He loved having her beside him, but although he still wished that she would magically fall in love with him—especially as he'd rescued her from a dire fate—she was as spiky, unreachable and mysterious as ever.

Cym was soon eating and sleeping normally; whatever trauma she'd faced in the Sydian camp she stored deep inside, where no one could reach. Alaron wanted to comfort her, but she refused to even acknowledge that anything had happened—it worried him, but what could he do? He couldn't voice his feelings, and he knew she wouldn't want to hear of them even if he could. Their relationship had quickly reverted to their usual amicable teasing and banter, friends, but a little distant—more like brother and sister than the lovers he so desperately wished they were.

Foolishly, he'd confessed to her that he'd not just saved Anise from the massacre but he'd kissed her too, and now she teased him mercilessly about what she'd dubbed "the Great Anise Affaire"— almost as if to avoid thinking about her own narrow escape from the Sydians.

"You're practically married to her, Al. I hope you're learning our language. Parli Rimoni, signor?"

"Huh? No! I'm not married to her! I'm just—" Unable to define exactly what he felt, Alaron's words evaporated.

After a few moments he remembered that he currently had the perfect comeback: "Anyway, you were two seconds away from being a Sydian bride."

That shut her up. For a while.

Alaron peered furtively from the cave-mouth. The view was spectacular: a massive gorge which cut through granite, running for miles from northwest to southeast, cutting the Pontic Peninsula in two. Gydan's Cut was one of the great wonders of the world. The carefully censored versions of the Ordo Costruo texts which were used to teach geography and the other sciences in the Arcanum spoke of the Cut as a place where the Yuros "plate" had fractured relatively recently—by which they meant less than a million years ago. The claim annoyed the Church, which believed that Kore had created all of Urte only ten thousand years ago; the Sollans were no less angered, as they had their Smith God forging Urte around forty thousand years ago.

Despite its theological impossibility, the Cut was truly majestic: a watery defile that seemed to go down forever, with white waters constantly boiling far below. The dense bushes which overhung the cliff tops were a blaze of color in their autumnal red and gold livery. The skies were filled with birds and the air was misty with spray. And to the east, Alaron could just make out the spires of Veiterholt Bridge.

The Veiterholt was the Ordo Costruo's first major engineering feat: a mile-long bridge spanning Gydan's Cut, linking Pontus to the proposed site of Northpoint. There was a fortress at either end of the massive stone span which arched gracefully over the narrowest point in the Cut, which in some places was a dozen or more miles wide.

Somehow, they had to find a way to cross the Cut, which would be no easy task, as the waters were an impassable torrent of white water churning far below. Alaron had come to the conclusion that he'd probably end up ferrying the lamiae across the channel one by one on his skiff and he was about to turn back and reenter the caves when he heard a shrill cry from above.

When he peered upward he was alarmed to see a giant winged beast swooping overhead. On its back was an armored man with a cloak streaming from his shoulders. Another followed, with blond hair streaming behind her as she spiraled down to the level of the cliffs and raced along the rim.

His nails dug into his palms as he recognized the woman who'd so casually stabbed Ferdi.

The Inquisitors were here.

He waited to make sure they hadn't found the cave entrances. As he watched the two fliers gliding hither and thither, buffeted by the updrafts, he heard sounds behind him and turned to see Kekropius's face bobbing toward him as he undulated up the cave's sloping floor. He had Cym on his back, her bare legs gripping his snaky hips. Alaron raised a hand warningly and put a finger to his lips, though the noise of the Cut's churning waters made the gesture irrelevant.

"Inquisitors," he hissed, jabbing a finger skywards, and Kekropius swayed to a halt, his face losing its welcoming smile.

Cym slid from his back and scrambled to Alaron's side. He was faintly relieved to see her fully clothed; she'd threatened to go bare-breasted in solidarity with the Lamiae women, and he'd not been entirely sure she was joking. The Lamiae women were genuinely mystified over this fascination with feeding glands—not even their males understood it.

"What have you seen?" she whispered.

"Two of them—they're the same group that attacked your father's caravan."

Cym bared her teeth. "Let me see them."

Kekropius put a warning hand on her shoulder. "No foolishness, Cymbellea. They must not detect us."

Cym bit her lip. "They won't," she promised.

Kekropius went to warn his people while she and Alaron crawled back to the entrance. They'd been living beneath trees or within caves for so long that open sky made Alaron nervous now. He slid in beside Cym and they watched as four more Inquisitors appeared over the next hour, landing near the cliffs. They fed their steeds before feeding themselves, then one brandished a wooden staff.

"Relay-stave," Alaron breathed in Cym's ear. "They're reporting in."

By midday, there were three more venators present, including another woman, this one with a sour, pasty face who reminded Alaron of a female Gron Koll. Malevorn Andevarion was among them, and just the sight of him made Alaron tremble with rage and fear. Then a big windship loomed overhead and the Inquisitors bustled about, working ropes and sails to lower the craft onto the stone shelf right at the edge of the Cut. They lashed the ship down securely as the wind and rain rose in intensity.

Alaron could see Malevorn and the blond woman herding their winged steeds into the trees and tethering them up. They were barely a hundred yards away.

"Someone on their ship has been scrying me for weeks," Alaron said. "I think the distance has protected me, but now they're right on top of us I've got to put some solid rock between us."

"We'd better move everyone to the lower caverns," Cym agreed.

He glowered down at the Inquisitors. "Kore's blood, I'd love to go down there and hack those bastards to dog-meat."

"We all would, Alaron. But they'll be mostly pure-bloods. We have to be realistic—the only thing we can do is hide until they move on."

He sighed heavily. "I know. It's just . . ." He stared down at Malevorn Andevarion. "Why is it that some people who deserve nothing get everything?"

"It's just the way of the world—anyway, who says he has everything?" She backed away from the cave-mouth and straightened.

She looks lovely, he thought. Even with the face tattoo and in travel-worn clothes, Cym would always be his definition of beauty. Despite having the Inquisition on their very doorstep, he braved the question he'd been asking himself for years.

"Cym, if I'm not what you want, and Ramon's not what you want . . . what do you want?"

She lifted her eyebrows. "As if you two twerps are the sum of all manhood." She sighed, reached down and pulled him to his feet. "Alaron, I want someone who walks like a king and shines like Sol. I want someone with poetry on his lips and majesty in his voice. I don't know if I will ever meet him, but when I do, I'll know. There won't be any doubts or questions. I'll just know."

"People like that don't exist," he said sourly. He pointed at Malevorn. "Except that prick."

"Oh, Alaron." She put her arms about him. "You're my dearest friend, and I do care about you. You just don't make my heart go *boom*. I'm sorry." She peered over his shoulder. "And that creep down there does nothing for me at all."

"Good. Let's go. I'm sick of looking at him."

The Inquisitors showed no immediate signs of moving on, so the lamiae stayed in the lower caverns. It was as well they had moved into the deeps so quickly, for the Inquisitors found the upper caves soon after landing. They searched thoroughly, but Naugri had covered their tracks using Earth-gnosis to conceal the passages that led to the clan's new hiding place and the skiff had been taken to the deepest cavern. Moving on was out of the question, until the Inquisitors were gone.

The solid rock shielded Alaron and Cym from scrying, so although they didn't know it, the Inquisitors would have to rely on physical clues if they were to find their quarry. Clearly they remained oblivious to the fact that their quarry was so close.

The snake-folk found an underground pond they could fish, but even so, after nearly a week the clan was beginning to run low on food. Outside it was cold and wet, and the clouds hid the full moon that rose in the middle of the month. While the venator riders left on patrols each dawn, the windship crew took the opportunity to make running repairs on their great vessel. Men from the nearby Veiterholt Fortress came with fresh timbers and canvas, and their voices and hammers echoed through the woods, ringing out against the constant thunder from the Cut.

The ninth day of waiting finally dawned clear. The Inquisitors' attempts to scry Alaron were entirely predictable—once at dawn and once again at dusk—and Alaron avoided them easily enough by staying deep underground at those times. That morning he and Cym crawled to a vantage point they'd found overlooking the windship. Only three of the venators remained, so five of the eight Inquisitors were out on patrol.

As they watched, another two left in a carriage—probably to go to the Veiterholt, Alaron guessed—leaving just one Inquisitor on board, a morose-looking youth with a fervent air about him. He was arguing with a fat priest, who Alaron stared at intently, wondering why the face was familiar, until he realized it was another old Turm Zauberin classmate. Boron Funt.

It must be Funt doing the scrying: they're calling in people who know me. It was an oddly flattering thought, to be personally annoying so many Inquisitors.

Then the windship's pilot started walking around the hull, making the keel glow as he replenished its power.

"They must be readying her for flying again soon," Alaron whispered.

Cym nodded, then suddenly turned to him and grinned. "Hey, you know what?"

He recognized that smile. It meant trouble. "What?"

"That's an awfully nice ship."

Boron Funt stomped away, fuming. Brother Filius was an oaf—no, he was worse than that: he was an arrogant fool. In his narrow world there was only his precious order—he had absolutely no idea of the difficulties involved in scrying a vigilant quarry, let alone how draining it was. Funt felt constantly tired—not to mention the fact that he was positively wasting away on military rations, all the while he was frazzling his mind seeking that Kore-bedamned lunker Alaron Mercer.

Take this morning, for example: he'd been pounding away for *hours*, all to no avail, with not even a sniff of Mercer's first veil. That was the demoralizing thing: there'd been not even a *hint* of contact. Filius thought it should be easy, but he wasn't an Air-mage; he knew *nothing* of scrying.

Scrying is like fencing in the dark, Funt thought. *You have to be hyperaware, straining every sense for the other's presence. Well, no wonder I'm exhausted.* It was hard, even for a pure-blood, and getting any sort of contact outside about sixty miles was nigh impossible.

Then once you'd found them, you had to pierce their wards to make full contact. The first veil of wards protected distance. The second veil protected direction, the third prevented visual contact, and the last prevented sound. There were all manner of shields that could block scrying—so could simply being underground or in a building—Hel, even dirt tossed in the air could break a weak connection. Water distorted it, and so did fire. Mercer might be nothing but quarter-blood merchant-scum, but he'd been trained at the best Arcanum in Noros.

Over the past three weeks he'd managed to pierce Mercer's first veil three times, just enough to know that he was alive—but for days now he'd not even managed that. Each veil was harder to penetrate—and when he did get anything, it usually alerted the target, which meant he always lost the scent at that point. At least it showed he was getting somewhere, but Filius refused to see it that way.

The windship pilot was outside, replenishing the keel. The poor fellow was probably more exhausted than he was—windships were taxing beasts, as Boron recalled from his days at the Turm. He was so grateful to be in the clergy and above such mundane tasks. There was a raucous laugh from up on deck, where the six human members of the crew were repairing the sails and ropes and timbers. He hated all their talk of Pontus and the women there, filthy talk. He felt upset, and hungry. Why hadn't he been taken on the visit to Veiterholt? He scowled, even as his mouth watered at the thought of the meal they would even now be enjoying. *No one realizes how much I'm doing for this mission*, he grumbled to himself.

He was about to take himself back to bed for a well-earned rest before his next scrying attempt when a dazed-sounding voice called from the edge of the clearing, "Hello? Hello the ship?"

Funt stopped, utterly stunned, and waddled to the rail of the windship and peered down. "Mercer?" he gasped. "*Alaron Mercer?*"

Unbelievably, his quarry of the past three months was standing below on the grass near the edge of the cliff. He looked awful: coated in mud, damp and disheveled, one hand on his sword and the other clutching his bloodied side. He had lost a boot and his bare ankle was wrapped in bloody, muddy bandages. He was limping pathetically.

He was carrying a scroll-case.

Boron gaped. *I've done it! I've worn him down—I've broken him! What's he carrying?—is that it? Is the rumor true?*

Brother Filius appeared beside him, staring suspiciously. "This is him?" he muttered. Gnosis-light began to glow about him. "This reeks of a trap." He drew his sword. "Beware!" he shouted to the crew, who'd frozen in surprise at the first shout. "Watch every direction."

The six crewmen clattered to the deck, their eyes wide as they tried to face every side at once.

"Throw down your weapon," Filius shouted at Mercer, who complied at once, as if in a daze.

He's dead on his feet. He probably hasn't slept properly in months— not since I first broke through his defenses. Funt moved forward. "He is my prisoner, not yours."

Filius threw a contemptuous look at Funt over his shoulder and snarled, "Stay where you are, you piece of lard." He leaped easily from the windship to the land and strode toward Mercer, pulling Mercer's blade to his own hand with telekinesis. It was an ill-made thing; he barely looked at it before tossing it over the cliff into the seething waters below with a nonchalant shrug. "Drop whatever it is you're holding," he shouted, indicating the scroll-case.

Funt held his breath. Was this the thing Adamus and Malevorn had hinted at? The actual Scytale of Corineus? *Can I let it fall into Filius's hands?* He braced himself and followed Filius over the ship's rail, wincing as he landed heavily in the wet moss.

"Please," Mercer said in a plaintive voice, "sanctuary, for bringing you this—"

Filius snorted. "I dictate terms here, you fool. Put it down or I'll skewer you."

Mercer went to comply, but Funt called, "Wait! The Crozier must have that case."

Filius glanced sideways. "Commandant Vordan controls this mission, not the Crozier."

"Adamus Crozier outranks the Commandant."

"In the field, the Inquisitor has precedence," Filius rapped back. He stretched out a hand and used telekinesis to wrench the case from Mercer's hands, then backhanded him with the same power, almost sending him off the cliff.

He looked around, gripping the case, triumphantly. "Secure the prisoner," he told the nearest crewmember.

The sailor, a lanky man with a wispy beard, looked hesitantly at Alaron. "He's a mage," he replied doubtfully.

Filius hissed impatiently and thrust a finger at Mercer. A mage-bolt blasted the fugitive off his feet. Whatever shields he'd been using were completely ineffectual and he collapsed, quivering and whimpering. Filius followed up with a gnostic web that engulfed Mercer, then vanished inside him. Mercer was evidently too far gone to resist the mesmerism-gnosis.

"There," Filius announced, "he's helpless for a few minutes. Tie him up. I'll place a Chain-rune on him when you're done."

The wind-sailor grabbed a coil of rope and edged forward while Filius ignored Funt and turned his attention to the scroll-case. He rattled it experimentally, then looked at the priest. His eyes held a challenge: *If you want this, you're going to have to try and take it off me.*

Funt realized that he didn't have the courage to try.

Filius flipped the lid from the case and tipped the contents into his hands. He looked at the plain, unadorned rod of wood. Boron Funt did too, looking puzzled. Was this truly the prize they'd been seeking? It looked nothing like what they'd been told of it at the Arcanum.

Then an unknown mental voice, one Boron didn't know, cried, <*Go!*> and a rush of bodies poured up over the lip of the cliff.

Huge reptile-men with snake-bodies instead of legs swarmed toward them brandishing weapons, and the air was suddenly filled with flying spears. Behind them the windshipmen shouted in alarm as voices roared in the woods and the foliage came alive.

Funt swatted away the spears, shielding himself desperately as the windsailor beside Mercer went down beneath a fanged horror with a female torso and paired snake-legs that wrapped about him.

But then he shook his head as if to clear it: he and Filius were not mere men; they were magi—*pure-blood* magi! They could fight back! As if coming to the same conclusion, Filius started to blaze away with lethal gnosis-fire. Funt used Air-gnosis on the first of these creatures to come at him, easily swatting it off the cliff. Then he poured mage-fire into the face of another—but to his stunned amazement, it shielded, not so well that it didn't take a Hel of a blast that charred its skin and boiled one eye, but still it kept coming, its heavy sword battering against his shields. Its bared teeth were pointed, and two fangs jutted out like those of a viper.

Funt took a step back . . . just as a hand erupted from the earth and gripped his ankle.

All at once the earth was boiling. He fell backward and glimpsed the pilot-mage, going down beneath a pair of snakemen who came right out of the earth. One leaped on him and he slammed his hand at it, releasing a narrow burst of force that struck the beast beneath the chin and almost ripped its head off. It collapsed onto him, sliding off his shields as he tried to roll clear. In the background, he heard venators squealing and tearing at their rope bindings.

Then the rest of the beast that had gripped his foot lifted itself from the ground, its jaws wide and teeth bared, and ripped through his shields. Fangs punched through his robes and into his calf and he yowled in pain and anger as his lower leg went numb. He flailed about, using his good leg to kick himself free, and crawled backward from the thing as it rose over him. It was massive, built like a wrestler, with a shock of snaky hair. It roared inchoately and lunged at his foot, its mouth widening, then snapping shut over his ankle.

Funt screamed as bones crunched, and something fell from the snake-monster's mouth as blood sprayed. The numbness climbed his body.

The venators screamed again. One ripped free into the air and flapped away, trailing a stream of blood, then a spear thudded into its breast and it dropped like a stone. The rest of the venators were torn down by a pile of inhuman figures.

Beside him, Filius was shouting Scripture as fire blazed from his hands. Boron saw more snake-men twist away from him, convulsing. There were half a dozen bodies collapsed about him. Out of the corner of his eye he saw Alaron Mercer climb unsteadily to his feet; he barely deflected a combined blast of fire and lightning from Filius— but that distraction was enough for a female snake-creature to lunge at the Acolyte from behind. She latched into his forearm and bit down before he slapped away—but the damage had been done.

Filius howled as his bare arm immediately began to discolor. He staggered dizzily, spewing fire in random directions, his shields faltering. More of the snake creatures threw themselves at him, and within seconds Filius was spitted on three spear-shafts at once. His shrieked prayers became whimpers as he thrashed about for a moment, and then went limp.

Funt tore his eyes from the Acolyte's dead body, trying to work out why he couldn't feel his left foot. Then he saw the reason, and he felt a sob bubble up his throat. The foot was gone and blood was fountaining from the stump in great gouts, soaking the ground. *This isn't happening*, his brain told him.

Just as suddenly, it wasn't. He was in the training ground at the Turm Zauberin. *I've fallen off my horse, that's all.* "Fetch Magister Yune," he called, the words coming out oddly high. "I think I need a healer." He looked around for someone to help him.

Oddly, his friends were nowhere to be seen. There was only Alaron Mercer, of all people. "Help me," he whimpered as the merchant's son stumbled toward him, smiling inanely. "Mercer, help: I think I've hurt myself."

A dozen alien faces loomed over him: bestial faces that had no place in this dream. He erased them, focusing only on Mercer, who was carrying a leather scroll-case, one he vaguely recalled as being important. But it wasn't as important as his poor foot.

"Help me, you cretin," he snapped at Mercer.

"I blocked both his attacks," Mercer said, his voice sounding distracted. "I've never done that before."

Imbecile! He has to help me! I fell off my damned horse! Or . . . something . . . "I seem to have hurt my foot," he groaned, wishing he sounded a little manlier just now. But he could, couldn't he? He could *order* Mercer to do it. He was a pure-blood, after all. "Stop babbling, Mercer," he snapped. "Fetch Mistress Yune! I've hurt myself."

"Two spells at once . . . and I blocked them. It was as if the danger cleared my mind of doubt. I felt . . . fantastic."

He felt the numbness climbing his leg into his midriff. "Please, Mercer," he whimpered. "My foot—"

Mercer seemed to notice him at last. "Why are you here, Funt?"

"To find you, you moron! Where's Magister Yune?" Agnes Yune had always been kind to him. She'd given him sweets, especially when he was homesick. He'd been homesick a lot. He'd always thought of her as a kind auntie. "Please, it's beginning to hurt."

"Can we eat him yet?" something growled.

Funt cringed away from the fierce voice and focused on the merchant's son again.

"What happened to Poulos?" Alaron Mercer said in his ear. "He went missing three weeks ago. Did your friends find him?"

Poulos? I've never heard of any Poulos. What happened three weeks ago? "Where's Magister Yune, Mercer? I don't feel well."

"Poulos looked like Hypollo here: with snake-hair and lizard-skin."

"Oh, that thing? Dranid killed it and we fed it to the venators. Hel's sake, Mercer, fetch Aggy Yune!" His voice was faltering. Somewhere close, a lot of somethings were gorging on fresh meat. He could smell the iron stink of blood; he could hear the ripping of flesh. "Where are my friends?" he asked plaintively.

Mercer said softly in his ear, "You never had any."

He opened his eyes as Mercer straightened and walked away. He was surrounded by reptilian faces, creatures from nightmare. His fantasy of Turm Zauberin evaporated. Filius was being torn apart limb from limb and devoured raw. So was the pilot-mage. He could hear the human crew pleading for mercy.

"Mercer, please . . ."

"He's all yours," said Alaron Mercer, without looking back.

The venators had flown south that morning, so Alaron and the lamiae took the stolen windship north first. They flew very low, to keep out of sight of Veiterholt Bridge and its fortresses, then turned northeast, aiming for the coast south of Pontus. The remaining crewmen worked the sails under the close supervision of Naugri and a dozen other lamiae who were proficient in Rondian. They were made to describe everything they were doing, instructing their captors as they went along. They had the look of men trapped in a nightmare, wanting desperately to wake up as soon as possible.

Alaron took the tiller. Windships were much tougher to fly than skiffs, but the same principles applied. The lamiae barely fit aboard, but somehow they managed, filling the cabins and crews' quarters with the females and offspring while the males stayed on deck: thirty-four adults and two dozen children on a ship that would normally house no more than two dozen people. They had no pilot-mage, but many of the lamiae had Air-gnosis; they were already stationed below and constantly feeding the keel gnosis-energy.

Their first priority was to reduce the chances of being followed. Alaron ordered anything personal to be chucked straight into the Cut, to cut down the Inquisitors' ability to scry the ship. It meant disposing of a treasure-trove of weapons and armor, not to mention diaries, prayer-books, and jewelry, but the Elders were rigorous in scouring the ship of anything the Inquisitors might be able to trace. The only thing they kept was one of the pilot-mage's charts. The ship itself could be shielded using energy from the keel, and Alaron ensured those were fully empowered.

It was hard to erase Boron Funt's final screams, but Alaron was determined not to forget these were the bastards who'd killed Muhren and Mercellus and Ferdi and Poulos and all those helpless Rimoni. He'd lost his breakfast into the Cut, and after that, he'd shaken himself and done his best to pull himself together. He'd not been able to stop himself from feeling sorry for poor delusional

Boron Funt at the end—he'd never expected that—but he couldn't Chain-rune a pure-blood. There had been no choice.

If he'd shown any remorse for the death of poor Poulos, I might have tried to stop them, but he didn't even care. Poulos was just a freak to him . . .

Once all the personal effects had been disposed of, Alaron turned his attention to rendering the ship itself proof from scrying. He worked with Ildena and the strongest of the Air-magi to create wards, leaving Cym to use the main cabin as a surgery, repairing the worst of their injuries.

We defeated two pure-bloods and a mage-pilot who must have been at least a half-blood. He smiled grimly. He was proud of the lamiae. They'd lost eight warriors, but considering what they'd been up against, it was a stunning victory. *We could even have taken down a couple more . . .* Then he smiled at himself: "We" was a man-made race of constructs. His people.

"Something amuses you, Milkson?" Kekropius called from his position near the stern, where he was watching over *Seeker*, trailing the windship on a long rope.

"I was just thinking that I feel more akin to your people than to those Inquisition bastards."

Kekropius acknowledged his words with a faint tilt of the chin. *Pride.*

Above all, he thought of the moment when he was shielding from the pure-blood Acolyte. He'd known that he was likely to be attacked, had already imagined the ways he might shield, but there was only so much one could anticipate. When the Acolyte had used both fire and pure energy together, sheer terror had crystallized his mind, and somehow he'd managed to deflect both attacks.

I wish I could remember exactly how I did it. That must be how a trance-mage feels all the time . . .

Cym emerged from the cabin, looking shaky, and went to the rail. The Vlk tattoo on her brow was more prominent than ever against the pallor of her face. She'd been trying to help burned lamiae all morning, but he could see it wasn't going well. She looked utterly drained, and completely distraught.

As he watched, she shuddered, gripping the rail, and stared down at the rolling lands below. This high up, they could see for miles, but there was still no sign of the sea. There was a big compass set below the tiller, with a gnostic map made of shifting lines of light set into the crystal face. The Elders were poring over the device with great excitement. Their goal felt tangible to them now, for the first time more reality than dream.

Alaron walked over and stood next to her, resting a hand on her shoulder.

"I can't save his other eye," she murmured. "He's half-blind, and just wants to die."

He winced, wishing he could do more, but healing was something he had no affinity for at all.

"What now?" she asked dejectedly.

He forced an encouraging smile. "We're going to the Promised Land."

"And where is that, exactly?" Cym asked, not unreasonably.

"Pretty much wherever in Antiopia we like. It needs to be somewhere coastal, within reach, so that means Dhassa or Javon, maybe."

Cym might never have had geography lessons, but her well-traveled father had taught her the shape of the world. "The coast of Javon," she suggested.

"Just what I was thinking. Kekropius agrees. He's going to persuade the Elders."

"Can you find it?"

"That compass and map device will take us right there."

"The Inquisition will follow us," she said tiredly.

"If they can—but I've heard venators can't stay aloft for long. If we go out over the ocean, there will come a point where they can't follow us, even if their scrying can find us." He couldn't help smiling.

"Until they get another ship," Cym reminded him.

"Oh. Yeah." He felt foolish all of a sudden. "Hadn't thought of that."

She raised an eyebrow. "Sol et Lune! All this competence you've been showing has had me worried. It's nice to know the old Alaron is still in there."

"Cheers. So, what are you going to do about finding your mother?"

"I'm not sure. I'm a Hermetic Water-mage with a very limited education, remember? I'm no good at Clairvoyance." Everything Cym had learned was down to Alaron and Ramon slipping out of the college at night to go through their own lessons with her. There were huge gaps in her skills. "I'm going to start trying, though."

"That's dangerous," Alaron warned. "A poorly cast scrying can attract all sorts of things—it could lead the Inquisitors straight to us. Your mother and grandfather will most probably be in Hebusalim, and that's occupied by the Rondian Army."

"Then what do you suggest?"

"We take the lamiae to Javon, then you and I take *Seeker* to Hebusalim. Once we're closer, it will be easier to find her. I've got some ideas."

"You always do," she said fondly. "You're nothing if not tenacious." She turned aside, as if complimenting him made her uncomfortable. She jabbed a thumb toward the human crewmen. Four of them were sleeping fitfully, but the other two were talking to a small cluster of lamiae, demonstrating knot-tying techniques. The men were so petrified of their captors that they obeyed all commands instantly with glassy-eyed obedience. "What's going to happen to them?"

Alaron shrugged uncomfortably. "I don't know. They want to go home, obviously. But I don't think we could survive a storm without their experience, so we have to keep them with us for now." He gestured at Mesuda and Reku, huddled beneath the masts, watching the humans with glinting eyes. "Ask them."

"I did earlier," Cym replied. "The Elders won't risk news of their existence getting out." She shuddered. "I think they mean to kill them once we reach safety."

Probably. Alaron felt helpless. "I suppose you can't blame them. The lamiae had human souls grafted into specially grown lizard bodies: they were created to be slaves. They were penned up and bred like animals; they were experimented on. They are what the Pallas magi made them."

"I know." Cym dropped her voice. "I understand all that—I'm Rimoni, I know what it is like to be an outcast. But these sailors are just men who were in the wrong place. They're not even in the Inquisition. They're just windshipmen whose ship got requisitioned."

"My Da says the Inquisition only uses fanatics."

"For soldiers, maybe—but look at them: they're petrified, but when they talk about sailing the skies, their eyes light up, just like yours did. If they're fanatical about anything, it's flying."

Alaron swallowed, watching the animated expression on the face of the sailor speaking to the listening lamiae. "I suppose. It's not my decision."

"But you have influence."

He exhaled. "All right, I'll talk to Mesuda."

Cym rubbed at the ridged lines on her brow. "Thank you." She forced a smile. "You're more like a man every day. It's unnerving."

Alaron grinned. "Just don't tell me I'm like my Da."

"Your father is a good man," Cym said seriously. "Where is he, do you think?"

"Somewhere in Dhassa? Safe, I hope. Da's pretty smart."

"He and Papa were such good friends," Cym said sadly. Her eyes misted over and she turned away, wordlessly.

Alaron knew to let her go.

Malevorn knelt with what was left of his fellow Acolytes. They were just five now: Dranid, Raine, Virgina, Dominic, and himself. Commandant Vordan knelt a few paces before them as Adamus lit the pyre to burn the gnawed remains of Brother Filius, Boron Funt, and the windship pilot-mage.

All of them had been slaughtered and half-eaten. The windship was gone, including the crew—live meat for these beasts, no doubt. There were five dead venators, leaving only four. All of their personal possessions were gone.

Their collective fury hung about the glade like a red mist.

"Father Kore, take the souls of these your servants," Adamus Crozier prayed. "Forgive them their failing, and accept them in your service in the hereafter. This we pray."

"Forgive them their failing," they echoed. Any Inquisitor who died at the hands of the enemy—*any* enemy—was deemed a failure.

Fuck that. Malevorn glared sourly at the pyre. *They lost our windship! I hope demons bugger them for eternity in Hel.*

This defeat was an outrage not known to the Order since the Noros Revolt. They all felt it, the shame. He glanced sideways at Dranid's stony face, at Virgina's shocked pallor, at Dominic's disbelief, and Raine's simmering fury. He related most closely to her reaction, he noted. Beneath their utterly different exteriors, he was coming to realize that they were the most alike here. They were both driven, and neither cared who or what perished, so long as they got their way. She had no airs and graces, just earthy, animal desires. They'd screwed again while on patrol, and he believed she might be coming around to Adamus's faction.

He glowered at Vordan's sickly gray face. The disgrace lay heaviest on the Commandant himself, something Adamus Crozier had not been slow to emphasize. It was Vordan who'd ordered them to widen the search, leaving their windship so weakly guarded.

We knew from that creature we tortured that there were more than forty adult snake-men, all with gnostic powers and some intellect. They've eluded the Inquisition for twenty years or more, yet you treated them like mindless savages. You're a fool, Vordan. What happened was your fault.

The funeral rite ended with the bloodied bones of the three dead magi ablaze. Adamus Crozier swung around to face them and thrust a stiff finger at Commandant Vordan. "By the power vested in me by the Church of Kore, I name you, Lanfyr Vordan, unfit for command. You have lost four of your Fist, and two auxiliary magi. You have failed in the mission set you by the Holy Church. I arrest you in the name of Corineus, and bind you over to the Courts of Piety in Pallas."

Vordan's already ashen face drained of all remaining color. The Courts of Piety had the power to utterly destroy a family, even if one person had transgressed, and they rarely showed clemency. The Vordan family would be utterly impoverished and forever dishonored. Malevorn found his own gut tightening: not from sympathy, but in remembrance that this fate had almost been his own. When his father, Jaes Andevarion, was disgraced in the Noros Revolt, only his suicide had prevented the Courts from taking such retribution on the family.

"My lord Crozier," Vordan croaked, "this command was yours, not mine." A hush filled the glade, as if even the rushing waters below had faded into silence.

Adamus gripped his crozier and lifted his head contemptuously. "We've all heard you claim eminence over me in the field, Commandant. Mine the guidance, yours the command: you've said so in hearing of us all. You cannot hide behind another, and it shames you to try."

Vordan looked about him: at Elath Dranid, his friend and champion for twenty years. Dranid showed no emotion. His eyes went to his lover Raine, who slowly and deliberately stroked Malevorn's arm. Any hope the Commandant still might have harbored winked out.

Adamus spoke again. "Lanfyr Vordan, I discharge you from command, and appoint Elath Dranid in your place."

Malevorn hid his disappointment. Dranid was always going to be appointed; he had the seniority. Any other outcome was unrealistic. *My time will come . . .*

Vordan's eyes glassed over as Adamus ripped the badge of command from his tunic and handed it to Dranid.

The new Commandant kissed the Crozier's ring, then growled, "Fist, to me," as he came to his feet. He lifted his fist to his breast, and thumped it once. "Farewell your former Commandant."

The Acolytes made the salute as Vordan drew his sword, kissed the hilt, then held it out for Dranid. The former Second took the Commandant's blade, kissed it also, and replaced his own blade, which he sent spinning over the edge of the cliffs into the maelstrom below.

As Vordan drew his personal dagger, his family blade, Adamus Crozier stretched out his hand for the weapon. Malevorn held his breath. This was Vordan's last chance to redeem himself—to save his family from the powers of the Courts by taking the same path as Jaes Andevarion.

Death or dishonor.

Vordan reversed the blade and rammed it into his own heart.

Raine sucked in her breath, her eyes eager as her lover swayed, blood blooming around the blade's hilt. Dominic gasped girlishly. Virgina and Dranid remained stony-faced. So did Malevorn, though the moment had been oddly chilling.

This is how powerful men lose.

Adamus Crozier smiled as the iron-faced Commandant crumpled at his feet. He bent and made a gesture that only a mage would recognize, burning away Vordan's soul so that there was nothing left to pass on to Kore's hands. There would be neither Paradise nor Hel for Lanfyr Vordan.

Then he looked up and met Dranid's cold eyes. "Commandant Dranid, ready your Fist. We have heretics to hunt."

25

SACRED VOWS

Safia

Safia was a poetess of the ancient world during the reign of Fustius II, the 7th Rimoni Emperor. She was renowned for her beauty and her talent, and was the first woman to be appointed as Poeta di Laurelae to the Imperial Court. However, her residence there ended in scandal when she was found in the bed of the empress. The term "safian" has been applied ever since to women who desire other women. Though Safia was banished, it is said that the empress visited her often in her luxurious "prison," a villa near Taphe, only ten miles from the Summer Court in Pallas.

ANNALS OF PALLAS

Brochena, Javon, Antiopia
Zulqeda (Noveleve) to Zulhijja (Decore) 928
5th and 6th months of the Moontide

Gurvon Gyle waited in the bell tower of the Sollan chapel that overlooked Piazza Giannini, the place where the Dorobon made their public pronouncements. The piazza had been the city's olive oil market, but now it was hung with blue and white Dorobon flags and pennants. Soldiers paraded in formation before the steps of the chapel, keeping away any but those Dorobon and Gorgio adherents invited for the occasion. Trumpeters and drummers were standing at attention, awaiting the signal to proclaim the coronation of the king.

Gyle glanced at Hesta Mafagliou, who was gazing down at the piazza, her eyes unfocused, her lips moving constantly, in communion with a dozen or so spirits stationed about the surrounding buildings. She'd spent all night conjuring demons and placing them into the bodies of birds to be her eyes and ears.

So far, nothing untoward had happened. The Jhafi were simply ignoring the ceremony, not rioting, as Octa Dorobon had feared.

Gyle went back inside the chapel, to the little balcony overlooking the inner sanctum. Bronze Sol et Lune faces still gazed out from the walls, but the Sacred Heart of the Kore had been placed upon the altar and a Kore Crozier now presided over the chapel. The man had been sent by Pallas to convert the Javonesi to the Kore. *Good luck with that*, he thought drily. Others had tried before him; they had all failed utterly.

"By the holy power of Corineus, who intercedes on our behalf with almighty Kore, I invoke the Sacred Heart," cried the Crozier, whose chosen name was Eternalus. "I call upon the Blessed Three Hundred to witness this great moment. I convey the sanction and approval of Emperor Constant Sacrecour and his Sainted Mother to this coronation."

His words echoed about the small chapel. Gyle could see Octa Dorobon, her face displaying every feeling as she watched, torn between distaste at the humble setting and grim satisfaction at the importance of the moment. This was her triumph: the coronation of her son to replace the husband she'd lost on the throne her family had won and lost and won again. Of course, it was also the moment when legally she gave up control of her son, and her conflicted feelings were also writ large across her visage.

Poor bastard, to have to call her "Mother," Gyle thought, turning his attention to the son.

Francis Dorobon was clad all in gold, gold thread embroidered onto gold silk, with only a blue and white quartered shield on his breast interrupting the radiance of his garb. His hair was immaculate, his face composed and filled with pride. His sword glowed with gnosis-light. In the darkened chapel, he shone like one of Kore's own Angels.

"Behold, the symbol of royal supremacy in this kingdom," Eternalus Crozier intoned, displaying the Javon crown. He then swept into a recitation of Francis's lineage. Gyle ignored Olivia Dorobon's discreet wave and focused on Cera Nesti instead. Something in the girl's demeanor had been troubling him these past few days. There was a lightness in her step that had not been there since her father the king was murdered.

Her skin looks healthier. Her eyes have a new radiance. She treads lightly where before she trudged.

There was no news from the outside world that might have lifted the girl's spirits. So he was left with one thing. *Fool,* he told himself scornfully as he studied the way her lips were parted in a secret smile.

Fool is too mild a description for what I am.

She had let him kiss her.

He hadn't meant any such thing to occur. He had meant only to brief her about the coronation and the ceremony that would follow. "They will use your presence to show their power over you," he warned. "Do not be provoked, no matter what they do or say. It's not worth it."

"I'm not stupid, Magister," she'd reminded him, flashing a faint smile that confused him. He'd been puzzled why she was so cheery about all this.

"Cera, this is important. Octa wants you dead. She does not want Francis to proceed with his marriage to you or Portia Tolidi. She's afraid she's losing control of her son, and she will lash out at you."

"You'll look after me," she'd said, cocking her head just so, in the way that showed her to best advantage. Had she been practicing in a mirror? Somehow it had made his throat catch. "I know you will."

He'd not often been truly lonely in his life. Normally he dealt with solitude easily, but very occasionally, it bit him hard. The first time that had happened had been during the Noros Revolt, in the months before the massacre at Knebb. That loneliness had been born of the war and the loss of his lover, a period of utter desolation that had ended the night Elena Anborn had come to his tent.

His second period of aching emptiness—that was right now.

He liked to portray himself as a man who walked alone, a man who needed no one else—but that wasn't true, and he wasn't one to lie to himself. He needed someone, not so much to bed—though that was certainly part of it—but to talk to. That had been Elena's magic, the thing that bound them so close together. Sex was like eating, he did it because at times he needed to, but it was that meeting of minds he really craved.

And right now, the only person with the wit, intelligence and perception he needed was this young woman, Elena's protégée. The irony was part of the allure, he was sure of it, but that didn't make it less real. Only a fool did not acknowledge his own needs and desires.

His manipulations meant Cera still mistrusted him, but over recent weeks he thought the barriers had been coming down, as much on her side as his. She was drawn to him, by their kindred souls, he knew it—and he wanted her. If that meant betraying Francis Dorobon, he would do it: to protect her, and bind her to him. He could feel his body beginning to yearn for hers. It didn't matter that she was not as beautiful as Vedya or Portia; her mind was the stairway to her soul.

"I will look after you," he'd promised her. "We are both under threat here. We need each other."

She'd shivered when she met his eyes. Had that been fear, or the acknowledgment of desire?

"Magister—"

Her voice had brought him back in the room. "Call me Gurvon, Cera."

She'd smiled shyly and slowly flicked a tress of hair from her face in a motion so graceful it froze him. "Why do you risk yourself to protect me?" she'd asked—and that she spoke of state affairs and not of passion only enflamed him further. She was truly a woman with a heart and mind like his own.

"One must always keep options open," he'd told her seriously.

"So I am just a long-odds bet, in case the leading horse falls?"

"No. I find the Dorobon repulsive," he had said, his voice a whisper that would not carry to where Hesta might be watching. "It is only politics that has me aiding them at all. There are far worthier causes."

She'd taken his cue. "Alliances can change," she'd breathed. "Gurvon."

He'd thrilled at the sound of his name on her lips, and it had encouraged him to continue, "How can I go back to Yuros after this? The emperor does not welcome those he owes. Far better if I had a sanctuary here."

She'd stared up at him, so close to him he could smell the flowery, musky scent of her body. "Would you truly betray the Dorobon? For me?"

I could betray anyone, but the reasons would always be dictated by logic. "For you, perhaps." He'd reached out, caught her chin, tilted her face upward, and covered her mouth with his.

Her lips were achingly sweet, and she hadn't pulled away. Only iron discipline and the nagging suspicion that Hesta might be watching had kept him from more—that, and the fact that she still must go to Francis's bed as a virgin.

"All is well," Hesta whispered in his ear, bringing him back to the coronation. He hid his surprise that she'd gotten so close to him without his knowledge.

She is dangerous in her own way. I should be more wary of her.

He lifted a hand in acknowledgment. Mara and Sordell were with Endus Rykjard, laying plans. Hesta was his only experienced backup here in Brochena. Young Mathieu Fillon was strong, but he was young and as yet unblooded, and Madeline Parlow was useless in a fight. He had to rely on Hesta more than he liked, but so far she'd risen well to the task. She shouldn't be here, though, and she shouldn't be speaking aloud. Gyle thought she looked tired from the constant drain on her gnosis caused by so many active spirit-bindings—but that's what he was paying her to do.

He answered her mentally, letting his irritation show, *<Do not even whisper in here: the acoustics are very pure. Stay focused on your demons until the king is back inside the palace.>*

<No one is going to attack,> Hesta sniffed. *<The only threats are already inside.>* She indicated Octa and her faction.

<It's not Octa I'm worried about right now. It's Elena. Get back out there.>

The Lantrian made a sly face. *<The Nesti girl is growing up, isn't she?'>*

<She's a child.>

<She was Queen-Regent, child or no. She is intelligent, and values intelligence in other people. She's waking up, becoming a woman. I wonder if Francis will appreciate her?>

Gyle scowled. *<If I want your advice on young women—>*

<You have only to ask.> Hesta winked impudently. *<I'm an expert, remember?>* she smirked and sashayed away.

As Gyle silently fumed, his eyes went back to Cera. It certainly rankled to see the girl wed to another, but marriages weren't forever, whatever the vows said. And he still had several cards to play, including Timori, whose whereabouts he'd been careful to keep from anyone else in his team.

Francis was now kneeling before Eternalus Crozier, who was raising the crown over his head. "Francis Louis Dorobon, rightful Marquis of Sendon and Verussy, by the power vested in me, I crown you King of Javon." He lowered the crown, newly remade to fit snugly, onto the head of the young man.

Nineteen. That's ludicrously young for such a delicate role.

Francis was the same age as Cera, of course—but she had been twice the ruler Dorobon would ever be. His eyes strayed back to her: standing alone at the end of the third pew, isolated, vulnerable, her eyes glassing over. She would be remembering her father and mother, thinking of her sister and brother. He found himself wanting to shield her from this, for nothing more than the gratitude in her eyes.

If the Dorobon turn on me, I could raise this whole land against them, if it was in her name.

He watched only her as those present cheered their new king, then filed forward to kiss his ring. They made her do it too, in her plain violet dress that made her look more like a servant than a princess. They hadn't let her wear her coronet, nor any jewelry; nothing but a bridal veil. Portia Tolidi was similarly attired. They awaited the second ceremony to come; the wedding, which would be conducted in private because of Octa's fury that it was to happen at all.

Now the moment was come, he wasn't truly sure he wanted it either.

Only a fool did not acknowledge his own desires.

It was raining . . .

Travelers had told her it rained all the time in Yuros, but Cera had only ever lived in Javon, where it rained just twice a year, in Noveleve and Febreux: once going into winter and again coming out. At those times torrential downpours filled the lakes and flooded the plains. The Keshi called it the Yagmur; in Lakh it was the Monsoon.

Traditionally, the Yagmur was a cause of celebration. Even under Dorobon occupation and after the loss of so many men, those celebrations went ahead.

She could hear the drums pulsing through the city where the Jhafi thronged, white-clad men in some of the squares, brightly clad women in others. It was one of only two festivals where the women could shed their bekira-shrouds in public, and only then as long as no men were present. She remembered her mother taking her and Solinde dancing some years, whenever duty permitted. Those had been some of the happiest times of her life.

This year, she could only listen from her darkened room and yearn.

She stifled a yawn and stared down at the rain-lashed city, wishing she could take Portia and dance with her amidst all the other women. She had risen at dawn to pray in the little masjid attached to the palace, the same one her mother used to take them to, to pray to Ahm. The palace was silent, in contrast to the streets outside. *The dreary Rondians cannot compete with our vitality*, she thought with a smile.

There would be no official duties until evening; there was nowhere she needed to be. She missed the meetings, the intense discussions that shaped the kingdom. Now she was nothing, just a bargaining chip—or a broodmare. She pulled her left hand from under the covers and stared at the heavy, uncomfortable ring on her left hand. The Dorobon crest marked her as Francis's possession. Immediately after the Dorobon's coronation, she and Portia had been taken to a small Sollan chapel where drui Prato had married them both to Francis under the Javon protocols. She'd pretended in her mind that she was marrying Portia instead.

Then Francis had taken them both to his suite, and while Portia watched, he had taken her maidenhood. Portia's presence had made it bearable, despite the pain and humiliation of being made to kneel and be taken from behind like a cow. But at least she hadn't had to look at him, his repulsive face and pallid, fleshy skin. It had hurt, but not so much, and he'd apparently mistaken her grunts of discomfort for pleasure. He'd been pleased with her bloodied loins and had taken the stained sheet to the door to show those waiting. Then he'd banished her, so that he could have his way with Portia. There'd be no bloodied sheets there.

I am a woman and a wife. It was odd, but the thought meant nothing to her. Nothing did, except Portia.

Their stolen moments were all the sweeter for the danger, and the difficulties in contriving them, slipping at midnight into Portia's bedroom, trusting Gyle's word that no one now watched them. Most nights Portia wanted only to sleep or to simply be held—they had made love on only three occasions—and those little rejections hurt when Cera wanted her so badly. Her days were full of desperate desire, a need that burned inside so intensely she thought she would immolate. She'd always scorned love-struck girls, but now she was one, and she could scarcely bear it. Knowing her passion was only partially returned was another torture—but when they were together, nothing else mattered.

She could not believe a being so lovely would consent to lie with her; she could not believe that another's mouth and tongue could elicit such pleasure from her. And to let her do the same, to taste the spicy hollows of her skin? That was beyond price . . .

And afterward they talked so freely, shared things she'd never told another soul, whispering softly in each other's ears until all the time had slipped through their fingers and the charade must begin again.

I love her. I want to be with her forever. Her suspicion that Portia lay with her only out of pity and friendship was a pang she could bear, for now. *She will come to love me fully in time,* she told herself; she would even have prayed for it, if she had thought that there was any god who might grant such a wish.

Today King Francis was off with his friends, Gyle included, hunting lions. She was pleased Gyle was away, for playing with his affections felt deadly dangerous. He wanted her, she knew that, even if that meant cuckolding the king. So far she'd managed to hide her utter loathing of him, let him think she was being brought around, but she knew she could not do that forever.

No doubt Octa and Olivia were indulging in yet another bout of gluttony and excess in the royal suite. They would doubtless already be on the way to intoxicated—they would drink all day until they finally collapsed insensible sometime around dusk. There was no one living here on the top levels except Portia and her. Marriage hadn't changed the arrangement of the bedrooms, and that was absolutely fine by Cera.

Finally! The moment she'd been waiting for arrived: Tarita gave a discreet rap on her door, then pattered away. Of course her little maid knew—but if she judged, she didn't condemn. Cera erupted from her bed and scurried from her room to the next in the blink of an eye. The parlor door was open, affording a view of an unmade bed and a long, lithe body sprawled naked among the sheets, a tangle of russet hair vivid against white skin.

Cera lost her breath momentarily.

Portia looked up with hooded eyes. "You are insatiable," she complained, wriggling to make room in the bed.

Francis Dorobon's entourage wound its way slowly back into Brochena, through the kenars, the Jhafi slums, at the edge of the city. The column was large enough to dissuade attack, something that was becoming a greater threat of late. Two patrols had been ambushed

and murdered last month. Fenys Rhodium and Sir Teris Grandienne's response had been brutal: they'd sealed off the area where the
attacks had taken place and burned it to the ground with gnosis-
fueled fires, slaying hundreds of men, women, and children who'd
almost certainly had nothing to do with the attacks.

I could have taken you straight to the men who did it, Gyle mused.
But he was more than happy for the Dorobon to engender more
hatred for themselves.

Now the column of mounted men wound through the streets,
four tawny mountain lion pelts hanging from poles as prizes. The
hunting had been good and Francis well amused. He and his friends
had hunted enthusiastically for ten days, and laughed and cavorted
drunkenly every evening. Gyle had never been quite included—he
was not of their lineage—but Francis openly sought his guidance,
and he was treated with respect.

"Gyle," King Francis boomed, trotting his horse up beside him
and slapping his shoulder. "Excellent sport, my friend! We must do
it again soon!"

"There are other beasts also worthy of the chase, your Majesty,"
Gyle replied, and regaled Francis with descriptions of the local deer,
wild tuskers, and carnobirds, the giant flightless eagles that lived in
the mountains. A new expedition to the southeast was mooted.

"There is always good meat to be had in Javon, if one knows
where to hunt," he added, temptingly.

Francis glanced about him then leaned closer. "My friend, getting out of this damned court lifts my spirits. I know I shouldn't
say so, but I do not feel wholly in control here still. My mother's
confidantes are constantly badgering me about this or that." He
faked a yawn. "They bore me. Mother thinks I am still a child,
and Fenys Rhodium and Terus Grandienne take their cues from
her. I am a crowned king, and twice married, and still Mother
tries to suffocate me. How can I get her to step back and give me
room to breathe?"

Gyle smiled inwardly. Such conversations with Francis were
becoming more frequent, and he was relying more and more on
him for advice.

"A king must trust his advisers," he said carefully, "and family is important, of course, but they are not the only source of wisdom."

"Marrying my sister Olivia would make you one of the family," Francis said slyly.

Good grief!

"The affairs of the kingdom take all my energy, sire," Gyle replied hurriedly.

"Ha! Not all of them, my friend! Don't think I'm not aware of your clandestine relations with her." Francis didn't sound disapproving, just amused. "I would not have thought you and she well matched, in truth."

Gyle smiled in the friendly way that Francis liked. *I must be careful not to insult his sister, but the last thing I want is to be saddled with her.* "It is just a sometime thing, sire." He dropped his own voice. "I believe she sees it as a rebellion against your mother."

The king laughed briefly, then looked around again to ensure they were still out of earshot before asking seriously, "You would not accept if I offered you her hand, then?"

"Milord, with all respect, I doubt I will ever marry. My work does not permit such arrangements."

"A shame," Francis mused. "I would like to formalize our alliance." He snickered softly. "And it would give Mother apoplexy." He glanced up at the fortress as it came into view and his face brightened. "And now my lady awaits."

"They both await," Gyle reminded him.

Francis looked across at him and as if sharing a confidence, admitted, "The Nesti girl does not move me. Her skin is too dark and she has no gaiety. No . . . spark." He sniffed. "I don't like her smell—garlic and curry-leaf. But I do my duty, and she does hers."

"Get her with child, sire." Gyle made a crude gesture. "The Nesti are half-pacified already by your marriage to Cera. A mage-child will bind them to you."

"She comes on heat next week." He chuckled lewdly. "I shall plow her diligently, and name the child Gurvon." He clapped Gyle on the shoulder. "But meantime, I have a finer mount to ride. The Tolidi girl is besotted with me, you know—she's insatiable." His eyes went up to the towers of the palace. "I tell you, Mother still talks of saddling me with some trollop from her circle, but I'll not put Portia aside, no matter what. Whatever other wife my mother foists upon me can put up with that, or I'll not have her. I'm king now: I make the rules!"

Portia Tolidi was harmless enough. Gyle said encouragingly, "Your lady mother has perhaps forgotten what it is like to be young. She will loosen her reins upon you in time," he added, twisting the knife subtly.

Francis scowled. "My mother doesn't understand me."

"Mothers seldom do." *Actually she reads you like a book, my dear Francis. As do we all.* "I daresay she will tire of Javon soon enough. I am sure she will return to Yuros once she feels you are secure." He watched the young man deal with the implication that his kingship was still insecure.

"Sooner rather than later, I hope," Francis growled. He glanced back at his coterie of young friends. "My friends are fine fellows, but they don't understand politics like you and I, Gyle." He dropped his voice. "My mother fears you. She thinks that you have more influence over me than she does."

"Her jealousies are unfounded, my lord King," Gyle lied. "You are your own man."

"I am," King Francis agreed fervently, as if by saying so, he might make it true. "Mother's friends think they rule me." He bit his lip. "I wish I was free of them. But Mother . . ." He sniffed angrily. "I cannot just send them away."

"Lord King, you cannot send them away *yet*, but you can work around them. The Nesti used to have a council that effectively controlled the kingdom. Create your own council—then gradually exclude your mother's people. Take control."

Francis's eyes lit up. "I could . . ." Then, "Could I?" Gyle could already see the young man's mind jumping from the notion of freedom to a shirking of responsibility. "All those boring *duties* . . ."

He restrained himself from rolling his eyes. "My lord, rulership need not be a burden. Appoint a few trusted people to advise you, and then direct everything through Don Perdonello to implement your decisions." *My good friend Francesco.*

"Him? I don't like him."

"He's the most capable administrator in the realm, your Majesty. You can rely on him to carry out your will and not to burden you with *unnecessary* matters."

"But if I alienate my mother, we will appear divided—the people may see weakness." He dropped his voice. "I have only ten thousand loyal men."

You have far fewer than that, boy. "Then get the Nesti onside. Get Cera with child. Treat her well in public and the Nesti will come around. They are still powerful and free. Bind them to you."

Francis considered. "I suppose she isn't utterly unattractive, for a mudskin. I've had uglier women. And I'll still have Portia." He smirked. "Your idea of having several wives was a good one. You really should try it yourself."

Cera woke from a hazy midafternoon dream, a doze brought on by sheer boredom. Portia had been closeted with Francis Dorobon since the hunt had returned, leaving Cera neglected and lonely again. She hadn't been summoned at all, and the thought of Francis and Portia together was sheer misery.

She rolled over and lay on her side staring at the wall. A pale angel sang silently upon the tapestry while a knight and lady knelt at her feet. The Amteh Scriptures held that angels had no gender, but this angel had always looked female to Cera: strong and pure and womanly, with a severe determination that reminded her of Elena. She wished gloomily that her former champion was with her, even if she probably hated her now.

I would kneel at her feet and beg forgiveness. Then together we would slaughter these Dorobon pigs.

A hand touched her shoulder and she started, opened her mouth, and—

—a knife of pain thrust through her mind and she stiffened, choked, and tried to cry out. But an insidious lassitude filled her like venom and instead she found herself staring vacantly as she fell into a state of complete inertia.

A lugubrious female face with a gold Lantric nose-ring and two luminous deep-set eyes rose over her. It was the woman she'd seen in her rooms—Gyle's spy. She wanted to scream, but she couldn't remember how. Then an accented voice filled her skull and obliterated all possibility of thought or action.

<Be still, girl. Utterly still . . .>

"Hello little safian," the Lantric woman said aloud. "Did you have a sweet dream? Time to wake now, and do your duty."

Cera tried to call for help, but the only thing that came from her mouth was one faint word: ". . . duty . . ."

The woman smiled brightly. "Yes, duty. You must do as I say, exactly as I say. The kingdom depends on it."

". . . kingdom . . ."

"Exactly. Cera, you must go to Gurvon Gyle's room. Tell him that Francis neglects you. That he leaves you unfulfilled. Tell him how much you need him."

There was no choice, no option. Cera felt a liquid warmth flow from the woman's eyes, a pulse of heat that traveled down her spine and into her loins. She shivered with the longing to be taken and used. Her skin prickled and flushed with the heat, her nipples hardened painfully and she groaned. ". . . need him . . ."

"Exactly. You want him in you—you want him so badly you would risk all. He feels the same way, my dear, I assure you. He feels exactly the way you do."

The woman deftly loosened the laces at the front of Cera's nightgown, then pulled out a little vial and dabbed something clear onto each nipple. "He wants to suckle you. He wants you."

". . . wants . . ." The word filled her head, imparted meaning to all that was happening. She tried to kiss the Lantric woman, desperately needing to be held and loved. ". . . wants . . ."

The Lantric woman caught her hands, laughing huskily. "No, no, my sweet. Save your passion for Gurvon. Think how sweet it will feel."

The woman stood her up and smoothed down her hair. "Go to him like this, with the smell of the bedroom on your skin and your hair tangled. Now hold still." She smeared something over Cera's lips. "Don't lick your lips, whatever you do. Let him kiss them first."

". . . kiss . . ."

"Look, little safian. Here is your maid. She's going to help you find your lover."

Cera turned her head as Tarita walked stiffly into the chamber and took her hand. Her eyes were vacant.

". . . lover . . ." Cera went to kiss the girl, but the Lantric woman caught her.

"No, no. Save your kisses for Gurvon, my dear. Then all of Paradise will be yours."

A kiss.

All the long days of Francis's hunt, Gyle had thought long and hard about that one kiss, the one he'd stolen from Cera Nesti's lips. Or had she offered it? His memories were oddly blurred about that moment. It had felt like both.

He was still in his traveling clothes, just unbuckling his sword-belt, when there was a soft rap upon his door. He called a challenge, then his heart double-skipped at the sound of *her* voice.

"My lord Gyle?"

He was across the room and had disabled his wards and opened the door before his mind could engage. He looked past her at the corridor, where Tarita, her maid, waited attentively.

"What?" He looked down, at Cera and caught his breath. She was a disheveled vision of young womanhood, plucked from his fancies. "My queen?"

She looked dazed, and fresh from the bedchamber. Her hair was a bird's nest and she was clad only in a thin nightgown. He could see the shape of her body through the flimsy fabric, could see the line of her cleavage down the poorly tied front. "Cera? You cannot walk the castle like this." All his instincts screamed warnings of entrapment.

I should call for servants, I can't be seen with her like this . . .

"Gurvon," she breathed, and her eyes bored into his. "I've been longing for you to return."

Great Kore . . .

He looked at Tarita, who smiled, and made a small hand-gesture, one he would not have thought she knew. It meant "All is well" in the hand-speech of the Lantric Silent Tongue. Mustaq al'Madhi's gang used that tongue.

Tarita must be his spy . . . Is this a gift to me? A peace offering?

Tarita winked, and walked stiffly away.

He stared after her as Cera's hands slowly reached for his face. For a second he stalled, then he pulled her inside and locked and warded the door again. "Cera? You shouldn't be here! You belong to Francis and—"

She kissed him, and the words died in his mouth and in his brain. As his lips locked onto hers, she ground herself against him. Her dusky musk filled his nostrils and the sweetness of her mouth filled his, her saliva faintly bitter and utterly intoxicating. He gripped her shoulders, then her waist, and almost overbalanced as he lifted her awkwardly and carried her to his bed. The rational part of his mind clamored warnings, but all the blood in his body was pumping to his groin. His mouth was fizzing with her taste, then a weird sense of dislocation began. He lowered her to the covers, wrenched dizzily at his own clothing as she looked up at him with desperate eyes and tugged her nightdress open, baring herself to him.

His eyes went from her face to her breasts.

He fell on her, caught her right nipple in his mouth and suckled hard, and she moaned and writhed as the room dipped and weaved about them. It was dizzying—and suddenly frightening—

His mind caught up with him, and with it the familiarity of that taste on her lips and breasts. *His tongue was fizzing.* The sensations of swirling and falling intensified. And her eyes were unnaturally glazed over.

How the Hel would Tarita really *know the Silent Tongue?*

By then it was too late.

His doors disintegrated in a blast of energy, his wards obliterated by pure-blooded gnosis, the backlash blasting his synapses. He tried to pull himself from Cera's arms even as she groaned beneath him. But his limbs were like jelly, his cock the only rigid part of his body. His mouth was so numb he couldn't feel his tongue.

Poison . . . on her skin . . .

A cloud of barely discernible figures burst into the room, and between one heartbeat and the next, there was a dagger resting over his heart. He looked up into the eyes of his betrayer.

Hesta Mafagliou's long, razor-edged stiletto pricked his skin. The steel was aglow with mage-fire. "Don't move, boss," she said quietly, radiating calm. Her nose-ring glittered in the flames of the torches as half a dozen magi from Octa Dorobon's contingent swarmed inside. "We all have our price," she added softly.

He managed to push himself off Cera, who looked dazedly about her, then her hands went to her mouth and she rolled into a ball to cover herself. She began to shake.

He sought desperately for a way out of this, to preserve himself, but Hesta's blade pricked a little deeper and she shook her head.

<*Damn you—*>He tried to talk, but his tongue lolled and he drooled helplessly. <*What was your price . . . Hesta—?*>

"An Imperial pardon. Lucia wanted you removed with minimal disruption, so she sought me out. I have a pardon, and they will return my estates in Lantris. My disgrace never happened. I am clean again."

<*You'll always be what you are . . . Your next lapse will see it all taken away again . . . Lucia gives no gifts.*>

She shook her head. "I am too old for love and lust now, Gurvon. I won't fall again." She cut his periapt-cord and pocketed the gem deftly. "They stone adulterous women here, do you know that? Men they just berate and send on their way . . . unless they rukk the queen. In that case . . ." She made a lopping gesture toward his neck.

<*I . . . am Imperial Envoy . . . I cannot be arrested . . .*>

"You said it yourself, boss. Lucia gives no gifts. She gave Octa the orders herself." Hesta clucked smugly. "I know where Mara hides, and which of the Dorobon magi is housing Sordell. I've already gutted Fillon. I've told them where to find Timori—thought you'd kept that secret, didn't you? You've no cards left to play."

Damn damn damn . . .

He lifted his eyes to meet hers, barely clinging to consciousness as the poisons spread through his body. *<You've sold yourself for a lie, Hesta. Society will never forgive you, regardless of what Lucia gives you.>*

"Money buys everything, Gurvon. You know that. This is making me very rich." Hesta licked her lips. "I'm going to be known forever as the one who brought you down."

26

Uneasy Peace

Affinity

The mage can be known by his affinities for certain studies or crafts. The other aspects of the gnosis are relatively uniform, but it is in the ability—or inability—to master aspects of the studies that a mage's distinctive style becomes apparent, and in which their greatest power and vulnerability lie. Even the most powerful magi have studies they are unable to wield, as no man is perfectly in balance with all aspects of his world.

Huw Blund, Andressea, 627

Mount Tigrat, Javon, Antiopia
Zulquda (Noveleve) to Zulhijja (Decore) 928
5th and 6th months of the Moontide

"I have a present for you," Elena said as they ate one night in early Noveleve. She produced a pouch and tossed it to Kazim, who eyed it warily before opening it hesitantly. She realized that she was holding her breath, wanting him to be pleased with the gift.

Things were not the same between them—how could they be? Gnosis-training mind-to-mind was too great an intimacy; secrets neither would have willingly shared with another were given involuntarily. The Gnostic Colleges maintained distance between teachers and pupils, but that couldn't be the case working at the accelerated speed she and Kazim were. Mind-to-mind learning was more intimate than sex; the bonds and ties it left were sticky and persistent, like trailing spider webs.

An observer would have thought them less close, not more. Kazim had moved to a different floor, taking a smaller cell where an initiate monk had slept. They washed their own clothing, trained physically separately once more, in case the constant proximity became even more claustrophobic. They only shared meals, and then all their conversation was of the gnosis—but despite their efforts to keep some degree of space between them, internally, the training was wrapping cords around their two souls.

This had only been possible because Kazim had truly consented to learn. He opened his mind, and filled it with all she taught. There were basic gaps she had to fill in swiftly so a chance encounter with a low-blooded mage wouldn't destroy him. Then she moved on, developing his repertoire: shields and wards; ways to lock down doors and windows; spells for hiding from normal sight and from mages' sight; how to communicate mentally over distance; exploring his affinities.

He tried as hard as he could to restrict the amount of gnosis he used, to hold off the day when he simply had nothing left. But as days passed he felt himself becoming weak—not physically, but magically, for the final resources of his stolen gnosis were being bled away by their training. The energies first released by Meiros's soul and then replenished by Wimla's death were almost gone, and his morality and humanity forbade him from replenishing.

Elena approved, of course, but it meant that he was growing weaker even as his skill increased. And he'd told her that fighting the longing to kill and replenish was hard. It showed on his face sometimes.

But there were joys too, and tonight was one. He opened the pouch and pulled out a sapphire the size of a fingernail. His eyes goggled. "What is this?"

She smiled at his stunned pleasure. His smile was a wondrous thing; it lit up his face.

"It's a periapt gem," she said, "the sort easily attuned to Air-gnosis." She tugged her own into view: a similar stone. "Sapphires work particularly well with Water and Air."

"Ispal Ankesharan would wet himself!" he exclaimed. He didn't need to explain; she knew his history as well as he himself did now—she knew who Ispal Ankesharan was, almost felt she'd met him.

"But I can't accept such a thing," he said sadly. "It is too much."

"It's worth a lot to a trader," she admitted, "but its value is much higher to a mage. You'll burn through energy more slowly—you'll be able to go up against a trained mage on an equal footing. I need you to have it, if we're going to work together. Without it, any one of Gyle's gang will defeat you."

He still looked uncomfortable as he dangled the gem in his fingers. She reached out and clasped his fingers around it. "Take it, Kazim. It is yours."

They both stared at their clasped hands, hers pale, callused, and lined with the first signs of aging; his big, dark, and smooth. For an awkward moment their eyes met.

"I am not complicated," he'd told her once. He wasn't, but the things happening to him were.

She let go. "You'll need to tune it to your gnosis. I'll show you how."

He exhaled heavily, as if coming to a decision, then spread the cord and lowered it over his head. He looked up at her with his big, wounded eyes. "Sal'Ahm," he said softly.

"Thank you for taking it," she replied. She studied him. The smile had transformed his face. She would have loved to see it again.

Instead he sighed and said, "How do I tune it?"

"Channel your gnosis through it, as gently as you can. It takes time—hours, days even—before the flow becomes natural. But it's worth it, trust me. It will allow you to burn less energy."

He looked hopeful, but the following days proved her wrong. The periapt made no difference. On reflection it made sense: a periapt boosted renewal of gnosis, allowing spells to be cast more intensely, but as a Souldrinker he simply could not replenish. It made her wonder if their relationship was doomed.

Despite this setback they began to make plans. It was late Novel-eve, and Kazim's training was progressing well. He felt more comfortable with taking instruction now, in combat at least. The gnosis was a different matter; she suspected it always would be. His affinities were basic and his gnostic style would never be subtle, but he was very strong in a simple but extreme way. His spells might be straightforward, but they were brutally effective.

"When will we go to war?" he asked from time to time, feeling his eagerness to rejoin the fray return. Finally, she gave him a direct answer. In Janune, the cooler temperatures would make travel more bearable . . .

As Noveleve ended, the north wind began to blow cooler around the mountain, giving Kazim a hint of what winter would be like here, so high above the plains. They were low on fresh meat, so Elena took him to the river upstream from Shimdas village. He'd fished before in Baranasi, dangling lines into the muddy, sluggish flow of Mother Imuna. This river was very different. It wound through the dried-out land like a wriggling snake, changing course by the season. Right now it was broad and shallow, awaiting the autumn rains, but there were plenty of places to fish.

But first, Kazim wanted to bathe. He left Elena beside the largest pool and walked upstream until she was hidden by a fold in the land, then stripped and waded naked into the water. It was colder than he had expected and his skin started tingling as he waded deeper. He found that he was already subconsciously scanning with the gnosis, seeking life; a few fish were near, just small things. He ducked under and launched himself into the deepest part of the flow.

He swam blindly for a few seconds, then came up, spluttering, enjoying the bracing chill. It was so much cleaner than the Baranasi waters—though Mother Imuna was supposed to be the world's purest river, its purity was very definitely spiritual, not chemical. This was completely different: fresh, natural, clean . . .

Movement caught his eye and he realized he'd swum past the mound he'd picked to hide him from Elena. He was a little shocked to see her, sixty yards or so downstream, also wading into the water, straight-backed and completely unselfconscious in her nakedness.

She was standing sideways on to him and he found himself studying her cautiously, curiosity overcoming his disapproval. She had
strong shoulders and a flat, straight waist, not in the classic hour-
glass shape women should have. Classically, Ahmedhassan women
were supposed to be wider at the hips than shoulders, and she was
not . . . but he could see that did not mean she was not a woman.
Her bottom was narrow, but it was rounded, and her breasts were
just as he'd imagined them: small and high, and so firm they barely
jiggled as she moved. She'd unbound her hair and it fell about her
face in a pale cloud, hiding her eyes. Her belly and breasts and bottom were utterly white, like snow, which made her look unnaturally
bare, as if an extra layer of skin had been revealed.

She sank beneath the water, and he did too, to wash the image of
her body from his mind's eye, but it didn't work. He caught another
presence: another living mind, one so alien and hungry that he surfaced, recoiling in fear, and started searching around for the threat.
Then he realized what he'd sensed was a catfish, lurking in the lee
of the far bank—a big one, waiting ravenously for its lesser kindred
to pass.

He glanced back at Elena, sitting in the shallows some way away,
washing her arms and legs. Her tiny nipples were pink, he noticed,
and erect from the cool water. The sight caused his cock to stiffen, and
she suddenly raised her head and looked directly at him, as if sensing
his attention. She lifted her chin, didn't trouble to hide herself.

He ducked back under the water to avoid her challenging eyes.
Something else was threatening their delicate balance now: physical desire. She was, for all her strangeness, still a woman and not
without her own allure. Irritably, he pushed the thought away and
sought a distraction. He tried to still the waters about him as he
swam and sent his senses questing out, seeking the catfish. A plan
formed in his mind, a way to prove himself . . .

There—

He was good at swimming, as he was at all things physical. He
worked his way upstream of the catfish, then floated toward it,
barely having to move, letting the current take him. *I'm just a little
fish*, he told the silent darkness beneath the bank. *So tasty . . .*

The darkness heaved and jaws careened out of the shadows, lined with rows of needle-like teeth. He quailed in alarm as jaws wider than his head clamped onto his leg and a massive body thrashed about, shaking him like a doll. He shouted in pain, stunned at the sheer size of the creature, which was so much greater than he'd anticipated. His vision spun as the jaws clenched tighter, burying the razor-sharp teeth hooked in his thigh deeper. As pain went shrieking through his body he grabbed onto his gnosis and blazed away at it in terror, using the Air-gnosis lightning she'd taught him, desperate to get this monster off him. The water boiled about him in a vivid white *CRACK!*, and then the biter was gone, leaving him reeling about in the still-churning water, desperately trying to regain his feet, but failing—

He fell backward as his legs gave way, and the sky swirled above.

"*KAZIM?*" He could dimly hear something thrashing through the water, and realized it was Elena calling. Her voice sounded full of fear. "*KAZIM!*" she cried again as his skin started fizzing and livid patches of fire danced before his eyes. He could hardly feel a thing.

"Holy Kore, what have you done?"

Elena's face appeared above him, flushed and fearful, distorted and alien as the colors in his eyes ran and pulsed. All he could do was stare up at her, dazed, then the pricklish buzz receded and a wall of pain struck him down, a rolling boulder of agony that pulverized him.

He sank back into the water.

Kazim awoke to darkness—a damp cloth wrapped over his eyes. Apart from that, as far as he could tell, he was floating in water. *Am I in the river still?* He remembered that brilliant flash, and the burning, boiling agony that followed. And he remembered Elena's voice.

What happened?

His skin felt . . . *numb* . . . there was nothing else, really: no sensation except for a deep itching. But something in the totality of the darkness frightened him.

"Elena?" His voice was a hoarse croak.

"I'm here, Kazim." Her voice was filled with exhaustion and worry.

"Where—?"

"We're at the monastery. You're going to be all right, I promise you." Her hand touched his shoulder and he felt her breath on his face. "I'm here," she repeated. She sounded rather like Tanuva Ankesharan—his Lakh "mother"—did when one of her brood fell ill.

"What happened? How—?" He had a thousand questions, and no idea which should be asked first.

"Hush. Sleep now." Her voice made it a command, and he couldn't disobey.

When he woke next it was still dark. His skin itched like crazy. He wasn't lying on his back in water anymore but on his front on a mattress, and as far as he could tell, he was still naked. Cloth still bound his eyes—he could feel it—and everything was dark. He tried to reach his gnosis, but he couldn't, and the feeling of helplessness that gave him was frightening.

"Elena?"

No reply.

"ELENA!"

He heard running feet as she cried, "I'm coming!"

She hurried in and asked anxiously, "What is it?"

He felt immediately ashamed at his small panic and admitted, "It's nothing—I woke up, that is all." His limbs felt leaden, but at least he could feel them. He groped around for a sheet. "Where are my clothes? Why is my face bandaged—?" He swallowed as a new fear struck him. "My eyes—?"

"Will be fine," she answered firmly. "Lie still, you idiot." A sheet settled gently over him. "I was just letting your skin breathe—it'll heal faster that way."

His hands flew to the bandage about his face. "But—?"

She caught his wrists firmly. "Leave it," she said sharply. "They are mending well, but they need rest."

"Am I blind?"

"No, no—you're not blind, but it will take a little time for your eyes to fully recover."

He forced himself to do something like relax. "What happened?" he whispered after he had calmed himself a little.

She snorted. "You just about killed yourself. What on earth made you use electrical energy in water you were actually *swimming* in yourself?"

He had no idea what she meant. "Electrical energy? What is that? I only wanted to catch a fish—"

She choked back a laugh. "Kore Almighty!" He felt her lean over him, felt the weight of her elbows beside his shoulder. "You idiot! Don't you know that—? *Sol et Lune*, you didn't know, did you?" Her voice went up an octave and she sounded close to hysteria. "It's all my fault—I should have taught you—"

"I was just trying to lure out the fish, then blast it with lightning," he interrupted her. "But he was bigger than I thought—"

"Ha! Was he ever! He was almost as big as I am. If you weren't a mage you probably would be dead. He'd have held you under until you drowned. Biggest damn catfish I've ever seen," she added in an impressed voice.

"In Baranasi they sometimes catch catfish as heavy as oxen," he told her. "But I never thought there would be something so large here." He cursed. "Shame it got away."

She laughed again. "Oh no it didn't! You put enough energy into the river to kill every fish within a hundred yards, and then some." Her voice dropped. "Water and lightning together are very powerful: the water feeds the lightning. The only reason you're still alive is that you were the originator of the blast and that softened its impact enough that all you suffered were burns." She patted his cheek. "You're lucky I'm a healer. You've lost most of the skin from your torso and legs, and you would have been blind if I hadn't gotten you under treatment immediately."

He felt his skin prickle with retrospective fear and had to calm his breathing as she went on, "Three layers of skin I've had to slough away—but don't worry: I've smoothed the skin pigment so there aren't any blotchy patches. You're a work in progress, but I think you'll be back on your feet in a few days."

"How long was I . . . ?" He paused, almost afraid to ask the question, but she patted his shoulder reassuringly.

"Asleep?" she finished for him. "Almost two weeks." She poked him lightly. "You do look a little odd, though, now that you're white-skinned."

"*WHAT—?*"

Strong but gentle hands restrained him as he tried to push himself upright. "Calm, Kazim, calm. You need to relax and rest if you are going to get better quickly. Don't worry, you'll soon get used to it—I have." She laughed slyly. "Would you like some catfish stew?"

When she did finally let him pull off the bandages, of course his skin wasn't white at all; that had been her idea of a joke. It was certainly paler than it had been, though. All his chest hair was gone, and his legs were hairless too, but his head and beard were fine—because they'd been out of the water, Elena said.

The light hurt his eyes at first, but she had been ministering him closely, feeding him with healing-gnosis and gradually unwrapping the gauzy bandage, letting a little more light in every day so that his eyes could accustom themselves bit by bit to raw daylight. She made sure he had a sheet draped over his body all the time now, even though he knew that she'd not just seen every inch of him, but she'd been washing him and cleaning up his waste. The embarrassment was almost overpowering.

"I owe you my life again," he said, more bitterly than he'd intended.

"Well, sorry about that," she responded caustically.

He floundered. "No, no, I didn't mean—" He tried to rephrase it so it sounded less insulting. "It's just that all I seem to do is owe people."

"It must hurt, to be indebted to a ferang jadugara, huh? How nefari does that make you?"

He winced. "Many lashes."

Her eyebrows went up and her lips quivered in that indignant way she had, but for once she didn't launch into another diatribe of criticism. "Lashes? The Kore haven't burned sinners at the stake for a long time." She thought about that, and then added fairly, "Apart from during the Crusades."

"Better to purge the flesh than burn eternally," he quoted. Though his memory of the exact words was hazy, Haroun had said something of the sort to him once. He wondered where the Scripturalist was—was he even still alive? He wiped his eyes and they stayed clear this time, though the dim room seemed horribly bright still.

"And the women are lashed also?"

He shook his head. "If a nefara woman knowingly pollutes another man, she is stoned."

"Why are women always treated worse than men?" she asked sourly.

He shrugged. "It is just how it is. Ask a Godspeaker, not me."

"I've had enough debates with priests to last my lifetime," she said dismissively. "They are all liars—some of them even know they are."

He made a warding gesture in case an apsara was listening. Ahm's angels watched every act and recorded every sin, the Godspeakers taught. "You should not insult holy men."

She sighed heavily and sat beside him, propping her elbows on the bed as she often did. Her blond hair, tied back, gleamed like platinum. She looked both mildly irritated and amused. "Anyway, Kazim Makani, the only thing you owe me is thanks. I don't store debts."

"You would not survive in Baranasi. Debts are what they trade."

She smiled at that, which pleased him enough that his own mouth twitched involuntarily.

"Oh look," she teased. "The stern warrior smiled." Her eyes were warm, but she looked away shyly. "La, I shall let you wash yourself, now you don't need my help anymore." She stood up and bustled away, as if she too found the little moment of intimacy too much.

"Elena?"

"Mm?"

"Thank you."

She smiled. "Debt paid."

Then she was gone.

Spin, block, and dance away. *Bang, bang!* The staves of tempered wood bashed together. Lunge and go! Elena felt an exhilarated buzz in her veins as she executed the movements perfectly, and a flash of admiration at the way Kazim stayed with her. Then his stave was flashing at her face, even as he dropped and lashed his lead foot sideways.

"Uhh!" she flipped sideways, let the motion flow with her gnosis, spiraling through the air and out of his reach above the pond. She was wearing a red ribbon on her arm to show that she was bleeding, but to her surprise Kazim hadn't declined to practice with her. It gave her hope: she might actually be getting through to him, maybe changing his views.

"Cheat!" He slashed at her, but couldn't reach, even though he leaped at her from the lip of the bridge railing. She laughed and righted herself in midair.

He scowled. "You know I can't reach you." He put his hands on his hips. "Come back down, you craven ferang."

His remaining gnosis had been burned out by the catfish incident. He said that the hollowness inside him felt like a cancer, but the yoga helped him deaden it. He no longer laughed at her meditation training.

"Come get me," she teased, twirling her weapon.

"You promised: no magic."

"I had my fingers crossed." She grinned at his annoyance. "Catch me if you can."

He came over the edge of the bridge in a single bound, roaring at the effort. His stave flashed at her—damn, but he was fast these days!—but she managed to block, even though she almost lost her grip at the strength of his blow. His gnosis might be gone for now, but his body was fully operational. He trained bare to the waist now, having announced that he needed to regain some color, and she'd threatened to do the same, making him blush furiously.

Bang! Thrust and move, duck and run. He was backing her into a corner. She tried to go left, then had to arch her back and pull herself in, desperately trying to put her body out of the way of his stave as he blocked off her escape.

Shit, I'm trapped . . .

Thwack! She blocked a low kick with her own stave, but she couldn't move her planted feet quickly enough, leaving her open to his blow. Her free hand flashed upward and shields flared, battering his stave away.

"Cheating bitch!" he roared, and threw himself at her. His body was twice her bulk; he flattened her shield and bore her down, his weight knocking the air from her lungs. One hand grasped her wrist, trapping her hand, and as his stave went flying he grabbed for her periapt. "Got you!" he crowed.

She tried to flip him off as the hand seeking her periapt tore through her buttons and grabbed.

Then he went utterly rigid, his face changing in an instant from triumph to horror as he realized that his hand was not holding a gemstone, but a mound of soft, silky flesh. "Uhh—"

"Easy, tiger," she panted. His weight on her felt . . . *too damned good*. But he'd accidentally scratched her skin and that was smarting. "Get off," she said peevishly, when it became clear that he'd frozen in embarrassment.

For an instant it was as if he'd not heard her. His eyes were filled with lust, and then with something worse: the hunger in his gaze that rose whenever the Souldrinker side of him threatened to take over. The latent dread that she might one day have to kill him or be killed herself flashed across her brain.

Then he exhaled, and was himself again.

"Ahm's Light, I'm so sorry," he gabbled, jerking his hand away as if she was diseased.

He stood quickly and backed off as she tugged her tunic closed. "I'm so sorry, I didn't mean to—" His face was scarlet.

She bunched the tunic and knotted it shut, feeling both foolish, and very relieved. "It's okay, Kaz—it's nothing, really. I'm surprised it hasn't happened before."

"I just wanted to take your periapt so you couldn't cheat again."

"I know—it's all right." She sat up. "You beat me fair and square." She traced the line of blood on her breast, swathing the little wound in soft light, cleansing and sealing it.

He took in what she'd just said and slowly beamed: a radiant smile that gave Elena goose bumps. "I did, didn't I? Fair and square."

"Don't get cocky." She rubbed the back of her head ruefully. Being smacked to the stones then crushed by someone twice her size had left her more than a little battered. She reached a hand up to him. "Just try not to grab my tits again, right? Now that *would* be cheating."

He stammered another apology, then clasped her hand and pulled her upright, carefully averting his eyes.

Get dressed, Ella, before the boy dies of embarrassment.

"Let's finish for the day," she offered. "It's getting late. Your turn to cook."

He kept his face averted, but she didn't mind too much: he had a nice profile, and his torso was a beautiful array of toned muscle under bronzed skin. She felt like she was radiating heat herself, and some of that was flooding to parts of her body she didn't want to think about just now.

From the door, she turned back and called, "Kazim?"

He turned and faced her. "Ella?"

Ella . . . He'd not shortened her name before. She felt a little flutter of pleasure and pain at the way he said it. *We're so close, but the barriers are still there*—she felt such an urge to rip them down. "Kaz, you do see it, don't you: that these rules and punishments are how they control us? They don't come from God. They are nasty little strictures invented by men to enslave other men."

Like the rule that says I'm nefara, and so you won't see me as a woman . . .

His face tightened as if in pain. "Ella, this last year, I have lost almost everything—my home, my family, my fiancée, and now even my fellow warriors. Everything has been torn from inside me, one by one, and there is nothing left now but a tiny flame, surrounded by God's mercy. It hurts me when you question that."

She winced at the bleakness in his voice. "The Jhafi Amteh don't even have the concept of nefara. I'd never heard of it until I met you."

He shook his head sullenly. "Then they are heathen also. You cannot pick and choose the laws of Ahm, Ella. You are either faithful totally or not at all."

She rolled her eyes. "Damn it, you're in a cage and you don't even see it." She recalled other arguments, with Kore priests and Sollan drui, cunning debaters with glib tongues and faultless reasoning who could explain any crime as God's will.

She stomped away, abruptly sick of the whole subject.

Kazim lay on his mattress in his darkened room. Through the small square window the night sky glittered with stars. The mountain winds caressed the leaves of the vines that clad the outside stonework. The cooler weather and daily rain had stirred fresh vigor into the vegetation, bringing it back to life. In Lakh tales, romance always blossomed during the rainy season.

He rubbed his palm on the sheet again, as if trying to wipe away the memory of her breast under his hand. Despite the later argument and his pent-up frustration at their bickering, it was that moment he was carrying with him into the night. He felt like he was teetering on the edge of some unspeakable fall.

She is nefara: utterly nefara. She had boasted of it—admittedly, while she was drunk. *Lies. Theft. Murder. And unnatural acts—she said so herself.*

But still he couldn't help but picture her lithe body as he'd seen it that day in the river, could imagine her lying beneath him, moving with him as they coupled. The mental images were driving his cock to new extremes of rigidity.

If she walked through my door now . . .

His mind went *YES!* as his door swung open.

But it wasn't Elena, come to drag him into Shaitan's fires.

It was Jamil, with his finger to his lips.

27

Mother, Daughter, and Widow

Hermetic: Animism

Some there are that even speak with beasts, hear and smell and taste as beasts, and even take their forms. There is no limit to the deviancy of the Magi.

THE KALISTHAM,
HOLY BOOK OF AMTEH

Strange though it may sound, I feel closer to Kore in beast-form than at any other time.

SENDARA GARRYN, BRICIA, 791

Javon Coast, Antiopia
Zulqeda (Noveleve) to Zulhijja (Decore) 928
5th and 6th months of the Moontide

Smoke rose lazily from the funeral pyre which lit up the surface of the river carving its way through the valley. The low hills all about them were purple with heather, and lush grasslands all but choked the flow of water on this wide delta. The song of passing rose from fluted alien mouths, carrying through the still night air.

Mesuda and Reku, the two Eldest, had died, and every lamia mourned. Mesuda had gone first, dying within a few minutes of landing in the promised land on this chosen place, here on a river delta five miles inland from giant falls on the west coast of Javon. *The Promised Land.* The sheer power of her emotions had ruptured her aged heart.

Reku had finally been granted the title she had craved for so many years, only to die that same night, so now Kekropius was Eldest, and his first job was to preside over the double funeral of the first two lamiae to die in their new home.

Alaron found himself weeping, affected by the sorrow of all about him. Mesuda had been almost kindly, though she'd always put the clan's interest far above his own. He had even come to respect Reku—and he'd proven himself to her in the end, he was sure of that. He'd visited her just before the end and she'd gripped his hand and smiled at him as she nibbled his thumb in jest. He'd even miss her—a little, at least.

Cym reached out and took his hand. They were standing next to the Rondian windshipmen, whose fate was still undecided. Kekropius was trying to work out an oath that might be compelling enough that he could afford to let them go, though there was considerable dissent on the matter.

After he'd finished his words of farewell, Kekropius joined Alaron and Cym. "This place is perfect," he told them, his voice heavy with emotion. "No humans come here. The nearest settlement that the map on the windship shows, this 'Lybis,' is more than one hundred miles inland. There is plentiful fresh water and game, even land for cropping, if we can learn the art of it. It truly is the Promised Land." He laid a hand on Alaron's shoulder. "This is all thanks to you, Milkson."

That's enough about the milk. "I was just lucky you were there when that Inquisitor found me," Alaron said, the high emotion of the moment making him feel rather uncomfortable.

"It was a happy day for everyone." Kekropius smiled, flashing his fangs. "Except the Inquisitor. So, what will you do now?"

"We have to find my mother," Cym interrupted before Alaron could respond.

"Where is she?" Kekropius asked. "Can we aid you in any way?"

"We're both as bad as each other at Clairvoyance," Alaron admitted. "I think we're going to need Ildena's help again. It's nearly three hundred miles to Hebusalim and the sea's in the way, as well as mountains."

He turned back to Cym. "You've not seen your mother since you were a baby—you don't even know what she looks like." He hated to sound so pessimistic, but as he'd told her over and over again, he doubted they'd be able to do it, even with the lamiae's help.

Cym pulled up her sleeve to reveal a tarnished silver bracelet. "She left me this when she handed me to my father. She took it from her own wrist."

It's just a trinket—who knows if your mother had any emotional connection to it? But I found you with a wooden doll, so who knows?

"It's worth a try," he said, trying to instill some enthusiasm into his voice.

They tried scrying for Justina Meiros that very evening. Alaron sat cross-legged in a circle on a hill overlooking their encampment, together with Cym, Ildena, Nia, and Vyressa. Ildena cradled her distended belly protectively; she was due any day now.

Kekropius sat to one side, trying to placate Fydro, who was concerned the exertions might harm his wife and their unhatched offspring, even though Alaron was fairly confident that scrying carried no physical risk to her.

"We're just testing," he told her. "You don't need to work hard—just be careful not to overexert yourself, okay?"

Nothing happened, and after half an hour Alaron was about to give up when he suddenly recalled something Magister Fyrell had once said: to find a blood relative, one could use actual blood.

After persuading Cym that the spell needed just a few drops, not a flagon of her blood, he pricked her finger with the tip of his knife and carefully dripped three drops into the water in the scrying bowl. Behind his closed eyes he watched as the gnosis links surged and carried them outward like a web of light. He had no idea which way they were going, for their inner vision blurred from host to host: the spirits of the air and the ghosts of the living.

Then, abruptly, those spirits became fewer and fewer, and he and the lamiae had to push harder to find the next. Ildena's hand became slick with perspiration and he could feel sweat running down his own brow.

We can't keep this up much longer . . .

Then they struck a ward and they all shouted in shock—

<*Hold on, stay together,*> he sent to the lamiae women.

They struck the second veil, and Cym cried aloud, "Mother?"

A hesitant, stunned mental voice responded, "*Child?*"

Alaron felt Cym's tears as if they were his own. The ward-veils opened all at once and they saw a woman in a blue mantle, standing in the middle of a cylindrical, open-roofed chamber made of stone. Waves crashed and gulls shrilled.

Cym shouted, her voice hoarse, "*Mother! It's me! It's your Cym—*"

"*Sol et Lune!*" The mental image surged closer, revealing a pale, aristocratic face with a haughty nose and harsh mouth. Justina Meiros's diamond eyes filled with tears and her lips trembled. "Cymbellea? Truly?"

Isle of Glass, Javon Coast, Antiopia
Zulhijja (Decore) 928
6th month of the Moontide

Ramita Ankesharan was cooking, a magic she understood more clearly than any of Justina's gnosis lessons. She had chosen a recipe her mother had taught her and was lightly roasting spices over the gnosis-heated element while soaking chunks of defrosted chicken in the yogurt she'd made herself. Her body felt lethargic and off-color, as if she was starting a slight fever. Winter was coming. The air was palpably colder outside now, and it seeped into the stone that enclosed them. The sunlight through the skylights barely lit the chamber, and the gnosis-lights felt wan.

As she entered the seventh month of her pregnancy, Ramita felt like she'd doubled in size. Her belly was so swollen she could no longer walk but was reduced to waddling everywhere. In the mirrorglass her face was pudgy; she looked like her mother. That made her cry.

She barely heard Justina as she came down the stairs, but when she did look around she cried out in alarm. The jadugara was clinging to the railing; she looked as unsteady as a drunk. Her first thought was that she'd been at the opium again, despite all her promises, but then she saw Justina was almost blinded by tears.

She took her frying-pan off the heat and hurried over to her, crying, "Justina, what is it?"

Justina stared glassily at her, then let go of the railing and collapsed into Ramita's open arms. She staggered, and only her involuntarily summoned Earth-gnosis gave her the strength to guide Justina to the nearest chair. Justina collapsed into it and began to cry anew.

Ramita knelt beside her, growing increasingly alarmed. "What has happened?" she asked. "Justina, what can I do?"

After several moments, Justina gasped out, "My daughter—"

Ramita stared. It took her a minute to work out what Justina was saying, but then her mind took her back to the sad tale Justina had told her, of bearing a daughter, and giving the child away to the father. Was she having some attack of remorse?

"I am sure she is well," she began, but Justina cut her off.

"She contacted me," she whispered hoarsely. "*My daughter contacted me.*"

Ramita went cold all over, terrified. All the lessons Justina had pounded into her, of being wary of the tricks and traps other magi might set, of false contacts and cruel games, set off warning bells inside her head. Why would this semi-mythical daughter contact her now, when she was a fugitive, hunted? Her mind went instantly to Alyssa Dulayne, who knew all of Justina's secrets and vulnerabilities. Concocting some lie to lure Justina out would be child's play to her.

"Are you sure it was her?" she demanded skeptically.

"I gave birth to her," Justina said. "I *know* her."

"You had her only a few months," Ramita pointed out. "Do you know her now?"

Justina made a conscious effort to gather herself. "I know my own child." She wiped her eyes and met Ramita's probing stare. "I hear what you are saying—I do. But it was her, I would swear it."

"And what are her loyalties to a mother she has never met?" Ramita replied. "She was raised in Yuros. Why would she contact you now?"

"She's in trouble. She has something the Inquisition wants." Justina seized Ramita's hands. Fear spread over her face. "I cannot let those bastards take my daughter. I must protect her."

Ramita licked her suddenly dry lips. "What did you tell her?"

Justina looked away. "I told her to come here."

Ramita stared. She had spent night after night in overpowering loneliness, fending off Huriya's whispers, though she longed so much to open up and talk to someone—*anyone*. And now, Justina had cast aside prudence—on a whim! It filled her with an anger that surprised her.

She rose to her feet and shouted, "How *dare* you? We are here to guard your father's unborn children! You swore to protect them, and now you risk everything for your own selfish wants?"

Justina's eyes flared. "She's my daughter! She needs me, for the first time ever, she *needs* me!"

"You think only of yourself!"

Justina's aura flared red and her hand whipped across—

—and Ramita caught it. She didn't know how; she made no conscious move, but reflex and the weeks of training took over. She clamped her stone-hard grip about Justina's skinny wrist and held on.

As Justina snarled and gathered her energies, Ramita sent her skidding across the room, armchair and all, not even considering the "how." As woman and armchair thudded against the wall, the wooden frame of the seat cracked and Justina's body was thrown back into the padding.

"Don't you *ever* hit me," Ramita shouted.

Justina stared at her, stunned, as the armchair broke apart, leaving her sprawled in the wreckage. They glared at each other from opposite sides of the room as the air crackled with unresolved energies. Then sanity returned.

In all their training they had carefully avoided direct confrontation, but she clearly regarded herself as the stronger. That brief flurry of activity had taken less than a second and they'd both been acting without thought, but the winner had been clear. Ramita had never been stronger than anyone in her life—she'd not fought physically since she was about eight. She barely recognized herself.

Justina exhaled and visibly calmed herself.

Ramita watched warily for some underhand counterblow, but none came. "You have put us at risk," she stated.

Justina hung her head. "I know. But she *needs* me."

What will I do, when my children call my name? Ramita unclenched her hands. "I understand. It is done now." She cradled her belly. "What do we do now? When will she arrive?"

Justina acknowledged the placatory words. "In a few days. They have a windskiff."

"*They?*"

"There is a *boy* with her." Justina said the word "boy" as if it meant "noxious parasite."

Ramita smiled at that.

Justina scowled. "I am sorry for striking you."

"You didn't," Ramita reminded her. "You only *tried* to."

Dhassa, Antiopia
Zulhijja (Decore) 928
6th month of the Moontide

Huriya sat facing the circle of Souldrinkers, who were hanging on her every word. They were all Hermetic magi, the exact opposite of her. She couldn't shape-change, but they couldn't do the mindwork she could. Though she was jealous of their bond, she was not jealous of them. She was who she was.

"I have been calling to Ramita Ankesharan, using Mesmerism to make the call more alluring," Huriya said. "She is hiding somewhere with Justina Meiros. I can feel Ramita listening to me, even though she doesn't respond. She is not very skilled in Clairvoyance; she fails to realize that just by listening, she creates a link."

"Is it enough to find her?" Perno asked in his deep voice.

"Not yet. She has strong wards. But it reveals certain things." She glanced at Zaqri, who smiled deferentially at her, but with no warmth. She wanted him, but he didn't want her—that had never happened to her before. Her resentment of Ghila, the leonine pack leader's mate, deepened.

Sabele had summoned Zaqri's pack after many days in the wild to follow up the new clues Huriya had found. They were all naked and dirty and they looked even wilder and more bestial than before. They'd ignored all other foodstuffs save for raw meat, and Huriya realized many of them were barely human now. Only the older ones had managed to find their human voices again.

She was very glad that animism was not a strong affinity for her.

She looked around the pack now and reported, "I get a vague impression of direction and distance. She's somewhere north or west of here."

The pack looked at each other.

"Javon?" Ghila suggested.

"Is this reliable?" Hessaz wanted to know.

Sabele's cracked voice filled the circle. "Huriya's gift is not in clairvoyance. She is primarily a Mesmerist. It is the hypnotic quality of her sending that is drawing Ramita Ankesharan in. I am monitoring what she is doing, as well as divining. The spirits cannot sense Ramita, but they perceive Justina Meiros at times, when she asks questions of them. Justina is not the diviner that I am—I can trace her mind in the ether. Her mental touch always moves southwards, which is consistent with someone north of here."

"The Zhassi Valley?" Ghila suggested.

"Perhaps." Sabele clapped her hands. "We will move into the mountains north of the Gotan Heights. The Rondians have advanced beyond there now and they have left only a few garrisons behind. We can move relatively openly."

"The Hadishah are at Krak di Condotiori," Zaqri put in, his bass voice making Huriya quiver.

"I do not think the Hadishah need to know of this matter," Sabele replied, and Huriya filed that thought away for a later date, when she might need to drive a wedge between her mistress and Emir Rashid.

"Well done, Huriya Makani," Zaqri said approvingly, making her glow.

"She is learning," Sabele said in grudging praise.

The next day they set off on their journey north. Half of the pack flew on ahead, while the rest, mostly the younger ones, accompanied Sabele and Huriya, who traveled by camel-cart. The beast-magi moved in human form so that they could remind themselves of who they really were. Huriya wished Zaqri had stayed too. She knew full well that this was not love, just an infatuation such as she'd felt for Jos Klein, but even admitting that to herself did not help much. She had always bounced emotionally from one male to the next, even as a girl trading secret kisses for sweets in Aruna Nagar market—but that did not make it easier to take being thwarted with equanimity.

It took them two weeks to get to the Zhassi Valley, easily avoiding the occasional Rondian patrol: they were poor-quality troops with no magi, no threat at all. Near the high pass into Dhassa they found some caves, and at Sabele's order, they set up base there. The old jadugara appeared to know the place well.

Throughout the journey, Huriya sent out her mental hooks, trying to lure Ramita in with reminiscences of their wonderful life together, professions of sympathy, of pity, of undying love, pleading for her forgiveness and offering pretend news of Kazim. She tried everything she could, and sometimes she just *knew* that Ramita was listening, but still she couldn't coax a response. But every day the sense of direction grew stronger, and now other sensations were creeping in: wind and water. She could almost feel Ramita's hair lifting in the breeze. She could almost smell . . . *salt.*

"Near the sea," she told Sabele.

After a couple of days' rest they traveled north and hit the Dhassan coast northeast of Hebusalim, hundreds of miles east of Southpoint, in a place where no one at all lived. The pack captured and tamed wild horses, which they rode alongside the camel-cart where Huriya had to endure Sabele's constant nagging presence. She was horribly jealous, but she had never learned to ride. Being tied to Sabele felt increasingly inhibiting . . . *But I still need her,* she told herself

The seacoast was awe-inspiring. Massive cliffs of some white stone defended the land from the sea. Though the water thundered far below, still they could taste the tang of the spray on their lips and misty clouds billowing all the way along the coastline.

Sabele sent Perno to a secret place to retrieve a windskiff, in case she and Huriya needed to travel swiftly. Huriya's certainty increased: Ramita was near, she *knew* it. But though the pack searched for miles in either direction, Noveleve waned and still Ramita and Justina eluded them.

Their frustrations grew.

Finally, they had the breakthrough they had been seeking—in a unexpected form.

Sabele and Huriya were huddled over the brazier, listening to the night air, when they felt someone's mental voice carry out across the ether. The faint, almost inaudible cry came from the northwest, where there was only water, and it vanished immediately.

But it was unmistakably a mage's voice. *<Mother,>* the unknown voice called, *<guide us in.>*

If they had not been so near and listening so closely in this remote place they would never have heard it. And if they'd not heard it, they would never have attached any significance to the brief flare of lightning that cracked across the northern horizon. But together, it was enough.

Sabele caught Huriya's hand. "There! *There!* She's not *beside* the sea: she's *in* it!" The old jadugara lurched to her feet in excitement and shuffled to her maps. "Ha! See? The Pillars of the Gods! That is the only place north of here they could be! She is hiding among the Pillars!"

Ramita was almost moved to take Justina's hand, to try and calm her. The white witch was in a positive frenzy over the discovery of her daughter. She spent the days waiting for her arrival in a frenzy of cleaning, though she'd never paid the slightest attention to such domestic trivia before. She flew into rages over the smallest things, and was generally unbearable.

Just after dusk on the third day came the call Justina had been awaiting, just as they were about to leave the platform and go below, fed up with the freezing-cold high winds shrieking around the pillar of rock. It was raining, and the storm-tossed sea met the low cloud that filled the sky.

<Mother, guide us in!>

Justina squawked like a startled hen. "*It's her!*" she announced in a flurry of excitement and raised her hand. She sent a vivid bolt of lightning into the sky, not the first such bolt that night, but the others had all been natural, and Ramita had been frightened that one might strike the very place where they stood. Justina's bolt smote the heavens like a sword on a shield.

Then they huddled together on the balcony, shielded themselves from the rain and watched the skies. Ramita clutched her belly and tried to keep her body temperature from falling as the night came on.

Justina was clad in her usual heavy mantle. There were dark circles beneath her eyes, but other than that her porcelain face was unreadable. Ramita had put on a sari to mark the occasion of this auspicious meeting. Justina was scandalized by her naked belly, but she refused to change: a bared pregnant belly was an honorable thing at home.

I am Lakh. Let them deal with it, she thought crossly.

Then out of the night it came, a dark shape like a giant bird that soared in on the winds. Justina lit a gnosis-light in her hand, illuminating the top of the pillar, and the windskiff swooped toward them. Ramita glimpsed pale faces, wide-eyed in the darkness: a young man, wrestling with the sails, and a black-haired girl fighting the tiller. They looked terribly young.

At last they managed to position their craft over the stone circle and lower it to the surface despite the buffeting winds. Then the skiff touched the stone, and Justina flew to its side.

"Cymbellea!" she shrieked, and enveloped the girl at the tiller in her arms.

Ramita hung back, watching mother and daughter curiously. Justina was sobbing, but her daughter was all business. It was the exact opposite to what she'd anticipated, and it gave her a new insight into Justina Meiros's nature. The jadugara might hide her emotions, but that didn't mean she was without emotion; she clearly craved acceptance from someone she could call family.

The girl looked just like her mother: cool and composed, the center of her own universe. She wondered how long it would be before they were at each other's throats.

For now, though, Justina clung to her almost pitiably, fretting at the girl's strangely marked forehead, patting her hair, offering her an arm, though her own legs were as unsteady as a newborn colt.

Almost as an afterthought, Ramita glanced at the boy. He was neither tall nor broad, though he was still taller than her. He looked awfully young, and he had none of the certainty that Cymbellea did. His face was pale; though it was not a weak face, it had an unfinished look to it, with plenty of baby fat in his cheeks. He looked competent enough, though, lashing down the sails firmly before lowering packs over the side. He wore a sword easily, and he managed to work without tangling it about his legs.

"Mother, please," Cymbellea said after a moment, pushing out of Justina's embrace. "Can we get the skiff undercover and get out of the rain?"

Justina regained enough composure to open the doors and help the two young people drag the windcraft to one side; there was not enough room to stow the skiff up here, and it was too stormy to make them fly it down to the lower landing site. Ramita went to pick up one of the packs, but the Rondian boy hurried toward her. "Hey, I can look after those," he said anxiously before his voice trailed off as if he doubted she understood his words.

He's never seen a Lakh before.

"Fine," she said shortly, let the bag drop and waddled away in a huff. *They probably think I'm the maid.*

In just a few minutes, they were all inside. The boy and girl had been wrapped in leather raincoats, with scarves knotted about their throats. Justina showed them to their rooms below and allowed them time to change while she alternately fretted with her hair and wept. Ramita had to do everything: mulling the wine, seeing to the simmering curry, heating the room. Finally, the two guests reappeared, clad in loose-fitting Rondian men's garb: pants and long-sleeved shirts with buttons at the front. They stood awkwardly facing Justina. The boy was cradling something in his hands, a leather bag about two feet long.

"Mother," Cymbellea said into the silence, "this is Alaron Mercer."

Ramita frowned. The name Mercer rang bells with her for some reason, but she could not say why; the memory just would not come.

The boy ducked his head. "Uh, Lady Meiros," he said, his face coloring.

Justina frowned at him. "I do not know your family, young sir."

"My mother is—uh, was—an Anborn."

Justina's face flickered with interest. "Elena Anborn? The Javon queen's champion?"

Alaron shook his head. "Tesla, her elder sister."

Justina's face lost some of its animation. "Oh. And 'Mercer'?"

"My father . . . Uh, he's a trader. Not a mage."

Justina looked at him as if to say, "What is a Kore-bedamned merchant's boy doing with my daughter?" Justina's daughter had herself been conceived of a non-mage, but a boy of similar parentage was obviously not good enough to be with Cymbellea. Ramita felt a twinge of sympathy for the young man. Her own father was a trader, a most honorable profession, in her view.

"Alaron is a good friend, Mother." Cymbellea was composure itself.

"Do you know my Aunt Elena?" Alaron asked into the silence.

"Only by reputation," Justina replied, her face revealing that the woman's reputation was no small thing. Ramita wondered who she was. "I have no news of her, I'm afraid."

The boy looked disappointed. He shifted the bag in his grasp uncomfortably. "Nor I, ma'am."

The room fell silent again.

Before the two children—which was how Ramita thought of them, although they were probably older than she was—concluded that she really was just the maid, Ramita decided she was going to have to do her own introductions. "Namaste. My name is Ramita Ankesharan-Meiros."

Cymbellea blinked. "*Meiros?*"

"I was married to Lord Antonin." She gave Cymbellea her most winsome smile. "I think that makes me your grandmother."

Alaron stared about the table, not quite believing with whom he was sharing it. That Cym was here with him was amazing enough; he'd never found her less than incredible. She'd been at the center of his heart for too long for him put his awe aside. She might not love him, but she gave meaning to his existence just by being near.

Her mother drew his eye the most: Justina Meiros, a figure of legend, if not for her own deeds, but by association. She was the only living daughter of Antonin Meiros, the Bridge-Builder himself, and that made her some kind of demi-goddess at the very least. She looked like Cym too, a glimpse of what Cym might become.

Except that he could never imagine Cym being so cold-faced and close-mouthed. Justina Meiros looked like someone who'd lost too much, until mourning what could have been had become a lifetime's habit. Her mouth was forever pursed in silent sourness, and she seemed only to see the negatives. When Cym began to explain how she and Alaron had come to be here, Justina had only had criticisms to make. Verelon and Sydia were bleak and primitive wastes, and Pontus a cesspit. Everything was wrong, everywhere.

Occasionally his eyes went to the little woman from Lakh. At first he'd thought her plump, then realized that she was heavily pregnant. Her costume was outrageous! It looked like she'd wrapped herself in a long multi-colored bed sheet—and it actually left her stomach bare. Quite barbaric. He felt sorry for her. She seemed pleasant enough, but way out of her depth. She must have just conceived to Lord Meiros—unbelievable in itself, given the man's age—only to have him die on her and now she was obviously a fugitive, quite dependent upon Lady Justina's charity. He couldn't place her age. She was tiny and her face was smooth, but it had a maturity and firmness that made him think she must be much older than him. It must be hard for her, a non-mage, bearing Meiros's children.

That the mighty Antonin Meiros was dead had thrown an immediate pall over the table. Cym was stunned, although she'd never met him. She'd clearly placed great store in being of his line. Justina sounded quite lost when she spoke of her father. The tiny Lakh woman seemed on the verge of tears too, to his surprise. For himself, he'd been having enough trouble thinking of Lord Meiros as a real person; he belonged in stories, not life.

Justina explained how she and Ramita came to be here, fugitives from a broken Ordo Costruo. They had no news of the outside world, or how the Crusade progressed, and Alaron's confidence in coming here began to wane.

"Uh, when is your child due?" he asked Ramita during one of the increasingly long gaps in the conversation.

"The second month," she replied in her thickly accented Rondian.

"Febreux?" he clarified. She waggled her head side to side, a strange gesture he'd never seen before, but it appeared to mean *yes*. "Um, it's a shame that . . ." He trailed off, realizing that he'd been about to say something stupidly insensitive about her dead husband. Silence filled the room again as he flushed bright red.

Well done, Alaron. Another brilliant conversational gambit.

Her voice uncharacteristically wary, Cym started, "Mother, I need to tell you something." And she launched into the tale of the lost Scytale, not naming it, just calling it "an artifact."

Alaron watched Justina's eyes narrow as the tale progressed: from General Langstrit and his trail of clues, to breaking into the Governor's Palace, that frantic night in Norostein that had cost the lives of the general and Alaron's mother, and their flight across Yuros and the Bridge . . .

Justina grew more and more agitated as she listened, and as Cym's story drew to a close, she asked, "Where is this 'artifact'?" Her eyes went immediately to the bag lying on the table beside Alaron's right elbow.

He glanced at Cym. *I guess this is where we find out if this was the right thing to do.*

He picked it up and handed it to Justina Meiros.

She pulled the bag open and removed the cylindrical leather case. She stared at it curiously, then pulled the cap from the top. She lifted the rune-carved pottery to her eyes and read them with a puzzled frown.

Finally she looked at Cym. "What is this?"

Alaron was a little surprised that she didn't already know. He opened his mouth, then closed it again. It was Cym's place to tell her mother. He glanced sideways at Ramita, who was also looking blank.

Cym's voice was tentative. "Mother, this is the Scytale of Corineus."

The look that came slowly across Justina Meiros's face was impossible to read; there were just too many emotions. Amazement certainly, and shock: total shock. And fright even—but not ambition or greed, to Alaron's enormous relief.

She put it down and stared at it, made no attempt to pick it up again. Her mouth opened and closed a dozen times as she sought words.

"How?" she gulped at last.

Cym gestured at Alaron. This was his story now: it had been his thesis, the piece of work that had torn his life apart. His ridiculous theory, that the Noros Revolt had been triggered not by a rebellious king, but by three Noros-born priests and one outrageous theft. It felt unbelievable, even now that he'd been proved correct.

He couldn't blame Justina Meiros for shaking her head as he spoke; he was too, and he'd lived through it.

"I wish Father were here," Justina muttered into the silence when he finished.

Eyeing this brittle, closed-in woman, Alaron found that he was wishing the same thing.

After that, it was as if they were all too awestruck to speak. No plans were proposed, no decisions reached. As the evening stretched on into even larger silences, he yawned ostentatiously, scooped up the Scytale and announced that he was going to bed. Cym came with him and they took to the stairs together. He was longing to soak in hot water, and the little Lakh woman had said there was a bath below with hot water available from a tap. This miracle he had to see.

"Well?" he called softly to Cym as she went to her room.

"Well what?" she replied coolly, tossing her hair.

"Have we done the right thing?"

Her eyes narrowed. "Of course."

He found that he couldn't quite agree. *These two women are as lost as we are.*

Ramita watched the two young people leave, sipping the last mouthful of the one cup of wine she'd allowed herself. She'd not understood most of their story, other than that this "Scytale" was somehow important, so once they were gone, she asked Justina about it.

The jadugara answered absently: it contained a recipe to grant people the gnosis. It took a while to understand everything this meant—after all, she'd become a mage just by conceiving; what did it matter that there were other ways? Then she thought about a world in which everyone became a mage just by sipping a drink, and it was as if all the air had left the room.

At first she wondered whether her husband had somehow foreseen this; that this was all part of his plan, but this was unlikely. He would have said something of it, surely? So it could only be coincidence: she, apparently potentially the strongest mage in the world, was now one of four people possessing the greatest artifact in that world. If it was not pure coincidence, then every mage with the skill to cast a divination would be here with them. No, her husband had not brought this thing here; the gods had.

"Justina," she asked softly, "what are we going to do?"

Justina appeared to be so stunned that she did not even object to the word "we." She said blankly, "I don't know. Kore's Blood, what can we do?"

Ramita recognized that the question was rhetorical: Justina Meiros did not ask the likes of her for an opinion. But she offered one anyway. "Let's take it to Vizier Hanook. We could found a new order of Lakh magi."

Justina looked as if she'd rather eat vomit, though she constrained her a reply to a crisp, "I don't think so."

Then she began to talk wildly of recruiting suitable candidates— only women, because women were by nature more peaceful and trustworthy than men. This was news to Ramita. Some of the most aggressive and larcenous people to grace Aruna Nagar Market were women. Most men were like lambs compared with Vikash Nooradin's wife, to name but one. But in Justina's mind, she and her new sisterhood could force an end to the wars.

It sounded foolish to Ramita, not at all something Antonin Meiros would have done. *I miss you, my husband, more than ever.*

"The boy seems clever," she observed. Naïve and nervous, certainly, but growing into a good man, she decided.

"The little troll better not think he has any hope of marrying my Cymbellea," Justina snapped.

"He knows this. They are only friends."

"How would you know?" Justina asked waspishly.

I may be only a market-girl but I know how men and women look at each other. "It is clear: she has nothing but friendship for him, and he knows this."

"Hmm. Well thank Kore for that. A merchant's son . . ."

"I think he is a nice boy," Ramita remarked, mostly just to annoy Justina, though she thought her words true.

"Huh." Justina finished her wine with a gulp. "Sol et Lune, what am I going to do?" She poured herself another drink. Her eyes were glazed from shock and the onset of intoxication.

Ramita stood and left her to it. "Don't worry, Daughter," she called over her shoulder. "I'll think of something."

<Did you hear it?>

Malevorn started as Raine's mental voice filled his head. *<Hear what?>*

Her mental touch caressed his mind. It was a slick, slimy touch with a tang of her own juices, both repellent and alluring. *<Mal, I thought I heard someone call, somewhere away to the east.>*

He looked in the direction she was indicating, but there was nothing there but sea, for hundreds of miles.

They'd lost valuable days waiting for Adamus to secure them a new windship in Pontus, but for the rest of the week since Vordan's death the Fist had been furiously hunting. The new windship was now slowly following the line of the Leviathan Bridge, providing them with a cell base. It was big enough for the four remaining venators to sleep on the decks, and it had come with three pilot-mages and a squad of soldiers. It must have cost a fortune—or would have, if Adamus actually used money; as it was, the word *Inquisition* turned out to be currency enough.

Malevorn and Dominic had been flying in a spiraling pattern broadly following the line of the Bridge, circling every windship they saw to check it wasn't the one stolen from them. Each day saw three or four other windcraft traversing the ocean, laden with supplies if going south and plunder if returning to the north.

Malevorn searched the Bridge from up here—though it was still little more than a dark line with white water bursting about its pillars—seeking a place to land. It was dusk and his venator was exhausted, barely able to do more than glide.

<East of here? There's nothing out there,> he returned.

<Exactly,> Raine purred. *<It was a young woman's voice, I swear it: she called out "Mother, guide us in." It could be the girl we're hunting.>*

Mother, guide us in. He felt a twinge of excitement. *She might be right.* *<Where are you?>* he called, suddenly keen to see her. *Perhaps she and I can find this thing ourselves?*

<I'm south of Dawn Island. My bird is exhausted.>

<Are you alone?>

<I've got the Virgin with me.> Her mental touch became more intimate and secretive. *<She heard it too, and is calling Dranid.>*

Damn. <*Thanks for telling me,*> he called, sending a little mental caress of appreciation. He felt her squirm hungrily at the touch and she sent back a lewd fancy that made his blood smolder. He wanted her, but circumstances kept intervening. They were never paired on a mission, and it was beginning to feel like a deliberate thing. Was Dranid trying to drive a wedge between them?

<*See you at the next rendezvous,*> he sent. But then Dranid's gruff voice filled his mind, summoning them back to the ship. Clearly their new Commandant thought Raine's clue worthy of further attention.

They'd been scattered over miles of empty ocean, but after Dranid's call they gathered again on the new windship, the *Magol*—named after a giant of Lantric legend—at midday the next day. The ship was circling the massive tower on Dawn Island. The light atop the great pillar of stone was too bright to look upon directly; it lit Adamus's soft face luridly as he brought them up to date.

"Sister Raine has served us well," he told the gathered First. "She was on the eastern beat when she heard a gnostic call: a female, strong but untutored. I am confident it was Cymbellea di Regia. She was calling to someone she addressed as 'Mother.'" He licked his lips. "Our patience and resolve will be rewarded, brethren. We are going to fly east from here, toward the Javon coast. This time, the hunt will not be for naught."

Malevorn glanced around the circle. Dranid was all conviction, and the others were lost in the increasingly rare feeling of triumph. *And sure, I'm pleased too. But who the Hel is this girl's mother?*

28

THE CITY OF GOLD

Shaliyah

Is there a place on Urte which approaches the glory that awaits us in Paradise? Yea, the city of the prophet Aluq, Shaliyah the blessed, Shaliyah the holy, Shaliyah the beautiful. All who dwell there live in the undimmed light of Ahm.

THE KALISTHAM,
HOLY BOOK OF AMTEH

Peroz, and the road to Shaliyah, Antiopia
Zulqeda (Noveleve) to Zulhijja (Decore) 928
5th and 6th months of the Moontide

The character of the heat had changed. The air was perfectly still, and subtly charged. High clouds scudded across from the west, but at ground level there was no wind at all, other than that summoned by the Air-magi to power their wind-vessels. Distant lightning storms had become a nightly show, but there was no rain yet.

The southern army was not so much fighting its way across Kesh as shitting and fucking its way across: the arrival in Peroz had enabled them to restock their supplies, but it still meant a change of diet for the legionaries, for they'd finished the last of the Yuros stores. The unfamiliar Antiopian fare meant a new wave of stomach upsets—Legion camps had a foul stench at the best of times, but this was worse than anyone could have anticipated. And because disease was rampant among the city's refugee-swollen populace, the soldiers were confined to camp—but the ever-resourceful legions managed to procure women who had been vetted and cleared by the healers, so it wasn't long before their tents were operating as normal.

The demand for poppy increased too, driving the price up even further. The temptation to cash in was ever-present in Ramon's mind, but his plan—and his constant dream of his mother's freedom—required him to restrain that urge, and Kip's forceful reminders of his promise did the rest. Keeping the small group in the know from betraying them took a great deal more intimidation, but between his threats and the presence of the giant Schlessen, they managed. He suspected Storn might be selling a little on the side to prevent the whole ruse from collapsing, but in the circumstances he had little choice but to turn a blind eye.

Peroz was a large city, one of the biggest they had yet seen. A river ran through the sprawling mass of poorly made mudbrick buildings, and all life revolved around its sluggish flow, though it was by now little more than a trickle, and undrinkable, if you actually looked at the riverbed, a stinking morass of silt and debris. More than half a million people dwelled within the walls like ants in a mound, and the whole place was encircled by refugee camps, filled to the brim with suffering and sickness. Duke Echor's first order was to send the refugees west, and the Thirteenth, still at the rear of the advance, met these pathetic columns, human tides of misery stumbling along under the lash of their guards, as they marched into the city.

That day Ramon, Kip, and Severine were waiting beneath the balcony of a wrecked farmhouse, watching a khurne rider trotting toward them. The way Seth Korion held himself told Ramon all he needed to know. *A rukking waste of time.* He glanced at Severine, who was groggy with lack of sleep.

"He listened," Seth told them after he'd dismounted and led his khurne to where it could graze the sparse dried-up weeds that passed for vegetation in this hellish land. He sat down on one of the rickety chairs and looked around at the group. "He told me that I was observant. He was very interested, he said."

Kip spat. He'd long since stopped shaving—there was no spare water and he was fed up with the constant cuts—and his ragged blond beard and hair were bleached to white-gold by the sun, but his skin was darkening. "So what is he going to do about it, eh?"

"I don't know," Seth admitted miserably. "The Duke told me I was not to speak of this with anyone else—not even Duprey."

"Did you tell him about us?" Severine asked timidly.

Seth shook his head.

"Good," Ramon said lightly. "That way the Inquisitors will come for Seth first."

Kip chuckled at that, but the general's son sniffed morosely, not at all certain that such a thing wouldn't happen. "He told me to keep my eyes open, and to let me know of anything else I learn."

"That's something," Ramon said, more to make Seth and Severine feel better than with any real conviction.

Severine met his eye. There was a bond between them now, from sharing this intrigue and the fact that he had actually supported her. "Perhaps if we can find more evidence, he will step in," she said.

"The Inquisition are beyond all authority," Seth said. "Even I know that." He stood up. "I need to pray."

As he stumbled away, Severine said, "He is friends with the chaplain. They pray a lot." Her voice was heavy with sarcasm.

"Frand is as big a wimp as he is," Kip remarked, wrinkling his nose.

"Tyron Frand's all right," Ramon said. "He's scared of women, but he's basically decent."

Severine sniffed wetly. "I don't like either of them."

"I'm sure it's mutual." Ramon watched as Seth Korion's khurne came at his call, then swiftly carried him away. "You know what? I got a look at Duprey's new maps last night after the staff meeting. We're on the edge of almost three hundred miles of desert. There are maybe a dozen waterholes on our route, but there's no vegetation at all. Just sun and sand."

Kip picked up his canteen and slugged some musty warm water. "Yar. Our men are exhausted. It takes weeks to fully recover from a long march at the best of times. We've come five hundred miles or more already with hardly any rest."

"Duprey said some of the legates asked Echor to delay the march on Shaliyah, but the duke's informers say Salim's gold will be shipped to Mirobez soon, so we're marching in two days."

"It'll take us the whole of Noveleve to reach Shaliyah," Kip estimated.

Ramon glanced at Severine. "There will be no refugees in the desert. Maybe your visions will stop."

She turned to him. Her eyes looked desolate. "I hope so," she whispered.

The camp was settling in for its final night outside the mudbrick walls of Peroz. The Thirteenth was just one small group amid the great serried ranks of tents, indistinguishable from a distance. Ramon was taking his turn infusing the keels of the legion's wind-skiffs. Somewhere in the distance he could hear Argundian drinking songs, and further away, the rhythmic rattle-drums of Estellayne. A few night birds called out, the remnants of the shrieking dusk cacophony. There were no trees left. The army had cut down the few groves for firewood, and burned every bit of scavenged furniture too before resorting to the dried dung the natives relied on. They'd drained three of the city's six main wells to refill the water-caravans, not caring that their depredations were leaving the people of Peroz to face extreme privation once the army had left.

Ramon was more concerned about his scheme than how the natives would fare. He was due to make another payment to his investors before they left, and this time some of them were demanding gold instead of his promissory notes. He had no wish to be parted from the thousands of coins he'd amassed so far, and he was now isolated from any contact with the Yuros merchants who'd provided most of his last batch of new investors. He was beginning to wonder if the time had come to destroy the opium and vanish with the money, but extrication would be difficult, and although he had amassed more than three hundred thousand gilden, that was still short of the amount he calculated he needed for his plan.

So for now he would hold on, awaiting the one last big injection of money his plan needed: like Duke Echor, he was counting on the Sultan's gold to solve all his problems.

"Ramon." Severine Tiseme's voice reached him a few seconds before she appeared, wrapped in her traveling cloak. She touched the keel. "I'll help."

He blinked. *A helpful Severine? Unprecedented!* Though in truth, there was something between them now. It was just a question of what that was, and what they might do with it. She was certainly pretty, even exhausted as she was, with those great black circles under her eyes. And he actually sort of liked her. But he didn't *trust* her, not by any stretch of imagination.

"I'm nearly done," he lied, but she snorted impatiently, closed her eyes and reached out her left hand. A powerful surge of gnosis poured into the keel and it was replenished in a fraction of the time it would have taken him. Without another word she moved on to the next, Ramon hurrying behind her, and repeated her actions, until the little fleet was almost glowing with power.

"Now, come with me," she ordered, and strode away, making her way purposefully through the ranks of tents toward the city.

He scurried to catch up and grabbed her shoulder. "Where are we going? Did you have a vision?"

"No, I cast a Divination and it told me to find a certain place." She took his hand impatiently and pulled him after her.

He stopped dead, asking, "What place? Severine, where are we going?"

She put a finger to her lips, hushing him, and murmured, "Just follow, Ramon—I'm going to show you."

They had to use the gnosis to aid their vision as she led him through the darkness into the maze of city alleyways, slipping cautiously past the houses of the Keshi. The city was supposed to be under curfew, but the further into the narrow, twisting lanes they went, the less this was enforced. They had to evade prowling gangs of youths, angry little mobs of Keshi armed with knives and home-made clubs. Once they came upon a murdered legionary, lying facedown in the dust. He had a slit throat and no purse, but Severine didn't spare him more than a glance.

Finally they came to a tall building near what sounded like a livestock market. Severine looked around and once she was sure they had not been seen, pointed to the crumbling stone stairway built onto the back of the house and leading to a shadowed doorway.

They climbed the steps into the deserted building and Severine led them to the front windows as confidently as if it were her own home. When Ramon tried to question her she turned and fiercely hushed him, until he threw up his hands and nodded his acquiescence, and proceeded to follow her without further comment.

The windows opened out over a square. Severine pulled up her hood and made sure her hair was tucked out of sight before creeping forward, beckoning Ramon after her.

They pressed against each other in the cramped space and peered down onto the dimly lit plaza, where a horse was lying on its side, squealing. It took a moment for them to realize it was in the throes of giving birth. Then something glinted on its head, and Ramon realized that it wasn't a horse birthing; it was a khurne.

Interesting.

Then he looked at the men standing around the thrashing creature and felt his heart leap into his throat.

The animal was surrounded by the members of Siburnius's Fist. Delta, the bald branded mage, was standing there too, just a little outside the circle, and he was watching the khurne's labor with fierce concentration, his eyes gleaming, even in the darkness. The Inquisitors were also watching intently. No one was paying any attention to the shadows—after all, who would *dare* attack Inquisitors?

It took a while, more than half an hour, before the new foal emerged. Though it was hornless, it was somehow not quite a horse but something other, something alien. It thrashed about, shrieking in fear at the men who surrounded it, terrified by this new world, by the lights and the movement. Its mother watched it, prostrate with exhaustion, unable to do anything as the creature tried to stand on wobbly legs and fell, wrenching its head around.

The bald mage came forward, intoning something in a low voice, speaking too quietly for Ramon and Severine to work out what he was saying. The newborn khurne watched him coming closer and began to panic, but then calmed and lay there transfixed.

Animagery, Ramon guessed. Severine, pressed close up against him, was trembling too, he realized. He linked fingers with her and squeezed.

The man reached out, holding something in his right hand. It was pulsing green and purple, glowing through the flesh, revealing his skeletal digits.

<*That's the gem he uses when he kills,*> Severine whispered into his mind. <*It glows that same color when he does it*>

Delta bent down and touched the khurne colt between the eyes with the gem, and all at once it flared, a dazzlingly bright flash that illuminated the square like a great bolt of lightning, bathing all those watching in its putrid colors.

The colt's head fell onto its chest and it started shaking.

What in Hel's name—?

Severine squeezed Ramon's fingers so tightly he began to lose feeling in them, but he didn't pull away; he needed the comfort of another's touch as much as she did. They stared as the little construct—*is it still a construct if it is actually the born offspring of a construct?*—thrashed about weakly, its limbs still shaking as it tried to toss its head. It was still caught in the gnostic glow.

Delta spoke—in fluent Keshi, to Ramon's great surprise. The mage's melodious voice carried easily in the otherwise silent night.

Ramon turned to Severine and pulled her head close. As quietly as he could—if they could hear Delta that easily, surely he could hear them?—he whispered, "He said 'Get up.'"

First the colt twitched at the branded mage's words, then on awkward limbs, it rose to its feet and stood obediently.

More Keshi spilled from Delta's lips.

"'Walk,'" Ramon translated, grateful for his easy facility with foreign languages; his paterfamilias had always encouraged language lessons, both at Turm Zauberin and since.

The little khurne staggered forward, its legs akimbo.

"'Walk in a circle, then stamp three times.'"

As they watched breathlessly, the colt did *exactly* what the mage ordered.

The implications hit them both at once, and Severine closed her eyes and pressed her face into Ramon's shoulder, stifling a sob—so she didn't see what happened next: the man standing beside Siburnius turned to the Fist Commandant and shook his hand. As he stepped into the light, Ramon saw a face he knew, though he'd only ever seen it at a distance, on the parade grounds or at the head of the army, leading the march.

Duke Echor Borodium of Argundy.

<*We've got to go,*> Ramon whispered in her mind. He pulled her away from the window and held her to him until she stopped shaking. <*We can't be seen here—we really can't.*>

They crept out, barely daring to breathe, and made their way back through the empty house and into the alley. They'd gotten barely a block away before Severine began to babble, "*Tell me I saw wrongly! Tell me they didn't do that! Tell me it's not true!*"

Ramon shook her gently, trying to quell her growing hysteria. "Hush," he whispered, stroking her arm, desperate to stop her from falling apart. "Listen, Severine, I *know*, okay?—but we're not safe here, do you understand? We've got to get well away from here."

Severine shook him off, straightened her back and wiped her eyes. "I'm all right," she whispered hoarsely, though she sounded anything but all right. "Just get me out of here."

She looked around, trying to orient herself, but clearly her brain couldn't cope with such detail. He took her hand and led the way back through the city streets to the army camp.

They found a broken-down, deserted stable on the edge of the camp. It had obviously been some kids' hideout before the army had arrived—the mudbrick walls were covered in obscene Keshi graffiti and date stones littered the ground around the poor excuse for a firepit dug into the middle of the floor. They'd become almost inured to the stench of human excrement in camp and barely noticed the piss-soaked walls. The wooden roof beams were long gone, and shattered tiles covered the floor, but they kicked them into a pile to create a clear space on the floor and sank to their haunches facing each other.

"They're killing refugees and using their souls to inhabit the khurnes!" Severine burst out in a frantic whisper, barely able to keep the volume down. She reached for Ramon's hand. "And probably the hulkas too! Ramon, we have to tell the Duke—*Seth* has to tell the Duke! He can—"

"Shush." He put a hand over her mouth. "Listen, Severine, Echor already knows—*he was there.*"

She froze, and he told her what he'd seen.

She listened, not interrupting, stunned, until he'd finished, shaking her head in utter disbelief. Finally, she stuttered, "Then . . . every khurne . . . every hulka . . . they all . . . every one of these . . . these *creatures . . . they all contain a human soul . . .*"

"And the war hounds—the ones Seth described in his father's legion too, no doubt," Ramon added. "They're all possessed by the souls of people." He swallowed. "They must have begun it during the Second Crusade." He looked down at their linked fingers. "Severine, I may be only a Silacian familioso mage—but I know evil when I see it."

"Who can we go to?" she whispered.

"When the man at the top is involved? I don't know. I can't begin to imagine."

"We have to do something." Severine's voice was steeped in fear and doubt.

"Not here, and not now," Ramon started. "Maybe when we're back in Yuros—although if the Inquisition is involved, I cannot think of anyone who'll want to touch something like this with the end of a lance-pole . . ."

Severine's eyes welled up with tears. She lurched over to him, shaking, and clutched him blindly, wrapping herself in his arms as she had in the deserted house. All he could do was try to stifle the sounds of her despair as he held her close to his chest. As she cried out her pain and terror in huge, body-racking shudders, her whole body quivering, he held her, patting her back, feeling completely ineffectual, but trying to give her some kind of comfort.

When at last she stopped crying, she whispered in his ear, "I don't want to be here. I want to go home." Then she pulled his head to hers and kissed him desperately.

Something inside him went still in surprise. She was most of the things he despised: a rich Rondian princess who thought she was the center of the universe; a self-important, condescending snob—or at least, she had been. The trauma of her visions had been stripping that away, layer by layer, revealing the raw, almost skinless soul beneath, with no filters to block out what she was daily confronting. He pitied her that, and he found himself grudgingly admiring the self-belief that made her pugnacious and principled enough to want to resist this evil. She was growing up in front of him.

And she was more than comely, even right now, when she was little more than great bruised eyes and skin and bone held together by sheer desperation . . .

And taking advantage of that desperation would be the act of a churl.

He pulled away and said quietly, "Severine, you don't want me—"

"Don't you tell me what I don't want," she replied, reaching for him again. She started to pull his clothing apart, then gave up on that and lifted her own robes to her waist, spreading her legs and revealing herself to him, even as he surrendered to the inevitable. Despite his concerns about taking advantage of her, his member had gone rigid at the first touch of her silken flesh.

She pushed him flat on the ground, then lowered herself onto him, groaning hungrily in his ear as her warm, damp tightness enclosed him. She rolled him over until she was underneath him and lifted her hips upward to meet him even as he pulled away, then pushed back inside her. She gasped with pleasure and rose to him again, and he sealed her mouth with his, trying to concentrate on anything but the feel of her, running through the table of affinities in his head and trying to hold off, even for just a few moments more, but then she wrapped her legs around his hips and moaned into his mouth and he came, emptying himself into her in great convulsive gouts while she grunted in unison.

They went still and lay locked around each other, panting softly, for long moments, until she opened her eyes and blinked as if to say, "Oh, it's you."

They stayed like that, exploring each other's face in the dim light of the rising moon. Outside, the noises of the camp went on, the singing and drumming, the whickering of the horses and the low-ing of the cattle of the wagon-train.

"Get off, you fool," she whispered finally.

He slid out of her, his semen-slick member shrinking. He shifted his weight and put an arm across her chest, pinning her down. "Wait," he whispered. "The night isn't over yet."

She wrinkled her nose. "Rukk off. I've had what I want."

He shook his head. "But I haven't—nor have you, not really." He put his hand on her mound, and then slid a finger into her, and she quivered, sucking in her breath. So he did it again, and again, until her desire to leave melted away. She moaned softly, a sound like pleased surprise, and started gently rocking her hips to his rhythm, and as she writhed under his ministrations he studied her face, enjoying her agonized, ecstatic expression as she came for him.

Afterward, she lay looking up at him, her face filled with radiance as if she were made of moonlight. Slowly she propped herself up on one elbow and kissed him, slowly and deeply.

"Thank you," she whispered. "No one's ever done that for me before."

"You're welcome," he said, rolling onto her and slowly pushing himself into her again as she gazed up at him with a look of exultant surprise.

This time they took it slowly, and made their pleasure last.

Pallacios XIII was still the last in the column as they set out for Shali-yah. The narrow desert road forced the legions into single file until the army was strung out over several miles. Mages and legionaries alike wrapped themselves in headscarves and covered every inch of bare skin as they clanked through the desert under the rising heat. The sand reflected and radiated the sun's fire, sending it throbbing through the poor soldiers who were boiling in their heavy armor.

Each day was identical to the last, a trial and a purging, as if they were being hammered on Kore's anvil. Peroz vanished behind them as if it had never been, and the desert swallowed them up.

Echor left two of his twenty-one legions behind to garrison Peroz, and sent a further three south to invest a fortress near Vida. Duprey begged to be part of the desert crossing, much to Ramon's disgust. Storn's wagons now carried as much opium and coin as they did food and water, and he lived in perpetual fear of exposure.

The windships sent to reconnoître their destination reported that Shaliyah was fortified and garrisoned, and there was no sign that Salim was about to retreat. It looked like someone was at last prepared to stand and fight, and that thought alone lifted the morale of the whole army. After so long on the march, the prospect of taking out their fury on an actual enemy was intoxicating.

Despite this, Ramon was convinced the march was showing every signs of disaster. Two days into the march half the beasts of burden came down with some sickness that rendered them incapable of moving. Investigation revealed poison in the feed, but by then it was too late; that was the price of complacency. When they found the first three watering holes on the route were entirely dry, with nothing left but hard, cracked beds of silt, the men began to talk of curses.

There was one blessing: after Peroz the visions that had been plaguing Severine ceased and she began to sleep through the night—something Ramon knew at first hand as he slept wrapped around her on her narrow cot. She made no attempt to hide their relationship: he was sharing her tent and that was that. It earned her sneering contempt from Renn Bondeau and lewd snickering among the rankers, but she didn't care—if anything, Ramon was more bothered by their social inequality than she was. He thought perhaps that she simply hated being alone at night—or maybe her overwhelming craving for a child, which was a sure way out of this nightmare, was overpowering all other motivations . . . but the sleep and lovemaking had restored her color and removed the dark circles under her eyes, and a restored appetite for food had also started to restore her natural curves.

"So, you are in love, yar?" Kip commented one morning as they prepared to march. The sun was barely up, but already the heat lay over the camp like a blanket. Severine was long gone to her post at Duprey's side, relaying his messages to the other farseers.

Ramon wasn't really sure how he felt about her. He had come to like her, to enjoy her company, now she wasn't being so haughty all the time—but they could still end up squabbling over nothing. Was that love? He had no idea. He ignored the question and jabbed a finger toward the southern horizon, where a distant figure mounted on a tall beast—a camel, probably—was watching the camp. "Keshi."

Kip peered blearily; he was a little shortsighted. "How many?"

"Just one, amici, but that's the third morning in a row."

Seth Korion and Tyron Frand walked past them to the edge of the camp, peering at the lone rider. They had become close, the pair of them. Now they were loudly arguing about the merits of some poet or other—rukking poetry was all they ever seemed to talk about.

Ramon and Kip turned to watch as a troop of Estella cavalry rode out toward the Keshi scout. He waited until they were halfway to him before lazily turning and trotting slowly away, leaving the Estella to return empty-handed, but deeply relieved that they hadn't been forced to gallop in this heat. The Rondian rankers jeered them, until a tribune stepped in to shut them up.

"Is Sevvie pregnant yet?" Kip asked, returning to his original line of questioning. "Or should I take a turn?"

Ramon chuckled and said, "No. And no! She bled last week— she's not fertile till the full moon, so all our efforts since that first night have basically been for fun. Getting a bit of practice in, you know?"

"How is it that the only pretty girl in this whole wertlos camp is with a runt like you?" Kip teased. "What's wrong with her?"

Ramon tossed the content of his empty cup at him. "She's crazy," he said with a laugh. "So obviously we're well matched."

"Yar, you said it." Kip leaned closer. "Is she still having her bad dreams?"

"No, not since Peroz."

"Then the Kirkegarde aren't following us anymore. Or they've run out of victims." He turned away and spat. "How many of those poor verdamnt refugees Echor marched back will end up like those we saw? Or *inside* something?" He looked about him furtively, then dropped his voice, even though no one was paying them the least bit of attention. "I am glad you told me, but I can't even look at the hulkas now without thinking of how they're made."

"It makes me want to steal Seth Korion's khurne and set it free," Ramon admitted. "I've never known a worse thing—Pallas have really outdone themselves with this. It's the evilest thing I've ever heard of."

Kip agreed grimly, but there was nothing any of them could do, and they knew it.

The second week of the march brought more dried-out watering holes, and their own water-barrels began to empty worryingly fast. The tribunes set Water-magi to probing the ground around and below the waterholes, but none of them could say how or why the water was gone. They had no idea whether this was normal in this desert land, and no one had thought to bring native guides.

The windships were seeing more and more Keshi camel-cavalry. They were coming up from the south, traveling light in groups of a dozen or so. The first combat casualties came when a group of Estella horsemen with no magi support ran into one of these Keshi groups. The Keshi archers proved deadly, slaying half a dozen of the Estellan riders before they fled.

The army shrugged off the lesson; no magi had been involved so it didn't matter.

Duprey pulled his own magi together and asked those with any Water-gnosis to try and augment their supply. This was a dangerous thing he was asking. Creating water was a torturously slow, draining exercise, and it generally left the mage dangerously dehydrated. Frand, Korion, and the healer Lanna were the most adept at Water-gnosis, and they worked doggedly at the task as the week of the waxing moon unfolded.

Meanwhile Severine was kept busy relaying messages between the battle-magi and passing everything on to Duprey. Some nights she and Ramon were so tired all they could manage was a chaste kiss on the cheek before collapsing into the deep, dreamless sleep of exhaustion, but as the full moon rose, Severine roused from her lethargy, pulling Ramon onto her again and again.

Ramon hated her desperation to quicken. She told him she would not ask him to formally acknowledge any child; all she wanted was a discharge, and her blazing need and the question mark it left over their relationship was an unacknowledged tension—but in spite of that, he willingly plowed her, again and again, and every day felt his dependency on her growing. He liked how they were together; he felt witty and funny and ironic and strong when he was with her.

I'm a fool, he admitted to himself. *I'm falling for her, idiot that I am.*

The army crawled forward, moving more slowly with every passing day. As the water-wagons emptied they were abandoned alongside the road and the beasts that pulled them butchered for meat. Encounters with enemy scouts seldom resulted in much more than the exchange of arrows, but they were becoming increasingly frequent. The windships flying the long patrols still reported growing enemy forces in Shaliyah.

At the end of the third week, as Ramon was riding with Storn, word fizzed through the column: the advance guard had reached the city. Relief was palpable on every face and the legionaries picked up their pace. There was a low ridge ahead, already lined with the battle standards of the other legions who'd arrived ahead of them.

As the Thirteenth got closer, they could hear cheering, a distant rumble that grew and grew. Finally it was their turn to top the rise, the last in line, and look out over the shallow, wide valley. Below them stretched Echor's army, his Argundian legions at the core, the Estella arrayed on his left, to the north, where an exposed plain gaped. The remaining legions, those from Bricia and Andressea and Noros, were arrayed to the right, on the southern flank not far from the tail-end of a line of low hills. An old ruin of some sort topped the closest hill, and it was to that flank that Duprey waved his men.

As they made their way along the ridge, the men of Pallacios XIII could see on their left the great city they had come so far to sack.

Shaliyah was a gleaming marvel. It was built around a small lake, the shimmer of which could be glimpsed beyond the walls—those walls themselves were made of some kind of shiny flecked stone that glistened in the setting sun like pure gold. The domes of the Dom-al'Ahm and the turrets of the massive palace shone so brightly Ramon had to squint.

Figures robed in white filled every inch of the walls. The west-facing fortifications ran for at least a mile from the gatehouse at the center of the defenses, curving about the lake and ending with a fortress at either end.

"Thank Kore," Storn said fervently, striking his right fist to his breastplate. "Thanks and praise."

They had arrived. The army was a scarlet tide, pouring into the valley.

After marching for seven hundred miles, footsore and increasingly under-supplied, they'd finally found the enemy. The legionaries pulled off their helmets and waved them in the air as their cheers rolled down the valley and echoed from the hills, bouncing off the walls of the city. Here was where the war would begin: right here. Nature had been a formidable opponent, but she had been overcome. The enemy would surely be an easier foe.

29

SALTWATER AND BLOOD

Myths and legends of the Scytale

No artifact is so shrouded in mystique as the Scytale of Corineus. Some say that just to touch it grants immortality—or a vision of Corineus's face; or godhood. Some say it is a weapon; others believe that it grants communion with Kore, and the wisdom of the ages. The superstitions of the common folk know no limit.

ORDO COSTRUO COLLEGIATE, PONTUS

Isle of Glass, Javon Coast, Antiopia
Zulhijja (Decore) 928
6th month of the Moontide

Alaron woke early and lay for a while listening to the sounds of this strange place. At first it was eerily silent, but then he could make out the never-ending dim pounding of the waves on the rocks below. He could feel the almost imperceptible trembling of the tower of stone. *I bet this place has stood for thousands of years*, he reassured himself nervously.

He dressed quickly, strapped on his sword out of habit and went out into the hall. All of the doors were closed, so he took the stairs back to the main living room, where he was met by the scents of heavily spiced cooking. The little Lakh woman was in the kitchen, and three pots were simmering on her stove. Thankfully she wasn't wearing that outrageous attire that left her pregnant stomach uncovered. He'd thought he was immune to female weirdness after months of bare lamia breasts, but a bare pregnant belly was just wrong. But she was crammed into a plain shift—well, simple, rather than plain, for the cloth was alive with colorful decorative swirls and patterns, a cacophony of color.

Now, what was her greeting word? "Uh . . . Nam-stay?" he tried.

"Namaste," she corrected brightly, looking up and smiling at him. Her teeth were beautifully white against her dark skin.

He noticed again how small she was—apart from her enormous belly, of course. She only came up to his chest, and he wasn't overly tall. But he liked her demeanor: her eyes were smiling, but patient. She had a kind of dignity and self-sufficiency that made her seem almost middle-aged, though her clear skin looked too youthful for her to actually be middle-aged. She'd displayed flashes of temper last night, too, so she was no doormat. He wondered how old she really was.

"Uh, nama-stay—er, Ramita, right?" She waggled her head in that weird Lakh nod. It was kind of charming, he decided. "That's a nice name."

She smiled. "Thank you. Your name . . . it is amusing. Very barbaric, but sweet."

"Alaron? It's just a name."

"In Keshi, al'Rhon means 'Goat.'" She giggled. "Although I am sure you are not a goat," she added consolingly.

Great, I have a stupid name in Keshi. He made a face, looking around for something to eat. "Is there any bread?"

"Bread? You mean roti? I can make some." She waved a hand toward an oven.

"Ah, sure." He wondered what foreign bread would be like, then told himself, *It's bread, how different can it be?* "What's cooking?" He checked out the pots as she named them: foreign dishes he'd never heard of, all some kind of yellow or brown gloop, smelling of every spice he could ever have imagined. There were no proper breakfast foods like cheese or eggs in sight, so she had to be cooking for lunch or dinner.

"Um, can I help?"

"I don't think so," she replied with mild condescension. "Please, relax."

He leaned against the bench. "So, um . . . you're a Lakh." He dimly knew the place existed from geography lessons, but that was about it. *It was massive, and full of Indranicans . . . people like her,* he guessed.

She waggled her head again and said, "I am from Baranasi, on the holy river Imuna." Her voice held a lilt of longing.

"How old are you?" he asked curiously.

"It is not proper to ask," she said, sounding amused.

Oops.

"Uh, I'm nineteen," he offered by way of apology. He'd had his birthday a few days before they stole the windship in Gydan's Cut, but he'd forgotten all about it at the time.

She waggled her head. "I am sixteen."

He blinked. *Sixteen, and seven months pregnant? Great Kore . . . she'd probably been just fifteen when she married.* He couldn't stop himself from blurting, "Really? You're *so* young."

She smiled prettily, taking his incredulous comment for a compliment. "Thank you." She patted her belly. "I'm having twins," she said proudly.

"How do you know?"

Her face went sad. "I just know," she said softly. Then she *tsked* and went back to her cooking, producing flour from somewhere and creating wet dough, then kneading and rolling it. "I will make roti now," she announced.

"Shouldn't we wait for the others?"

"Lady Justina does not get out of bed until much later." She stroked her belly again. "My babies and I cannot go without for so long." She waggled her head again, confusing him even more because he didn't think she mean "yes" this time, more something like "this is true."

"Cym likes to sleep late too," Alaron told her. They looked at each other and he knew she was thinking the same as him: *like mother, like daughter.* They both smiled at once, and he decided he rather liked this little woman, Ramita, young widow of the world's greatest mage.

She made him breakfast, a bizarre meal of spiced gloop she called "curry," something white and spongy she named as "rice," and the roti: which was most definitely not proper bread. It didn't rise at all, and it contained all these strange seeds and yet more spices—but weirdly, it all tasted pretty good. However, the curried gloop went through him in ten minutes and he spent the next thirty minutes stuck in the privy. His mouth was burning too, almost as much as his ass.

After that he stuck to rice and water, which at least filled his belly. Ramita ate all the food with evident relish, and was visibly trying to suppress her mirth at the plight of his nether region.

"Do not worry," she said kindly, patting his arm. "Many ferang struggle at first to eat proper food."

"*Proper?*" he retorted. "It almost killed me!"

"You will get used to it." She wagged her head, giving it yet another type of meaning, something like, "I know best."

I have no intention of getting used to it.

The room grew a bit dimmer and when he looked up at the sky-light, he noticed it was beginning to rain. "Do you think I can move the windskiff to your other landing space," he asked? "Lady Justina said last night that I should, if the wind's not too fierce."

"Of course," Ramita replied. "I will need to open the lower gates for you."

When he went up, he found the wind was manageable. It was the work of minutes to get the skiff aloft. In the daylight, he could see that this pillar rose hundreds of feet above the highest waves—but the spray was incredible. It was only because he knew what he was looking for that he managed to make out the smoothed space below, and the dark opening in the rock.

Despite the buffeting winds he managed to get the craft down safely, though he was quickly tiring from exerting gnosis that wasn't a strong affinity. Finally, he lowered the sails and pulled the mast out of its socket, before pulling it into the opening. He found himself on a smooth stone floor, beside a deep-looking pool with myriad large fish swimming in it. *Interesting—*

Ramita was standing beside the doors, and he was about to ask her about the fish when she did something quite startling.

She turned the big doors with a gesture of her hands and they boomed closed, then sealed.

His jaw dropped. *"You're a mage?"*

She waggled her head, and now it meant *"Yes"* again, with strong overtones of *"You've only just realized?"*

"From bearing my husband's children," she told him, her head erect as if daring him to be shocked.

"Oh." *Of course—Mistress Yune told us about pregnancy mani-festation, didn't she? And of course that would happen to her, even though she's not Rondian . . .*

"Uh . . . that must have been a shock for you."

She cocked her head. "You have no idea."

He's like a big puppy, Ramita thought as she watched Alaron fussing over the skiff. He folded the sails properly before stowing the mast, and only then did he go to the pool and start peering at the fish. He behaved awfully immature at times, as if he'd been sheltered from difficult things, but then he'd reveal something about himself that really took her aback—like that his mother was dead. And though his voice was filled with longing whenever he spoke Cymbellea's name, something in his manner suggested he knew that she was quite out of his reach. She knew Lakh boys who would have been bitter about such a thing, but he appeared to be quietly accepting—that was no small thing in itself. It hinted at a strong but under-stated kind of manliness, like her father had. He would grow to be a good man, she thought.

Poor boy. This Cymbellea doesn't appreciate what she's got.

"You are very old to be unmarried," she observed.

He threw her a look. "Not really. We don't marry until we're nineteen or twenty."

Holy Parvasi! No wonder Yuros is underpopulated!

"Then you are betrothed?"

He blushed, as if this wasn't a normal question, then started, "Sort of—" which he quickly changed to, "Not really, no."

"Ask him about Anise," Cym called as she emerged from the stairs, holding a towel. Alaron ducked his head shyly, which made the two young women smile at each other.

Cym peered at the pools. "Is there a bath with no fish in it?"

Ramita pointed at the smaller pool, then led Alaron back upstairs to the lounge. Shortly after a freshly washed Cym arrived, Justina joined them. Neither looked like they'd slept much. They appeared to expect Ramita to cook for them, but she decided she was okay with that. Alaron—*what a funny name!*—looked as if he wanted to stay well clear of them, so she showed him to the library, then took herself back to the kitchen.

Parvasi, let mother and daughter find understanding, she asked the goddess as she busied herself with her pots and pans.

Seeing the two women together made her miss her own family dreadfully and she found her eyes misting over several times as she made lunch. They were such a dreadfully long way away. She worried over whether the promised money for her pregnancy had ever been sent. Were they safe? Were they happy? Had Jai gone home with his Keita?

Queen of Heaven, watch over them all, she begged.

"Um . . . are you all right?" Alaron said. He had reappeared, a book clutched in his hand, looking at her concernedly.

She was immediately flustered. "Don't creep up on people," she scolded him, then regretted it and said apologetically, "No, no, I am fine. I was just remembering my home."

"Were you a princess in Bara-what's-it?"

She sniffed. "No, and all the happier for it. I am from Aruna Nagar Market. It is the best place in the world."

He looked at her disbelievingly. Perhaps he thought that whatever cold and primitive place he came from was better, she thought irritably. *Just let him say so!* But he disarmed her with a quiet question. "Do they know of Yuros there?"

"Yes. They say it is filled with afreet."

"Afreet?"

"White-skinned demons who eat children."

"I don't eat children," he said gravely. "They're too fatty."

It took her a moment to work out that this was a joke, but once she did she laughed involuntarily. *He is a nice boy.* It was fun to have someone to talk to, even if he was just a ferang. "What will you do with your Skittly-thing?" she asked him as she used the gnosis to defrost the meat, then reached for the largest knife to chop it into thin slivers.

"The Scytale?" He exhaled heavily. "I don't know. I thought Cym's plan was good: she'd give it to her mother, who'd give it to her father, and Lord Meiros would solve everything. We've been hiding and running so long we never even heard that he was dead. If we had, we might never have come so far."

"The mother and child, they would still have sought each other," Ramita replied confidently. "I know families: we can't keep away from each other."

"I have no family—no brothers or sisters, that is. Just my father left, now. And Aunty Elena."

"I have three brothers and two sisters, and three more who died, including my twin," she told him. "And Huriya too."

"You lost a twin? What's that like?" he asked with guileless insensitivity.

She decided she didn't mind. "Jaya died when I was five. She was a loudmouth, she talked all the time." She waggled her fingers, smiling. "*Jabber-jabber.* I missed her for a long time, but our family is so big, no one can be lonely for long. Huriya became my twin—she took Jaya's place, in a way. I still sometimes miss Jaya, but it was a long time ago."

"Who is Huriya?" he asked, mangling the pronunciation.

"Trouble." Ramita pursed her lips. "We have had a falling-out."

"I'm sorry."

"Don't be. She eats people like you for breakfast."

He made a face. "Literally? Like an afreet?"

She squealed with laughter. "No! It is just one of your Rondian 'figures of speech.'"

"Phew." He grinned: "I've just been traveling with a group of creatures who really do eat people for breakfast!" And he proceeded to fascinate her by telling her the strangest story, of men with snake-tails who had trekked across the whole world seeking refuge. She didn't actually believe him, but it was so absorbing she almost burned the food.

"You are an outrageous liar," she scolded him good-naturedly.

"No, it's all true," he protested. "The lamiae are as real as you or me."

"It is true," Cymbellea, walking into the kitchen. "I can vouch for it all."

"Then your lands are even more primitive than I have been told," Ramita declared.

The Rondians found this amusing, and Ramita decided all people must think their land the best. "Are you ready to eat?" she asked politely.

Alaron made another attempt to eat her "curry." She'd reduced the spices for his benefit, but it was still far too hot for him—and for Cymbellea too. They had the palates of babies. It was very funny, though, the looks on their faces as they gasped for water, then fled toward the privies. Justina, who had been eating proper eastern food for all her life, was similarly amused.

Once everyone had settled down, they took advantage of the rain clearing away to go to the top level and enjoy the sun. The viewing platforms offered views of the sea, and the other pillars, which fascinated Alaron and Cymbellea.

After a while Cymbellea and Justina went to another platform to talk. They lowered their voices, clearly arguing, while Alaron just stared out across the water, paying them no attention. *Perhaps he is thinking of this "Anise,"* Ramita mused. *He's a little lovesick, I think.* She smiled wistfully; it reminded her of all those years of being in love with Kazim, and terrified her parents would arrange for her to marry someone else—and in the end they had, of course, just not someone she could ever have imagined.

But I miss you, my husband. Every night, I wish again that you were here.

"Look at the size of that gull," Alaron said, breaking into her reverie. "It's *massive.*"

They all peered at the huge seabird. It had a fierce yellow beak, and its wings were as wide as a man is long. It circled the pillar and called aloud, a harsh shrieking noise, then veered away toward the south, climbing as it went. The cloud was low, especially to the west where it was rolling toward them on the wind, tumbling and boiling like an oncoming storm.

"It was some kind of albatross," Justina called from the next balcony, "but bigger than any I've ever seen." Her voice had a worried catch to it. "I should have killed it."

Ramita looked at her, surprised. "Why?"

Justina pointed upward, at a flock of dark shapes. The giant gull was speeding toward them. "Because I am beginning to think it might not have been a real bird."

Ramita clutched her stomach, which quivered with kicking feet. A lump of fear caught in her throat.

"Let's go below," Justina snapped, pulling back her hood. "Now!"

Almost as if they'd heard her, the giant birds peeled off and dived toward them, shrieking a challenge as they came. And even worse, a giant wooden ship emerged from the cloud-banks to the west of them. Six huge flying creatures glided menacingly alongside it, and her heart started thudding as she saw they had armored riders.

Ramita reached inside her for that semi-tangible well of strength her body now harbored: the gnosis, the devil-magic, her husband's final gift to her. Her lips fluttered in prayer as she backed toward the stairs.

Darikha-ji, be with me. Our enemies are here.

It's Malevorn's lot, Alaron realized at once, as the venators shrieked and swooped toward them. His skin prickled with heat and sweat and his whole body trembled. He thanked the impulse that had seen him wear his sword, and he drew it as they all retreated to the central landing area atop the pillar. "Lady Meiros, what is the most defensible place here?" he called to Justina. The air around Cym's mother was alive with wards, and lightning crackled at her fingertips.

"Get below and prepare to seal the doors," she shouted. Then she thrust a hand toward the windship and the clouds blazed with vivid jagged light. A fork of energy erupted from her and blasted the forecastle of the ship—or would have, except for a web of blue light that absorbed the energy in a burst of sparks. The venators shrieked, rearing up with wings billowing, and then began to surge forward.

Then the giant gulls were between them.

Alaron blinked as he realized two things: one, that the birds were changing into winged people as they flew, and secondly, *that they were attacking the windship.*

"Who are they?" he shouted. *Perhaps they're here to help us—?*

But that vain thought died as one peeled off and shrieked toward Justina, who effortlessly blasted it from the skies.

Cym grabbed at his shoulder. "Come on," she shouted as her mother sent another bolt of lightning into one of the shapeshifters. A blinding flash revealed its bones, then it disintegrated and fell from sight. Then someone howled a spell and a wooden skiff dropped from the clouds. Fire almost enveloped them, testing Justina's wards to the limit, but her web of protective light flashed blue to white, imprinting itself on his retinas against the boiling blackness of smoke and fire.

"Daughter, get below!" Justina cried, and he caught her involuntary thought: <*That fire was of Ascendant-strength.*>

Kore Above, an Ascendant! Alaron grabbed Cym, and ran for the stairs. Ramita was ahead of him, her eyes bright with fear, but she was composed, not panicking. She immediately shot upward in his estimation; he himself was terrified.

"Get inside," he told the two women, taking it upon himself to hold the door open for Justina. Or to close it if she didn't make it. The sky about the pillar was alive with shapes swirling through the smoke and blazing light. There was lightning bursting among the giant gulls, and more of them were falling from the sky, and then he saw a venator plummet straight toward him as a raking blow shredded its right wing. The rider leaped clear and struck the rim of the stone wall; he nearly bounced off it, but somehow managed to cling on.

Alaron blazed at the armored man with his own mage-fire, but his efforts only struck shielding wards. Then he glimpsed the man's face: *Malevorn!*

He heard Justina shouting defiantly as the great windship filled the air above. She threw a blast of fire that burst around its rigging, setting the sails on fire, and three windshipmen dropped from the vessel, their uniforms ablaze as they fell, one striking the stone with a sickening crunch, the others thudding into the decks of the vessel.

Justina backed toward the door as mage-bolts battered her shields.

"Get inside, my Lady!" Alaron shouted. "Please!"

She was obviously reluctant to obey him. Her eyes and hands were ablaze with fury—but then two more venators landed safely on the rim, and one lunged at her, its maw opening. She blasted it full in the mouth and as it recoiled, instantly dead, its death-throes threw off its rider, a pale young man who looked utterly terrified. The other reptile caught a gull-woman in its mouth and bit down, snapping her spine before tossing her aside. The Inquisitor-rider thrust at Justina with his lance, but the spearhead glanced harmlessly off her shields.

Alaron turned back to Malevorn, just in time to duck a bolt of energy that struck the lintel, leaving a blackened smear marking the place where he'd stood a moment before.

Justina flew past him, then whirled to slam and seal the doors.

"They followed us," Cym howled, her voice full of anguish and self-recrimination. "They traced my calling—they must have!" She looked like she wanted to tear her own eyes out. "It's all my fault!"

"Silence, daughter!" Justina snapped. She threw more energy into the wards about the doors, which were throbbing from successive gnostic blows. "There is only one other way out of here: the lower gates. Go and ready your skiff."

"We can carry four!" Alaron shouted. "No one gets left behind." His mind raced: the skiff was demasted: *Why did I do that? Fucking tidiness! And why are the attackers fighting each other?*

He thrust these wild thoughts aside and focused on the now. "We can all fit!"

"On that little twig?" Justina said scornfully.

"How did you get here?" Cym demanded.

"We flew on a carpet," Ramita told her, "but it is in the storage area above." She clutched at her stomach. "My children," she said. "They cannot have my children."

Justina looked at Cym. "There is an Ascendant out there. Take Ramita below and ready the skiff. *Do it.*"

Her face hardened as she turned to Alaron. "The boy and I will buy you time."

Alaron swallowed. *Kore's blood, she means for us to die so Cym and Ramita get away.*

"No, Mother!" Cym shrieked. "Please, we can all go!"

A series of gnostic blasts made the doors above shudder. The wards turned molten for a moment, but still they held.

Ramita, the calmest person here, took Cym's arm and pulled her toward the stairs. "Come. We have to ready your vessel."

"We can all get out," Alaron said aloud, willing it to be so.

Then the skylight shattered, glass cascaded over them and all of Hel burst in.

Ramita felt panic blossom inside her for the first time as the transparent ceiling high overhead on the western side of the lounge cracked and huge shards of glass started to plummet down. They struck the rock and shattered further, cascading out in all directions: a devastating wall of jagged chunks that could rip a person apart.

She was standing closest as the glass fell, and without quite realizing what she was doing, she screamed, "No!" and her gnosis burst from her like a vast, pulsing wave. She had no idea what she was trying to do—it was just sheer force, pure energy—but it froze the first onslaught of the broken glass in midair, holding it there. She realized she could feel it battering against her involuntary ward, like she was being punched, but somehow she weathered it, holding the sheet of lethal shards from them until it lost momentum and, with a deafening crash, rained harmlessly to the floor.

She reeled backward and fell against Alaron, who clutched her while staring, and the look of helpless dread on Justina's face had changed to wonder . . .

Then two shapes dropped through the hole in the roof. The first, a powerfully built white man, died instantly as Justina's gnosis, a brilliant blend of fire and lightning, blasted him. His blackened body fell with a crunch into the broken glass. Then a white-haired hag floated into view and hurled Justina back with an imperious gesture, as if the daughter of Meiros were nothing but a child.

Is this an "Ascendant," like my husband? Ramita stared at the old woman, who snarled like an animal and hurled a torrent of broken glass. Justina's shields held, just, though stray shards broke through, ripping at her mantle, drawing blood from her arms and legs. Behind her, the door bulged as their other attackers renewed their assault.

Ramita had no particular plan, but in blocking the glass, she'd been reminded of what Justina had told her of the stuff: it was composed of sand, super-heated by Earth and Fire-gnosis: her prime and secondary elements.

She picked up a big shard of glass with telekinesis and hurled it at the crone. It shattered impotently against her shields, but it made the crone turn toward her.

Her mental voice filled Ramita's head. *<Be still, Ramita. I don't wish to hurt you,>* she said in Lakh.

Ramita's jaw dropped. *She knows me?*

More people, naked men, some dark like her, some with skin as pale as Alaron's, dropped through the hole above into the chamber: they were all half-human and half-beast. A dark shape swooped toward her, a man with the wings and face of a bat, and Alaron blazed fire at it. The man-bat-creature thudded sideways, hitting the floor and bouncing once before lying still. But he had no time to relax, for a jackal-headed woman went for him almost immediately, forcing him to defend himself with his sword.

The doors shuddered again, and with her gnosis-sight Ramita could see that Justina was trying to hold it while fighting off the old crone. She also saw that the old woman's shields were gathered to her front, which gave her a clear angle of attack. She gathered more glass and threw it with all the force she could muster, just as Justina threw a mage-bolt. The accidentally synchronized attack proved deadly effective: shards of glass punched through the old woman's shields, one large piece lodging deep in her right thigh. Others ripped at her side, stripping her skin to the bone.

The old woman shrieked and collapsed yowling—which clearly shocked the beast-people. By now there were five enemies inside the chamber, but they all hesitated as the old woman fell, except for the jackal-woman, who had seized Alaron and borne him to the ground—she snapped at his face, but he twisted and threw her off. There was blood on his shoulder and running from his nose. Another of the beast-men was trying to rake Cym's flesh with long, filthy nails, but she threw him from her furiously. Two more of the shape-changers were still frozen in shock.

But Ramita recognized the fifth foe: *Huriya Makani,* her erstwhile best friend, the girl who had been as close to her as her dead twin.

"Hello, sister," the Keshi girl called as she dropped from the roof. Her voice was filled with barely contained bloodlust. She landed astride the old woman and pulled the glass shard from her thigh. The wound had partially sealed over, but the witch-woman looked glassy-eyed, barely aware.

"You!" Justina strode toward Huriya, both hands coming up as mage-fire gathered in her fists. "Get behind me, Ramita," she snapped. Then she focused on Huriya alone. "You opened the door for my father's killers."

Ramita's hand went to her mouth. *No!*

Huriya just smiled. "Oh, that wasn't me. That was my brother's lover who let in the Hadishah."

Justina stopped. "What are you saying?"

Huriya's face twisted nastily. "It was Ramita who let them in."

That split-second was all that it took. An instant when Justina's face went wild, her shields forgotten, her gnosis lost as her eyes sought confirmation in Ramita's face.

The nearest of the two unopposed shape changers, a golden vision with a lion's head, blurred inside Justina's guard. With one slash of his claws he tore out her throat. She arched over and fell, her head almost detaching as blood gushed through the air like an after-image.

Beside her, Cym howled in denial and threw herself bodily at Lionhead, but he swatted her aside as if she were nothing. Only Cym's instinctive shields prevented her from sharing the fate of her mother, but still she was hurled bodily against the wall. She slid down it to the ground, stunned, unable to do anything to stop Lionhead as he leaped onto her and pinned her down.

Alaron was scrambling to his feet. Ramita was staring at the almost headless body of Justina Meiros as her eyes flickered and went dull. Blood pooled about her in a steady flow. In that moment, Ramita was utterly helpless—but no one came at her. All eyes were suddenly on Huriya and the crone.

Huriya gripped the glass shard she'd wrenched from the hag's thigh, though it sliced open her hand, then in one fluid motion, she plunged it through the old woman's chest and kissed the woman's lips, inhaling with a look of ecstasy on her face.

Alaron grabbed Ramita's shoulder. His eyes went from Huriya to Lionhead, who started to roar, his claws at Cym's throat. Alaron shouted, "*No!* Please, *don't!*" and Ramita felt the young Rondian's hand clamp her arm. He wrenched her behind him and, brandishing his sword, cried despairingly, "Please, don't hurt her!"

Lionhead pulled Cym's throat to his mouth, menacingly, and all the while Huriya continued to kiss the dead woman. Her eyes rolled back in her skull and she moaned with pleasure, as if she were experiencing the most blissful of sexual peaks.

Sweet Parvasi, what has she become?

Jackal-woman and the other two shifters, who were now in human form, stalked toward them, naked and bloody. "Yield," Jackal-woman rasped.

Ramita and Alaron were about to obey when the door exploded inward and an armored Inquisitor burst into the room, followed by a flood of soldiers.

Oh Hel. Alaron shoved Ramita, shouting, "*Go, go!*" He saw an Inquisitor going for Lionhead while the first rank of the soldiers made straight for the disturbing dark-skinned girl hunched over the dead witch.

Dokken, he thought. *Souldrinker.* It was the only thing that made sense. He'd heard of them of course, but he'd never been sure if they were real, or just scary myths to frighten young magi. *So not legends then,* he thought wildly to himself.

The room was filled with fire and screaming, and bodies hitting the floor.

<*Cym, Cym, Cym!*> he called, unable to see anymore, but he'd have to trust that she'd heard him. He ran after Ramita, caught her arm and half-carried her down the stairs, looking behind him every now and then—but it wasn't Cym who came after them but one of the shapeshifters: Jackal-woman.

Some stupid remnant of chivalry had stopped him from trying to kill her earlier, but in a sudden burst of protective fury he forgot that; he fed the gnosis into his blade and punched it straight through her shields. A foot of steel burst out through the back of her chest and she slid to the ground with a bewildered, naked look on her face. Blood bubbled from her mouth.

No one else followed.

"Get below!" he called to Ramita, who scurried into her room even as he sprinted to his. He snatched up his pack and thrust the Scytale into it, then went back to the hall, calling again for Cym. Ramita was still in her room and he screamed at her to hurry as he peered through the smoke now billowing from above. But still the Rimoni girl didn't appear.

He counted thirty nerve-racking seconds until Ramita emerged, clutching a bulging carpet-bag. But although he could hear the shapeshifters and Inquisitors ripping each other apart above him, no one came.

Cym is up there. He was desperate to charge back upstairs and find her, but it felt like suicide, and he had to protect Ramita and the Scytale. She began to waddle to the next flight of stairs, the one leading to the lower doors, and before he followed her, he locked and warded the doors behind him. They were halfway down the stairs when he heard and felt that door blasted open.

"Mercer!" someone roared.

Malevorn Andevarion—no, no, no—!

Ramita jerked to a stop. "Let me!" she shouted in his face. He had no idea what she meant to do, but she turned and made a vicious gesture with her hand.

The ceiling collapsed with a deafening roar into the stairwell behind them with a crash that blasted through them both. Dust and smoke spewed everywhere.

He gaped at her. *Great Kore, she's strong . . . but—Oh Cym, how will you get out now—?*

"Now," Ramita snapped, "we go."

He ran down the last few stairs to the skiff and threw in the pack containing the Scytale while Ramita threw open the sea-doors with a single peremptory gesture. Her words were lost in the tumultuous sound of the sea roaring below. Spray and mist immediately concealed the opening.

Somewhere in the dust and dark above he heard Malevorn's voice, shouting faintly. *Rukking Hel! He survived?* A torrent of earth and stone flew over them and struck the far wall. *Shit, he's coming!*

Alaron whirled and grabbed the mast two-handed, and went to ram it into its socket. He kept praying that somehow Cym would appear, having miraculously gotten herself out of this impossible situation. There was a second stairwell on the opposite wall. He was desperate for Cym to burst through it, but instead, an armored warrior erupted from it: a blond woman with a face of utter perfection, her eyes as cold and dead as corpse.

He recognized her instantly: she was the Inquisitor who had killed Anise's brother Ferdi. She came straight at him, reaching him before he'd really registered her presence, and brought her sword hacking down at the juncture of his shoulder and neck.

Reacting instinctively, he blocked with the mast, and her blade cleaved it in two as effortlessly as if she were cutting butter. The top bit sheared off and spun toward the doors.

"Yield, heretic!" she shouted, hacking at him again, and he threw himself down just as her blade sliced the air above him, barely missing him. Before he could recover she kicked him in the chest, sending him sprawling onto his back. He gasped for air, and had barely a moment to draw his blade before she was on him again.

Steel rained down on him, blow after blow, ripping his sleeve, slicing his face open from left eye to jaw.

As his left eye filled with blood, he raised his sword in desperation, but before he could swing it she kicked his hand and sent his sword clattering away.

She shouted triumphantly, reversed her own blade with a showy grip-reverse and raised it high to impale him.

He tried to gather his gnosis for one last blast, though he could barely feel it—

—then the sheered-off mast punched through her back and out between her breasts and she shuddered and staggered forward. She crashed toward him, and he barely managed to roll clear in time—but he did.

He stared wildly around him.

Ramita had thrown the top section of the mast from twenty yards away with the force of a ballista, powerful enough to punch through a pure-blood's shields.

But that's impossible—

He climbed shakily to his feet and ineffectually wiped the blood from his eyes, wincing at the pain of his cut face. Then he sheathed his sword and hurriedly rammed what was left of the mast into the socket, then began to drag the skiff toward Ramita, all the while trying to control his shaking.

The Lakh girl was just as unsteady. She kept staring from her hand to the impaled Inquisitor, her eyes round with fear. "I didn't mean to—"

"Thank Kore you did!" he shouted. "Come on! We've got to go!"

Booted feet hammered on the stairs, too heavy to be Cym. He heard Malevorn again. "Mercer," his old enemy snarled from somewhere above. "Stand and fight, you stinking coward."

Alaron's blood boiled. *I've stood toe to toe with you for half my life, Andevarion, even though I've lost every time. I've never backed down from a fight with you—don't you dare call me a coward.*

But one look at Ramita, clutching her belly, her expression terrified, quelled any impulse he might have had to stay and fight.

She's carrying Meiros's children. I've got the Scytale. We've got to get out of here.

He finished dragging the skiff to her. As mage-fire flashed down the stairs, his shields crackled and blossomed about him. "Get in!" he shouted at the Lakh girl and she complied as heavier bolts of energy bloomed about him.

His shields wavered, but somehow he held them together. Malevorn emerged from the dust clouds about thirty yards away, a bloody sword in hand. He'd lost his helm along the way, but he still looked parade-ground perfect as he strode toward them.

The world seemed to move slower about him, as if every second was twice as long as normal. He lifted his hand and sent an assault that was a bewildering blend of overwhelming fire, shards of stone from the rock fall and a telekinesis grip to hold Alaron helpless in place as he died.

He could—maybe *should*—have frozen in terror, and died then and there. But he'd been fighting Malevorn for years. Losing—but fighting. He knew what to expect. He'd never been able to stop it before, but he knew what was coming. And just as at Gydan's Cut, his instincts responded before he'd consciously willed himself to move.

It was as if his mind had fractured into separate brains: one part of him activated the Air- and Water-gnosis of the skiff while another fed his shields. Still another carried him fully ten yards in one bound to land in the center of the skiff, well clear of Malevorn's telekinetic grip. It wasn't that he was stronger than his enemy's blow; he was just no longer where it fell. He used his own telekinesis to propel the skiff away from his attacker, and now Ramita saw what he was doing and helped to pick up the skiff and hurl it forward. Her strength was truly alarming, but right now it was keeping them both alive.

Fire blasted out behind them as Malevorn came after them, filled the air in their wake. His gnosis-blasts washed over the craft, but they failed to ignite it, as the Water-gnosis Kekropius had melded into the timber protected the little vessel. But now Malevorn was moving like the wind itself. His sword was raised as he hurtled toward Alaron in a flash, and suddenly he was just yards away.

Ramita, standing behind Alaron, gestured, shouting aloud, and a wall of force picked up Malevorn and threw him bodily back into the chamber. Alaron saw his nemesis' mouth go wide with shock as he vanished back into the dark chamber, then their skiff was propelled out over the edge of the landing platform and into the air. He glanced up, saw the Inquisitors' ship ablaze in the sky above, while lightning and fire still flickered at the top of the pillar of stone. Then the skiff tilted and they plummeted toward the ocean.

Still his fractured mind did not relent. "Cover!" he shouted, letting his brain translate the word from thought into gnosis, and canvas unrolled around them in an eye-blink, enveloping the hull and closing about them as sylvanic-gnosis sealed the gaps, an instant before they nose-dived into the depths.

30

AN IRREVOCABLE CHOICE

Apostasy

Which is the greater sin: to insult your neighbor, or to insult Kore? The answer of course is that the sin of slighting Kore is the greater, for in slighting Kore you slight all men.

FURUS MITER, CARDINAL OF THE KORE, PALLAS, 589

What is sin? Sin is whatever I decide it to be.

SERTAIN, FIRST EMPEROR, PALLAS 610

Mount Tigrat, Javon, Antiopia
Zulhijja (Decore) 928
6th month of the Moontide.

Elena woke to a dagger pressed to her throat, then rough hands grasped her arms and pulled them tightly behind her. She gasped for air and was reflexively gathering her gnosis to fling her attacker away when a fist hammered into her stomach and she bent in half as pain sheeted through her. A volley of pulverizing blows to the face knocked any kind of coherent thought out of her, and she reeled in pain, her senses blurred. She dimly sensed three of them, one holding either side of her, the one with the fists now staring into her eyes. His face was blurred, as if seen through wet glass: a vicious scarred Keshi with pitiless eyes.

<Kaz—>

Her mental call ended in another savage blow and she all but blacked out. She thought there was a fourth man now. His cold hand gripped her forehead. He spoke aloud, in Rondian. "Enough, Gatoz. Let me . . ."

Then gnostic energy roiled from the newcomer's fingertips, knives of burning steel carving her brain to shreds while constrictor snakes of power wrapped about her soul, choking her. She tried to scream, but nothing came. Throbbing darkness closed down her sight, then her nerve-endings, and on and on it went as she tried to rally her gnosis to fight this other man, but he was too strong for her. Their silent struggle went on forever, until she had nothing left—nothing at all. No gnosis. Nothing.

Chain-rune. He's rukking Chained me. Oh dear God . . .

She closed her eyes for a long while, seeking calm, but she failed. She felt defiled, more utterly ravaged than if the intruders had taken turns fucking her. *That'll be next.* She tried to move, but the darkness took her down again.

When she became aware again, no one was near, though conversations buzzed somewhere in the distance. She pulled herself from the lure of oblivion by the barest of margins, drawn by a vaguely familiar voice.

I know that man . . . It took a while, but at last it came to her: *Stivor Sindon.* She opened her eyes and found him bending over her. She flinched involuntarily. His was the Chain-rune, she realized.

Sindon lifted her chin. "Well, well: the notorious Elena Anborn. Do you even know what price Mater-Imperia has set on her head, Gatoz?"

The scar-faced Keshi, Gatoz, glowered at the Magister. "She belongs to the Hadishah."

"I'm not claiming her, just making a point."

Kazim! Where's Kazim? What have they done with him?

She didn't have long to wait to find out. They picked her up and frog-marched her, still clad in her bloodstained nightdress, into the dining hall. Her eyes flew from face to face: Keshi men with hooded, blankly hostile eyes. Then she saw Kazim: standing beside the window with his arm around the shoulder of an older Keshi.

The betrayal tore at her. "*You traitorous two-faced bastard!*" she started, and he spun around, his face changing, but what to she didn't see, because Gatoz whipped around and punched her full in the face. Her nose broke, spraying blood everywhere as her head flopped sideways, and then with exaggerated slowness the shadows leaped from the corners and filled her head.

"No!" Kazim thrust Jamil away and tried to reach Gatoz. "Stop it!" For a second he thought Gatoz's blow had broken her neck, so limply her head lolled, so bonelessly she sagged in the arms of the men holding her.

You traitorous two-faced bastard. Her words seared through him. But she didn't understand—he'd been pleading on her behalf. Jamil had said she would be given a chance . . .

"Gatoz, you promised—"

Jamil caught his arm and held on to him, dragging him back, but Kazim threw him aside. He hadn't even realized that he was now bigger than his friend until that instant. He strode toward Gatoz.

The Hadishah commander turned to face him. "I promised nothing."

"But Jamil—"

"Jamil said what I told him to say." Gatoz flickered a glance over his shoulder. "Take the woman to a secure room and chain her up."

"She's on our side," Kazim protested hotly, trying to go to her, but Gatoz blocked him.

He thrust his face at Kazim and snarled, "Boy, you've been with her for four months. Where does your loyalty lie?"

Kazim glared at him, eyeball to eyeball. "To my captains," he growled through gritted teeth. "But—"

"Silence!" Gatoz barked, spraying him with spittle. "Go to your quarters, boy."

"But—"

Gatoz's palm lashed his cheek and he reeled, seeing stars. "I said *silence!* Do we need to Chain you also?"

Breathing heavily, he fought the urge to strike back. Around him the other Hadishah were watching him with hard faces and narrowed eyes. Only Jamil's face held any sympathy, and even that was muted.

He stepped back and made obeisance to Gatoz. Then he walked from the room, feeling like an utter coward. Out in the corridor, he saw the two men dragging Elena toward the storerooms. He turned to follow when someone put a hand on his shoulder. Jamil had followed him out.

"No, Kazim," he murmured, "don't. She's not worth it."

He turned to face his friend—his *blood-brother*—as his mind churned sickly. "You told me she would be safe," he whispered. It had been the first thing Jamil had said to him when he'd realized what had happened. Dhani the shopkeeper had gotten a message through somehow, and his Hadishah comrades had found him. He'd been overjoyed—until Elena's predicament became obvious.

His cheek throbbed from Gatoz's blow.

Jamil was watching him warily. "Kazim, she was never going to be allowed to remain free: surely you realize that?"

"No—no, I didn't. You promised me, brother!"

Fool! I didn't think it through, though it's so damned obvious a child could see it. Rashid doesn't want Rondian allies. Even Sindon is tolerated only for convenience.

Still he tried to bargain for her safety, for her sake and for his. "She has sworn to kill Gurvon Gyle—she's on the same mission as us!"

Jamil shook his head. "Not here, lad." He pulled Kazim toward the nearest door, which led to a scriptorium that he and Elena had never bothered to use. It was open to the skies and strewn with windblown debris, but it was empty and it had a door, which Jamil now closed.

Kazim faced his friend and spoke as quickly as he could, hoping something—*anything*—would sway him. "Listen to me, please: Alhana is *not* our enemy. She wants the Crusade defeated as much as we do. She knows Gyle's weaknesses. We need her to succeed on our mission. You've got to help me persuade Gatoz."

"Keep your voice down. Listen, Kazim, things have changed. Gyle is no longer a target now. An accommodation has been reached. We're only here to bring you home."

Kazim clutched the window frame, trying to steady himself from the feeling that the floor was shifting beneath his feet. "You've reached a *what*? He's our *enemy*."

"And also the enemy of another enemy," Jamil said quietly. "A deal has been made."

Kazim felt a wave of physical sickness, and he was overwhelmed by a feeling of utter powerlessness.

I told Dhani how we could be found without asking Elena if I should. She'd have known it was stupid. I've betrayed her with my own idiocy.

He turned away, blinking furiously. Hatred of both Crusade and shihad swirled inside his belly.

He looked at Jamil and tried again. "She has saved my life, brother. Twice. Even though she knows who and what I am."

Jamil blinked. "You told her that you are Hadishah? That you are *Souldrinker*?"

"Of course—she was training me. She knows everything about me, and I about her. She's not our enemy. She should be our ally."

Jamil shook his head and said firmly, "We never reveal ourselves to outsiders except under orders."

Kazim rolled his eyes, barely repressing his temper. "Jamil! You're my friend—you have to help me save her!"

"Save her?" Jamil looked at him pityingly. "We don't *save* Rondian women. If she is fertile, she will be taken to the breeding cages. If not, we'll cut off her head and burn the body. Those are the only paths her life will now take."

Kazim fought the urge to scream until Jamil paid attention and *listened* to him. "What about Alyssa Dulayne?" he rasped. "Rashid makes exceptions for her." *And we all know why.*

"Rashid is an emir. He does as he likes." Jamil put a hand on his shoulder, and Kazim had to restrain himself from throwing it off. He knew his friend was trying to help him—but he wasn't trying to aid Elena, so he was not his friend at all.

"Kazim, go to your quarters," Jamil said quietly. "Accept whatever punishment Gatoz gives you. Please, do not disobey him. He'll have your head on the pike beside this jadugara's if you defy him again."

Breathe in. Breathe out. Kazim hung his head. *Sweet Lord Ahm, I know he's wrong. But I need to be alone now. I need to think.*

He said slowly, "All right." He would feign repentance. *For now.* "Where is Haroun?" he asked distantly.

"He's with the skiff. We kept him back from the raid in case things got feisty. Do you want to see him?"

"I need someone to help me understand this."

Jamil frowned. Piety wasn't something either of them was prone to. But Kazim had been through a lot these past months, and he accepted the words at face value. "I'll send him to you."

"Then what?"

"Back to Halli'kut. We have the Ordo Costruo prisoners there, in breeding cages. It's where we'll take your woman, if she's fertile." Jamil cocked his head curiously. "Is she?"

The thought of Elena, caged and forced to bear children until she died, was nauseating. Everything about her—the way she walked, the way she talked, the way she lived and fought—she was all about freedom. Confinement would be a slow death sentence. *But if I say no, he'll tell Gatoz and they'll kill her.* "She bleeds every month," he said truthfully.

"Then Gatoz will likely let her live. She's older than we like, but she's a half-blood; she should still produce three or four magi-children for us. When does she bleed?"

Kazim's memory for such womanly matters was hazy at the best of times. "I think she bleeds with the new moon," he said. That was now.

Jamil grunted. "Good. We'll have her in the Krak di Condotiori before she ovulates again." He looked at Kazim with something like sympathy. "Listen, Kaz, I know it's hard to see a woman you've been bedding treated this way. Ahm Himself knows I find the breeding cages an ugly necessity. But it's for the greater good." He exhaled thickly. "I was born in one, remember?"

"I wasn't bedding her," he replied stonily. "She is nefara."

Jamil raised an eyebrow, then shrugged. "None of my business," he said skeptically. "Come, let's get you into your room before Gatoz comes looking for you. He's going to want a strip of your hide for standing up to him in front of the men."

Kazim let Jamil lead him back to his room, but he pushed him away when he tried to enter. As he heard the door bolted behind him he started fuming inside.

Even Jamil doesn't trust me now. Or maybe he thinks he's protecting me.

He sat on his bed, feeling useless. He flexed his hands in front of himself, studying his palms. The delicate, hard-earned pact he shared with Elena seemed vital now, in ways he couldn't even describe to himself. If he could not persuade Gatoz that she was more use to the shihad as an ally than a slave, she was destined for a slow death locked in a cage where she would be subjected to multiple rape and repeated pregnancies until her womb was no longer any use, and at the end, death without burial . . . and if she did not quicken—

He silently promised her that he'd save her from such a fate, one way or another.

He had no idea how much time had passed when he finally heard the bolts on his door drawn back. It was dark outside, the new moon a thin arc covering half the sky. As Gatoz entered, his hands crackled with energy, and all the candles in the room flared to life. Kazim was suddenly conscious that his own gnosis was burned away; he was near helpless against even the least of the men here. The emptiness inside, the hollow space where his gnosis had been, echoed inside him.

Gatoz stalked toward him. "Well, boy?"

He looked up, trying to quell his desire to lash out. "What?"

"You've been here four months. What have you been doing?"

What indeed? Kazim explained in as flat a voice as he could— *keep it factual, don't sound attached to her*—starting by relating how Elena had rescued him when he was dying from Mara Secordin's venom, how they'd found they both wished to kill Gurvon Gyle and so had agreed to work together.

"We were almost ready to move," he added. "She has showed me her Rondian fighting and gnosis skills. We were planned to return to Brochena at the turn of the year and carry out our mission."

Gatoz pursed his lips, looking as if this were all interesting, but quite irrelevant. "Gyle is no longer a target," he said baldly. "We were preparing to move back into Kesh when your message reached us. We flew here as soon as we heard."

Kazim swallowed and tried to frame one final plea. "She's on our side, Gatoz. I swear it." But if Gyle was no longer a target, he knew Gatoz would ignore him. "Gyle is still an enemy," he repeated.

"Of course he is," Gatoz agreed. "But he is not our target for now." He put a hand on Kazim's head as if he were talking to a child. "Listen, boy, Rashid favors you, for what you might become. But all I see is a feckless child who is sulking because he can't play with his toys. If a soldier refused to pick up his sword and insisted on fighting with his bare hands instead, it would not be tolerated, would it? Nor would he last. Rashid says you can be an asset, and therefore we tolerate you." Gatoz dropped his voice to a menacing growl. "But it's pissing me off. You hear me?"

Kazim hung his head.

"I do not tolerate the sort of shit you give out from anyone, but Rashid says I must. That's a shame, because I'd like to punch your pretty face in."

And I'd like to cut your throat. Kazim couldn't stop himself from glaring back at the other man, wishing he had a weapon—any weapon—

Gatoz poked him in the chest. "I'm prepared to think the white witch has warped your head. Maybe you don't even know how wrapped around her fingers you are."

"It wasn't like that," Kazim said hoarsely.

"Then how was it?" Gatoz asked him. "Jamil says you didn't even fuck her." He snickered. "Then again, she probably doesn't want some mudskin's lingum inside her precious white yoni."

Kazim found himself trembling with the effort of not lashing out. "She's not like that—"

"They're all like that, boy," Gatoz scoffed. "Women are like crows, they pick at a man until there's nothing left but bones. They're only good for one thing." He spat on the floor. "Think on it, boy. Are you with us or not? Because we're flying south to war and Rashid expects you to be with us, and filled with holy fire. I wouldn't let him down if I was you."

Kazim hung his head. "Am I a prisoner?"

Gatoz appraised him carefully. "Until someone can use mysticism-gnosis to check the inside of your head, I've got to treat you as suspect, so for tonight, you're going to stay in here." He straightened, looking around, then with a gesture, sealed the windows shut with glittering wards that flared, then faded to invisibility.

"You don't need to lock me in," Kazim said, hating how small his voice sounded.

"Boy, I think I do. And I'm the one who decides." He strolled nonchalantly toward the door.

Kazim hung his head. From the bottom of what felt like a pit of despair, he asked, "What will you do to Elena?"

An ugly look crossed Gatoz's face and he paused in the doorway. "She's got the only yoni in this dump and I'm going to use it." He cocked his head and smiled at Kazim. The smile never reached his eyes. "And knowing you're pining for her will just make it all the sweeter."

Red-hot hatred blazed behind Kazim's eyes, so fierce he could barely see. How he kept from leaping at the man he could not tell. "She's on blood-purdah," he started babbling, seeking any excuse that might stop Gatoz from defiling her. "She is polluted—she is nefara. Your soul—"

Gatoz looked at him in surprise, then roared with laughter. "You believe in that shit?" he hooted derisively. "Boy, when you're a little older, you'll see the lies of the Scriptualists for what they are." He backed away, measuring Kazim with his eyes. "Don't do anything stupid, boy. Think of where your future lies."

Then he was gone and the door bolt clanged behind him. As Kazim watched the door in despair, light flared about the frame: Gatoz had added a gnostic seal for good measure.

Kazim was trapped. He sat alone in the darkened room, fresh tears glistening in the candlelight.

Elena surfaced in a wet sea of pain. Her face felt like a mallet had been taken to it, and her stomach muscles throbbed where she'd been punched. For a few moments four lights floated unsteadily in front of her before resolving into two candles high on the opposite wall. She tried to pull her arms to her chest, but manacles held them spread apart. She could rise maybe six inches off the pallet before the tautness of the chains prevented anything further.

She sagged back, panting. Two flies were crawling across the dried blood on her face. She shook her head, and they lifted off for a moment, then buzzed back down and settled again.

No. Please, no—not this.

Clearly Kazim had contacted his Hadishah friends. The last sight of him, his arm slung companionably over the shoulder of one of her captors, tore at her soul. She'd invested so much in the boy—and she would have sworn they were beginning to understand each other. She hated to think that she could have been wrong about him.

I saved his life—not once, but twice. How could he have done that—?

But Cera did the same, her callous memory reminded her, and her heart sank. There must be something in her that was wrong, that everyone she cared about would betray her . . .

She groaned and tried to move her legs, but they were bound too, one foot to either bed-post, holding her legs spread apart. She didn't need to imagine what came next.

She could almost hear Gurvon's voice: *"Well, old girl: this is what you get for trusting people. What happened to you? You used to be the most cynical bitch alive. Still, it's only what you deserve."*

The door opened and Magister Stivor Sindon came in, wrapped in a thick velvet cloak, his pate gleaming, his chubby, bearded face looking faintly amused. He settled on a chair beside the bed and lit a pipe. "So, Elena Anborn. You've come down a long way in the world."

"Get me out of this and I'll work for you," she said. She didn't expect for a heartbeat he'd do that, but she had to at least go through the motions.

He puffed at his pipe for a moment as if contemplating her offer, then the wry smile on his face dropped and he said coldly, "Don't insult my intelligence, Elena. You're worthless to me. And I certainly never liked you."

She gave up the pleading immediately. "Totally mutual, Sindon."

"Ah, that's more like the Elena Anborn I know." He tutted amiably. "Gatoz will be here shortly. I've let him know you're awake." He made a faux-distressed face. "The man's an animal. Pure appetite. And always hungry."

She looked away. *I won't beg.*

"What I don't understand is *why*, Elena. Clearly you and Gyle had the Nesti tied up between you—don't bother trying to explain why you went to the trouble of aiding both sides last year, I'm sure it's too devious, even for me. But why did you vanish when our attack on Gyle failed in Julsep?" He sighed when she didn't respond and asked, "So have you genuinely fallen out with him this time, eh?"

She stared into space, wishing the man gone, wanting nothing more than to get this messy rape and murder thing over with. She'd always known her life would end like this. It was part of the game, after all.

Sindon rattled on, "The boy, Kazim Makani: you know what he is, don't you? He's *Dokken*. He murdered Antonin Meiros and drank his soul—he's got power to burn and then some. I expect you already know this. Did you intend to make him your pet assassin, to get back at Gyle?"

No. I took him in out of curiosity, and then I began to care, she admitted to herself. It wasn't something she would ever say out loud. Then she wondered, *Is it better to love foolishly than not to love at all?* Except it wasn't love, was it? It was just another might-have-been on the way to an unmarked grave or a midden for hungry jackals.

The door opened and Gatoz strode in.

She winced at the sight of him. He oozed brutality.

Gatoz flicked a finger toward the door, indicating Sindon should leave; he didn't bother to speak a word. The Ordo Costruo magus threw Elena a look that was completely without sympathy, then left.

Gatoz locked the door behind him with bolt and gnosis, then came and stood over her. He didn't speak, not even to taunt her, and his silence was in its own way more frightening than any threat or promise of violence or death. Men who talked could be swayed. But this one had that peculiar look to him; he was both fanatic and pragmatist, a man for whom the cause was everything and the means irrelevant. She'd met men like him in the Kirkegarde. They'd made her blood run cold.

He pulled from his belt a long, wickedly curved knife. The well-honed blade gleamed in the candlelight as he used it to flick up the hem of her nightshift.

He stared at her cleft in silence for a long, long time, then he raised his flinty eyes and she could feel them crawling over her like a physical sensation. His hatred—that he *despised* her—was clear, and so too was his brutal strength. He would make this hurt, and he would feel no guilt in doing so.

"You don't have to do this," she said in his language, trying to pitch her voice somewhere between pride and pleading, to appeal to his better nature.

"No, I do," he replied. His voice was low, level, completely objective. "It is both expected and required."

He slid closer, pushed her thighs apart and sniffed her, then pushed her hem up above her breasts and examined the muscles of her stomach, prodding with the hilt of his vicious dagger.

"Let me tell you why. While we investigated Kazim's disappearance, we spoke to many Jhafi. All praised you, for *deigning* to take our part. I saw little girls in the street, waving sticks and shouting, playing at being Alhana the White Witch. They truly wanted to be *you*."

Good for them, she thought, unable to tear her eyes from the blade as it caressed her belly.

"You are a sickness, Alhana. A woman's place is very carefully defined in the Kalistham, and for stepping outside those boundaries—and for encouraging others to follow—for that alone you deserve to be brought low. That you are magi, white, and a godless infidel only adds weight to the need to publicly destroy you. We must make any woman who thinks of your fate shudder. So that is what we will do."

The low, seething fury behind his lifeless voice crushed her. She felt her face empty of color as sick fear took over. It was as if he saw her degradation as some divinely decreed task.

"What—?" She choked on the question, and couldn't finish the words. After all, she already knew . . .

He reversed the dagger in his grip and showed it to her. "Tonight, I am going to use you as you have never before been used. A woman's place is on her back, in service of her man. The only words that will leave your mouth will be in praise of my manhood, and cries of pleasure. You will gyrate your hips for me like the whore that you are, and you will seek to climax when I do. Should you reach that release, I will refrain using this blade on you, but should you not climax as I do, then I will carve off a part of your body—your ears, or your nose, or your scalp, or an eye, perhaps. You need none of those to bear children for the Hadishah."

Oh Kore Oh Kore please please please help me please save me—

"And when we are done and you are pregnant, I will parade you, a mutilated horror, through the streets of Javon as an example to all young Amteh women: this is what becomes of females who seek to elevate themselves." His eyes bored into hers. "So do I need to tell you more of what will happen if you resist?"

She shook her head mutely. Her belly was churning and her raising panic was barely contained.

"Excellent."

He placed the blade on the table beside the bed, and then slowly began to unbuckle his belt.

Kazim stared out the window at the night. If he raised his hand to the open window, light crackled and pushed the digit away: the wards were there to keep him in.

Think of where your future lies.

Was this his future now? Was he to be nothing more than a plaything of powerful men who would reward or punish him as they saw fit? Men who would enslave a woman, even one who shared their goals, just to breed more killers; men who would manipulate him and twist his every desire to their own purposes; men who had not earned their great gift but been born with it, but who nonetheless strutted about as if they deserved worship.

Gatoz and Rashid are no better than the Rondian magi, he admitted at last.

He could not wipe Elena's face from his mind: that last look, betrayed and confused, frightened—*helpless,* when she never was helpless. Superimposed over that was the sight of her, sword in hand as they trained: poised and alert, perfectly balanced, infinitely capable.

I lost Ramita.

I don't want to lose Elena too.

And that led to the thought he truly could not face: of Gatoz, and what he would do to her. He felt his blood sizzle in his veins and found himself groping around for a weapon—any weapon . . . But of course they'd all been taken from him.

This is the trust they have in me . . .

The bolt outside drew back amidst a small flash of energy and the door opened. He wanted it to be Jamil, offering to help, but instead it was Haroun.

Succor for my soul, he thought with a new cynical bitterness that shocked him so much he almost expected Ahm to strike him down—but all that happened was that Haroun said something in a low voice to someone outside and the door shut again. New wards flared—presumably set by a guard-mage outside, the part of his brain that could still analyze noted.

Haroun approached cautiously. "Kazim, my brother." He seized Kazim by the shoulders and kissed both cheeks. He looked genuinely distraught at this situation. "What has this jadugara done to you?"

Kazim shook his head. "Nothing at all."

Haroun looked troubled. "Brother, I doubt you would even be aware of how different you are, but I must tell you: you are not the Kazim we love."

He dismissed the notion instantly and instead asked, "Can a nefara woman be redeemed?"

Haroun's eyebrows lifted, then he frowned and his face took on the familiar look of studied intensity he reserved for the deepest of theological questions. "Of course a woman of the Amteh can be redeemed—but I must presume you are talking about this jadugara, this Ahlana woman, yes?" He smiled sadly. "That is impossible, my brother. Those spawned by Shaitan are beyond Ahm's love."

"But you've told me that Ahm loves all Creation—"

"All of *His* Creation, Kazim. The spawn of Shaitan are outside of his ambit. They are less than the mud in the fields, less than the shit from a cow's bowels. They are pollution itself. Such is the being with whom you have been consorting."

Kazim nodded slowly, sadly. He noticed that Haroun's eating knife was missing from his scabbard: another indication that he really was a prisoner here. The darkness closed in on him.

"Kazim, I will plead your case," the young Scriptualist said gently. "Gatoz will understand that you have been bewitched. I doubt you will even be flogged. An example will be made of the Rondian whore, of course—perhaps her limbs will be lopped off; that will not impair her breeding, but it might be sufficient retribution for her perfidy."

Kazim swallowed a mouthful of bile. "Thank you, Haroun," he croaked. "You've made everything clear to me now." *Utterly clear.*

"I am here to serve, Kazim." Haroun preened a little. "Magister Sindon will be here shortly to examine your mind. If what the jadugara has done to you is simple, he may even be able to restore you himself."

Kazim put his arm around the skinny Scriptualist's shoulders as if in affection and said softly, "Thank you for coming."

Haroun beamed with pride as Kazim slid his arm around further. And *wrenched*.

Haroun's neck snapped audibly. His face lost the smile and went slack. His eyes started losing focus as his body sagged into Kazim's arms. Kazim lowered him to the ground, covered his mouth and nose with his own mouth and inhaled. He tasted something dry and smoky in his mouth and sucked it down, and kept inhaling as sensations flooded him, a scarlet tide of memories drawn from the failing body . . .

A brutish father and a protective mother . . . Bullying brothers and a sister who was too pretty for her own virtue . . . Escape, to a masjid, learning at the feet of the Scriptualists, wanting only to belong . . . Rape at the hands of two soldiers in a back alley, a suicide attempt . . . Examinations and praise, sudden elevation . . . Watching those two soldiers being crucified on trumped-up charges, and the first inkling of power . . . being set to watch a promising young boy from Aruna Nagar, a Keshi boy, who could run like the wind . . .

Kazim swallowed, and felt the hollow inside him where the gnosis waited fill up. "Thank you, brother," he whispered bitterly. Everything Haroun had ever been to him was a lie. "Thank you for *everything."*

Haroun ceased to exist. The cloud of memories and consciousness dissipated into pure energy which Kazim gulped down, taking it into himself until it became *potential,* became gnosis, straining for release.

He dragged the body behind the door then washed his face in the basin and composed himself, drawing a mental map of the monastery from his memory. He could guess where they'd taken Elena: the secure cellar with the heavy door. The sapphire periapt still hung from his neck—he'd never taken it off, though it was of no use to him.

She gave it to me . . .

It weighed on his neck like an unfulfilled promise.

Lessons from the Hadishah on how to move silently, how to kill, even without weapons, combined with lessons from Elena on use of the gnosis. He'd never had the energy—or the inclination—to learn any more than how to defend his mind and body from other magi, but he could feel the *potential* for more. Whatever he unleashed might not be elegant or precise, but he would make sure it was *potent.*

He was halfway to the door when the wards flared again, the bolt rasped and it swung open. He darted to the side, behind the in-swinging door, and grasped the only thing to hand: a candle from the wall holder. He pinched it out.

A man stepped through: Magister Sindon, come to fix his mind, shielded and warded and already speaking as he approached: "Haroun, are you finish—?"

Yes. Haroun is finished.

It wasn't a complicated attack: Kazim simply filled the candle with telekinetic gnosis so that it would keep its shape, then whipped it around the door, through the Magister's unfocused shields and straight into his left eye. All the way in.

The Ordo Costruo man gasped faintly and deflated to the floor, the candle stuck in his eye socket. Kazim was over him and flying at the guard-mage in one movement. He'd assumed the guard was magi because of the wards that had flickered on and off, so he took no chances: he blazed away with the same lightning he'd nearly killed himself with at the river, blasting it through the Hadishah man's shields before he could gather them properly. The electricity earthed on the man's armor and as Kazim watched, he jolted then thrashed and spasmed, while the metal armor went from cold gray to a white-hot flare in an instant. The man clattered against the wall and slid to the stone floor, still shaking.

Some poor woman had been kept in a cage so that this man could be born. A woman like Elena. He'd known this in the back of his mind, but until now he'd never really *thought* about it, never taken in the whole truth of what that meant.

The scimitar and dagger he pulled from the smoking corpse were still crackling with energy, and he fed them with more as he flitted along the corridor, the image of Gatoz violating Elena spurring him on.

He got to the stairs going upward undetected and silently flowed up them, gathering his cloak and hood about him to conceal any flash of skin.

Footsteps...

He ducked into a doorway, the privy doorway, and let someone pass, then emerged behind the man and while he slammed the dagger through his back into his heart with his right hand, his left arm went around the man's face, smothering his coughing gasp. He winced as the man bit, hard—his last conscious act—leaving a faint imprint of teeth, even through the thick cloth of his cloak. He pulled the body into the privy and even as he shut the door, the room had already filled with the stench of voiding bladder and bowels. He had no idea who the man was, or if he'd even met him before, but he had been in his way. He considered taking more energy, but found he didn't need to. It appeared that one soul—any soul—was enough to replenish his gnosis completely.

He moved onwards, striding purposefully.

The final corridor was before him. The dining hall was there, and from the noise, it sounded like most of the Hadishah were there. Cooking smoke wafted down the corridor along with the chatter of voices and the clatter of plates. He walked past, hood up, and hoped no one looked in his direction. No one did.

Once clear of the dining room, he pounded down the spiraling stairs into the monastery's storage rooms, pulling himself to an abrupt halt at the bottom. His caution was repaid; when he peered around the corner he saw a man there, some fifteen feet away. He was clearly a Hadishah mage, for he was playing a gnosis game with his dagger, balancing the tip on his fingertips and making it spin, first one way, then back again. A barred door was at his back.

Kazim composed himself, gathered more energy and *reached*.

The man juggling the dagger never even felt the attack: one instant he was using his gnosis to flip his dagger from finger to finger; the next, it was ripped from his control and punched into his own throat. He choked on blood, the air in his throat bubbling wetly, and slid down the wall. His eyes went to Kazim as he tried to fight the blood-loss, repair the wound, but Kazim worked the strands of force with all his strength in a sawing movement and the blade wrenched sideways, left and right, left and right, until he felt the man's spinal cord snap. The lights went out in his eyes before the blood jetting out of his neck had petered out to a trickle.

He crossed the remaining distance, stepped over the body and placed his finger on the door-handle. He could feel the tingle of power there: strong, but not Ascendant-level strong, and therefore not strong enough. He inserted his own power into the flow of forces, just as Elena had taught him, and was a little surprised at how easily he disrupted the ward. It fizzled out with a sharp "pop," and he wasted no time in launching himself through the door.

Elena had her eyes closed when the door crashed open, but her eyelids flew up as a cloaked and hooded figure burst into the chamber. Gatoz was unbuckling his belt, but in the intervening second between breaking in and attacking, somehow the Hadishah captain managed to draw his sword.

Not that it availed Gatoz. The newcomer had lightning crackling down the blade of his own sword and she saw the energy leaping between the blades as they clashed, saw Gatoz jolting, his limbs jerking involuntarily with each parry. The Hadishah man howled as there was a brilliant flash and he was thrown backward, slamming into the far wall of the room with a loud *crack!*

But Gatoz was not done; he launched a left-handed bolt that seared the air about the newcomer's head—but the man was *fast*, arching his body away from Gatoz's blast, which sprayed fire over the wall. His hood fell back and she saw Kazim, his face enraged, teeth bared, and eyes wide, and for the first time since she'd been shaken awake, all those hours ago, she felt a surge of hope—and *pride*—as Kazim—her *blood-brother*—leaped at Gatoz, slashing down hard as the Hadishah man tried to adjust his shielding to cope with the lightning. Their blades crashed together again, the clanging steel echoing about the room.

They were both big men, and both were fast, and their skills had been fed by practice and augmented by gnosis. But Kazim had been training with her for months now, and he had been working very hard. She could clearly see the differences between the boy he had been and the man he now was: Gatoz bucked, while Kazim flowed. Kazim danced, while the other man merely fought. Though Kazim's gnosis-attacks were clumsy, his defense was not. Gatoz tried to blast at him and was shielded with a grace that obviously surprised him—but not her. For her, there would be only one winner.

But it wasn't happening fast enough. She heard shouting, and the thunder of footsteps on the stairs, and shouted, "Kazim, they're coming!"

He heard her and immediately launched another attack at the increasingly beleaguered Gatoz—but the man was no fool, and instead of trying in vain to hit Kazim, he was concentrating on defense, buying time until his men could arrive, content to be driven back and back until he was pinned against the far wall. The boots were closer, though they'd slowed—someone was urging caution, obviously—but still only seconds remained.

She cursed her helplessness and cried, "Kazim, get me out of this!"

There was no finesse in what he did; he just flung out his left hand in her direction, and a wall of force struck the bed like a hurricane wind. The bed flew sideways and upward at bone-wrenching speed, just as the door opened and two Hadishah spilled into the room. It struck them like a runaway wagon, crushing the first against the wall and knocking the other backward into his fellows outside. She caught a flash of bewildered faces as they shouted out in shock, then the head- and tail-boards splintered. She almost wrenched her left arm from its socket, but Kazim's brutal spell had worked: the frame had broken and she was able to pull her right arm free, though it was still chained. Seconds later she had kicked her legs free too.

She glimpsed a flash of steel—Gatoz's dagger, lying where it had fallen on the floor—and she snatched it up just in time as the next Hadishah vaulted the bed. He landed on his feet above her and thrust down, trying to skewer her through the belly, but she twisted her body away and his blade buried itself in the mattress. She contorted back and slashed the tendon behind his ankle and the man shrieked and fell. She buried Gatoz's knife in his chest, just to be sure.

Then Kazim bellowed in pain and her eyes whipped around. He might have saved her, but he had been catastrophically distracted in doing so and Gatoz had taken the opportunity of his moment's distraction to plunge his sword into Kazim's side.

The Hadishah snarled in triumph as Kazim's left hand flew to the blade jammed in his flesh.

And held it there.

She saw Gatoz's eyes bulge as he realized what Kazim was doing. His sword was stuck in his foe's body and his knife was sticking out of the Hadishah Elena had just killed—he had no weapon left. Kazim ignored the pain of the wound and drove his own scimitar up under Gatoz's ribcage, then he twisted it and, very slowly, pulled it back.

The Hadishah let go of his sword as his legs began to sag.

Elena could see the massive effort Gatoz was making to ward off the oncoming darkness—*die you pig die*—but then she heard someone else pushing his way over the broken bed and she spun around to find a man in full armor standing there, staring into the room, looking horribly conflicted.

He looked at her and as their eyes met, his face hardened.

She yanked in vain at the one remaining chain still binding her to the broken headboard, though her damaged shoulder screamed in protest. *Damn this fighting with no gnosis!*

There was no time to retrieve the dagger. She whipped her free arm around, caught the chain and whirled it, lashing out at the newcomer, who caught it easily on his sword—but he hadn't been expecting it to wrap about his blade the way it did. She tugged hard on it and yanked him sideways as he swore and tried to wrench the weapon free. He barely noticed Kazim approaching—until her blood-brother's blade punched in under his right armpit and into his chest.

The other Hadishah standing in the doorway about to enter the room lost his nerve and started backing away.

Kazim wrenched Gatoz's blade from his own side and a great gout of blood stained his tunic, but he ignored the wound as the man he'd stabbed tottered, then sprawled across the mattress at her feet, his eyes glazing over. Instead Kazim made for the door, where the retreating attacker was backed up against his fellows. Freed from any need for stealth, he raised his hands, channeled his gnosis and spewed flame into the corridor.

The effect was devastating, and Elena heard its effect as she ducked to escape the searing heat that backwashed into the room.

There was a clamor of agonized shrieking, but the voices stopped almost as quickly as they had begun. She heard body after body clatter to the ground.

Her skin was wet with sweat and the close air heavy with smoke and the taint of burning flesh. She looked up at Kazim and started, "Kaz, we've got to get out of here. The smoke—"

He wasn't looking at her; he was leaning over the armored man lying at her feet, a middle-aged warrior with a world-weary face. "Brother," he said softly, "I'm sorry."

The man opened his mouth and blood bubbled up among his words. "You chose her. Don't ever call me brother again."

Kazim's face contorted in momentary sadness, then all emotion left his face. As Elena watched, he bent over the fallen man and kissed his bloodied lips as he died. To her horror she realized what she was seeing: a Dokken, drinking souls. Then he straightened, and his eyes were glazed and disoriented. She was almost too frightened to move.

Abruptly he blinked, and was *Kazim* again. He picked her up in his arms and with one swift tug, pulled the last chain out of the headboard. He cradled her against him like a child, and she could feel his own heart was hammering and he too was sodden with sweat. She clung to him, shaking, as he blasted a breathable path through the smoke with Air-gnosis.

They emerged to find the monastery ringing with silence. He put her down gently on a bed—her own bed—and she collapsed there, shaking with relief.

He hadn't said a word, not since the armored man he'd killed had withdrawn his brotherhood.

He did that for me.

"Kaz?" she asked gently, "Are you all right?"

He stared at her as if seeing her for the first time, then his eyes narrowed. He looked dangerous, and she fought not to flinch as he demanded, "Did you do things to my mind, to make me love you?"

She stared up at him. *Love?*

His voice was trembling with emotion. His hands were trembling with restrained violence.

What lies have they told him?

"Did they tell you that? Kazim, for four months we've fought like cat and dog! We've spent half the time screaming at each other and the other half trying to beat each other to a pulp—does that sound like *love* to you?"

He stared at her, and his eyes suddenly welled up. "No," he choked out, "no, it doesn't."

Unbelievably, she felt a bubble of laughter escape her throat. "Of course, maybe I'm just rukking useless at charming people."

"You are," he told her. He scrubbed furiously at his face. "So why is it that I just killed my friends for you?"

She gulped for breath and her heart stuttered, then it pounded on again, painfully hard. She had an overwhelming urge to wash all the blood and smoke and death away, to make *him* clean again—but all she could do was cling to him in her bloodied nightshift and try not to collapse.

Eventually, some kind of control, even decorum, reasserted itself between them. He looked around for her cloak, plucked it from the hook and wrapped it around her. Once she was decently covered, he looked at her again, this time with a bleak sadness in his eyes.

"I was a fool," he said simply. "I thought they would welcome you, for your aid against Gyle. But they've reached an *accommodation* with him."

Have they? Gurvon, you devious prick!

"Did Gatoz—?"

She shook her head. "You were on time. Like an answer to a prayer."

He flinched at that, as if the thought of her prayers was unwelcome. "Have they done anything else to you?" he demanded.

"They placed a Chain-rune on me," she told him. "It won't fade just because the caster is dead." She reached out and took his hand and pressed it to the middle of her chest. "You need to reach inside me and disrupt it—as if it's a locking ward you're opening. It'll hurt me, but only a little, and I'll soon recover."

He closed his eyes and laid both hands on her chest, and then she felt a sharp popping sensation, like a small explosion. She gasped, but the pain quickly faded and she immediately felt her gnosis begin to flow again, replenishing her like water reviving a withered plant.

"Thank you," she whispered. She straightened her nose, rejoicing as her healing-gnosis flowed unimpeded. "Thank you so much."

He squeezed her hand, then stood. "I need to find the rest of them."

"Wait," she told him, "let's heal you first. It'll be quicker in the long run." She quickly stopped his bleeding and loosely sealed the wound in his side, then she filled the water bowl from the ewer on the nightstand and charged the fluid with clairvoyance-gnosis. She scanned quickly, going room to room, from the top of the monastery to the bottom, seeking signs of movement or energy.

"I'm not getting anything," she muttered, "but they could be using runes of hiding."

"We'll check every room," he replied. His eyes still looked bleak.

She admired his determination as much as she pitied his loss. She seized his hands and looked up into his eyes. "Kazim, I don't know what to say—you came for me." Her voice was filled with wonder. "I don't even know why—"

She saw him swallow.

He did it because he loves you, you idiot.

He composed his face and met her eyes. "What Gatoz was going to do to you—it was wrong—and the others just stood aside, even Jamil. So I had to stop them." He looked away. "How can they claim to oppose evil when they do these things? You can't clean floors with a bucket of blood."

It sounded like something from the Kalistham. She couldn't have put it better if she'd tried.

"I hate what the Crusade is doing to my land," he went on, "but the way the Hadishah tries to resist—that is *wrong*. Our own people live in fear of us. There has to be another way. I thought the shihad would be pure, but it's been corrupted. It's not holy anymore—maybe it never was. How can you find paradise by killing innocent people?"

She squeezed his hands and said quietly, "If you wish it, we can end our pact, Kazim. No debts. You could go home—"

"I have no home anymore," he told her. "I have no home left but you."

No home left but you. She stepped into his arms and hugged him tightly, struggling to control her own tears, while he stroked her hair and promised naïvely stupid things about keeping her safe.

31

HEADS WILL ROLL

Morphic Gnosis

There is much that is laudable about morphic-gnosis, includ-
ing the ability to improve oneself physically to improve lon-
gevity, strength, speed, and appearance. Within this Craft lie
the seeds of a better human being. But why do we continue to
teach our young magi how to take another's form, when to do
so offers such obvious criminal purpose?

SENATOR RANN DEVEREU,
PALLAS LEGISLATURE 776

Brochena, Javon, Antiopia
Zulhijja (Decore) 928
6th month of the Moontide

Cera was marched from the dungeons and up into the palace, flanked
by two soldiers whose gauntleted hands were clamped upon her upper
arms. Armed men were everywhere, and the occasional Dorobon
courtier—Octa's people, not Francis's. She'd been in her cell for hours
with neither food nor water, and she felt dizzy and ill. She dimly recognized where she was: a small parlor on the ground floor. The Lantric
woman was waiting for her again. The soldier let her go and her limbs
failed her, leaving her groveling helpless on the floor.

"Leave us," the Lantric mage snapped, and the soldiers immediately did as they were ordered.

"You did this," Cera snarled.

The woman smirked. "I did. I, Hesta Mafagliou of Lantris. You're only human, girl; *I* am a mage. I can do whatever I want with cattle like you."

Cera buried her face in her hands. "I'll tell them. I'll—"

"Tell who?" Hesta said scornfully. She bent over and wrenched Cera's hands away from her face, then slapped her. The blow made her head ring. "Shut up, girl. You will say exactly what I wish you to say." She pulled Cera's face to hers. "Or I will also betray your little finger-and-tongue sessions with Portia Tolidi to Octa Dorobon and your precious safian lover will die alongside you."

Cera's words of defiance turned to dirt in her throat. "No," she choked.

Hesta pursed her lips, and for a moment at least she looked faintly sympathetic. There was pity in her voice as she said, "Believe me girl, I know what you're going through. I too had my world pulled down around me for a love others see as unnatural. It's not fair, but what is? In the end, life is a struggle, and the winner takes all. I would make a corpse of all the world to have back what I lost."

Cera tried to look away, but the woman's eyes and mind latched onto her like the tentacles of a river-squid. "This, little queen, is what you will tell the tribunal . . ."

Sometime later the soldiers came again and half-carried, half-dragged Cera into the midst of many seated men: Amteh God-speakers and Sollan priests; the Kore bishop, Eternalus Crozier, and more. Some were familiar—she saw Acmed al'Istan, who had sat at her council table, and Drui Ivan Prato, her childhood confessor—but they all looked at her as if she had sprouted demon horns.

Eternalus Crozier rose to his feet, as the doors slammed shut. "Cera Nesti, you are accused of adultery with Gurvon Gyle, murderer of your father. How do you plead?"

I'm innocent, she tried to scream, but instead, she said, "Guilty," the word coming out with the exact intonation Hesta had implanted when she had spoken it into her skull. More words followed, and she let them spill out, not even bothering to listen to herself: made-up stories of lurid couplings, straight from Hesta's imaginings. Her eyes bled tears.

"You are also accused of plotting with Gurvon Gyle to usurp the realm and overthrow the king. How do you plead?"

"Guilty."

Why not? If I have to die, let that prick join me.

Eternalus Crozier's voice was dispassionate; Acmed's eyes condemning; even gentle Ivan Prato's face was filled with disgust.

There was little else to be said. Under Amteh law she could be stoned, but the Crozier showed her mercy, of a sort, by condemning her instead to a Yuros-style beheading.

No one pleaded for her or on her behalf.

First, though, came the paperwork. All afternoon they put before her scrolls filled with the details of the lies Octa Dorobon had contrived to implicate her enemies: secret meetings, names she barely knew, people she'd never met—magi of Gyle's contingent; Francis's friends, even a mercenary captain called Endus Rykjard.

That gave her a momentary spark of hope that soon Dorobon and mercenary would be at each other's throats, but that died as the litany of made-up accusations went on and on. They even named officials based in Pallas, but she no longer cared. She confessed to everything they wanted.

The documentation finally completed, she was led back to her narrow cell.

Eternalus Crozier accompanied her to the door of her cell without uttering a word. Only as he opened the door did he finally break the silence. "Do you wish to confess your sins before you die?"

"I am Sollan," she replied, as defiantly as she could. "Your God is nothing to me."

His face twisted nastily. "Then you will suffer for eternity in Hel regardless," he told her. "The headsman will be here in ten minutes."

She blinked. "What? But the law—" The law demanded three months between sentence and execution of the condemned, in case grounds for appeal were found.

"You are beneath the law. Prepare yourself for death."

They entered together, the two Dorobon women: Octa waddling triumphantly, Olivia a lesser shadow in her wake. Gurvon was chained to a wall of the cell, battered and bleeding. Three ribs had been broken, and his face had been pummeled to rawness. Every breath was agony. His ears still rang, and blood and snot encrusted his face.

"Well," boomed Octa jovially. "What a sad comedown, Magister Gyle! Look at you: all broken, and about to lose your head. We've decided not to wait until morning. Every second that you are alive makes me nervous. Tradition can go fuck itself: I want you dead now."

She snapped her fingers, and a hooded executioner marched in, ax in hand.

"Mommy, do I have to watch?" Olivia said, wrinkling up her nose.

"Yes, dear, you must," Octa said nastily. "You were prepared to bed him, so you can jolly well watch him die."

Olivia pouted. "It was just *rukking*, Mother. I didn't have anything to do with his plots and plans—he never even *mentioned* them."

He could hear the undercurrent of fear in her voice.

"Of course not. Gurvon Gyle was hardly going to confide in a silly chit like you, my dumpling. No one would ever think that."

"Thank you, Mother," Olivia gushed. She looked on the verge of tears, but he didn't for a moment think they were for him.

"There, there. He was never really interested in you, darling child." Octa patted her daughter's cheeks. "He was just using you to try and win poor Francis's trust, all the while conniving with that evil Nesti minx behind our backs. If he had other lovers we'll find them and we'll chop off their heads too."

The headsman unlocked his manacles. A Chain-rune shackled Gyle's gnosis, and his body was a throbbing mess. Escape was not a possibility. The moment his wrists were released from manacles he collapsed to his knees, jarring them painfully.

"Just because someone slept with Gurvon doesn't make her a traitor," Olivia said worriedly.

"It does if it suits me, darling," Octa purred.

She knew about everything Olivia had done; he could hear it in her voice. But family was different. Excuses could always be found for family.

Octa clicked her fingers and another guard came in, carrying a heavy canvas bag. When Octa gestured, he opened the bag and tipped it over, so that the contents were able to fall to the floor. The two heads that rolled from it thudded wetly against the stone. Mathieu Fillon, and the mage Sordell had inhabited. He wondered if Sordell's scarab was just a smear on the floor somewhere, but he didn't have long to brood on the question, for there was a noise in the corridor outside, then another jailer came in, rolling a big block of wood into the center of the room. It had a notch in it, and it was encrusted in blood both old and fresh.

An executioner's block.

Gyle stared at it, the unreality of this moment creeping over him. *Is this really it? After all these years, and all I've done? It can't be—*

"Get it over with, man," Octa growled, and at her command the executioner hefted his great ax. She groped for a leather bag of coin dangling at her waist and jingled it enticingly. "Take his head off in one blow and you get the lot."

The guard shoved Gyle into place, then retreated to a spot behind Olivia. The headsman bowed to Octa, positioned himself between her and his subject and kissed the blade against the back of Gyle's neck, measuring the blow.

No, there must be some angle, he thought desperately, seeking something, anything . . . But his pain-numbed brain was churning too slowly, nothing was connecting.

"Mater-Imperia wants me alive," he pleaded.

"Of course she doesn't," Octa tinkled merrily. "She gave me permission herself, minutes ago. She respects you too much to delay your death."

She looked at the headsman. "Do it now."

The ax swung.

Francis Dorobon sat alone on his balcony, wondering what the future held for him. *I'm King, I'm still King.* He clung to that thought. *But Mother is going to rein me in again.* He cringed inwardly. For just a few weeks, he'd truly felt that life would be as he wanted it—*finally.* He'd been hunting and drinking and dancing with his friends, living like carefree rulers of the world. He had Portia, the most beautiful woman in existence. What did he care what that Nesti bitch and Gurvon got up to? As long as she didn't end up with Gurvon's child in her belly, he didn't give a shit.

But Mother didn't see it like that, oh no! This was her excuse to reclaim all the ground he'd fought so hard to win. That waddling tyrant who dominated every waking moment of his life would shunt him aside yet again and do whatever she damned well liked.

It's all Gyle's fault—he's a fucking spy! How could he be so rukking stupid as to get caught like this?

The central truth of his life was reasserting itself: *no one took on Mother and survived.* The mere thought was foolishness, suicidal idiocy, and Gurvon Gyle deserved to die for not realizing it. He'd miss the man's wit and understanding—but he wouldn't miss Cera Nesti at all, though who knew what her execution would trigger among her people. The Nesti would need to be crushed now, and he was by no means sure he had enough men to do it.

At least I still have Portia. Though he was cross that she'd tried to plead for Cera's life.

He tried to put aside his fears for the future and to think about the things that gave him pleasure, but the same reality kept on intruding: he was losing control again, and Mother was going to rule his life forever.

"Lord King?" A woman's voice, a heavy southern Yuros accent, intruded on his unhappy thoughts.

He flinched; he hadn't realized anyone was so close. "Who are you?"

The woman was a big-nosed, sad-eyed Lantrian clad in a shapeless black robe. She had a nose-ring, and her iron-gray hair had been tied back in a severe bun.

"My name is Hesta Mafagliou," the woman said. "I work for your mother."

"What do you want?" he asked timidly.

"I have been sent to tell you that the queen and Magister Gyle are about to be executed. Cera Nesti's family will be told that she was struck down by fever. A period of mourning will be declared. No one will know of your shame."

"Shame?" he echoed hollowly, then re-found his temper. "There is no shame on me. I am the King. A king cannot be shamed."

Hesta Mafagliou regarded him steadily. "Yes, my King."

Her eyes judged him—all of their eyes would judge him: the soft-cocked King of Javon, cuckolded by his chief adviser. His mother had warned him—*because Mother always knows best, damn her.*

He gripped his periapt, longing for someone—anyone—to lash out at. "You're the one who found them together, aren't you?"

The hooded eyes twitched. "I did, my King."

"You should have come to me!" he shouted at her, "not gone running to my mother!"

"Your mother already knew—" the woman began, then stopped. She'd miscalculated, and she knew it. She backed toward the door.

Mother knew—it's a set-up. We've all been had, by my damn mother!

"Get out!" he shouted. "Get out of my sight!"

The Lantric witch backed away. "My lord King, I'm sorry—"

A bulky shape filled the space behind her. "Mother?" Francis began.

"Hesta," the newcomer rumbled. "I've been looking for you."

The ax blade arched through the air. It crunched through flesh and bone, and the head thudded wetly to the floor.

Gurvon Gyle stared at the goggle-eyed shock only just registering on Octa Dorobon's face, as her head bounced in the straw like a dropped pumpkin and rolled to a standstill beside the execution block. Her body remained upright a second longer, then crashed sideways.

Behind her, Olivia opened her mouth to scream, but the sound became a gurgle as the guard behind her punched a taloned hand through her back, gripped her heart and squeezed it. She shuddered, helpless agony on her face, then she too fell facedown to the ground, landing on her mother's carcass.

Her killer's face altered, various faces forming then faltering and giving way to the next, until she settled on her own: the androgynous face of Coin—or Yvette, if there was a difference—a skinny white youth of indeterminate gender.

Yvette wiped her hand clean on Olivia's skirts and grinned at him.

"Gurvon, are you all right?" Rutt Sordell asked from within the body of the executioner. "Can you stand?"

He tried, though he couldn't take his eyes from Octa Dorobon's severed head, still trying to speak, even as the features were going slack. He gripped the block and gingerly pulled himself upright. The walls were swaying and pulsating around him. "Get this rukking Chain-rune off me," he croaked, his throat dry and gritty as he started fighting to clear his head.

"I'll do it," Coin offered, her voice shrill with concern—for him, he realized with a start. "It'll take a pure-blood to do it." She reached out and gripped his shoulder, her eyes going blank. He tentatively let go of the wall and clung to Coin instead.

Images filled his mind as the pain washed over him: a knot of energy wound about him, and an amorphous liquid presence started tearing it apart. Coin's face lifted to his even as she ripped apart the last bindings on his gnosis.

"Thank you, Yvette," he panted, meeting her eyes, and then, "Where is Mara?"

Sordell grinned. "She's going after Hesta. Come on, Gurvon, we have to hurry."

"And Cera Nesti?"

Coin patted his arm. "In her cell. We have to get to Francis before Eternalus or Rhodium find out what's happening." She looked up at him, smiling. "Can you stand?"

He nodded slowly. His voice filled with genuine gratitude, he said, "Thank you. Thank you both—all of you."

The two magi facing him met his look with devoted eyes and he realized he didn't know how to deal with that. *They actually* care *about me. They took a stupid risk in staying and trying to rescue me— and they pulled it off.*

He wasn't used to nontransactional relationships.

"You are true friends," he told them, though he was unsure what he even meant by those words.

Sordell and Coin smiled harder, so hard he wondered if their faces might split.

"Mara?" Hesta Mafagliou's face bulged with fear—no, more than fear: utter, absolute terror.

The woman who'd stepped into the room was not his mother, Francis realized. He'd never seen this obese creature with thick cords of red hair twined about her head before. She might have been his mother's bigger, heavier—and much more frightening—sister. She filled the space absolutely, even as it seemed to swell to accommodate her. When she smiled, she revealed rows of triangular teeth.

This is going to be to the death, he realized, moving swiftly to the far corner, *and I'm in the middle of it . . .*

Francis had barely taken in the newcomer—*Mara?*—when Hesta's hands went up and lightning crackled from them, jolting the larger woman, who went into a mad spasm as she was thrown backward against the closed door by Hesta's attack. But she didn't go down. Instead she began to *alter*, her mouth widening and her shoulders, head and neck fusing together as she changed into something that was less than half human She growled heavily and began to push against Hesta's blows, walking forward as if wading upstream.

Hesta threw even more energy into her mage-bolts, shrieking for aid as she did so, but no one came, and Francis could see her attacks were having little real effect on the other woman. It was as if this Mara felt no pain. She pushed off from the door as Hesta's attacks wavered and she sought for a new attack, something that might be more effective. The obese woman's flesh was burned and bleeding, but she took one step, then another, and then surged toward Hesta, her eyes flat and empty.

Hesta shrieked again, and now the air shimmered with half-seen figures—spirits or demons—that tried to claw Mara, but the giant woman came on regardless, ignoring her half-seen assailants as they started to fasten onto her. She couldn't shake them off, but Francis saw that she quickly gave up trying, concentrating instead on reaching, *reaching*—

—and making contact at last. Her hand touched Hesta's wrist, her fingers locked around it and with one powerful jerk she snatched the other woman into her arms. Hesta screamed, a long, despairing wail, as Mara's mouth opened wide, and then, impossibly, even wider.

The screams were cut off abruptly, and Francis tore his eyes away.

For a few seconds all he could hear was the sound of a beast, gorging. He ran from his corner to the balcony and tried to shut off the opening with a gnosis-wall. He cowered there, shaking and mewling for mercy, fearing for his own life, for surely he must be next on the beast-woman's menu.

At last he heard feet pounding along the corridors and voices crying out—was that Terus Grandienne, shouting his name? Francis had never thought to be relieved to hear that man's voice, but now he shrieked out for help, even as that immense, ghastly woman reared up on the other side of his magical wall. Her face was a leering, half-human thing of teeth and blood; her bloodlust was up, her hunger barely sated. For a moment she pawed at his wards, then she turned back into the room as Grandienne burst inside. She loomed over the knight before Francis could work out whom to warn.

32

A Storm in the Desert

Shaliyah, Kesh, Antiopia
Zulhijja (Decore) 928
6th month of the Moontide

It was dawn, and the whole of Duke Echor's army was alive with activity. From the Estella cavalry in the north to the Thirteenth, perched below a promontory in the south, in a the dried-up river-bed. Every man was sharpening his weapons, packing up his possessions, hauling provisions, shouting instructions, and *waiting*.

There was that tang—the stench of fear, no matter how invincible the men felt themselves to be—as the army readied itself for battle. Men would face themselves today, and would learn what they were: killers, or cowards—or something better than either.

Legate Jonti Duprey strode through the milling tribunes and jabbed a finger at Ramon. "Sensini, what is this?" Severine was with him, as his liaison, and she was making all kinds of warning faces, but she did not dare to mentally communicate with Ramon, not with the legate standing right next to her.

Ramon composed his face. "What is what, sir?"

"This!" Duprey pulled him aside, waved his tribunes away, including a worried-looking Storn, and thrust a piece of paper into Ramon's face. "Why have I been given a promissory note with *your name* on it?"

Ah. Okay, bound to happen sooner or later. Ramon straightened up and put on his most confident mask. "Sir, the tribunes and I have devised a promissory system for the march so that valuable bullion is not constantly being circulated. It keeps the risks of banditry and corruption down, sir."

"Or at least centralizes it," Duprey growled. "One of the legates used this note to settle a gambling debt."

Ramon blinked. He'd never thought the notes would have currency outside the traders. *Oh well, in for a fennick . . .*

"Sir, the notes are essentially just a convenient means to facilitate the movement of money. To us. The legions have used them for years."

They haven't, but Duprey wouldn't know that . . . would he?

Duprey studied him. "Have they really, Sensini? And yet Nyvus believes this to be most irregular."

Ramon threw a glance at the dapper little aide and contemplated assassination.

Duprey exhaled heavily. "I'm going to have to report . . ." His voice trailed away. He cocked his head, looking puzzled, and said, "*To us*, you say? Who exactly is 'us'?"

Got you. "That's exactly the right question, sir! Since Sagostabad, the Tenth Maniple of the Thirteenth has essentially become the banking and distribution center for the southern army." He put on a modest, not-quite-innocent smile. "We charge only a nominal fee, to cover expenses."

Duprey cast a wary glance around him to ensure they weren't in danger of being overheard and moved closer. "A fee?"

Behind him, Nyvus was visibly straining to hear. Over Duprey's shoulder, Severine was glaring at Ramon.

I guess I should have told her before now.

"Sir, we charge one percent on each transaction," he lied glibly. He'd gotten his story ready to cover this eventuality long ago. "The fee has of course been going into the coffers of the Thirteenth. Sir, *you*—er, I mean, *the legion*, of course—now has eleven thousand gilden in your war-chest."

Duprey's eyes bulged. "Eleven *thousand*?" he said weakly.

Ramon was puzzled for a moment, until he remembered that eleven thousand gilden used to be an exciting amount of money for him too. *Now I'm theoretically worth nearly four hundred thousand...*

"Sir, is there a problem?"

"No, no, not at all," Duprey squeaked eventually. "Carry on, Sensini." He visibly took several deep breaths. "Wait—there's a storm coming and Prenton isn't back yet. Take the other skiff and scout the southern quadrant."

Ramon saluted. "Yes, sir."

"And Sensini—" The thought of all that money had almost turned Duprey's eyes to coins. "*Carry on.*"

Nyvus, standing behind the legate, heard that. He scowled darkly. Ramon winked at him and saluted his commander. "Understood, sir."

He hurried away, but not before hearing Severine make an excuse and set off after him. He got into the tent just before her, but she grabbed him and when he turned to face her, hissed, "Ramon? What the Hel are you doing?"

"Sevvie, calm down, will you? It's just a little arrangement I've set up with the tribunes—"

"Hah! Duprey might have backed off, but he's not stupid, and neither am I. You're raising a counterfeit currency while you hoard all the gold in your back pocket! You'll be hanged for this."

He stared deeply into her eyes and suddenly burst into a great grin. "You *care*."

She snorted irritably. "I'm your *lover*, rodent. Why haven't you told me?"

"'Lover,' as in 'love'?" he asked.

"Don't get above yourself. It's 'lover' as in 'willing receptacle for your bodily fluids.' *Why haven't you told me?*"

"For your protection."

"Like fuck—you're pocketing all manner of coin and not telling me—after all we've done together—"

"I distinctly recall being told how far beneath you I am—and not just once!"

She pouted, then abruptly turned on the charm. "You know I don't mean that, darling. You know I care for you. Truly." She stroked his chest. "So how much have you got stashed away, dearest?"

"'Dearest'?"

"As in 'most expensive.'" She nuzzled his face. "How much?"

He shrugged. "The abacus doesn't count high enough."

Her eyes bulged. "You're incredible."

"As in 'has no credibility'?"

She smiled artfully. "You know I *do* care, Ramon."

"You're a Tiseme. I don't even exist."

"Shhh—that's just not true, Ramon. I like you, you know that. You stood by me against the Inquisitors, and you've made this whole nightmare just about bearable. You make me laugh, and you make me come. And now you've got money. Doesn't that feel like destiny to you?"

"Cow." He snatched up his flying leathers and stomped out of the tent.

"Ha! You care as much as I do!" she shouted after him, while the entire legion stared.

"Yeah?" he called back over his shoulder. "I have no idea how much that is. Do you? Maybe you can calculate how much on an *abacus*!"

The wind whipped Ramon's hair as he flew through the upper reaches of a fogbank that had stubbornly refused to dissipate as the morning wore on. He barely noticed; all he could think of was Severine. His feelings had been growing by degrees for weeks now, but every time it began to feel real, as if they were truly in love, something happened to destroy the illusion, and he had no idea what was true or not.

She's using me. All she wants is a pregnancy and some money and that's the extent of her feelings, he told himself—but was that all?

Half the time they were battling it out as if they were punishing each other for being the wrong race, the wrong religion, the wrong class. Sometimes he'd go out of his way to upset her, just to prove how different they were. But other times, when they were lying curled around each other in the aftermath, their sweat drying on each other's skin, being together was bliss.

We'll take this damned city and I'll find somewhere comfortable for her, slip her some coin before I run away. Her visions have stopped. There's not going to be a battle. She'll be fine.

Shaliyah lay to the north of him, a pile of white stone shimmering in the sunshine, but beyond it, the storm clouds were gathering, growing darker by the minute. Thunder rumbled overhead.

Other Rondian skiffs were flitting above the city, and he could dimly make out the mental calls of the pilots, marveling at the architecture below them. But the fog was getting thicker around him and low clouds were drifting into his path, and it wasn't long before he realized he'd lost sight of the city and the army and everything else. Normally just being up in the sky soothed away all his worries, but today he just kept refighting his argument with Severine, only this time working in his best insults.

It didn't make him feel any better.

Occasional gaps in the clouds revealed glimpses of the dirty brown ground, rock-strewn wastes interspersed with areas that were pure sand. Despite the fog, heat radiated in the air.

He wiped at his face, then started as a dark shape skittered through the mist away to his left. As it dipped toward him, he realized it was another skiff.

<*Hey, seen anything?*> he called absently.

There was no reply from the newcomer. He peered at the other craft as it circled closer; it had a rakish look, and a triangular sail, which was unusual. The pilot was wrapped in dun-colored desert robes, with only a slit revealing dark eyes. He thought the pilot-mage might be female.

<*Hablas Estella?*> he sent, and when that elicited no response he tried, <*Parli Rimoni?*>

The other pilot flinched visibly, then waved at him tentatively. She was definitely female. He pulled his craft into a parallel trajectory to hers and edged closer, until they were only a few yards apart, skimming the top of the fogbank.

"Hey," he shouted out. "Which legion are you from?"

She looked him up and down, then glanced up, and he followed her gaze to see two more windskiffs closing in on them from the south, the direction of the city. They both had that same triangular sail, and he wondered if it made them faster.

He gave a thumbs-up to show he'd seen them, then looked down as a momentary gap in the fog revealed an expanse of desert floor—

—which was crawling with men: white-robed, steel-clad men, rank upon rank, marching in serried columns barely fifty feet beneath them.

They were heading toward the southern end of the Rondian lines.

Shit! Salim's got a whole rukking army out here! He swore violently and gestured wildly at the other pilot-mage to make sure he had her attention. <*Sol a mio!*> he sent. <*Look at them all! We've got to warn the Duke!*>

She met his eyes, raised her hand as if to confirm—

—and blazed a mage-bolt at him.

Rashid Mubarak stood with Salim III, Sultan of Kesh, in the high turret of the gatehouse of Shaliyah, staring out across the narrow plain, which was fast filling up with ranks of Rondian soldiers. The heathen had never come so far east before, right into the very heartland of Kesh. But this was no accident. Whenever the Keshi had given battle before, it had been an act of desperation, little more than throwing men into the path of the invader, and it had been like piling kindling on a fire.

This time, the strategy was different. This time, they had deliberately lured the enemy to their doorstep.

"They have come, as you predicted," Salim noted. "Our gamble takes shape."

Salim was tall, and in his midtwenties. He was a soft-spoken, cultured man, a man of principles, but capable of swift and ruthless action. He was not a mage, of course, but he was nonetheless formidable: his body had been trained for battle and his mind to resist mental assault—though if he did come under direct attack, the day was probably already lost, for Salim's value was in his intellect, and the love all his men had for him.

Rashid had never lacked ambition, but he knew full well that becoming Emir of Halli'kut was the highest station to which he could realistically aspire without becoming a tyrant. Though he was a three-quarter-blood mage, he knew he would not last a day should he try and usurp Salim's throne; his own people would cut him down before Salim's even reached him.

He had realized this at an early stage in his career and curbed his ambitions accordingly. He served Salim, wholeheartedly, and unto death. To be finally free of the Ordo Costruo and able to do so openly was a gift in itself.

"We are ready, Great Sultan."

"This is Shaliyah," Salim reminded him. "After Hebusalim, Shaliyah is the holiest of holies, the refuge of our people. This is where the Prophet first began to teach. Failure is not an option."

Rashid gestured toward the Rondian lines. "They have taken our bait. The city is ready. We have enough food and water stored to last three summers. We have enough arrows to slay them all twenty times over."

"Lack of arrows and provender has never been the problem in the past," Salim reminded him. "It is the lack of the gnosis."

Rashid bowed again. "I am here, and all of my Ordo Costruo. All of those we have bred who are old enough to serve are here also. Each and every one stands ready to give their lives, Great Sultan." Rashid studied his overlord. Was he truly ready to dare the unthinkable and take on the Rondian army head-on?

"Our scouts report that Duke Echor has sixteen legions: eighty thousand men with two hundred and forty magi. Can we defeat so many?"

"My lord, we have thrice their number, and a horde of Ingashir, and even Lakh elephant-borne warriors. They are all attacking from inside the storm itself. We almost match them, mage to mage. It has to be enough."

"They say you must outnumber them five to one," Salim replied steadily.

"If you have no magi, lord. Many of ours may be weaker in blood, less well-trained, but they will keep the Rondian magi busy. Trust in the storm my Ordo Costruo have conjured; such workings, once begun, cannot be stopped. It will be devastating." Rashid hesitated. "And we have our allies, Great Sultan."

Salim studied the emir in return. "These—what did you call them?—these 'Dokken.' These 'Rakas.' We can trust them?"

Rashid was slow to respond, but eventually he said honestly, "The Dokken have been the secret enemy of the magi since the gnosis was gained—and that includes our own magi. Sabele would as soon destroy me as any Rondian mage. They may aid us now, for this shihad, but eventually they will turn on us. Eventually they will have to be dealt with."

"I would like to meet this Sabele."

"She is away in the north on some errand, Great Sultan, but her warleader is here. Arkanus is of Yuros, as most of them are, but he has been living in secret in Mirobez for many years. He has brought more of his Rakas here than I ever knew existed. There are hundreds." Rashid couldn't keep the worry from his voice when he admitted, "Some may be more powerful than I."

Salim looked at him and smiled. He placed a hand on Rashid's shoulder. "You have my trust, my friend. You know that. You will find a way to contain them. This will be our greatest victory."

Rashid bowed low. "We will not let you down, Great Sultan."

Salim looked out over the plains, at the distant lines of the enemy. "We have brought Echor here. It is a gamble, but that is the nature of war."

Rashid's mind went back over a year, to that dimly lit room in Pallas, when his enemies had agreed to place a third of their own forces beneath his blade. He could still scarcely believe that Emperor Constant—or more particularly, Mater-Imperia Lucia—could be so ruthless. He shuddered a little as he recalled the callous way she'd asked, "Emir Rashid, if we give you Duke Echor and all his men, can your people destroy him?"

And now we are about to find out.

"This is our hour, Great Sultan," he said confidently.

"Then let us unleash our fury."

The gnostic attack took Ramon utterly by surprise, and only the training imbedded into him at Turm Zauberin saved his life. As the brilliant energies crashed into him, his shields rose instinctively and repelled the worst of the blow, though it still scorched clothing and skin and seared his vision. For a few seconds he found himself dazed, and the windskiff faltered and started drifting aimlessly, only the gnosis already imbued in its prow keeping it from tumbling toward the earth.

He shook himself, tried to rattle his brain back to awareness, and poured more energy into the little vessel. It started to rise, but still he could see nothing through the shifting fogbank.

<*What the Hel?*> he sent, too stunned to comprehend why another mage would assault him. *Is it because I'm Silacian?*

Another bolt hammered into his back, but this time he was ready and easily repulsed it. The woman pilot-mage shouted aloud, and this time he recognized the language.

Sol a mio, she's Keshi! His mind reeled at the sheer impossibility of it all: *They've got magi! They've got the gnosis!*

Then the other pilot-mages replied to her, and their shouts started ringing across the sky as they joined the pursuit.

His vision cleared and he returned fire, aiming not at the mage but at her upper mast, where he hoped her shields would be weaker. It worked: his mage-bolt burned through the ropes lashing her sail to the mast, the triangular sheet of canvas tore away and fell over her and she started screeching furious imprecations as she tried to free herself. The bottom of the sail was still tied to the boom, which was making it even harder for her to struggle out from under the heavy folds. As she wrestled with the waxed material, she unbalanced the little craft and it slewed sideways before losing all momentum. It fell away behind him as he soared onward.

Her companions were closing in though, so Ramon couldn't risk staying to finish her off—not when a whole secret army—an army with *magi!*—was headed for Duke Echor's oblivious right flank, where the Thirteenth were stationed.

He pulled the wind into his sails and fled, and as the two other Keshi windcraft dived after him, he sent his thoughts questing forward, filling them with as much intensity as he could manage.

<Severine, hear me!> Calling her name crystallized all the emotions inside him and pulled him past all the trivialities of *Do I? Don't I? Does she? Doesn't she?* They all resolved into a single thought: *I have to warn her!*

He knew instantly that she would not hear him, for his mental voice had crashed into a gnostic veil cutting off all communications from the aerial scouts to the army. Such veils took a long time to prepare, and a whole heap of skill and experience.

They've got some rukking powerful magi—and they knew *we were coming!*

For a second a second horrible thought hit him: *The Keshi captured Alaron and took the Scytale.* But then the immediacy of his peril took over. Another blast of energy struck his shields: the other Keshi pilots were closing in on him. They must be pulling as much air into their sails as he was—maybe even more, for they were catching up with him. He gritted his teeth, decided he would have to risk plowing into the earth and dived down into the fog, skimming the spears of a regiment of Keshi soldiers who bellowed in shock as he appeared above them.

They reacted immediately with a salvo of arrows that battered his shields, and then he was past them. The Keshi pilots were now almost level with him and he had to fight hard to keep his sense of direction as they played hide-and-seek in the roiling mists. Distances flew by as they exchanged ineffectual mage-bolts, and then, quite abruptly, he was out of the fog and into clear sky. Below him were the plains of Shaliyah, spreading for miles.

It had been—what? Two hours? Just two hours ago he had left on patrol, and in that time, the whole world had changed.

They have magi!

The plains had also changed: now they were full of fighting men.

Duke Echor had positioned his army so it was arrayed north to south, facing the city, which was currently disgorging rank after rank of Keshi, marching in good order, armored and bristling, and fanning out in well-rehearsed precise formations as they streamed toward the Rondian lines. There were uncountable numbers of them massing at the northern flanks, preparing to attack.

Duke Echor's army was arrayed to counter them, and as Ramon surveyed the deployment, it struck him that the duke could not possibly have been aware of the forces in the mist at the southern flank. He'd been out-thought and outmaneuvered. This was not supposed to happen. And neither were enemy magi supposed to exist.

We're in trouble . . .

Worst of all, from up here Ramon could see a great yellow-brown cloud on the far horizon, rolling in from the north like a massive boulder. A fierce wind was beginning to pick up too, and with a start he realized what he was looking at: a legendary Keshi dust storm. He'd heard that the natives believed afreet were responsible for sucking up the sands of the desert and hurling them across the plains, but whether magic-made or natural, this was not a good time for one to strike. He was beginning to think it was no coincidence.

He was just looking behind him, trying to spot his pursuers, when the first breath of the northerly hit him, buffeting his little craft. He turned her across the wind, trying to hold her steady, when he heard more Keshi cries, and the enemy skiffs shot out of the fog behind him—

To his surprise, rather than converging to take him down, the two Keshi windskiffs appeared to give up, for they wheeled and headed back toward the city at full speed. He exhaled in relief. It looked like the thought of facing a properly trained Rondian mage full-on was still intimidating . . .

Then he turned to face forward again and immediately realized why the enemy mage-pilots had fled. It was nothing to do with the innate superiority of the Western magi; the desert storm had to be moving impossibly fast, because in the few seconds he'd been looking away, it had blotted out half the sky. The wall of darkness was rolling inexorably toward the northern flank of Duke Echor's army. Lightning flickered in its bowels.

It's going to dump all over us. I've got to land before it hits . . .

He hauled on the sheets and dragged the tiller about, setting course toward the banners of the Thirteenth and traveling at a reckless speed. He suddenly realized that he was the last Rondian skiff still in the air. There was a sandy space before Duprey's command group and he plowed into it at breakneck speed. The moment he touched the ground, he was out of the skiff and running toward Duprey. The legion commander was shouting orders as his frontline maniples formed up. Ramon burst through the ring of men, shouting, "Legate! Legate Duprey! The enemy are in the mist in front of us, *and they have magi!*"

Everyone turned toward him. *Impossible* was the word in every mouth, but he did not give anyone a change to voice it.

"It's true, sir, I swear!" he shouted. His eyes went to Severine as he cried, "We have to warn the duke!"

"Wait, calm down!" Duprey replied, raising a warning hand to stop Severine. "What are you saying? Are there renegade Ordo Costruo here?" They'd all heard rumors of defectors.

"There were enemy mage-pilots—*Keshi!* Three of them chased me!—and they have *thousands* of soldiers on the ground—"

"Catch your breath, Sensini," the legate ordered. "You're panicked."

He said it as much to steady those around him, Ramon thought, but the words still stung. "*Rukka mio!* I am not panicked! They're out there, huge numbers of them, and they have magi!"

He heard the whispers running like wildfire through the ranks as those in earshot passed the news back. Tyron Frand looked worried, but Renn Bondeau and the Andressans were dismissive. He didn't care about them, but he could see Duprey closing up his mind.

"I have orders to anchor the right and hold," the legate said firmly, "and that is what we will do."

They were all standing on a rise below the cliffs where the wagons were placed, overlooking the dried-up riverbed, and as the legate spoke, Ramon realized the fogbank was drifting closer—almost as if it were alive. *Or controlled.*

"Sir, I saw Keshi footmen, coming right at us. We've got to wheel right and set to defend," he tried again.

"Sensini is spooking at shadows," Renn Bondeau snickered. "Ten to one it's a herd of camels and a flock of birds."

Ramon flushed. "Legate Duprey, please! They'll be here in minutes."

Duprey gazed at him steadily. "My orders are to hold here, and advance when the enemy break. I will follow those orders until they are countermanded! Return to your post." He glanced up at the ridgeline behind the legion. "Your place is with the baggage."

The implicit insult burned, as did the looks on the faces of the other magi. He bunched his fists, turned to Severine. *<Do you believe me? Or do you just think I'm a fool too?>*

<Of course I believe you,> she sent back, though he was sure he could hear doubt in her mental voice. *<I'll try and scry into the fog.>*

Duprey turned away and addressed the gathered tribunes and magi. "We will deploy as ordered. This changes nothing, gentlemen, not unless Sensini's report is verified. We will array for pursuit, not for defense. All of you, get to your positions now!"

Rufus Marle echoed the orders with a feral snarl, driving the men and magi away, his natural bloodlust clearly rising at the thought of a fight. Bondeau, Korion, and the rest of the magi exuded their normal sense of invincibility. Even Kip was looking at him skeptically.

<We're in big trouble,> he sent to the Schlessen. *<Be ready.>*

<I'm always ready,> Kip responded with a jocular swagger.

<I mean it, Kip. They're coming!> He turned back to Severine. *<Be safe,>* he exhorted her.

Her face was torn. *<I know you saw something, Ramon. But I have to stay with the commander.>*

<Don't let him get you killed.>

<He doesn't want to die either. You be careful too.>

<I love you.> he said. In that instant he was being totally honest.

She flinched. *<Don't toy with me.>* She hurried away, not looking back.

He bit his lip, but let her go.

After a moment he ran back to the skiff, leaped in and took it to the ridgeline above, where Storn and the Tenth Maniple waited. The ridge wasn't terribly high, but it still afforded him views over the whole battlefield. *Our front line should be up here, not down there— but Echor obviously thinks he's untouchable. He thinks he doesn't need tactics, just magi.* The winds were still rising and the sand in the air was beginning to sting. Sol knew how much damage it would do when it hit the southern flank with its full force.

Storn hurried to his side and reported, "We've got the wagons unhitched—"

"Then hitch them again," Ramon snapped at him. "*Now*. We need to be ready to move them."

The tribune blinked. "What? But—"

"I know you've only just unhitched them, but you need to listen to me, okay? So just do it."

"The men won't like it, sir."

"The men will like it plenty when they realize what's happening. The enemy is out there in that fog, Storn: they're hiding there, waiting for us."

Storn peered into the oncoming mist and sniffed, then looked puzzled. "It's not moving with the wind, sir," he started.

"Tell that to Duprey," Ramon grunted. He looked south, to the broken fortress at the near end of the line of hills, about a mile away. "Get that skiff loaded onto a wagon: there'll be no more flying today. If we need to pull back, we make for that ruin to the south."

Storn frowned. "Rondian legions don't retreat, sir—we never have to."

Ramon ignored that. "Have we got anyone scouting to the south? We don't want to find a bunch of Keshi up our rukking asses."

"Col's out there—and look: Korion's been ordered to take his cavalry south, to screen our flank." He pointed away to the right.

Ramon peered along the tribune's finger and saw a khurne rider far in the distance, at the head of a line of horsemen. *Perhaps Duprey at least half-believed me . . .* He fervently hoped so. "Then the Lesser Son had better keep his eyes peeled, because I saw Keshi out there." Ramon dropped his voice. "What about our *special consignments*, Storn?"

Storn looked about him warily before whispering, "All safely under wraps, sir. I have the promissory notes on my person. The gold and poppy are in the lead wagons. One of Echor's staff was sniffing round while you were gone, but I fed him a line and he went away."

Ramon bit his lip. *That's all we need . . .* He looked at Storn and said firmly, "We'll deal with one problem at a time, Tribune. Let's get the wagons re-hitched and the lines set up. I want men above that dry riverbed, where the cutting climbs to this plateau—if the enemy break through Duprey's men, that's the only place we'll have any chance of holding them."

"Rondian legions don't break, sir. It doesn't happen."

Ramon strode along the ridge until he was overlooking the cutting, where a river had carved a path from the heights to the plain. The cliffs might not be that high, but they were surprisingly precipitous behind the Thirteenth. He stared out over the battlefield, straining his eyes to get some idea of what was happening. It was hard to tell, but it looked like something might be happening away in the north. He could definitely see lightning—and was that the invisible concussion of gnosis being unleashed?

Even as he watched, a great mass of Keshi flowed forward like a dark shadow over the sand and struck the Rondian north flank. They recoiled in a cloud of billowing dust, and a cheer went up all along the lines, including among the watching men of his own maniple. For a few moments he felt his breathing ease. Perhaps he'd underestimated the might of their own forces.

But still the fog crawled closer to their position.

We're right where the Keshi expected us to be, Ramon thought nervously. *And they've got magi—how many? How skilled? Enough to make a storm and prime the weather to suit themselves? We've just got here, most of the men haven't even rested from the march. The Keshi must be fresh, well fed and watered, and well rested . . . we have eighty thousand men and two hundred and forty magi—how many do they have?*

At that, another highly unwelcome thought intruded: *Would Emperor Constant lament if we're all wiped out?* Duke Echor's army was almost entirely made up of vassal states—and looking at it from Pallas's perspective, if the potential threat to the Crown that Echor posed was dealt with, the loss of the few Rondian legions would surely be acceptable.

For a moment he even wondered if the emperor had actively set this up. *But to do that he'd have had to practically invite Salim to his planning sessions . . . and that's impossible, surely?*

"*Holy Kore!*" Tribune Storn exclaimed as the fogbank disgorged rank upon rank of Keshi infantry. He looked at Ramon with sudden fear, his earlier confidence wavering visibly. "You were right, sir!"

Si, thanks very much for noticing . . .

As each Keshi unit emerged from the mists they burst into song—prayers to Ahm, Ramon guessed—while above the noise of thousands of voices chanting to their god came the whip-crack voices of their officers. Trumpets brayed, and the Keshi forces surged forward.

Ramon watched the great wave of screaming men hurtling toward Duprey's lines, and then raised his head and scanned he entire battlefield. That sight was repeated all along the southern flank of the Rondian battle-line, and still the enemy continued to pour out from the mists.

To his credit, Duprey reacted instantly. Within seconds, with Severine using her gnosis to relay his orders, Duprey's officers were wheeling their units into defensive formations, packing shields. But the Rondian legions had been issued only with light javelins instead of the heavy pikes they would normally deploy for defending. Though the lines reset swiftly, precious moments had been wasted, during which no archers fired to disrupt the enemy. And quickly though the men responded, the lines had not managed to fully interlock before the first waves of Keshi soldiers struck them.

The sultan's white-robed infantry stormed forward, bearing their distinctive circular shields. Some attacked the Rondian front line while others ran toward the gaps in the ranks, seeking to get through and circle behind. It looked like there were too many for the Rondians to contain—the din of their battle-cries made it sound like the world was filled with them—and then their arrows began to punch home, stinging clouds of them launched from behind the front ranks, raining down like sleet.

But terrifying as the massed Keshi attack was, the battle-magi of the Thirteenth knew their job. From his vantage point, Ramon could see Secundus Rufus Marle and Renn Bondeau, the magi with the lead maniples, below him as they cast shields overhead, domes of pale light that warped the air and slapped aside the storm of arrow shafts. Barely a single arrow penetrated.

The rankers responded with javelins, with a blast of telekinesis lending extra force to the thrown spears, and the front rank of Keshi tumbled to the ground, spitted.

But still the enemy kept pouring onward.

As the oncoming Keshi came within range of Marle and Bondeau, the magi lifted their hands, working in concert, and fiery orange liquid washed over the advancing infantry. Ramon could feel the rush of heat from where he stood, two hundred yards away and thirty yards higher, then truly awful bloodcurdling screams rose over the war cries. He flinched, and his nails gouged his palms. Fire was a hideous weapon, and he felt like he was hearing every individual, agonized shriek.

Marle and Bondeau did not rest. They followed their flames with Earth-gnosis, making the ground itself ripple until the Keshi were tripping over each other and sprawling among those already slain by spears and liquid flame. Then lightning crackled and the onslaught wavered as groups of armored men were blasted apart by searing mage-bolts. The Keshi died in their hundreds in the successive waves of fire and lightning.

So far, so much as you'd expect, Ramon thought: *Rondelmar victorious*. But when he tore his eyes from the conflict below, he found the distant scenes were far more worrying. The sandstorm was enveloping the northern flank—and he could have sworn there were distant dark shapes moving in the yellow-brown clouds of sand and earth.

It takes weeks to create precisely the weather you want, so they would have had to know exactly where we were going to be, to the very day—and weeks in advance. How can they possibly have known—?

Then out of the east, flying serenely above the Keshi army, came a fleet of windships, each with that distinctive triangular sail. And now those sails bore the crescent and scimitar of Salim. They were aloft despite the oncoming storm . . . His jaw dropped. *These Keshi are truly insane . . .*

Ramon physically felt the doubt and fear that struck all down the Rondian line as the rankers suddenly realized that for the first time in their lives, they were facing an enemy with gnosis. The Rondian windships rose as if in answer, sails hastily unfurling to meet this new threat, but as if the appearance of their own gnosis-wielders had given them heart, the Keshi soldiers roared their approval and surged forward with renewed vigor. Mage-bolts flew, but now they were coming from both sides, all the way along the line—*and there were more flying from the east than from the west.*

How can they have so many magi?

As Ramon stared in horror, he saw individual mage-duels breaking out all over the place, distracting the Rondian magi from protecting the rankers. The overwhelming Keshi numbers began to hammer against Echor's lines, and the Rondian line buckled inward as masses of the enemy hurled themselves bodily at the interlocked shields of the thin front line.

"We'll hold 'em, sir, you'll see," Storn muttered, but when Ramon looked at him, the tribune was gripping his reins as if his life depended upon them.

Beneath their vantage point, the attack on the Thirteenth was coming apart. These attackers didn't appear to have any magi support, which meant the Keshi were simply target practice for Rufus Marle and Renn Bondeau. But they were holding the legion in place, preventing them from going to the aid of the center.

Ramon could no longer see the left wing of Echor's army, for it had vanished into yellow-brown sand cloud. He'd been told what these desert storms were like: hundred-mile-an-hour winds blasting sand so hard it stripped flesh from bone. The Rondian windships were already being thrown across the sky; it was obviously they were faring far worse than the enemy craft in the alien conditions.

If you knew the storm was coming, could you prepare yourself to fight in it?

It was certainly true that the enemy appeared to be somehow immune to the power of the sand-filled winds. Ramon could see and sense gnosis being expended all over the battlefield as the enemy windships reached the duke's lines, and started targeting individual mage-pilots. Every time he saw one of the tiny figures emitting gouts of light, he felt the rippling power prickling his skin. Echor and his staff were high-bloods, raised in Argundy and trained to war—but there was no mistaking the overwhelming and unexpected power being deployed against them. And an unwarded legionary could die in a fireball as easily as a Keshi.

He watched, appalled, as all along the Rondian lines, gaps appeared and hordes of Keshi punched through.

"The duke'll plug the holes," Storn repeated feverishly. "You'll see."

As if to vindicate his words, one of the Keshi windships suddenly burst into flames and plummeted to earth—but it plowed into the lines of an Argundian legion, killing dozens of men before it shattered into splinters. And that was only one ship; more and more came on, mage-fire flickering among the sheets of arrows that poured down from above.

Ramon turned his attention back to the ground immediately below him as another assault smashed against the front ranks of the Thirteenth. Bondeau strode to the fore and on his own managed to throw the attack back with a massive burst of Fire-gnosis. All around him arrows crackled to nothing and the Keshi nearest to him went up like torches, filling the air with the stench of cooking flesh. The men cheered as those Keshi still living fled.

Maybe it was worth having you along after all, Bondeau you prick ...

Then another surge of energy took his breath away: it was distant, but incredibly powerful. It took him a moment to work out what had caused it—and then he realized that the dust-storm had struck the center of the Yurosian line. The Rondian magi must have been trying to hold it back, but to no avail, for the magic that had set the storm in motion worked the same way as rolling boulders down a mountain: once it was in motion and had picked up momentum, it was almost unstoppable.

Even as he reached out with his gnostic senses, trying to find out what was happening, the Rondian magi's efforts failed—and then he didn't need to focus his senses to feel the shrieking of thousands of men as the sandstorm ripped through the lines, tossing men aloft like ants before completely engulfing them. His gnostic senses gave him a fuller picture as he sought to scry what was happening: he saw and felt men panicking, burying their faces as the unnatural dust-storm filled nostrils and throats with sand, blinding eyes, and scouring skin and flesh. The thousands of soldiers in its path were literally being flayed alive . . .

That's going to keep coming up this valley until it rolls over the top of all of us and eats us alive . . .

There were Keshi attackers in those dust-clouds, he would swear to it, and other things too. He could see the enemy windships were manipulating their strange triangular sails now to lift themselves clear of the storm, and those Rondian craft that had managed to get into the air were dropping straight to the ground again before they were wrecked. But still there were large shapes looming out of the dust-storm itself: giant beasts with wicker structures on their backs, filled with archers and magi, all protected from the elements in ways the Yurosian rankers weren't. As they came they wielded their weapons with ferocious intent, pouring arrows and mage-bolts down onto those rankers blinded by the sand and reeling from the almost-living dust-storm. Ramon had to fight back the nausea as he worked out the full extent of this hidden slaughter, feeling first one legion go under, and then another. All along the line the Keshi magi were engaging their Argundian and Estellayne counterparts. Though most were outmatched in skill and blood-rank, still they kept the Rondians occupied, allowing the Keshi infantry who outnumbered the Yuros-born rankers three or four or five to one to keep pushing and pushing until their greater numbers told.

The Thirteenth and its near neighbors were still managing to hold the line. The legions had other advantages—better armor, better discipline, more training; their heavy equipment suited a close press better than the looser formations and more individualistic fighting style of the Keshi. But that could take them only so far: they had no strong places to defend, no fortifications to narrow the front against the sheer numbers they confronted. The reserve maniples were now engaged, individual units swallowed up as a vast and savage brawl developed. This was far from the pristine classroom conditions where most of the magi had learned their craft; this was hack and stab or die. The rankers were being overwhelmed by men who appeared not to care if they lived. They had the prayers of the Kalistham on their lips even as they threw themselves at their enemies and died in their hundreds, their thousands.

Ramon looked at Storn. "Tell Duprey he's got to pull out."

Storn looked at him. His eyes were wide, disconnected. "The Thirteenth is holding," he maintained stubbornly. His armpits were soaked in sweat and his lower lip trembling. "We're holding."

"We are. The rest of the rukking army isn't. Send a rider."

"Echor's got reserves," Storn argued.

"That's an order, Tribune."

"You don't know war, sir," Storn replied, babbling. "Sometimes it can look bad—worse than it is. The thing is not to panic."

"The thing is not to rukking die," Ramon countered. He closed his eyes and sent a call arrowing out. *<Sevvie! Where are you?>*

<Ramon? Are you all right? We can't see anything down here.> She sounded overwhelmed. *<It's awful!>*

He longed to just magic her away. She was made for parlors and parties and pretty dresses, not for this nightmare. *<Tell Duprey to pull back. We can defend the hills to the south. The whole army needs to move south.>*

It was as if she hadn't heard him. *<We've lost contact with the next legion. I've more contacts coming in.>* She shut him out, but he could sense her exchanging thoughts with other farseers down the line.

He hissed in frustration. "I'll go myself," he told Storn. "Duprey won't shift."

The thought of his only mage leaving him galvanized the tribune and he grabbed Ramon's arm. "Sir, I'll send someone, right away." He shouted orders to a messenger while Ramon turned his attention back to the battle below.

Fifty yards below them, down the treacherous slope, visibility faded as the dust turned the day to a gray-brown twilight. He began to lose any sense of what was happening further down the line. There was only enemy all around them. He saw Bondeau hurling fire, breaking up another attack, and Duprey shouting for calm. He could just make out Severine, still with the legate, relaying his commands.

He tried to call to her again but she was sending, to someone further north.

<*Sir,*> Ramon shouted, projecting his voice into Duprey's mind, <*you've got to move. We're losing, sir!*>

Duprey whirled and looked up at him. <*Sensini! Get your men down here! We need help!*>

<*Sir, you have to move back. I can see what's happening, and we're about to be overwhelmed.*>

Duprey's temper exploded. <*Get your men down here to reinforce the line or I'll have you arrested!*>

Severine burst in. <*Sir, I've lost contact with High Command.*>

Duprey whirled and both shouted and sent, <*Then find them again, girl! Kore's Balls, I'm surrounded by rukking babies!*>

Ramon sensed Severine's mind reel from what was virtually a mental assault, but Duprey barely noticed; he was casting about for some way to save his men. More arrows sheeted from the gloom and the eerie cry of the Keshi sounded again, the battle-prayer of Ahm carried triumphantly on the winds. The ground began to rumble, the pounding of many, many hooves.

Ramon cursed. <*Sevvie, you've got to get out!*>

<I can't,> she wailed, then shut him out again, bending all her thoughts to trying to contact Echor's aides.

Ramon held his head in anguish and for a wild moment contemplated swooping down and snatching her away. Around him, the rankers of the Tenth Maniple watched him, their faces shaky. *I've got to stop worrying the men,* he thought, but it wasn't easy to look calm when you knew things were falling to pieces. *They can see what I see, and they're not stupid.*

It occurred to him that he should fix that.

"Storn! Move the Tenth Maniple twenty paces backward!"

"What?" The tribune looked mystified.

"Just do it!" He was beginning to think that Storn wasn't the man to deal with this sort of situation either. He doubted anyone in the army was. *Has anyone here ever been on the losing side in a battle?*

Below him the disaster continued to play out, though only the gods knew what was truly happening now, for the sandstorm had enveloped the center, cutting off almost all visibility. Behind him Storn was shouting orders, and slowly the Tenth Maniple began to shuffle back, even as they craned their necks, trying to keep watching as the disaster unfolded below them.

"Move them back another ten!" he shouted at Storn, conscious of all the ears and eyes on him. Now they couldn't see the battlefield, they were taking their cues from him.

Right, look calm, damn it. Keep it simple. Do the obvious.

"Ready the supply wagons for moving," he told Storn loudly, trying to sound like he knew what he was doing, though really, he was making it all up as he went along.

"Hitch up the oxen and horses again. Let's get the stores clear of the storm. We're going to shift them to that old fort to the south of us. Move!"

Following orders seemed to relieve the rankers: someone was in charge, and action made them feel like they were doing something positive, that they had some control. Ramon clung to that feeling too, despite the evidence of everything he could see below. *Someone will do something! Papa Sol, let it be so!*

"Get someone out to Seth Korion's riders," he told Storn. "Tell him to come west and guard our flank." *If any Keshi cavalry get among us, we'll be in all kinds of shit.* "Move it!"

As the Tenth Maniple went to work behind him he went back to the rim of the ridge, wondering what he could do. *We're a legion of hard-assed mutineers,* he reminded himself, *but all I've got are the sappers and supply men. Rukking wonderful.*

But so far they were doing just as they ought: beasts were being led to wagons, newly erected tents were being pulled down and packed up . . .

And all the while, the dust storm rolled closer.

Ramon could make out groups of enemy magi now, as they began to move into support of the Keshi on this flank, seeking to engage individual Rondian gnosis-wielders in duels. Rufus Marle had come under attack; as he started trading mage-bolts with several Keshi magi, his protection of his maniple faltered, just as Ramon had seen happening all the way down the line. The surging wall of howling Keshi hit the front rank, which buckled, wavered, and reformed as desperation lent the legionaries newfound strength. They hurled the enemy back in desperation, but all the time they were being pushed steadily against the base of the slope behind them. The battle was now boiling at the foot of the small cliffs at his feet.

This is it.

<Sevvie?>

<I'm here,> she called back, and now he could see her, huddled in Duprey's shadow while the legate blasted away at the wall of Keshi that were threatening to crush them against the rock wall beneath Ramon's vantage point. She was only sixty yards away, but it felt like miles. *<What do you see, Ramon?>*

<I see that we're all rukked if we don't get out!> he shouted back. *<Tell Duprey he must retreat!>*

He saw her tugging on Duprey's sleeve, pointing upward, and at first the legate seemed to berate her, then at last it looked to Ramon like he was coming to his senses. He began pointing about him, directing centuries to his left and right, ordering them to pull back to either side of the low cliffs and seek places to climb. He looked upward, toward Ramon, cursing inaudibly, then he grabbed Severine's shoulder and shouted something into her face. The girl looked stricken, then she rallied.

She kissed Duprey's hand, which Ramon thought strange at first, and then he understood. *Someone's got to give the rest time to get out of there.*

He closed his eyes and muttered a prayer to Mater-Luna, because only the Queen of Madness was going to get them out of this.

Severine soared upward on Air-gnosis, mage-bolts and arrows deflecting from her shields as she landed at his side. She was in tears, and he had to force himself to resist the urge to throw his arms around her.

Instead, he made himself focus on the practical. "Get to the baggage train, secure your things," he shouted. "We're pulling back to that fort. And tell Seth Korion—I've sent a messenger, but who knows if he's found him in this Helish mess."

She nodded mutely, then fled toward her tent. When he watched her go, it was with a feeling that if he closed his eyes, he'd never see her again. Then the first tendrils of the sandstorm struck, whipping a swirling, stinging blast of dust over him, and he lost her in the haze.

Papa-Sol, he prayed with all his heart, *look after her.*

He spurred back to the defile, where men of the Fourth and Fifth Maniples were streaming up, marching at double time even as they hunched over, seeking some protection against the searing winds. More men were coming from the north, broken units of other legions, still disciplined, but on the edge of flight. He waved them southward.

The entire valley was obscured now, shrouded in shadows, but the Keshi seemed immune to the conditions, emerging like ghosts from the swirling dust, wailing their unearthly prayers, and selling their lives dearly. He saw them hit Duprey's front line again, and felt the gnostic concussions as the legate tried to do the work of a legion. Others tried to aid him: Marle was there, swearing and cursing as he blasted away, and now he could see Coulder and Fenn, the two magi from Brevin, and one of the Andressan magi, though he couldn't tell whether it was Hale, Gerant, or Lewen, and that bothered him, for he felt he ought to know who was likely to be selling his life so dearly, allowing as many of the Thirteenth as possible to escape.

But they were almost out of time.

"Sir? We have to go." Storn plucked at his sleeve. "I'll put our wagons in the van. We'll get the stash out, sir."

"Food and water, Storn," he replied automatically. "If we get out of this, the last thing we need is that damned poppy."

Storn's face fell. "But we've got hundreds of thousands of gilders' worth," he whined.

"Abandon them—" He stopped, and then said quickly, "No, wait, I've got an idea."

"We can save it?" Storn's eyes filled with hope.

"Absolutely! Bring the wagons to the ridgeline, quickly as you can, man!"

"Here?" Storn looked left and right. "Why?"

"You'll see." Ramon felt energy coursing through him. The Thirteenth was completely nose-deep in shit, but he'd had an idea—something that might buy them a little time—and that was something to cling to.

It took several minutes to get the wagons hitched up and wheeled over to the cliff. He gestured to where he wanted them, then turned and checked on the rest of the Thirteenth, streaming away south, running as fast as armor and burdens permitted.

Below him, Duprey and Marle's maniples still held the riverbed defile, but yard by yard they were giving ground, and some of the Keshi were beginning to look up at him.

"What do you want us to do sir?" Storn asked as his men gathered about the carefully positioned wagons.

Ramon dragged his eyes from the chaos below and looked at the tribune. He worked out the correct spot first, then he showed it to the men. Then he told them what to do.

The men looked at him, completely bewildered, and Storn's mouth gaped open. "But, sir—it's worth *thousands* . . ."

Ramon laughed grimly. "Just do as I say, Tribune, and exactly when I say so."

It became a matter of time and timing. There weren't that many enemy magi here yet, but the number of white-robed Keshi soldiers was rising all the time.

Ramon watched as Bondeau extricated his maniple, wheeling it to the left and up the long slope to the north of their position, right into the shadow of the oncoming storm.

Meanwhile Kip's maniple, the Ninth, were already there, parting to let Bondeau's exhausted men through, then closing behind them. The Schlessen battle-mage was singing, his guttural bass ringing down the valley. With his helmet gone and his blond hair flowing free he looked every inch the barbarian as he faced the pursuing Keshi. He'd discarded his shield somewhere along the way and had just his giant Schlessen zweihandle, the famous two-handed sword of the northern tribes. Even from where he watched, Ramon could see gnostic energy crackling along its long blade.

As the Keshi struck, Kip launched himself at them, dragging his men behind in a whirlwind of brutal fury. Ramon could sense Kip drawing on Earth-gnosis for extra strength, and he could see the result, for with every blow he was cutting men in half, shearing straight through armor, sword-blades and spear handles and all. He was like a giant straight out of his people's legends. But just as he began to hope that Duprey and Marle might take advantage of Kip's efforts and win free from the bottom of the ridgeline, the hammer fell.

The Keshi ranks parted to allow through a shrieking wave of cavalry, held in reserve by the Keshi commander until just this opportunity. The riders made straight for the exhausted men and magi clustered about Duprey just as a bunch of gnosis-wielding enemy joined the fray.

Some of the newly arrived Keshi started countering Duprey's defensive spells, while others attacked, mind to mind. As Duprey's magi defended, the Keshi cavalry, lances lowered, thundered straight into the locked shields of the rankers.

Outnumbered and facing the charge, without magi protection or even pikes, their javelins gone and arrows spent, the rankers were overwhelmed. The Keshi riders hammered right over the top of them, spitting men like pigs or tossing the bodies aside, then flailing and slashing down on the reeling soldiers, the hooves of their mounts doing as much damage as the riders' blades. The noise was horrifying and the iron reek of blood filled the air as friends and foes alike fell in droves.

Then the first enemy reached the magi. Coulder, facing to his right and trying to keep a man from Duprey, never even saw the scimitar that took him in the back of the neck and almost decapitated him.

Fenn howled as if his own child had died and let his wards drop for just an instant—but that instant was time enough for a lancer to slam through a gap and ride him down. As the two battle-mages from Brevin fell, Duprey sent mage-bolts left and right, screaming his defiance.

Ramon turned to the men about him. "*Ready? Now!*"

They lit the first package and hurled it below.

The opium Ramon's maniple had been diligently hoarding for the past few months was "cooked" by the suppliers before delivery: boiled until purified and dried out. Now it was essentially flammable flakes, all ready to be smoked. It took a push with both Air- and Fire-gnosis to get the effect he needed, but in just a few seconds they had filled the narrows below with clouds of burning opium. At first it had little effect, and then all the men below—by now mostly Keshi—were collapsing, choking, and coughing. They poured more and more of the toxic powder into the narrows and set it alight as the surviving Rondians staggered from the clouds and fled to the left, trying to link with Kip's Ninth Maniple.

The enemy magi immediately tried to counteract the toxic cloud, but Ramon was Arcanum-trained, and he held the poppy-packed air together, keeping it from becoming dissipated, either by their own frantic workings, or by the gathering winds as the heart of the storm rolled inexorably closer. He fought with all that he had, and as he did, he felt lives wink out below him as they were overcome by the poison fumes.

To think men actually smoke this stuff by choice!

To think I almost traded in it . . .

He put aside that flash of guilt. For now there were lives to be saved, and he pushed every ounce of his gnostic strength into keeping his lethal cloud intact, even as enemy magi ripped at it from all sides.

And it was working: he was buying the extra minutes needed for the remains of Marle's and Duprey's rankers to escape and flee to the south. They were staggering out of the smoke, dazed and weaving, but Kip's men seized them and pushed them on their way.

The following Keshi infantrymen who made it through were just as disoriented and were mercilessly dispatched.

Then no more Rondians emerged; he'd done enough. The weight of all the enemy magi focusing their counterspells against him began to tell, and the rising winds started to rip at the cloud too, until with a final groan, Ramon was forced to release his gnostic workings and let the smoke go. In seconds the rising gale had torn it apart and swirled the poppy flakes away.

Revealed below was a sea of enemies, thousands of them, all staring up at him. The steep cliff prevented them from coming straight at him; instead they turned and started running to his left, heading for the riverbed where Kip's men held the new rear guard. The Ninth Maniple were suddenly the only thing preventing the enemy from pouring onto the upper plain and running amok among the fleeing men and the lumbering supply wagons.

The Keshi were storming heaven with their hymns as they surged up the slope, each trying to outstrip the rest as they sought to be the hero to take down the giant barbarian.

The first Keshi was wielding a scimitar and shield, and Kip called to his gods as he swung the zweihandle and brought the six-foot blade crunching through the man's blade, shield and helm. The next tried to spear him, but Kip stepped to the right of the lunge and hacked the man in half. The next two tried to take him together, one on either side, but they were hammered back by a burst of carefully marshaled telekinesis, then their heads flew off, effortlessly severed from their necks in one fluid swing. Then Kip's rankers, taking courage from their mage, closed about him, forming a new line. More Keshi were coming, but Ramon could see that they weren't totally alert; they must have been exposed to his drug-cloud.

"*Ycha bei Minaus!*" Kip was shouting. "*Ycha bei Minaus!*"

Si, you are a bull-headed god, no doubt—but I've still got to get you out of there! Ramon thought as he spurred his horse along the ridge. He began pouring mage-bolts into the oncoming Keshi and they stopped and looked upward, trying to pinpoint this new threat. Their hesitation caused their advance to falter, and Kip's men stopped retreating. The Schlessen must have been caught in the toils of bloodlust, because incredibly, he screamed an order to advance—it was an act of utter madness, but it lifted his men, who took up his stentorian cries. "*Minaus! Minaus!*" they screamed—soldiers always loved war-gods, even foreign ones.

Ramon watched as fear struck the Keshi, who suddenly believed that they were caught at the front of some massive counterattack, led by an insane barbarian. The first ranks faltered, their prayers wavering, and they started involuntarily backing way—then they turned and ran back into the dust clouds below.

Kip's men whooped, and began to go after them, but Ramon screamed at the Schlessen to stop them.

"Kip!" he shouted, trying to attract the barbarian's attention as he spurred his horse down the slope. "No—no! Kip, don't chase them! You've got to get your men out of there!"

But the Schlessen didn't hear him. His eyes were wild and the blood was pumping fast through his veins as he waved his zweihandle and screamed, "*Yar! Yar! Ycha bei Minaus! Attacke! Attacke!*"

"Neyn, you idiot! Kip! Get the Hel out of there!" Ramon slammed a mesmeric spell at the Schlessen's brain, trying to puncture the battle madness. "Pull back, you fool!"

For a few moments it looked as if Kip and his men were going to ignore him and charge straight back into the unholy mess below, but then sanity—or Ramon's spell—prevailed.

Abruptly, Kip exhaled and blinked several times, as if banking the fires burning in his eyes. He raised a hand to halt his men and shouted, "Yar!" acknowledging Ramon's order. "We go!"

He waved his men back up the slope, though Ramon thought he looked almost disappointed to be leaving the fray with Keshi still alive. The men with him were as reluctant as their battle-mage to leave the field.

Ramon spurred his horse down the slope to meet his friend. "Don't lag, amici! There's a whole lot more of those bastido down there!" *<Is this a proper war yet, you great lunkhead?>*

"Yar, this is a proper war now," Kip announced grimly as he reached Ramon and reached over to grasp his hand. "About time, yar?"

"Si, amici," Ramon snorted. "And we've just been royally rukked over."

Kip laughed aloud. "Yar, it's been one giant *arschficke*." He raised a hand and gestured, setting his rankers on the path southward. "But my Bullheads stayed strong," he added with gruff pride. "They're almost as good as a Schlessen warband."

"As you say—but can they run?" Ramon called. "See that fortress? It's about a mile south, I reckon. That's where you've got to be before that rukking storm hits us!"

They both turned back and looked up. If anything, the storm appeared to be slowing, almost as if it had somehow been set to linger over the center, right where Duke Echor was.

And that might just be the saving of us, Ramon thought. "Let's go." He tugged on Lu's reins. "Save me a good spot in the castle."

"See you there, mein freund," Kip agreed as he sheathed his zweihandle. He leaned across and slapped Ramon's thigh. "Don't wait too long yourself, yar?"

"I won't." Ramon waved him off, then attended to his own responsibilities. It was time to ensure his own motley collection of storemen and clerks escaped this catastrophe too.

"All right, men, it's time for us to get out of here," he shouted. He brandished his sword and cried, "Come on—let's go!"

As the men about him began to run, he pointed his own horse's head south and spurred it hard.

He could see Bondeau had his maniple halfway across the plains, closely followed by the remnants of Marle's command, those who'd managed to scale the dune ridge while the legate bought them time to escape. On the hill to the south was the broken-down fortress, the only possible sanctuary in sight. The wagons were spread out across the plain, and the men too, as everyone ran for cover. He estimated there were two thousand men, less than half of the legion—but then he saw a dark shadow to the west, and his heart sank.

Cavalry, flanking the line and cutting toward them . . . If that's not the Lesser Son, we're completely rukked.

"Faster!" he shouted to the men about him, though it was unnecessary; he wasn't the only one to have seen what was coming for them. "Move yourselves!"

The remnants of the Thirteenth ran like all Hel was on their tail.

Dust on the Wind

The Deserts

It is said in The Kalistham that the deserts are a punishment for the sins of the world. For every sin, Ahm weeps a tear that becomes a grain of sand. The Keshi say that the world is filling up with sand, for man is eternally sinful. But through the agency of the Ordo Costruo, gardens flourish now in Kesh, where once there was desert. Grain by grain, ignorance is defeated. It is for such works that we exist as human beings.

ANTONIN MEIROS, HEBUSALIM, 854

Isle of Glass, Javon coast, Antiopia
Zulhijja (Decore) 928
6th month of the Moontide

The skiff broke the surface and the membrane of canvas and gnosis that had protected them, allowing them to keep breathing, popped, letting a gust of fresh air wash over them. Then another wave towered above them, soaking them. Alaron shouted aloud and the bubble reformed as they went under again. Though it bulged alarmingly, somehow it held, despite the power of the waves. He tapped into the power the lamiae had poured into the keel, kept the bow down, and headed forward, praying all the while.

Next time they surfaced, he was ready. He used sylvan-gnosis to feed buoyancy into the keel, and as the pillar receded, he found they could actually float. The waves, though gigantic, weren't breaking, and though the movement had both Ramita and him vomiting, the skiff remained upright and above the waves. Until they could get aloft, it would suffice.

His mind was still buzzing with a thrill he'd never expected to know. For a few seconds back on the landing platform he'd reached trance-gnosis again—and this time more completely than he had in Gydan's Cut. Desperation and terror were achieving what years of lessons and practice had never managed, and proved he really did have the ability to use different aspects of the gnosis simultaneously. But any sense of triumph he might have felt was obliterated by what had been left behind. Justina Meiros was dead. And Cym—*Cym!*—if she wasn't already dead, she was in the hands of one enemy or another . . .

As they were swept away by the fierce currents the Isle of Glass behind them was receding at a frightening pace. They could see the Inquisitors' windship was still aloft, but its mast and sail had been burned away and it was moving sluggishly. It looked like none of the venators were left. All the shapeshifters had vanished inside the massive pillar.

We got out, but Cym's still in there . . .

He felt tears well up again, and this time he couldn't stop them. Cym was lost and her newfound mother was dead, and he could not go back without destroying what little her loss had gained.

He clutched the Scytale to him.

Ramita, sitting in the bow, her eyes fiercely protective as her hands caressed her bulging belly, whispered, "I'm sorry." She was barely audible above the thunderous seas, but he knew what she'd said.

There was nothing he could say; he could only add his salty tears to the surging waters that bore them away.

Ramita stared around her. The little skiff flared with protective shields every time they went under and she was barely wet, despite a dozen immersions. Already the Isle of Glass was far behind them as the open sea swept them along on massive surging waves.

She could not escape the image of Huriya, her sister no more, devouring the soul of the old woman . . .

All you gods, what has she become?

And Justina was dead.

Dear daughter, be at peace.

But worst of all was the guilt: one simple truth had unpicked Justina's defenses with awful precision.

I let Kazim in. I killed Antonin, and now I've killed Justina.

She buried her head in her arms as they were swept onwards, into the darkness of the trackless seas, cradling her unborn children and praying for survival, for their sake if not for hers.

Cym opened her eyes, disoriented by the smoke and darkness. She was lying facedown on cold stone and her whole body ached abominably, especially her right shoulder; that was where she'd struck the wall. It was only because she'd managed to get her shields up in time that she'd even survived that impact.

She went to move, but couldn't. Something heavy, a weight pressing into the middle of her back, had her pinned down. She twisted her neck, trying to see, and found herself gazing into the face of a lion just a few inches away. Its panting breath was hot on her flesh.

She tore her gaze away from its blue-eyed stare and realized that the head sat on the shoulders of a majestic human body—a man's body.

This is the one who killed my mother.

And it was more than likely that he was about to kill her too. What had the Keshi girl said to her mother that had left her defenses so fatally wide open? The words had been in an unknown tongue, but what words could have left her mother—a mage of such power and such experience—so utterly defenseless?

Now she could see other shifters moving about her. Most of them were kneeling before the feet of a diminutive Keshi girl, kissing her hands and feet. Cym thought the girl's face was a strange mixture, both regal and common at the same time, but she appeared to be inordinately proud of herself, for she was preening and giggling at the same time.

Then her eyes fell on Cym and she said something—one word, a name, maybe?

"Zaqri—" she called again, and this time Lionhead shifted to face her.

She spoke again, a liquid stream of Keshi.

Lionhead is called Zaqri, Cym noted. *He killed my mother . . .*

Zaqri stood, and his face changed, until it became that of a ruggedly handsome blond man with gleaming blue eyes. Cym tried to move as well, but she was drained by gnosis use and battered from being crushed beneath him. She barely had the strength to lift a hand. All she could do was lie there, helpless, as Zaqri moved gracefully over to the young Keshi girl and knelt at her feet. He bent and kissed them, and words passed between them, and then he returned to hunch over her, a single hand pressing her back down. He was still naked from the battle, a vision of masculine power and grace. And he was drenched in her mother's blood.

"Girl," he said. "Who are you?"

They speak Rondian . . .

She shook her head in surprise, and an involuntary moan escaped her lips as she tried to squirm away from him. She had to drag her eyes from the majesty of his gore-covered body.

He seized her chin and pulled her head around to face him. "I will Chain you if I must, little girl." His huge hand rested on her forehead and suddenly he was inside her brain. His gnostic strength was truly frightening. *<See? I am far stronger than you, Rimoni.>* His mental touch was as masterful as his body—he was decades older than her, she sensed, and yet he was in his prime.

Though he terrified her, she made herself be defiant. *<You killed my mother.>*

<And your people slew my mate,> he countered bitterly.

They stared at each other unflinching. Then something broke inside her. *<Is . . . is my mother inside you?>*

He shook his head. *<Only her energies. I am stronger now than I ever was.>*

<Is she . . . aware?> she asked tremulously.

<Gone,> he replied, with no attempt to soften the blow. *<Only a memory.>* He gripped her shoulders and spoke aloud. "Open to me girl, or this will hurt."

She had no choice, she realized; she opened her wards and let him into her mind. He was like a torch in a darkened room, and he filled her absolutely, his lion face shining like the sun. *Like Sol.* She couldn't have resisted, even if she had tried.

His leonine visage studied her very carefully as she forgot how to breathe. Then he caught a thought she could not protect; his eyes went wide and he looked away, wonder in his expression, his hands shaking with excitement.

He left her mind and said softly, "My Queen, I have learned something."

Huriya walked slowly back to him. "Yes?" she asked, dropping her own voice to a whisper.

Cym could only just make out his words as he bent his great head to Huriya's ear. "The Inquisitors came here seeking an artifact—you have Sabele's memories; you will know the Scytale of Corineus."

Huriya's eyes went round as saucers. "You're sure?"

Zaqri's hand gripped Cym's chin. "This girl has held it in her hands."

Cym's heart sank as she looked from Huriya to Zaqri. The Keshi girl was unnerving, with her aura that was both ancient and corrupt. But Zaqri frightened her more. Her mind went back to something she'd said to Alaron recently, an articulation of all her girlish longings: "I want someone who walks like a king and shines like Sol. I want someone with poetry on his lips and majesty in his voice. I don't know if I will ever meet him, but when I do, I'll know. There won't be any doubts or questions. I'll just know."

And I do know, for he is Zaqri.

But he killed my mother. So I must do the same to him.

Under her breath, she whispered the sacred oath of vendetta.

The Fist—what was left of it—knelt in a prayer-circle on the fore-deck as the windship crawled east on a cold breeze, heading toward the distant cliffs. There were more ghosts than survivors now, and even Elath Dranid's usually stolid face was haunted by failure and loss. He had been so certain in battle; now he looked lost. The three other survivors wore that same look of oppression, of defeat and disgrace on their faces.

Malevorn glared down at his signet, feeling the weight of his family's need weighing on his shoulders. As a child he'd been the one to find his father's body; now that memory blurred with Vordan's last moments.

If we do not succeed, we will be joining them both in Hel.

That he was even here himself was a minor miracle. Realizing he was trapped on the lowest level of the stone pillar, he'd had to clamber out, using Earth-gnosis to ascend the treacherous slope. He'd hailed the remnants of the Fist and they'd only just managed to extricate him before the winds shoved the hulk of the *Magol* out over the seas. But there was little comfort in rescue, and little brotherhood between the survivors gathered about him. Dranid had retreated into himself; he was clearly inadequate for the challenges of leadership, despite his martial prowess. Dominic had never seemed so much like a bleating lamb. Only Raine's simmering fury reassured him. He knew how she felt; she, like him, would visit a world of pain on those who'd thwarted them. He didn't care what it took, but Alaron Mercer and that mudskin with him were going to *suffer*.

We've had our asses thrashed by Souldrinkers. We let Alaron-Kore-be-damned-Mercer escape us with the greatest prize on Urte. There will be a reckoning.

They had jury-rigged a sail to the stump of one of the *Magol's* masts. Dominic's only notable contribution so far to this whole damned trip had been to start the masts regrowing, using his otherwise useless sylvan-gnosis. Nonetheless, they still were crawling landward at a walking pace. Of the two-dozen men-at-arms they'd taken into the fray they had only half a dozen left, and only one pilot-mage. All the venators were dead too. Malevorn Andevarion's fury was barely containable.

Faces swam before him: Vordan, dead by his own hand. Brothers Alain and Jonas, both cut down by Jeris Muhren. Seldon and Filius, butchered by constructs. Boron Funt, brought in to scry a college-mate and slaughtered by those same creatures. And porcelain-faced Virgina, skewered on a broken mast. Had Mercer done that, or had it been the mudskin girl? She'd hurled him backward like a toy, he knew that, and he'd have her guts for it. But who *was* she?

Adamus Crozier joined them. He stood beside them and laid his hands on Malevorn's and Dranid's shoulders. "My brothers and sister in Kore, we have been punished—not by our enemies, but by Kore Himself. We have been weak, and we have strayed from purity. Spiritual weakness has led to martial weakness. No more. We have a clear goal before us: the capture of this thief Alaron Mercer, who has betrayed the empire and thrown in his lot with Rimoni and mudskin scum. We are going to find him and we are going to make him sorry he was ever born."

Kore, let it be so.

"Now listen. You all know we hunt the Scytale of Corineus itself. You know what it does, and what it could mean: a rival Ascendancy; leading to the destruction of all we hold holy and pure. We have no choice: we must not stop until we have regained it."

Mount Tigrat, Javon, Antiopia
Zulhijja (Decore) 928
6th month of the Moontide

Elena set the sails of the skiff so they were poised to unfurl as soon as they'd risen high enough to catch the wind. Kazim stood in the bow, surrounded by their possessions—some clothing, their bed-rolls, all their stores, weapons, and armor.

She met his eye.

Time to go.

They could not stay here on Tigrat, of course: the monastery was compromised—and she just wanted to be away from the place. No matter; she had another refuge in mind. Shepherds kept huts on the high summer slopes; they went deserted through winter and she knew of one less than a day's flight from here. They'd labored throughout the rest of the night, gathering everything they would need and piling it into the skiff. Staying busy helped to keep the horrors at bay too—and kept her from crawling back to the sanctuary of Kazim's strong arms and hiding there forever. It was his very solidity that gave her the courage to go on—but it also reinforced their growing mutual dependency.

Kore help me, I want him. But it shouldn't be now. Not so soon after . . . all this blood.

How they'd not fallen into each other in the aftermath of the battle she scarcely knew. Perhaps because of the stink of death that hung in the air here; the miasma of destruction. But the bond between them was as palpable as the winds that whistled through the old ruins.

"Where are we going?" he called.

"I've another hideaway set up northeast of here," she called. "It's not far—or so nice, I'm sorry."

"Why are we flying in daylight?"

She held up two fingers. "One: the Hadishah might come back sooner than we expect. Two: we'll be flying through the hills in winter; there'll be no one around to see us."

"What will we do next?"

Her mood became grim. "We're going to wage war on the Dorobon. Training is over. It is time for us to join the fray."

He nodded, accepting her words easily.

He saved my life. He killed his sworn blood-brothers for me. I'm in his debt forever. Her eyes drank in the rakishly heroic face and the sheer size of him, and reflected that he was still a boy despite his size and power. He was barely twenty-one. She could see the man he might become, though: someone she could come to care for. They'd shared too much, forged bonds neither could now put aside.

Ella, Ella, Ella . . . you've got maybe ten years of relative youth remaining, and then what?

It doesn't matter, she told that chiding inner voice. *Ten years is a long time when you don't know whether you'll even survive this rukking war.*

That thought didn't make her sad, though; she'd always felt most alive when everything was up for grabs—even her heart. Especially then.

"Are you ready?" she called. "Then let's go!"

"Hold on!" Kazim shouted, and called the winds. The sails billowed as the hull lifted, and at last they were on their way. He felt his heart lift as the skiff rose under his—*his!*—power. The Air-gnosis churned from him like blood pumping from a fresh wound. The faces of the colleagues he'd killed last night haunted him, drawn on the backs of his eyelids, although the only regrettable death was Jamil. Gatoz he would have killed a thousand times over, and Haroun . . . well, the Scriptualist had exchanged his humanity for dogma somewhere along the way. The others he'd barely known, but they had been complicit in Gatoz's crime. They were not fighting the same shihad that he was; they were nothing more than brute killers and that was all. They would have killed for any cause.

He was different. He needed an ideal. He needed his personal shihad to be pure.

There was a giddy feel to the day as they uprooted themselves and moved on. They had burned the enemy skiffs, and he was relieved to see Molmar had not been one of the pilots, though they barely knew each other. There was no one left in the world now who cared about what he did. Except Elena. In the end, he'd done it all for her.

When he'd cradled her against him and helped her through the shock of what they'd experienced, he'd desired her more than any other, even Ramita—but they'd been so caked in blood, and he wanted things between them to be pure too.

We will find a place where a mountain stream flows and I'll wash her clean.

He didn't know where they would end up, or what they would do when they got there—kill people, probably; Dorobon soldiers, certainly. And people like Gurvon Gyle or Gatoz, as many of them as they could take down.

Faces popped into his head: Ramita, of course, bringing with her a regret and guilt that would never leave him. Jai, her brother, and his, by blood-bond: *Where are you, brother? If I could do this clairvoyance thing Ella talks about, maybe I could find you?* And Huriya—*But do I even want to find you, little sister?* He paused, and then thought, *But if there's a way back for me, maybe there is for you, Didi?*

He had never been one to dwell on the past. This past year he'd crossed the world to do something terrible, and it had been worse than he'd thought it ever could be. It had been the darkest time of his life—but now he could see a way out: a path to follow, like looking at the trackless wastes and seeing a star. For now, that was more than good enough.

He looked back at Elena. Her face was alight with a glow he'd not seen before. She was still utterly unlike everything he'd ever thought a woman should be, but that didn't matter anymore. For now and for the foreseeable future, they would face the world together. They would find a way to set it to right.

The sky was calling. His shout echoed through the ruins: "Let's fly!"

Brochena, Javon, Antiopia
Zulhijja (Decore) 928
6th month of the Moontide

Francis Dorobon sat on his throne, staring down at the three figures kneeling before him in chains.

Fenys Rhodium, Terus Grandienne, and Eternalus Crozier hung their heads.

I've got three of the most powerful men in the world on their knees before me. He was exultant.

"Mercy," Magister Rhodium begged.

Francis looked at the fat magus and was reminded only of his mother. *She's dead. She's dead. She's dead. And the world still turns!*

He glanced at his two queens: Portia, a vision of loveliness on his right, and Cera, a dour presence on his left. He decided that he would have them both tonight, right after the banquet, to remind both who was master.

If Gyle wants the Nesti girl, he'll have to earn her.

Pleased at the thought, he glanced sideways at his Chief Counselor. Gurvon Gyle was resplendent in the purple of an Imperial Envoy, though Francis thought his furtive face looked strange under the bright lights of the court. He was moving awkwardly, the result of the severe beating he'd been given.

"Are there grounds for mercy, milord Gyle?" he asked, just to hear the answer out loud.

"There are none, my King," Gyle said solemnly. "These men connived to usurp your just rule and to make you into a puppet of their convenience. They have all confessed."

They had indeed, after being captured with the loss of scores of men, then Chain-runed and tortured until they were ready to confess to anything he desired. None of them could walk now, and their fingerless hands were still dripping blood on the marble floor of the throne-hall. He had had to use Endus Rykjard's mercenaries to secure their capture, and there were now as many condotiori here as Dorobon legionaries, and more mercenaries were coming up from the south; Gyle had promised there would be enough to properly secure Javon in Francis's name.

"Then let there be no mercy," Francis shouted. "Bring out the executioner!"

This kingdom belongs to me.

Then he remembered Olivia, and turned to her. "You don't need to watch this, dear sister."

For an instant, Olivia stared back at him, her face blank, as if she wondered why he thought her so squeamish. Then she surprised him by shaking her head. "I'll stay, brother," she said, her eyes on Gurvon Gyle, as they had been ever since she had entered the room. Seeing Mother die had doubtless been traumatic for her, but she was showing an inner strength he'd never suspected of her. And the eyes she cast on Gurvon Gyle were full of devotion.

It's a whole new world for us both.

"Gurvon, my friend." Endus Rykjard's bright teeth shone in the twilight. "Imperial purple looks strange upon you."

Gyle shrugged. "I'm adaptable, Endus; surely you know that." He struck a pose. About him were gathered his depleted circle: Mara and Rutt, both deadly, and both apparently devoted to him. Pretty little Maddy Parlow, who'd kept Timori safe from Octa's clutches. Coin was already in place, secure in her newest role. She too looked at him with needy eyes. Perhaps they all just needed someone to channel their talents? *All some people ever want is a purpose; they'd sell their souls to the man who gave them one.* They were each, in their own way, followers rather than leaders. They needed him to lead, and so they were his.

Rykjard poured wine for each. "So, my friend, you are now the most powerful man in Javon. My congratulations."

"It is also thanks to you, Endus."

The mercenary captain shrugged self-deprecatingly. He'd been exceedingly well rewarded for his steadfast treachery. "Deliver on your promises, Gurvon. That is all I ask."

Gyle smiled. "What news from the south?"

"Adi Paavus has left Korion's army and marches for the Krak, and the other mercenary commanders are deserting and racing to join him. We'll seal ourselves in Javon, then put the squeeze on little Franny."

Gyle smiled at that, and they shook hands. "To the Kingdom of the Condotiori," he said.

Rykjard raised his cup in a toast. "I'd drink to that."

Gyle grinned about his circle of subordinates. "My friends, we're going to ransack this kingdom."

Shaliyah, Kesh, Antiopia
Zulhijja (Decore) 928
6th month of the Moontide

Ramon Sensini stared through the narrow windows of the ruined fortress. The men of the Pallacios XIII and the remnants of half a dozen other legions huddled all around the courtyard and filled every bit of room in the place; each one of them was wrapped in cloaks and cowls and veiled like the Keshi against the sandstorm that howled among the ruins. Those who were trying to sleep did so sitting up.

Ramon had woven an Air-gnosis barrier over the window to allow him to use it, but it was draining him and he knew he'd have to take it down soon. Though it was midafternoon, it might as well have been midnight, so dark was it outside. A dirty brown gloom filled the air, clogging his mouth and nostrils, eyes and ears with grit. His eyes were weeping sand and his throat was scraped raw, though that was as much from shouting as the desert storm. But at least there was no chance of an enemy attack right now.

"Anything?" Severine asked, her voice hollow.

He shook his head.

"We got away," Renn Bondeau repeated dazedly. "I can't believe it."

Ramon glanced from the white-faced Palacian to the equally stunned Schlessen. Kip's face was red-raw from the sand blasting at his fair skin. He shook his head again, this time in disbelief. *We got away this time—but for how long?*

He looked across at Seth Korion. The general's son had brought his cavalry in the very nick of time, driving back their pursuers and allowing the Thirteenth to reach this temporary haven. He was now the ranking mage, and that made him by default Legate of the Thirteenth. Not that there was anyone to ratify that promotion, for Severine had been unable to contact any of Duke Echor's magi. They had no way of telling whether the army was simply hunkered down beneath the sandstorm, or if it had been swept away, massacred by the unexpected Keshi legions. But the air had that unmistakable reek of death and disaster.

"*Got away?*" Severine echoed dully. "They *slaughtered* us like sheep. We're thousands of miles away from the Bridge, and the enemy have *magi*. We haven't *got away* from anything."

"My father will save us," Seth Korion said, attempting defiance.

Ramon stared at the young man, and found himself unexpectedly filled with pity. *Your father probably set this up*, he thought—but he couldn't voice that thought, not when they had so little hope to cling to.

"Now what?" Bondeau asked hollowly.

Korion looked helpless, and so did Severine. Even Kip shrugged. They all gazed about the room, and then, strangely, their eyes settled on him: Ramon Sensini, the Silacian guttersnipe. He had never even dared dream such a day might come when people looked to him for answers.

"What now?" he answered slowly. "Now we have to get home."

"But how?" Korion breathed, as if Ramon might actually have a workable plan.

Ramon rolled his eyes. "Lesser Son, you're going to have to take command. You're the senior officer." He noticed Bondeau open his mouth as if to dispute this, then he closed it. No doubt the Rondian would be trouble at some point, but for now he looked too stunned to argue.

Ramon forced a faint smile. "But don't worry: I'll do all the thinking. I have a plan."

He'd thought they might argue, shout him down—but all he had to say was: *I have a plan*, and that was enough; he was, unofficially, in charge. The details could wait.

There was little said after that. They were all drained and exhausted, and they needed to rest, even if sleep was going to prove impossible with the horrors of the day still fresh in their minds. He found Severine a blanket and covered them both with it as they sat with their backs against the wall. Eventually she stopped shaking. He stroked her cheek and thought how lovely she still managed to look, even begrimed by dust and sweat. "Are you all right, amora?" he whispered.

She looked up at him, tears in her eyes, and lifted her hand to his face. "Ramon, I'm carrying your child."

Halli'kut, Northern Kesh, Antiopia
Zulhijja (Decore) 928
6th month of the Moontide

Kaltus Korion sat astride his horse, overlooking the walls of Halli'kut. He liked to be alone at moments like this before battle; he found it focused him to sit there by himself, facing the enemy:

one hero, about to bring his wrath down upon the dark hordes before him.

So it was with some annoyance that he saw General Rhynus Bergium climbing the hill toward him. He sighed in vexation, until he noticed that the general was carrying a messenger scroll.

The general proffered the scroll to his commander and stood back to allow him some privacy when he opened it.

Korion pushed the walls of Halli'kut from his mind, examined the seal—that of Emir Rashid—and broke it open.

The message was brief, just twelve words.

The army of Echor Borodium has been destroyed. The bargain is fulfilled.

"Where did this come from?" he asked Bergium.

"An enemy rider handed it to one of our scouts," Bergium replied, eyeing the scroll curiously.

Korion handed him the scroll.

The general read it, blinked, and read it again. Then he smiled. "Congratulations, Lord General. The command of the Crusade is yours once more."

Kaltus Korion closed his eyes, letting the setting sun kiss his face. "It always was, Rhynus." He chuckled softly. "What a glorious day."

Well done, Belonius Vult! Your plan worked. What a shame you're too dead to enjoy the moment.

"Will we still attack tomorrow?" Bergium asked.

Korion opened his eyes and gazed down on Halli'kut. "Of course. The real war has only just begun."

THE END OF BOOK TWO OF THE MOONTIDE
The story continues in:
UNHOLY WAR

DRAMATIS PERSONAE

The Scarlet Tides

As at Junesse 928

In Yuros
Imperial Court, Pallas

Emperor Constant Sacrecour: Emperor of Rondelmar and all Yuros
Mater-Imperia Lucia Fasterius: the emperor's mother, a Living Saint
Cordan: son of Constant, heir to the throne
Coramore: daughter of Constant
Lord Calan Dubrayle: Imperial Treasurer
Arch-Prelate Dominius Wurther: Head of the Church of Kore
General Kaltus Korion: Commander of the Armies of Rondelmar
General Rhynus Bergium, Korion's second-in-command
Adamus Crozier: a bishop of the Kore
Natia Sacrecour: Constant's imprisoned elder sister

RONDELMAR

Echor Borodium, Duke of Argundy: uncle of Emperor Constant
Boron Funt: a priest-mage

THE EIGHTEENTH FIST OF KORE'S HOLY INQUISITION

Lanfyr Vordan: Inquisitor and Fist Commander
Dranid: Fist Second
Alain: Fist Third
Raine Caladryn: an Acolyte
Filius: an Acolyte
Jonas: an Acolyte
Virgina: an Acolyte

Seldon: an Acolyte
Dominic: an Acolyte
Malevorn: an Acolyte

THE LAMIAE

Kekropius: an Elder male
Kessa: mate of Kekropius
Mesuda: an Elder female
Reku: an Elder female
Hypollo: an Elder male
Naugri: a male
Fydro: a male
Ildena: wife of Fydro
Nia: a female
Vyressa: a female
Poulos: a male

THE TWENTY-THIRD FIST OF KORE'S HOLY INQUISITION

Ullyn Siburnius: Inquisitor and Fist Commander
Delta: a mage

NOROSTEIN, NOROS

King Phyllios III: King of Noros
Governor Belonius Vult: Imperial Governor of Noros
Eli Besko: a Norostein counselor and mage (deceased)
Captain Jeris Muhren: Watch Captain
Vannaton Mercer: a trader
Tesla Anborn-Mercer: mage, wife of Vannaton Mercer (deceased)
Alaron Mercer: mage, son of Vann and Tesla
Gina Weber: daughter of Jos, Council mage
Pars Logan: a veteran of the Noros Revolt
Clement: Council secretary
Olyd Krussyn: a Council mage
Gron Koll: a Council mage (deceased)
Blayne de Noellen: a mage

Silacia

Mercellus di Regia: head of a Rimoni gypsy family
Cymbellea di Regia: Rimoni gypsy, daughter of Mercellus
Anise: a Rimoni orphan
Ferdi: Anise's brother
Signor Torrini: a landowner
Alfonso: a Silacian farmer
Pater-Retiari: a criminal clan-lord

Turm Zauberin Arcanum, Norostein

Lucien Gavius: Principal of Turm Zauberin (Arcanum College)
Darius Fyrell: a tutor at Turm Zauberin
Agnes Yune: a tutor at Turm Zauberin

Gurvon Gyle's Gray Foxes (based in Noros)

Gurvon Gyle: a mercenary captain and spy
Rutt Sordell: a mage, whose soul is currently lodged in the body of Elena Anborn
Mara Secordin
Yvette ("Coin"): a child of Mater-Imperia Lucia
Mathis Drumm
Glynn Nevis
Hesta Mafagliou
Mathieu Fillon
Madeline Parlow

In Antiopia
Pontus

Giordano: a Silacian trader
Regina: Giordano's daughter

The Thirteenth Pallas Legion (Palacios XIII)

Jonti Duprey: Legate
Rufus Marle: Legate-Secundus
Baltus Prenton: Windmaster
Lanna Jureigh: Healer

Tyron Frand: Legion Chaplain
Severine Tiseme: Legion Farseer
Seth Korion: a battle-mage
Renn Bondeau: a battle-mage
Tomas Coulder: a battle-mage
Bevyn Fenn: a battle-mage
Hugh Gerant: a battle-mage
Evan Hale: a battle-mage
Rhys Lewen: battle-mage
Fridryk Kippenegger: a battle-mage
Ramon Sensini: a battle-mage
Nyvus: Dupre's aide-de-campe
Storn: Tribune of the Tenth Maniple
Coll: a scout of the Tenth Maniple

SYDIA

Gul-Vlk: chief of Vlk tribe
Hyr-Vlk: chief's son
Drzkir: head shaman of Vlk Sfera
Myrlla: a Vlk Sfera mage
Gilkria: a Vlk Sfera mage

ORDO COSTRUO (MAGE ORDER BASED IN HEBUSALIM)

Antonin Meiros: Arch-Magus (deceased)
Justina Meiros: Antonin's daughter
Rene Cardien
Rashid Mubarak, Emir of Halli'kut
Alyssa Dulayne
Taldin
Stivor Sindon
Francois Vertros

HEBUSALIM

Tomas Betillon: Imperial Governor of Hebusalim
Ramita Ankesharan: Lakh widow of Antonin Meiros
Captain Faubert: master of the windship *Fleur-Rouge*

In Javon

Cera Nesti: Queen-Regent of Javon
Timori Nesti: Crown-Prince of Javon
Solinde Nesti: Princess of Javon (deceased)
Paolo Castellini: a Nesti guard commander
Harshal ali-Assam: a Jhafi noble
Francesco Perdonello: Chief of Royal Bureaucracy
Acmed al-Istan: an Amteh Godspeaker
Pita Rosco: Master of the Royal Purse
Luigi Ginovisi: Master of Revenues
Seir Luca Conti: a Rimoni knight
Comte Piero Inveglio: a Rimoni nobleman
Seir Lorenzo di Kestria: a Rimoni knight (deceased)
Ilan Tamadhi, Emir of Ihtemsa
Seir Rico di Kestria: a knight (elder brother of Lorenzo)
Seir Maxi di Aranio: a knight
Borsa: Nesti family nursemaid
Tarita: a palace maid
Ivan Prato: a Sollan drui
Mustaq al'Madhi: a criminal
Endus Rykjard: a mercenary commander

THE DOROBON MONARCHY

Octa Dorobon: widowed matriarch of Dorobon Family, pretenders to the Javon
    throne
Francis Dorobon: son and heir of the Dorobon line
Olivia Dorobon: daughter of Octa and sister to Francis
Magister Rhodium: a mage
Sir Terus Grandienne: a mage-knight
Eternalus Crozier: a Kore bishop
Alfredo Gorgio: a Rimoni lord of Hytel
Portia Tolidi: a noblewoman of Hytel, sister of Fernando
Fernando Tolidi: a nobleman of Hytel (deceased)

In Kesh
Sagostabad

Salim I, Sultan of Kesh
Wimla: a Krak di Condotiori maid

Among the Hadishah

Kazim Makani: a Souldrinker and assassin
Jamil: a mage assassin
Molmar: a Hadishah skiff-pilot
Gatoz: Hadishah mage and commander
Talid: an assassin
Yadri: an assassin
Hamid: a Hadishah trainee
Arda: maid to Alyssa Dulayne
Haroun: an Amteh Scriptualist

Elsewhere

Sabele: a Souldrinker seer
Huriya Makani: a Souldrinker, sister of Kazim
Zaqri: a Souldrinker
Ghila: a Souldrinker, wife of Zaqri
Perno: a Souldrinker
Hessaz: a Souldrinker, wife of Perno
Arkanus: a Souldrinker warleader

In Lakh
Teshwallabad

Tariq, Mughal of Lakh
Hanook: Royal Vizier

Baranasi

Ispal Ankesharan: trader
Tanuva Ankesharan: Ispal's wife
Jai: Ispal's son
Keita: Jai's lover

From the Past

Johan Corin ("Corineus"): Messiah of the Kore

Selene Corin ("Corinea"): sister and murderer of Johan, personification of feminine evil

Hiltius Sacrecour: late emperor, grandfather of Emperor Constant

Magnus Sacrecour: father of Emperor Constant

Alitia: deceased first wife of Emperor Constant

General Arkimon Robler: a renowned Noros general

General Jaes Andevarion: a disgraced Rondian general

Olfuss Nesti: a deceased King of Javon

Jarius Langstrit: a Noros general

Fraxis Targon: a deceased Inquisitor

APPENDICES

Time line of Urte history

Year Y500BV*:   Approximate beginning of the Rimoni conquest of Yuros.

Year Y1:   Beginning of the reign of Emperor Sertain, and new calendar adopted.

Year Y380:   The dissident Corineus and his followers engage in "The Ascension of Corineus." Corineus dies, but three hundred survivors led by Sertain gain the gnosis and begin the conquest of Yuros. Another hundred under Meiros forgo war and journey eastward into the wilderness, and a further hundred "moon-tainted" survivors go into hiding.

Year 382:   Sertain is crowned first Rondian Emperor in Pallas and establishes Sacrecour dynasty that still rules in Pallas. In time Rondian rule extends across almost entire continent of Yuros.

Year 697:   First windships from Pontus "discover" Antiopia and its ancient and thriving civilizations. Trade links develop, and eventually, plans for a linking bridge are developed by Meiros and his order of peaceful magi, the Ordo Costruo.

Year Y808:   The First Moontide: the Leviathan Bridge is completed by Meiros and opens for the first time.

Year Y820+:   The Second Moontide sees Rimoni natives flood into Ja'afar (Javon) in large numbers, where they buy land and establish themselves. As they gain political control, civil war develops, but is averted by the "Javon Settlement" formally adopted in 836. The monarchy of Javon becomes democratic and is legally tied to the necessity for mixed racial background.

---

*(BV = Before Victory)

Year 834:   A Keshi invasion of northern Lakh establishes the Amteh in Lakh, and a dynasty subservient to Kesh (the "Mughal" is a Keshi ruler of Lakh territories).

Year Y880/881:   The Seventh Moontide: the most successful Moontide trading season in Hebusalim, and the revelation that the Pallas debt exceeds revenues. Crown credit crisis resolved by underwriting of crown debt by merchant bankers Jusst & Holsen.

Year Y892/893:   The Eighth Moontide: trading is disrupted by a series of atrocities by both Amteh fanatics and Kirkegarde knights.

Year Y902:   "The Year of Bloody Knives": Emperor Hiltius is assassinated and his son-in-law Constant becomes emperor. Adherents of his elder daughter are arrested and executed after a reported coup attempt.

Year Y904/905:   The Ninth Moontide and the First Crusade: the Rondian Emperor Constant sends his legions into Hebusalim. His armies are permitted to cross the Bridge by the Ordo Costruo; they defeat the armies of Dhassa and Kesh. The Rondians establish the Dorobon monarchy in Javon and plunder Sagostabad. The Rondians leave a garrison in Hebusalim to resist reoccupation.

Years Y909/910: The Noros Revolt: King Phyllios III of Noros refuses to send tax and tribute to Pallas, provoking a military response. Despite promises of support from neighboring states, Noros is isolated and finally defeated in 910 when the last armies under General Robler surrender.

Years Y916/917: The Second Crusade: Rondian legions are reinforced in Hebusalim. They defeat the Sultans of Dhassa and Kesh and plunder as far east as Istabad. Again they withdraw to Hebb Valley as the Bridge closes.

Year Y921:   Rebellion in Javon results in the Dorobon monarchs fleeing into exile and the establishment of the Nesti monarchy. Olfuss Nesti becomes king.

Year Y926:   The Eighth Convocation of Amteh declares Shihad upon the Rondian invaders.

Year 927:   The next Moontide will begin in 928. The Third Crusade is declared by Emperor Constant, and preparations for war accelerate in both continents. Note: Antiopian chronology is counted from 454 years earlier than Yuros, so Y927 is A1381.

Time and Dates in Urte

The world of Urte uses a lunar calendar, and due to the size and influence that the moon has on both continents (or perhaps because they were once joined) they have essentially the same calendar, though they use different names for the months. There are twelve moon-cycles in a year, each 30 days long, making the lunar year 360 days. The solar calendar is a few hours longer, meaning that every few years an out-of-calendar day is recommended by the Ordo Costruo to the Emperor of Yuros and the rulers of Kesh, which is widely observed. The months are as follows:

Month of Year	Season	Yuros Name	Antiopian name
1st month	Spring	Janune	Moharram
2nd month	Spring	Febreux	Safar
3rd month	Spring	Martrois	Awwal
4th month	Summer	Aprafor	Thani
5th month	Summer	Maicin	Jumada
6th month	Summer	Junesse	Akhira
7th month	Autumn	Julsep	Rajab
8th month	Autumn	Augeite	Shaban
9th month	Autumn	Septinon	Rami
10th month	Winter	Octen	Shawwal
11th month	Winter	Noveleve	Zulqeda
12th month	Winter	Decore	Zulhijja

There are five parts to the lunar cycle, each roughly six days long, creating five six-day weeks. They are: New Moon, Waxing Moon, Full Moon, Waning Moon, and Dark Moon. The weekly holy day is usually the last (or first) day of the six-day week; generally no commercial work is done and the day is divided between religious observance and relaxation.

The days of the week are as follows:

Day of Week	Yuros Name	Kesh name	Lakh name
1st day	Minasdai	Shambe	Somvaar
2nd day	Tydai	Doshambe	Mangalvaar
3rd day	Wotendai	Seshambe	Budhvaar
4th day	Torsdai	Chaharshambe	Viirvaar
5th day	Freyadai	Panjshambe	Shukravaar
6th (holy) day	Sabbadai	Jome	Shanivaar

The time is measured using sand-timers, and the hours are rung by a man assigned to staff the tallest tower of every city, town and village. There are varying numbers of hours to the day and night: at the instant of dawn, a bell is struck, and then again every hour until sunset, when a different (lower-toned) bell commences. Depending upon the season and latitude, a day might contain as many as sixteen daylight or nighttime hours or as few as eight, but a day always totals twenty-four hours. Due to variability in quality of timing devices and vigilance of timekeepers, the timekeeping can be quite variable. The hours of the day are named as follows:

- Sunrise is the first hour: Day-Bell One
- Midday is typically Day-Bell Six
- Sunset would normally be considered Day-Bell Twelve, or Night-Bell One.
- Midnight is typically Night-Bell Six.

The Primary Religions
of Yuros and Antiopia

Sollan
(Yuros):

The Sollan Faith was the dominant religion of the Rimoni Empire and evolved from the sun and moon cults of the Yothic peoples that spread from the northeast prior to the formation of the Empire. Sol is the male deity and progenitor of mankind, together with his wayward wife Dara, or Luna, who is associated with the moon. The Sollan faith is kept by priests known as *drui* whose primary function is to keep records, advise communities, and observe the seasonal rituals. The Sollan faith was outlawed by the Rondian Empire in 411 following the establishment of the Kore. It still thrives in parts of Sydia, Schlessen, Rimoni, and Pontus, and also among the Rimoni of Javon.

Kore
(Yuros):

The Church of Kore was established alongside the conquest of Rimoni by the Rondian magi. It believes that Corineus, the leader of the group who discovered and consumed ambrosia and gained the gnosis, was the son of God (or "Kore"). The Church elevates people of mage-blood (i.e., related to one of the 300 Ascendants who led the conquest of Yuros by the Rondians) and holds that Kore gave the gnosis through the death of his Son. The Kore is the prime religion of Yuros, except where Rondelmar does not hold sway (parts of Sydia, Schlessen, Rimoni, and Pontus). The Kore is male-dominated and places religion and the magi above secular society.

The Kore promises eternal life in Heaven for the faithful, a status that magi automatically gain, but ordinary men can aspire to. The wicked burn in Hel, a fiery underworld ruled by an evil spirit called Jasid (though never named, as that is believed to be unlucky).

The Kore promises eternal life in Heaven for the faithful, a status that magi automatically gain, but ordinary men can aspire to. The wicked burn in Hel, a fiery underworld ruled by an evil spirit called Jasid (though never named, as that is believed to be unlucky).

Amteh (Antiopia): The Amteh Faith developed in the deserts of northern Antiopia and is principally associated with the Prophet Aluq-Ahmed of Hebb, who rose to importance in approximately A100 (Y450BV). His new teachings, collected in the *Kalistham*, superseded preceding religions based upon propitiation of gods that may have been related to the Omali faith. It is highly male-dominated and demanding of both time and conspicuous worship. The only deity is Ahm, a male Supreme Being. He reigns in Paradise where only the faithful go. The wicked are condemned to a place of Ice ruled by Shaitan, the eternal enemy.

The modern (Y900+) Amteh Faith has its center in Sagostabad (Kesh) and holds sway in all of the northern lands of Antiopia and even parts of Lakh following the Keshi invasion and establishment of the Mughal line in Y834. There are some breakaway sects, notably the Ja'arathi, a more liberal sect that does not follow the more restrictive practices of Amteh (it separates secular and religious jurisdiction, does not require women to wear a bekira-shroud, and allows widows to remarry without consequences). It has a following among the wealthy and the intellectual élite. The Ja'arathi claim their path to be a more accurate reading of the original teachings of Aluq-Ahmed.

There are also several fanatic Amteh sects, the most notable being the infamous Hadishah, outlawed by the Sultans of Dhassa and Kesh but harbored in Mirobez and Gatioch and widespread in the north.

Omali (Antiopia): Founded in Lakh in prehistory, the Omali faith posits one Supreme Being (Aum), who is both male and female and can manifest in many ways, but principally as the gods and goddesses of the Oma. The Omali assign specific virtues to the different Oma, and there are at least fifteen major deities and hundreds of minor ones.

The Omali believe in a cycle of death and rebirth called *samsara*, in which the same souls are reborn time and again into new lives, until they perfect themselves, attain a state called *moksha*, and become at one with Aum. The prime deities are collectively known as the Trimurthi and encompass three male deities, the spirits of creation, preservation, and destruction.

The Omali religion is the dominant faith of Lakh, despite the military conquest of northern Lakh by the Amteh-worshipping Mughal dynasty 100 years ago (around Y834)

Zainism (Antiopia):   Zainism is believed to be derived from Omali and the teachings of a man called Zai of Baranasi (whom the Omali believe to be an incarnation of Vishnarayan the Preserver). He preached removing oneself from worldly forces to seek spiritual, intellectual, and physical perfection. Zainism's tenets still include the cycle of *samsara* and the seeking of *moksha*, but renounces worldliness. Zainism remains a fringe cult, but due to its liberal attitudes to gender equality, sexuality, the arts, and its martial techniques, it has a following among élites.

THE GNOSTIC ARTS

Basic Theory: The Magi teach that when a person dies, their soul leaves their body. This disembodied spirit usually lingers for some time in our world and therefore has powers of movement and communication. The Scytale of Corineus enabled the magi to tap into these powers without having first to die, giving the mage "magical" powers in life.

Mage's "Blood":   The child of a mage inherits powers equal to the average power of their parents: so a full-blooded mage and a non-mage would produce a half-blood with commensurately half the basic gnostic strength of the pure-blood. The "blood-rank" of magi is therefore determined by their percentage of mage-blood.

Note that the children of Ascendants are not as powerful as their parents: consuming ambrosia generates greater power than can be inherited genetically.

Ascendants: Those who survive drinking ambrosia are Ascendants, and they wield the highest powers of the magi. The ambrosia is risky, however: not everyone who drinks the potion is strong enough to take the mental and physical strains; there is a strong likelihood of dying or becoming insane

Souldrinkers: Magi descended from "God's Rejects" can access and maintain the gnosis only by using the energy of consumed souls. They are a secret sect that are held by the Kore to be wholly evil.

Magi and   Magi are prominent in Yuros society, and because of their
Society: skills, they generally do well financially, as well as acquiring great status and influence. They have special status in religious worship. They are expected to set the moral example and personify Kore's teachings.

Both male and female magi have fertility problems. There is great stigma should a female mage bear a child to a man considered beneath her and/or out of wedlock. Males have more license and father many mixed-blood magi out of wedlock, but this is limited by their poor fertility.

| Gnosis and Law: | The use of gnosis is carefully controlled by the Church and the Arcanum (the fellowship of magi who control education and policy). Some Studies (especially within Theurgy and Sorcery) are closely monitored, but all gnosis is capable of misuse. |

The Facets of the Gnosis

There are three facets to the gnosis: Magic, Runes, and Studies.

| Magic: | Magic is the use of basic magical energies, such as discharging energy at an enemy (a "mage-bolt"), lifting or moving an object with gnosis (kinesis), mind-to-mind communication, or protecting oneself with gnosis (shielding). |

| Runes: | These are a series of symbols from the old Yothic alphabet (the "runes"), assigned for convenience to specific gnostic abilities. The symbols don't have intrinsic power; they are merely a form of shorthand for magical abilities. Some are assigned to general-use powers (like the Chain-rune, or wardings), and others represent powers accessed only through Studies (see below). |

| Studies: | These are the most sophisticated applications of gnosis, and even the best and most talented magi are usually only capable of using two-thirds of them, as their minds are conditioned to perform some tasks better than others. There are four Classes (or Fields) of gnosis and within each Class, four specific Studies (meaning there are sixteen Studies in all). The combination of Studies that a mage finds himself able to use is determined largely by personality (or "affinity"). |

| Class Affinity: | There are four Classes of gnosis; a mage will normally find they have more affinity to one than others, and therefore antipathy toward the opposing Study: for example, Thaumaturgy is the antithesis of Theurgy, and Hermetic the antithesis of Sorcery. |

| Elemental Affinity: | Each mage will also have an affinity to an element that will shape how they operate. This combined with Class-affinity will determine the abilities that mage will excel at, those they will merely be functional at, and those they cannot perform at all. |

A mage who has an "absolute affinity" has supreme mastery over a Study. It requires single-minded devotion to one Study for which they already have a strong affinity (in both Class and element). A mage with absolute affinity often has a narrower selection of Studies at which they are proficient.

The Classes (or Fields): Thaumaturgy: the manipulation of the prime elemental forces: earth, water, fire, and air. Earth and Air are held as antithetical, as are Water and Fire. This is the simplest Class.

Hermetic: use of gnosis on living organisms, divided into Healing (restoring someone to normal), Morphic (altering "normal" forms), Animism (emulating and controlling creatures), and Sylvanism (manipulating plant matter).

Theurgy: use of the gnosis to affect the mind; divided into Mesmerism (influencing other minds), Illusion (deceiving the senses), Mysticism (communion of minds), and Spiritualism (projecting of the spirit).

Sorcery: dealing with other spirits; divided into Clairvoyance (using the "eyes" of the spirits to observe other places), Divination (using the "eyes" and knowledge of spirits to predict the future), Wizardry (control and use of spirits), and Necromancy (communion with the recently dead).

The Studies

Thaumaturgy: Fire: an aggressive Study; gives a resistance to fire and an ability to douse flame. This Study is primarily used by the military, as well as in metal-working.

Air: a versatile Study that gives the ability to fly and also to manipulate weather. It is widely used in commerce and by the military.

Water: the ability to shape water, to purify water, to breathe water, and to use water as a weapon at times (the more skillful have been known to drown a man on dry land).

Earth: the ability to shape stone is valuable in construction. Earth-gnosis is also widely used in mining, hunting (tracking), and smithing, and has even been used to create or still earthquakes.

Hermetic: Healing (Water-linked): restoring flesh to its normal undamaged state. It can be applied against illnesses and viruses as well. It is regarded as unglamorous.

Morphism (Fire-linked): the manipulation of the human form can be used to enhance (or deplete) musculature or appearance, right up to taking on the appearance of another person. Often used to gain special endurance for a task. The most feared use—to disguise oneself as another person—is illegal. It cannot be sustained for long periods.

Animism (Air-linked): can be used to enhance the senses, to command the behavior of other creatures and even to take on beast-form oneself. Many applications, both in civilian and military context.

Sylvanism (Earth-linked): can be used to enhance or deplete wood and plant material. Often used in construction of buildings, tools and transport, in both peace and wartime. Wide use of potions and unguents for temporary Gnostic affects.

Theurgy: Mesmerism (Fire-linked): this is the use of mind-to-mind interaction to aid, dominate or mislead another. Can be used to strengthen another's determination or sense of purpose, but more infamously used to manipulate and mislead.

Illusion (Air-linked): the ability to produce false sights, smells, tastes or sounds to deceive others. Can also be used for protection from the same, to deceive attackers, and to entertain.

Mysticism (Water-linked): the communion of minds, permitting rapid teaching, deep-probing of minds to restore lost memories and to heal mental disorders or calm anxiety. Can be used to link the minds of magi to enhance the power of gnosis-workings by sharing energy.

Spiritualism (Earth-linked): the ability to send one's spirit out of the body, where it can then travel long distance and use limited gnosis once there. Used in communication, also in scouting and similar.

Sorcery: Clairvoyance (Water-linked): the ability to see other places, the distances being determined by the skill and power of the mage. It can be blocked by concentrated layers of earth or water, and certain other restrictions.

Divination (Air-linked): questions can be asked of the spirit world, which will then give information (often captured in visual symbols) and will allow the mage to predict a probable outcome based on the known information. Unreliable and subject to distortion by personal bias and knowledge gaps.

Wizardry (Fire-linked): the ability to summon a spirit and control it, either in its natural spirit form or within a body supplied by the caster. Perilous, due to hostility of spirits, and considered theologically dubious. Can give access to all other Studies secondhand, so widely used to achieve indirectly effects provided by other studies.

Necromancy (Earth-linked): the ability to deal death through forcing the spirit to depart; can also be used to communicate with the recently dead, and even to bring a spirit back to reanimate a dead body. Its acceptable uses are to question the recently dead on crimes related to their deaths or to help a spirit "pass on" (exorcism), but reanimation especially is illegal and other uses are morally and theologically dubious.

Gnosis Affinity Table

Below is a Mage Affinity table.

STUDIES	EARTH (element)	FIRE (element)	AIR (element)	WATER (element)
THAUMATURGY (The manipulation of inanimate matter)	Earth-gnosis	Fire-gnosis	Air-gnosis	Water-gnosis
HERMETIC (The manipulation of living matter)	Sylvanism	Morphism	Animism	Healing
SORCERY (the manipulation of spirit beings)	Necro-mancy	Wizardry	Divination	Clairvoy-ance
THEURGY (the manipulation of mind and spirit)	Spiritualism	Mesmerism	Illusion	Mysticism

How to use the table:
- All magi have a primary affinity to a Study, and/or to an Element. Most have an affinity to both, and many have a weaker secondary affinity.
- Any affinity creates a blind spot to its opposite:

FIRE	EARTH	THAUMA-TURGY	THEURGY
AIR	WATER	HERMETIC	SORCERY

Fire and Water are opposites   Thaumaturgy and Sorcery are opposites

Air and Earth are opposites   Hermetic and Theurgy are opposites

- So a person with affinities to Fire and Sorcery will be strongest at Wizardry and most vulnerable against Water-gnosis.

Glossary

Rimoni

Alpha Umo: First Man; an expression meaning the leader of a group of men

Amici/Amica: Friend (male / female)

Amori/Amora: Love(r) (male / female)

Arrivederci: Farewell

Buona Notte: Goodnight

Castrato: Castrated man; in the Rimoni Empire it was common to castrate boy singers and male servants.

Cojones: Testicles

Condotiori: Mercenary

Cunni: A woman's genitals (obscenity)

Dildus: A colloquial word for a penis

Dio: God

Donna: An unmarried woman, the equivalent of "Miss"

Drui: A Sollan priest

Familioso: A term for a family clan that runs criminal activity in a town

Grazie: Thank you

Pater: Father

Paterfamilias: Head of the family (male)

Rukk/rukka!: Fuck! (obscenity)

Rukka mio!: Fuck me! (obscenity)

Safian: Homosexual woman

Si: Yes

Signor/i: Gentleman/gentlemen

Silencio: Silence

Keshi/Dhassan/Jhafi

Afreet:	Evil spirit of the air in Kesh mythology
Bekira-shroud:	Loose-fitting black over-robe worn by Amteh women
Dome-al'Ahm:	Amteh place of worship.
Eyeed:	The three-day festival after the Holy month of Rami
Fatwah:	A religious death sentence decreed against those who have offended Ahm
Godsinger:	A person assigned to call the faithful to prayer
Godspeaker:	A senior Amteh priest and scholar
Raki:	Rice-based spirit, known in Lakh as arak
Scriptualist:	An Amteh priest
Shihad:	A holy war decreed against a people or place for religious reasons
Souk:	Market
Wadi:	Dried riverbed

Lakh

Achaa:	Okay or Yes or Very well
Arak:	Rice-based spirit, known in Kesh and Dhassa as Raki
Babu:	"Big man," a word for a local community leader
Baksheesh:	A tip or a bribe or a gift, depending upon the context
Father:	Father
Bhai:	Brother
Chai:	Tea, usually heavily spiced with cardamom, cinnamon, mint, and other herbs and spices
Chapatti:	Flat bread
Chela:	A trainee Omali priest or sadhu
Chod!:	Fuck! (obscenity)
Chodia!:	Fucker! (obscenity)
Dalit:	An "untouchable"; the lowest, most menial class of Lakh society
Didi:	Sister
Dodi Manghal:	The predawn meal before wedding
Dom-al'Ahm:	Lakh (originally Gatioch) word for an Amteh temple

Dupatta:	A scarf worn by women with a salwar, and often used to veil the face from the sun or for modesty
Fenni:	A rough and cheap spirit distilled from wheat
Ferang:	Foreigner
Ganga:	Marijuana
Garud:	A bird-deity; the steed of the God Vishnarayan
Ghat:	Terraced steps leading down to water, used for worship and washing in Lakh
Gopi:	A milkmaid
Guru:	Teacher or wise person
Havan Kund:	Part of the wedding ritual, where the couple separately and together circle a fire, performing ritual words and actions
Haveli:	Walled style of house with an inner courtyard common among the well-off of Lakh
Jadugara:	A witch or wizard
Jhuggi:	Slums, shantytowns where the poor dwell
Lingam:	Male sexual organs
Mandap:	The holiest place in a shrine, and the consecrated place where wedding vows are exchanged in a person's house (which is blessed to become a temporary shrine)
Mandir:	Omali Shrine
Mata:	Mother
Mata-choda:	Motherfucker
Mela:	A fair
Nehin:	No
Pandit or Purohit:	Omali Priest
Pooja:	Prayer
Pratta:	A religious ban; e.g. the Blood-pratta that bars a menstruating woman from male company
Rangoli:	Decorative floor-paintings
Sadhu:	Itinerant Omali holy man
Salwar Kameez:	A pull-over one-piece dress worn with drawstring baggy pants and a scarf (dupatta)
Siv-lingam:	Religious icon representing the penis of the God Sivraman and his consort's yoni.
Tilak:	A prayer-mark on the forehead

Vridhi Pooja:	Ancestor prayers
Walla:	"Fellow," usually associated with a job, e.g., a chai-walla is a tea-boy
Yoni:	Female sexual organs

Acknowledgments

Writing books is actually a team sport. I'm very lucky to have a group of wonderful supportive people who have contributed to this one.

First up, many thanks to Paul Linton for slogging through the first completed draft and providing so much valuable feedback. Likewise to my fabulous agent Heather Adams and her partner Mike Bryan, without whom none of this would be happening.

Huge thanks to Jo Fletcher for her guidance, expertise, eye for detail, continuity, and what works. Much gratitude and respect. Also thanks to Nicola Budd and the rest of the JFB/Quercus team, Emily Faccini for the maps, and Paul Young, Jem Butcher, and Patrick Carpenter for the cover.

And of course, love and mega-thanks to my wife, Kerry, for going through every draft and giving her insights, opinions, time, and support to make sure this book was written.

Love and hugs to my children, Brendan and Melissa, to my parents and family, and all my dear friends for just being yourselves.

Thanks to the two Doctors of Wittertainment for the word "braffing." And hello to Jason Isaacs.